THUNDERSTRIKE
& OTHER STORIES

WARHAMMER
AGE OF SIGMAR

THUNDERSTRIKE
& OTHER STORIES

RICHARD STRACHAN • ERIC GREGORY
DAVID GUYMER • GAV THORPE • C L WERNER
DARIUS HINKS • ROBERT RATH • DALE LUCAS
JAMIE CRISALLI • ANNA STEPHENS
DAVID ANNANDALE • MICHAEL R FLETCHER
DAVE GROSS • BEN COUNTER

BLACK LIBRARY

A BLACK LIBRARY PUBLICATION

'Shiprats' first published in
Black Library Events Anthology 2017/18 in 2017.
'The Neverspike' first published in
Black Library Events Anthology 2018/19 in 2018.
'The Sea Taketh' first published digitally in 2018.
'Bossgrot', 'Blessed Oblivion', 'Strong Bones' and 'The Garden of Mortal
Delights' first published digitally in 2019.
'The Serpent's Bargain' first published in *Inferno! Volume 4* in 2019.
'Blood of the Flayer' and 'The Siege of Greenspire' first published in
Oaths & Conquests in 2020.
'Buyer Beware' first published digitally in 2020.
'Ghastlight' first published in *Direchasm* in 2020.
'Watchers of Battle' first published in *Inferno! Volume 5* in 2020.
'Mourning in Rainhollow' first published in *Inferno! Volume 6* in 2021.
This edition published in Great Britain in 2021 by
Black Library, Games Workshop Ltd., Willow Road,
Nottingham, NG7 2WS, UK.

Represented by: Games Workshop Limited - Irish branch,
Unit 3, Lower Liffey Street, Dublin 1,
D01 K199, Ireland.

10 9 8 7 6 5 4 3 2 1

Produced by Games Workshop in Nottingham.
Cover illustration by Alexander Mokhov.

See Black Library on the internet at

blacklibrary.com

Find out more about Games Workshop
and the worlds of Warhammer at

games-workshop.com

Printed and bound by CPI Group (UK) Ltd, Croydon, CR0 4YY

Dear Reader,

Thank you for buying this book. You stand on the precipice of a great adventure — welcome to the worlds of Warhammer Age of Sigmar.

Herein you will find a host of great stories that explore the Mortal Realms — a fantastical landscape of mighty heroes, strange beasts, wizards, terrifying monsters, bloodshed and betrayal. Here, rampaging armies clash in brutal conflict, dauntless explorers test their mettle and their swords amongst the cavernous ruins of ancient civilisations, and wild magic causes the dead to rise again.

With this book you will undertake a journey through these realms and meet some of the many characters that inhabit them, pointing the way to even further adventures — recommending your next reads from the extensive and ever-expanding Black Library range.

So strap on your sword or ready your wizard's staff and let us begin. You have but to turn the page...

CONTENTS

THUNDERSTRIKE

Richard Strachan

CHAPTER ONE

If there was one thing Captain Holger Beck hated about the swamps – even more than the bloodthirsty mosquitoes, the over-bearing heat and the stink of filthy, brackish water – it was the light. Filtered through the feathered branches of the paperbark trees, it fell from the sky like a foul miasma, gloomy and sick. It gave everything a queasy, submerged look, and constantly peering through it was beginning to give him a headache.

Holger looked out from the raft over the choked wetlands and felt his heart sink. They were poling along a narrow channel that cut between the glades, the surface of the water carpeted in a thick green scum. On either side of the channel the swollen boles of the swamp mahogany trailed beards of moss into the water. They looked like faces staring at him, he thought, like creatures uneasily mashed together from all the muck and filth of this awful place. He turned away. Every now and then he could hear the rippling flop of a leopard eel slipping below the surface, the slow and menacing drip of the recent rain pattering through the leaves.

Something screeched in the distance, hidden in the mists. Holger sighed. A mosquito landed on his neck with a flicker and he slapped it into a bloody paste.

'It's a man's life in the Freeguild,' Sergeant Huber said. She raised an eyebrow, an ironic smile on her face. 'Isn't this the kind of adventure you signed up for, sir?'

Huber's collar was unbuttoned and her sleeves rolled up, her breastplate stacked with all the others at the centre of the raft. The rest of the platoon was sprawled out exhausted in the heat, mopping their brows with sodden kerchiefs or staring dejectedly into the shadows across the water. On either side, two guardsmen dipped poles into the stagnant water and propelled them slowly onwards. The water slopped over the lip of the raft, oily and dark. Holger looked back at the rafts that were following behind, another dozen or so carrying his whole company deeper into the Mirkmere Swamps. He could see the glint of metal, the faded green of uniforms, but he couldn't even see the rearguard, the light was so dim.

'I didn't take a commission in the Iron Bulls so I could have *adventures*,' he said. He uncorked his flask and took a careful sip, feeling it burning in his chest. *Only enough firewater left for another day or two, damn it.* 'I took it for a nice uniform, a quiet bit of guard duty, and plenty of opportunities for playing cards and drinking in the officers' mess.'

'And then the siege happened,' Huber prompted him.

'And then the siege happened...'

He shut his eyes, tipped the flask to his mouth again. No matter how long ago it was, the memories still lashed him with their original force. Lieutenant Holger Beck of the Iron Bulls had spent the best part of the Siege of Excelsis hiding in a tavern cellar off the Pilgrim's Way, head buried in his hands as he tried not to cry. The smart new uniform, the polished steel breastplate, the officer's sword at his hip – none of it was worth a cuss when the enemy were at the gates. He had slipped away as the first arrows fell, as the Ironweld cannons had started firing with a sound like holy thunder. He didn't think of himself as a coward, Holger Beck. He was more of a realist, and the idea of matching himself against the awful things that had fought their way into Excelsis had been just too fantastical a concept for him to entertain.

Armoured orruks slavering for war, ogors and daemons... He shivered. Thank Sigmar he hadn't had to witness the worst of it.

'Still, it all worked out in the end,' Huber said cheerfully. 'The lone survivor of your platoon, all those medals, the promotion. Your own company.'

'Yes,' he sighed again. 'It all worked out beautifully.'

'I must confess,' a voice said at his side, 'that it pains me to hear you talk in such cynical tones, Captain Beck.'

Holger turned to see the priest standing there with a strained look on his face. Caspar Hallan was young, ascetically thin, his hair shorn down to the scalp. He had the sort of flinty, uncompromising look in his eye that had always made Holger nervous. He bobbed slightly as the raft buckled over the water. As far as he could tell, Caspar was as close to being a fanatic as you could get without actually grabbing a copy of *Intimations of the Comet* and ranting your way into the wilderness to convert the heathens. Holger had always been highly suspicious of men who were that certain in their beliefs – they tended to be the ones who got you killed.

'Mere soldiers' banter,' Holger said. 'The life of a guardsman is a hard one, I'm sure you'll agree, and our humour occasionally tends towards the dark.'

'We must not make light of our mission, however,' Caspar said. Unlike the sprawling troops, he hadn't even loosened a single button against the heat. 'The brave settlers missing from Palmer's

Creek, from Dezraedsville and Junivatown, deserve better. They deserve our zeal, our courage, our faith!'

'They'll get all three,' Holger said. 'We'll find out what happened to them, I promise.' He glanced at Sergeant Huber and shrugged. 'As much as I can promise anything in this benighted place.'

Caspar drew himself up and stared with unyielding fervour into the dripping murk.

'There is nowhere in the Mortal Realms that can be considered benighted while the light of Sigmar is there to illuminate it.'

'And what brings you with us?' Huber interrupted. 'This is a military expedition, not anything to do with Sigmar's Temple.'

'The ministry of Sigmar's priesthood is wherever his justice needs to be meted out,' Caspar intoned. Holger couldn't tell if he was quoting scripture or not; everything the young man said felt like it came from a parchment or a scroll. 'Nearly a thousand of the faithful have vanished from these settlements, brave crusaders spreading the light of Excelsis deeper into the Mirkmere, and I would be on hand to offer spiritual succour wherever it is needed. Succour,' he added, patting the hammer at his belt, 'and righteousness.'

The reports had been coming in for weeks now, of homesteads and settlements utterly deserted, their inhabitants vanished, as if swallowed up by the swamps. Contact had been lost with Fort Harrow, and concerns had even reached the office of the High Arbiter in Excelsis. Holger shook his head and traipsed to the back of the raft, stepping over his soldiers' feet. He had no doubt that all those settlers were dead. Leopard eels were the half of it; there were flense-fish in these waters, he was sure, razorspines too. Even bloaters. Any number of disgusting diseases, any quantity of poisonous fruit. Bogs, quagmires, quicksand. No matter what Caspar thought, it wasn't just the faithful who joined these crusades out into the wilderness; it was those too poor or too stupid to see any other way of surviving. You take folk who've spent their lives grubbing about the slums of Excelsis and drop them in the middle of the Mirkmere Swamps, what do you expect to happen? You could barely see five feet in front of you in here. They'd only built the rafts because the trails were so choked and overgrown it would have taken them weeks to cut their way through.

Holger sighed for what felt like the hundredth time that day. Sigmar knew what had happened to those people, but where was the sense in sending a full company of Freeguild into the swamps to look for them? And a full company that was led by none other than the Iron Bulls' least enthusiastic officer, for all that?

'Just my luck,' he muttered bitterly.

He squinted through the rising mist at the rafts coming up behind, raising his hand to signal them.

'We'll have to stop soon,' he said to Huber. 'Evening's nearly on us, and this damned mist is getting worse. It stinks like corpses. We'll press on to Fort Harrow in the morning.'

'Take us in to the bankside,' Huber told Corporal Fischer.

The corporal angled his pole to push the raft to the left, and soon they came under the lowering canopy of the woe trees. The shadows were deeper here, danker, the mud oozing into the water. A whooping, almost mournful cry came from deeper in the swamps. It rose and then broke apart, fading into a careful silence.

Holger could see the other rafts following up behind and bumping into the bank. He stepped out into the mud and slogged his way up towards the treeline, where lank ropes of ivy dropped from the canopy overhead. The undergrowth was thick with bindweed and scrub. The swamps were full of these patches of raised ground, hummocks of mud that were like islands in the shallow waters. He could see Lieutenant Weigand further down the bank chivvying his platoon from their raft, and the other platoons beyond them – all of them struggling with their weapons and

17

equipment, the helmets and breastplates, firearms, swords and shields, ration packs.

What a waste of time... he thought.

He turned to call on Corporal Fischer to start setting up camp. Fischer was standing there under the low sweep of a woe tree, one hand resting on its trunk, the other trying to pluck something from his mouth. For a minute it looked like he had something caught in his moustache, and then his knees buckled and he sank into the mud.

'Fischer, what do you think you're doing?' Holger said. 'Get on your feet.'

He stepped forward. A *snick* in the air, the whip of something passing his face. He turned and saw Lieutenant Weigand with an arrow sprouting from his eye, his mouth open and a look on his face of vexed amazement. He toppled from the bank, and with a splash disappeared into the slimy water. Holger looked back at Fischer, slumped against the tree. His eyes were like glass. An arrow had passed through the back of his neck and was jutting from his jaw.

Holger turned to Sergeant Huber, who stood there with her mouth open, her hand on the hilt of her sword. Half the other guardsmen from the company were still on their rafts, the other half milling about uncertainly on the bank. There was absolute silence, broken only by that same strange whooping call far out across the wetlands and the glades, which rose once and then melted off into the mist.

Holger swallowed. 'Huber?' he whispered.

'Yes, captain?'

'...What do we do?'

There was a sharp hiss, like falling rain. A dozen guardsmen hit the mud, riddled with arrows.

Someone screamed. There was the scrape of drawn swords, the damp thud of arrows striking shields. Hoarse shouts of command, steel clashing against steel. A guardsman stumbled past and col-lapsed in the undergrowth with a knife buried in his neck.

Holger threw himself into a hollow between the bloated roots of a tree. Groaning, screams, the splash of water. He risked a glance over the edge of the root and saw a dark shape slip past, lank and wiry, a long blade in its hand. He saw one of the guards-men from Third Platoon stagger past with his guts hanging out, blood pouring from his mouth. He choked, dropped, fell face for-ward into a brackish puddle. The mists swam like a rolling tide, the gloom broken only by a few columns of watery light falling down from the canopy.

'God-King save me, save me, please!' Holger hissed.

He scrambled over the roots and slipped into the slime, rolling, hauling himself up, running. An arrow smacked into a trunk be-side his head.

'Huber! Where are you?'

He ducked, tripped again, smacked his head against a stone. He scrambled into a spume of razor-tipped fern, the stink of rot and blood in his nose. He was heading deeper into the swamps, but there were screams still ringing from the bank, and if Holger Beck knew one thing it was to run away from where the fighting was fiercest.

'Oh Sigmar, please,' he whispered. 'I swear, see me through this and you'll have the most faithful servant at your command!'

He ran on, scurrying from cover to cover. When he glanced back, the channel of water had been swallowed in the mists and the screams and cries were dying away. He'd lost his sword some-where, but no force in the Mortal Realms would have made him go back for it.

Slowly, for the next agonising hour, Holger crawled forward inch by inch through the putrid water, weaving his way through the swamp weed and the fern, trying miserably not to make a sound. Insects clicked and whirred in the air around him; creatures slithered away through the muck. Water dripped down his collar. The darkness drew in and he started to shiver.

He started and stifled a scream when he saw a pale face peering at him from the undergrowth, but it was only the priest, Caspar Hallan, huddled in the mud.

'Damn it, you scared the life out of me!' Holger spat.

Caspar's thin face was drawn with fear. There was a long, shallow cut down one cheek, blood dripping onto the torn collar of his robes.

'Captain Beck...' he said in a hoarse whisper. 'What... those things, they... Did you see them, Beck? *Did you see what they were?*'

Holger swallowed and shook his head. He risked a glance over his shoulder. Was that laughter he could hear? A liquid cackle, burbling off into the fens.

'We have to go back,' Caspar hissed, staring into the darkness. 'For Sigmar's sake, we have to go back...'

'I don't think Sigmar's listening out here, priest.'

'Then what do we do?'

'We make for Excelsis – it's our only hope now. Get back to the city, warn them if we can...'

Or, he thought, *just hide away in the lowliest backstreet tavern we can find and never breathe a word of what happened here...*

A shadow dripped across Caspar's face. The priest's eyes went wide with horror, and his mouth opened to scream. A dank smell enveloped him.

Holger spun around, but then all he saw were stars.

CHAPTER TWO

'It's the light,' the old priest said. He raised his face to the wash of colour as it fell from the stained-glass window: Sigmar, resplendent, casting a comet into the void and illuminating the realm entire. 'Don't you find, my lord? Even under these Cursed Skies, a little light gets through. That's where my faith resides.'

'I've told you before, Jonas,' Actinus said. 'I'm a knight, not a lord.'

They were sitting on a bench at the front of the chapel, the Knight-Relictor and the priest. It was a humble place, a small stone temple to the God-King, one of the first to have been built when Excelsis was founded all those decades ago. In the years since it had been swallowed up by the slums, the cramped alleyways and the tall wooden tenements of the Veins, where the dirty streets were carpeted in glimmerings, the blackened shards of prophetic magic cut from the Spear of Mallus. A deadlier addiction than drink, Actinus had heard. It gave what no mortal could live without for too long: hope.

'Of course,' the priest said. He laughed softly and clapped his hand to Actinus' pauldron. 'You must forgive me, but you all look like lords to me. Touched by the God-King's fire, how could you be anything else to mere mortal men?'

Actinus nodded, his face unreadable behind his skull-plate mask. It was early, as bright as it could be in these darkened days, and the torches were still unlit. The temple had only a narrow nave and could seat no more than twenty worshippers. It was quiet most of the time. Actinus liked it that way. He liked the cool silence of the little chapel, the plain functionality of the altar, the wooden benches, the undecorated walls. Simple, unadorned. This is what faith should be, he thought. He liked this old priest, Jonas, who tended Sigmar's altar with all the calm certainty of a gardener pruning his roses.

He couldn't say what had first brought him here. A morning when his uneasy sleep had sent him patrolling the more insalubrious parts of the city, perhaps, or when his dreams seemed to need the quiet and the silence in order to settle once more in his mind. He had seen the comet carved above the old wooden doorway of the temple and had stepped inside, and immediately all the riot and disorder of Excelsis had fallen away.

The city had suffered terribly in the siege. Whole districts had been swept away as the maddened followers of Kragnos breached the gates. Thousands and thousands had died, but the work of rebuilding seemed scarcely less anarchic.

It is all a tumult, he thought. *Everything is in flux. And I am here in this form with no clear grasp of my purpose.*

He heard then, like some faint echo on the edge of sound, the screaming of his comrades. He saw shards of lightning flattened on a black sky, clouds roiling like the deeps of a troubled ocean. Behind his faceplate, Actinus closed his eyes.

Jonas' dry laugh degenerated into a fit of coughing. When it was over, he sat back on the bench and wiped his eyes.

'Forgive me,' he said. 'The spirit is willing, but the body grows weak.'

'I worry I take up too much of your time, Jonas.'

'Not at all!' the priest laughed. He swept out his hands. 'Do you see a line of parishioners beating a path to this altar? No, this is an old place, long forgotten. There are other temples in the city, more than enough to cater to the citizens' spiritual needs. We are little more than a jewel in the mire here.'

He glanced at Actinus and rubbed his unshaven jaw.

'I must confess though,' Jonas said, 'it remains a mystery why you seek out my company. One who has walked with Sigmar himself surely has no need of a human priest. Not that I don't enjoy our little talks, of course.'

Behind the mask, Actinus smiled. 'Simplicity is its own reward,' he said. 'And I find that… there is much that falls away from me when I enter this place.'

'Much that troubles you?' the priest said. He peered at Actinus' face, as if behind the sigmarite faceplate he could see the human features, in all their vulnerability.

'Perhaps. Much that preys on my mind.'

'You talk, I'm sure, of fallen comrades.'

'You're perceptive, old man,' Actinus said.

'I've been a soldier in my time,' Jonas said. 'Long before I was a priest. I've had soldiers in here, crying for dead friends. I know what it's like to lose a comrade in arms. It's a loss that can never be filled, formed as it is of grief and guilt both. But I understood that for your kind, well… death is not the end, is it? You return, reforged by the will of Sigmar?'

'It is so,' Actinus said. 'And yet… there are times when the new form we take is perhaps not what we expected.'

'Indeed so,' Jonas said, nodding. 'I had noticed… I've seen many of the Stormborn in this city, over the years – warriors from the

Knights Excelsior, the Astral Templars – but it seems there are some that I no longer recognise amongst you. Armours and chambers unknown to me. New forms indeed.'

Actinus shifted on the bench, which creaked ominously beneath him. The priest's words were true, but they made him feel obscurely uncomfortable. He was of the Thunderstrike Stormcast, lit by Sigmar's grace and refined by Grungni's genius, and they were the response to conditions across the realms that were only degrading. There had been centuries of war since Sigmar first launched his crusade against Chaos, but the wars had only become more vicious. After all the destruction and violence meted out to Excelsis, to admit that there might be worse to come would only place a burden of distress on the old man.

'But these lost comrades,' the priest went on, 'have not returned as you yourself have returned?'

'No,' Actinus said. 'Not as far as I can ascertain.'

He heard their screams again, their souls sundered in the wind of the Cursed Skies, while he shot arrow-bright for the forges of Azyr. The bright city, the seat of Sigmar's grace. A grace he had somehow earned, while his comrades had not. He reached out with his mind towards the moments of his previous death, but his soul recoiled from it. It was too raw a thing, too painful.

Turillos, he thought. *Bravest of men, with your twin blades flashing. Bold Khellian, quick to anger, your loyalty as unbreakable as your bond. My friends, forgive me...*

'It is true,' Jonas said, 'that the God-King fashions his tools to his purposes. It is not always given to us to understand why.'

'Indeed not,' Actinus said. 'We must be wielded as he sees fit.'

Jonas cackled again. 'Aye, so they say. Not much of a comfort at times though, is it?'

He struggled to stand up, groaning, his legs trembling. Actinus stood and held out his arm, the massive gauntlet like an adult's hand holding a child's. Jonas chuckled again to see the comparison. For most mortals, to be in the presence of a Stormcast Eternal was overwhelming, but this old priest seemed unmoved. Perhaps that was another reason why Actinus found himself drawn here. To be the subject of awe was often something that bred only contempt, and he would avoid that if he could. He helped Jonas walk over to the altar, the priest moving with a slow, shuffling tread.

'You said you have guarded the sacred relics in Holy Azyr?' Jonas asked him. 'The reliquaries of Sigmaron?'

'It is so,' Actinus said. He tapped his armoured fist to the censer on his belt. 'I carry with me some of those relics, the bones of great martyrs and saints.'

'Then this might interest you, good sir knight.'

The old priest reached with a trembling hand and took from the altar what looked to Actinus like an ordinary knife. He passed it with reverence to the Knight-Relictor. It was a sword, Actinus realised, a standard blade for a mortal soldier, which in his armoured hands seemed absurdly small. The blade was notched here and there, but it still held a decent edge.

'There is nothing special in the blade itself,' Jonas said. 'One of many churned out by the city armouries before the siege, but that sword belonged to a young soldier of this parish who died fighting in the defence. His mother, one of my few parishioners, brought it here and laid it on the altar, in sorrow and in gratitude for her son's sacrifice.'

'What was the soldier's name?' Actinus asked him.

'His name was Aldert Sommer. A good lad, a common guardsman. None too special, if the truth be told, just an ordinary boy. But he was willing to lay down his life for Excelsis when the time came. I want you to have it,' the priest said. He looked at Actinus with craft in his eyes. 'Take it with you on your next campaign. A relic, not of a great saint or martyr, but of an ordinary young man who gave in the end all that he had to give. It is holy, in its way. I hope it will help you.'

Actinus turned the sword over, watching the dull blade catch the light as it streamed through the stained-glass window, a wash of red and gold and blue. Long accustomed to the sacred reliquiae of Sigmar's holy city, he didn't have the heart to tell Jonas that the sword felt undistinguished in his hands. It was the cast-off weapon of a soldier who had no doubt died in some squalid and desperate fashion – crushed by falling masonry, speared by some daemonic grotesque that far outmatched him, or trampled by the bestial hordes of Ghur as he tried to run away. It was not the weapon of a martyr, but of a scared boy pressed into service because he had no other choice.

But it was not given to everyone to be a hero, Actinus thought; and then the screams of the Cursed Skies screeched once more into his memory.

'Thank you,' he said. He tucked the sword into his belt. 'I will take heart from it, I'm sure.'

'See that you do, and may it be a blessing to you. A keepsake, from a place where you are always welcome.'

Actinus bowed his head. The care of souls was part of the Knight-Relictor's duty, a sacred task which mere mortals couldn't possibly understand, but he was beginning to think that this old priest had insights into the subject which might have eluded him. Jonas might not grasp the very soul-stuff of Stormcast warriors as they fell in battle, but, in his way, he was adept at shoring up the spirits of those in his care. It was easy for Actinus to forget what he had once known as a mortal. There was always so much more to remember.

'Ah,' Jonas said as Actinus helped him back to the bench. 'We have another visitor – it seems this humble temple is becoming something of a refuge for your kind, Actinus!'

The Knight-Relictor looked down the nave, and there, standing illuminated in the narrow stone doorway, was a huge Stormcast Paladin in resplendent gold armour, intricate and ornate, more like a statue than a living thing. It was one of the Lord-Imperatant's praetors, Actinus knew, the champions sworn to their liege's service in his personal bodyguard. They spoke with the voice of the Lord-Imperatant himself, and if Lord Taranis had sent one of his praetors, then the reason must be grave.

'Knight-Relictor,' the warrior said. So deep was the soul-bond between the bodyguard and his liege that in the praetor's voice, like an echo or a memory, Actinus could hear Taranis' gruff and forthright tones. 'My lord requires your presence.'

Actinus turned to the priest, who sat there on the bench in placid contemplation. He rested his hand on the hilt of the blade Jonas had given him.

'I fear it may be some time before we meet again, my friend,' Jonas said. 'Sigmar go with you.'

'And with you,' Actinus said, '...my friend.'

CHAPTER THREE

It was as easy to assume they were building the city from scratch as repairing the damage it had sustained in the siege. As they left the dingy, mist-shrouded alleyways of the Veins and skirted the eastern wall, cutting across the Pilgrim's Way as it stretched on towards the Abbey of Remembered Souls, Actinus marvelled again at the scale of the devastation. The celestial magic of Lord Kroak, the Slann starmaster, had reversed much of the damage in the aftermath of the assault, but even this long after the siege there was much to repair. Entire districts had been cast into ruins, buildings toppled like toys, rickety hovels and soaring tenements cast down into kindling. Great trenches had been gouged into the city's streets. Palaces and merchant halls alike had been sheared down to their foundations, and covered passageways and arches had been cracked open to the broiling sky. This part of Excelsis was far removed from the grand avenues and civic spaces of Squallside and the Noble Quarter, but it had suffered just as badly none the less. Wherever Actinus looked, there were people scrabbling amongst the ruins, collecting bricks, working in red-faced crews to lift wooden spars and beams from underneath the rubble, or to gather shards of broken roof slate and stack them in listing piles. A faint haze of dust arose from the work of reconstruction.

'Such industry,' he commented to the praetor. 'Such zest for rebuilding what they have lost.' The champion said nothing. Almost to himself, Actinus continued, 'It fills the heart, does it not, to see ordinary men and women setting themselves to such a task.'

Encouragingly, Actinus saw that the iron laws of commerce were still in operation. Framing the littered squares, or gathered around the empty plinths of toppled statues, were market stalls and pedlars hawking their wares, ale sellers, flower girls, pie merchants, scrap-and-bone men, the ever-present traffickers in cut-price glimmerings. Coin must change hand, and it would take more than the near destruction of the city to prevent it. There was a kind of vigour in this, he thought. Trade and dealings, people haggling for bargains, the face-to-face discourse of the streets. It was admirable.

As they reached the barbican that squatted its twin towers over the bastion's eastern gate, Actinus glanced back towards the city's western side, where the Spear of Mallus loomed like a mountain in the harbour, circled by the floating towers of the Collegiate Arcane. A vast shard of the world-that-was, plunged into the deeps of Excelsis Bay, the Spear was the source of all prophecy and foresight in the city. The tiniest shaving from it could give hope to the desperate, a glimpse of what might yet be, no matter if that hope were false or not.

Actinus turned his gaze right, where he could see the brooding pile of the Consecralium glaring down on the bay from its promontory above the water, a blunt fang of black iron and gunmetal stone – the grim fortress of the Knights Excelsior. They had been hard-pressed during the siege, Actinus knew, blockaded in their Stormkeep by Slaaneshi cultists and their daemonic allies. Their casualties had been immense. He glanced up at the parched blaze of the skies above the city, a whirlpool of black cloud and eldritch light, flashing and churning as if struck by hidden storms. He wondered how many had made it through. Back to Azyr and the Anvil of the Apotheosis… How many of their souls screamed there still, wrapped in the coils of that unholy madness?

The barbican was formed of two square towers of black stormstone, each ten storeys high and flecked with arrow-slit windows. At the top of each tower was a sequence of barbettes for the Ironweld volley guns and rocket batteries, the blunt muzzles of which Actinus could just see nosing out towards the parched lands beyond the city walls. A stairway led up the side of each tower towards the Neck, the narrow road that ran around the inside of the city walls. A company of Bronze Claws was drilling on the parade ground in front of the keep, marching smartly to the barked commands of its officer. The soldiers' weapons looked clean and well kept, Actinus thought, their uniforms worn but decently maintained. As the two Stormcast warriors passed by, the company came to a crisp halt and offered them a salute.

'Hail, lords!' the officer cried. His face looked strained and nervous.

Actinus raised his hand to his chest in recognition, but the praetor did nothing.

'They salute for you,' Actinus said as they passed the parade ground. 'The mortal soldiers. You owe them respect for the respect they show you, at the very least.'

'Lord Taranis is waiting in the keep,' the praetor said, again with that faint echo of the Lord-Imperatant's voice.

Actinus gave a cold smile. He wondered how old this praetor really was. Forged and reforged, returning always to serve his master, and each time with a little more of his master's soul taking the place of his own… They were old beings, the praetors. Great champions in an eternal brotherhood who would lay down their lives without a moment's hesitation in the defence of their lord, but who were reforged only when a sufficient number of them had died, so the bonds of brotherhood were never broken.

Warriors out of time, Actinus thought. *Decades could have passed since this one last set foot on the Mortal Realms.*

The keep had suffered only superficial damage in the fighting, and that had soon been repaired. When they passed under the portcullis of the southern tower, they entered a bustle of activity – adjutants rushing past with requisition orders, Freeguild officers directing troops down the Neck to reinforce other parts of the bastion, groups of grumbling duardin engineers scowling over plans and schematics.

The praetor led Actinus through a narrow doorway at the other side of the tower and up a spiral staircase to the guardroom at the top. Lord-Imperatant Taranis stood there by the embrasure, peering down through the narrow window at the spread of dead land beyond the walls of Excelsis, still littered this long after the siege by broken weapons and burial pits. His armour, a pale gold so polished it was almost white, glowed in the light of the torches that lined the walls. He stood there with his head bare, his helmet resting by the table on which he had spread out his maps of the city and the surrounding lands. His thick black hair, flecked with grey, was swept back from his forehead, the strong chin marred by a thin scar that feathered down from his cheekbone to his jaw. Taranis turned to the praetor as Actinus entered.

'Thank you, Castor,' he said. The praetor nodded and took up position on the other side of the guardroom, where two more praetors stood at attention by the fireplace. No fire had been lit, despite the damp chill in the barbican; a Stormcast Eternal had no need of such comforts.

'He speaks with your voice, my lord,' Actinus said, making

obeisance, 'and yet seems willing to keep his own counsel. These are old souls who attend you, I can tell.'

'In one way or another, they've been in my service since the Realmgate Wars,' Taranis said. His face was grim. 'And it would not do to have this discussion beyond the confines of this chamber where mortals could overhear.'

'Of course, my lord,' Actinus said. 'I did not mean to question your purpose.'

Taranis stared frankly at him, his eyes flashing deep with sparks of fire. He allowed himself a smile.

'I've never known a member of the Relictor Temple who didn't relish questioning his commander's purpose,' he said.

'I wouldn't presume to do so,' Actinus said.

Lord Taranis turned again to the narrow window, gesturing with a sweep of his gauntlet at the wild lands of Ghur: the swamps and savage plains, the low, creeping hills of Thondia.

'We may guard only a small section of the city here, Knight-Relictor, but you know as well as I do how close to the edge Excelsis is. That the city was saved is a miracle in itself, but even now the beasts of this realm take heart from our troubles. Orruks mass to the north, further up the Coast of Tusks, as they always have. Those miserable spider-grots still make the Forest of Gorch their stronghold, and in the city itself the Nullstone Brotherhood has not been as fully extinguished as we would like the citizens to think. Cultists within, enemies without, and colonies far out in the swamps falling silent... And these Cursed Skies broiling in the deeps above us, like a sword above our heads.'

'It is why we are here,' Actinus said simply. 'The Thunderstrike Stormcasts have been forged for these new trials.'

Taranis sighed, glancing at his maps. 'Aye, so it seems... and the trials will be sore indeed, I am sure.'

He gestured Actinus over and speared a finger at a map of the wilds, the Morruk Hills and the Mirkmere Swamps to the south-east of Amberstone Watch, largest of the settlements Excelsis had established beyond its walls.

'Crusades have been sent out into this wilderness to the south-east,' he said, 'colonies established along the line of the swamps here, and in the shadows of the hills. Small-scale settlements, no more than a few hundred colonists each, some mortal soldiery to protect them. Contact has been lost with all of them.'

'All?'

'Palmer's Creek, Dezraedsville, Junivatown,' Taranis said. 'And Fort Harrow deep in the eastern reaches of the swamps.'

Actinus looked down at the map, the sliver of Thondia on the edge of the city, the vast and untracked wilds beyond it.

'Survivors, refugees?' Actinus asked. 'Has anyone brought word back?'

'None,' the Lord-Imperatant said. 'Some huntsmen who ply the swamps report that the settlements are utterly deserted, not a sign of life. A company of Freeguild from the Iron Bulls were sent into the swamps three weeks ago. They too have vanished.'

'A concerning development,' Actinus mused.

'The High Arbiter is certainly concerned,' Taranis said, striding from behind the table, his sable cloak billowing out. 'The people are barely in check, and news of this sort would surely push them over the edge. Hysteria, riots… They are desperate, as I'm sure you have noticed.'

Actinus glanced over the map, the leagues that lay between the city walls and the deeps of the swampland – a foul place, he had heard, of bitter fens and sucking quagmires, wreathed at all seasons in a stinking brew of bog-mist and vapour.

'These are dangerous lands,' he offered. 'It's possible the settlers and the Freeguild troops were simply… devoured? The wilds of Ghur are as deadly as the creatures who call it home, it is said.'

Taranis shook his head. 'The coincidence feels too neat. For them all to disappear without a single trace, not a single sign of violence... *Something* is out there, Actinus. I would ask you to find it.'

'I am at your command,' he said.

'We can ill afford to let another threat build on our borders, while we remain so stretched. I would have information at the very least. You will take a small strike force with lieutenants you can trust. Make for Fort Harrow and track down that missing Freeguild company, if you can. Find out what happened to those settlers and discover what's lurking in those swamps.' Taranis turned to him, his jaw set. 'Bring them Sigmar's justice, if need be,' he said.

'It will be done.'

Actinus bowed and turned to go, already thinking of who he would recruit for the mission. He paused at the doorway.

'May I ask, lord, why you have chosen me for this task?'

Taranis smiled as he addressed himself once more to the spread of maps.

'It is said you spent much of your time amongst the people, Knight-Relictor, wandering the streets, sitting in the temples. You have... an affinity with the mortal citizens, would you say?'

Actinus considered this. It was not something he would have framed to himself in this way, but he acknowledged the truth of the Lord-Imperatant's words. His own mortal life was many years past, as insubstantial to him as a dream, but when he walked amongst the people of Excelsis he felt some faint echo of those an-cient, everyday experiences: the feel of the blood in his veins, the emotions surging under the surface of life. The feeling as night fell of another day achieved. They were lost things, no longer grasp-able by him, but no less precious for all that.

'I suppose so, my lord. I couldn't say why exactly, but their presence raises my spirits. For all their frailty, the mortals have a strength that is often overlooked.' He glanced to the slitted window, the wilderness beyond. He could hear the faint hammering of construction in the city beyond the barbican. 'Their ambition, their sense of hope. All is torn down around them, and yet their first thought is only to rebuild. They have keen souls, brighter than you would think. Even the worst of them.'

'We are here to destroy Sigmar's enemies and to defend his empire,' Lord Taranis said, nodding. 'And what is Sigmar's empire but the people who live in it?'

Actinus touched the hilt of the blade in his belt, the sword the old priest had given him.

'The temple is not the building,' he said softly. 'It is the people who meet in it.'

Taranis frowned. 'Is that scripture?' he asked. '*Intimations of the Comet*?'

'No, my lord,' Actinus said. 'Just something a friend once told me.'

They formed up on the parade ground where the Bronze Claws had marched the day before. Twenty Vigilators stood at the front preparing to move out, festooned with ropes and pouches, their armour less restrictive and better suited for their role as scouts and pathfinders. In silence they checked their weapons and equipment, sheathing their swords and axes, stowing the bolts for their crossbows. Behind them, impeccably ranked, was a unit of Vindictors, shields harnessed to their backs for the march ahead, swords hanging from their belts. Following these, the hammers to the Vindictors' anvil, were two small units of Annihilators and Vanquishers, the heavy infantry, siegebreakers and champions all, who would shatter any opposition foolish enough to stand against them.

A small force, Taranis had said. It was so, but as Actinus emerged from the barbican and stowed his own weapons, checking the relic censer was secured to his belt, he would have ranged this strike team against anything the Mortal Realms could throw at them.

They were starting early, leaving the city with the dawn. Above, strained and filtered through the maddening turmoil of the sky, the light of Sigendil, the High Star of Azyr, pulsed weakly in the riot of the clouds. Beyond the parade ground, across a dusty, shattered square piled high with rubble, the ruins of the city began to glow in the haggard light. Saw-edged, uneven, they were blurred by the haze of dust that still lingered in the streets, looming in the smog like the bones of some stupendous beast glimpsed across a shadowed plain.

'This feels like using a hammer to crack a nut,' Leta said at Actinus' side. The Knight-Judicator rubbed thoughtfully at the scar that twisted across her upper lip. 'Are you sure we need so many warriors just to find a few mortal homesteaders and some missing troops?'

'It was no mere handful of soldiers that went missing, Leta. A full company of Freeguild have vanished in those swamps.'

'Freeguild,' she snorted derisively. 'Probably still stumbling about with their maps upside down. What can you seriously be expecting to fight, anyway? A few fen-toads and bloaters? The orruks don't go near the swamplands, and from what I can see they've taken a beating in this part of Ghur. Shame we missed it...'

'The Lord-Imperatant commands and we obey,' Actinus said. 'And it always helps to be prepared.' He signalled the Freeguild guardsman by the barbican gate to open the portcullis. The great gate began to howl against its grooves as it was slowly unshackled from the ground. 'Lord Taranis believes there is more to these disappearances than we might assume.'

'And who am I to question it?' Leta said. She grinned, the scar stretching her lip into a sneer, and ran her fingers through her close-cropped black hair. 'I'm looking forward to loosing a few arrows at targets that can actually fight back. Ripper!' she cried suddenly. 'Strix!'

She slung her golden bow across her shoulder and gave a piercing whistle for her two gryph-hounds to come to heel. Racing across the parade ground, the beasts loped quickly to her side, their sleek black and blue feathers ruffled with elation, beaks clacking, savage claws raking the dust beneath them in their haste to be off. Leta smiled indulgently at them, reaching down to scratch their heads.

'They're like me, Actinus – they can't stand being cooped up in this city any longer. They long to fight!'

'Take the Vigilators out then,' he said. 'Blaze us a trail to the edge of the swamps, and we'll follow close behind.'

Leta cried for the scouts to follow her and jogged towards the open gate, her cloak rippling out behind her. Ripper and Strix bounded after, screeching with excitement. Together, the Storm-cast warriors sprinted into the wild lands beyond the city, turning to head south, where the distant Mirkmere was slung low against the horizon, a dark smear like a streak of grime.

'Pellion,' he called. The Knight-Vexillor stood in front of the Vindictors, his helmet under his arm and a look of iron resolu-tion on his slender face. Pellion had always seemed so young to Actinus, and he wondered again at the means and manner of his first death. What had called him into the ranks of the Stormcasts? It was a subject few of them liked to discuss. He would almost have said the Knight-Vexillor seemed untried, but he knew that any Stormcast reforged into the Thunderstrike must have a mighty soul indeed. 'Unfurl your banner.'

Pellion nodded curtly and snapped the pennant out, the great cloth of gold and blue bolstered by a lightning bolt of sigmar-ite. The golden threads that spelled out their battle honours were woven from infinitesimal filings taken from the Anvil of the

Apotheosis itself, and despite the early hour and the weakness of the light, the banner shone like a kindled flame. Prayers to Sigmar trailed from the pennant on parchment scrolls, fluttering in the sultry breeze that gusted through the bastion gate.

'Take us out, Knight-Vexillor,' Actinus said. 'We head for the Mirkmere.'

CHAPTER FOUR

He knew it was only a dream, but that did not make it any less terrible.

He was on a blasted plain, and the skies above were churned with black, like ink coiling through clear water. Tendrils of lightning broke and scattered against the clouds. The air shivered with the screams of the dying, the wet work of blades, the brutal percussion of war. He was choking in the dirt of some great depression, the ground fringed with dry weeds and the staggered columns of soaring mesas on either side. The fighting had thrown a huge cloud of dust into the sky, staining the light a strange coppery red, so all the desperate warriors below seemed bathed in blood.

Men and women swirled in the dance of combat, hacking and cutting, stabbing, dying. They fought with sword and hammer, spear and axe, tooth and claw. He saw Turillos still holding his twin swords, kneeling, spewing blood, a spear plunged through his chest. He saw Khellian staring at him, her skull caved in, half her teeth smashed out. Her mouth opened to speak words she could no longer form. As she toppled forwards, Actinus pulled a blade from his side, screaming with agony. He dragged the helmet from his head and the kiss of the air was like a furnace. Then a shadow was over him, a black sheet that smothered all his sight. He reached for the light – and then he *was* the light, they were all the light, stabbing up towards the diamond brightness of Sigendil, the holy star, so frail up there, so far away.

He heard them screaming, their souls crying out as they streaked into the iron clouds – the Cursed Skies, which held them still, while he went on to glory.

'Actinus?'

'I'm awake,' he said. He was groggy, his eyes still burning with that light. He turned his face away and reached for his helmet. 'I was just resting. I wasn't asleep.'

'I believe you,' Leta said, smirking. 'I wouldn't blame you if you were, though. We've been at this three days straight.'

'What's wrong?' he said. 'Has anything happened?'

He stood up from where he had been sitting against the trunk of a moss-shrouded tree. The rest of his troops were strung out around the clearing, a shallow hummock of land on a slight rise above the swamps that was ringed with mahogany and bullrushes. Some of the Stormcast warriors were cleaning their weapons or trying to scrape the worst of the mud from their armour. Others stood on guard, the Vindictors with their shields drawn, their weapons in hand. He saw Pellion sitting alone by his banner, which he had planted in the mud beside him. Even in this dank, grey-green light, it glowed with purity and purpose. Actinus took up his sword, his hand reflexively straying to the censer on his belt.

'Nothing's wrong,' Leta told him. 'Not yet, at any rate, although there's always time.' Her longbow was still strung over her shoulder. 'You seemed agitated – I thought it best to wake you.'

'Thank you,' Actinus said. The dream was still there behind his eyes, but fading now, losing definition. No more than a faint memory. 'I dreamt of old comrades... old friends, long gone.'

He shook his head. Like a painting made of coloured sand, the memory broke apart.

A thick, cloying mist had laid itself against the swamp, disguising the paths they had been following across the standing water. It smelled acrid, unnatural, with a faint scent of burning hair.

'We should press on,' Actinus said. 'I don't like the look of this mist – it's going to make everything more difficult.'

Leta stared off across the water to where the wetlands were choked with blackgum and fern, and by great coiled spans of cordgrass and bramble. The dense swamp vapour threaded through the vegetation. Insects thrummed around it, agitated, their iridescent wings flashing an oily green. Frogs croaked and water dripped from the vines that trickled down from the canopy above.

'There's nothing natural about this mist,' she said carefully. 'I sense great evil in it. Someone works this against us...'

'Then you should be cheered,' Actinus said. He gathered up his weapons.

Leta smiled at him, eyes narrowed. 'And how do you figure that?'

'Because it means that Lord Taranis was right, and you will soon have some targets for your bow that are capable of fighting back.'

'Ha!' Leta cried. 'Was that you actually making a joke, Knight-Relictor?' She thumped her fist to his pauldron with a clash of sigmarite. 'I can't tell – you're normally as dry as the Great Parch in Aqshy. Well, if so, then every cloud has a silver lining after all.' She raised her head and whistled, and from deep in the tangled bowers of the swamps came an answering screech. 'Ripper and Strix will show us the way, if the Vigilators haven't found us a path already. Come, Actinus. After that long "rest" you should be as raring to go as my gryph-hounds!'

For two days they had slogged through the swamps, marching from the heathlands on the eastern edge of Excelsis to the borders of the fens further south, and then into the Mirkmere's humid interior. The Morruk Hills had lain ahead of them, slightly north, low and slumped things capped with fume and vapour, like the funeral barrows of ancient kings. The mist spilled down into the swamplands beneath, where the bare and saturated land, a chilly moor of reeds and rough ground patched with stagnant water, soon gave way to more tangled bogs and mires. Before long, the Stormcasts were wading through rivers of mud and slimy water that reached up to their thighs, their golden armour bespattered with filth in the grey, uncertain light. Slack ponds bubbled like a reeking stew around them. Insects droned imperturbably through the dense air: glossy-backed beetles as big as a fist, dragonflies that looked carved from chalcocite.

'I'm beginning to feel sorry for the mortals who came this way,' Leta said, huffing her way through a rattling clump of bullrushes. 'This can't have been easy for them.'

'Nor for us.' Pellion grimaced as he crushed a leech in his fist. It burst with a rancid stink, and he flicked the remains from his fingers. He held the banner rigid above his head. 'It gives you more respect for the common soldiery, I have to admit.'

'Not to forget the ordinary men and women who made it out this far,' Actinus chided them. He waded on slightly ahead of his comrades, the long line of Vindictors strung out behind them, with the Annihilators and Vanquishers bringing up the rear. He could hear the splash and slobber of their feet hiking through the muck. 'Common or otherwise, these were mere citizens braving the wilds to build their settlements. Many of them will have gone unarmed. Men and women and children,' he said, as if to himself, 'matching themselves to the savage lands of Ghur with no more than faith as their armour.'

From the ragged edgelands they entered the Mirkmere proper, the choking miasma of the swamps. Tall stands of pond cypress lurched into the sky, shutting out the light. Ropes of bindweed and bramble were laid across the paths like traps. Channels of water crept between hummocks of wet ground, with here and there solitary outcrops of standing stone or the broken trunks of trees forming a kind of route they could follow. Everything was carpeted in thick moss and lichen, and fronds of fungus quivered like agitated flesh as they passed. The light was pallid and sickly. Thick black shadows lurked in the undergrowth, in the over-hangs of the swollen trees. The air was dead, inert, every sound muffled in the mist. From far across the swampland they could hear strange and melancholic cries, despairing, and from nearer at hand came the low susurrus of the insect world, a permanent whisper. Fifty miles they had covered in their first day.

'Onwards,' Actinus said. They could cover thirty more before the light failed.

His dream still lingered as they set off deeper into the swamps. It lay there on the edge of his recollection. As they marched on, the Vindictors slinging their shields across their backs and pro-gressing single file into the stagnant water, Actinus picked idly at it, pulling the threads this way and that, focusing on one part or another before discarding it and trying to see the whole picture from a different angle.

He wasn't even sure how much of it was real. He knew Khellian and Turillos had been real; they lived in him still, vivid and alive, their faces vibrant to his memory. He could close his eyes and see Khellian's tapered jaw, the dark eyebrows, the lock of black hair looping down across her eyes, the sides of her head shaved to reveal the Ghurish tattoos imprinted on her scalp. He could see Turillos with his swords across his back, laughing, that great world-shaking boom, his black skin smouldering with an inner fire. Actinus didn't doubt them for a moment. What gave him pause was that dusty plain, the mesas rising above them, cutting out what light fell from the broken skies. There was something insubstantial about that place, vague and sketched in. What battle had they been fighting? What enemy was against them? Actinus could not even say how long ago it had been. All he could remember was the corposant blur of the lightning, the Anvil like lava beneath him, the agony of reforging. Then the long years tending to the censers and the reliquaries in Sigmaron, preparing himself for this return.

There was no history behind him, he thought. There was not even memory. There was only pain, and these vague impressions of sacrifice.

'Everything must be taken on trust,' he muttered to himself. 'It is all we have.'

He held his hand to the censer, feeling the cool certainty of the relics within. He must have that same certainty. His soul must not burn as the souls of his comrades burned. It must be like a cool and vacant flame, untroubled, inextinguishable.

'You said something, Knight-Relictor?'

He found himself marching alongside Pellion, in the centre of the Stormcast force. Like most of the troops, although unlike Actinus himself, the Knight-Vexillor had taken off his helmet against the clammy heat and had hooked it to his belt. Sweat trickled down his forehead. He held both hands to the banner, wading purposefully forward through the slime. He didn't even move a hand to brush the vines from his face as they passed beneath but ducked his head and let them carry over him instead.

'Forgive me,' Actinus said. 'An old habit, talking to myself. Leta says it's because I want the guarantee of an intelligent conversation, but I would never be so presumptuous to say as much.'

Pellion laughed, but the laughter seemed forced. They marched on in silence, Actinus looking ahead into the tangled shadows, listening to the creaking of the branches, the slop of water, the rattle of the insects. A long whooping call came from somewhere far off in the scrub. It trailed away into a shallow cry. A bird, perhaps, he thought.

'You carry yourself somewhat apart from the others,' Actinus observed. 'You do not get on with your comrades?'

Pellion looked shocked.

'I would lay down my life for them!' he spluttered. 'Without question, without doubt, I would–'

'Yes, yes,' Actinus said, holding up his hand. He smiled behind the skull-plate. 'I understand. You're a hero unparalleled, ready to sacrifice yourself at a moment's notice, and so on. Sigmar should be blessed to have such a champion... But there's a world of difference between honour and friendship, Pellion. I know the look on your face, because I feel it often enough on my own.'

The Knight-Vexillor clenched his jaw and looked away.

'And what look would that be?'

'The strain of solitude. The burden of command. All things thrive in companionship, but we are called apart all the same. A Knight-Relictor must be free to walk between all the souls of the chamber, without favour, and a Knight-Vexillor must stand as a solitary rock, banner raised high, while the chamber surges around him. They can be lonely roles to inhabit.'

Pellion's shoulders gave an almost imperceptible slump.

'The honour is greater than I ever would have imagined,' he said, 'but I confess, the burden weighs heavily as well. I miss...'

'Yes?'

Pellion frowned, as if doubting his own words.

'The simplicity of being but one warrior amongst many,' he said. 'Where your responsibilities stretch no further than the comrade at your side.'

'There are other burdens too, I sense,' Actinus said. He glanced at the young knight beside him, his furrowed brow, the doubts that so clearly ranged across his face. 'I believe I feel them myself. You question why you were taken to be reforged as one of the Thunderstrike, when others equally deserving were not.'

Pellion nodded and lowered his voice.

'It's a burden of greatness that I do not feel,' he confessed. 'Is that what I'm supposed to think, that I've been chosen by Sigmar, even beyond those who were chosen to join the ranks of the Stormcast Eternals in the first place? The honour is great, but it feels an insult to old friends to assume myself worthy of it.'

'Well,' Actinus said, resting his hand on Pellion's shoulder. 'As a wise man once said to me, the God-King fashions his tools to his purposes. It is not always given to us to understand why.'

Pellion smiled wanly. 'That at least is something I haven't lost.' He nodded towards the swampland ahead, the stew of roots and vines, the mist that rolled and broke apart as they passed through it. 'Even in a place like this, I know Sigmar sees all. He has his plan.'

They marched on in silence for a while, Pellion to Actinus' eyes now holding the banner straighter, higher, his shoulders back. Eventually, the Knight-Vexillor glanced to Actinus' belt, the sword that hung there.

'I wanted to ask,' he said, 'about the Freeguild blade you carry. It seems a curious sidearm for a Knight-Relictor?'

Actinus patted the hilt. 'Ah, I doubt when it comes to it I'll be relying on this in battle,' he said. 'No, this is… To be honest, I couldn't say. It's no more than a favour perhaps, to the wise man I mentioned earlier. A token of remembrance.'

Pellion smiled. 'Leta warned me that you were cryptic.' He laughed, genuinely this time, and Actinus was pleased to see the cares smoothed free on his face. 'I'll enquire no further.'

Actinus inclined his head in thanks. He kept his hand on the blade. Why *had* he brought it with him? Just because Jonas had gifted it to him, and he didn't want to disappoint him? He was sure it was not a relic, no matter what the old man had said. In his censer he had a fragment of thigh bone from a Sigmarite priest who had single-handedly defied an Exalted Deathbringer in the depths of the Realmgate Wars. That was certainly a relic; centuries of veneration had made it so, if nothing else. Was it enough then just to *believe* that something held the sacred fire to make it worthy of reverence? Time sacralises all things, it could be said.

'Hmm,' Actinus mumbled. 'It could be, it could be...'

Pellion glanced at him but said nothing else, and then his train of thought was broken. As they came near a spread of firmer ground, elevated above the dank sheets of standing water, the Prime from the Vigilator contingent came splashing back to the head of the column.

'Knight-Relictor,' he cried. 'You should see this, up ahead.'

'What is it, Cadmus?'

'We've found one of the human settlements,' he said, looking grave. 'It's as we feared...'

CHAPTER FIVE

It was a small place, no more than a scattering of huts around a muddy central square – a scrap of civilisation planted in the depths of the wilderness. None of the houses was higher than a single storey. At the front of the square stood a trading post and a small temple. Further back there were cramped rows of housing, each hut abutting its neighbour. Doors listed from broken hinges. Windows were shattered. Some of the huts had been reclaimed by the swamps and were wreathed in bindweed; Actinus could see many of them already tipping slantwise into the greedy grasp of the mire. There was a smell in the air of dead, abandoned things, of mould and damp and rotten food. Overlaying everything was the stink of the swamp-fog, the smell of burnt hair, scorched bone, death.

'Palmer's Creek,' Actinus said. It was utterly deserted.

He knew the crusades into the wilderness were establishing more permanent settlements – tough, fortified towns planted on key nexus points of geomantic energy – but there was nothing in Palmer's Creek that suggested anything other than the failure of hope over experience. Amberstone Watch, for example, would prove a formidable outpost in time, but there was something pitiful about this place. He felt his throat thicken at the thought of the pilgrims who had tried to build here, the crushing realisation they must have felt that they had made a mistake. Or perhaps he was being too harsh on them. They had set up their temple, they had built their trading post, and they had thrown up their houses. Maybe they had set their faces to the swamp instead, and defied it for as long as they could?

The Stormcasts moved in, cautiously. The Vigilators fanned left and right, crossbows primed, short blades in their left hands. The Vindictors gathered around a squat and irregular pillar in the middle of the square. It looked to Actinus like the raw material for a statue, a representation of the village arbiter, perhaps, or even of Sigmar himself. Daubed on the side of the menhir was a crude glyph, the suggestion of fierce eyes, a leering mouth. Actinus looked on it with distaste.

'Greenskins?' Leta said at his side. Her bow was now charged in her arms, thrumming with restrained power.

'I don't recognise the design,' Actinus said. He ran his armoured fingers across the stone, smearing the glyph. 'Ashes,' he said.

'The orruks have tribes unnumbered, not to mention the grots. It could be something we just haven't encountered before. It could even be Sylvaneth. The tree-kin have no love for those who encroach on their sacred spaces.'

'Possibly...'

'Knight-Relictor!' Pellion called. He was on the other side of the square, standing outside the smashed doorway to one of the huts. He had rested his banner against the wall of the building and now beckoned Actinus over.

Actinus had to stoop to pass through the doorway. It was dark inside the hovel, the packed-earth floor still soft and springy underfoot. The shutters had been closed, but the window glass lay in shards across the ground. The tables and chairs had been roughly thrown aside, but otherwise there were no signs of violence – no blood spatters on the wall, no bodies, no splintered furniture from any fighting.

Pellion crouched to scoop up some tattered cloth: a Freeguild tunic, in the forest-green colours of the Iron Bulls. One sleeve was ripped, the buttons were missing, and the tunic was smeared in grime.

'One of our missing company?' Pellion said.

Leta, standing in the doorway, peered into the gloom and grimaced.

'This is a waste of our time,' she said. 'There isn't a hope in the underworlds that any of those troops are still alive. Not out here.'

'And yet,' Actinus said, 'one of them made it this far back.' He looked at the windows and the listing door, scanned the ground at his feet for signs.

A cry rent the air from the other side of the settlement.

Actinus sprinted from the hut, Leta and Pellion close behind him. The cry had degenerated into a despairing sob, and as they crossed by the plinth in the centre of the square he saw Cadmus dragging two men back into the village from the scrub on its outskirts. They were struggling against the Vigilator-Prime's iron grip. Although Cadmus was doing his best to be gentle, the men screeched and cried as if the Stormcast warrior were intent on their murder. Cadmus, a forthright fighter at the best of times, was losing his patience.

'For Sigmar's sake!' he muttered. He shook them both. 'Stop your bleating – I'm not going to hurt you!'

'Let them go, Cadmus,' Actinus said. He stood with his arms spread out, palms open and empty, Leta and Pellion taking careful position on either side of him. He could see the other Vigilators dispersing into the undergrowth on the edge of the settlement, in case the captives tried to run.

Cadmus freed his grip on their arms and slowly stepped back as the two men sprawled in the dirt. One of them, young and as thin as a reed, with a crazed look in his eyes, tried to scramble back into the scrub with a frantic scream, but Cadmus grabbed him and set him back beside his fellow. He buried his face in his hands and started crying.

The other man glared at them warily through a tangled fringe of black hair. He had a month of straggly beard on his chin, and his cheeks were hollow with hunger. A livid scar was drawn against his brow, fresh and still weeping. He knelt there, hands splayed in the dirt, looking as if he were just waiting for the signal to run. His shirt was heavily stained with mud and sap, with a patch of what looked like old blood on the torn collar. He was wearing Freeguild breeches, Actinus saw.

'We mean you no harm,' Actinus said. 'You see us, don't you? You see what we are?'

The black-haired man slowly nodded his head. He was shivering, although whether with fear or cold, Actinus couldn't have said. He considered removing his helmet and going bareheaded like the other Stormcasts, but decided against it. There were certain standards to keep up, after all. What was the Relictor Temple without a little mystery?

'My name is Knight-Relictor Actinus, of the Taranite Chamber, the Hammers of Sigmar,' he said. He indicated the others. 'This is Vigilator-Prime Cadmus, Knight-Judicator Leta, and Knight-Vexillor Pellion. We have come from Excelsis.' He peered at the man. Was he even taking this in? 'We have come to rescue you.'

The black-haired man said nothing, only stared at them with that same feral glare. The younger man uncovered his face and looked up at them. He shook as he raised his hands to rub his face.

A twitch spasmed in his cheek and plucked at his lips. His mouth cracked open. A few of his teeth were broken. He was gurgling.

No, Actinus realised. He was *laughing*.

The laugh tore at his throat, bubbling over his lips like vomit. He raised his trembling hands to the heavens and screeched like an animal, eyes wild.

'Praise them!' he cried. 'Praise them with great praise, we are saved! We are saved!'

The officer's name was Holger Beck, the captain of the Iron Bulls company that had been sent to investigate the disappearances. It was hard for Actinus to believe, but the younger man, Caspar Hallan, was actually a Sigmarite priest. He had lost his robes at some point in his ordeal and was instead garbed in a filthy shirt and a tattered loincloth. The Freeguild tunic they had found in the hut was Holger's; both men had been resting there when they heard the Stormcasts approach and had run off into the scrub rather than risk seeing what came near.

'Ignore him,' Holger said, shovelling food into his mouth as they sat in the temple. He nodded at Caspar, who was sitting by the altar, muttering to himself with a lopsided grin on his face. The priest had seemingly no understanding of his surroundings. 'He lost his mind a good while back. Didn't you, Caspar?' he called. The priest giggled and shook his head. 'Don't bloody blame him. There were times I nearly felt I was losing it myself.'

The temple was curiously untouched, something else that surprised Actinus. If the settlement had been taken by greenskins, then he would have assumed a base level of desecration, vandalism and looting. Instead, the plain wooden building still had its complement of benches, its simple altar. The prayer books may have been mouldering in the heat and the damp, but otherwise they were untouched. Curious, he thought. Most curious.

Actinus and Leta sat with them, while one of the Vigilators brought more food. The scouts carried iron rations to sustain themselves in the wilderness: hard tack and dried meat, but better than a gourmet meal to the Freeguild captain as he filled his belly. He guzzled a flask of water, a look of ecstasy on his face.

'Can you tell us what happened?' Actinus asked him. Caspar gave a muffled shout, and quickly covered his mouth. He started weeping. Holger swallowed and wiped his lips with the back of his hand. His jaw trembled. 'How far into the swamps did you make it? Did you see any sign of the settlers?'

Holger shook his head. 'We tried pressing through the scrub on the path from Excelsis, as you did,' he said, 'but it was too difficult. We tracked further north until we met the channels coming out of the Morruk Hills, lashed some rafts together, poled down the swamp water towards Fort Harrow from the west. Bypassed the settlements here, but we thought we might double back and reach Junivatown before heading on to the fort.'

He clasped his hands together to stop them shaking.

'Gods, then...' He drew a breath. 'Then we were hit.'

Actinus watched him closely. The fear on his face was unmistakable. As he closed his eyes, Actinus knew the captain was reliving every moment of his torment.

'What hit you?' he asked gently. 'Did you see what they were?'

'Ghosts, I thought at first,' Holger said with effort. He rubbed a hand across his stubbled jaw. 'Pale, wavering in the gloom, like haunted faces peering at us, screeching... But they were real enough, solid enough to hold a blade and string a bow. I didn't get a good look at them at first.' He glanced at the ragged priest, still weeping by the altar. 'I tried to lead some of the survivors back towards the rafts, tried to make a fighting withdrawal...' He coughed. 'Anyway, in moments we were overwhelmed. Something knocked me out, and when I came to, we were all chained together, forced on through the swamps in the torchlight. They weren't swamp spirits – I could see that. More like...'

The priest shrieked, raising his hands to the temple ceiling. Actinus couldn't tell if he was laughing or weeping.

'They were spirits, spirits of the dead!' he howled. 'Spirits of swamp and glade, come to punish us for encroaching on their sacred ground. Yes!'

'They were orruks,' Holger whispered. 'I'm sure of it. But not like *any* I've ever seen before. Lank, dripping things, loping through the mire as if they were born to it. Swimming through the water like frogs, faces painted white, some of them holding these shields with these *awful* leering things painted on them... And the way they moved us, the way they *talked*... I couldn't understand it, but you could tell they were making plans, that they had a strategy of some kind.'

Leta leaned over and muttered to Actinus, 'That doesn't sound like any orruk I've ever met.'

Actinus nodded. 'Continue, please,' he said to Holger.

'That night march was one of the worst moments of my life,' he said. He had put down the plate of food, but he grasped the flask as if it were a cup of firewater and his life depended on it. 'Any stragglers were hamstrung and left in the swamp to die, eaten by the leopard eels. They thrashed us on with cudgels, and if you cried out, they'd cut your throat. I know greenskins are a brutal race, but this was something else. This wasn't even cruelty. It was just... it was just pragmatism.' He looked up under his tangled fringe. 'A total indifference to life.'

He went on. 'The next day we reached a camp of some kind, deep in the wetlands to the north, raised up on reed beds with these floating outpost islands all around it. They put us in cages. There were civilians there as well, settlers from the towns we'd been sent to investigate.'

'How many?' Actinus asked.

'It was hard to tell – a hundred, maybe? Maybe more, maybe less. More than half my company was dead, and there were only about a hundred of us left. At night they dragged some of us out to fight, two at a time. A ring of torches, a bone knife tossed between you… If you refused, they cut your hands off and ate them in front of you. Everyone fought after that. I fought, Sigmar help me…' He raised the flask to his mouth and took a deep draught. 'They were laughing, if you could call it laughter. Hacking and gurgling away to themselves, sitting beyond the torchlight, just these pale wavering faces grinning at us.

'I don't know how long we were there, days maybe. They hadn't fed us, had barely given us water. I thought we were going to starve. Then, one evening at dusk, they opened the cages and dragged about half of the survivors out, civilians and soldiers, shackled them all together. And then… then they–'

The captain choked, dropped the flask and covered his face. His shoulders trembled as he forced down the sob. Actinus was moved; the courage it took to relive such horrors should not be underestimated. Very gently, he placed his hand on Holger's shoulder.

'Come, my friend,' he said. 'The worst is over now. You are safe.'

By the altar, the priest rolled onto his side and howled with laughter. He raked at his face with hands like claws.

'We must depart!' he screamed. 'Make penance for our outrage, beg forgiveness of leaf and vine!'

'Pellion,' Actinus said. 'Perhaps you could take the priest and find him somewhere to rest. Your presence, the presence of your banner, may comfort him.'

Pellion nodded. Gently, he stooped to pick the shivering mortal up from the floor and carried him out of the temple.

Holger had regained himself by this time. His face was a mask.

'They bound the others together,' the captain said again, 'and then they cut out their tongues, one by one. That's the image I'm left with,' he said quietly. 'That pile of severed tongues, glistening in the torchlight...' He shook his head. 'They marched them off into the swamps, heading to Sigmar knows where. Sacrifice, meat for some awful feast – I dread to think. And then one of them, one of the orruks, loped over to the cages and grinned at us, those horrible yellow tusks, the white paint flaking on its face. It mimed eating, you know? Dipping its fingers to its open hand and raising them to its mouth. And it said, in something like our speech, some horrible parody of it, it said, "*'Ungry?*" And it... it picked up all those tongues, and threw them into the cages!'

He looked at Actinus. His face was drawn with horror.

'I hadn't eaten for *days,*' he said. 'Do you understand? Sigmar forgive me, but I hadn't eaten for *days!*'

They camped for the night in the remains of Palmer's Creek. Leta was for pressing on immediately and bringing these monstrous greenskins to battle, but Actinus knew that the mortals would not manage another step without proper rest. Even so, the Freeguild captain had been incredulous when he heard of the Stormcasts' intentions to advance. His cry had echoed through the temple.

'I've lost near three hundred men to these swamps! We need to go back to Excelsis *now*, don't you understand? Not tomorrow, not at first light, but right now!'

'Don't you crave vengeance for your comrades?' Cadmus had said. He hadn't quite managed to mask his disdain. Actinus had held up a palm.

'Be reasonable,' he said. 'Captain Beck has been through an appalling ordeal. He is weary. We will rest here tonight and make our decision in the morning.'

Now, as the huts and hovels of the settlement slumbered in

the eerie flicker of the torchlight, Actinus and Leta walked the bounds, ensuring the guard was alert for any encroachment. Some of Cadmus' Vigilators had formed a picket out in the scrub, while Hektor's Vindictors patrolled the central square. The Annihilators and Vanquishers were further back by the temple, ready to respond with a flank attack should anything make it through.

The night pulsed around them like a living thing, close and sultry. Moths as big as their hands raggedly fluttered through the air. Water dripped from the ivy that strangled the huts, and from somewhere far off in the glades came that same hooting, whooping call Actinus had heard the day before. Not a bird, he was quite sure of that now.

'You believe the Freeguilder's story?' Leta said. 'He strikes me as a coward, who ran away as soon as the fighting started. There were probably no more than half a dozen orruks from the Shatter Shins, who'd strayed into the swamps by mistake. The rest of his tale is just the phantoms of his fear getting the better of him, or he's made it up to cover his dereliction.'

Actinus demurred. 'Captain Beck strikes me as a man who has been profoundly frightened. I doubt if he is inventing this ordeal, or even exaggerating it as much as you think.' He thought for a moment. 'He is not a brave man, no. But nor, I think, is he a coward.'

'Only a coward would run from a prison camp and leave his men behind,' Leta scorned. 'What sort of leader does that?'

Holger had told them of his escape, prising his way out of his cage at night, with Caspar by his side, soon after the other prisoners had been led away. Actinus acknowledged Leta's point: a true leader does not leave his troops to die in his stead, while he seeks safety.

'Even so,' he said, 'you judge him too harshly. He is a mortal man, while we have Sigmar's lightning in our veins. It is not given to everyone to be a hero.'

'Hmm,' Leta grunted. 'Where is he now anyway? Sloped back off to Excelsis?'

'He is asleep in one of the huts,' Actinus said. 'He has no intention of travelling alone.' They had made a full circuit of the settlement and arrived again at the porch of the temple. Actinus nodded to Helican, the Vanquisher-Prime, who stood by the temple's doorway. The massive Stormcast warrior held his two-handed blade upright by the pommel, the sword planted in the ground. Immobile, resolute, like a statue in his stained golden armour. 'He has been wandering in the wilds for weeks, and it's a miracle he still lives. Sigmar evidently watches over him.'

A foetid breeze uncurled across the settlement, ruffling the torchlight. Shadows writhed across the square. The trees beyond the settlement shivered, their leaves scraping together with a sound like a blade being sharpened.

'And that?' Leta said, nodding towards the pillar in the centre of the square. Actinus looked; he could see the priest, Caspar, his rags like a grave shroud, picking his way past the wary Vindictors, muttering to himself. 'Does Sigmar watch over him too?'

The two knights stood there and watched as Caspar paused by the pillar, a look of holy wonder on his face. Slowly, very slowly, he reached out and dabbed his fingers at the glyph. With more urgency, laughing softly to himself, he smeared the glyph away until his hands were covered in pale ash; and then, gleefully, he smeared the ash across his face. Flecked by torchlight, he turned to them and waved across the square, his face like the grinning visage of some tormented gheist.

'I'm afraid,' Actinus said, as the priest capered off into the darkness, 'that is a question to which I do not have the answer.'

CHAPTER SIX

Dawn leaked across the Mirkmere as if ashamed of itself, creeping over vine and bower, over the matted roofs of the huts and hovels of Palmer's Creek. Dark shadows faded to a lighter grey, and the sickly greens and yellows of the swamp were revealed in all their pallid glory. A thick fume had risen overnight, billowing in across the stretches of standing water and making the whole village seem no more than a sodden island floating in a sea of fog. Actinus crossed the square, noting the smeared glyph on the central pillar. He passed by the Vindictors as they checked their weapons and prepared for the day's march, nodding to Hektor, who clashed his gauntlet to his breastplate.

'The night was quiet?' Actinus asked.

'As the grave,' Hektor said.

'Just as well we're not in Shyish then, or I would be worried.'

Hektor laughed, and Actinus allowed himself a thin smile.

He stooped to enter a hut on the other side of the square. Holger Beck was sprawled out on a rough mattress on the floor. He looked exhausted. His eyes were sunken in their dark sockets, and his face was lined and drawn, his clothes still ragged and stained with mud. He sat up as the Knight-Relictor entered, blocking out the light from the doorway. Actinus noted the spasm of shock on his face, the usual human reaction whenever confronted with Sigmar's chosen. No matter how used to it they were, it was hard for a mortal to disguise their natural fear.

'I would ask if you had slept well, if the answer was not so obvious,' Actinus said. He stood back from the mattress, not wanting to loom too closely over the captain. 'At the very least, I hope you managed to get some rest.'

'Better than I've had for weeks,' Holger muttered. 'Although it feels I'll never have a good night's sleep now for as long as I live.'

'And your companion, the priest?'

Holger rubbed his eyes. 'I don't know. I've had no sign of him since yesterday. I don't think he sleeps any more, in any case. The nightmares...'

Actinus pictured Caspar grinning in the darkness. He thought of that blasted plain under the copper light, his friends dying around him.

'Well,' he said. 'I'm sure he will turn up over the course of the day.'

Holger looked at him with an anxious expression. 'You've made your decision?' he asked. 'We're going to head back to the city?'

'I'm afraid not,' Actinus said. He looked around for somewhere to sit, but apart from a rickety wooden table the hut was bare, and he doubted if it would hold his weight. 'We must press on into the swamps until we reach Fort Harrow.'

Holger's face creased, and for a moment Actinus thought he might actually cry. He clasped his hands together as if he were praying.

'For the love of Sigmar, we must go back to Excelsis,' he pleaded.

'If you're determined to go on, then at the very least give me an escort back!'

'I cannot stretch my force too thinly, Captain Beck. I'm sorry, but if what you say is true, then I will need every warrior at my disposal. There will be no escort.'

'Then what in the name of the gods am I to do! Stay here on my own? I'll be dead the moment you leave!'

Fear gave him courage; Holger snapped up from the mattress and thrust a finger at the Knight-Relictor. It reached no higher than his chest.

'It's all right for you! You and the other Stormborn, you've the power of the gods in you – none of this is any more than a walk in the bloody park! What about me? What can I do – what can flesh and blood do against all this... this *horror!*'

He collapsed onto the mattress, wringing his hands. Sweat had broken out across his face, thick, cold droplets of fear that trickled down into his beard. His bottom lip was slack and trembling.

'I'm a coward,' he whispered. 'I've always been a damned coward – I don't deserve my rank in the slightest. You know,' he said, looking up at Actinus, 'I spent most of the siege hiding in a bloody cellar. I ran away from my unit then, and I've done it again now. I left everyone to die while I saved my own skin.' He covered his face in his hands. 'I am afraid,' he mumbled. 'I just don't want to die.'

Actinus stepped forward and crouched before him.

'It is not given to us to decide when we live and when we die,' he said. 'We have only one choice, and that is to face death with courage and dignity, or with disgrace. Twice you have chosen to dishonour your regiment and dishonour your soul. Let the third choice be the one that redeems them all.'

He took the Freeguild blade from his belt and passed it to the captain, hilt first.

'This is a sacred relic from one of the temples in Sigmaron,' he said. 'It was given to me by a priest I know, a great man and a great servant of Sigmar. Take it, please. I believe it will help you.'

Holger uncovered his face and looked up. With a shaking hand he reached for the sword.

'A relic?'

'It belonged to a young officer called Aldert Sommer,' Actinus said. 'He was much as you are – untried, selfish perhaps, not a brave man. But during the siege, when the moment came and his comrades and his city were threatened, he drew on a well of courage he didn't know he possessed. His men were dead around him, he was alone, but he held the bridge at Stormstone Cross as long as it took for his regiment to withdraw, when the first breach in the bastion was made.'

Holger held the sword gingerly, gazing down at the blade.

'Stormstone Cross,' he said. 'I know it well… A nice part of the city. There are cloistered gardens there, by the canal, a very pleasant little tavern next to the bridge called the Lock and Key…'

'Aldert would not have had time to take in the sights. He was outnumbered ten to one, but he fought with every ounce of his strength until he was cut down. He saved the lives of hundreds of men and women. He was a hero,' Actinus said, squeezing Holger's shoulder. 'And his heroism sacralised that blade. I give it to you now, to aid you in your struggle. Use it, Captain Beck. Draw strength from it. Honour it.'

'I… I will,' Holger said quietly. He breathed deeply and seemed to settle himself, the sword clutched in his hand. 'I can make no promises, but I will do my best.'

'That is all any of us can do.'

'Thank you, my lord.'

Actinus smiled to himself as he stood. 'I am no lord,' he said. 'I am merely a knight.'

He left the hut, and as he walked back across the square he

thought: *A lie it may be, but... after all, a lie can still profit the good if it is employed in the service of truth...*

He found Leta on the edge of the settlement, standing where a dirt path petered out into the waterlogged soil. Sprigs of wiry grass stabbed up through the layering of slime, and the vines hung heavy from the canopy, coiled in ivy. Cadmus' Vigilators were preparing to head out, in advance of the main contingent, and they slipped past the Knight-Judicator as she stood there calling Ripper's name into the depths of the swampland. Strix sat by her side, chittering nervously and clacking his beak.

'Leta?' Actinus said. 'We'll be moving out shortly with the main force. Is everything all right?'

She scratched impatiently at her scar, still staring out into the creeping fog. Her golden armour was stained with grime and glistened with a covering of dew. 'Ripper's been missing since last night,' she said. 'The two of them went hunting after dusk, and only Strix came back.'

Actinus looked out onto the brooding veil of mist. Here and there he could see a patch of thorny scrub, a twisted tree lurking in the gloom. As he watched the Vigilators set out, he saw that the swampland was more stable on this side of the settlement, less of a quagmire, and the water only came up to their knees. That was something, at least.

'Should we be worried?' he asked. Leta shook her head.

'He can take care of himself, but even so... it's unusual.'

'The priest has gone missing as well,' Actinus said. 'Captain Beck hasn't seen him since yesterday, although given what we saw of him last night, I'm unsure whether we should be concerned.'

Leta turned to him, frowning. 'I don't like it,' she said. 'Any of it. If you twisted my arm, and if you promised not to tell Pellion, I could be forced to admit that I'm very slightly uneasy.'

Actinus gave a dry laugh. 'Only very slightly though, I'm sure.'

Just then, drifting dolefully across the swamps, came that same low, whooping call he had heard three times already. Leta looked at him, her eyebrow raised. Actinus could hear the soft splashing of the Vigilators as they moved off through the mist.

'Do you think they're watching us?' Leta asked, her voice low. 'Whatever they are?'

'Almost certainly,' Actinus said. 'Still, we have little choice but to carry on as planned. We'll make for the east, bypassing Junivatown, and then head up to approach Fort Harrow from the south. If there are any survivors from Captain Beck's company, or from the settlements, they will have gathered there, I'm sure of it.' He turned to go. 'We'll have an end of this,' he said. 'One way or another.'

The mist thickened as they marched, bringing with it a stench of rot and sulphur. The land around them was just a vague backdrop draped with weeds and dripping with water. Greasy black birds unravelled from the trees above them and clattered off deeper into the swamps, screeching at their trespass. Leopard eels slithered through the mire, no more than a humped crest breaking the surface of the water. For the most part they kept a wary distance, but deeper into the morning Thestis, one of the Vindictors out on the flank, was dragged under by two of them working in concert. There was a splash and a muffled cry, and then the swamp water foamed with blood. After a moment of thrashing chaos, Thestis emerged with one of the eels skewered on her sword, the other gliding off into the shelter of an overhang near a copse of mouldering trees. She grinned, her sword dripping with slime.

'First blood!' she cried. Actinus raised a fist in salute.

Although the Vigilators still forged ahead, seeking the best paths through the mire, the remainder of the Stormcast force moved closer together, their pace dictated by Holger Beck's less forth-right speed. The swamp water only came up to the Stormcasts' knees, but for the captain it was nearer his waist, and he had to wade through holding Actinus' elbow for balance. Actinus had held back to accompany him, not wanting the mortal soldier to feel abandoned in the midst of what must have seemed to him a troop of demigods. He had the relic sword sheathed in his belt, Actinus saw, and he had done his best to tidy up what remained of his uniform. In the absence of its buttons – 'Stolen by those monsters, though gods know what for,' he'd said. 'Coin, no doubt.' – he had tied the tunic together with twine. He was a captain again, Actinus thought. Though his company was gone, he would try to honour them in this, if nothing else.

'Still desperate to get back to the city, Captain Beck?' Actinus asked him, as the Freeguilder staggered on at his side.

'I've been desperate to get back the minute I received my orders to leave,' he grumbled.

'Are you Excelsis-born?'

Holger bridled, thrusting out his chin. 'I may have been born in Squallside, but my family are Azyrites, if you must know,' he said. 'We're no Reclaimed, we're of a right and proper lineage.'

Actinus bowed his head. 'No offence was meant,' he said. 'For us, lineage is perhaps something left behind when we are forged. We forget how important it can be for some.'

'What were you before…' Holger asked, tentatively. Actinus glanced at him and he looked away, swallowing. 'I apologise,' he said. 'The question must be insensitive. I didn't think…'

'Not insensitive,' Actinus told him. He reached out an arm to lift a vine that trailed across their path. 'Just not one I can answer. It is different for all of us, but the process of reforging can make our memories like dreams – strange, and sometimes hard to grasp. Personally, I choose not to dwell on it.'

Holger nodded. He looked chastened, somehow, Actinus thought. As if he had peered too closely at a mystery best left unsolved.

'You're all very different from what I thought you would be,' the captain said. 'I've rarely seen any of you up close, and you always seem so... well, so terrifying, if I had to be honest. But you, Knight-Relictor, you seem much more human than I would ever have assumed.'

'We are what we are,' Actinus said quietly. 'And I will take that as a compliment.'

Holger stumbled suddenly, flopping forward in the swamp water.

'Damn it all to the underworlds and back!' he spluttered. He grimaced and wiped a string of weed from his jaw. 'You know I once heard a duardin engineer back in Excelsis talk about how they could drain these bloody swamps, some machine or other they could use to just... I don't know, to just suck the water out. The Kharadron will have some engine that could do it, I'm sure.'

'Where would they put it?' Pellion said, approaching. He marched slowly on Holger's other side, his banner still raised high and clipping the ragged ceiling of the canopy. 'The water, I mean. Once they've sucked it all out.'

Holger airily waved his hand. 'I'll leave that bit to the duardin engineers. Pour it into the ocean at Excelsis harbour for all I care.'

'These swamps alone are near a hundred leagues in all directions,' Actinus said, mildly. 'No one holds duardin engineering in greater respect than I, but I doubt even their ingenuity could manage such a feat. Alas,' he said, holding out his hand as the winged spear of a dragonfly alighted briefly upon it, 'I fear they will always be with us.'

'More's the damned pity,' Holger grumbled.

'I don't know,' Actinus said. He looked at the swaying foliage, the sullen waters and the dripping beams of the swamp mahogany, the flash and scatter of frogs and reptiles slipping out of their path. 'In the right circumstances, there is beauty to be found here, I'm sure.'

'Perhaps, Knight-Relictor,' Pellion offered, 'it has just been well hidden in all this mist?'

Actinus laughed. Holger snorted and shook his head.

'This is far from any natural mist,' he said. 'Those creatures brewed this up, I saw them. A great big stinking cauldron in the middle of their camp, and some monstrous orruk savage slopping all sorts of bits and pieces into it. Poisons, elixirs, body parts, and I don't know what else. That's how I escaped – the smoke hid me as I slipped out into the swamps.'

Pellion scowled and looked at Actinus. 'There's sorcerous intent in it,' he said. 'I have no doubts there.'

'All this from one cauldron?' Actinus said. 'I find that hard to believe.'

Holger bared his teeth in a grin that was part black humour, part creeping fear.

'Maybe there's more than one,' he said. 'Did you think of that?'

'Knight-Relictor!' a voice cried out of the mists ahead. A moment later Cadmus came splashing through the waters. There was a scream further off, not of fear or terror, but of unbridled rage. Actinus felt his heart lurch and he drew his sword.

'Cadmus,' he said. 'What's happening?'

The Vigilator-Prime, his helmet secured to his belt, looked appalled. He glanced back the way he had come. There was another scream, a string of bellowed invective. Actinus recognised Leta's voice.

'You'd better see this,' Cadmus said.

'Lead the way.' Actinus disengaged himself and turned to Holger. 'It may be time to draw that sword, Captain Beck,' he said. The Freeguilder blanched, and with a trembling hand unsheathed the blade.

They ploughed on through the muck, the rearguard Vanquishers warily hefting their great two-handed swords, the Annihilators their bludgeoning hammers and shields. Actinus sprinted ahead, as fast as he was able through the sucking mud.

The mists parted around him. Further on he could see a dim tableau of Vigilators arranged around a solitary tree, a spindly blackgum capped with a froth of serrated leaves. Leta was there, and she had drawn her bow. She aimed off into the shadows that surrounded them, the nocked arrow glowing with celestial fire and casting an eerie glimmer on the scene.

'I'll kill you all!' she hissed into the mist. 'I'll pin your filthy hides to the walls of my chambers, you scum! I'll kill every last one of you!'

'Knight-Judicator,' Actinus said firmly. 'Compose yourself. Are we under attack?'

'Not yet,' Leta cried. Her teeth were bared, the great scar across her mouth savagely twisting her lip. Sparks danced in her eyes, the flicker of lightning. Strix circled her legs, agitated, chittering to himself. 'They taunt us, Actinus! Look what they've done!'

He stepped past her. There, nailed to the tree, his legs broken and twisted around to point off towards the north, was the corpse of Ripper, her gryph-hound. His head had been cut off, and the poor creature had been disembowelled. Long ropes of intestine looped down to the mud at the base of the tree. Above the gryph-hound, painted on the bark in its blood, was another of the leering glyphs they had seen back in Palmer's Creek.

'Look what they did,' Leta said. She lowered her bow, and her face was like iron. 'Promise me, Actinus. Promise that you will not hold me back, when the time comes.'

Actinus glanced off into the gloom that surrounded them, the creeping mist that sat like a lid on the swamps. Everything seemed quiet now, poised, as if waiting. His eye was caught by something slipping back into the shadows, far across the water – a glimpse of a pale face, masked in white. Caspar, he thought. Or something else entirely…

'We will go on,' he said to Cadmus. 'North now. Fort Harrow is not much further.'

He looked at Leta. 'I promise,' he said.

CHAPTER SEVEN

They pressed on, wary now, until the dusk began to fall. The darkness drifted in through the canopy of the trees and the light began to fall away. Beyond the shuttering mist and the branches above them, Actinus could feel the Cursed Skies churning in their malevolent haze. He wondered how his Stormcast force would seem from that elevated perspective, to Sigmar himself perhaps, peering through the murk. Would they appear in all this vast and deadly profusion as no more than a speck of gold glinting in a field of mud? Or would they seem as Actinus knew them to be, like a light forging through the darkness, casting back the shadows wherever they appeared?

He glanced round at Pellion with the banner held high, Leta with her unslung bow, her scarred face set in a steely grimace, Hektor and his Vindictors marching with resolute tread, hacking through the brush. None of them were deterred. Even Captain Beck, struggling to keep up, his new sword held with both hands upon the hilt, had in many ways risen to the moment. He still looked scared, his eyes darting to the shadows in the undergrowth, but his jaw was set. He was still here, still pressing on. That had to count for something, a point of credit in the ledger of his soul.

'It won't be long now,' Actinus said to him. 'Fort Harrow is near.'

They marched on for a few more hours into the darkness, the Vigilators no longer ranging so far ahead but keeping closer to the main contingent. Eventually Actinus saw a glow up ahead, a faint amber haze that was diffused by the vapour of the mist, sparkling in the black glades almost like the sunrise. About twenty yards on, at the limit of visibility, he could see Cadmus and his Vigilators strung out along the treeline before a wider clearing, all of them crouching in the undergrowth with their weapons drawn. He crept closer to them, Holger by his side.

'The fort is just ahead,' Cadmus said in a whisper, 'on the other side of the clearing.'

Actinus squinted into the swamp-fog draped across the beaten ground before them. He had the dim impression of wooden walls about twenty feet away across an apron of cleared land, a palisade lashed together from sharpened stakes and tree trunks, rising from the mist like a breaker in the sea. Torchlight wavered at the top of the walls, and here and there he could see shadowed figures standing at watch. There was a wooden gate built into the wall and a ditch running around the circumference of the fort. The wood was stained black with moisture, and although the clearing itself was utterly silent Actinus could hear the drip of water off in the undergrowth behind him, the gurgling croak of bloaters and the rustle of swamp rats. No noise came from the fort, neither the clink of steel from pacing sentries nor the quiet grumble of soldiers passing the time.

Leta sidled up on Actinus' left, pushing Holger out of the way. Strix bounded close, snarling, but she calmed him with a word.

'The fort looks unscathed,' she whispered. 'No signs of any violence.'

'One of my men has scouted round the other side,' Cadmus told them quietly, 'and there's nothing there either. The walls are intact, no breaches, no damage.'

'Then whatever happened to the settlements has bypassed Fort Harrow,' Actinus mused. 'Does that seem likely, I wonder?'

'Well, I don't like it for one,' Holger muttered. He gripped his sword and stared past the Stormcast warriors into the fog. 'Something's not right. If they were expecting trouble, there should be more troops on the walls.'

Leta scoffed at his side. 'What do you suggest we do then, captain – run away?'

Holger scowled, and Actinus held up a hand for silence.

'Like it or not, here we are,' he said. 'Very well then, let us make ourselves known.'

He stood up and stepped out of the treeline, slowly crossing the beaten ground with his hands open at his side. Behind him, fanning out across the clearing, the rest of the Stormcasts emerged from the swampland.

'I am Knight-Relictor Actinus Astrapon, of the Hammers of Sigmar,' he called out, high and clear. 'In the name of Sigmar and Lord-Imperatant Taranis, open your gates and give us entry. We are friends.'

Warily he watched the crest of the palisade, where the silhouettes of the sentries stood. His words vanished into the mist. The sentries did not react; they were just shadows on the cusp of the firelight, smears of darkness against the golden fume of the lamps.

'Do you hear me?'

There was a faint cry then, wailing softly over the walls. Another, and then another – indecipherable, anguished.

'There are people in there,' Holger muttered. He stood by Actinus' elbow, as if he wouldn't risk being even a pace away from him.

'Then let us go and introduce ourselves,' Actinus said.

He drew his sword, signalled to the Vindictors to advance. Hektor calmly ordered the formation and the Stormcast warriors unslung their shields, fanning out into a line ten wide and two deep. Actinus dragged Holger back into the lee of the phalanx, following as the Vindictors marched towards the gate, the Annihilators on the left flank and the Vanquishers on the right. Cadmus sprinted off to join his Vigilators, covering the rear in skirmish order.

Actinus stared up at the shadows of the sentries, fifteen feet above them, willing them to move, to issue a challenge – anything. But they stayed as they were, slumped forward, leaning on the sharpened stakes of the palisade, and as they approached the walls he could see why.

They were all dead. They were just corpses impaled on stakes, their spears and swords lashed to their wrists, steel helmets rakishly askew on rotting heads.

'By all the gods...' Holger hissed.

'Are you seeing this, Knight-Relictor?' Leta called. She had her bow drawn, blazing arrow aimed at the dead men on the walls.

'I see it,' Actinus said.

The wailing continued, a frail cry rising over the blackened walls.

'The gate is barred,' Hektor called. 'Do we force a breach, Knight-Relictor?'

'Bring it down,' Actinus said. He turned as he walked, scanning the shadows on the other side of the clearing, the latticework of weeds and branches, the tangle of the dripping vines. Inside his helmet, he could feel the sweat trickling down his forehead. Every moment he expected an arrow to come lancing out of the dark, a spear, a bellowed war cry, but nothing came.

The Vindictors stepped up their pace as they approached the gate, sprinting now, shields out-thrust, and they smashed into the swamp-rotten wood. The twin doors of the gate burst back upon their hinges with a splintering crash.

The Vindictors funnelled through and re-formed into a wide semicircle on the other side of the stockade. Actinus calmly followed, striding past them. As the rest of the Stormcasts entered he cast his eyes around the remains of Fort Harrow.

A pall of smoke clung to the ground. There was a stink of excrement and rotting flesh. Around the interior of the walls stood storehouses, barracks, officers' quarters, squat single-storey huts little better than the hovels they had seen in Palmer's Creek. The middle of the fort was an open space perhaps a hundred feet across, dominated now by two vast enclosures of marsh wood, in which dozens of men and women were trying desperately to break out – the survivors, Actinus saw, of Holger's company. They wept and screamed with weakened voices as they saw the Stormcasts, some of them trying to gnaw their way through the bars, others covering their heads with their hands and wailing all the louder. The bars were smeared with filth, some foul and luminous poison that had already claimed a dozen of them, their bodies littering the ground. It looked as if they had all been there for some time.

'Free those people at once,' Actinus commanded. 'Get that gate closed and barred.' He looked up at the walls. 'And get those bodies down and buried.'

He reached for the censer on his belt, taking strength from it, peace. He looked up into the bleak and fuming sky until his heart had stopped hammering in his chest and his fury had abated.

'My liege,' he whispered. He closed his eyes. 'Sigmar, guide my arm in this venture, and let these people have the justice they deserve.'

Hektor broke the locks on the cages with the rim of his shield. The captives staggered out onto the parade ground, some collapsing in the dirt, others flinging themselves at the greaves of their rescuers, weeping. The Stormcasts shared out what rations they had brought with them, passing round skins of water. Cadmus sent two of his troops to search the barracks and the storerooms for more supplies.

Actinus looked on the survivors. The orruks, or whatever they were, must have dragged them here from their camp deeper in the swamps, laying them out like bait in the centre of the fort. They were starved, half mad, their uniforms rotted to little more than rags. He and his Stormcasts had freed no more than fifty mortals here, he saw, and of that number only half looked capable of fighting. Captain Beck's company had been near three hundred strong when they set out. The settlements, assuming they were all as deserted as Palmer's Creek, must have numbered a thousand souls between them. They were all gone, devoured by the Mirkmere Swamps, and by all the awful things that lurked within them.

He watched his troops gently freeing the bodies from the top of the wall, passing them down and laying them out on the edge of the parade ground. Actinus stood over them and uttered a prayer.

'Lord Sigmar, by the hammer and the throne, take these souls into your care and watch over them in the underworlds where they now dwell. Give them peace.'

His attention was broken by an angry shout over by the cages. He turned to see a young woman in the remains of an Iron Bulls uniform, bald patches in her scalp where her hair had been ripped out, launching herself at Captain Beck. Although a head shorter than him and barely able to stand up after her ordeal, the woman floored the captain with a savage blow to the chin.

'You stinking craven!' she screamed. She leapt at him, raining blows on his head until one of the Vindictors hauled her back. 'You left us there to die, you bastard!'

Holger rolled onto his side, trembling, his face covered in blood. 'I'm sorry!' he cried. 'I had no choice!'

The woman kicked and struggled in the Vindictor's grip. 'You could have helped us escape! You and that damned priest, only thinking of your own worthless skins!'

Actinus approached. At a signal, the Vindictor released her. The woman's fury was already spent; she slumped to the ground and pressed her fingers to her eyes. Her face was covered in bruises, her cheeks hollow. Holger was sprawled in the mud across from her. Actinus helped him to his feet.

'One of your former comrades, I assume?' he said.

'This is Sergeant Huber,' Holger told him. He looked at her warily, and she glared up at him with hatred.

'If there was only one thing that gave me hope all the weeks we've been stuck here,' she sneered, 'it was the thought that you were starving to death in those swamps, or that you'd been torn apart by the eels, or worse. After everything that's happened, to see you stroll in here with Sigmar's finest is almost more than I can stand.'

'I'm sorry,' Holger said. He couldn't meet her eyes. 'I truly am. I took the chance, but… I couldn't have freed the rest of you. We would all have been discovered, and then what? We'd be standing with our comrades on the walls of this fort now, or they would have cut our tongues out and dragged us off to the gods know where. Please, Huber, believe me – I truly am sorry.'

Sergeant Huber hawked up a glob of saliva and spat at Holger's feet.

'*That* is how much your apology is worth to me,' she said, in a cool, calm voice. 'And if we make it back to Excelsis, I swear to all that is holy that I'll see you court-martialled for dereliction of duty. You'll swing for this, Beck.'

'There is time enough for that once we reach Excelsis,' Actinus told them. 'Let us ensure we can get there in the first place, and preferably in once piece. And–'

There – that whooping call, rising up across the mist-fumed glade. And again there, on the other side of the fort; and there, behind them, until suddenly it felt as if that plaintive, hooting cry were pealing in every corner of the swamps at once, blending and rising to a bitter crescendo, until it faded away into the huddled silence and left no more than an echo behind it. Everyone in the centre of Fort Harrow, Stormcast and mortal alike, stopped to listen, and with bated breath waited for it to return.

Actinus was the first to speak into the silence. 'Vigilator-Prime?'

'Yes, Knight-Relictor?'

'I'd advise you make the gate secure. As quickly as you can.'

CHAPTER EIGHT

He stood above the gate and watched the darkness, and he was sure the darkness was watching back. Lights had been kindled beyond the walls, the flames of torches somewhere far off across the stands of swamp mahogany. Actinus could hear the splash of water out there, but whether it was the dread fauna of the Mirkmere or something else entirely, he couldn't say. He leaned against the spiked palisade, sword in hand. It was difficult to man the whole perimeter of the fort with so few troops. The Stormcasts had spread out as much as possible, but Actinus had gathered more of his warriors at the sector near the gate. Cadmus had repaired the bar as best he could, and the Freeguild had piled broken crates, barrels and carts against it, but beyond this they could do little more. Their shields would be their best defence.

It had been over an hour since the calls had echoed across the swamps. An hour of waiting and preparing, steeling themselves for whatever would come next. For the Stormcasts it was no great ordeal, but for the mortals it was another thing entirely. Actinus glanced round at the surviving members of the Iron Bulls and the Fort Harrow garrison, who milled about uncertainly on the parade ground. Some sat with their heads in their hands. Others paced uneasily, unable to settle. A couple of dozen troops in ragged uniforms, half-starved, with a scavenged collection of inadequate weapons from the looted armoury... They had taken some heart from the proximity of the Stormcast troops, but when the fight came down, there would be little relying on them. The soldiers had emphatically rejected Captain Beck's authority and had organised themselves around Sergeant Huber instead, who sat on a camp stool sharpening her blade, a look in her eyes of almost deadened hatred.

Beck, drifting uncertainly between his comrades and the Stormcast contingent, came idling across the hard-packed square and sat at the bottom of the wooden stairs.

Actinus sighed. He felt obscurely depressed. Captain Beck had disgraced himself, it was true, but at the same time he was trying to atone for his actions. He was still here, and that had to count for something. And yet, he looked on his former comrades with a mixture of guilt and resentment and kept himself apart, and they looked on him with utter contempt. There was no middle ground between them, no hope of forgiveness or redemption. Not even common danger could make them see common cause.

Leta, with Strix at her heel, came striding along the walkway at the top of the wall, pushing past one of the Vindictors. Since they had barred the gate, she had been prowling the palisade looking for targets in the depths of the swampland. She had wanted to fire at those smears of light as they wavered in the gloom, but Actinus had stayed her hand. There was no sense in frittering themselves on piecemeal attacks. They must strike like lightning, in one overwhelming blast.

'There's no sign of any movement on the other side,' she said. She nodded at the treeline across the apron of dirt ahead of them. 'The swamps to the north look sparser, thin, more like fenland than this jungle. If they attack,' she said confidently, 'they'll attack here.'

'Agreed,' Actinus said. 'More cover from the dense foliage, only a short sprint across the flat ground to the gate. It can only be twenty feet from here to the trees – it could be covered in moments.'

Leta sighted along her bow, flaming arrow drawn back. 'I only wish they would. I'd pick off a dozen of them before they'd made it a yard.'

'Ah, but we still don't quite know who "they" are now, do we?'

'Orruks,' Leta said, 'without a doubt. I've been talking to the survivors, and from their descriptions I can't see what else it would be. Their behaviour–'

'–is unusual, I concur,' Actinus said. He peered at the treeline. A dash of white, the suggestion then of something withdrawing into the greenery, heading deeper into the mists. He wondered what had happened to Caspar Hallan, whether the priest was alive or dead. He hoped alive. 'There is a strange certainty to what they do, a precision or intent. Not at all the mindless rampage we might have expected from their kind. But then Ghur is an exceedingly large and varied place, and I doubt if even Sigmar knows the full extent of the creatures that dwell in it.'

There was a flutter somewhere behind him, on the other side of the fort, the flat *thunk* of metal struck by a solid object. Actinus turned to look back over the parade ground, to the palisade on the northern side.

One of the Vigilators toppled backwards from the viewing platform, falling fifteen feet to strike the ground with a crash. There was an arrow protruding from the hard leather between his helmet and his gorget. Actinus heard Cadmus crying out an order, and within moments the whole northern sector of the fort was being peppered with a rain of shots – thick barbed arrows smacking into the sharpened stakes, skidding from the Stormcasts' armour, soaring high over the walls to lance the beaten ground on the other side. The Vigilator who had been struck was writhing in the dirt, spitting blood through the mouth of his faceplate.

The Freeguild scattered, seeking the shelter of the walls, where they crouched with their swords and spears in hand. Some of them were wailing with fear. Atop the walls, Actinus saw the Vigilators rising to shoot back, skimming bolts over the palisade.

'Looks like we were wrong!' Leta cried, leaping down from the wall to the parade ground below. 'They're hitting the southern wall!' She sprinted across the dirt, bow in hand, swamp-stained cloak rippling out behind her while Strix streaked ahead.

'Leta, stop!' Actinus cried. 'It could be a feint, it's–'

Light, and fire. Sound burst and broke apart, leaving him with only a high, persistent whine in his ear. He felt himself raised up, soaring through the air, his sight a blurred cascade of light and darkness, of burning white and red and the deepest, Stygian black. He was weightless, and for a moment he thought he was searing back through the maelstrom of the Cursed Skies, back to Azyr and Sigmaron, to the Anvil. He'd failed. Body and soul rent asunder, to be forged once more in the eternal flame.

He hit the ground like a thunderclap, the breath beaten from him, blood in his mouth. The whine in his ear fractured into an almighty roar, a cacophony of screams and cries, the ring of blade-work. After a moment he realised he was on his back, staring up at a broiling sky flecked now with smuts and ashes.

Turillos, my friend… Khellian…

No, he thought. Not yet. He was still alive.

He rolled over and shakily gained his knees, using the point of his sword to lever himself up. He'd managed to hold onto that, at least.

He turned and looked back. Where the gate had stood there was now nothing but a smoking crater. The whole section of wall on that side of the fort was a splintered ruin, the sharpened stakes charred black and burning, the palisade shattered by some incredible explosive force. The parade ground was wreathed in smoke, choked by the fog that crept in over the breach. Actinus saw half a dozen of the Vindictors lying dazed on the ground, thrown back from the walkway around the palisade. One of them tried to stand, his arm and half his face missing, his armour torn apart by the blast. Actinus, still stunned, tried to call out to him, but as he stood there the warrior toppled backwards and broke apart in a searing flash of lightning, the spear of his soul lancing up to pierce the Cursed Skies above and seek refuge in the heavens.

A shadow lithely skipped through the broken walls, shrouded by the smoke. There was something burning in its hand. Actinus had an impression of a loping, sinuous beast, gnashing its jaws, red eyes dancing with pleasure. It was utterly silent. It paused and threw the burning thing, dancing back as the spark sailed over the fume towards the stunned Vindictors.

'Get out of the way!' Actinus screamed at them. 'Run!'

He tried to stagger forwards, but then the spark burst apart in a blinding flare, a gout of flame and smoke that threw him backwards. Even through that terrible fire, he could see the lightning strikes, the souls of his comrades shooting up to the sky.

The clash of weapons, the cries of command. Most of the southern wall was ruined, but there was fighting on the north palisade. Actinus turned, sword at his side, and through the smoke he could see the signs of struggle on the walls: black shadows flowing around the glint of tarnished gold.

'Leta!' he cried. 'Pellion! We need to reinforce the south wall now!'

He stepped forward – only instinct saved him, the flicker of something in his peripheral vision. Without thinking, he raised his sword, point down, and caught the swing of a blade against the crossbar. The blow staggered him backwards, but in moments he was on guard, pivoting to meet the threat, at last coming face to face with what had been stalking them through the swamps for so long, what had captured the settlers of Palmer's Creek, what had cut the Iron Bulls apart and imprisoned the survivors for weeks of the cruellest sport.

'Yes…' Actinus said, weaving slowly side to side as he took its measure. He swallowed the blood in his mouth. 'You're an orruk, all right…'

It was a head shorter than him, hunched, with a low-slung jaw, its gangling limbs sinewy and powerful. The orruk snickered and gurgled at him, red eyes flickering with malice. It held a rough-hewn hide or leather shield in one hand, painted with that same leering glyph Actinus had seen so many times now – like a screaming face, the eyes glowing with some weird swamp-luminescence. The spikes that fringed the shield were smeared with some festering slime, against which the orruk wiped its primitive blade. It was wearing only the stinking rag of a loincloth, but its skin, more grey than green, was decorated with crude tattoos, painted designs and strange, disturbing symbols. The creature bared its sharp yellow teeth in a sickly grin, its canines more like tusks.

It was like no orruk he had ever seen. Instead of rushing in with roars and bellows of rage, it merely matched his stance and followed his movements, seemingly with a sharp and sinister intelligence. The orruks of the Ironjawz or the Bonesplitterz clans were little better than animals, crude and aggressive beasts that lived for war. This thing though… this was different. It raised its chin at him, red tongue protruding between its teeth, almost as if it were taunting him.

Well, Actinus thought, there would be time enough for sober appraisals later.

He lunged forward with his blade, splintering the orruk's shield with his first swing, drawing back and aiming a backhanded blow at its head. The orruk yelped and skipped to the side, ducked, came in with three quick stabs that Actinus easily parried. It jumped back to dodge his cut, but then jumped forward and caught him off balance, smashing its shield boss into his faceplate while it cut low and fast across the back of his knee. Actinus staggered, pivoting so the slash only clipped his greaves. He swung his sword from high to low and tried to cleave the thing in two at the shoulder, but again his blade only met the foetid air. The orruk rolled under the swing and leapt up to try to stab him through the sternum. Actinus caught the edge of the blade on his gauntlet and threw it aside, risking a glance at the northern wall, where he saw the Vigilators struggling hand to hand with the orruks who had scaled the palisade. Sigmar alone knew what was happening behind him.

'Enough!' he cried. As the orruk darted in for another stab, he flipped his blade and smashed the pommel into the creature's jaw. It howled in pain, eyes blazing, and Actinus stamped the side of his armoured foot against its shin. He felt the bone crack, saw the orruk gasp, eyes wide. Before it could even utter a cry, he swung his sword and sent its head spinning off into the gloom.

He kicked the body aside. The barracks were ablaze. The northern wall was swarming with orruks – lank, loping things quick with blade and spear, darting in as the Vigilators struggled to hold them off. On the south side, the Vindictors, much depleted by the explosions that had forced the breach, had formed a shield wall and were slowly pushing the orruks back. Dozens more scuttled through the broken wall, trying to force the Vindictors to retreat, but even before Actinus had the chance to rush over and lend his blade, he felt the ground tremble beneath him.

Out of the shadows, like a golden battering ram, utterly unstoppable, came the phalanx of Annihilators. Shields out, hammers raised, they thundered into the mobbing orruks near the broken gate with a grinding flash, scattering bodies, kicking up gouts of blood and mangled limbs. The orruks screeched in terror and bounded back into the shadows beyond the breach, leaving their dead and wounded behind. Actinus watched as the Annihilators calmly dispatched them, crushing skulls with one swing of their hammers, spattering their shields with blood.

He saw Pellion standing in the middle of the parade ground, banner high, the threads of the Taranites' battle honours glowing. Pellion's face shone with an expression of the utmost reverence, transported even in the midst of this blood and horror.

'Keep that banner flying!' Actinus cried as he ran for the northern wall. He saw Holger Beck cowering in the lee of the storehouse, his hands clamped over his ears. His sword, the relic blade, was lying on the ground beside him. As his eyes met the Knight-Relictor's, he cringed and looked away.

'Get up and fight,' Actinus shouted. 'Raise that sword unto its holy purpose, Captain Beck!' He saw Sergeant Huber and some of the other Iron Bulls by the wooden stairs that led up to the walkway on the north wall. Five of them were struggling to bring down one of the orruks, Huber howling with battle madness as she plunged her blade into its eye and out the back of its head. 'If you will not, then give that sword to her,' Actinus cried, 'for she will make better use of it than you!'

By the time he reached the wall, the orruks were beginning to slip away. He leapt up the stairs three at a time, Leta above him firing shot after blazing shot into the fenlands beyond, a black smear of shallow lakes and waterways glinting now with the harsh light cast by the burning fort. Her face was smeared with blood and dirt, her armour scratched. Strix, haring about the walkway by her feet, looked as if he had been feasting on the dead, his face and neck feathers soaked in gore.

'Have you ever seen orruks using grenades?' she cried. 'Where did they get those? From the Kharadron? Those are duardin-make, surely?'

'There are many unanswered questions here,' he said.

He wiped his blade on his cloak and took in the situation as quickly as he could. The sounds of battle had died down. The orruks had left dozens of their dead behind, but the Stormcasts had taken severe casualties. Five of the Vindictors had died in the explosion that forced the breach, and at least half the Vigilators perished on the northern wall. The fort was a ruin, the north palisade little more than a smoking wreck.

Actinus looked to the skies, at the faint feathering of light as the dawn began to break. He looked at the burning barracks, the settlers forming a chain to pass buckets from the well in a vain effort to douse the flames.

'We can't hold this fort as it is,' Actinus said. 'The damage is too severe. We don't have sufficient troops.'

'Agreed,' Leta said. She slung her bow across her shoulder, but her keen grey eyes still scanned the fenlands beyond the wall.

'We don't have enough food for the mortals, and we have no way of informing Lord-Imperatant Taranis of our predicament.'

'We'd be boxed up in here,' Leta said, 'until the orruks overran us. Which I'm beginning to think was their plan all along.'

'We need to break out, make a fighting withdrawal back to Excelsis. It's our only hope.'

He looked down from the wall at the smoking barracks, the remaining Freeguild soldiers cleaning their weapons and tending their wounds.

Leta leaned towards him and said, quietly, 'It's near a hundred miles back to Excelsis. We could manage that march without rest, but the mortals won't. Most of them will die.'

'I know,' he said softly. 'But I fear we have no choice. We die here, or we die out there.'

His face burned behind the skull-plate mask. He longed to remove his helmet, to feel the cool air on his skin. But if the decision
must be made, then let it be made by the Knight-Relictor – rigid
in his faith, implacable.

Inhuman.

CHAPTER NINE

They passed through the wreckage of the gate and marched quickly across the open ground, the Vigilators taking the lead, the Vindictors covering their rear, and the Annihilators and Vanquishers on either flank. They passed through the treeline, sloshing once more into the filthy standing water, and plunged back into the murk of the swamps.

The civilians and the surviving Freeguild took up position in the centre, staggering on as well as they could at the Stormcasts' punishing pace. Many of them took heart at being near Pellion's banner. Undimmed even in the sultry drizzle of the morning, it glowed with all the holy purpose of High Azyr. All who looked on it felt new strength in their veins.

At the front, the Vigilators hacked through the creeping vines and cut down the spiny thatch of bullrushes and swamp grass, clearing a path they could all pass through. There would be no misdirection now, no circuitous routes – their only chance was the speed of the march, and the straight line back to Excelsis.

Holger Beck, as ever, positioned himself by Actinus' side. The Knight-Relictor was aware of him huffing and panting at his elbow as he strode along, the Freeguild captain trying his best to keep up. Even now, in this extremity, he kept himself away from his former comrades. Actinus glanced over his shoulder and saw Sergeant Huber, grimly determined, wading through the green pools and the sucking mire behind him. There was a battered, glazed look in her eyes, but for once she wasn't glaring at her captain. She had adjusted, Actinus thought, even if Beck had not. She knew that what mattered now was survival, nothing more.

He regretted his outburst during the battle, as Holger had cowered in the shadows covering his ears, but Actinus was curiously depressed that the captain hadn't drawn heart from the blade he had been given. Even when every sword could have made a difference, he had not stood up to fight. Perhaps Actinus had misjudged the captain. He had thought him a weak man who only needed encouragement, but maybe Leta was right after all; he was a coward, nothing more. It was dismaying. Sigmar's empire may have been the people who lived in it, but those people needed to be like iron to survive and prosper.

'Keep up, Captain Beck,' he murmured. 'We must not tarry.'

Beck, his face glassy with sweat, nodded shakily and carried on.

The day deepened, the light grew dim, and the mortal soldiers began to falter. The mud, the weeds, the lank vines and the stinking water were taking their toll. The fort was now a distant memory behind them, but the endless expanse of the Mirkmere felt more constricting than those four walls had ever done. Leopard eels were beginning to circle the column, and Actinus could hear bloaters croaking and groaning in the undergrowth around them.

Near dusk, some of the guardsmen began to collapse. Most of the younger troops had been taken away in chains by the orruks, leaving only the older veterans that were running on their last reserves. They were hardy fighters, but even the most dauntless had their limits. In twos and threes they fell to the side, so exhausted they couldn't even cry out for help. The column ploughed relentlessly on, Actinus briefly stepping aside so he could offer them Sigmar's mercy. None took it. They looked at him in despair, their eyes, their haunted eyes, pleading with him to take them. *And yet I cannot carry them all*, he thought. *I cannot…* He would nod and place his hand on their shoulders, willing their souls to Sigmar's care, and then a hundred yards further into the pestilent glades he would hear them screaming in the distance. The leopard eels, he told himself. Or worse…

All through this the orruks had shadowed them, pricking the flanks of the column with arrow shot, firing off thick barbed bolts that splintered in the body and were almost impossible to remove without causing deeper injury. The bolts were smeared with a poisonous filth, and although the Stormcasts could weather the infection, even the smallest cut was enough to bring the Freeguild soldiers down. The column as it passed left a trail of its dead behind it.

The painted faces on the orruks' shields glowed and shivered in the bushes on all sides, fading away, reappearing, accompanied always by that same whooping shriek. Some of the settlers began to cry with fear, pushed beyond the limits of their sanity, only too clear what would happen to them if they fell behind. The Vindictors moved to the flanks of the column, trying to protect it with their shields, but there were too few of them to make a real difference.

On the column marched, wading through the sucking bogs and cloying mires, hacking back the great coils of bramble, the clinging vines that blocked their way. The swamps burbled and squawked around them, foul leathery birds crying from the branches, toads softly barking from rotten stumps, the ever-present insects fizzing in the brew of swamp gas and fog.

'They're massing on the right flank!' Hektor called out, pointing with his hammer. The light was beginning to fail. They had reached a spread of firmer ground, a sequence of raised hummocks fringed with thick, spiny grass. 'They're going to attack!'

'Column!' Actinus shouted. He could see the orruks gathering in the undergrowth, masking their movements between the thick stands of cypress and hickory. 'Shields to the front!' He touched the censer on his belt, felt the surge of cool and certain faith in him. *Not yet,* he thought. *Not yet…* 'And ready your weapons!'

The column halted, pivoting as the storm of arrows increased. The orruks were screaming in the brush now, rattling their shields. Leta unleashed a firestorm on them, blazing the undergrowth with her holy arrows, the remaining Vigilators picking off any survivors with their crossbows.

'Watch the rear,' Actinus commanded. 'Pellion, raise your banner that they may be blinded by our faith.'

He saw it first, a black orb sailing out from the undergrowth, trailing a ribbon of pale smoke – one of those cursed incendiary devices. Where in the name of Sigmar had they got these from? As it arced towards them, Actinus shouted to take cover behind the Vindictors' shields, but Hektor had seen the danger at the exact same time. The Vindictor-Prime leapt forward, catching the fiery orb against his shield and knocking it into the mud. He threw himself on top of it, and in the rending flash of its explosion he was blown to pieces.

'Hektor!' Leta cried. With a despairing snarl she whipped her arrows through the brush, plucking orruks from their feet, piercing shields and skulls alike.

Actinus, half blinded by the explosion, groped in the darkness for Hektor's soul as it sheared off towards the heavens. He felt the celestial energy that had filled Hektor's form, that resonated through the ornate craftsmanship of his armour and the vigour of his Stormborn body. It burned there like a brand, unquenchable. Guiding it with all the fury he could muster, Actinus rebounded that energy off towards the orruks as they spilled from the undergrowth, immolating them with a burning, golden flame. The Soul Blaze, the killing burst – it was Grungni the Maker's mark upon them, the celestial power of Azyr now weaponised and wielded by the Relictor Temple into a final act of holy and purifying vengeance. The orruks, blinded by the light, screamed as the flesh was scorched from their bones. Pellion's banner seemed to burn all the brighter, and as the orruks retreated into the undergrowth, the surviving mortals managed a rousing cheer.

'They're fleeing!' Holger said, waving his sword above his head.

'They'll be back,' Sergeant Huber muttered. 'Knight-Relictor?' she said, turning to him. 'We can't continue like this – we need to rest for an hour at least. None of us are going to make it back to Excelsis otherwise.'

'Agreed,' Actinus said. 'We've gained a moment's respite and may as well use it. Tell your troops to rest while we guard them.'

The hour turned into two, then four. The night passed without incident, and the quieter it was, the more Actinus was minded to let the mortals rest as long as they needed to. They had covered more ground than he would have thought possible, but the cost had been great: Hektor dead, his force whittled further down, the surviving Iron Bulls now no more than a ragged company on its last legs. As the swamps thrummed with suspicious life around them, the stinking mists creeping closer over the waters, he sat in the mud and allowed himself to close his eyes. He didn't sleep though. He would not allow himself sleep, and the dreams that always followed.

My old friends, he thought. *It will not be long now. I will be with you again soon…*

CHAPTER TEN

They found the priest early the next morning, cowering in the reeds on the edge of the cleared ground. Strix had snapped into the bullrushes and caught him by the ankle, dragging him into the clearing as the mists rose and broke apart in the weak dawn sunlight. Caspar howled and scrabbled at the dirt, trying to claw himself back into the undergrowth.

'What have you found there, Strix?' Leta boomed, grabbing Caspar by the scruff of his neck and hauling him to his feet. 'Priests hiding in the bushes, eh? They'll do anything to catch you out in a blasphemy, won't they?'

He was half naked, filthy, strewn with pond scum and dressed only in a mouldering loincloth, his face still smeared with ash. He had used a knife or a sharp stone to carve crude versions of the orruk glyphs into his skin, and blood was trickling down his chest. His face was even more haggard. His eyes danced madly in their sockets. Leta threw him to the ground, to a shout of anger from the Freeguild troops. One of them, a handgunner with a

bristling moustache and a swollen black eye, stepped forward and
kicked the priest in the stomach.

'Near three hundred good troops lost, and you survive, you
maggot!' he spat. 'Where's the justice!'

There was a chorus of bitter approval. Sergeant Huber looked
on with relish, while Caspar, grovelling in the mud, held up his
hands, beseeching.

'Spare me!' he whined. 'The lords of bog and leaf are angry! The
spirits of the water, fey dwellers of the blackgum and the vine! You
must plead for their forgiveness, as I have pleaded!'

'He's out of his mind,' Huber cried. 'He's abandoned Sigmar –
he thinks those monsters are something to be worshipped!'

'Hang him!' 'String him up!' 'Drown him in the swamps!'

The Freeguilders formed a bristling mob around him, screaming
for punishment. Caspar knelt and grovelled before them.

Actinus strode forward, pushing his way through the mob. The
Freeguild troops shrank before him. Leta stood there on the edge
of the circle, impassive, looking on the scene as it unfolded.

'What's the meaning of this?' Actinus said. 'This man is hurt,
half dead with starvation.'

Sergeant Huber rounded on him, rage making her voice shake.

'He's as bad as Captain Beck, another one who ran off and left us
to die!' The crowd of soldiers grumbled their agreement. 'For all we
know he's been leading the orruks to us. You heard what he said –
he thinks they're gods or spirits. He's been driven mad by this place!'

Actinus helped the priest to his feet. Caspar trembled beside
him, teeth bared through a wispy tangle of beard.

'Nonsense,' Actinus said. 'The orruks know perfectly well where
we are. They led us to Fort Harrow, hoping to trap us there and
destroy us, and they follow close on our heels now. They have
never lost sight of us. This man had nothing to do with it.'

'What of Ripper?' Leta called out. Her hard and unyielding

gaze met Actinus' eyes. Strix growled dangerously at her heel. 'The priest disappeared at the same time, and the next morning we found Ripper nailed up in the swamps. He had something to do with it, I know he did.'

Actinus stared at her, unspeaking. The voices of the others died away. He felt the tension between them tauten like a wire, stretched to breaking point, but after a moment Leta's gaze faltered and she looked away.

I see your soul, Knight-Judicator, he thought, *and it is a thing of mercury and fire. But do not overstep the mark...*

'Look at him,' he said. 'Do you honestly believe this man could have been a match for your gryph-hound?'

Leta, eyes burning with anger, stared off into the black waters. 'No,' she admitted.

Actinus turned to the crowd. 'If this man has lost his mind in this place, then who here can say that they have not felt themselves pushed to the same brink? He deserves our pity. He is no threat to us.'

He looked down at the priest, shivering there on the dank ground, stinking of the brackish water. Whatever he had once been, a priest, a messenger of Azyr's word, a wielder of Sigmar's hammer, he was nothing now. He was little better than the beasts that called this place home.

Jonas, my friend – that all priests of Sigmar should have your spirit...

'Go, and be at peace,' Actinus said softly. 'Follow us if you want to return home, but I will not force you either way. You have suffered much, I feel.'

And with those words, blinking wildly, his head twitching, Caspar Hallan bounded off into the waters of the glades and was lost in the rising mist.

'Gather your gear,' Actinus commanded the Freeguild troops. 'But we must travel lightly now, and at speed.'

* * *

It was getting brighter, but the mists were thickening. The dripping glades of the swamps seemed to press in on them. The light, filtered through the canopy, bathed them all in a washed-out green. The Stormcasts soon looked as if they were stained with verdigris, like a line of copper statues left from some dreaming time of myth. As the sun rose, sallow beyond the Cursed Skies, the swamps began to thrum again with life: the click and buzz of insects, the sense of fecund things surging around them.

The soldiers took up their weapons. The surviving civilians dragged themselves to their feet with piteous groans, slapping mosquitoes, wringing water from their clothes. The remaining Stormcasts checked their gear and took up their positions, the Vindictors already wading out into the scum and peering through the pallid swamp gas ahead.

'One more day should do it,' Pellion said.

'Another day like yesterday?' Leta said, coming near. She unclipped her cloak and let it fall into the black waters, discarding her helmet, her gauntlets, onto the sodden dirt. The longbow in her hands still gleamed with holy fire, a streak of gold, undimmed.

'We have no choice,' Actinus said. 'We go on, or we die.'

Leta gave a sharp nod. Actinus thought he saw the trace of a smile on her lips.

'Well,' she said, 'let's try not to do that then.'

'Have faith,' Pellion said. His face, normally so sombre, broke into a grin. He shook his banner. 'Even in this fell place, the light of Sigmar burns. And we are that light, are we not? Then let us burn all the brighter in his name.'

The day that followed was one of the most desperate actions Actinus could remember.

The mist came in great clammy banks, steaming across the water, smothering the undergrowth. Trees lurched out of the gloom, lagged in creeping bindweed. The Stormcasts stepped up their pace, the formation more of a mob now than a column, and as they thrashed through the glades the orruks harried them every step of the way. Barbed arrows spun out of the murk on one flank, piercing Stormcasts and mortals alike, and while their attention was drawn, groups of orruks with cruel swords and crude shields rushed in from the other flank and tried to cut them down.

Each time this happened the column staggered to a halt, spinning to meet one threat, pivoting to blunt the other. The Vanquishers, no more than half a dozen of them left now, strode out with a roar and hewed the orruks to pieces with their great two-handed blades, slicing through shields like paper, cleaving heads and limbs. Always the orruks would retreat though, quickly fading into the shadows and fog – and then, as the column lumbered into motion again, the arrows would rain down on them once more. All the while, the glowing faces the orruks painted on their shields peered at them from the weeds, accompanied by a fearful shrieking.

'They fight like skirmishers,' Leta panted as she ran beside Actinus. She snapped off a burning shot from her bow, the bolt arcing off into the scrub. 'Like partisans. If we could just bring them to open battle…'

'They fight to their strengths,' Actinus countered. 'As is only right. We are in their element now.'

'Again, if you pressed me,' Leta said, shaking her head, 'I could be forced to admit that it might have been a mistake to come here.'

'And yet here is where we find ourselves, all the same.'

Leta laughed, bounding ahead with Strix on her trail, her arrows falling like lightning in the mist.

Hours passed. On they went, splashing through the filth. Some of the mortals stumbled over submerged roots and crashed down into the water with a feeble cry, too exhausted to get up. Others who straggled behind were plucked from the column by arrow shot. The Freeguild troops ran blank-eyed, hoarse, utterly hollowed out by their exertions – and still they went on, for the whooping cacophony of the orruks around them was enough to put steel into their legs and a furnace in their lungs.

Actinus, wherever he could, stopped to lift the fallen and get them on their feet again, bringing the most exhausted closer to the aura of Pellion's banner, where the holy light refreshed their senses and gave them new heart. When orruks slipped past the barrier of the Vanquishers on the left, he drew his blade and cut them down, parrying thrusts on his gauntlets, stabbing, slashing, staining the swamp water with gouts of red.

'On!' he screamed, pointing with his sword. 'Onwards, do not stop!'

The Stormcasts were relentless. With hammer and shield they blunted each assault; with sword and crossbow they took a grim toll, and whenever one of them fell at last, brought down by weight of numbers or by an opportune shot, Actinus harnessed their celestial energy and sent it scorching out into the orruk lines with a bellowed prayer. A few moments were gained, a brief respite for the column to cover lost ground – but then the shrieking in the bushes would start again, the stinking mist would thicken, and the arrows would fall once more: a hard and merciless rain.

Midday, sunlight lancing through the canopy in transparent spears. The fume of swamp gas flowed around them, the mist and fog brewing in the depths. Cadmus, limping, an arrow shaft sticking from his hip, leaned against a gnarled cypress. He had lost his helmet miles back. His armour was battered and dented.

'We've come off the trail,' he groaned as Actinus approached. An arrow clacked neatly into the wood beside his head and he ducked, crouching in the green water. There were only two other

Vigilators left now, and they kneeled on either side of the tree, trading shots with the unseen orruks in the scrub. Leta stood proudly just beyond them, arrows flecking the water on either side of her, skimming off her armour to patter into the mud. Calmly, she drew and released, drew and released, each celestial arrow searing into the gloom like a lance of fire.

'Keep coming!' she shouted at the capering shadows. 'I need the target practice!'

Actinus turned to Cadmus. 'If we keep heading west, we should reach the plains beyond Excelsis one way or another,' he said. 'We'll be out of the swamps at least.'

'Aye,' Cadmus sighed. 'But the orruks keep pushing us north each time they attack. They know what they're doing – they're guiding us back along the line of the Mirkmere. They're trying to turn us around, I'm sure of it.'

'They're cunning creatures,' Actinus muttered. 'I'll give them that.'

'This damned mist, it's getting worse,' Cadmus said. 'If we could clear that they'd only have half the advantage they do now.'

Actinus ran his fingers over the relic censer on his belt.

The time has come, he thought. He whispered a prayer.

The flame kindled inside the censer cup and set the relic burning. The thigh bone of that warrior-priest who had defied a champion of Khorne in centuries past and struck him down with faith alone...

The holy incense trickled from the reliquary. Soon it was billowing out in a cloud that sparkled with motes of golden light. Everyone who breathed it felt they were drawing a lungful of fresh mountain air rather than the smoke of conflagration, and where the incense touched the swamp-fog it seemed to press it back, breaking it apart into threads and tendrils that drifted through the reeds, a veil torn away to reveal the greasy profusion of the swamps around them: the drifting, stagnant water carpeted in weeds, the listing trees, the brittle stalks of the rushes and the saltgrass.

Actinus could hear the dismay in the orruks' cries as they scuttled further back into the shelter of the foliage. He closed his eyes. He felt the pain of this, even if he saw the sense in it. This was the extremity the forces of the God-King had reached – to immolate the holiest of relics, to buy victory with the destruction of what they most venerated.

Such a daemon's bargain, he thought. *And yet, what choice do we have now?*

'They're retreating!' Leta called. She snapped off two more shots, turned to grin at Actinus as he stood up from where he had been crouching. 'If you can hold this mist back another few hours, we can make it out of here. We can–'

The first arrow caught her in the back of the neck, the thick, barbed point splintering through her throat. Leta dropped her bow and raised her hands to it, choking, eyes strained and frantic, the second arrow then sailing in from a thicket of reeds no more than twenty yards away and slamming into the leather under her arm, piercing the gap between her plates. She crashed forward. Actinus leapt up to catch her and together they sprawled in the water, Leta coughing blood, clawing at her throat. Strix gave a skirling howl, his eyes blazing red. As Actinus tried to pull Leta into the shelter of the cypress, the gryph-hound leapt from rotten log to reed bed and launched himself into the scrub. Actinus could hear the orruk screaming, the savage snap and rend of Strix's beak.

'Help me!' Actinus cried, but when he turned, he saw that Cadmus' eyes were glassy, his breath shallow. The poison on the arrows had weakened him too much, and the blood loss was too great. He neared death. Actinus dragged Leta into the cradle of the tree's exposed roots, next to the Vigilator-Prime. Gently he laid her head back. Her lips were flecked with blood; it gushed from the rent in her throat.

'Killed… by an *arrow*…!' she choked. She grasped his hand, tried to smile through the pain. 'The damned *irony* of it…'

He looked wildly around. A dozen small skirmishes surrounded him: Vanquishers struggling on the fringes of the column with bands of orruks – Helican, the Vanquisher-Prime, roaring his battle cry as he cut them down; the Annihilators, lacking the space to build up momentum for their devastating charges, forming an inviolable phalanx with the surviving Vindictors in the centre. Iron Bulls troops fought where they could, hacking and slashing with their scavenged swords. He saw Holger Beck, his blade in hand, crying out and wildly swinging at a capering orruk, before Sergeant Huber leapt in to impale it through the back. The water around them was slick with blood and floating bodies.

'My bow,' Leta groaned in Actinus' arms. She reached for it. He saw it glowing beneath him in the stagnant water, three feet down, and plunged his hand in to bring it up. He pressed it into Leta's hands. He could see sparks of lightning flickering around the rim of her gorget. It would not be long now. Beside her, still blinking, Cadmus struggled for breath.

'Get back, Actinus,' she said, blood trickling down her chin. Her eyes were fading, her face as pale as paper. 'Let me… one more time…'

She drew the bow with the last of her strength, and its aethereal arrow was brighter now than any Actinus had ever seen before – lambent, like white fire burning in the deep. She loosed it with a sound like lightning. Actinus craned to see it pierce the brooding sky, a blast of holy light that burned far beyond the drear canopy of the swamps.

Her death was on her now. As the flicker of the lightning strengthened, Actinus stood back and muttered prayers for her dissolution.

Her body broke apart. Cadmus, sprawled there in the roots of the tree, flung his arm across his eyes. Actinus reached with his soul and felt the light inside her burning, the celestial energy that had coursed through her and kept her whole, and as her soul lanced back towards the heavens he threw that energy with a scream of blinding rage towards the orruks who pressed in on all sides, immolating them, burning their foul flesh and turning them to no more than columns of black ash that dissipated on the fertile breeze.

Strix squawked and howled as they moved out. The gryph-hound wouldn't leave the blackened trunk of the cypress where his mistress had died.

'We'll stay together,' Cadmus called, raising his crossbow, still slumped in the roots of the tree. His breath was ragged, his eyes dim. 'We'll hold them off... won't we, Strix?'

The gryph-hound, perched up on the swollen roots, gave a mournful call. Cadmus put an arm around his neck. Actinus raised a hand in salute and turned to go, wading on through the bloody water, bitterness in his heart.

An hour later, looking back, he saw a spear of lightning reach its pale fingers up towards Azyr.

CHAPTER ELEVEN

They made their last stand on a bank of rough ground, at dawn the next day.

Black water lapped amongst the reeds and the bullrushes. The smoke from the relic censer had burned away, and in its absence the mists resurged towards them, like storm clouds rolling in across a bitter sea. In its depths they could see the loping forms of the orruks, gathering like flense-fish around a wounded prey. There was something exultant in their whooping cries now, their cruel laughter, the rattle of their painted shields. The moment was drawing near. The column, no more than half a day from the edge of the Mirkmere, could not go on. They had reached the end.

Actinus, bleeding from a dozen wounds, set the shields of his Vindictors in a rough semicircle. Helicon held back his Vanquishers behind them, the Annihilators ready on the right flank for a final, suicidal charge. The Freeguild troops, no more than a dozen left, were now resigned to death. They gripped their weapons in shaking hands, some of them barely able to stand, all of them willing to sell their lives dearly.

'You entered these swamps on a crusade for Sigmar,' Actinus cried out to them, standing by Pellion and his banner. 'You will leave them as martyrs, a prayer on your lips and hymns in your hearts!'

The orruks screamed ahead of them, massing in the bowers. A chill drizzle began to fall. There was the sound of something huge and ungainly crashing through the undergrowth deeper in, grunting, lowing like some maddened beast. Bolts flicked out of the shadows. Red eyes glared and danced. Yellow teeth glinted in wide and mocking grins.

'Here they come!' Holger shouted at Actinus' side. 'By all the gods of each and every realm,' he muttered, cringing into what passed for a fighting stance, 'look on me now and keep me safe, I beg you!'

'Sigmar does not promise you safety!' Actinus bellowed. An arrow flashed from the fog and skimmed across his breastplate. 'Sigmar does not promise you life! Sigmar promises only *justice*, and the hand that wields it!'

He raised his sword. 'For Sigmar! For Sigmar and Taranis!'

The orruks came swarming on, shrieking and cursing, bounding through the water in a great splashing tide, some swimming in the deeper places to throw themselves on the Stormcast rear. Actinus threw Holger to the side as the line broke, swinging up, cleaving an orruk from chest to shoulder, pivoting, swiping out again with his sword, a flash of teeth and brains on his blade. An elbow back to smash a jaw, reaching in to rip out a lolling tongue. Ducking, stabbing, the hilt of his sword red with blood.

'Khellian!' he screamed. He cut left, brought the pommel up to hammer out an orruk's teeth, reversing the blade, slicing it through a belly, guts coiled on the ground.

Khellian falling, her head caved in...

'Turillos!'

His breath booming hollow inside his helmet, a crunch in his ribs as a sword hacked into his side. He gasped, looked up, head-butted the orruk and felt its cheekbone snap, hammering in with the sword until the arm dropped to the sunken mud, splitting its chest open on the backswing.

Turillos, sliding down the shaft of the spear, spewing blood...

'For Sigmar!' he screamed, voice hoarse, broken.

He felt the blade go in, lancing into his side. He clamped it there with his gauntlet, pulling the orruk off balance, snapping in with the sword to slice its legs off below the knee. He hauled himself up, panting, bleeding, and stamped down on its face, again and again, until the skull split, brains jetting out to stain the water grey.

The lightning smeared against the dark clouds, that risen hell, the madness of the sky, while I go on to glory...

'To glory!' he cried. 'To the death!'

Around him, mortal and Stormcast were screaming, hacking, possessed by battle madness. He saw Holger slipping, falling on his back, sword extended, a hulking orruk howling as it fell down the blade. He saw Sergeant Huber leaping onto the back of another orruk, teeth clamped to its neck, savaging off a mouthful of flesh. He saw the Annihilators thundering like an avalanche into the swamps on the left, smashing apart a mob of orruks before they could cross the glades and attack. Helicon, singing a prayer, his blade broken and a mound of dead at his feet, lightning already leaking from his wounds. Civilians screaming, cut to pieces, the water around them red as a butcher's yard. Orruks slinking through the mists, arrows flying, a fume of blood.

A bolt punched into his shoulder, piercing the plate. He dropped back, three orruks rounding on him, shields up, those grotesque glowing eyes glaring at him. He splintered the first shield, reached in and threw it aside, sword up and plunging into the orruk's throat. The second beast cut in wide, its blade shattering on his armour. Actinus punched out with his fist and laid its cheek open, grappled with the third. Its sword went into his stomach, grinding on the plate. He punched down, broke its wrist.

That blasted plain, ringed with red dust, the Cursed Skies boiling above us. My friends, I will be with you soon…

Two more bore down on him, snickering. His fingers were numb, his sword in the mud at his feet. He felt his soul boiling in him.

'Taranis,' he mumbled, voice weak. 'Sigmar…'

He dropped to his knees. The orruks came on, swords raised, laughing.

'Orruks…' he said. 'Or are you? What are you?'

His sight was fringed with shadows.

'*Hur-hur!*' one of them cackled. Its mouth framed brutal speech, tongue licking those yellow fangs. '*We'z Kroolboyz, we iz,*' it hissed. '*Throatsnikkaz. And you'z ded, storm-lord.*'

'Not a lord,' he sighed. He grappled with them, heaving himself to his feet. 'I'm… I am a knight…'

Jaws open wide it raised the blade, and there was nothing but a sly cruelty in its dull red eyes–

Blood sprayed into Actinus' face. He staggered backwards as the orruk went down, splashing into the water, clutching its throat. The other turned and swung, and as Actinus fell to his knees he saw Holger Beck brandishing the relic blade, the sword smoking with gore.

'Get back!' he screamed, hacking down, frenzied, clattering the orruk's shield from its grip. The beast champed its jaws and leapt backwards, but Holger lunged and speared it through the heart. As the orruk slid off the point of his sword, he ran to Actinus' side.

'For Sigmar's sake – for *my* bloody sake – don't die!' he said.

Actinus managed a dry laugh. 'I'm afraid I can make no promises, Captain Beck. But help me to my feet, and we'll see.'

Holger pushed him upright, matching his mortal weight to the Stormcast's armoured bulk. He stooped to pick up the Knight-Relictor's sword. Actinus took it from him, feeling some strength flow back into his arm. His wounds ached, bleeding freely. Pellion was behind him, sword in one hand, banner in the other, the cloth of gold and the blazing sigmarite still shining like the light of heaven.

A few scattered troops, fighting back to back, a throng of desperate settlers huddled in the dirt, waiting for the end; it would not be long now. They had been lured in, tempted by the missing settlers, the vanished company of troops. Now the snare was finally closing in on them.

'My friends,' Actinus said. The blade was slick in his hand from the blood that ran down his arm, the orruk bolt throbbing in his shoulder. 'I have had the honour of fighting with you. Now, let us share the honour of dying together, in righteous cause.' He turned to Pellion. 'This, Knight-Vexillor. *This* is the burden of greatness. This is why we were chosen.'

The orruks prowled the margins of the glade, hissing in the mist. Further in came that same crashing thunder, the crackle of broken vines and shattered trees, the huffing of some monstrous beast. And then it appeared.

The mist parted before it, as if cringing from its touch. On either side, folded in tight to its body, were great leathery wings that rippled and twitched, trailing through the filth. Its head was as big as a man, at the end of a long, sinuous neck that whipped and curled around the margins of the glade, the low-slung jaw racked with slavering teeth, yellow eyes peering through the murk in search of prey. The smell that came off the creature was the stench of a corpse-pit, and when it opened its mouth to shriek Actinus staggered backwards. Sitting there at the base of its neck, saddled ten feet off the ground between the great beast's muscled shoulders, was an orruk warlord festooned with trinkets and fetishes, its body painted in swirling runes.

The warlord gave some harsh command in its grating language, pointing with its spear at the dauntless warriors before it. It laughed, long and loud, crowing at them, leaning forward in the saddle with a look of hideous amusement on its face. The carrion-beast shrieked at them again, slithering forward. Behind it, in a cautious advance, came the orruks of the Mirkmere Swamps – the Throatsnikkaz, the spirits of the water, fey dwellers of the blackgum and the vine…

Actinus raised his sword.

'I give you the honour of dying first,' he called to the warlord. 'You and your pet.'

The orruk roared with laughter, but before Actinus could attack there came a howl from behind him and Holger sprinted across the hummock of wet ground, sword raised high. His face was flushed with madness, his teeth bared. He threw himself forward, facing up to the blunt, fanged maw of the carrion-beast, swinging wildly with his blade until he had hacked a bloody smear across its snout. The creature reared back, screaming, eyes like pools of dead water, the warlord desperately gripping the horn of its saddle to stop himself from falling.

'Iron Bulls!' Captain Beck cried. 'Iron Bulls, for Excelsis!'

He lunged in again, slashing at its chest, gagging on the stink of its blood – and then Sergeant Huber was leading the last of her troops forward to support him, a tight knot of soldiers bearing swords and spears, splashing their way through the putrid water.

'To the captain!' she called. 'To Captain Beck!'

The beast snapped down and grabbed Holger in its jaws, its savage teeth piercing his chest and shoulder. He screamed, and blood gushed from his mouth. With a flick of its head the creature sent him flying through the air, crashing into a spray of ferns. Huber roared, her voice cracking, the Freeguild stabbing the beast in a dozen places even as the orruk warlord stretched to hack them down.

The orruks, initially stunned by Beck's crazed assault, regained themselves and burst across the island of raised ground towards them. Actinus staggered forward, sword up. His right arm was numb. Pellion was at his side, chest heaving, a vicious cut across his eye. A handful more, the last survivors.

'They will fit our names to your banner,' Actinus wheezed. 'And even if the banner is lost, one day it shall be found, I swear. Our comrades will avenge us. We will take our place in the roll of the honoured dead!'

Come then, he thought, the orruks getting closer. *Bring me to the end of my purpose in this place… Bring me to the light once more.*

It was like the risen sun, burning away the mist and the foetid darkness. Azure, blinding, a wash of gold that burned in from the west and bathed the Stormcasts in its refulgence. Actinus blinked against it.

The orruks, mobbing near the patch of open ground, fell back in confusion, lank arms raised to shield their eyes. The warlord's carrion-mount, bleeding from its wounds, unfurled its rugged wings and shrieked, the bodies of the savaged Freeguild troops scattered in the shallows at its feet. As the orruk boss tried to thrash his warriors onwards, Actinus could see the form that strode purposefully through the light. He laughed, and his wounds were as nothing. His sword was a feather in his hand. His soul burned inside him.

Leta's arrow, he thought. *It has brought salvation. It has brought the light.*

Lord-Imperatant Taranis, bareheaded, his face a mask of cold and tempered wrath, stood there with his ornate greatblade resting on his shoulder. His praetors flanked him, and behind him marched the golden host of the Taranite Chamber – phalanxes of Vindictors, shields and hammers raised; Vigilators in skirmish order, springing through the mire to outflank the orruks to north and south; the battering ram of the Annihilator contingent, and the massed champions of the Vanquishers. Hundreds of warriors, the Thunderstrike come to place the hammer of justice on the baleful darkness of the swamps.

'Knight-Relictor,' the Lord-Imperatant said, his voice booming across the waters. 'Can you still fight?'

'Always, my lord,' Actinus said. 'Until the end.'

'Then do me the honour of joining me in battle,' Taranis said, raising his blade. 'Let us show these scum the full extent of Sigmar's reach.'

Actinus clashed his sword to his breastplate, and behind him the survivors of his force roared in triumph.

'The honour will be mine, my lord,' he said.

EPILOGUE

The Veins were quiet as he approached the temple, his feet ringing on the cobblestones. The bustle of the afternoon had faded to a cautious dusk, and there were only a few pedlars out selling their wares, a handful of beggars lying in the alleyways. The tottering tenements reared above the streets, some of them braced with scaffolding as all the work of construction continued. Actinus looked up into the narrow strip of sky just visible between the rooftops. It still fumed with eldritch cloud up there, the bitter veil of the Cursed Skies, but Jonas had been right; a little light did still get through.

The temple was quiet, as always. His feet scuffed on the dun sandstone as he passed along the nave, between the lines of simple wooden benches. Above the altar rose the stained-glass window, Sigmar burning in the void. Actinus raised his head and pressed his hand to his heart.

He stood by the altar and took Holger's sword from his belt, placing it with reverence on the brushed stone.

After the battle, hooting their distress, their warlord dead and his stinking steed hewn to pieces, the surviving orruks had disentangled themselves from the fight and had slipped back into the mists and the fell shadows of the Mirkmere. As the Vigilators guarded the perimeter, Actinus had searched through the bodies until he found the Freeguild captain, lying broken in the weeds. His shoulder had been ripped open, and the carrion-creature's blade-like teeth had punctured him from throat to hip. And yet he still held the sword, blackened with the creature's blood. On his face had been an expression of firm and unyielding resolution.

Sergeant Huber had limped over to him as Actinus crouched in the mud. Her face was battered, one hand pressed to a wound in her side.

'I never thought I'd live to see it,' she said. 'Captain Beck, a hero.'

Actinus gently removed the sword from the captain's cold grip. He tucked it into his belt.

'None of us are made heroes,' he said, standing up. He winced at the pain of his injuries. 'It is something we have to choose instead.'

He looked around to see Stormcast warriors helping the survivors, passing food to the settlers, some of them slinging the bodies of the dead orruks into the water. Lord-Imperatant Taranis, his blade cleaned of orruk blood after the fearsome toll he had personally taken, was ordering the dispositions for the march back to Excelsis. They were so close to the edge of the swamps; they had made it so far, close enough for Leta's warning arrow to be seen from the eastern bastion. So close.

'I suppose the company is yours now, sergeant,' Actinus said. 'I imagine a promotion will be due for this.'

Huber, looking sickened, stared at the carnage around them, the swirls of blood in the black water, the body parts, the spilled guts and severed heads.

'What company?' she said, simply. 'I'm all that's left.' She looked at the Knight-Relictor. 'All my friends are dead.'

'My sympathies,' Actinus said, as he moved away. He glanced up at the fringe of the canopy, the rucked sheet of dark cloud above. 'To survive is a burden that cannot be shared.'

Now, as he stood by the altar, he heard a scuff of feet from the sacristy. A door opened and a young priest appeared. He was pale, bookish, black hair beginning to thin at the crown. When he saw Actinus he gave a cry of shock and threw himself to his knees.

'My lord!' he stuttered. 'One of Sigmar's chosen! You honour us with your presence.'

'Please,' Actinus said softly, 'stand. There is no need for such obeisance.'

'Of course,' he said, getting to his feet, his voice quavering.

'Where is Jonas, the priest who serves this temple? I would talk with him, if I may.'

The young priest bowed his head.

'Forgive me, lord, but he has passed away, taken into Sigmar's grace. He was an old man. His time had come.'

Actinus looked away. He stared up at the stained-glass window, nodding.

'Of course. I understand.'

'My name is Pieter, if it please you, sir. I serve this temple now.' Although he could not quite meet Actinus' eyes, he glanced to the sword on the altar. 'If there is anything I can help with, it would be the greatest of honours...?'

'This?' Actinus said. He looked at the sword. 'I bring this for the benefit of the temple. It is a great relic, a holy weapon used in Sigmar's cause. Jonas gave it to me, and I in turn gift it back to you, more sacred than it was before.'

The priest flushed with shock. Reverently he reached out for the hilt of the blade, not quite able to bring himself to touch it.

'My lord! This is too much, for a humble place such as this!'

'Nowhere is too humble for Sigmar's grace,' Actinus said. 'This blade belonged to a man called Holger Beck, a captain of the Iron Bulls. He stood undaunted against the darkness. He saved my life. He was a hero. Remember him.'

Actinus turned to go. The priest tore himself away from the sword and called back down the nave.

'But surely, for a relic of such holiness, it deserves to be in High Azyr?' he cried. 'In the presence of the God-King himself?'

'No,' Actinus said. He turned at the door and looked back. The altar was struck by the soft red and golden light as it fell from the window. 'Let it remain here, where it can be seen. Let it remain among the people.'

YOUR
NEXT READ

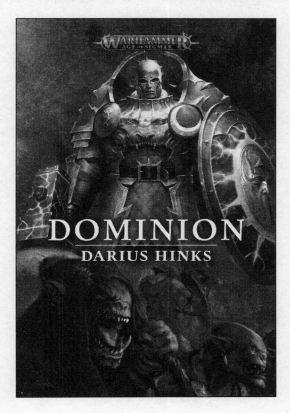

DOMINION
by Darius Hinks

In the Realm of Beasts, savagery reigns. As the forces of Destruction beat at the gates of Excelsis, sellsword Niksar Astaboras is embroiled in a journey across the hostile wildlands that could yet preserve Order in the Mortal Realms.

BOSSGROT

Eric Gregory

'It's the wrong way, innit?'

Gribblak opened the visor of his helm and squinted through the rain to survey the valley. His skrap was an avalanche before him, but it was falling in the wrong direction, falling *back*, a tide of grots and squigs and troggoths crashing towards Gribblak and the safety of the foothills.

His cave-shaman, Oghlott, fidgeted. 'They's leggin' it, boss.'

'I en't told 'em to leg it.'

'All respect,' Oghlott said, 'they's bein' chopped to bits.'

Gribblak's visor creaked down over his eyes again. He left it down this time, stared at his shaman through the eye slits. Oghlott was a keen enough shaman, but given to glumness. Now and then he needed some conviction slapped into him. Gribblak smacked the other grot's back.

'That's rot. They's just got to shape up.' He cupped his hand around the grille of his helm and shouted, 'Go back, you half-gitz! Shape up and go back!'

The dusk light was muted behind the clouds, and the freezing rain was picking up, turning to sleet. Out of the roiling clash bounded a clump of squig-riders, the grots clinging to their panicked mounts. Squig-breath fogged the air, and the beasts crashed through the outlying yurts of the enemy encampment like red fists pounding muddy slush.

That looked mighty fine to Gribblak. Smashing the camp, driving the roving 'umies away from King Skragrott's territories – it was the whole point of this raid on the valley nomads. These weren't even the cleverest 'umies. A bunch of blood worshippers, by the look of their banners. Fools enough to worship the mess inside 'emselves; fools who had wandered too far into Skragrott's claim.

So why was Gribblak's skrap running away?

He glanced aside at Oghlott. The shaman clutched his robes tight against his body, anxious or cold or both. Braids of roots and cave-fungi swayed from his neck as he shivered. Maybe…

'Give us a Dincap,' said Gribblak.

Oghlott's frown deepened. 'Why–?'

Gribblak snatched a deep-purple mushroom from the braid around the shaman's neck, opened his visor and swallowed the fungus whole. The moment the flesh of the Dincap touched saliva, it began to vibrate.

His throat thrummed and his guts shook as he swallowed the mushroom in a gulp.

Being a boss was about words. Anyone could see that. The boss-gods of the realms – the bloated pus-bag gods and big rat gods and shiny gold git gods – you didn't see them out here scrapping. You didn't see them at all. They were stories. They were words in the heads of their warriors.

The big bosses knew how to put the right words in the heads of their mobs, and that was why they won. That was Gribblak's way, too, and it had got him this far: boss of Gobbolog Skrap.

And it was going to take him further. Maybe Gorkamorka had taken a bite out of the Bad Moon, but Gribblak was going to eat the whole thing.

He was going to be the boss of gods.

'OY!' he shouted, and his voice reverberated down the valley. The Dincap's vibration in his stomach and chest and throat gave him the voice of a hundred grots, the voice of a riot.

'OY!' he shouted. 'LOOK 'ERE.'

In the muddy, rain-lashed valley below, the stampede of his skrap slowed. The eyes of his grots turned up to him; even the cave-squigs hesitated and turned around, confused. Now that the fighting slowed and Gribblak commanded the attention of the valley, he could see that the 'umie nomads looked up to him, too, clad in their crimson armour and furs, axes and butcher's knives in their hands. A thrill of pleasure ran across his scalp.

Look at 'em all, looking at me!

Gribblak imagined how he must have appeared to these common grots and 'umies, his lunar helm gazing down like the Bad Moon itself. Proper majestic.

'YOU LOT,' he thundered. 'SHAPE UP AND SHOW 'EM WHO'S BOSS!'

The grots of the skrap looked back and forth amongst one another. Now Gribblak raised an angry finger towards the enemy line.

'AND *YOU*. COWARDS! SEND YOUR BEST AND I'LL GIVE 'IM A POINTY ENDING.'

The entire valley seemed to hesitate as Gribblak's words echoed. The sleet drummed against his armour, and satisfaction welled in his chest.

This was how you did it. This was how fights were won. You didn't need to go down in the mud and actually stab an 'umie. Inspire your skrap, goad the other side, and watch the show – that's how gods did their business.

And then it stormed out of the fog of dirt and snow and flesh: the 'umie blood-boss.

It *had* to be the boss. Its armour was stained the colour of sunsets, and steam rose where the rain fell on its skin. It rode a beast like nothing Gribblak had ever seen, metal and sinew clenched around hellfire; the eyes blazed, and slag-spittle dripped from the jaws. The warboss' axehead burned, too, an otherworldly crimson borne aloft like a torch. A wreath of skulls hung around its neck.

The 'umie clutched a wriggling grot by the waist – a fanatic still gripping his ball and chain. The blood-boss raised the grot to its mouth and tore his head from his neck, then hurled the limp body aside and emitted a garbled, throaty scream.

The hooves of the beast burned the ground where they fell. The blood-boss crashed through the skrap's already tattered line and made straight for Gribblak.

'Leg it,' he squeaked, and his tinny alarm echoed across the valley. 'LEG IT!'

The blood-boss stormed past a troggoth, and the troggoth's arm – still wielding a stalactite plucked from an old lurklair – whirled into the air. Squigs scattered from the front lines, screeching their distress and bounding into the hills. And the sleet turned to hail.

Gribblak ran. He was already unsteady, breathing hard inside his helm as the ponderous thing bobbed with every step, but now he was slipping in the mud, and pellets of ice threatened to knock him flat. 'Oh please oh please oh please,' he panted, and his own voice thundered all around him, 'OH PLEASE OH PLEASE OH PLEASE.'

The cave mouth was close. From his perch in the crags of the foothills, he could wriggle into the damp, dark safety of his caverns. Squeeze his way into a narrow passage where no fire-eyed 'umie monstrosity could follow.

But the blood-boss was quick, and Gribblak couldn't turn his head to see how close it was. He couldn't see much of anything, ahead or behind. He was almost to the cave mouth, wasn't he? He tried to blink away sweat and sleet. The ground was shaking, or he was – then something *massive* slammed him in the back and he went skidding through the mud.

'*Please,*' he screeched. 'I en't boss of 'em! Don't kill me! I en't bossgrot!'

And his throat vibrated, and his helm thrummed, and the words sounded all through the quicksilver valleys in the northern reaches of King Skragrott's claim:

'PLEASE! I EN'T BOSS OF 'EM! DON'T KILL ME! I EN'T BOSSGROT!'

He hardly knew he was talking, at first, he was so lost in his terror. He wanted to move, to run, but he was frozen where he lay. Was he dead? The rain drummed on his armour. He heard his own words playing around him, his own begging, and another voice, too.

'Shut up!' said the voice. 'Just a squig.'

Gribblak looked up at his cave-shaman. Grimacing down at him, Oghlott gripped his arm and hauled him upright. 'Up,' he hissed. 'Shut up and run, go!'

He ran. And as he scrambled towards the cave mouth, an echo of his begging chased him:

'I EN'T BOSSGROT, I EN'T BOSSGROT, I EN'T BOSSGROT...'

A lot of bosses liked to boast that they'd never taken a shanking, but that wasn't Gribblak's way. You had to reckon your losses, he said, in order to know who to blame.

Once the shakes had died down and he felt fit to hold court in his Reckonin' Room, Gribblak set his Gobbapalooza to work up a ledger of the damage. Oghlott recited the totals:

A full two dozen fanatics. A contingent of snufflers. Seventeen squig hoppers, and most of the squigs. Two Dankhold troggoths.

One gargant named Hurg. A coterie of stabbas that no one actually remembered joining the skrap, but whose remains were present and who had definitely themselves suffered a stabbing.

'And,' Oghlott finished, 'morale.'

The boss and his counsellors sat around the fossilised toadstool that served as a round table. Luminescent mould lit the lair a sickly blue.

'Who?' Gribblak asked.

Oghlott hesitated. 'Wot?'

'The last one. Whoizzit? Mor–'

'Mor-*ale*.' Oghlott pursed his lips. 'The fightin' feelin' in the mob.'

Gribblak frowned and rubbed his eyes. 'Is these the gitz I got to hold Skragrott's claim?' he asked no one in particular.

Several of the Gobbapalooza – his shroomancer and scaremonger and boggleye – exchanged glances. Hazzlegob, the scaremonger, munched absently on what looked like a small bat's wing. He stuffed the wing through the mouth-hole in his Glareface mask, which was painted to make him look like the primal enemy of all grots: the great burning face in the sky, bright-death incarnate, Glareface Frazzlegit.

'I got to show the Loonking I'm *keen*,' said Gribblak. 'Show 'im I got this skrap in hand. But they got no stick-it-to-it, do they?'

'No stick-it-to-it,' repeated Hazzlegob glumly. He was the only one who answered, but he didn't seem entirely attentive.

Gribblak had tried to be a good boss, a kind boss. A lot of grots wanted to rule with an iron claw, to command fear and timid obedience, but that wasn't Gribblak's way. If you lived on your skrap's fear, you'd lose everything the second someone scared 'em more. What you wanted, what you *really* wanted, was unqualified adoration. Or failing that, some grudging respect. Gribblak thought he'd done right and proper by his mob – he gave 'em a place in the deep and dark, let 'em carouse a bit in between raids...

But maybe he'd gone too easy on 'em. Let 'em get soft. Some of these young grots hadn't seen real scrapping since they were wee spores, and perhaps not even then. The moment they hit a band of blood-drunk 'umie daemon worshippers, they turned tail and ran.

'We got to get 'em fit and fighty,' said Gribblak. 'If you fall off the squig, you got to get right up, stab it in the eye and show it who's in charge. We got to throw 'em back in a fight.'

Oghlott the cave-shaman glanced across the table at the members of the Gobbapalooza. 'Once we heal up, build the mob back up a bit–'

'I en't talkin' later. I'm talkin' now.'

The chamber was quiet. The glowy moulds flickered.

'Now,' said Oghlott.

Gribblak smiled. He expected his counsellors were feeling pretty awestruck by his boldness of vision.

'It's got to be now. Give 'em a win 'fore they got time to get all mopey 'bout tonight. And 'fore Skragrott gets wind we took a shanking, starts to think we's less than keen.'

'When,' said Oghlott carefully, 'is *now*? And what fight do we got to throw 'em into?'

Gribblak felt such a surge of pride in his new plan that he spread his arms in a flourish of revelation.

'Tonight! The Glinty Crown!'

King Skragrott's territories had steadily expanded since his founding of the loon-city Skrappa Spill and the vast outlying network of lurklairs in the Yhorn Mountains. But in the northerly reaches, his Gloomspite hordes had hit a snag.

On the peak of Mount Pizmahr: a fortress hammered into an iron mountain of Chamon. Mob after mob and skrap after skrap had laid siege to the fastness, and each had been repelled. Not just repelled, but decimated. The fortress was cold and silent and flew no banners – no grot knew who held it, or why. But whenever a skrap approached, the massive cannons on the ramparts thundered, and even the finest mobs were broken.

A great Glinty Crown on the peak of Pizmahr, its cannons winking a taunt in the light of day. And a prize that the King of Grots hadn't yet added to his pile.

If he could give Skragrott the Crown, any little missteps or embarrassments would be forgiven, forgotten. Surely he'd ascend to the ranks of the king's most favoured generals alongside the likes of Izgit or Warrblag. The skrap would get its pep back – everyone would win!

'No,' whispered Oghlott.

The cave-shaman usually had a downcast look to him: tired or dour. But his demeanour was changed now. He met Gribblak's gaze, and his tone was resolute. Some decision seemed to have worked itself out behind his eyes.

Gribblak blinked. 'Wot?'

'*No*,' Oghlott repeated, more firmly this time.

'You en't allowed to say no,' said Gribblak, more puzzled than angry.

''Ts sayin' no. The skrap'll riot. You try to send 'em on some death-wish blunder 'fore the moon has set on the *last* rout, these gitz'll tear you limb from limb and eat your tongue to shut you up. They'll rip us *all* up just to be safe.'

The moulds on the wall brightened, as if in response to Oghlott's raised voice. Gribblak sat back on his toadstool stump, aghast.

'They'd never. They adore me. Even the meanest gitz got some grudgin'–'

'They do *not* got some grudgin' respect for you,' Oghlott spat. 'Not before, and sure as Gork's fist not now. Not after the raid on the Corroded Hills, not after that awful sortie with the stunties and the time we lost a lair to some tree-aelves. Not after you ran squealing from the 'umies where any git could hear...'

The memory floated up out of his guts unbidden: *Please! I en't boss of 'em! Don't kill me! I en't bossgrot!*

He shook his head to dislodge the words. The valley had been noisy. No one had paid him any mind.

'Stop talkin' rot,' he said. 'This skrap is mine. I built 'em up with my own hands. I know what's best for 'em, and they *know* I know what's best for 'em.' He stood up. 'You lucky I don't shank you.'

Oghlott looked to the assembled Gobbapalooza, and all save for Hazzlegob – who had fallen asleep – nodded their support.

'We's all tried to do our jobs,' said Oghlott. 'But if we got to stop you to do right by the Loonking and the skrap, that's what we goin' to do.'

His counsellors stared at him, unified and obstinate. The mould-light flickered again, and each of their eyes glowed red in the dark.

Gribblak had been afraid of a great many things in his day, but never his own Gobbapalooza. None of them were very fighty taken alone, but together they commanded an awful brew of shroom-spells and hallucinations and danksome magics. He backed out of the Reckonin' Room slowly.

'*You en't boss,*' Gribblak hissed. 'Y'hear me? By sun-up you'll see. I'll take the Glinty Crown and this skrap'll call me bossgrot and cheer. Mark my words. By sun-up.'

And with that, he turned and ran from his own skrap.

He needed a disguise.

In battle – or *near* battle – Gribblak was unmistakable. The plates of his prized boss-armour were layered with growths of war-fungi, and the bright yellow lunar helm put him a head above the other grots. The get-up always made him feel a bit more like a boss: he stood tall and heavy and looked out from behind the face of the Bad Moon itself.

But the armour was also a bit of a pain. The helm was cramped and unsteady, and its visor wouldn't stay up. The vambraces were sufficiently heavy that he had to grunt and strain to raise his arm and point at stuff, especially as a battle wore on. And while the crop of mushrooms growing across his armour were appealingly colourful and helped clear his head for wily tactical calculation, they also smelled like the troggoth dung in which they had been cultivated.

When the skrap was at ease in their lurklair, Gribblak wore a different sort of dress: robes and sashes of the finest make a grot could get, dyed the colours of squig-skins and glow-moulds. Around his neck he wore the fangs of Chamonite ore-beasts bigger than gargants.

So he was always unmistakable.

Gribblak hurried away from the Reckonin' Room and through the windy lurklair passages that led to the common grot-holes. Puke pooled on the ground, and the leftover parts of half-eaten cave wyrms were strewn about everywhere, as if they'd been hurled at the cavern walls. The stench of both mixed with spilled brew.

Gribblak knew the skrap got rowdy, but this was ridiculous.

At his feet he found a grot passed out with his arms wrapped around a stalagmite, his black Moonclan robes splayed around him.

Aha, Gribblak thought.

With his new, pilfered hood pulled low over his eyes, Gribblak made his way through the tunnels of the lurklair and into the Ruckus Pit. The gitz had spent an inordinate amount of time equipping the chamber with massive kegs built into the walls. Everywhere, stalagmites were festooned with shroom-chains. Glowing spore dust drifted through the air, giving off a faint light. Teeth and chunks of bone fashioned into dice littered the ground; the stench of bodily waste was thicker, and grots were passed out here and there in heaps.

Ordinarily, the noise of the Ruckus Pit echoed through the lurklair at all hours. But the mood was subdued now – a low music of mutters punctuated by the occasional bitter laugh.

If Gribblak knew one thing for certain, it was that his skrap adored – or grudgingly respected – him. And though he couldn't fathom why Oghlott and his band of back-stabbers would believe otherwise, he was going to have a mighty fine time showing them just how loyal his gitz could be.

In disguise, Gribblak would walk among his ordinary grots. He would speak with them of their hopes and dreams, and plant the rumours of a glorious plot soon to unfold at the hands of their boss. Then, when the ground was prepared and the time was right, he would reveal himself as Gribblak and announce, with maximum drama, the siege of the Glinty Crown.

He couldn't wait to see the look on Oghlott's face.

Doing his best to walk like a common grot, Gribblak approached a cluster of gitz gathered in a circle. It looked like they were play-ing some dice-chucking game. As he came closer, he could make out fragments of the grumbled conversation.

'–fine and good but *I'd* pull out his tendons, to start.'

'Tendons. Mm.'

No one paid Gribblak much mind as he joined the circle. The dice-chucking game, he found, wasn't quite a game. Instead, the grots were trying to prod two runty squigs into a fight by half-heartedly throwing bone-dice at them.

A lot of bosses liked to mix with the common grots when they weren't fighting – have a few mouldroot brews, act like a regular git – but that wasn't Gribblak's way. You could pretend all you liked, but the fact was your leaders had one job, and your front-line grots had another. Maybe you could buy cheap affection with a shared drink, but a proper boss cultivated real love, real power, real command, all by drawing lines. Gribblak knew he was right about that – it was all the proper gods' way – but it meant he hadn't spent much time talking to his mob.

'Howzit 'ere?' Gribblak asked. He tried to sound like his idea of a common grot, and a little inebriated. 'You's drinkin' anyfink good?'

No one answered for a while. The smallest grot fidgeted with an emblem of the Bad Moon. 'Just the swill wot's left,' he said. He looked up at his friends and resumed the previous conversation. 'I 'spect *I'd* work up a kinda grinder for 'im. Put 'im through nice and slow, turn 'im into a kinda paste.'

A grot with one eye nodded approvingly. 'Nice one, Vork. We oughta put you in charge.'

'I heard a rumour,' Gribblak broke in, 'dat da boss has some kinda proper plan to put Gobbolog Skrap on top. Right where we's belong, eh?'

The one-eyed grot paused mid-throw, narrowed his remaining eye. 'Aye. Right where we belong. What's your name?'

Gribblak hesitated. 'Hob... blangle,' he said. 'Hobblangle.'

Vork grunted. The one-eyed grot threw his dice, caught one of the tiny squigs on the head. It squealed and flopped into the other animal, but they didn't seem to want to fight. 'I'd like to hear what the boss'll have us do now, then.'

'Well,' Gribblak said, 'I 'ear he's keen to take a *big* prize. Maybe even da Glinty Crown.'

'I'll bet 'e is,' snorted Vork.

'Reckon 'e aims to give us a win. Show us we's a sharp lot of–'

'You boys remember,' Vork interrupted, 'when we lost a lair to those *trees*? Trees in a cave. I never.'

The others laughed darkly.

'We get shanked,' Vork sighed. 'Over'n over, we get shanked.' He shook his head and threw his Bad Moon emblem at the larger of the runt squigs. The medal smashed the beastie's head and left a luminescent pink goop on the cavern floor.

'Aw, c'mon, Vork,' someone said.

Gribblak tried not to let his consternation show. With this group of grots, at least, he was going to have to be a little more inspirational than he'd anticipated.

'I wonder,' he said, 'wot you's hopes'n dreams are – for after we take the Glinty Crown?'

'Y'know,' said the one-eyed grot, 'we was just talkin' through that. Rankar here was thinkin' we oughta tie the boss' arms and legs to four squigs and send 'em all running to the four winds. And I like that for a dream, but I'm really intrigued by Vork's put-'im-through-a-grinder idea.' The one-eyed grot stared at Gribblak, his eye unblinking. 'You?'

Gribblak shivered. 'I want a drink,' he said quietly.

Vork grinned. 'I'll bet.'

Trying not to look too out of sorts, Gribblak backed away from the circle and hurried deeper into the Ruckus Pit, pulling his hood further over his head.

His thoughts wheeled like he'd eaten a bad toadstool. That was proper seditious talk from the dice-throwers. But it was just six gitz, right? Six gitz didn't make a skrap. And these front-line grots were notoriously unreliable. You had to watch 'em every second.

In the farthest corner of the Ruckus Pit, where it was darkest and most danksome – and where the largest keg stood – Gribblak spotted his top bounder trio, known in the skrap as the Squigwind. Between the three of them, they'd been riding for six seasons, which was a prodigious and frankly improbable amount of time for anything to survive mounting a squig. The Squigwind was held in awe by the rest of the skrap – given all the best grub, the best grot-holes, the best trophies (though it had been some time since the skrap had occasion to take trophies). They were exactly the sort of voices Gribblak wanted to hear, and wanted to speak for him. Respected. Influential. With the Squigwind behind him, the rest of the skrap was sure to fall in line and march on the Glinty Crown.

The trio sat along the spine of some long-dead subterranean beastie. The nominal leader, Ralgog, smoked an elaborate pipe of stunty make and stared at nothing, while the spore-twins Habble-grob and Grobblehab played a pilfered snare drum and lyre, or at least thwacked the instruments at intervals. The thwack-song was slow and disjointed and unpleasant to the ear, but – perhaps on account of the musicians' status in the skrap – no one complained.

'Oy!' Gribblak called, waving to the Squigwind. 'Howzit 'ere, bounderz?'

Ralgog didn't look at him. 'Zog off.'

It had been a good long while since anyone had told Gribblak to zog off from anywhere. For a moment, he was speechless.

'I got – I mean, a rumour's goin' round y'might want to hear,' he managed.

The bounder Grobblehab slapped a discordant twang of irritation from his lyre and threw it to the ground in anger. 'They said *zog off*, didn't they?'

'Now you stopped Grobblehab playin',' Ralgog growled.

'I–' Gribblak started.

'*I want to hear the music,*' Ralgog spat. 'Go away. Or I'll gut you.'

It was as though something in the air had gone rank and thick and bitter, and every grot Gribblak talked to had breathed it in. But that only made his plan more important. He resolved to stand firm.

'Rumour is,' he pressed, 'boss is goin' to lead us on a siege of the Glinty Crown 'fore sun-up.'

'Ahh. I see what's goin' on here.'

Gribblak froze. 'You do?'

Ralgog waved away Gribblak's rumours like a faint odour. 'Don't y'worry, little grot. He tries anything that stupid, we'll feed 'im to the squigs.'

'I 'spect we'll feed 'im to the squigs anyway,' Habblegrob added in sing-song, banging the drum to each syllable of *an-y-way*.

'It's past time,' Grobblehab agreed.

Somewhere in Gribblak's head, a voice was beginning to scream, and he wasn't sure he would be able to shut it up. He could feel the shakes starting up again, and he was desperate not to let that show – inside his robes, he gripped his own wrists and tried to hold himself together. The Squigwind was just a bunch of big-headed gitz with mouths full of rot, he told himself. Their pride was bruised; they didn't mean what they said.

'You en't really goin' to feed 'im to the squigs, though,' he said quietly. 'You wouldn't. He's the boss.'

There wasn't a chance for the Squigwind trio to respond. Into the Ruckus Pit marched a grumbling, clattering, stomach-turning procession. Flanked by two Dankhold troggoths – one missing an arm – and their attendant trogg-herders, Oghlott and the Gobba-palooza entered the chamber, banging a piece of scrap metal like a bell.

'OY!' Oghlott shouted, Dincap-amplified. 'NOW HEAR THIS. GRIBBLAK WANTS TO MAKE US FIGHT AGAIN TONIGHT. HE WANTS TO SEND US TO THE GLINTY CROWN TO DIE. BUT WE EN'T GONNA STAND FOR IT. WHO 'ERE THINKS 'IS TIME IS UP?'

The grots in the Ruckus Pit roared their approval.

'Grind 'im up!' shouted Vork.

'Let's feed 'im to the squigs!' called Ralgog.

Gribblak couldn't stop the shakes now. His whole body trembled; his hands shuddered in his robes. The screaming voice in his head made it hard to think straight. *This skrap is mine. I built 'em up with my own hands.* Were the words in his head, or was it his own voice screaming?

Gribblak hurried towards the lurklair tunnels farthest from his back-stabbing cave-shaman, and for the second time that night, he fled from the grots he was meant to command. And all the while a voice screeched, *You'll see, I'll show you, you'll see.*

* * *

Frantic, hands shaking, he tried to strap the vambraces to his wrists. Latch the greaves. Usually he had someone to help him with his armour, and these irksome echoes kept sounding in his head:

I en't bossgrot, I en't bossgrot, I en't bossgrot...

Stupid. Gribblak tried to shake away the past. Fumbled the last armour-strap through its loop and put on his moon-helm.

You'll see, he thought. *I'll take the Glinty Crown and this skrap'll call me bossgrot and cheer.*

The armour-stash was quiet, except for the shifting, slobbering sounds of nearby squigs in their paddocks. All the grots were in their holes, licking their wounds, or else plotting revolt with the Gobbapalooza. Gribblak took up his slicer and made for the stables.

He was still shaking, and his thoughts were still a storm, but Gribblak moved with a new clarity of purpose. He opened the stable gates and stepped towards the sound of gnashing in the dark.

In the Gobbolog Skrap, a bounder of the Squigwind was held in awe for riding an ordinary cave squig and surviving the season. But there were madder and more deadly mounts.

Among many of the skraps most favoured by King Skragrott, it was customary for bosses to keep a mangler: two giant cave squigs chained together. Each of these monstrosities had grown to the size of a troggoth, or larger, and together they were a tide of destruction, two hungry disasters that hated one another.

Up to now, Gribblak hadn't actually ridden his mangler. But now was the time. He was boss. This was his place. He opened the cave-mouth gate, then opened the paddocks.

What followed was a blur. The darkness filled with thundering squig-flesh; Gribblak grabbed hold of a rein and held on as the mangler squigs rammed into the walls of the stable, smashing the other paddocks and releasing the rest of the smaller cave squigs.

Then the mangler jerked in the opposite direction and they were outside, tumbling at an absurd velocity through the Yhorn foothills, night air whipping Gribblak's skin.

Summoning all the strength in his shaky limbs, Gribblak climbed the leash and seized the harness and goad atop the larger of the mangler squigs. They touched ground and then leapt, again and again, creating a jerky, bobbing rhythm. Muddy slush flew as they bounded forwards; trees snapped and branches scritched across his helm. Gribblak looked above and below, looked for anything to guide him.

And there it was: the Bad Moon.

The grinning light shone down and lit a path towards Mount Pizmahr and the Glinty Crown. Gribblak exhaled in awe, then renewed his grip on the harness and goaded the mangler squigs north, towards the Crown.

For a wonderful moment, they answered his reins, or at least moved in the direction he harassed them into moving. He soared through the night under the light of the Bad Moon, and he raised his lunar helm high, and in spite of the madness and sick-making speed, his shakes stopped.

This was it. The peace of perfect command. This was where he belonged. He fixed his gaze on the fortress atop Mount Pizmahr and grinned.

Then, with a *crack*, muzzle flashes lit the face of the mountain. The Bad Moon fell behind the clouds, and fire streaked at him through the sky.

The cannons on the ramparts of the Glinty Crown thundered, and it was as if an entire mountain were shooting flame at him. A shot must have hit the larger mangler – it yowled and surged forwards when it touched ground, somehow faster and angrier than before.

The fortress grew closer, closer. He could make out torches on the ramparts – what looked like 'umies.

They were moving too fast. His eyes teared up; he couldn't see. Another shot cracked, and it must have stopped one of the manglers this time. He lost his grip on the harness and now he was in the air, hurtling faster than he'd ever moved, tears in his eyes and his stomach in his throat, a lone grot in the night sky.

He woke to the sound of 'umies.

There was an ugly cadence to their speech. Their words were like stones in a wall, dull and neat and all in line. But you could catch the gist of 'em.

'–a single rider?' said one voice.

'I shouldn't think so. I have encountered the creatures a great many times, and I have never known them to act alone.'

'Perhaps it was inebriated.'

'Oh, indubitably. But I'll guarantee that more of the filthy little sots are to follow.'

Gribblak was face down on damp straw. Night breeze still cooled his skin in the spots his armour didn't cover. He got to his knees, blinked, opened his visor, looked around.

He was under the stars, still. The sky was purpling to dawn. Underneath him, a thatched straw roof. The roof was inclined, and he had to work to keep his footing as he stood.

Below lay... well, it looked like an 'umie village. He'd seen – and razed, or *tried* to raze – plenty of little townships like this back in his early raids as boss, back before everything went to rot.

The first voice was speaking again. 'To be frank, lord, I am uncomfortable firing the cannons while the instrument is tuning. The crew report... strange sights. Faces in the powder, lord. Tongues in the cannon fire.'

Gribblak looked out over the village. It wasn't quite the same as the 'umie settlements he'd seen before, now he looked closer. The buildings were crowded together, leaving only a web of narrow alleys between them. The village was surrounded by thick walls and cannon emplacements. And in the centre of the settlement was a vast machine of rings and spheres, twice again the size of the house he stood atop, golden and seeming to speak to every sense at once, shine-hum-vibrating and leaving a copper tang in his mouth and nose. Understanding struck him all at once.

The Glinty Crown. His mangler had hurled him into the Glinty Crown.

Alone.

Gribblak crawled to the edge of the thatched roof and glanced down at the owners of the voices. The 'umies were both covered head to toe in silver armour and red regalia, but what really seized Gribblak's attention were the blastas and fire-sticks strapped to their belts and backs. He felt the shakes starting to return. These were some of the most heavily armed 'umies he'd ever seen. Soldiers in the same armour marched through alleys across the village, fire-sticks at the ready.

'Your objection is noted, captain,' said the 'umie with the biggest feather in its hat. 'I will report your crew's sightings to the battlemage. But I recommend that you master your discomfort. It is unlikely that the Collegiate wizards will interrupt the night's trials on the Orrery.'

'Yes, lord.'

The 'umies parted, and Gribblak exhaled. He looked up to the Bad Moon for reassurance, but the sky was empty now. No grin, no guiding light.

And that was about right, wasn't it? Coming here had been stupid, stupid. He couldn't break a fortress himself. His whole skrap couldn't have survived the first thirty steps of a march on those cannons.

Oghlott was right. He was a git. He'd never been bossgrot, not really: he was a stupid git, and grots had listened to him for a while, and now they didn't.

He was a stupid git whose luck had run out, and he was on his own.

Gribblak whispered a plea to the Bad Moon. 'Let me live,' he whispered, 'let me get outta here, and I'll just take what I get forever after. But let me live.'

The night was silent, except for the shine-hum-thrum of the golden machine and indistinct 'umie orders in the distance.

'Right,' said Gribblak. He was on his own.

First, he needed to get off the roof. Then he could sneak through the alleys, make his way to the top of the ramparts, avoid the gunnery crew, and climb down Mount Pizmahr.

He took a deep breath.

Below the edge of the roof, about a body-length down, was a cart full of straw. Gribblak scooted over the edge of the roof feet first, kicking to find a foothold on the cart. He misjudged the step, slid off the edge, hit the cart and fell onto the cobbles of the alley with a loud clang of armour on stone.

'What was that?' came the voice of the 'umie with the big feather. Gribblak scrambled under the cart as its footsteps neared. Four more pairs of feet followed shortly behind, and Gribblak watched the armoured boots approach.

'I saw one. One of the little sots. I would swear on it.'

'Heads and fingers steady,' said the 'umie boss. 'We *cannot* have any stray fire, understood?'

The boots stopped by the cart. Gribblak bit the insides of his cheeks and gripped his wrists, and tried to stop himself shaking, fearful of his armour ringing against the cobblestones.

But it didn't matter. Slowly, the captain peered under the cart. There was nothing for it.

'Yaaaaa!' screeched Gribblak, and leapt out at the captain. He grabbed the 'umie's head and gripped its helmet; the 'umie stumbled backwards, dropping its weapon and batting at its own helm. The other soldiers raised their fire-sticks uncertainly.

'*Do not fire!*' the captain shouted. 'Do not fire! Hit it with the stock! Get it off me!'

Gribblak dug his armoured claws into the captain's eyes, eliciting a scream from the 'umie, then hurled himself from its shoulders to the spot where it had flung its fire-stick. The weapon was a lot to lug, but he could just manage to carry it with both hands. The 'umie soldiers decided to disregard their captain, spraying fire all around Gribblak as he rounded the corner and dived into another alley.

Which way were the ramparts? He tried to remember the view from the roof, but he couldn't quite place himself. He passed what looked like a blasta-stash, an 'umie mob-hole. In one doorway, an armoured soldier blinked and reached for its fire-stick as Gribblak raced past. The line of 'umies in pursuit was growing.

He weaved left and right, zigged and zagged. Where were the drink-houses, the game-houses? He'd seen plenty of 'umie villages. There should have been big, dumb uggos stumbling out of taverns and puking in the streets. There should have been swindlers and night's-watch and angry card games and midnight music – all the messy life that turned to screaming when a Gloomspite raid caught a town unawares in the dead of night.

Instead, the Glinty Crown was all soldiers marching in rows and that awful shine-hum-thrum. Where were the spore-'umies and wrinkly-'umies? What kind of village was this? There was something wrong about the place. He thought again of stones, dull and all in line.

He emerged into a courtyard, and realised he was running the wrong way entirely. Before him was the great golden spinny machine, all spheres and rings. *Orrery*, the 'umie captain had called it. Around the instrument were gathered 'umies in robes of black, adorned with astronomic patterns in gold. The robes almost reminded him of a common Moonclan grot's.

The Orrery was bright-loud-heavy. The copper tang sharp on his tongue. The robed 'umies turned to regard Gribblak, and their eyes blazed white.

In the centre was a light as bright as death and hot as annihilation. He swore he saw eyes in the fire, eyes and a gaping mouth. He saw his scaremonger's mask before him, and every scare-story he'd ever heard as a little spore-git returned to him at once.

'Glareface,' he whispered.

Gribblak raised the fire-stick and shot at the Orrery. He wasn't sure what happened next. The recoil knocked him on his back and dislocated his arm. The muzzle flash was light and thunder but it was also a face, and the face vomited more faces, which vomited more faces. The faces weren't grot or 'umie or anything else that made sense, and they licked the world with tongues of fire. He was pretty sure the fire-stick wouldn't have done that in a normal place, but somehow it didn't seem all that strange here, now, in the loud-heavy-bright aura of the Orrery.

Behind Gribblak, his 'umie pursuers opened fire. Their muzzle flashes made faces, too, and bright hairline cracks opened in the spheres of the Orrery, in the faces of wizards. The light in their eyes and mouths shifted from white to a pulsing rainbow.

The world was breaking. Gribblak got up, spun around and dived under the legs of his pursuers, back into the dull, cold alleys of the Glinty Crown. Gritting his teeth against the pain in his arm, heaving his armour forwards with every step, Gribblak did what he did best:

He ran.

In the wake of Gribblak's flight from Gobbolog Skrap, Oghlott was left with no choice but to abandon the lurklair. The paddocks were smashed and the tunnels were swarming with squigs, so the surviving grots made their way outside, into the foothills. It was the first real moment of cheer the skrap had shared in ages. The troggoths were grumpy to be awake, of course, but the grots laughed about Gribblak's flight and the various means by which they would kill their old boss when they found him.

For his part, Oghlott was almost gratified by the necessity. Of *course* Gribblak had ruined the lurklair as he left it – *of course*. Further proof that the Gobbapalooza made the right choice in deposing him.

For the first watches of the night, the craftiest grots fashioned effigies of Gribblak and entertained themselves by flattening or shredding or burning or eating them. They scanned the horizon and kept half-joking watch for Gribblak, should he attempt to return. Some discussed who would be the next boss, glancing sidelong at Oghlott, who was careful to make no claims on boss-dom. He had an idea that the leadership of the skrap ought to arise out of common agreement, but he was still working out how to put this to a mob of boisterous, intoxicated gitz.

As the night wore into morning, the grots of Gobbolog Skrap grew less boisterous, but more intoxicated. They'd started eating more potent mushrooms out of boredom, and many watched the horizon purple in a bleary stupor. Having nothing better to do, and having plenty of choice fungus on his person, Oghlott joined them.

And then something strange happened. The sky bloomed, its purples unfolding all at once into blues and pinks and reds and greens, a rainbow corona that expanded to encompass the sky.

In his fungal haze, Oghlott couldn't be sure for how long this unfolding in the sky carried on. It might have been minutes; it might have been hours. Then, as abruptly as the colours had opened, they collapsed into a single point on the peak of Mount

Pizmahr. The Glinty Crown erupted in a column of flame that made a false daybreak.

Yelps of fear arose from the grots who were awake. Oghlott shielded his eyes.

It was late, and he was severely inebriated, and time shifted tricksily. An hour might have passed, or a night. At first, the cave-shaman thought he was hallucinating. But no, there he was, trudging through the woods towards him:

Gribblak.

One arm hung limp at his side, and the other lugged an 'umie fire-stick. The visor of his moon-helm was broken off, the yellow paint was scorched. The bonfire of an 'umie fortress burned on the mountain peak behind him.

He staggered towards Oghlott, panting hard, and hurled the helm from his head. The grot underneath was bloodied and squinting through a puffy eye, but it was unmistakably Gribblak. Oghlott looked back and forth from Gribblak to the ruins of the Glinty Crown to Gribblak again.

'You was right,' Gribblak gasped. 'I en't bossgrot. Never was. It oughta be you.'

Much of the skrap was passed out, but the ones who were awake and gazing at the horizon drifted closer to see what was happening. The scaremonger, Hazzlegob, left off chewing the head of an owl to stare at Gribblak.

'I en't interested in fightin' or runnin' no more,' said Gribblak. 'So you know. You don't got to hunt me down. I'm finished.'

Hazzlegob swallowed part of his owl. He removed his mask, briefly considered the crude Glareface scowl, and pointed at the blaze on Mount Pizmahr.

'You do that?'

Gribblak looked back at the destruction and frowned.

'Oy!' said Hazzlegob, sudden and sharp. A nearby pile of grots startled awake. 'Boss 'ere's burned down the Glinty Crown all by hisself.'

More of the skrap began to gather. 'I never seen Skragrott do nuffin' like that,' one said.

'I never seen a herd of troggoths do nuffin' like that.'

'You 'member those rumours in the Ruckus Pit?' said a one-eyed grot. 'I 'spect we got it wrong. I 'spect the boss was sayin' he'd take the Crown on 'is own.'

'If 'e can do that, 'e oughta take the crown. The real one.'

The talk was moving too quickly for Oghlott to follow properly. Gribblak seemed to feel the same, looking confusedly from speaker to speaker.

''Ere's to the boss–'

'Down with Skragrott–'

'The Bad Moon's high!'

'Give 'im a crown–'

More and more grots gathered, staring at Gribblak and the horizon in awe. The little grot looked helpless in his armour, dragging his 'umie fire-stick. In his numb fungal haze, Oghlott wasn't sure what to feel. Despair? Relief? Resignation? What he did feel, as the skrap chanted around him, was an unnameable brew of the three. Snufflers and bounders and herders and every other sort of grot stomped over the effigies they'd made earlier to get a look at their returned leader.

'Hail Gribblak!'

'High King of Grots–'

'Touched by the Bad Moon–'

'Hail to the bossgrot!'

The mob cheered, and behind Gribblak, the sky burned. He looked questioningly at Oghlott. 'I'm bossgrot?'

The cave-shaman shrugged.

'I *am* bossgrot,' he repeated, and it wasn't a question this time.

Gribblak surveyed the assembled mob, squared his shoulders, stood a little taller and raised his voice. 'I killed the Glareface, y'know. Got 'im right in the eye.' He grinned.

'D'you want to hear the story?'

YOUR
NEXT READ

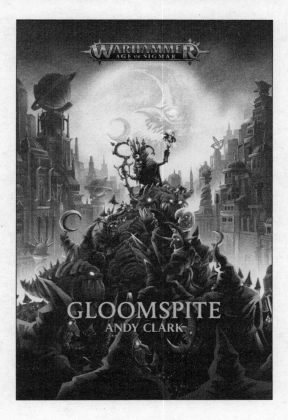

GLOOMSPITE
by Andy Clark

The Bad Moon looms over the city of Dracothium, and Watch Captain Helena Morthan knows it bodes ill for the town. Can she and grieving warrior Hendrick Saul defeat the plans of the Gloomspite Loonking and save their people?

THE SPEARS
OF AUTUMN

Richard Strachan

The ridgeline levelled as the horsemen reached the summit. The land fell away below them into a rich meadow speckled with white flowers, where a silver stream cut across the grass and disappeared into the broad gilt spread of the autumn forest in the distance. Belfinnan could see the mist rising amongst the trees, the branches mantled in red and gold, the shadows that lay thick against the trunks.

Arduinnaleth, he thought. The Blessed Woods, as was. But now no longer. Now no more than a place of dread and secret sorrow...

The forest spread out against the horizon, from one end of the Sundrake Plains to the other, a wide blanket of russet and brown. Far to the south Belfinnan could see the conical peak of Cuithan-nan Tor, like a crown rising from the trees, but to the north the edge of the forest was lost in the rising mist. His horse, Gyfillim, shied nervously under him.

'There, lad, there,' he said. 'Take heart. There are worse trials ahead, I'm sure, than this stretch of woodland.'

Behind him, the Spears of Sariour spread out along the ridge: five hundred Dawnriders, their proud stallions barded in white plate. On each steed sat an aelf clad in the panoply of war, with a bright lance tucked into the holder at their stirrup. Their blue pennants and the curving crests of their helmets waved in the soft breeze that murmured across the grass, bringing with it the scent of leaf mould and dust from the distant trees.

'I do not like this, lord,' Bethyn said at his side. She twitched the reins to bring her steed in line. 'Arduinnaleth is a cursed place, they say. Even in Xintil the rumours reach us. Few who enter come out unscathed.'

'Myth and folklore.' Belfinnan grinned. He turned his smile on her. 'And even if it were hard fact ground out by long study, I would care not. This is the route ahead of us. There is no other.'

'We could pass around,' Bethyn suggested. She pointed off towards the north. 'There's a road that skirts the forest and would bring us back in time to the right path.'

'Aye, and in how much time?' Belfinnan said. 'Stonemage Y'gethin has struck his banner and called for help, and Belfinnan the Brave would not tarry in providing it. We must reach the Temple of Ultharadon as quickly as we can.' He laughed. 'And the last to arrive owes the rest of us a round of drinks!'

He reached across and slapped her shoulder. Bethyn sagged in her saddle and rolled her eyes.

'Brave hearts and bright blades, Bethyn,' he said. 'Let the forest fear us, rather than the other way around.'

'Of course, my lord,' she sighed. She glanced to where the troop had ranked up in crisp order, awaiting Belfinnan's command. The sunmetal of their lances gleamed like starlight. She lowered her voice and leaned in closer.

'Not all of us have the hearts of veterans though,' she warned. 'We lost many in Shyish, and the new recruits are untried. The

dangers ahead of them are sore enough, surely, without putting
them to a further test?'

Belfinnan frowned and looked away. The sky was blurred with
cloud, a trailing spread of grey that seemed to reach with drear
tendrils down to the tips of the brooding trees. The regiment
had performed miracles in Shyish, fighting with skill and valour
as the Lumineth made their strike against Nagash. But Bethyn
spoke the truth; their casualties had been heavy, and of the new
recruits there were many who had yet to experience the blood
and madness of combat. Especially against an enemy as pitiless
as the Ossiarch Bonereapers...

He shuddered, and twisted around to disguise it. He saw again
the grey Shyishan plains, the miserable amethyst skies, the champ-
ing skulls of the Ossiarch infantry in their endless phalanx. The
whirl of swords and falchions, broken spears, aelven blood spilled
in the unforgiving dust... He looked at his riders again. One
young aelf near the left flank trembled with apprehension, as if
the dark mass of Arduinnaleth were an enemy host drawn up
before them.

Now there's one close to the edge of it, he thought. Aye, untested
indeed... But the test cannot come soon enough.

'We go on,' Belfinnan commanded. 'An hour wasted on the way
is an hour less to defend our homes.' His face was fierce and certain. 'Let us fear no darkness before darkness itself veils our eyes,
for there is plenty of time for caution when we're dead.'

'They fell to the Thirsting God during the Spirefall,' Ceffylis said
as he rode. He shook his head, as if he couldn't bring himself to
believe such folly. 'The aelves that used to live here. Once, the
healing arts were brought to perfection in Arduinnaleth, but then
they turned from healing to the study of pain.' He glanced at the
trees and touched the rune on his breastplate: *Senlui*, the breath of

the wind. 'Fell tales of torture and sacrifice darken these woods…
What madness drove them, what spite?'

Beside him, his horse picking its way through the leaf-litter,
Dyfeth laughed. The sound seemed to flatten out in the silence of
the forest, stirring nothing in Ceffylis' breast but a dull foreboding.

'I don't believe it was ever that bad,' Dyfeth said, with a confidence Ceffylis was sure he didn't feel. 'And it was so long ago.
You've been listening to old wives' tales, Ceff.'

'The scholars say it too! Those who study those dark days. My
father said–'

'Your father's a farmer on the Xintil plains,' Dyfeth said, as if
he were explaining it to a child. 'What would he know about it?'
He laughed again, more easily this time. 'Put away such fancies,
we'll soon be at war! Turn your mind to the Bonereapers instead,
and the thrashing we're going to give them!'

'You weren't in Shyish either, Dyf,' he said. 'Don't act the veteran.'

Dyfeth looked put out. 'Veteran or not, we've got Belfinnan the
Brave leading us – the dead men don't stand a chance! He crushed
the barbarians at Silent Meadow without breaking a sweat, he's
the best blade in Xintil.'

Ceffylis nodded queasily and looked around at the grey columns of the trees. Straight and branchless, frothing out into a
wide canopy of orange and gold far above them, they marched
off endlessly on either side, rows and rows like the serried ranks
of an ancient army. Some listed with age into their neighbours.
Others were tall and arrow-straight, looming over the aelves as
they rode through the forest. Their grey bark seemed to shine
with a leaden, spectral light.

There was no sound other than the crunching progress of the
Dawnriders as they rode across the carpet of dead leaves, no birds
singing in the branches, not a breath of wind. The regiment picked
its way along a shallow trail, heading ever east towards the rumour

of Ultharadon in the distance: the holy mountain, the seat of the temple where Stonemage Y'gethin had sent out the call for aid. Aid, against the dread legions of Nagash, the Bonereapers...

Ceffylis felt his stomach lurch.

'Still,' he said, warily. 'Nothing good ever comes from being overconfident.'

He started in the saddle and looked around wildly. He had heard a breath mutter briefly in his ear, as if someone had whispered over his shoulder, but when he turned there was nothing there. Only the ranks of the trees stretching away into the shadows, the curling mist that lingered in the hollows and drenched the fallen trunks. No breeze, nothing...

'You heard that too?' Dyfeth said. His grey eyes were hard behind the slit of his helmet. He clenched his jaw.

'The whispers of the dead,' Ceffylis said quietly. The leaves tumbled around them in a drift of dust. 'The aelves of the Blessed Woods linger.'

Dyfeth spurred his horse forward.

'Then stay and chat with them if you like,' he said, scowling. 'I want no part of it.'

Ceffylis watched him ride further up the trail. He brought his own horse to a halt. The rearguard cantered on ahead of him, the sound of their passing soon swallowed up by the heavy shadows and the thick leaves that littered the forest floor. A leaf dropped from the high canopy, and in the silence it crashed to the ground like a falling rock.

A line of sweat trickled from his scalp. He clasped his lance, felt the horse under him shy slightly, grumbling in the quiet. He was suddenly weary, tired from the long leagues they had already covered and the thought of the miles they still had to go. And for what? he thought. For war against the Bonereapers, the worst of Nagash's armies. He hadn't been with the others in Shyish, but the veterans told sour tales of that dread enemy, tales so grotesque he could scarce believe them. They tore the bones from your corpse, it was said, and used them to build new soldiers for their ranks. They snatched the very soul from you and stuffed it screaming into their troops...

'Teclis save me,' he whispered. He missed his father. He missed the calm and placid acres of the farm where he had grown up. The spear felt hollow in his hand, as flimsy as a child's toy. The armour felt ludicrous on him, like a costume for a mummer's ball. It smothered him, its weight threatening to drag him from the saddle. Better a plough, he thought. A plough and rough-spun clothes for the fields.

Underneath him, Tuicellin, his horse, began to skitter and whinny, darting to the side as if reading his mood. Or as if distressed to have such a coward on his back.

Ceffylis...

He whipped around. Something trailed in the mist behind him, a puff of smoke blowing apart on the breeze. But there was no breeze here.

Ceffylis, son of Ceffyllam...

'Who's there?' he cried.

Soon to die on the plains of Ymetrica...

'I will not die,' he muttered. He clenched his teeth and hugged Tuicellin with his knees, the horse bucking under him, whickering with nerves. The sweat was cold on his back now, and his fear was a ball of ice in his stomach. 'I will not die in this place.'

The mist and the leaves seemed to conspire then, to breathe together and whisper in the shadows, and as he stared into the darkness he thought he saw a haggard aelven face carved out of smoke. Leering, laughing at him from behind the trunk of a swaying tree.

'Leave me be,' he whispered.

He flicked the reins and Tuicellin leapt forward. He could see the rearguard up ahead. He looked back, but the shadows of the forest were empty behind him.

The Dawnriders camped for the night in a spread of clear ground near the centre of the forest. A cold circle of pale light was all they could see of the evening sky above them. The ground was covered in a soft, grey grass, and scattered throughout it were the jumbled foundation stones of ruined buildings, last relics of the aelves who had once called Arduinnaleth home. Ceffylis felt a strange repulsion from those stones, and so he built his campfire towards the edge of the clearing, where the shadows under the trees lingered. He tethered Tuicellin and saw to its fodder first; like any Dawnrider, he had been trained to put his horse's needs before his own. He patted the beast's flank and gathered sticks for his fire. He lay down on the grass, his helmet and his lance at his side, and listened to the low murmur of his comrades talking around their own campfires. He could hear Lord Belfinnan's bright voice calling out from the other side of the clearing.

'On occasions such as this,' he cried, 'I always feel that a little poetry is the perfect accompaniment...'

There was a chorus of groans from his oldest comrades, the steedmaster's laughter chasing them as he began his recitation. Ceffylis drowsed near sleep, staring into the flames of his campfire. How could he be so cavalier, so full of mirth, in such circumstances?

I am not like him, he thought. I do not have what it takes to be a hero.

Belfinnan the Brave, victor of the Shadrian Crisis when he was younger than Ceffylis was now. The greatest horseman in Xintil, the finest blade. Legends accrued around him the moment he got up in the morning, it seemed. And where did they all march to now, but to give aid to an even more forbidding name – Carreth

Y'gethin, stonemage of the Temple of Ultharadon, one of the greatest warriors in Lumineth history. What was Ceffylis compared to them? A pebble next to a mountain, a scared boy who jumped at shadows and whispers, while these aelves duelled with the gods themselves.

He had grown up on the edge of the Xintil plains, where the Spears of Sariour often trained. Many a day he had spent as a young aelf, staring in awed wonder at the majesty of the Dawnriders as they passed his father's fields, the glint of their armour, the proud bearing of their steeds, the strength of their arms. He had striven since those days to join their ranks, and now here he was, a rider in the company of Lord Belfinnan himself. A rider who did not deserve such honour.

He rolled over and saw Dyfeth a few yards away, sitting by his own campfire, talking easily with Gwen'allin from First Lance. She drew out her lyre and strummed a gentle chord, singing softly to herself while the flames crackled next to her. Dyfeth glanced over but Ceffylis closed his eyes and pretended to be asleep.

Why did they not feel as he did? They sat there in easy comradeship, singing to calm their souls, while he tormented himself like this. He could hear the leaves falling beyond the clearing, the drift of dead things relinquishing their grip. The green season was turning across the continent. Autumn prepared to throw its russet cloak across the lands.

Like us, he thought. The Lumineth came through the fire of the Ocari Dara into a quick green spring. But now autumn is upon our race at last.

Everyone said it. In hushed conversations, in keen-eyed glances between old friends, they admitted the truth. Even Dyfeth felt it, despite his bluster. The Bonereapers could not be defeated. Death itself could never die, and Nagash would only be held back for a little while. They would all die in this war, even as the leaves of

Arduinnaleth died, and the autumn drifted into a cold and un-forgiving winter.

He woke suddenly and felt the touch of a chill breath against his skin. He screwed his eyes shut and reached in his mind for the first rung of the Teclamentari, trying to settle his mind and smooth out his soul.

His campfire was no more than a smattering of embers. He felt cold, although he had drawn his cloak around him before falling asleep. He sat up, rubbing some life back into his hands. There were leaves scattered around him, a trail of crisp red and yellow that led into the depths of the forest. He felt icy fingers around his heart. His breath began to quicken, pluming in the cold air.

Your death is near you now, Ceffylis, the whispers said. Harsh and insinuating, wheedling and clear, they drew around him like a bitter breeze. *Turn and run, boy. Save yourself, coward, from the doom that will claim you.*

'I am not a coward!' he hissed.

Coward… no more than an untrained boy. But the wise man runs from folly.

The voices rolled and chuckled around him, thin as paper.

The coward lives, while heroes die in pain and misery.

He felt his voice catch in his throat. He thought of his father suddenly, bent-backed as he tended their fields. He imagined him shielding his eyes to watch the messengers pick their way along the cart track as they brought news of his son's death: Ceffylis cut down, his body looted for its bones on some bloody Ymetrican field. The harvest would be coming in soon, he thought. His father would need help; he couldn't manage on his own. He needed his son.

Run, save yourself, save those that you love… Tarry not, or the swords of the dead will pierce you.

He could barely take a breath, he was so cold. He looked around the clearing where his comrades slept, wrapped in their cloaks and blankets, their fires crackling low. Around the edge of the clearing, the Dawnriders' horses dozed gently, some standing, some at sufficient ease to lie down.

Is it just me? he thought. *They come for me because they know I don't have the courage to go on. They see me for what I am... I am not a warrior, not a hero.*

He seemed to see the smoke-wreathed field of battle before him, the marching legions of the dead, their blades stained with aelven blood. He shuddered and closed his eyes.

Quickly, the decision made almost before he realised it, he packed his few things and rolled up his blanket. He saw cold faces lurking in the trees, watching him with amusement. Cold aelven faces, scarred and broken. They pulsed and faded in the mist, and their dead eyes followed him as he crept silently across the clearing. A few of his comrades grumbled in their sleep, but none woke up to see him leave. Good; he could not have borne the shame of being witnessed. By the time anyone missed him he would be miles away. He swallowed hard and felt tears pricking at his eyes. He was no warrior. He was nothing but a farm boy, deluding himself that he could ride with legends.

Yes! the voices muttered around him. He felt cold fingers brush against the back of his neck. *Do not look back – leave these aelves to the mercy of the dead... None will leave Arduinnaleth alive... None will leave Ymetrica now.*

Quickly and quietly he fitted the bridle and drew Tuicellin from the edge of the clearing. True night never fell in Hysh, and although the sky above was masked in cloud, there was enough light to show him the trail they had followed yesterday. He held his breath and listened. A guard would have been set around the camp, but he was sure he could slip by them unheard.

'Come, Tuicellin,' he whispered. He stroked the horse's neck and led it by the reins. 'Let us be quit of this place at last. Let's go home.'

He was no more than thirty yards from the clearing when he found Lord Belfinnan; or rather, when Lord Belfinnan found him.

The steedmaster was sitting casually on the trunk of a fallen tree, helmetless, his long legs stretched out before him while he whittled a stick with his camping knife. He looked up at Ceffylis with wry amusement, as if they had done no more than cross paths on a pleasant spring morning.

'I wouldn't recommend this place for a midnight stroll,' Belfinnan said, easily. 'The shadows are thick on the ground, and it's hard to see where to put your feet. Although I've no doubt Tuicellin would know the way home – our horses always do.'

Ceffylis blanched. Shame and horror burned in him. He felt his face flush, and his words as he tried to speak came out in a panicked stutter.

'My lord! I swear, I wasn't... I didn't mean...'

'Ceffylis, isn't it? I saw it in your face, lad, before we entered the forest. "There is one," I told myself, "who is close to breaking." I thought you might slip away, when the chance presented itself.'

Ceffylis looked into the steedmaster's blue eyes, so cold and clear, a hard gaze that would not falter. There would be no lies that could deceive him, he knew. He would only want the truth.

'I bring dishonour to the regiment just by being here,' Ceffylis said quietly. 'I am beset by fears I cannot master.'

'The whispers in the woods?' Belfinnan asked him. 'Pay them no heed. They are no more than the voices of dead aelves who poisoned their souls a long time ago, bitten with rage and sorrow and resentment. They would say anything to turn a faithful soldier from his path.'

'They only speak a truth I can barely admit to myself!' Ceffylis protested. The shadows crawled around them. The leaves fell like a dying rain, a soft dry patter amongst the trees. 'I am a coward. I am frightened, lord. I'm frightened for my father, left behind, and I'm frightened of what awaits us at Ultharadon.'

Belfinnan nodded, as if none of this surprised him. He stood and laid a hand against Ceffylis' shoulder.

'You think I'm not scared too?' he said earnestly. 'Every one of us here feels the dread of war and fears the sorrows to come. It is natural. It is honest, and admitting it is not a flaw.'

Ceffylis looked up. Despite everything, he was scornful.

'Even you, lord? Belfinnan the Brave? Forgive me if I don't believe you. You won the field at the Shadrian Crisis when you were younger than I am now, and I don't see you creeping away shamefacedly in the night!'

Belfinnan glanced away, his mouth a tight line. He let go of Ceffylis' shoulder. He seemed to diminish as he stood there, the proud and dashing aelf deflating into a troubled soul that wrestled with a terrible decision. When he spoke, his voice was bitter. He stared off into the darkness as if seeing again a sight too awful for him to contemplate.

'The Shadrian Crisis, aye...' he said. 'That's where my reputation was made...' He shook his head and something of his former bearing came back. 'Sit down,' he said. Without waiting for Ceffylis to answer, Belfinnan sat once more on the fallen log. After a moment, uncertain, Ceffylis joined him. Belfinnan took a flask from his belt and unstopped the cork, drinking deeply.

'Let me guess what you know about the Shadrian Crisis,' he said. 'The steedmaster, Lord Aquilith, was killed in the first charge. The Godseekers quickly surrounded us and all hope seemed lost. But then, Belfinnan the Brave, a mere boy, rallied the Lumineth troops and led the breakout on the flank. But he didn't stop there – no, as if touched by the martial genius of Tyrion Himself, he looped around and split the Godseekers' army in half. Revealing a genius for war astounding in one so young, he led charge after counter-charge, and destroyed the Slaaneshi forces piecemeal, until not one of them survived. And so the war was won.' He grinned and offered the flask. 'Does that sound about right?'

'It isn't true?' Ceffylis said. 'But everyone knows that story – it's legendary. They say you were wounded in a dozen places and still fought on.'

He cautiously took the flask, inhaling its scent. It was sharp, piercing, like hot sunlight, but mellow too, like a meadow cast in a blanket of sweet flowers. He took a careful sip and coughed.

'Gods, what is this?' he spluttered.

'Liquid courage,' Belfinnan laughed. The sound was like a bright bell pealing on a summer's day. 'A dozen wounds, indeed...' He shook his head. 'The story's half true. That's the problem with legends – they always grow teeth in the telling.'

'Then what really happened?'

'You truly want to know?' He gave a sour smile. 'Well, when the Godseekers attacked, I ran away.'

Nothing he could have said would have shocked Ceffylis more.

'I don't believe you,' he said, but when he looked into Belfinnan's eyes he saw that the facade had fallen away. No more bluster, no more insouciance. The mask had been removed.

'What would you prefer to believe?' Belfinnan said. 'The legend? Or the truth?' He took the flask and drank. When he spoke again, his voice was as dry and quiet as the trees.

'When Lord Aquilith fell, we were thrown into confusion. The charge buckled, half our front line collapsed. I was on the left flank, and we could see the whole advance beginning to falter. That's a sight that can trouble the heart of the bravest aelf, believe me. One rider begins to turn away, and then the next, and then the next, and before you know it the whole regiment is in headlong retreat. The Godseekers fought like daemons, although they were no more than aelves and men. Their chariots, those great bladed wheels, scything through our ranks...'

He squeezed his eyes closed. When he opened them again, they were like shards of ice.

'I turned and ran. Most of us did. I spurred Gyfillim and rode like fury, but when I looked back I could see my friend, Emyris, riding hard towards the Godseekers, screaming, couching his lance. The whole flank had collapsed, but he went on, alone, and his spear was as bright as the light of Hysh itself. Teclis knows, but he was brave...'

'What did you do?' Ceffylis asked.

'I felt ashamed, as you do now. I had known him my whole life, and we had been friends since we were children. Gods, but we weren't much more than children then... It wasn't for glory, or for victory, that I turned around. It was for my friend. I was desperate and afraid, but I knew I couldn't let him die alone. If need be, I wanted to die beside him.' He smiled and corked the flask. 'I could do that much, at least, if nothing else.'

'But you turned the tide?' Ceffylis said. 'You won the field.'

'I did. As I turned, so did others. As I charged, so did my comrades. Soon the whole regiment was following my lead, breaking through the Godseekers' flank. And then the rest, as they say, is legend.'

Ceffylis looked at his feet. 'What happened to Emyris?' he asked, although he already knew the answer.

'He died,' Belfinnan sighed. 'Cut down by a Godseeker's blade. Unheralded, unmourned by any except me.'

'He was a hero.'

'No,' Belfinnan said sharply. He gripped his arm and his eyes were fierce. 'He was an aelf who did his duty, that's all. That's all any of us can do, though the odds are against us and the stakes are as high as you could possibly imagine. Take your fear, Ceffylis, and embrace it. It will not leave you, but if you acknowledge it and respect it, then it will not master you either. This I promise. Do what you have been tasked to do, for none of us can do any more than that.'

'I will, my lord,' he said, and under the steedmaster's burning gaze he meant it. He pictured Dyfeth, lying in the dirt, frightened, wounded. He thought of Belfinnan himself, surrounded at the last, selling his life as dearly as he could.

I will not let him fight alone, he thought. I will die beside him, if need be.

Belfinnan slapped his shoulder. Something of his old mood had come back. The mask had returned to his face, and he was once more the dashing warrior who laughed at death.

'Go on then, lad. Get yourself some sleep. We've a long ride tomorrow. I can't promise the fighting ahead of us will be anything but hard, but if you stay true to your friends, you cannot go wrong. I swear it.'

Ceffylis led Tuicellin back through the trees, those silent sentinels, back across the clearing. His campfire still smouldered, as if he had never left it. He tethered his horse and quietly settled himself down to sleep. The whispers of the woods drew away, as pale now as the memory of winter in the depths of summer's plenty.

They were just words, he thought. Just the voices of aelves that had lost all chance of duty and sacrifice, condemned to fade into the shadows and silence of this autumn place. They could not touch him now.

They left the forest early, brooding Arduinnaleth, chill and austere. The shadows seemed to bleed out onto the heathland from the narrow ranks of trees, and as the Dawnriders guided their horses onto the plains, they felt the last cold whispers fading away behind them. A few leaves scattered out onto the grass, gold and brown and yellow, and the clean air that blew across the plains carried with it the crisp hint of the changing season.

Belfinnan looked back at the woods. There amongst the trees he thought he saw the cold, sad faces of the dead – but just for a moment. As the light rose and the clear sunlight fell, the faces drew away. He thought of Emyris then, choking in the grass, and he held his hand to the rune on his breastplate. How many years had it been? And he felt the shame burning in him still.

He saw Ceffylis riding proudly near the head of the column, his lance held high. He spurred Gyfillim closer.

'You see that?' Belfinnan said. He pointed off to the hazy distance, where the flat green land met the blurred horizon. There, in the centre of the line, was a dark mark like a blunt spearpoint. 'Ultharadon. The Holy Mountain. That's where we're heading.' He turned and cried to the regiment. 'Onwards! Y'gethin's temple has the finest cellars of zephyr-wine this side of the Shimmersea – and if that doesn't spur you on, nothing will!'

He laughed and thrashed the reins and leapt forward across the grass. The wind tearing past him was a faint and sluggish thing compared to the speed of Gyfillim.

Onwards, he thought. Let our spears fall like autumn leaves, but always on, ever on, to the very end… To glory, and to our friends.

THE SEA TAKETH

David Guymer

'Oh, ware the day the fishing folk come,
To no barrier will they concede,
Their lures will entice both the strong and the frail,
And lo will the good fishes bleed...'

'What is that ditty she sings?'

Ingdrin Jonsson had no idea at what age humans considered their offspring to be competent adults, as per Artycle Nine of the Kharadron Code, but the girl was as winsome and waifish a thing as he could imagine, and so he addressed his question to the father.

''Tis an old song, Master Jonsson,' Tharril bellowed, his words timed to the rhythm of his oars and the crash of spray across his back. 'Her ma sang it to her, as my ma sang it to me.'

'It gives me the creeps.'

'Any honest song should.'

Jonsson clung grimly to the port gunwale as freezing saltwater sprayed his face. It was not like plying skyborne currents. His dusky beard stuck to his skin and to his light sky-captain's leathers. He could taste the ocean on his breath. Holding fiercely to the slimy wood, he peered back into their star-speckled wake. The surface of the ocean bulged and receded, as though something vast and primordial breathed. Where waves crested, they caught starlight. Where waves sank, they folded under, taking that captive light back with them to the depths. The oceans were realms within the realms, forgotten by time, history and gods. Ancient magic dwelled there, unformed, untouched by hands mortal or divine since the formation of the aetheric cloud itself. With every precipitating crash against the hull, he was reminded of its elementalism. With every tug of current on the keel, Jonsson conceded a little more that he had placed his fate in the hands of a dark and unruly god.

> *'They crave what's within,*
> *'neath flesh and 'neath bone,*
> *Sparing only the young...'*

Tharril was effectively enthroned in the wooden prow of the boat, an oar in each hand, controlling the boom of the lateen sail with a pedal-like noose of rope about his left foot. Beneath the bench there was a massive warhammer, and in his lap, a spear. Tharril and his folk were fishermen, but there were plenty of fish around Blackfire Bight that would consider a single-sail like this one small prey. Jonsson too was armed, a skyhook on a strap across his shoulder and a privateer pistol loaded in his holster.

Thalia, the girl (Jonsson had also heard her father call her 'spratling' or oft times just 'sprat'), sat against the starboard gunwale, across the centre line from Jonsson. A plaid net lay in sodden folds over her knees as she sang her ballad, extricating wriggling fish as long as her arm or longer. Silver, nightshade blue and bone white shimmered under starlight as they flapped and squirmed, only to disappear into buckets of cold brine. Jonsson watched as she pulled another fighter from the net. Smaller, this one, its tail barely reaching her elbow with her hand clamped expertly about its gills. She tossed it over the side.

The ocean accepted its return with a faint splash.

> 'And when they grow old and grandchildren forget,
> That will be the day when the fishing folk come.'

Jonsson wondered if he was paying Tharril and his girl too much to sail him out there, if they were just going to pursue a normal day's take along the way.

'Why do you throw back the small ones?'

'They are young,' she replied.

'But why?'

She shrugged. 'You just do.'

With a grunt, as disturbed as much by the company of the odd girl as by her brute of a father, Jonsson prised his fingers from the gunwale and leant forwards. His chest of equipment had been stowed inboard.

With exaggerated care because his hands were numbed with cold and shrivelled by salt spray, he worked the combination lock and lifted the lid. Unrolling the now-wet fleece packing, he assembled his zephyrscope and arktant.

Bringing the rubber eyepiece to his eye, he trained it on the twinkling dot of Sigendil. The night sky might vary from realm to realm, and even within a realm, and with the movements of Ulgu-Hysh within the aetheric cloud, but the beacon star of Azyr was a fixed point in every sky. With one eye on the High Star, he manipulated the sliders on his arktant to account for the position of the local constellations.

'Can you hold this thing steady?'

'Ha!' Tharril barked, rowing.

'*Bokak*,' Jonsson swore, as a sideswipe wave spoiled his measurements.

'What are you doing?' Thalia asked.

'Taking a position, girl.'

'Why?'

'Because!'

'I thought Kharadron lived in the sky.'

Jonsson sighed. 'Aye, girl, we do, seeking our fortunes on the aether winds.' He leant across the open chest and winked. 'But every now and again, some careless soul drops something.'

'You are looking for treasure?'

'It won't look for itself.'

The girl sniffed, with the iron rectitude of the very small. 'No one takes from the sea.'

'Good. It'll still be there then.'

'No one takes from the sea.'

'What about these?' Jonsson nodded towards the nets and buckets full of splashing fish.

'That's what the sea gives.'

Her deathly earnestness brought a snippet of a smile to Jonsson's face. 'A sour face like that aboard an aether-ship is almost always a sign of something trapped in the ear. Very serious if left untended.' He reached out as though to tug on her ear, but then pulled his hand back with a flourish at the last moment, presenting her with a copper comet and a toothy grin.

She frowned.

'Hah!' said Jonsson, slapping his thigh. 'Would you see that? Somebody raised this girl right.' He passed one hand over the other, the copper coin disappearing. Then he unfurled the palm of the crossed hand to reveal a larger, golden coin. The girl's eyes lit up, as if in reflection. 'A quarter-share, from the aether mints of Barak-Thryng, girl. Legal tender under any of the six great admiralties.'

'Take the coin, spratling,' grunted Tharril. 'Afore he makes it disappear again.'

Jonsson winked as the girl scraped it off his palm.

'What's that?' she said.

Jonsson followed her gaze down.

'Now *that*,' he said, patting the hard object that lay safe beneath the second layer of fleecing, 'is something that will really amaze you.'

Jonsson's heavy boots thudded to the ocean floor. His legs bowed, his shoulders bunching, the monstrous pressure of the sea bottom crushing down on the weak points of his armour. The rigid plates of the deep-sea-adapted arkanaut suit creaked like a metal pipe being squeezed by a gargant.

'Oh, ware the day the fishing folk come.'

He turned on the spot, ponderous as an armoured beetle. His headlamp sent a speckled beam into the pulverising blackness. Bubbles issuing from the seams in his armour and the rings of his air hose – a mile of collapsible metal flexing from the back of his helmet towards the surface – cut up his light. Every one was a tiny mirror held up in the completeness of the dark.

'Ingdrin Jonsson isn't afraid of the deep!'

He lowered his skyhook warily.

Almost nothing lived at these depths.

He knew of the merwynn and the kelpdarr, fiercely isolationist and protective of their territories, but even they rarely plumbed beyond the sunlit layer. The great beasts that preyed on such folk, lurkinarth and kalypsar and the like, prowled the richer waters of the coastal regions and shipping lanes accordingly. The ocean floor was a desert.

Spiny encrustations of rose-coloured coral glittered everywhere his lamps passed.

There was nothing here.

Bracing himself against the awesome weight of water on his shoulders, he thumped down to one knee. Bubbles and silt puffed up around the armoured joint, but the cloud stayed compact and low. With his beams angled tight to the opalescent reef around him, he ran his gauntlet over its surface. He had never seen a mineral like it. His light seemed to be trapped by the structure of it, spreading outwards through veins of denser crystal. Piece by piece, the reef lit up, and street by colonnaded street, the turrets and spires of a drowned city was lifted out of darkness.

'Tromm...' he breathed, bubbles squirming through the gaps in his mask.

The structures were of coral and lime, as if grown out of the reef itself, the lustre of nacre gleaming from monuments and domes. There were high towers. Great bridges. Palaces. Walls. Statues of what looked like aelves stood sentry over squares and gardens, armoured in opulence in pearl and shells and mounted upon monstrous piscine steeds. For all its obvious former glory, however, the place was a ruin. Pallid, light-shy vegetation strangled the life from the great works, the camouflaged wings of bottom-feeding rays rifling through the debris that littered the grand avenues.

'Aighmar.' Jonsson stared over the coral-lit city with something like reverence. 'Lost city of the Deepkin aelves. I found it.'

'Their lures will entice both the strong and the frail.'

Jonsson gripped his skyhook and looked back. His helmet could not freely rotate about his shoulders. It took a moment.

'And lo will the good fishes bleed.'

Behind him again.

'Who's there?'

He plodded around another half-circle, bubbles exploding from his helmet's seals as he cried out in alarm. While his attention had been fixed on the lambent city of the aelves, the blunt nose of something gigantic had emerged from one of the larger hollows in the reef. Jonsson did not see much. A dull flash of cartilaginous teeth. A silvery ripple of gills. Then there was an explosion in the water, spined fins seething, monstrous grey muscle writhing, and the beast was surging from its lair towards him.

He reacted on a hair trigger. It saved his life.

In a storm of bubbles, the heavily adapted aether-endrin bolted onto his shoulders pushed him up and back. Shudders ran through the water as the beast's jaws crashed shut on the effervescence where he had just been.

Jonsson got a horribly good look.

The beast was as long as a short-range gunhauler, grey as battle-damaged iron. Its eyes were glassy yellow knotholes of alien hunger.

With a powerful stroke of the tail, it twisted into Jonsson's bubble trail, dorsal blade-fin carving the water as it closed the distance, fast. Jonsson swung his skyhook between them and fired. The harpoon launched in silence, a red cloud billowing from the side of the monster's snout.

The beast thrashed in pain and fury, almost ripping the skyhook, still tethered to the harpoon by a taut length of steel chain. Jonsson pulled the release bolt before the gun was ripped out of his hands and the chain twanged off towards the wounded creature. Jonsson drew his pistol from its thigh holster. He had no expectation that it would fire under water, but it was all he had left.

The monster jerked about the middle, gnashing at the chain that its own movements flicked tauntingly over its head, missed, and drove its head through a coral wall. The reef crumbled around it, blood fountaining as the coral worked the harpoon embedded in the beast's snout like a well pump, and something in its animal mind said 'enough'.

It swam away, churning a thin river of red with its tail.

Jonsson let out a relieved breath.

That had been an allopex.

'You have the best bad luck of any duardin born, Ingdrin Jonsson,' he told himself.

He had never heard of an allopex hunting alone, and a school of them could bring down a krakigon.

'They crave what's within, 'neath flesh and 'neath bone.'

With a snarl, he swung his pistol towards the source of the voice, twisting his head prematurely so that he was looking into the back of his helmet. He almost laughed when he realised. It was the air hose. That girl, Thalia, must have been sat near the inlet, singing. He gave the base of the hose a rap as his boots sank inexorably back towards the ocean floor. 'Nothing to fret over,' he said loudly, hoping that his voice would carry back up. 'Just like I promised.'

But when he started towards the ruins of Aighmar, he did so quickly.

There was blood in the water.

One night and another day later, Thalia had a knife in her hand, blood as far up as the elbow.

She sighed, opening the ghoulish bream from mouth to tail and emptying its guts into a pail. She enjoyed filleting. Normally. She liked the sliminess of the fish in her hands. She liked the smell, the sound of the brothing pot bubbling inside, waiting for the tail fins and the heads, listening to the hens in the back patch clucking their goodnights.

She squinted across the shingle to where the sunset was slowly turning the ocean an amethyst-tinged red. The water was placid, as still as the brass mirror that da had never removed from ma's dresser. It looked bigger to her somehow, swollen. Waves lapped at the pebbly promontory, like the village cat at the fish juices on her fingers.

She blinked herself awake, realising that she had been about to nod off. Right there on the porch step, her chores unfinished. She shook her head. The air was thick. Her eyelids felt like honey.

Stifling a yawn, she found herself facing in a direction that she had scarcely given a moment's consideration to before today. The inland road. It was the way to Toba Lorchai, the greatest city in all the realms next to fabled Azyrheim itself, or so her da had told it. Da had never been there though. Neither had she.

Jonsson had gone there.

Thalia had slept all night and most of the morning, but the Kharadron had been packing his chest into his strange metal caravan, pushing a clinking pouch into da's hand and disappearing up the inland road almost as soon as they had drawn the boat up onto the beach.

'A black wind in his sails,' da had said that night.

A sudden shriek from the direction of the water snapped her head up.

The sound lingered on the air for a moment before being abruptly silenced. She strained her ears, but could hear nothing but the crash and tumble of waves on the shingle. The tide was in too high, washing about the boat sheds and net stores. The sea was too red. Brown-and-white kelp bobbed with the action of the waves like bodies.

'Da?'

She bent down to deposit the un-gutted fish back into its bucket as an arrow thudded into the porch post in line with where her eyes had just been. She looked back at it, quivering in the split wood, and gasped, too shocked to scream.

A woman with a dripping shortbow stood waist-deep in the shallows, buffeted from behind by pliant waves. At first glance she might have passed as human, but she was not human. Wet robes the colour of an ocean under moonless skies clung to a slender physique, fish-scale armour cladding her forearms and torso. Her face, shoulders and midriff remained bare, her skin as pale as a dead fish's eyes. Thalia thought her beautiful, but it was a haunting, pitiless kind of beauty, the sort that would drive mere mortals to distraction and despair.

The woman nocked another arrow to her bowstring. She raised her bow to draw, sighting down the shaft. Thalia noticed with horror that she had no eyes. Just smoothed, perfect skin over shallow sockets.

From the first shot to now it had probably been about a second.

Thalia did scream then. She screamed and she ran.

Da would have wanted her to go inside and bar the door. That was what he had always told her to do when the dead and the drowned came. But that was not what she did.

The second arrow whipped past her face, splitting the wood nearer the bottom of the porch post, as Thalia leapt onto the loose stones and tore towards the pier.

Set at the lip of the promontory at the outskirts of the village, the pier served both as a wave breaker and as a mooring for a dozen one- and two-berth boats on its leeward side. It was also where da and the others would sit out and drink beer when the nights were warm.

She started to hear noises as she got closer.

Shouts. Metal.

Fighting.

'Da!'

She sped around the last cabin, a third arrow thudding into the corner boards at her heels, and saw it.

The jetty speared outwards into the still, swollen water, a zig-zagging half-bridge of wood, forested with masts and lines.

Eight women and three men – most of the adults in the village – were there on the boardwalk, hemmed in by an ever-circling tide of lissom warriors wielding two-handed swords. Like the bow-woman they were sightless. Like the bow-woman it did not seem to matter. The village had always prided itself on being well armed, and had been taught by harsh necessity how to use its weapons well. But they were accustomed to fighting off the seasonal deadwalker floods, enemies that could not flow around a cudgel or a spear-thrust like seaweed in the currents of a passing fish. These warriors seemed almost to be dancing rather than fighting, the huge blades in their hands willing partners instead of tools to be directed.

Old legends, myths and songs skipped through her mind. Frightful tales of the dark ocean and hungering aelves.

'Deepkin…'

Thalia picked her da out from the fighting.

Her heart almost stopped beating in relief.

Her da was as broad across the chest as the keel of a boat, browned by sun and sea, and caulked with scars. He could lift Thalia in one hand and cousin Rollin in the other, and throw them both, squealing, off the end of the pier. He was a champion, the God-King of her world.

With a roar, he smashed his warhammer into an aelf's chest.

The blow shattered the swordsman's armour. The aelf crashed to the decking a dozen feet back and did not rise.

'Da!' Thalia screamed in exultation, but he did not hear her.

His full attention was on his enemy.

Seawater was seething up through the planking of the jetty, causing the downed aelf's arms and head to lift up. Thalia gasped, for she was well used to the horrors of necromancy, but this was different. Wasn't it? Something compelled her to keep watching as a ghostly light shrouded the body. It seeped into the aelf's skin through the half-heart brand on his forehead, and mere seconds after hitting the deck a ruin, the aelf was vaulting athletically back to his feet. Armour hung off him, but the bruises over his ribs were already fading. He butterflied his moonlit blade.

Her da scowled and hefted his hammer.

Thalia's mind was racing, faster even than she was as she tore onto the boardwalk.

A very different-looking aelf warrior emerged from the sea on the crest of a solitary wave to be deposited onto the board-walk beside her da. His armour was scalloped and studded with jewels, heavier and finer than that worn by his warriors. His helmet was tall and fluted, inhumanly ornate, and entirely without any openings for eyes or ears. Only the mouth was visible and it was thin-lipped and cruel. In his hands, he bore a long-handled weapon with a serrated edge that fell somewhere between scythe and spear. A small lantern globe hung from its head. There was something about its light that pulled on Thalia, behind her eyes, inside her chest, that was desperate to take leave of her and be one with the source of that light.

The newcomer turned his spear, his *light,* towards her da.

His eyes softened as the light bathed his face. He lowered his hammer as though his arms could no longer lift it. He stared into the light. Something horrible and golden seemed to lift from his shoulders, streaming towards the aelf's lantern.

Then her da collapsed to the deck.

'Da!'

Small and desperately quick, Thalia darted through the melee, avoiding friends and hard-faced aelves both as she splashed onto the flooding jetty and threw her arms over her da. She shook him, crying, 'Da. Da! *Da.*' His eyelids quivered as if he were asleep and dreaming. His chest rose and fell beneath her body. Relief choked off her sobs. He was not dead. He was not dead.

She wiped the tears from her eyes, feeling the sting of seawater. 'Wake up, da.' Taking a shoulder in each of her hands, she shook him. 'Wake up!'

'I think that I am... feeling,' said the aelf with the light, looking down on Thalia and her da through the faceless metal of his helm. His lips remained straight lines, but he steepled a hand over the ridged plate of his breast and turned his blade aside. 'Pity. Sorrow.'

'It is understandable, soulrender.'

Another magnificently lithe aelven warrior strode down the boardwalk. She was perfect, a queen of austerity, dark-haired and pale-skinned, armoured in black, as cruel as the ocean waves.

'Away from the crush of blackness and cold, what can we do but feel as we were made to? Trust instead that soon it will be done, and that oblivion awaits us all beneath the waves.'

The one she had named soulrender lowered his head. 'It is rare to find such wisdom in the souls of the *akhelian*. The martial council chose well in electing you our queen.'

Thalia's lip was trembling, but she knelt defiantly upright between the aelf queen and her da, brandishing the inch-long filleting knife that was still in her hand.

'I like you, child,' the woman said, though neither her voice nor her face expressed any emotion. 'I would see my *namarti* children take souls like yours.' With a scimitar that glowed the colour of rose coral, she tilted Thalia's jaw so that their eyes met. 'My name is Pétra. Queen of the Mor'phann, protector of Aighmar and reaver of souls.'

Thalia was suddenly painfully aware that the sounds of fighting had stopped while the aelf queen had been speaking. A tear glistened in her eye, in defiance of her pride.

She wanted her da.

'Speak to me of the one that took from my ocean.'

* * *

Jonsson woke to the crash of waves.

He started, huge fists clamping around the leather steering grips of his endrin-cart and squeezing until both knuckles and leather were whitening. He breathed, letting the tension go slowly. Just a dream. Clearing the misted glass with a sleeve, he peered out at the bleakly forested hillside. The trees were stick-thin, sparse black leaves rustling with a sound like that of the distant sea amplified through a conch shell. It was dawn. He had allowed himself to sleep for too long. The expedition to Aighmar had wearied him more than he had admitted to the girl. But he had not been prepared to linger in that village a moment longer than he had to.

Cursing under his breath, he wiped the nightmare sweat from his palms on his trouser leg, and pulled open the door.

A rush of chill morning air displaced the stale, fish-breath odour that had been allowed to stew in the cabin overnight.

Too long.

Too, *too* long.

He clambered out, stretched his back, stretched his legs, then hurried around to the front of the cart to crank the endrin. Once the vehicle was awake and purring he hauled himself back inside and pulled the brake lever.

He made it another six hours before the endrin packed in with a wheezing sputter. He got out again, tense and muttering, to crank it one more time.

One last time. Another six hours ought to do it.

He stopped for nothing. Not for food. Not for drink. *Definitely* not for sleep. When the sun again began to sink below the barrow hills, he got out to light the lamps and climbed right back in.

Blackfire Bight was a vast and lawless expanse of grim hills, moribund coastline and bone-coloured sands, but it was neither banditry nor undeath that worried him.

He had already slept too long.

Jonsson did not know much about the sea-aelves. No one did. They were a myth, and in some cases even less than that, and from every scrap of information he had been able to uncover, they were quite brutal about ensuring that remained the case. *Deepkin*, some called them. *Idoneth*, those scant records suggested they called themselves. Some fragments of text claimed them to be descendants of the *cythai*, the first, mythical race of aelves to have been drawn into the realms by their creator, the god of learning and light, Teclis. Legends. If there was even a nut of truth to them, then the cythai had fallen a long way indeed. Such stories as existed in the inherited consciousness of coastal communities across the Bight were of settlements scoured overnight, ships vanishing, armies disappearing without a trace of an enemy, wars of migration as entire nations were driven inland by a sudden, inexplicable terror of the sea.

Jonsson did not know much.

He knew enough to move inland, fast.

He tried to avoid thinking of Tharril and the girl.

If Jonsson's mind was a keenly running endrin, then his conscience was that oil-stained bit of machinery that presumably did something of tremendous import, and which Jonsson had managed very well by never interfering with. He patted idly at his jacket pocket, cursing himself for giving the girl a whole quarter-share. What had he been thinking? What was she going to spend it on? He scowled. This was exactly what his old endrin-masters had always tried to teach him. Know every bit of your endrin. If you did not, then it was liable to hiccup at the most inconvenient of times.

The endrin-cart grumbled as it continued to climb.

Walls. That was what he needed. High ones. And guns. And an airship. Grungni, did he want his feet back on his airship. The Deepkin were coming for him, he could feel it in his water, and the one place nearby that was as far beyond the reach of an angry sea as it was possible to get was Toba Lorchai.

Skyport of the Kharadron.

Toba Lorchai was a thriving free port, a small city or a large town, depending on how one interpreted the finer points and artycles of the Code, and the stubbornly still-beating heart of Barak-Thryng's various interests in Blackfire Bight. While trade was administered (and, more importantly, taxed) by the admiralty, it was a stridently independent frontier port in most respects. The bulk of its labour force were human, which was true of many such ports across the realms, with a sizeable contingent of duardin craftsmen, traders and oath-soldiers, as well as a peripatetic community of orruks of a more mercantile bent. They traded in meat and in bone, and in the spoils of their constant warring on the restless lands of Skulldrake and Wither and Deathrattle Point. Most Kharadron authorities would have run the greenskins off long ago, but as long as there were other foes to fight – and Toba Lorchai had plenty – then their belligerence was an even greater boon to the town than their trade goods.

Its streets were gutters for the filth of the realm, its timber buildings climbing roughshod over the black rock of the hills and each other, as inconsiderate as the people that lived within them. Factionalism was rife. Kharadron and Dispossessed. Dispossessed and human. Orruk and absolutely everyone else. The detritus of brawls and base trades littered every doorway and corner. Draught animals that had to be blinkered and distracted with belled harnesses lest they go mad, lowed their distress in alleys. Giant vermin and hillfowl, war-bred beasts and skeleton birds, shrieked in cages. Smoke stuffed the winding lanes like a gag in the mouth.

It stank of cheap spices, night soil and endrin greases. It stank of ten thousand living, stubbornly still-breathing souls.

Jonsson thought that Toba Lorchai was probably the basest and worst den of iniquity in the eight Mortal Realms. If a fellow traveller or sage had told him authoritatively that it was, in all truth, the basest in all of creation then he would have been amused, but unsurprised.

But right then, that unpleasantly acidic burn in the back of his mouth was the taste of sanctuary. The timber stockade might have been ugly, but it was thick and it was high, and the populace, by virtue of being crooks and felons to a man, duardin or grot, were satisfyingly well armed. Better even than that, however, was the sheer freneticism of the markets, of the bawdy houses, of the excise forts and the smithies. It killed the sound of the sea that had been rasping in Jonsson's ears right up to the point that he guided his dying endrin-cart through the town gates.

Brushing off the yellow tobacco-stained fingers of an ancient and drunk-looking duardin offering to trade a tale for a coin, Jonsson pushed into the bustle.

Every grain of good sense was telling him to get back to his airship, but there was one duty he couldn't leave without observing.

The building that he was looking for was on the corner of a three-storey tenement in one of the most lightless and lawless wards of the lower city called the Greys. The skyports and grand houses of the Kharadron admiralties projected over the township beneath, like a gargantuan two-pronged fork suspended over their heads by the hand of Grungni himself. It cast large shadows and, situated right at the base of the old port's supporting columns, there were few places where they fell deeper than in the Greys. The building seemed to sag. Its roof drooped, its walls bulging imperceptibly. As if it were a plant withering for want of a ray of light. Its gritted windows displayed a piecemeal collection of faux-Nulahmian crockery and antique tableware. A spider-ghast grot stood on the porch step. His body had been painted entirely in lime white, except where carapace and mandibles had been scraped from the underlying green. He slapped a cudgel in his small palm, glaring menacingly at the handful of passers-by.

Most of the Greys' residents knew Murrag's place well enough to avoid it, but there was always the possibility that a stranger important enough to be missed might come innocently browsing for faux-Nulahmian crockery or antique tableware. The grot made sure that never happened.

Jonsson had known Murrag for decades.

When he had first deserted the venerable ironclad *Angrin-Ha!* (an incident involving a looted Nagashi idol and a few misplaced coins that the admiral had entirely overblown), it had been Murrag who had seen a place for him in her enterprise. Over the following decades, he had proven his eye for antiquities and his knack for acquiring them, generally from the cold hands of their former owners. The coin that had purchased him a small dirigible, the *Fiskur*, and a crew of his own, had been hers. Whenever he unearthed a treasure that he felt was too well protected for him to handle, he made sure that word was passed along, and she would find someone with more guns or fewer scruples. Any acquisitions that he did make went first through her. Always. It was an agreement he knew better than to renege on, even had he not been Kharadron with contractual obligation writ into his blood.

Aye, he knew Murrag well.

The miniscule enforcer glared at Jonsson as he approached. The insanely potent blend of narcotics that was currently hollowing out the grot's nervous system caused his eyes to cross and his head to jerk violently on his neck.

'It's me. Jonsson.'

'S-s-s-s.'

Jonsson was unsure what the grot was trying to say, but he shuffled aside obligingly. Jonsson pushed in the door.

To one who had never ventured inside (and most would have considered themselves lucky to be amongst that group), the shop would have seemed surprisingly spacious. The interior walls had been knocked down to leave just one large front-of-house area and a small living area at the back. The ceiling had been elevated, abolishing the second floor entirely. Jonsson was not sure what had become of the third floor. He had never been up there, nor seen any sign of stairs.

A handful of heavily intoxicated grots lounged about on chitin-stilt chairs that were small even to Jonsson, but in the context of this space seemed positively minute. It was as though they, the grots and Jonsson had all been shrunk and had ventured into a normal-sized room.

The effect was as disconcerting today as it had been the first time he had been admitted.

The grots largely ignored him, gazing in wonderment at the ceiling or eyeballing each other, a competitive spiderghast custom that Jonsson knew from experience could go on for days. One of them, however, was sufficiently lucid to lurch upright and stagger towards the knuckle-bead curtain that partitioned off the back of the shop.

Jonsson waited, fiddling nervously with his pistol grip. He did his best to ignore the ingrained fungal aroma. A muffled squawk and a *crunch* sounded from the other side of the curtain. He did his best to ignore that too.

'Ingdrin Jonsson.'

Murrag swept aside the curtain and, leading with the vastness of her belly, stomped into the shop.

The gaggle of opiated grots sprang suddenly to attention.

They saluted.

Murrag was the undisputed sovereign of all semi-legitimate and downright illegitimate business in antiques, artefacts and relics

DAVID GUYMER

in Blackfire Bight. Her word was law, her utterances waited upon
with bated breath, her needs, wants and every interest catered
to by any man who cared for the distinction between life and
death, rich or poor.

She was also an ogor. And huge.

Each of her arms was thicker than Jonsson's waist. Her hands
were like shovels, studded with bracelets and torqs that she wore
as rings. He had once seen her rip a man in half. Literally. *In half.*
And then eat him. Her gut was gargantuan. It was almost a second
entity, as if she had smuggled a handcart full of ripening produce
under the mountain of her skirts. Her eyes were jet-black spig-
ots, furrowed down into a slab of brow. Her hair was coarser than
goat's wool, braided and decorated in the Kharadron style. Her
appearance was brutal, but she was clever, very clever. When first
they had met, Jonsson had thought he would be clear of her debt
and free with her dirigible in a month. He had underestimated
her, as almost everyone did. Her insatiable greed was just another
manifestation of her ungodly hunger.

She was chewing as she entered.

Amongst unlicensed traders and petty crooks in every port of
the realms, an ogor bodyguard was the ultimate symbol of status.
The grots, then, had always been Murrag's idea of a poke in the
eye to convention.

'*Gnollengrom*, Lady Murrag,' said Jonsson, unclasping his hands
to give a respectful tug on his beard. He bowed.

'I always liked you duardin,' Murrag rumbled. 'So respectful.'

Jonsson bowed so low that his beard swept the floorboards.

'You are back so soon, Ingdrin. You found it then.'

Jonsson nibbled on his lip, trying to ignore the grumbling
noises coming from Murrag's belly, so powerful they were shaking
her skirts. 'Aye, lady, I did. Aighmar. Home of the Deepkin aelves
in Blackfire.'

She gestured Jonsson towards a side table. 'Show me.'

The table was scaled for the anatomy of an ogor, and Jonsson was forced to stand on a chair in order to tip the contents of his satchel over its top. Rings and chalices and blades and glittering chunks of coral spilled over the polished wood. Murrag picked through it.

'Aelves under the sea,' she mused. 'I had tasted the rumours. The Undying King hunts for them, you know? And the one with Three Eyes. Stealers of souls to one. Exiles of the Dark Prince to the other. They hide from them, but not from Murrag. She crunches the bone and gristle of legend and myth, devours through to truth inside.'

Jonsson bowed again.

'How did you find them?' she asked.

'We waylaid a sky-cutter flying the colours of Barak-Zon. Its own fault for straying so far from the patrolled lanes. Anyway, they had recently boarded and scuttled a Skryre clan ruinship that had been running repairs after a battle of its own. They didn't know what they had taken from its holds – not everyone reads Queek-ish – but it was a written record of a skaven invasion of Aighmar.'

'Records?' Murrag's brutalist features slipped into a broad grin. 'Not very... skaven.'

'Very detailed records too. The site was easy to find once I'd translated the skins. My guess is that they meant to pass them on to someone.'

'So, Nagash?' She licked her lips. 'Or Archaon?'

'I'd prefer not to think about it.'

The ogor picked up a blade from the loose pile of treasures to examine it more closely. It was a short sword, its nacreous blade and cross-hilt plain, but fabulously ornate around the grip – as if it were intended to impress by touch rather than sight. In Mur-rag's grip it looked like a supper knife.

'Pretty.' She looked up, hungrily. 'Is there more?'

'Aye, plenty more. There's a whole city down there. The skaven have picked it over, but for a race of scavengers, they're careless. You can send another crew though. I'm moving on.'

'Moving where?'

'Anywhere. Away. That was always our arrangement, lady. If ever I feel there's a prize I can't handle then I pass it on. No fee. No trouble. That's what I signed, and that's what I'll stick to.'

Murrag frowned down at him, the enormous muscles of her face shifting. 'The Deepkin scare you. Enough for *you* to tell *me* what our deal is.'

'They're coming for me. I can feel that they are. You as well now, I'm guessing.'

The ogor delivered a booming, stinking gale of laughter and gestured to her guards. They stiffened furiously.

'I feel very safe here.'

'I'm not joking.'

'Nor am I.'

Jonsson straightened. 'Well, then. I'll take my due, then I'll take my leave.'

Rubbing her belly with one hand, Murrag carefully separated out the trinkets from the coral shards and drew the former towards her side of the table, using the blade of the Idoneth short sword like an admiral moving ship tokens around a campaign map. Jonsson's heart sank to see the coral being pushed back towards him. The mineral was clearly a repository for some kind of aelf magic and must be worth a fortune to someone from the Collegiate Arcane, or even an Arcanite cabal for all he cared. He wanted rid of the stuff.

'Old things,' Murrag growled, stirring through the pile of jewelled conches and ornate weaponry with the pommel of her sword. 'That's what I buy. That's what I sell.' She grumbled something in a hissing greenskin language to summon one of her attendants. 'Cradz. Fetch the ledger. Five shares, made out for Jonsson.'

Jonsson gawped at her.

He could not sell his dirigible for five shares, even if Vorgaard, his pirate of a bosun, could have been persuaded to scrape off the rust.

'Get the rest of it where I can't see it,' said Murrag. 'I don't like the way it smells.'

There was something magical about gold. It was a long-standing physical principle amongst the aether-khemists and chirurgeons of the Kharadron that the placement of a sufficiently high denomination coin could cause a suppurating wound to close or a malignant growth to shrink. Meditating upon its glow could cure ills both physical and mental. Even just the weight of a coin in a duardin's pocket could make his cares evaporate, making his soul feel lighter by a ratio corresponding unerringly to the value of said coin. Jonsson might have expected the miraculous effect to become even more pronounced once he had passed through the various stairgates and customs forts into the skydock proper and could safely remove his hand from his pistol holster.

He felt no easing of his spirit.

And did not move his hand.

Something he could not tally, nor weigh out on a set of calibrated scales, had put his teeth on edge. The endrin of every patrolling gunhauler and monitor, of every skywarden and rigger, sounded to him like the roar of the ocean. From every street vendor and high-end duardin restaurant, the smell of decaying seaweed and saltwater made him want to gag.

The skyport was not the Toba Lorchai that most of its inhabitants knew, but it was the face that the admiralty lords would recognise. Here were the stone-built docks erected by the first pioneers of Barak-Thryng, long before the locals had come to build a settlement at its base. Here, shipping magnates and lords of industry of all races comported themselves in gowns, flocked by equerries and viziers, while ship captains strode about the port's wholesalers in armour.

After removing himself from Murrag's company – for the last time, with any luck – Jonsson had been of half a mind to pay a visit to a jeweller of his acquaintance in a last attempt at unloading the Idoneth coral before taking his final leave of Toba Lorchai itself. A master gemsmith of the Dispossessed, his acquaintance was as famed for his honourable approach to the business as he was for his eye for a gem.

Something persuaded him to err towards the direct route.

The thought of just dumping the coral on a bench or in a doorway somewhere and foregoing his profit never occurred – to do so would have been a flagrant violation of the Code, and Vorgaard, his bosun, would have stripped him of his captaincy had he even suspected him of such a crime.

Exchanging curt nods with familiar faces amongst the harbour watch, Jonsson hurried towards the docks.

The sooner he was a thousand feet above sea level with his gold and the Idoneth coral securely stowed away in the captain's cabin, the happier he would feel. He could sell it in another city. Preferably in another realm.

Then, maybe, he would feel ready to move his hand from his pistol's grip.

Across from the imposing granite portico of the endrinmaster's guildhall and bank, a fountain prattled. A scale replica of the Barak-Thryng ironclad *Thallazorn* spouted water from her gun turrets into a pool. The sound grated on Jonsson's nerves. A ring of metal benches surrounded the fountain. They were popular with lunching endrinmasters, but it was barely an hour after dawn, and there was only a handful of bleary-eyed longbeards nibbling on a belated breakfast.

Jonsson sat down.

It was only four thousand and nine steps from the Grundstok Gate to the docking tines, and he was practically a beardless scamp at a mere fifty-seven years old, but he was finding it increasingly hard going catching a breath. He exhaled slowly, looking up in astonishment at the stream of transparent bubbles that issued from between his lips and floated up towards the sky. Schools of skeletal fish shoaled about the equally astonished skywardens.

Trailing bubbles from his open mouth, he brought his gaze back down to port level, to where an allopex swam between the granite colonnades of the guildhall. The huge, grey-skinned sea monster was collared and bridled, barded in a rigid plate of darkly tinted shells. An aelf in elegantly streamlined armour and wielding some kind of net launcher rode in a standing saddle on the monster's back.

Jonsson's first thought was that he had gone mad.

The anxiety of his flight was bleeding into the reality of his five senses, his fear that the denizens of the deep ocean would come for him, and now he saw the ocean in all its horror right where it simply could not be. He would have laughed at his own broken mind had the beer-soaked endrinmaster on the bench beside him not muttered a drawled curse, tugged a volley pistol from the expanse of grey beard bundled up in his lap, and opened fire.

The hammer burst of shots snapped Jonsson out of his shock.

He jumped up smartly, drawing his own single-shot firearm.

The endrinmaster's salvo tore into the allopex's head. It crashed into the ground like a side of meat dumped from the back of a waggon, and crushed its rider's leg to the ground beneath its mass. The aelf screamed, seemingly more in anguish from being wounded, than from the pain itself. The endrinmaster casually walked over to the downed beast and shot the rider in the head, then belched an enormous bubble.

Throughout the great concourses and plazas of the skyport, the impossible was spreading. Everywhere Jonsson turned he saw his nightmare writ in powder smoke and charging bodies. Aelven warriors flowed down the main thoroughfare as though borne along on a flood tide, sweeping aside all before them, while in the air allopex knights and grim-faced warriors mounted on fangmora, eel-like horrors that coursed with sparking energies, converged on the endrinriggers working in their high nests.

The Kharadron of Barak-Thryng, however, were far from defenceless in their home port, even when assaulted unawares. Shots rang out. The leaden booms of skycannons. The rattling chatter of aethermatic weapons. Every food hall and warehouse in view that had been host to a captain and his entourage had become a casemate from which decksweeper volleys and fumigator fire raked the aelves and their bonded nightmares. In the sky, amidst the endrin rigs and aethermatic hoists, the Kharadron spat back at the aelven cavalry with drill cannon and rivet-fire. Shields of crackling elemental power surrounded the fangmora knights, deflecting most of the incoming projectiles. A second contingent, armed with energised spears, swept past the first before the lightning shields had fully dissipated, rushing towards the endrinriggers' impromptu redoubts with the fury of a wave.

Jonsson did not stop to watch.

'Grungni the Maker,' he breathed.

The old master belched another large bubble, which Jonsson took for typical longbeard disdain before noticing the arrow embedded in his chest. He pitched backwards and into the fountain with a splash.

Jonsson brought his pistol up as he quickly backed away, circling around the marble bulk of the fountain's scale model ironclad.

The aelves were advancing through the columns of the guildhall. They came with an eerie, floating gait, bounding rather than walking. It was as if they moved through water even as Jonsson, a hundred feet away from them, did not.

With a snarl, Jonsson aimed and fired.

The pistol kicked hard, annihilating an archer's shoulder and spinning him hard into the face of a column. The rest kept coming, loosing as they ran. Another old endrinmaster caught an arrow in the chin and in the eye, and dropped with a gurgle, his weapon unfired.

Jonsson did not even waste time reloading his pistol.

Toba Lorchai had been good to him. He would miss the place, it was true, but for him home had always been just a port of call. And the Code was very specific on the subject of lost causes.

Artycle Four, Point Five.

He turned and sprinted for the aether-docks.

The docks were Toba Lorchai's beating heart, its higher purpose and its soul. Three great prongs of granite, like a colossal fork, protruded from the crown of the hill, busy with aethermatic winches and cranes, sky-ships docking or embarking, loading or unloading. They were a hive at any time. If not for the incessant drum of gunfire and the eerie wailing of the aelves, then Jonsson might have been able to force his way into the cussing mob of Grundstok crew and longshoremen without noticing anything amiss.

A very large (and very well paid) garrison of Grundstok thunderers had responsibility for the docking tines, with a contingent of orruk mercenaries that fluctuated in strength depending on the perceived threats of the times. Fire-duels crackled into life as the aelves advanced on the docks. Howling mobs of green-skinned and war-painted orruk berserkers surged from the Grundstok stockades to engage the aelves hand to hand. The melees that broke out were ferocious. Seven-foot-tall orruks with bulging muscles hacked at the delicate aelven warriors in a frenzy. Scores of them fell in the first seconds of the charge, but the survivors neither cried out nor broke. They sang a flat, empty lament as they whirled into the attack with graceful, perfectly controlled strokes of their hefty blades.

The anarchy consuming the tines themselves was, if it were possible, of a different order.

Stevedores and endrinriggers fought one another for right of way. Harbourmasters bellowed red-faced at unyielding captains. Arkanaut companies beat terrified humans and duardin from their vessels' boarding planks with the butts of their pistols. Frigates and gunhaulers launched with their moorings still attached, ripping giant hooks out of the granite, crashing into the back of other vessels that had not yet cleared the dock, all of it conducted under the gale-roar of cold aether-endrins being pushed hard to full power.

Jonsson's own dirigible, the *Fiskur*, was smaller than most, a humble three-gunner with an aethershot carbine mounted in the prow, port and starboard, and a bow-chaser in the aftcastle. The collection of armour-plated spheres suspended over the deck within a girder of metal housed an old but well-proven aether-endrin. The winged blades of its propellers were already humming. A crew of seven were busy releasing the mooring lines and riveting the endrin-rigging for departure.

'Don't tell me you were about to cast off without me,' Jonsson shouted over the rising howl of the endrin, striding over the boarding plank mere seconds before an arkanaut companion with a torn ear and an eyepatch dragged it in from under him.

'As per Artycle Seven, Point Three,' said Vorgaard Hangarik cheerfully. The leathery-skinned bosun wore a crown that he had lifted from a Dashian tomb in Lyrhia at an angle he considered dashing, and which, on a duardin half his two hundred years, might well have been. He observed the frantic activity of his company with an unhurried ease, thumbs wedged under the belt that was buckled around his armour, sucking on the dry stem of an unlit pipe.

'Point Three pertains to the incapacity, insanity or death of the existing captain,' Jonsson panted.

'Well.' Vorgaard withdrew the pipe from his mouth and used it to gesture towards the violence that was slowly breaking through the Kharadron defences and spilling into the docks. 'What was any right-minded duardin to think?'

'I...'

Jonsson put his hands on his knees and coughed.

'You need a moment to catch a breath, cap'n?' said Vorgaard. 'I've got time.'

'Do we have clearance from the harbourmaster?'

'I wouldn't say *clearance* exactly.'

'Good enough.'

Blowing quickly and hard, Jonsson weaved through the arkanauts and hurried up the sheet metal steps to the aftcastle. He nodded to the turret gunner, and took the wheel.

Vorgaard followed him.

'Get my ship out of here,' Jonsson bellowed into the pole-mounted speaker-horn that was welded to the deck plating beside the wheel. 'Full power to the endrin. I want a thousand feet between us and the Deepkin before I can count down from the five aether-gold shares in my pocket.'

A raucous chorus of 'ayes' rang out at the promise of gold as the *Fiskur* lurched into a sudden climb. Jonsson gripped tight to the wheel, pulling the dirigible's course inland and upwards. The hull plating squealed and shuddered. The endrin-rigging emitted a long, tortured whine punctuated by bangs of stressed metal as the propellers dragged the ship away from the ground. The vast bow of an ironclad hove into their course. Grumbling under his breath, Jonsson hauled on the wheel, shaking his fist at his counterpart as the *Fiskur* sailed under the ironclad's keel and continued to climb.

Throughout it all, Vorgaard remained in a solid, wide-legged posture that he could hold unflustered through aether-storm or sky-battle. He cast Jonsson a sideways look.

'Deepkin, you say?'

Jonsson set his jaw. 'Aye.'

'The old legend?'

'Aye.'

'*Skat*,' Vorgaard swore.

'Aye.'

'I think we're out of it,' said Vorgaard, after a moment's silence.

Jonsson nodded and loosened his hold on the tiller, reducing the buoyancy in the aether-bags and levelling the pitch of the propellers. The dirigible eased off with her complaints as she levelled out of her climb, bar the occasional cough from the endrin that the endrinmaster quickly moved to tend.

He looked back.

The monolithic tines of Toba Lorchai were shrinking behind him. Even the gunhaulers and monitors that had been patrolling the sky lanes before the attack had been sprung looked small, coming about to add aerial support to the port's defenders as the *Fiskur* pulled ever further away. Just in time, Jonsson thought. He was not so high yet that he could no longer distinguish the dark, graceful tide of aelves from the splintering battle lines of the Kharadron and their allies. From up high it looked like a black sea coming in, sweeping away the sand fortresses and metallic pebbles that had been set up around the beach in its absence. They had already swept as far in as the tines. The fighting was even spilling over onto those ships still in dock, deck watches defending their gun ridges like the ramparts of a floating castle. Those that were not already fending off boarders redoubled their efforts to be aweigh, adding to the carnage in the slipways.

'Good thing somebody had the endrin running,' Vorgaard murmured.

'It looks as though they're sparing the township,' said Jonsson. 'Trust Murrag to get out of this in one piece.'

He looked away, sick, and stared at the matt gunmetal of the ship's wheel in his hands. He could not shake the dread that this was somehow not over, that the sack of Toba Lorchai was simply incidental. It was him the Deepkin wanted, he was sure of it. He did not know how they were following him, but he did not think they were going to stop here.

Perhaps he could return to the skyhold of Barak-Thryng itself. Or Azyrheim. Gods, yes. Let the Deepkin pursue him all the way there.

'New heading, bosun,' he yelled, spinning the wheel, the prow following it slowly to starboard. 'We're heading for the Azyr Gate at Glymmsforge.'

'Good idea,' said Vorgaard.

One hand on the wheel, Jonsson shrugged off his satchel, the coral a lumpen weight in the bottom, as if he had a spiked mace against his back, and tossed it to Vorgaard.

'Throw it overboard.'

The bosun tested its weight in his hand. 'Is it valuable?'

'Cite me later. Throw it overboard!'

'Aye, cap'n.'

Vorgaard walked towards the aftcastle battlements, the satchel drawn back for an overarm hurl into the wide, blue aether, but then stopped mid-stride. His arm dropped to his side and he just stared. Jonsson glanced over and swore.

'As aether is bloody light.'

In the sky dead ahead of their new course, in defiance of every scientific law that Jonsson cared for, there swam a gigantic armour-plated turtle. The behemoth was easily the mass of a fully gunned ironclad, but the throbbing waves of distortion rippling from the howdah mounted on its back made it difficult to make out in detail, or to accurately count the swarm of allopex and fangmora knights that ran abeam of it like gunhaulers escorting a dreadnought.

'A leviadon,' Jonsson breathed.

'Turn! Turn!' Vorgaard grabbed the wheel from him and bellowed into the speaker-horn. 'Port broadside. Aethershot carbine, fire. Skilli, why am I not currently deafened by drill cannon fire?'

The dirigible shook to a pair of tremendous booms, falling close enough together to be heard as one. The aethershot sailed into the diffraction cloud and to all obvious purposes disappeared. The detonation drill from the bow-chaser was not so easily waylaid. It burst in the vicinity, faceted loops of explosion rippling around the leviadon as if seen from the other side of an armoured window. A couple of fangmora knights dropped out of the sky – or sank, Jonsson was not sure – becoming increasingly visible as they fell away from the leviadon's protective field.

'Brace!' Jonsson yelled as something twinkled back in return.

A razorshell harpoon as long as Jonsson was tall crunched into the rigging, perilously close to the endrin housing. The impact lurched the dirigible to starboard, smashed Jonsson's face into the wheel, and sent him sprawling back to the aftcastle deck. He groaned. Voices fought for attention in his skull.

'Endrinmaster. *Wakaz!* To your post.'

'Fire! Fire!'

'Boarders aft.'

'Stand and repel.'

'All hands to the hold.'

The clash and clamour of steel brought him back around, the

scuff of armoured boots on metal planking. He jerked upright, reaching for his pistol. The repellent stench of something dank and rancid hit him halfway.

He blinked, looking up into the flat, noseless features of a nightmare with no right to exist beyond the blackest deep-sea trench. Its skin was rubbery and white, bristling with spined frills and venomous-looking barbs. It floated sinuously up and down, as if riding ocean currents that Jonsson, in his landlocked insensibility, was numb to. Its clawed fins raked Jonsson's beard with every down-movement, its triplet of tails coiling and unbunching on the deck.

An aelf woman sat bestride its back. Every part of her body, apart from her head, was encapsulated like a pearl within a shell of perfectly shaped black metal. Her skin was so gaunt and so pale that Jonsson could see the veins that webbed her face, and even make out the dark green of her eyes when she blinked. Her skin, her armour and her weapons all glistened with wetness, her voluminous dark hair billowing with unnatural buoyancy around the clamshell plates of her shoulders.

He could hear his crew fighting. Vorgaard, probably. Skilli in the turret. He grabbed up his pistol and swung it around. The aelf cut the barrel in half with a curt downstroke of her sword. It clicked as he pulled on the trigger.

'Boka–'

The aelf impaled him through the shoulder with the lance in her left hand, driving it through hard enough to pierce the metal of the deck, skewering him in place. The deepmare she rode opened its hideously alien mouth, but made no sound.

'Who... are you?' he said.

'Pétra. Queen of those from whom you stole.'

Jonsson shook his head vigorously, wincing as he pulled against the lance in his shoulder. 'I stole nothing. I found it. The city was abandoned. I claimed *galkhron* in accordance with Artycle Two, Point One of the– *Aaaarrgh!*'

Pétra released the butt of the lance and let it stand slack again.

'A thief's notion. To assert that a thing is unclaimed simply because it is untended.'

'My queen, here.'

Jonsson turned his head to look sideways along the deck. Vorgaard was sat up against the aftcastle wall, eyes closed, breathing shallowly as though asleep. His armour was unscratched. A tall aelf with a shining coat of armour scales and a helm that enclosed his entire face but for an expressionless mouth stood over him. He was the one who had spoken. He shook out the contents of Jonsson's satchel and held up the coral to his blank, eyeless mask. He appeared to sigh, a strange gesture when unaccompanied by any obvious outward sign of emotion.

'What have you done to my bosun?' Jonsson gasped.

The aelf ignored him.

'The lost shards of the chorrileum of Aighmar. I can feel the souls bound within.' His lips stiffened. 'I hear them wail.'

Pétra nodded, as though satisfied.

'The rest is in the township,' said Jonsson, pain making him gabble. 'I can show you who has them and where, in exchange for my life and my ship.'

The aelf queen regarded him with inexpressive eyes, a picture of untouchable beauty painted on a rock.

'I care not for the trinkets. Things can be replaced. Souls devoured by the Thirsting Prince are forever lost.'

Jonsson did not know what to say. How did you treat with creatures so alien in their values as the Deepkin aelves?

'Then… what do you want?'

'How did you learn about Aighmar?' she said.

'The city?' Quickly, Jonsson explained everything that he had previously related to Murrag, about the Barak-Zon sky-cutter, the skaven ruinship, everything.

'Then it is done,' said the helmeted aelf. 'We can return to the sweet annihilation of the senses and feel no more.' He lowered his scythe-like weapon, the light-globe swinging from its head emitting a curious pull on Jonsson's attention.

'No,' said Jonsson, trying to pull away, but for reasons other than the obvious one sticking through his shoulder, he could not. 'No.'

'You duardin are long-lived,' said Pétra coldly, hidden within the totality of the lure-light. 'Your soul will be highly prized. It will bring joy, of a kind, to the parent of a namarti who will otherwise wither in childhood and perish.'

'There's a whole city down there,' he protested. 'Thousands. You can't take them all. There will be those that remember you.'

Jonsson closed his eyes, but somehow he could see the scythe-wielding aelf's blank expression through the light. Pity. Sorrow.

And then there was nothing but the light.

Thalia hugged her knees to her chin and watched the waves break against the rocks. They were bodies, woollen and black, tumbling, ripping open, spilling their frothing white guts over the beach. She shivered, cold. She did not know what she was doing here, could not remember, only that she was alone. Her da had been taken by the sea, as her ma had been, long ago. The memory of the more recent event slurped and gurgled from her grasp, like wet sand from between her toes as the waves dragged it away to where her recollections of the older had long been submerged.

'And when they grow old and grandchildren forget, That will be the day when the fishing folk come.'

She looked back, along the deserted shoreline. To the inland road.

Because they were not the fishing folk.

They were the fish.

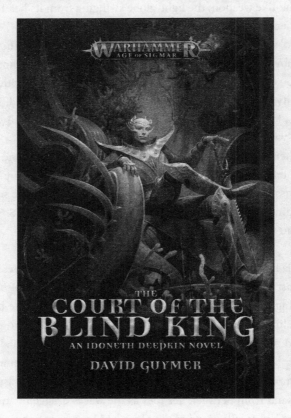

BUYER BEWARE

Gav Thorpe

A mawcrusher in full flight is a thing of brutal, terrible beauty. The bulge of powerful muscles driving its immense pinions up and down. The curve and recurve of wing flaps rising and falling with each beat. The spiked tail as it weaves from side to side, every twitch making small adjustments to the immense beast's trajectory. Ropes of drool trailing from sword-length fangs, each a stained-ivory slash against the dark tongue within the mouth, the bucket-like jaw opening wider and wider as the beast falls upon its prey.

This monster was a particularly dazzling specimen, bronze-like scales glistening against the ochre sky of the Ironpeaks of Chamon. Dark red stripes marked the upper scales and the crest that stretched back along to the fins of the tail, while the underbelly was mottled with a purple hue. Eyes like rubies peered out from beneath the heavy brow as the mawcrusher turned around a promontory of dark rock, its wing tip scraping through the last remnants of autumnal leaves, scattering red and gold flutters.

The magnificence of nature in its primal form was quite lost on the handful of stocky figures running full tilt down the mountain-side ahead of the descending behemoth.

They had divested themselves of their heavy aeronautic suits for this stealthy venture and were clad only in thick woollen under-garments from ankle to throat, varying in hue from the dark blue of panting, grey-haired-and-bearded Thorkki Longintooth to a somewhat beer-stained cerise worn by Nukduk, via outfits of sober beige, dazzling yellow and a regal purple. This last garment, further adorned with gold stitching of a sky-anchor upon the left breast, marked out the small group's leader, as did the ornately feathered wide-brimmed hat that he continued to hold atop the shaggy mass of black hair upon his head.

Karazi 'Fairgold' Zaynson, captain of the *Night's Daughter*. Pieces of dried leaf clung to the bushy falls of his dark beard, which had a reddish streak in the moustache and down the cheeks, a feature considered particularly fetching among the folk of Barak-Mhornar. In his other hand he held the handle of a bulging dark leather satchel, as did two of his companions.

There was not so much a path to follow down the slope as a slightly worn trail through the scattered bushes and twisted trees. The leaves were dry on the ground, crackling and billow-ing around the duardin as they pounded down the mountainside. Heavy breaths and the swoop of wings flung more arboreal de-tritus into the air, so that the slope became a shifting mass of dead foliage, sliding underfoot and gathering in drifts ahead.

'I tol' you they's never too far from tha nest!' shouted Rogoth, he of the sun-bright yellow undersuit. His locks and beard were as golden as his nether-wraps, flowing like streamers behind him as he vaulted a half-buried log.

'And I told you to keep running,' Fairgold growled back.

Ahead the mountainside appeared to become sky, the yellowish grass suddenly giving way to a haze of empty air. A jutting shoulder of rock barred the way, so that the group would either have to break towards the open side of the mountain or turn back up the slope.

'Where's the *Daughter*?' yelled Thorkki, face crimson between near-white beard and brow.

'Keep running!' bellowed Fairgold. He angled right towards the open slope where they had left the *Night's Daughter*. 'This way!'

'Yer a gold-drunk fool,' snapped Rogoth, heading left. 'This way!'

The other three duardin chased after their captain. A few heartbeats later Rogoth stumbled as his boot caught on a twist of root. He did not lose his footing, but the trip was enough for him to stagger to a halt for a moment. Fairgold slowed, head turning to look at his crew member.

A massive shadow engulfed Rogoth.

'Get down!' yelled Fairgold but it was too late. A moment later, jaws as big as the aeronaut snapped shut and the mawcrusher swooped up, leaving a splash of blood and shredded yellow where Rogoth had been. Nukduk gave a wail of despair and slowed down, neck craning as he watched the mawcrusher ascending. Fairgold skidded to a halt, heavy boots sending up dust from the dry mountainside. He took two steps back and grabbed Nukduk's arm.

'It's coming back,' the captain said, tugging. 'We've got to go.'

'Go where?' snarled Nukduk, digging his heel into the ground as Fairgold tried to pull him into a run. 'The *Daughter*'s gone without us!'

'They haven't gone nowhere, you flange-headed dolt,' insisted Fairgold, loosening his grip. Out of the corner of his eye he could see the mawcrusher wheeling across the slope, ready for another diving attack. 'Stay here if you want to end up like Rogoth.'

A glare at Thorkki and Zanna brought them after Fairgold as he gathered speed down the slope once more. Nukduk followed a moment later.

'Where are we going?' Zanna called, her braids like flails as her head whipped back and forth between the clifftop ahead and the descending mawcrusher coming from the left.

'Trust me,' said Fairgold.

He powered on, panting hard. A sudden gust lifted up the brim of his hat, flipping it from his head. He tried to turn and snatch it, but his short legs were not suited to such manoeuvres and he fell backwards, cradling the satchel to his chest on instinct as he rolled over. Zanna was nimbler, plucking the headwear from the air as it slipped past her. Back on his feet, Fairgold accelerated again, just behind his crew.

Out of the corner of his eye he could see the vast shadow of the mawcrusher approaching fast. Just a few paces from the cliff's edge the others started to slow. Fairgold drew in a deep breath. It was too late to stop now. Legs pumping harder than a ship's piston he caught up with the others, arms outstretched, and shepherded them to the edge.

As a group they leapt into the open air.

Rising below them was the *Night's Daughter*, her burnished hull and aether-gold cistern gleaming. Custom-built, she was longer than most shipyard vessels of Barak-Mhornar, her aether-gold tank and oversized skyscrew engines mounted lower and further rearward for speed. Where ships built for the battle line of the city fleet had bulging carbinades mounted in their prows, Fairgold's unaffiliated freegun vessel sported more crew room with shuttered firing slits in place of fixed pintle guns, currently bristling with weapons from within. It was a remarkable piece of work given it had been put together from a dozen different salvages and wreck raids. For a couple of heartbeats, Fairgold admired the vessel as he fell, before he and Zanna slammed into the side of the balloon-like aethertank while the other two aeronauts fell to the deck a little further below. Fairgold slid down the side of the cistern, fingers scrabbling at rivets and thick banding until he came to a stop. Zanna held on to the rail around the pilot's hatch above him, satchel in the other hand, captain's hat clamped between gritted teeth. He felt the whole ship throbbing as the engines powered it upwards past the cliff.

'Sorry!' Eskar Druadak shouted past Zanna from her piloting position. 'The cliff was going to break. Had to circle and wait. Didn't want that mawcrusher to see us.'

'Everyone else all right?' Fairgold called out as he allowed himself to carefully slide further down the aethertank until his foot touched a stabiliser fin. A chorus of half-hearted affirmatives broke the drone of the engines. A sudden wind as the *Night's Daughter* crested the cliff set the vessel swaying, and for a moment there was nothing beneath Fairgold and a long drop down to the cliff bottom.

The ironclad steadied as Eskar started to turn it away from the mountainside, but as she did so, Fairgold, face pressed against the bronzed tank as he clung on like a High Magnate holding a ha'penny, saw the mawcrusher swooping like a thunderbolt.

The company was already at quarters as the order to ready weapons rang across the ship. A score of aethershot carbines and pistols presented towards the mawcrusher from deck, firing slits and support stanchions, while the arkanauts at the main gun hurriedly turned their great cannon towards the incoming beast. It was still traversing when the first small-arms shots crackled out, dappling the *Night's Daughter* with muzzle flare. Bullets speckled the thick hide of the monster with little visible effect. Breech-cranks snapped and screeched as the aeronauts readied for a second volley. There would be no time for a third.

The main cannon boomed into angry life, setting the *Night's Daughter* shuddering from the serrated prow ram to the sky-rudders aft of the main screw. The jolt nearly threw Fairgold from his precarious perch, so that he was clinging on with one hand as he watched an explosion of shrapnel engulf the hurtling mawcrusher. It burst from the cloud of sharp metal and black smoke with mouth agape. Blood trailed from its face and left shoulder, and it rolled to one side as fresh carbine fire crackled below, a clawed foot lashing out as the beast swept past.

Engines now at full ahead, the *Night's Daughter* powered cloudwards, leaving the wounded monster to land lopsided at the clifftop, screeching its rage.

Picking his way to a support strut, Fairgold was about to slide down to the main deck when he saw flashes of blue sparks and a slick of dark smoke trailing from the gouge ripped into the side of the aether-engine by the mawcrusher's vengeful claws. Metal had parted like paper and a pipe hissed steam within. Even as he found footing on the deck, the captain could sense all was not well with his ship, a stuttering in the stroke of the engines.

Even so, his first thought was not for the ship but the endrineer below.

'Verna!' he bellowed into the smoke-filled chamber beneath the aethertank. The smell of burnt rubber and hot metal assailed his nostrils.

A goggled face smeared with grease appeared from the bank of vapour, a knitted beard-hammock protecting dark brown whiskers.

'She's fine,' said the duardin, wiping his oil-stained hands on a rag. 'Me too, thanks for asking. Busy.'

'What's the damage, Oggin?' asked Fairgold.

The endrinrigger sucked air through his teeth and shook his head.

'Not good.' He turned to call back into the hidden depths of the endrinroom. A muffled voice replied and Oggin repeated it for his captain. 'Couple of displaced packing glands... Thumbnail rupture on the eduction pipe... Splinters in the crossheads.'

Fairgold rubbed his beard thoughtfully, waiting for Oggin to continue. Nothing else was forthcoming.

'You dunno what any of that means, do you?'

'Nope. Except splinters, I know what they are.' Fairgold leaned past the assistant to address the mistress. 'How long? Can we make Breakward Stark?'

'I'll get us there, but we'll have to make do with endrin-shimmies until we land for proper repairs,' came the reply.

'You're the best!' Fairgold called before turning away from the hatch, to find himself confronted by Thorkki. The greybeard stood with fists on hips, brows knotted tighter than one of the rigger cables that held the endrin-tank in place.

'You still going to the orruks, after what's happened?'

'Why wouldn't I?'

'Rogoth is dead!' Thorkki shook his head, which set his beard to waggling fiercely from side to side. 'Don't that mean nothing?'

'It means nothing if we don't finish the deal,' snapped Fairgold. 'He'll still get his share.'

'What you gonna do with it? Stick it on a pile of mawcrusher sh–'

'Arrangements will be made!' barked the captain. 'All shares will be paid, in full, as promised.'

Thorkki grumbled some more but Fairgold pushed past, ignoring him.

'Eskar?'

The young pilot gave him a thumbs up from her position at the forecradle of the main superstructure.

'Already on our way, captain!' she called down. 'Quarter speed's the best we can do.'

Fairgold signalled his thanks and returned his attention to the rest of the crew, trying to find the right words. He failed. Everything that came to him, a usually gifted orator, seemed trite.

'Stand down from quarters, Thorkki,' he told his first mate. The greybeard hesitated and then complied, giving his beard a short tug of salute. 'Get some grub and rest, and then stand to again when we get to Breakward Stark.'

As the other duardin busied themselves, Fairgold moved to the starboard rail near the bow, staring ahead into the golden clouds at the horizon, the twin jutting peaks of Breakward Stark just about visible against them. About two hours, Fairgold reckoned, but his thoughts quickly moved away from the immediate future.

'I told him to go right,' he muttered to himself.

The *Night's Daughter* had never purred; it had too many craft involved in its parentage to boast the kind of engine you'd find in a thoroughbred ironclad. A growl, perhaps. More of a snarl, if one was being critical. And now it had a sporadic cough as the ship limped towards its rendezvous with jury-rigged pistons and whatever other endrin-based miracles Verna had enacted. Fairgold hadn't moved from the bow rail and the ship's company was quiet. The gate peaks of Breakward Stark were large ahead, while if he glanced back, he saw a smear of smoke in their wake, dispersing across the glimmering Ironpeaks.

It was nearly time.

'Thinking too much?'

He turned with a smile at the sound of Verna's voice.

'Maybe about the wrong things,' Fairgold confessed.

She had her endrin-suit on, thick black leather with ribs and plates of metal bound into it where a powered harness could be attached. While Oggin was usually sooty, oil-stained or in some other way marked by his labours, Verna had a knack for remaining almost spotless despite spending half her life below deck. Not that her haunt of choice wasn't without consequence – Fairgold could smell lubricant off her from ten steps away. Her light brown hair was pulled tightly back in a large plait but dozens of strands had worked loose, each trying to escape on its own trajectory.

She approached, assuming a businesslike expression that Fairgold knew would cost him money.

'Karazi...' When she used his birth name, he knew it was going to be a *lot* of money.

'What do we need to replace?' he asked with a resigned sigh.

'Main bracket head,' she said.

'I know that bit,' replied Fairgold. 'That's part of the hull, not endrinworks! You didn't mention it earlier.'

'Because I couldn't fix it earlier. Anyways, you'd have seen it, if you'd had a proper look where that bloody great gash in the side is. Like I haven't got enough to do.'

He stepped closer, arm snaking out for an embrace as apology, but she evaded with a twirl that almost decapitated Fairgold with her iron-threaded braid.

'Got to sort me tools,' she told him. 'Piston heads to remove, threads to cut, all sorts of delicate work. And you need to be getting ready to make the deal.'

Fairgold nodded and followed her back to the main deck. He stopped a moment to lay a hand on the ironwork around the main endrinroom. He could feel the occasional splutter, the deck juddering perceptibly with each missed beat. Verna had done her best work, now it was his turn to do his.

A bell clamoured into life along with repeated calls of 'All Hands! All Hands!' Booted feet thundered on iron steps and wooden decking as the ship's company, some twenty duardin in all, burst from below decks and dropped from hammocks slung from the main deck stanchions. Thorkki bellowed orders, relayed by his juniors, setting the crew to tidying away everything on the deck, readying the guns and their personal weapons.

When they were done they stood in several loose ranks in front of Fairgold, clustered on the forward section of the main deck.

'I've told you many times, there's no such thing as one big deal,' the captain began. 'We don't do getting rich quick on this ship. You might as well chase skymaids and cloudsilver if that's your thing.'

'Or legendary wrecks!' someone piped up from the back, but Fairgold could not recognise the voice.

'Looking for the *Night's Gift* is different,' he said slowly, scowling at the group as a whole. It was no secret that he wanted to find the remains of the infamous sky-ship, and he wouldn't have it held against him. 'That's family, not business. Anyway, this job is going to be one of the biggest deals we've made. It'll be tough, we've got to hold our nerve, and it means handling the orruks properly. Ten of you are coming with me. The rest will be guarding the *Daughter*. We get the map from the orruks, swift screws back to Barak-Mhornar and then it goes to the highest bidder at the Goldworth. And if the rumours of the Ironpeaks are to be believed, that map is going to be worth as much as an ironclad or more.'

As he rubbed his hands at the thought, Fairgold could feel the ship dipping as Eskar started to direct the vessel groundwards. Ahead the captain could see the twin peaks getting taller and taller. Nestled between them was a lush valley of forests, haphazardly hacked out in places by the orruks that lived there, reminding Fairgold of the pates of crew members that had saved a penny too much at the dockside barber's.

'Coming in a bit steep-like,' said Gorddo, head of the starboard team, turning to the others, who were muttering in similar discontent.

'We're losing trim!' shrieked Eskar from the piloting wheel above and behind Fairgold. She was so taken aback she forgot her studied Westdock-of-Barak-Zilfin accent. 'Not 'nough power, too much weight for'ard!'

The ship was quickly pitching forwards. Skyscrews whistled in protest while increasing creaks and groans from the super-structure warned of the strain as gravity fought the buoyancy of the aether-gold.

'Get aft!' bellowed Thorkki, waving the crew to follow as he started towards the endrin-block and aethertank.

'Aft, you sod-soled, jelly-kneed laggards!' Eskar encouraged from above.

The ship's complement bundled aftward, stumbling up the steep-ening deck. Fairgold staggered to the endrinroom hatch and grabbed hold of the frame.

'We need more power!'

'T'ain't no more,' Oggin called back.

'Then grab something strong and get ready for a bump.'

Fairgold turned to see what lay ahead. A sea of dark green and silver trees as far as the eye could see.

'Cap'n!' Eskar's call dragged Fairgold's eyes away from the rap-idly approaching treetops. 'I can't haul us up.'

He grabbed a rigging cable and climbed up as quick as he could, dragging himself over the rail of the fore-cradle to stand beside the pilot. She had one hand on the wheel and the other on the main pitch trim lever, looking as though she were wrestling two immense stone vipers.

'Aim for that gap,' said Fairgold, pointing towards a curving slash through the trees that could have marked a road. He grabbed the trim lever in both hands as soon as Eskar let go, turning to put his whole weight on it as ailerons and stabilisers fought mecha-nically to straighten themselves.

The nose lifted slightly and then, as the aerodynamics of the guide fins assisted the aether-gold, rose faster, but not so quick that they didn't crash through the foliage of the first few trees. In a plume of broken branches and scattered leaves they burst out across the cleared way, which was indeed a road of the very muddy and rutted variety.

'Steady off,' Eskar called down the speaking tube to the endrin-room, before lifting her voice to the rest of the crew with a bellow untoward for her petite size and generally refined disposition. 'Ballast up, you snail-wits!'

Rather more precipitously than they were used to, the *Night's Daughter*'s crew brought the ship to a halt, ploughing a deep but short furrow in the muddy road. As the sky-ship bobbed into a hovering position with its keel just above the ground, Fairgold gave Eskar a kiss on the forehead.

'We're here!' he called out and lifted off his hat with a whoop. 'Time to seal a deal!'

The air in the valley was thick with humidity and Fairgold was sweating inside his full suit by the time he had readied himself and descended the rope ladder to the ground. Wet mud oozed under his boots and flies buzzed from the trees to investigate this new intruder into their world. The air was tainted with sulphur from the surrounding volcanic mountains, which had recently belched forth a vast cloud of aether-gold vapours. If the rumours were true, a sky-seam had been discovered the likes of which Fairgold believed could fuel a fleet for half a season or more. Enough to sponsor another expedition to find the *Night's Gift*. Caught in the strange astromagnetic winds of Chamon, the aether-gold would soon disperse and it was a race against time to get the location from the orruks and back to Barak-Mhornar to sell it.

Their last calls of farewell ringing from the trees, Fairgold and his companions set off up the road, leaving the others to patch the damaged hull and finish the endrin repairs. Clad in bulky aethersuits, the contingent tramped up the road, heavy boots sinking into the mud.

'With a following wind we'll be back by nightfall, no problem,' the captain said cheerfully to his satchel bearers.

The orruk settlement was more impressive than Fairgold had anticipated – he had been expecting some hybrid of dung heap and salvage yard. The road, such as it was, had brought them to a wooden gatehouse set within a stockade of stripped tree trunks, each broader than a duardin. As he passed within, the captain saw a score and more dwellings had been built in a broad gash of hacked-down forest. Timber walls held up roofs of metallic leaves so that each appeared crowned with bronze and silver and copper. Smoke dribbled from the chimney of a solitary stone building set apart from the others; gangs of grots and a few humans laboured at piles of dirt beside it, while ingots of purer metal appeared on pulled sleds from the other side of the foundry. The handful of greenskin guides-cum-guards that had met the duardin on the rough road steered the group towards a longer, higher building than the rest, presumably the hall of the warboss.

'Slaves,' said Thorkki.

'Not our problem,' said Fairgold. He had seen the chains on the ankles of the humans and the whip marks on their backs. 'We'd join them if we tried anything.'

Indeed, the Kharadron contingent was outnumbered by at least a factor of ten, as armour-clad brutes stepped out of their barracks-like homes to stare at the trade delegation. They were expected, but that did nothing to soften the raw hostility in the eyes of the orruks as clawed fingers flexed on weapon hilts and fangs were bared.

'What if they decide just to rob us?' suggested Golkin.

'I was hoping we'd have the *Daughter* nearby to even the odds. Don't give them ideas.'

The interior of the chieftain's hall was dark, lit only by a firepit in the middle, beyond which sat the warboss on a great chair of stone and iron. In the gloom the creature seemed to be a towering statue of red and black metal. The escorts growled and snarled in the orruk tongue and then moved back to stand sentry with a pair of even larger greenskins at the door.

'Come,' rumbled the orruk. It lifted a hand ringed with gold and bones and beckoned them past the haze of the embers. 'Safe in my house.'

'We bring good news, mighty Orgaggarok of the Falling Fist,' said Fairgold. Like the orruk he spoke a trading language that was the bastard child of the celestial tongue of Azyr.

'Show me,' said the orruk, heaving his bulk upright. Like his minions he was clad in a full suit of armour, adorned with blades and spikes that made every part of his body a weapon. Standing, he was twice as tall as Fairgold. The captain was dressed in leather and steel harness and suit, but he was here to trade, not fight. The crew were likewise in their battle-gear, for 'purely precautionary purposes' as the captain had told them, and each carried a blade and pistol of some kind. Fairgold tried not to let his gaze be drawn to the mighty cleaverblade at the warlord's hip, which was almost as tall as he was.

At a gesture from the warboss two orruks appeared from the shadows, rolling the round of a felled tree. They set this down beside the firepit to use as a table. Fairgold noticed ruddy stains on the wood and hoped it was just looted wine, but knew he was trying to trick himself.

'Map first, if you please,' said Fairgold, not wishing to begin with any kind of concession.

'Oggin!'

The endrinrigger appeared out of the gloom at Verna's call, the pieces of a valve in his hands.

'Endrinmaster?'

'I said to put the sprocket cap back on the main exchanger before taking off the capitulating ring.' The *Night's Daughter*'s creator pointed at the offending part with a multi-headed tool. 'We've lost pressure in the flux chamber.'

Oggin pushed up his goggles and rubbed an eye with a thumb, leaving a grey smear over his eyelid like kohl.

'Why's the capitulating ring after the main exchange? That's not what it's supposed to do,' he asked, looking innocently at his mistress.

''Cos I built it that way, all right,' snapped Verna. ''S'quicker to swap the pressure taps over when you're trimming.'

'But then–'

'Isn't the time, rigger,' she cut him off. 'Go fetch a couple of hands, there's some manual pumping to be done.' Then, almost under her breath, she continued, 'Going to be late... Fairgold's not going to be happy.'

Compromises had been made. Three of Fairgold's crew brandished their satchels like shields as proof that he had the goods, while a scrawny grot held a rolled-up parchment as evidence of Orgaggarok's good intent.

With the chieftain was a smaller orruk that wore less armour but was bedecked in bone fetishes and other talismans. The warchanter, for such it had been introduced as, grunted and gabbled while gesturing wildly for some time. Flecks of saliva spattered the table-trunk and occasional green sparks flickered in the orruk's mad gaze.

'Hard work to find your sky-gold,' said Orgaggarok. 'Many head hurts and danger for Gorzbang. Strong Mork breath, yes?'

Fairgold took this to mean the aether-gold and the magical current that had conjured it from the Chamon winds.

'So-so,' he replied, waggling a hand. 'You know Mork. A breath for one is just a fart for another.'

The orruk's brow furrowed and red eyes pinned Fairgold to the spot. The chieftain's lip curled, revealing a dark gum and thick fang.

'Perhaps it is time for some disclosure,' Fairgold said quickly. He gestured to Thorkki and Snorrlig. Each opened their satchels and brought forward a leathery egg about the size of Fairgold's head. They placed them on the table, each held up by a rope quoit.

Orgaggarok flexed his hands appreciatively and bent forward to examine the eggs, tongue lolling from his wide mouth. He muttered something unintelligible.

'Fine specimens, delicately handled since acquisition, as promised,' said Fairgold, indicating the eggs with a flourish. He was wondering just how strong 'Mork's breath' was blowing. 'An orruk that owned such beasts would be a terror to behold and the envy of others.'

'Good,' Orgaggarok nodded. 'Blue lines and green patches means... prey finder? Good tracker. Brave. Loyal maw-krusha.'

'Yes? Rare? I mean, valuable. A very valuable addition to the stable of any warlord looking to pillage and plunder.'

The massive jaw shut with a crack and the orruk's murderous gaze fell upon Fairgold once more. A tentative claw prodded at one of the eggs.

Fairgold smiled as best he could.

'Is there a problem?'

Receiving the half-thumb ratchet claw from Oggin, Verna tightened the last fastening bolts under the piston line. She heaved herself out from under the bulk of the endrin-block and handed the tool back.

'I'll run the pressurisation test,' said the rigger.

'We'll skip it,' said Verna. 'Seals are all tight. It's going to take a while to get to full pressure as it is.'

'But what if...' Oggin mumbled into silence beneath Verna's unblinking but not entirely hostile stare. 'Right. I'll go tell Edra shall I?'

'There's a good lad,' said Verna, moving her attention to the main gauges. 'Quick as a Magnate's debt collector, if you please.'

As Oggin opened the door to the main deck it seemed to Verna that the sky was almost dark.

'A guide, perhaps?' suggested Fairgold, trying to ease the discussion along. 'Two mawcrushers is quite a bargain just for a map. If there was a guide to help us locate the aether-ore...'

A short and savage conversation erupted between the warlord and one of the other orruks. The tension caused sparks to start fizzing from the eyes of the warchanter.

'Gorzbang can smell Mork's breath for you,' declared the warlord, while next to him the warchanter twitched and dribbled.

Fairgold looked at the orruk shaman, who seemed about to explode. A smile slid onto the duardin's lips without effort.

'A generous offer. Very generous. But I would not dare keep one of your most powerful advisors away from you for such a length of time.'

The warchanter started to say something with a voice oddly screeching for an orruk, but a gesture from Orgaggarok had the magically volatile creature quickly dragged out of the hall by two burly enforcers. When they returned, they brought with them an orruk in a heavy apron of scaled skin over its armour. Evidently some kind of mawcrusher expert. A coiled whip hung at the belt of the apron. There was a fresh burst of fang-baring and snarls, followed by vigorous nodding from the beastmaster.

'These eggs old,' said Orgaggarok. 'Snarskab say so.'

'No, freshly plucked from the nest by my hand!' protested Fairgold. He thrust an accusing finger at Snarskab. 'I'll not have my word tarnished by such accusations.'

Orgaggarok tilted his head at Fairgold's theatrics and the duardin subsided with a bow.

'Please continue.'

'Old egg. Ready open,' insisted the warlord. A clawed finger prodded one of the eggs, which seemed to move back and forth of its own accord. The chieftain made a fist and then opened the fingers wide. 'Burst?'

'Hatch?' suggested Fairgold before he realised what he was saying. 'They're about to hatch?'

The captain kept his expression as a fixed smile but could feel his companions backing away slightly from the table. Fairgold rallied quickly.

'Not long to wait, eh?' He forced a chuckle. 'Means they are good, yes?'

The orruk considered this and then nodded once.

'Only two?' he rumbled, red eyes flicking to the third satchel. Fairgold glanced back at Hengirod, who was holding his bag as though it were a shrapnel shell with a lit fuse.

'Only one map?' Fairgold replied instinctively. Of course, there was only one map, but it was his nature to get every concession he could. Part of him wished his lips to stop moving but it was overruled by habit. 'There is still the question of a guide to answer. And, of course, the problem is that such aether-veins come and go. How am I to know whether the aether-gold will be there tomorrow, or the day after?'

The orruk rippled a lip, which might have been a smile or a grimace; it was impossible to tell. Fairgold held his nerve, meeting the gaze of the warlord while trying not to return any of the belligerence in its stare.

'Huh. Good map. *Two* clouds sky-gold,' said Orgaggarok. The warlord lifted up two clawed fingers. The map-bearer came forward and let the chart unroll, showing a roughly daubed but legible illustration of the region around Breakward Stark. There were two streaks of bright yellow: one above the mountains nearby and another closer to the coast of the Sea of Copperdust.

'Two sky-gold clouds, better than two eggs.' The orruk eyed the third satchel pointedly.

Fairgold took a breath slowly, trying not to look impressed. A second aether-vein! Not only would he cover the repairs to the *Daughter*, he could fund two expeditions to look for the *Night's Gift* too, and still have a small saving left over to procure a few shares in a promising company.

'Two for two seems like a bargain,' he began, but saw the furrowing brows once again and veered away from further haggling. 'But you have been most generous already and I am sure we can reach an agreement soon.'

He waved Hengirod forward. The other duardin deposited a third egg on the table before retreating swiftly, throwing nervous glances at the rest of the crew members.

'Three good,' snarled the orruk chief.

The beastmaster leaned forward, looked at the eggs for a few heart-stopping moments and then roared a few words to its lord. Orgaggarok responded with an interrogative snarl and there followed more fang snapping, grunting and pointing. The warboss stood so quickly he almost knocked over the table.

'Snarskab say eggs come from Iron Peaks!' bellowed the orruk. He thrust an accusing finger at Fairgold. 'Iron Peaks is Falling Fist land.'

'Is it?' Fairgold replied with all the false innocence he could muster.

'These my eggs. You take and sell to me. Thief!'

Fairgold grabbed a monstrous egg in each hand and held them up, making obvious his intent to dash them to the floor. Orgaggarok froze, beady red eyes flicking between the duardin and the eggs.

'It's still a good deal,' said the captain, taking a step back. The scrape of chairs and blades in scabbards sounded from other parts of the hall. Behind him, his crew laid hands on pistol handles and sword grips.

The orruk warlord bared dagger-teeth in reply.

'Catch!'

Fairgold threw the eggs – one to the chieftain, another to the beastmaster. As they scrabbled to catch the falling eggs, Fairgold dodged past the trunk-table and smashed his right fist into the face of the map-grot, pulling the parchment from its loosening grip as the diminutive greenskin toppled backwards.

Orgaggarok intercepted him as he turned. For the second time since waking up that day, Fairgold found himself staring into the flared nostrils of a monstrous creature that wanted to kill him. For the second time since waking up he found himself issuing the same command.

'Run for it!'

Before obeying himself, Fairgold flexed his right wrist in a particular way, activating the springload built into the arm of his drift harness. A one-use aethershot cane slapped into his waiting palm, trigger under his thumb. In an instant, the duardin captain moved his aim from warlord to egg, stopping Orgaggarok in mid-swing.

The ruse would only work for a heartbeat, but in that heartbeat Fairgold lifted his aim and opened fire, a spray of aetheric-propelled bullets ripping into the face of the beastmaster.

One of his companions fired, the crack of aethershot ruddily lighting the hall for a second. In the next instant, blades clashed and orruk shouts competed in volume with duardin curses. Orgaggarok swung his cleaver. Fairgold ducked, losing the tip of his hat-feather and the tiniest sliver of ear as the blade swept down and into the trunk-table. A heartbeat later, Fairgold had a blade in one hand and a proper pistol in the other. He fired at the red-armoured shapes around him, thrusting his blade without much thought as the melee spilled towards the firepit. He came face to face with a grot, who spat at him and then turned tail to run.

The orruks drew back, recovering from the surprise, giving the duardin a precious few moments to gather about their captain, a hedgehog of pointing swords and pistol muzzles. Huddled together they moved towards the door, at least a brace of pistols moving to confront any orruk that dared approach, discouraging further assault. Having levered his cleaver from the table, Orgagga-rok stomped forward, helmed head carving furrows in the beams of the ceiling. Faced with a wall of aethershot pistols he paused, snarling and snapping like a wakened guard hound.

With gesturing pistols, they waved the guards away from the doors and managed to negotiate their way across the threshold. Outside, dusk was settling fast. A few other orruks were taking an interest, but for the moment the sounds of fighting had not caused enough of a stir to rouse the rest of the settlement.

Fairgold looked around, scanning the sky above the wall for any sign of the *Daughter*. Ruddy dusk painted the air behind the peaks and twilight orange gave way to night blues in the other direction, equally devoid of sky-ship. He'd been hoping the others had turned up during the negotiations.

Eyes returning to the warlord as the orruk exited the hall, Fairgold called out.

'You've got the eggs! Nobody else has to get hurt.' Fairgold swished his blade back and forth a few times. 'Especially you.'

Orgaggarok rumbled a laugh in response, swinging his blade. 'But it fun,' the warlord growled back. 'Not kill you quick. Got fire nice and...'

The orruk trailed off, gaze moving up and away from the duardin. Fairgold felt a sudden chill as a long evening shadow fell across him. He half turned, laughing.

'The *Daughter*, by Valaya's bountiful bosom! Later is better than...' The captain's celebration was cut short as he saw not an armoured ironclad cruising over the wall of the stronghold but a monstrous reptilian with a scab-crusted face and shoulder.

Fairgold let out an un-duardin-like shriek and threw himself to the dirt as the mawcrusher swept down.

The raucous shouts of the orruks could have been surprise, panic or elation, or perhaps all three. The warlord brandished his cleaver and bellowed at the diving monster while his companions started converging on the hall from across the settlement.

'The gate!' snapped Fairgold, picking himself up. Ahead, the wooden gates were wide open but a crowd of grots were gathering around the massive capstan that would wind them shut. More grots on the towers hastily repositioned their bolt throwers and catapults to target the mawcrusher. Inside the stockade the beast crashed to a landing in front of the hall, hurt wing almost failing as claws scrabbled furrows through the dirt.

The duardin dashed as fast as they could towards the narrowing rectangle of woodland visible through the gates, Fairgold bringing up the rear as he glanced over his shoulder. Claw matched against iron, the mawcrusher and warboss slashed at each other with unbridled savagery, ripping armoured scales and metal plates from one another.

'Captain!' Thorkki's shout drew Fairgold's attention back to their own situation. A clamorous clanging from an alarm gong brought several dozen orruks towards the gate to help the grots. And the gap of the gate was now only wide enough for two abreast, closing fast.

A chorus of bestial shouts followed by a monstrous roar confirmed the battle outside the hall was still ongoing. Looking at the distance between his crew and the gate, Fairgold faltered in his stride.

'Ease off,' he told them. 'We're not going to make it.'

The others came to a ragged halt and unconsciously formed a circle as orruks pounded towards them from across the stronghold.

As blades were raised, a distant boom echoed across the treetops an instant before the blur of a shell slammed into the side of the mawcrusher, showering the ground and orruks with broken scales and bloody chunks of flesh. Duardin and orruk alike gave throat to their happiness as the *Night's Daughter* hauled into view over the peakward wall; the latter turned to angry bellows as aethershock torpedoes blasted the wooden wall into fire and splinters, the flaming blossom hurling grots and orruks high through the air. Carbine fire followed swiftly while rope ladders unrolled down the sides of the descending ironclad.

The duardin needed no encouragement from their leader and threw themselves towards the trailing ladders as the ship passed through the flame and smoke, pulling themselves up even as companions reached down to help.

Pistol and blade in hand, Fairgold watched their backs, turning slowly until he came to face towards the hall. The mawcrusher was still alive, but only barely. The confrontation had smashed away some of the pillars so that the front of the hall had collapsed, bringing down a wall and half the roof. In the corner of his eye Fairgold could see the flicker of flames where the stronghold wall used to be.

Past the twitching mawcrusher he saw the orruk chieftain. The warboss levelled his blade in accusation and bellowed something in the greenskins' guttural language. Fairgold needed no translator to recognise a bloody oath of vengeance when he saw one.

To his left and right orruks closed in, some of them falling to marksman fire from the *Night's Daughter*, others weathering the bullets with sparks and chips from their thick armour. The closest was almost within blade reach. Fairgold would have to turn his back to make for the ladders...

He held his ground, aiming his pistol at the closest foe.

'Grab my hand.'

Fairgold turned to find Verna behind and above him, drifting closer in full dirigible suit, aetherturbines buzzing loudly. She held out a gloved hand, the other encased in a handmade aether-shot rig that spat a hail of projectiles at the swarming orruks. As Fairgold holstered his pistol and grabbed hold, howls of anguish surrounded him, swinging blades missing his dangling booted feet.

The pair flew higher, soaring over the rising *Night's Daughter*. Shots from the greenskin war machines clanged against the hull and ricocheted around Eskar and the aethertank as she steered the ironclad up and away. Down in the settlement Fairgold spied the human slaves throttling grots with their chains before they made a dash for the gaps in the burning wall.

Verna guided them back towards the foredeck as the ship lifted out of range of the orruk war engines. She let Fairgold drop to the planks at the bow before attaching herself to a hitching ring on the outer hull.

Ahead the sun set over the wooded mountains, bathing the valley in ruddy gold. Even as the Breakward Stark disappeared in evening haze, Fairgold had a feeling that it was not the last he had seen of Orgaggarok and the Falling Fist.

'You were lucky none of us got killed,' snapped Thorkki. 'And for what?'

In his cabin with Verna, Eskar, Thorkki and a few others, Fairgold tightened a bandage round his arm where an orruk blade had nicked him in the scramble from the hall. Verna helped him tie the knot as he fumbled at the ends of the bandage with stubby fingers.

'For this!' crowed Fairgold, dragging a rumpled and slightly torn rag of parchment from out of his armoured jerkin. He unrolled it on the chart table and, with a broad grin, plunged a fat finger onto one of the streaks of yellow. 'There's aether-gold in them hills! Two clouds!'

'The map!' cried Thorkki.

'You didn't think we'd walk away with nothing, did you?' He gave Thorkki an admonishing look. 'When have I ever come out of a deal with hands as empty as an aelf's promise?'

'Well...' began Thorkki, but Verna cut him off.

'I'm sorry we couldn't get to you sooner,' she said, laying a hand on the captain's arm.

'If we had pushed any harder, the screws would have fallen off,' said Eskar. 'You should have seen her, dashing about like a mad thing to keep everything ticking over, keeping us all on our toes.'

'Of course you did,' said Fairgold, taking Verna's hand to give it a squeeze. 'I never doubted for a heartbeat that you'd be there.'

They shared a smile before he returned his gaze to the others.

'As you know, I never leave myself without an option or two,' Fairgold beamed. 'We've come out of this even better than I hoped. You see, there were four eggs in that nest, not three. We can find someone else that'll pay for a mawcrusher egg.'

'Where is it?' asked Verna.

'Nukduk's looking after it in the galley,' said Fairgold.

His gaze met that of Thorkki, whose eyebrows were slowly knotting in thought.

'That orruk told you they was really close to hatching...' said the greybeard.

As Fairgold bolted towards the cabin door, a hoarse shriek sang out across the *Night's Daughter*, followed by a drawn-out cry of alarm and the crash of falling plates and pans.

YOUR
NEXT READ

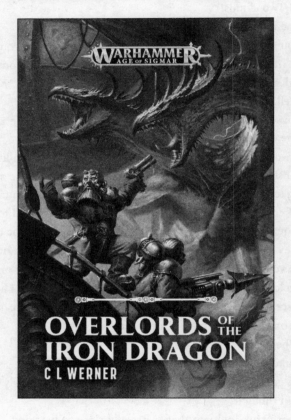

OVERLORDS OF THE IRON DRAGON
by C L Werner

Brokrin Ullissonn, a down on his luck duardin captain, has a change in fortunes when he finds an untapped source of aether-gold – but is the danger that awaits him and his crew worth the prize, or are they doomed to further failure?

SHIPRATS

C L Werner

Carefully, the heavyset duardin warrior raised his weapon. His eyes narrowed, fixating on his victim. He appeared unfazed by the gloom of the darkened hold, his vision sharp enough to pick out a marrow-hawk soaring through a thunderstorm. The duardin judged the distance, allowed for the air currents that buffeted the moored aether-ship and estimated how much strength to bring to bear against his foe.

The shovel came cracking down, striking the deck with such force that a metallic ping was sent echoing through the hold. Drumark cursed as the target of the descending spade leapt upwards and squeaked in fright. The brown rat landed on his foot, squeaked again, then scampered off deeper into the hold.

Furious, Drumark turned and glowered at the other spade-carrying duardin gathered in the *Iron Dragon*'s hold. Arkanauts, endrinriggers, aether-tenders and even a few of the ship's officers gave the angry sergeant anxious stares.

'Right! Now they are just begging to be shot! I am getting my decksweeper!' Drumark swore, not for the first time.

Brokrin, the *Iron Dragon*'s captain, stepped towards Drumark. 'You are not shooting holes in the bottom of my ship,' he snapped at him. 'We have enough problems with the rats. If you go shooting holes in the hull we won't be able to take on any aether-gold even if we do find a rich cloud-vein.'

Drumark jabbed a thumb down at his boot. 'It peed on my foot. Only respect for you, cap'n, keeps me from getting a good fire going and smoking the vermin out.'

'That is some sound thinking,' Horgarr, the *Iron Dragon*'s endrinmaster scoffed. He pressed his shovel against the deck and leaned against it as he turned towards Drumark. 'Start a fire in the ship's belly. Nothing bad could happen from that. Except the fifty-odd things that immediately come to mind.'

Brokrin shook his head as Drumark told Horgarr exactly what he thought of the endrinmaster's mind. No duardin had any affection for rats, but Drumark's hatred of them was almost a mania. His father had died fighting the pestiferous skaven and every time he looked at a rat he was reminded of their larger kin. It made him surly and quick to anger. This would be the third fight between the two he would have to break up since coming down into the *Iron Dragon*'s holds. Unable to find any aether-gold, the ironclad had put in at Greypeak, a walled human city with which Barak-Zilfin had a trading compact. The grain the city's farmers cultivated was well regarded by the Kharadron and would fetch a good price in the skyhold. Not as much as a good vein, but at least there would be something for the aether-ship's backers.

At least there would be if the rats that had embarked along with the grain left anything in good enough condition to sell. There were more than a few Kharadron who claimed that the *Iron Dragon* was jinxed and that her captain was under a curse.

Sometimes he found himself wondering if his detractors were right. This was not the first time Brokrin's ship had suffered an infestation of vermin, but he could not recall any that had been so tenacious as these. Whatever they did to try to protect their cargo, the rats found some way around it. They were too clever for the traps old Mortrimm set for them, too cunning to accept the poisoned biscuits Lodri made for them. Even the cat Gotramm had brought aboard had been useless – after its first tussle with one of the rats it had found itself a spot up in the main endrin's cupola and would claw anyone who tried to send it below deck again.

'These swine must have iron teeth.' The bitter observation was given voice by Skaggi, the expedition's logisticator. As he was tasked with balancing profit against expense and safeguarding the investment of the expedition's backers, every ounce of grain despoiled by the rodents stung Skaggi to the quick. He held a heavy net of copper wire in his hands, extending it towards Brokrin so he could see the holes the rats had gnawed. 'So much for keeping them out of the grain. We will be lucky if they do not start in for the beer next.'

Skaggi's dour prediction made Drumark completely forget about his argument with Horgarr. He looked in horror at Skaggi. An instant later, he raised the shovel overhead and flung it to the floor.

'That is it!' Drumark declared. 'I am bringing my lads down here and we will settle these parasites here and now!' He turned to Brokrin, determination etched across his face. 'You tell Grundstok thunderers to hunt rats, then that is just what we will do. But we will do it the way we know best.'

Skaggi's eyes went wide with alarm, his mind turning over the expense of patching over the holes the thunderers would leave if they started blasting away at the rats. He swung around to Brokrin, his tone almost frantic. 'We will be ruined,' he groaned. 'No profit, barely enough to pay off the backers.'

Drumark reached out and took hold of the copper net Skaggi was holding. 'If they can chew through this, they can chew their way into the beer barrels. Me and my thunderers are not going dry while these rats get drunk!'

The sound of shovels slapping against the floor died down as the rest of the duardin in the hold paused in their efforts to hear what Drumark was shouting about. Many of them were from his Grundstok company and looked more than ready to side with their sergeant and trade spades for guns.

'The rats will not bother the beer while they still have grain to eat,' Brokrin stated, making sure his words were loud enough to carry to every crewman in the hold. How much truth there was in the statement, he did not know. He did know it was what Drumark and the others needed to hear right now.

'All due respect, cap'n,' Drumark said, 'but how long will that be? Swatting them with shovels just isn't enough and we have tried everything else except shooting them.'

Brokrin gave Drumark a stern look. 'Others have said it, now I am saying it. You are not shooting holes in *my* ship.' The chastened sergeant held Brokrin's gaze for a moment, then averted his eyes. The point had been made.

'What are we going to do?' Gotramm asked. The youthful leader of the *Iron Dragon*'s arkanauts, he had watched with pointed interest the exchange between Brokrin and Drumark.

'I know one thing,' Horgarr said, pulling back his sleeve and showing the many scratches on his arm. 'That cat is staying right where it is.' The remark brought laughs from all who heard it, even cracking Drumark's sullen mood.

Brokrin was more pensive. Something Drumark had said earlier had spurred a memory. It was only now that his recollection fell into place. 'The toads,' he finally said. The newer members of the crew glanced in confusion at their captain, but those who had served on the *Iron Dragon* before her escape from the monster Ghazul knew his meaning.

'Some years ago,' Brokrin explained to them, 'we sailed through a Grimesturm and a rain of toads fell on our decks. They were everywhere, even worse than these rats. You could not sit without squashing one or take a sip of ale without having one hop into your mug.

'To rid the ship of her infestation,' Brokrin continued, 'we put in at the lamasery of Kheitar. The lamas prepared a mixture of herbs, which we burned in smudge pots. The smoke vexed the toads so much that they jumped overboard of their own accord.'

'You think the lamas could whip up something to scare off rats?' Gotramm asked.

Brokrin nodded. 'Kheitar is not far out of our way. There would be little to lose by diverting our course and paying the lamasery a visit.'

'Kheitar is built into the side of a mountain,' Horgarr said. 'Certainly it will offer as good an anchorage as the peak we're moored to now.'

Skaggi's eyes lit up, an avaricious smile pulling at his beard. 'The lamas are renowned for their artistic tapestries as well as their herbalism. If we could bargain with them and get them to part with even one tapestry, we could recover the loss of what the rats have already ruined.'

'Then it is decided,' Brokrin said. 'Our next port of call is Kheitar.'

The lamasery's reception hall was a stark contrast to the confined cabins and holds of the *Iron Dragon*. Great pillars of lacquered wood richly carved with elaborate glyphs soared up from the teak floor to clasp the vaulted roof with timber claws. Lavish hangings hung from the walls, each beautifully woven with scenes from legend and lore. Great urns flanked each doorway, their basins filled with a wondrously translucent sand in which tangles of incense sticks slowly smouldered. Perfumed smoke wafted sluggishly through the room, visible as a slight haze where it condensed around the great platform at the rear of the chamber. Upon that platform stood a gigantic joss, a golden statue beaten into the semblance of an immensely fat man, his mouth distorted by great tusks and his head adorned by a nest of horns. In one clawed hand the joss held forward a flower, his other resting across his lap with the remains of a broken sword in his palm.

Brokrin could never help feeling a tinge of revulsion when he looked at Kheitar's idol. Whoever had crafted it, their attention to detail had been morbid. The legend at the root of the lamas' faith spoke of a heinous daemon from the Age of Chaos that had set aside its evil ways to find enlightenment in the ways of purity and asceticism. Looking at the joss, Brokrin felt less a sense of evil redeemed than he did that of evil biding its time. The duardin with him looked similarly perturbed, all except Skaggi, who was already casting a greedy look at the tapestries on the walls.

The young initiate who guided the duardin into the hall stepped aside as Brokrin and his companions entered. He bowed his shaved head towards a bronze gong hanging just to the left of the entrance. He took the striker tethered to the gong's wooden stand and gave the instrument three solid hits, each blow sending a dull reverberation echoing through the chamber.

'Take it easy,' Brokrin whispered when he saw Gotramm from the corner of his eye. The young arkanaut had reached for his pistol the moment the gong's notes were sounded. 'If we aggravate the lamas they might not help get rid of the rats.'

Gotramm let his hand drop away from the gun holstered on his belt. He nodded towards the joss at the other end of the hall. 'That gargoyle is not the sort of thing to make me feel at ease,' he said.

'The cap'n is not saying to close your eyes,' old Mortrimm

the navigator told Gotramm. 'He is just saying do not be hasty drawing a weapon. Abide by the Code – be sure who you set your axe against, and why.'

Brokrin frowned. 'Let us hope it does not come to axes. Barak-Zilfin has a long history trading with the lamas.' Even as he said the words, they felt strangely hollow to him. Something had changed about Kheitar. What it was, he could not say. It was not something he could see or hear, but rather a faintly familiar smell. He turned his eyes again to the daemon-faced joss, wondering what secrets it was hiding inside that golden head.

Movement drew Brokrin's attention away from the joss. From behind one of the hangings at the far end of the hall, a tall and sparingly built human emerged. He wore the saffron robes of Kheitar's lamas, but to this was added a wide sash of green that swept down across his left shoulder before circling his waist. It was the symbol that denoted the high lama himself. The uneasy feeling Brokrin had intensified, given something solid upon which to focus. The man who came out from behind the tapestry was middle-aged, his features long and drawn. He certainly was not the fat, elderly Piu who had been high lama the last time the *Iron Dragon* visited Kheitar.

The lama walked towards the duardin, but did not acknowledge their presence until after he had reached the middle of the hall and turned towards the joss. Bowing and clapping his hands four times, he made obeisance to the idol. When he turned back towards the duardin, his expression was that of sincerity itself.

'Peace and wisdom upon your path,' the lama declared, clapping his hands together once more. A regretful smile drew at the corners of his mouth. 'Is it too much to hope that the Kharadron overlords have descended from the heavens to seek enlightenment?' He shook his head. 'But such, I sense, is not the path that has led you to us. If it is not the comfort of wisdom you would take away from here, then what comfort is it that we can extend to you?'

Although Brokrin was the *Iron Dragon's* captain, it was Skaggi who stepped forwards to address the lama. Of all the ship's crew, the logisticator had the glibbest tongue. 'Please forgive any intrusion, your eminence,' he said. 'It is only dire need which causes us to intrude upon your solitude. Our ship has been beset by an infestation of noxious pests. Terrible rats that seek...'

The lama's serenity faltered when Skaggi began to describe the situation. A regretful look crept into his eyes. 'We of Kheitar are a peaceful order. Neither meat nor milk may pass our lips. Our hands are not raised in violence, for like Zomoth-tulku, we have forsaken the sword. To smite any living thing is to stumble on the path to ascension.'

Brokrin came forwards to stand beside Skaggi. 'Your order helped us once before, when hail-toads plagued my ship. The high lama, Piu, understood the necessity of removing them.'

The lama closed his eyes. 'Piu-tulku was a wise and holy man. Cho cannot claim even a measure of his enlightenment.' Cho opened his eyes again and nodded to Brokrin. 'There are herbs which could be prepared. Rendered down they can be burned in smudge pots and used to fumigate your ship.' A deep sigh ran through him. 'The smoke will drive the rats to flee. Would it be too great an imposition to ask that you leave them a way to escape? Perhaps keep your vessel moored here so they can flee down the ropes and reach solid ground.'

Skaggi's eyes went wide in shock. 'That would cause the lamasery to become infested.' He pointed at the lavish hangings on the walls. 'Those filthy devils would ruin this place in a fortnight! Think of all that potential profit being lost!'

Cho placed a hand against his shoulder. 'It would remove a stain from my conscience if you would indulge my hopes. The death of even so small a creature would impair my own aspirations of transcendence.'

'My conscience would not permit me to cause such misery to my benefactors,' Brokrin stated. 'But upon my honour and my beard, I vow that I will not use whatever herbs you provide us without ensuring the rats can make landfall without undue hazard.'

'It pleases me to hear those words,' Cho said. 'I know the word of your people is etched in stone. I am content. It will take us a day to prepare the herbs. Your ship will be safe where it is moored?'

'We are tied to the tower above your western gate,' Mortrimm stated. He gestured with his thumb at Brokrin. 'The cap'n insisted we keep far enough away that the rats wouldn't smell food and come slinking down the guide ropes.'

'Such consideration and concern does you credit, captain,' Cho declared. He suddenly turned towards Skaggi. 'If it is not an imposition, would it be acceptable to enquire if the tapestries we weave here still find favour among your people?'

The question took Skaggi by such surprise that the logisticator allowed excitement to shine in his eyes before gaining control of himself and resuming an air of indifference. Brokrin could tell that he was about to undervalue the worth of Kheitar's artistry. It was a prudent tactic when considering profit but an abominable one when thinking in terms of honour.

'Your work is applauded in Barak-Zilfin,' Brokrin said before Skaggi could find his voice. The logisticator gave him an imploring look, but he continued just the same. 'There are many guildhalls that have used your tapestries to adorn their assemblies, and poor is the noble house that has not at least one hanging from Kheitar on its walls.'

With each word he spoke, Brokrin saw Skaggi grow more perturbed. Cho remained implacable, exhibiting no alteration in his demeanour. Then the high lama turned towards the wall from which he had emerged. Clapping his hands together in rapid succession, he looked aside at the duardin.

'I thank you for your forthrightness,' Cho said. 'Your honesty makes you someone we can trust.' There was more, but even Brokrin lost the flow of Cho's speech when the hangings on the walls were pushed aside and a group of ten lamas entered the hall. Each pair carried an immense tapestry rolled into a bundle across their shoulders. To bring only a few tapestries out of Kheitar was considered a rewarding voyage. Was Cho truly offering the duardin five of them?

Cho noted the disbelief that shone on the faces of his guests. He swung around to Skaggi. 'I have noticed that you admire our work. I will leave it to you to judge the value of the wares I would offer you.' At a gesture from the high lama, the foremost of his followers came near and unrolled their burden. Skaggi didn't quite stifle the gasp that bubbled up from his throat.

The background of the tapestry was a rich burgundy in colour and across its thirty-foot length vibrant images were woven from threads of sapphire blue, emerald green and amber yellow. Geometric patterns that transfixed the eye formed a border around visions of opulent splendour and natural wonder. Soaring mountains with snowy peaks rose above wooded hills. Holy kings held court from gilded thrones, their crowns picked out with tiny slivers of jade wound between the threads. Through the centre of the tapestry a stream formed from crushed pearl flowed into a silver sea.

'Magnificent,' the logisticator sputtered before recovering his composure.

'It gladdens me that you are content with our poor offerings,' Cho told Skaggi. He looked back towards Brokrin. 'It is my hope that you would agree to take this cargo back to your city. Whatever price you gain from their sale, I only ask that you return half of that amount to the lamasery.'

'Well… there are our expenses to be taken into account…'

Skaggi started. However good a deal seemed, the logisticator was quick to find a way to make it better.

'Of course you should be compensated for your labours,' Cho said, conceding the point without argument. 'Captain, are you agreeable to my offer?'

'It is very generous and I would be a fool to look askance at your offer,' Brokrin replied. 'It may be some months before we can return here with your share.'

'That is understood,' Cho said. He gestured again to the lamas carrying the tapestries. 'Pack the hangings for their journey. Then take them to the Kharadron ship.'

The unaccountable uneasiness that had been nagging at Brokrin asserted itself once more. 'I will send one of my crew to guide your people and show them the best place to put your wares.' He turned to Mortrimm. 'Go with them and keep your wits about you,' he whispered.

'You expect trouble?' Mortrimm asked.

Brokrin scratched his beard. 'No, but what is it the Chuitsek nomads say? "A gift horse sometimes bites." Just make sure all they do is put the tapestries aboard.'

Nodding his understanding, Mortrimm took his position at the head of the procession of lamas. Because of their heavy burdens, the navigator was easily able to match their pace despite one of his legs being in an aetheric brace. Brokrin and the other duardin watched as the tapestries were conducted out of the hall.

'Should I go with them, cap'n?' Skaggi asked. 'Make certain they do not mar the merchandise when they bring it aboard?'

'I think these lamas know their business,' Gotramm retorted. 'They are the ones who sweated to make the things and they have just as much to lose as we do if they get damaged.'

Unlike the banter between Drumark and Horgarr, there was a bitter edge to what passed between Gotramm and Skaggi. There was no respect between them, only a kind of tolerant contempt. Brokrin started to intercede when something Cho had said suddenly rose to mind. He turned towards the high lama. 'You called your predecessor Piu-tulku? Is not tulku your word for the revered dead?'

'The holy ascended,' Cho corrected him. 'Among the vulgar it is translated as "living god". You have yourself seen the ancient tulkus who have followed Zomoth-tulku's transcendence.'

Brokrin shuddered at the recollection. Deep within the lamasery there were halls filled with niches, each containing the mummified husk of a human. They were holy men who had gradually poisoned themselves, embalming their own bodies while they were still alive in a desperate search for immortality. The lamas considered each of the corpses to still be alive, tending their clothes and setting bowls of food and drink before them each morning. He thought of Piu and the last time he had seen the man. There had been no hint that he had been undergoing this ghastly process of self-mummification.

'I was unaware Piu had chosen such a path,' Brokrin apologised.

Cho smiled and shook his head. 'Piu-tulku did not choose the path. The path chose him. A wondrous miracle, for he has transcended the toils of mortality yet still permits his wisdom to be shared with those who have yet to ascend to a higher enlightenment.' His smile broadened. 'Perhaps if you were to see him, speak with him, you would understand the wisdom of our order.'

That warning feeling was even more persistent now, but Brokrin resisted the urge to play things safe. Something had changed at Kheitar and whatever it was, he would bet it had to do with Piu's unexpected ascension. Glancing over at Gotramm and then at Skaggi, he made his decision. 'We would like very much to meet with Piu-tulku.'

Cho motioned for the initiate by the door to come over to

them. 'I am certain Piu-tulku will impart much wisdom to you, but to enter his august presence you must set aside your tools of death.' He pointed at the axes and swords the duardin carried. 'Leave those behind if you would see the tulku. I can allow no blades in his chambers.'

Brokrin nodded. 'You have nothing to fear, your grace. Our Code prohibits us from doing harm to any who are engaged in fair trade with us.' He slowly unbuckled his sword and proffered it to the initiate. 'We will follow your custom.'

Slowly the three duardin removed their blades, setting them on the floor. Gotramm started to do the same with his pistol, but Cho had already turned away. Brokrin set a restraining hand on Gotramm's.

'He said blades,' Brokrin whispered. 'Unless asked, keep your pistol.' He brushed his hand across the repeater holstered on his own belt. 'We will respect their custom, as far as they ask it of us.'

Brokrin gave a hard look at Cho's back as the high lama preceded them out of the hall. 'If he is being honest with us, it will make no difference. If he is not, it might make all the difference in the realms.'

Drumark escorted the lamas down into the *Iron Dragon*'s hold. He had tried to choose the cleanest compartment in which to put the precious cargo, but even here there was the fug of rat in the air. 'This is the best one,' he said. 'You can put them down here.'

'You think they will be safe?' asked Mortrimm. Like the sergeant, he could smell the stink of rat. He looked uneasily at the bamboo crates the lamas carried, wondering how long it would take a rat to gnaw its way through the boxes.

'As long as there is grain, the little devils will keep eating that,' Drumark spat, glowering at a fat, brown body that went scooting behind a crate when the light from his lantern shone upon it. 'It will be a while before they start nibbling on this stuff.' He turned his light on the sallow-faced lamas as they carefully set down the crates and started to leave the hold. 'Tell your friends to get that poison ready on the quick. If we do not smoke out these vermin, your tapestries will be gnawed so badly we will have to sell them as thread.'

The warning put a certain haste in the lamas' step as they withdrew from the hold. Mortrimm started to follow them as the men made their way back onto the deck. He had only taken a few steps when he noticed that Drumark was still standing down near the tapestries.

'Are you coming?' Mortrimm asked.

'In a bit,' Drumark answered, waving him away. Mortrimm shook his head and left the hold.

Alone in the rat-infested hold, Drumark glowered at the shadows. The stink of vermin surrounded him, making his skin crawl. Instead of withdrawing from the stench, he let his revulsion swell, feeding into the hate that boiled deep inside him. Rats! Pestiferous, murderous fiends! Whatever size they came in, they had to be stamped out wherever they were found. He would happily do his part. He owed that much to his father, burned down by the foul magics of the loathsome skaven.

Drumark looked at the crates and then back at the noisy shadows. Despite his talk with Mortrimm and the lamas, he was anything but certain the rats would spare the tapestries. The vermin were perverse creatures and might gnaw on the precious hangings out of sheer spite. Well, if they did, they would find a very irritable duardin waiting for them.

Checking one last time to be certain Mortrimm was gone, Drumark walked over to a dark corner near the door and retrieved the object he had secreted there without Brokrin's knowledge. He patted the heavy stock of his decksweeper. 'Some work for you before too long,' he told it. Returning to his original position, he doused the lantern. Instantly the hold was plunged into darkness. Drumark could hear the creaking of the guide ropes as the ship swayed in its mooring, the groan of the engines that powered the ironclad's huge endrin, the scratch of little claws as they came creeping across the planks.

Gradually his eyes adjusted to the gloom and Drumark could see little shapes scurrying around the hold. Soon the shapes became more distinct as his eyes became accustomed to the dark. Rats, as fat and evil as he had ever seen. There must be a dozen of them, all scurrying about, crawling over barrels, peeping into boxes, even gnawing at the planks. He kept his eyes on the crates with the tapestries, all laid out in a nice little row. The moment one of the rats started to nibble at them he would start shooting.

But the rats did not nibble the crates. Indeed, Drumark began to appreciate that the animals were conspicuously avoiding them. At first he thought it was simply because they were new, a change in their environment that the vermin would have to become comfortable with first. Then one of the rats did stray towards the row, fleeing the ire of one of its larger kin. The wayward rodent paused in mid-retreat, rearing up and sniffing at the crates.

Drumark could not know what the rat smelled, but he did know whatever it was had given the rodent a fright. It went scampering off, squeaking like a thing possessed. The rest of the vermin were soon following it, scrambling to their boltholes and scurrying away to other parts of the ship. Soon Drumark could not hear their scratching claws any more.

Keeping his decksweeper at the ready, Drumark sat down beside the door. He stayed silent as he watched the crated tapestries, his body as rigid as that of a statue. In the darkness, he waited.

The wait was not a long one. A flutter of motion spread through the rolled tapestry at the end of the row. Faint at first, it increased in its agitation, becoming a wild thrashing after a few moments, the cloth slapping against the bamboo that enclosed it. Someone – or something – was inside the rolled tapestry and trying to work its way out. Eyes riveted on the movement, Drumark rose and walked forwards. He aimed his decksweeper at the tapestry. Whatever had hidden itself inside, it would find a warm reception when it emerged.

The thrashing persisted, growing more wild but making no headway against the framework that surrounded the tapestry. Whatever was inside was unable to free itself. Or unwilling. A horrible suspicion gripped Drumark. There were four more tapestries and while his attention was focused on this one, he was unable to watch the others.

Drumark swung around just as a dark shape came leaping at him from the shadows.

The decksweeper bellowed as he fired into his attacker. Drumark saw a furry body go spinning across the hold, slamming into the wall with a bone-crunching impact. He had only a vague impression of the thing he had shot. He got a better look at the creature that came lunging at him from one of the other crates.

Thin hands with clawed fingers scrabbled at Drumark as the creature leapt on him. Its filthy nails raked at his face, pulling hair from his beard. A ratlike face with hideous red eyes glared at him before snapping at his throat with chisel-like fangs. He could feel a long tail slapping at his legs, trying to hit his knees and knock him to the floor.

Drumark brought the hot barrel of his decksweeper cracking up into the monster's jaw, breaking its teeth. The creature whimpered and tried to wrest free from his grip, but he caught hold of its arm and gave it a brutal twist, popping it out of joint. The crippled creature twisted away, plunging back down on top of the crates.

Any sense of victory Drumark might have felt vanished when

he raised his eyes from the enormous rat he had overcome. Six more of its kind had crawled out from their hiding places in the tapestries, and unlike the one he had already fought, these each had knives in their paw-like hands. They stood upright on their hind legs, chittering malignantly as they started towards the lone duardin.

'Skaven!'

The cry came from the doorway behind Drumark. The discharge of his decksweeper had brought Horgarr and several others of the crew rushing into the hold, concerned that the sergeant had finally lost all restraint with the rats infesting the ship. Instead they found a far more infernal pestilence aboard.

The arrival of the other duardin dulled the confidence that shone in the eyes of the skaven infiltrators. The mocking squeaks took on an uncertain quality. Ready to pounce en masse on Drumark a moment before, now the creatures hesitated.

'What are you waiting for, lads!' Drumark shouted to Horgarr and the others. 'The bigger the rat, the more of our beer it will drink! Get the scum!'

The sergeant's shouts overcame the surprise that held the other duardin. Armed with shovels and axes, Horgarr led the crew charging across the hold. Their backs against the wall, the skaven had no choice but to make a fight of it.

As he rearmed his decksweeper and made ready to return to the fray, a terrible thought occurred to Drumark. The tapestries and their devious passengers had come from the lamasery. A place from which Captain Brokrin had not yet returned.

'Hold them here!' Drumark told Horgarr. 'I have to alert the rest of the ship and see if we can help the cap'n!'

The young initiate held the ornate door open for Cho and the duardin as they entered the shrine wherein Piu-tulku had been entombed after his ascension. The room was smaller than the grand reception hall, but even more opulently appointed. The hangings that covered its walls were adorned with glittering jewels; the pillars that supported its roof were carved from blackest ebony and highlighted with designs painted in gold. The varnished floor creaked with a musical cadence as the visitors crossed it, sending lyrical echoes wafting up into the vaulted heights of its arched ceiling.

Ensconced upon a great dais flanked by hangings that depicted the wingless dragon and the fiery phoenix, the living god of Kheitar reposed. Piu was still a fat man, but his flesh had lost its rich colour, fading to a parchment-like hue. He wore black robes with a sash of vivid blue – the same raiment that had been given to the mummies Brokrin had seen in the lamasery's vaults. Yet Piu was not content to remain in motionless silence. Just as the duardin had decided that the lamas were delusional and that their late leader was simply dead, the body seated atop the dais opened its eyes and spoke.

'Enter and welcome,' the thing on the dais said. The voice was dull and dry with a strange reverberation running through it. 'Duardin-friends always-ever welcome in Kheitar.' It moved its head, fixing its empty gaze in Cho's general direction. 'Have you given help-aid to our guests?'

'Yes, holy tulku!' Cho said, bowing before the dais. 'The tapestries have been sent to their ship, as you commanded.'

The thing swung its head back around, facing towards the duardin. It extended its hands in a supplicating gesture. The effect was marred by the jerky way in which the arms moved. Brokrin could hear a faint, unnatural sound as Piu moved its head and hands, something between a pop and a whir. He had seen such artificial motion before, heard similar mechanical sounds. The tulku was similar to an aetheric musician he'd seen in the great manor of

Grand Admiral Thorgraad, a wondrous machine crafted in the semblance of a duardin bard. The only blight on the incredible automaton's music had been the sound of the pumps inside it sending fuel through its pipes and hoses.

Whatever the esoteric beliefs of Kheitar, what sat upon the dais was not an ascended holy man. It was only a machine.

Piu began to speak again. 'It is to be hope-prayed that we shall all profit-gain from–'

Brokrin stepped past Cho and glared at the thing on the dais. 'I do not know who you are, but I will not waste words with a puppet.' The outburst brought a gasp of horror from the initiate at the door. Cho raced forwards, prostrating himself before the dais and pleading with Piu to forgive him for such insult.

Brokrin gave the offended lamas small notice. His attention was fixed to the hangings behind Piu's dais. There was a ripple of motion from behind one of them. Pushing aside the snake-like dragon, a loathsome figure stalked into view. He was taller than the duardin but more leanly built, his wiry body covered in grey fur peppered with black. A rough sort of metal hauberk clung to his chest while a strange helm of copper encased most of his rodent-like head. Only the fanged muzzle and the angry red eyes were left uncovered. A crazed array of pouches and tools swung from belts and bandoleers, but across one shoulder the humanoid rat wore a brilliant blue sash – the same as that which adorned Piu.

'Now you may speak-beg,' the ratman growled as he stood beside Piu. His hairless tail lashed about in malicious amusement as he smelled the shock rising off the duardin.

'Mighty Kilvolt-tulku,' Cho cried out. 'Forgive me. I did not know they were such barbarians.'

Kilvolt waved aside the high lama's apology. He fixed his gruesome attention on Brokrin. 'No defiance, beard-thing,' he snarled, pointing a claw at either side of the room. From behind the hangings a pack of armoured skaven crept into view, each carrying a vicious halberd in its claws. 'Listen-hear. I know-learn about your port-nest. Your clan-kin make-build ships that fly-climb higher than any others. I want-demand that secret.'

'Even if I knew it,' Brokrin snapped at Kilvolt, 'I would not give it to you.'

The skaven bared his fangs, his tail lashing angrily from side to side. 'Then I take-tear what I want-need! Already you let-bring my warriors into your ship.' He waved his paw at Cho. 'The tapestries this fool-meat gave you.' He gestured again with his paws, waving at the skaven guards that now surrounded the duardin. 'If they fail-fall, then I have hostages to buy the secret of your ship. Torture or ransom will give-bring what I...'

Kilvolt's fur suddenly stood on end, a sour odour rising from his glands. His eyes were fixed on the pistols hanging from the belts Brokrin and Gotramm wore. He swung around on Cho, wrenching a monstrous gun of his own from one of the bandoleers. 'I order-say take-fetch all-all weapons!' The skaven punctuated his words by pulling the trigger and exploding Cho's head in a burst of blood and bone.

The violent destruction of the lama spurred the duardin into action. With the skaven distracted by the murder on the dais, Brokrin and Gotramm drew their pistols. Before the ratmen could react, the arkanaut captain burned one down with a shot to its chest, the aetheric charge searing a hole through its armour. Brokrin turned towards Kilvolt, but the skaven took one glance at the multi-barrelled volley pistol and darted behind the seated Piu-tulku.

Instead Brokrin swung around and discharged his weapon into the skaven guards to his right. The volley dropped two of the rushing ratmen and sent another pair squeaking back to the doorways hidden behind the hangings, their fur dripping with blood.

Gotramm was firing again, but the skaven were more wary of their foes now, ducking around the pillars and trying to use them as cover while they advanced.

'We are done for,' Skaggi groaned, keeping close to the other duardin. Alone among them, the logisticator really had come into the room unarmed. 'We have to negotiate!' he pleaded with Brokrin.

'The only things I have to say to skaven come out of here,' Brokrin told Skaggi, aiming his volley pistol at the guards trying to circle around him. The ratmen were unaware the weapon had no charge and seeing it aimed in their direction had them falling over themselves to gain cover.

A crackle from the dais presaged the grisly impact that sent an electric shock rushing through Brokrin. The armour on his back had been struck by a blast from Kilvolt himself. Feeling secure that the duardin were distracted by his henchrats, he returned to the attack. The oversized rings that adorned one of his paws pulsated with a sickly green glow, a light that throbbed down to them via a series of hoses that wrapped around his arm before dipping down to a cannister on his belt.

The heavy armour Brokrin wore guarded him against the worst of the synthetic lightning. He turned his volley pistol towards the dais. Kilvolt flinched, ducking back behind the phoney tulku. As he did, the ratman's eyes fixated on something behind the duardin captain.

'The boy-thing!' Kilvolt snarled from behind Piu. 'Stop-kill boy-thing, you fool-meat!'

Brokrin risked a glance towards the door. It had been flung open and the initiate was racing into the hall outside, screaming at the top of his lungs. Immediately half a dozen of the skaven were charging after him, determined to stop him from alerting the other lamas about what was happening in Piu's shrine.

The ratmen made it as far as the door before a duardin fusillade smashed into them. Skaven bodies were flung back into the shrine, battered and bloodied by a concentrated salvo of gunfire. Just behind them came their executioners, Drumark leading his Grundstok thunderers.

The surviving guards squeaked in fright at the unexpected appearance of so many duardin and the vicious dispatch of their comrades. The creatures turned and fled, scurrying back into their holes behind the wall hangings. A few shots from the thunderers encouraged them to keep running.

'The leader is up there!' Brokrin told his crew, waving his pistol at the dais. 'There are tunnels behind the tapestries. Keep him from reaching them.'

Even as Brokrin gave the command, Kilvolt came darting out from behind the dais. His retreat would have ended in disaster, but the skaven had one last trick to play. To cover his flight, he had sent a final pawn into the fray. Piu-tulku rose from its seat and came lurching towards the duardin. There was no doubting the mechanical nature of the thing now. Every jerky motion of its limbs was accompanied by a buzzing whirr and the sour smell of leaking lubricants. Its hands were curled into claws as it stumbled towards Brokrin, but the face of Piu still wore the same expression of contemplative serenity.

'Right! That is far enough!' Drumark cried out, levelling his decksweeper at the automaton. When the Piu-thing continued its mindless approach, he emptied every barrel into it. The shot ripped through the thing's shell of flesh and cloth. In crafting his 'tulku' Kilvolt had stitched the flayed skin of Piu over a metal armature. The armature was now exposed by Drumark's blast as well as the nest of hoses and wires that swirled through its body.

Despite the damage inflicted on it, the automaton staggered onwards. Drumark glared at it in silent fury, as though it were a personal affront that it remained on its feet. While the sergeant fumed, Brokrin took command. 'Thunderers!' he called out. 'Aim for its spine! Concentrate your shots there!'

The thunderers obeyed Brokrin's order, fixing their aim at the core of the Piu-thing. Shots echoed through the shrine as round after round struck the automaton. Under the vicious barrage, the thing was cut in half, its torso severed and sent crashing to the floor. The legs stumbled on for several steps before slopping over onto their side and kicking futilely at the floor.

'And stay down!' Drumark bellowed, spitting on the fallen automaton.

Gotramm seized hold of the sergeant's arm. 'We have to get back to the ship! There are more of them in the hold with those tapestries!'

'Already sorted out,' Drumark declared. 'By now Horgarr should be done tossing their carcasses overboard. I figured you might be having trouble over here so me and the lads grabbed one of the lamas and found out where you were.'

Brokrin felt a surge of relief sweep through him. The *Iron Dragon* was safe. At least for now. He turned his eyes to the dragon tapestry and the tunnel Kilvolt had escaped into. Even now the skaven were probably regrouping to make another attack.

'Everybody back to the ship,' Brokrin said. 'The sooner we are away from here the better.' He gave Skaggi an almost sympathetic look. 'When we get back we will have to dump the tapestries over the side as well. We can't take the chance the skaven put some kind of poison or pestilence on them.'

Skaggi clenched his fist and rushed to the wall. With a savage tug he brought one of the hangings crashing down to the floor. 'If we have to throw out the others then we had better grab some replacements on our way out!' Catching his intention, Gotramm and some of the thunderers helped Skaggi pull down the other tapestries. The hangings were quickly gathered up and slung across the shoulders of the duardin.

'What about the rat poison, cap'n?' Drumark asked as they hurried through halls that were empty of either lamas or skaven.

'We cannot trust that either,' Brokrin told him. 'We must do without it.' He gave the sergeant a grim smile. 'I hope you remember where you put your spade.'

Drumark sighed and shook his head. 'I remember, but overall I would rather stay here and shoot skaven than play whack-a-rat with a shovel.'

YOUR NEXT READ

PROFIT'S RUIN
by C L Werner

Only the greedy and the desperate seek out the fabled sky-island of Profit's Ruin, for no Kharadron vessel has ever escaped its grip… Will Brokrin Ullissonn and the Iron Dragon be the first?

THE NEVERSPIKE

Darius Hinks

I glare at the ember-shot tide, listening to the hiss of the waves and the tick of my cooling armour. Escaping death is always so much harder than finding it. Returning from the underworlds has been like another reforging, another flaying of my soul. My mind is as fractured and distorted as my armour, but slowly my memory pieces itself back together. Every one of my retinue has fallen. My anger flares. They faltered. They failed. They paid the price.

'We fight. We Kill.' My voice cracks with rage. 'We win.'

I am standing on a shoulder of the Slain Peak, three hundred feet above the Ardent Sea, drenched in blood and caked in soot. I look like one of the ruins that litter the foothills below. The Realmgate spat me into the shallows and my warhammers are still smouldering where the god-wrought metal punched through the heat of the Ardent.

I whisper the names of the fallen, in accusation rather than benediction, then turn inland, spilling ash from my blue-green armour. From this height I can see the length of the valley. At the far end is a Stormkeep, silhouetted before the hammered-gold sky. Ipsala. Pride of the Zullan coast. Home to five glorious retinues of Celestial Vindicators, all of them veterans of the Realmgate Wars; the guardians of the Southern Wards. Two days' march. Then I will stand before warriors worthy of the name Stormcast Eternal. My own, vengeful kin. They will understand why I have returned. They would never fail me as the Hammers of Sigmar have done.

As I clamber down the slope, tongues of steam rush up through the blackened rocks, hissing and sighing.

'The Hammers of Sigmar did not fail you, Trachos. It was the other way around. You failed them.'

The accusation halts me in my tracks and my mind falls back to Shyish. My pulse drums as I recall pale, emaciated bodies, still smouldering in the ruins. Thin, broken limbs, grasping at smoke-filled air.

'I failed no one. The Hammers lacked steel.'

'You murdered those people.'

'I was relentless. As I must be. Those wretched souls *all* worshipped the Betrayer God. They bore the sigils of Nagash. None of them deserved mercy. The Hammers of Sigmar were blinded by pity. The fault was theirs.'

'What of their souls, Trachos? This is why you were made. You cannot simply abandon them.'

I limp down the slope, shaking my head, trying to rid myself of the wretched voice. I'd hoped to leave it in Nagash's underworlds. There's something unnatural about it. It's not simply my mind questioning itself – it's a distinct voice, ringing through my skull, accusing me.

'If you hadn't spent so long torching those huts, the Hammers of Sigmar would still be alive. You lost yourself in violence. You forgot what you were doing. The kill-fever took you.'

I clang my gauntleted fist against my helmet.

'*What do you think they'll say when you reach the Stormkeep? When you tell them how many men you've lost? What will you say when they ask you how it happened? How will you explain so many deaths? They will know, Trachos. They will know what's happening to you. Why would they send you back to Azyr? Your work is unfinished. They will send you back into the darkness.*'

I can't go back. Not yet. Not until I can be sure of myself. I struggle to keep my voice level.

'The Hammers of Sigmar are to blame for what happened. They should have burned the place down before I ever reached it. The gheists were already leaving their roosts. We had to go before–'

'*You're afraid to go back. You're a coward.*'

'Who are you?' I cry. 'Get out of my–'

A howl rips through the air, silencing me, echoing across steam-shrouded peaks.

I crouch, a hammer in each hand. It was the cry of a beast, a large one by the sound of it.

Something moves on the next outcrop, a monstrous shape, coiling through the clouds.

Someone bellows a war cry, deep and savage, almost as bestial as the howl that preceded it. There's a flash of light and a clang of metal hitting stone.

I look at Zyganium Keep. As soon as I reach it I can make my report and be gone. The voice in my head lies, but its presence troubles me. The gaps in my memory trouble me. I need to get home. I need to see the spires of Azyr and bathe in their holy light. I need to consult with the Lord-Celestant.

'*You're afraid.*'

'Never,' I mutter, but I know something is wrong. The voice is too clear. Too alien. Who is speaking to me?

There's another deafening howl and an answering battle cry,

followed by the sound of smashing rocks. I peer into the steam clouds. There's something big fighting in there. The peaks are juddering like they're in the grip of an avalanche. I look up at the jagged slopes. Perhaps there *will* be an avalanche.

'Run home, Trachos. Hide. Before you lose what's left of your mind.'

I curse and turn away from the valley and the Stormkeep, striding across the rocks towards the opposite crag, my boots pounding through the heat haze as I drop down into a crevasse and haul myself up the opposite side, climbing towards the sound of the fighting. Perhaps some of the Hammers of Sigmar made it back and are trying to reach Zyganium Keep? If there was a survivor, what might he say? My memories of Shyish are a shroud of screams and blood. What exactly *did* I do down there? *Could* some of the Hammers of Sigmar have survived? I did not see them all die. Sigmar's light fell from the clouds, slashing the gloom of Shyish, hauling some of their souls back to Azyr, but I could not count the blasts.

I look around. The Slain Peak is a famously treacherous place. Skin-roasting geysers erupt constantly from brazier-pits, and landslides are common, but the wildlife is the real threat. If one of my men is here, I'm duty-bound to help him, whatever he might have seen in Shyish.

The sound of fighting grows more frantic as I crest the ridge and rush through the clouds, hammers glinting.

I break through the clouds and stagger to a halt in shock.

I've reached a broad, bowl-shaped hollow, a few hundred feet in circumference and ringed with tusks of rock. There are three figures at its centre and none of them are Stormcast Eternals. The first is inhumanly slender and pale, an aelf, dressed in black, clutching daggers and weaving back and forth, nimble and quick, looking for a chance to lunge. At her side is something peculiar. For a moment, I struggle to name him. He's shorter than a man, but clad in so much scarred, chiselled muscle that he looks like a piece of the mountain. He's a duardin, I decide, with the fiery mohawk and beard of a Fyreslayer, but he's big – much bigger than any Fyreslayer I've seen before. He's as broad as an ox and his biceps are like tree trunks. I would have placed him as a great king or lord if he didn't look so deranged. He's wearing a patch over one eye and there's a single metal rune embedded in his chest, burning with the ferocity of a fallen star. The rune is the source of the light I saw through the clouds. Even without using one of my implements, I can tell that it's unlike the runes worn by other Fyreslayers. There's so much aetheric power radiating from it that the devices hung from my belt are crackling and humming in response.

The duardin is naked apart from a loincloth and, as his slab-like fists tighten, rune-light floods his frame, shimmering across his muscles and igniting a brazier at the head of his battleaxe. His gaze is wild and unfocused, and there's sweat pouring down his filthy, tattooed limbs. There's such a thick animal stink coming from him that I can smell it a dozen feet away. He lets out another war cry and pounds across the rocks towards his foe.

When I see what he's about to attack, I can't help but laugh. It's a drake. One of the stone-clad behemoths that thrive in the brutal heat of the Slain Peak. It's as tall as a watchtower and its spreading wings block out the sky, throwing us all into shadow.

The duardin must be insane. Even I would baulk at tackling such a colossus.

The drake opens its long, sabre-crowded jaws and spews a landslide, hurling rock and scree across the hollow.

I shake my head and turn to leave. The duardin is doomed. There's nothing I could do to help even if I wished it.

The duardin keeps roaring as the rocks smash into him.

I hesitate, looking back.

Dust and flying debris fill the hollow and, for a moment, I'm blinded. When the clouds fade, I laugh again.

The duardin is still standing. There are mounds of rock and gravel heaped around him, and he's shrouded in dust, but the drake has failed to injure him.

I shake my head. That blast could have levelled a fortress.

The aelf is hunched next to him and she seems unharmed too, protected by his bulk.

The drake hesitates, confused, as the duardin shrugs off the rubble and rushes forwards, rune-light sparking in his beard and pulsing through his veins.

The drake recovers from its surprise and screams. Then it rears on its haunches and spews more rock.

Again, the hollow fills with noise and dust. Again, when it clears, the duardin is unharmed, chin raised defiantly, infernal light burning in his eye.

The drake leaps forwards, landing with such force that the rocks beneath my feet slide away and I stumble down into the hollow.

It swings a tail the size of an oak, bringing it down towards the duardin's head.

There's a seismic boom as the duardin smashes the tail away, parrying it as easily as a sword-strike.

The drake stumbles, claws scrambling on the rocks, vast wings kicking up dust clouds.

As the drake struggles to right itself, the duardin runs across the hollow, bounds off a rock and leaps through the air, axe gripped in both fists and raised over his head.

The drake spews more rock, but the duardin is too fast, slamming his axe into its chest like he's attacking a cliff face.

The drake is about to launch itself into the air when the aelf sprints through the dust clouds and plunges her daggers into its leg. The blades are clearly no ordinary weapons. They cut through the drake's stone hide and the aelf has to dive away as black, steaming blood hisses from the wound.

As the aelf rolls clear, the duardin climbs higher, slamming his axe into the drake's jaw, knocking its head back.

I race for cover as the creature staggers towards me, ripping rock from the walls and thrashing its wings.

The aelf flips onto her feet and plants her blades in the drake's other leg and, as the monster falls, the duardin slams his axe into its skull.

There's another resounding boom as the drake hits the rubble-strewn ground.

When the dust clears, I find myself face to face with the duardin.

He's standing on the stone carcass, glaring at me with his single, infernal eye, axe raised and beard sparking, his whole body trembling with violence.

'Maybe we should gut this one too?' His voice is a low snarl. He glances from me back to the aelf.

I raise my warhammers and face him side-on.

'Wait!' cries the aelf, rushing forwards and grabbing the duardin's arm. 'He's one of us.'

The duardin grips his axe tighter. 'One of *you*, maybe.'

'He serves Sigmar.' She steps in front of him.

The duardin looks unimpressed, but allows her to speak.

'I'm Maleneth,' she says, still gripping her daggers as she approaches me. 'I belong to the Order of Sigmar.'

She's a Khainite. I've dealt with the Murder Cults before. Her blades are most likely edged with poison. I keep my hammers raised.

I nod to the duardin. 'And this?'

She gives me a strange look. I can't tell if it's a warning or a plea. Despite fighting beside him, she does not look comfortable in his presence. 'Gotrek.'

This close, he cuts an even stranger figure. The light is fading from the rune in his chest, but it's still fierce enough to give his face a hellish aspect. I notice that one side of his head is oddly weathered, as though scorched by acid. His only concession to armour is a metal pauldron on his left shoulder, but that's clearly borrowed, its design too crude to be of duardin manufacture.

'Show your face, manling,' he growls, narrowing his eye. His beard bristles as he barges past the aelf and squares up to me. He slams into my armour and I stagger. His head barely reaches my chest but I feel like a cart has thudded into me.

I remove my helmet and glare back at him.

He holds my stare; then, just as I think he's about to attack, he shrugs and turns away. 'Another prancing knight.' He mutters something in his own language as he heads back over to the fallen drake.

I look at the aelf. 'Does *he* serve Sigmar?'

'I serve no one!' yells the dwarf, without looking back at me. 'Least of all gods.'

I give the aelf a questioning look, but she holds up a hand, indicating that I should wait until he is out of earshot.

'What is that rune in his chest?' I ask when the duardin has reached the fallen monster.

She speaks in an urgent whisper. 'I need to explain,' she begins, but then I cut her off.

'What's he doing?'

The duardin has clambered up onto the fallen drake and begun hacking at the carcass, filling the air with sparks and noise. Incredibly, his axe cuts through the stone scales, severing chunks of hide and spilling torrents of black gore. Blood hisses as it splashes across the ground.

'We're going to perform a rite,' she says, sounding weary. 'He's going to fish out the innards and then I'll inspect them. Hopefully it will work this time.'

'This time?'

'Someone told him that only drake entrails can point us in the right direction, but we've tried five times so far and I've found nothing but half-digested herdsmen.'

I can't hide my shock. 'This is the *sixth* drake you've killed?'

She nods. 'If you only count the winged ones.'

I stare at the duardin. 'What is he?'

'Gotrek, son of Gurni. Apparently he was born in somewhere called the Everpeak and, if you believe what he says, he belongs to an earlier age than this – and another world, for that matter.'

I raise an eyebrow.

She still has that warning look in her eye. 'He's unlike any duardin I've ever met. He calls himself a Slayer, but he hates Fyreslayers as much as anything else we've encountered. They said he's one of their gods, sent to help them, but that made him even angrier.' She looks over at him. 'He's not keen on gods.'

She scowls at me. 'Look, I want nothing more than to be rid of him, but that's the Master Rune of Blackhammer he's got jammed in his ribs. It's more powerful than you realise. I'm sworn to return it to Azyr.'

'To Azyr?' My pulse quickens. An idea starts to form.

She nods. 'But Gotrek has other ideas.'

'Then kill him. If the rune is needed in Azyr, why have you left it in the possession of a lunatic?'

'Did you see what he did to that drake?'

'I know your kind, assassin. Brute strength is no protection against you. You could scratch him in his sleep and he'd never wake.'

'He never sleeps,' she snaps, but she looks away, suddenly unwilling to meet my gaze. There's more to their relationship than she will admit.

'You like him.'

Her face darkens and she tightens her grip on her knives. 'He's a fool.'

'But?'

She glares at me, her eyes full of vitriol. I can't tell if she's angry with me or herself. 'It's not just the rune. There's something strange about him.'

I keep looking at her.

She spits, her rage palpable. 'I can't explain it. He says there's a doom hanging over him and, after spending all this time with him, I'm starting to understand what he means. He's unstoppable. Something wants him to succeed. Or some*one*.'

I nod. I've seen such things before. Primitive savages, sure of their destiny, oblivious to the facts, tumbling headlong through life, gathering doe-eyed disciples until they finally crash, taking everyone else with them. The aelf is beguiled by him. She mistakes his wild momentum for destiny. She's in thrall to his fearlessness, not seeing that it's only born of stupidity.

Gotrek laughs as he snaps the drake's shoulder bones apart, filling the air with a black fountain.

'You said you're killing these beasts because you're trying to find somewhere.'

She nods. 'The Neverspike.'

The name gives me pause. I've heard it before, but can't place it for a moment. 'Why?'

'Because of some drunk in Axantis. He told Gotrek that there's an immortal there – someone who has been bound to the rocks by Nagash. The drunk called him the Amethyst Prince. And now Gotrek's got it in his head that, if this prince is an immortal, he must be from the same world he's from.'

My blood cools. 'I've heard of the Neverspike. Your drunk friend was right about the prince but the Neverspike is dangerous. It's a fragment of the underworld.'

She raises an eyebrow. 'Gotrek doesn't go anywhere unless it's dangerous.'

There's a thunderous slap as Gotrek rips the drake's stomach open and spills innards across the rocks.

'Aelf!' he cries, backing away from the wound, his arms drenched in blood and triumph flashing in his eye. 'What do you see?'

She hesitates. Still looking at me. Weighing me up. She wants me to leave. She's worried about what I might do to the Slayer. She's protective of him for some reason. It's the rune, I realise. She's worried I'll snatch the rune from under her nose. Then she'd have endured this boorish duardin for nothing. I smile as I follow her over to the mound of innards, my idea crystallising in my head. If the aelf can't take the rune to Azyr, I'll do it for her. No one could question my logic. What more important reason could I have for returning home? And then, in Azyr, I will rid myself of all these troubling memories and doubts. I will be renewed.

'You're doing it wrong,' I say after a few minutes of watching her poke at the sloppy mess, drawing bloody sigils and whispering pointless curses.

'What?' She looks up, her eyes flashing.

I take an aetherlabe from my belt and tighten the brass coil at its centre. Slender hoops whizz and click, orbiting its crystal dome until the gemstone inside starts to glow. I hold the device over the steaming intestines. Flies are already starting to gather but the mechanism is unaffected, picking up the aethionic currents with ease, whirring and clicking as its cogs fall into place.

The aelf's eyes widen. 'You're an ordinator.'

I ignore her, adjusting the device, closing in on the current.

Even the Slayer is intrigued. Some of the savagery fades from his face and I see a cunning I had not previously noticed.

'You're an engineer?' he says.

I say nothing.

He looks at me closely, then studies the various measuring instruments attached to my armour. There is a look of recognition in his eye and he mouths a few crude engineering terms.

I use my boot to move some of the intestines as the aetherlabe's teeth click into place.

I nod to a narrow ravine that leads from the hollow. 'The Neverspike is that way. You're only two days away.'

Gotrek laughs and slaps me on the shoulder, causing me to stagger. 'Finally! Someone with at least half a brain. What did I tell you, witch? We're almost there.'

He storms down the gulley, humming cheerfully to himself. His mood has changed in a moment from dour and fractious to eager and happy.

Maleneth is still kneeling in the drake's stomach, covered in blood. She looks at me in disbelief, then shakes her head and hurries after Gotrek, wiping the gore from her face.

'And this one?' says Gotrek, prodding another of my instruments with a stubby, spade-like finger.

We're hunkered in the lee of a scorched tree skeleton. Gotrek was keen to march through the night, but the aelf insisted we stop. The Slain Peak is even more dangerous in the dark than in daylight and the Slayer grudgingly agreed, still buoyed by the news we were close to the Neverspike.

'It looks like a connecting rod on a turbine,' he says.

He seems oddly knowledgeable about engineering. All his guesses are wrong, because he understands nothing about aetheric transference, but they are still *educated* guesses, based on a sound understanding of mechanics. I have never seen a savage so well versed in science.

'It's an adylusscope,' I explain. 'A kind of orrery. It tracks the cycles of the realms and all the other heavenly bodies.' I would not usually be so open with a stranger, but the duardin will be dead in a few hours, so I allow myself a little pride, describing the power of my cosmolabes and other surveying equipment.

'And this?' His eye narrows as he looks at the inverussphere.

'It reverses aetheric polarity,' I explain, knowing he won't have any idea what I'm talking about. I baffle him with descriptions of all my instruments, going through them one by one, amused by the disdain on his face. He tuts and shakes his head, muttering something about shoddy work, even though he could never conceive of the machines' complexity.

The Slayer has a sack filled with skins of ale and we've been drinking for over an hour.

'Not bad for a manling,' he grunts as I empty another skin.

'You've no idea who or what I am,' I say. 'I could drink this for days and still be ready to fight. My flesh was forged in the Anvil of the Apotheosis, not prised from the womb of...' I hesitate, struggling to imagine what he was prised from.

The rune in his chest glimmers slightly, flashing in his eye, turning it crimson. Then he laughs and throws another skin at me.

'Let's see,' he says, grabbing another skin for himself and poking at part of my armour. 'What does this do?'

The aelf is somewhere back down the gulley, taking her turn to watch for drakes, so I allow myself to relax. Since I started drinking, the voice in my mind has fallen quiet and I'm feeling a little more at ease. Once the duardin is dead, I can dig the rune from his remains and be on my way. My return to Azyr will be far more glorious than I had expected if the aelf is even half right about the power of the rune – and by the way my instruments are behaving, she is. The witch is a fool to have let the Slayer live so long. He openly derides Sigmar, along with every other god he knows the name of. He's an enemy of the God-King. And he's an animal. Just like the drake he left steaming in the hollow. All he cares about is which of us can hold the most ale.

After another hour of drinking, I begin to feel odd. Gotrek's face shifts in the half-light, swelling and leering like a gargoyle. 'What *is* this?' I say, frowning at the skin I was drinking from.

'The first decent ale I've found in this sweaty armpit you call a realm.' He wipes froth from his beard with a forearm that looks like a thigh. Beer glistens on his scarred skin.

I have the disconcerting feeling that I'm drunk.

Gotrek lets out a deep, rattling belch.

'I need to rest,' I mutter, falling back against the tree stump, feeling as though the mountain is swaying beneath me.

Gotrek grins, revealing a jumble of broken teeth, then slumps back against a rock, reaching for another skin, ignorant of everything beyond the satisfaction of outdrinking me.

'So now you're murdering duardin?'

I wince as I walk. My head is already pounding from the ale I drank last night and the voice in my mind feels like fingernails scraping across the inside of my skull.

I'm not murdering anyone. He wants to reach the Neverspike and I'm taking him there.

'You know what will happen to him if he approaches the Amethyst Prince. Nagash put him there as punishment for defying him. He's there as an example. As soon as Gotrek touches him he'll be ripped apart by death magic.'

If he dies, it's because he's a fool. A dangerous fool. And a blasphemer to boot. He talks of killing the gods. Who would blame me for letting someone so stupid destroy themselves?

'The witch.'

I look around. She's clambering up the slope behind us, her eyes locked on me. She has spent all this time in service to an impious lunatic and she has done nothing to take the rune. When the duardin is dead, I'll deal with her. My fingers brush against one of my hammers. I already have a good idea how.

'Manling!' bellows Gotrek from further up the slope. 'You've earned your beer!'

I pick up my pace, clambering quickly over the rocks to reach the Slayer's side. We're perched on a ledge looking out over another drop and the sight that greets me is horribly familiar. Another world has been smashed into this one: Shyish. The Neverspike is an icy, iridescent spear of rock that juts from the mountain, completely alien from the sun-bleached crags that surround it. The rock is shimmering and rimy, edged with patches of ice. It has no place in the Realm of Fire and the air knows it, billowing around the shard in flickering, static-charged spirals. If we had approached from any other direction, the Neverspike would have remained hidden from view. It is clearly the work of a divine intelligence. Even in Shyish, the shard would not have been a natural formation – it is a single curved talon of rock, and at its summit there is a tall alcove that looks like a shrine. There is a fire burning in the alcove, purple and blue, death magic, engulfing the figure within. It's impossible to see the prince clearly from here, so I take out one of my looking glasses and turn the shaft until the prince comes into focus.

I grimace. He's rigid with pain, but still alive, after all these long centuries. The flames are burning him, causing his skin to blister and peel, but he cannot die. His eyes are gone, melted into blackened sockets, and his flesh looks like living ash, crumbling and flickering in the blaze, but his agony is eternal – a warning to all who would challenge the so-called God of Death.

I hand the looking glass to Gotrek and he mutters something in the duardin tongue, shaking his head as he sees the prince.

The Slayer is minutes away from death. Nagash's magic will not preserve Gotrek as it has done the prince; it will simply immolate him. It fascinates me that he can walk so blindly to his death.

'Why do you seek him?' I ask. 'What do you want?'

'Vengeance,' he snarls, taking the looking glass from his eye and handing it back to me. 'The gods lied to me, manling. They promised me a worthy doom, then stole it from me. They brought me to your wretched realms with no explanation. So I'm going to make them bloody pay.'

I am about to explain to Gotrek that the Amethyst Prince is not divine, and never was, when I realise the absurdity of arguing with someone who thinks he can kill gods. The Slayer is insane. I knew it the first moment I laid eyes on him. I look at the rune in his chest. The ur-gold is forged to resemble the face of a deranged, psychotic Slayer. It looks almost identical to Gotrek.

I nod and gesture to a narrow bridge. It leads across a sheer drop to the Neverspike. It's a single, slender arch of stone, soaring across the chasm like a hurled rope, suspended by some unseen artifice.

The aelf joins us as we make the final approach, grimacing as the air seems to attack us, lashing and hissing around our faces as we cross the bridge.

We are only halfway across when shapes assemble on the far side.

'Aye,' laughs the Slayer. 'Show us what you've got.'

As we get nearer, I see that the figures are corpses – the remains of men and women, lurching from the rocks that surround the spike. They are charred beyond recognition but they move with silent purpose, gripping swords and axes as they shuffle onto the bridge. I mutter a curse as I see that the whole spike is spawning similar figures. There are hundreds of them struggling to their feet.

Gotrek roars in delight and thunders across the bridge, his axe flashing as he raises it over his head.

Maleneth hisses a curse and barges past me, drawing her knives as she sprints after him.

I take my time, slowly drawing my hammers as Gotrek crashes into the blackened husks.

He burns brighter than the prince, hacking and roaring through the crush. Blackened bodies fly in every direction, tumbling into the crevasse. Gotrek barely breaks his stride, carving a path through the undead husks with Maleneth keeping pace, lunging and stabbing.

By the time I reach the end of the bridge, dozens of the revenants have been hacked to pieces, but there are plenty left to attack me. I stride out onto the Neverspike, hammering corpses aside, smashing the sorcery from their lifeless flesh.

We fight towards the burning prince, and the battle is bathed in the violet light of his pyre. Gotrek grows even more excited, hacking through the throng with even more ferocity.

'Hurry, manling!' he cries, waving me on.

I oblige, picking up my pace. When Gotrek dies, I need to be close. The aelf is not a worthy guardian of the rune. I must be on hand to pluck it from his ashes.

As we approach the alcove holding the Amethyst Prince, it becomes hard to see. The death magic is dazzling, bleeding from the tormented prince and flashing through rows of shuffling corpses, scattering light like strands of purple lightning.

I have to shield my eyes as I battle the final few feet.

I'm so dazzled that it takes me a moment to realise Gotrek has turned to face me. He's silhouetted by the unholy blaze, but I sense that his mood has changed.

'What–?' I manage to say before he pounds the haft of his axe into my stomach.

I'm so surprised I do not prepare myself for the blow. Breath explodes from my lungs. I double over in pain. It's like being hit by a felled tree.

Before I can straighten up he hits me again, pummelling the side of my helmet and sending me sprawling across the rocks. My hammers slip from my grip and clang down the slope towards the bridge.

When I manage to sit up, my vision is blurry from the blow, but I see that Gotrek is holding my inverussphere. Fury jolts through me. It's an incredibly sacred device, capable of reversing the polarity of aether currents.

'Thought you'd kill me?' There's a grim smile on his face. He hacks down another revenant but keeps his eye locked on me.

I throw an accusing look at the aelf, then remember I didn't share my plans with her.

The Slayer laughs. 'Drunks always talk in their sleep. Especially pompous manling drunks who can't hold their ale.'

'What?' I gasp.

He turns and fights his way up to the blazing prince, ignoring the fury of the flames as he cuts through the rows of undead.

'I'm not interested in princes,' he cries, adjusting the inverussphere with surprising skill.

I curse as I stagger to my feet, fending off revenants with my fists. Gotrek wasn't drunk when I told him how my devices work; he was listening carefully to every word.

He looks at the sky. 'My quarrel is with the *gods!*'

He turns a cog on the inverussphere and punches it into the prince's twitching body.

The light flares, blinding me, then vanishes, plunging the Neverspike into darkness.

Magic rips through the undead, tearing them from their feet and hurling them towards the alcove, lashing across the rocks with such ferocity that I fall again, tumbling across the stones towards the prince, caught like a leaf in a tempest.

Cords of aetheric lightning smash against the Neverspike,

ripping the air with a deafening howl, rushing towards the alcove from the surrounding peaks.

Gotrek manages to stay on his feet, staggering but upright as the alcove becomes a vortex of shadows, smoke and body parts.

The Amethyst Prince howls in delight, finally freed from his torment, then disintegrates, obliterated like the rest of the undead, his ashes snatched by the whirlwind.

'Nagash!' howls Gotrek. 'The Slayer comes for *you!*'

He steps into the vortex, following the dead prince, bellowing a war cry as he vanishes from sight.

I try to crawl away, but the storm is too violent. I'm dragged, inexorably, towards the peak of the Neverspike.

There's a series of explosions as the Neverspike shatters, spraying amethyst lances into the darkness.

With a final, desperate lunge, I grab hold of the bridge, hanging on to a slender arch as rocks whistle past my head.

Then my fingers slip and I'm thrown forwards, my armour clashing against the rocks.

I hurl towards the vortex, surrounded by a storm of blackened corpses. Then the darkness takes me.

I howl as I feel the morbid chill of Shyish, soaking through my armour and eating into my arms. My memories clear, revealing in horrible clarity all the things I was trying to escape. But there *is* no escape from death.

As I fall I hear Gotrek, laughing and singing as he dives into the abyss.

YOUR
NEXT READ

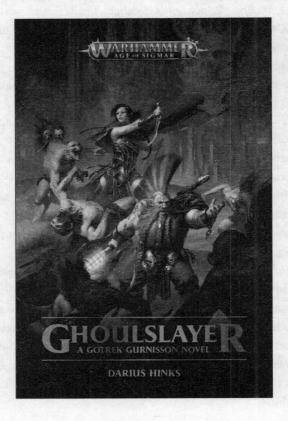

GHOULSLAYER
by Darius Hinks

Gotrek Gurnisson returns! His oaths now ashes, and branded with the rune of the god who betrayed him, the Slayer seeks the ultimate foe – the Undying King himself…

THE GARDEN
OF MORTAL
DELIGHTS

Robert Rath

Arise, all ye spirits, arise in the soul glade,
O children of the Everqueen, what dost thou see?
A foe-host has come bearing ember and axe blade,
To poison the water and butcher the tree.

Armour of ore they have pillaged from mountains,
And pelts of thick fur torn from unwilling beasts.
They come hence with daemons, both fair and befouled,
And ecstatic moans on the lips of their priests.

Grant them bitter welcome with stone-sword and
claw-root,
With borrowed earth-arms do we strike the first blow.
And soon we shall lay these gifts back in the soil,
All slick with the nourishing blood of the foe.

Hold fast, forest children, the Mirrored One cometh!
He cuts down our kinfolk, blades thick with sap-gore.
I weep at the sound of your pain-song and fear-dirge,
And reap lamentiri to sow you once more.

Hold fast, he comes!
He comes! Hold fast!
Do not break the song.

Wilde Kurdwen removed her claw from the dryad's root, unable to bear the dream-song. A season's cycle later, her last battle-chant still echoed in the souls of those she had failed.

They still sung, still striving to answer the war cry of their branchwych.

Indeed, the dryads twitched as they dreamed. Finger-branches clenched and released. Gnarled roots, planted deep in rich earth, twisted like running ankles. The flowers that bloomed from their chests, arms and legs shivered. From afar, it looked as though a flock of purple butterflies had alighted on their bodies, their petal wings opening and closing like eyelashes.

But there were no butterflies here. Nothing so delicate could live on this island.

Crouched, she could even imagine these sisters back in a Neos glade, their disquiet merely the natural, traumatic cycle of growth and regrowth. And indeed, many ripe fruits hung from these elegant spirits. Berries clustered around their throats like jewels on the neck of a high-born bride. Dark spices burst up through the cracked bark of their roots. And the feathery pollen stems inside the purple flowers would, after being pounded, dry into the finest sapphrin. They were blossoming, verdant.

Yet these dryads dreamed of battle. Of trespassers. Of blades stained amber by torchlight, of men with nets and kin cut down.

And they dreamed of axe blades chopping deep into their own flesh.

For these twitching, still-living dryads had no heads. Each one was decapitated, planted, a vehicle only for growth. New shoots emerged from the stumps of their necks – for dryads were resilient spirits – but soon the menial gardeners would come to trim them back.

They were not allowed to grow, for dryads themselves did not produce the fruit, spices or fine edible flowers. These delicacies came from the plants grafted on to their bodies – their shoots inserted into the living bark and wood-flesh with sharp knives and sealing wax – parasites that supped from the dryads' life force to make their branches heavy with culinary delights.

And no matter how much Wilde Kurdwen tried to fool herself in the quiet hours of night, there was no forest glade beyond this copse of headless spirits, only an obsidian wall that blocked the spirit-song.

High above, the branchwych saw the torches of warriors patrolling the battlements.

It was not a prison – it was a pleasure garden.

Red juice ran from the corner of his mouth, past his sharp chin and down a throat elegant as a swan's. A concubine dabbed at it with a war banner he'd prised from the hands of a dead witch aelf.

It was a petty pleasure, wiping his mouth with their sacred colours. But Revish the Epicurean lived for pleasure, petty or not, and he was old enough to know that the smallest experiences often brought the greatest joy.

He raised another tangberry and bit, rolling it in his mouth, tasting it with a tongue that split like a snake's. Days ago, he'd felt the stub of a third tip sprouting below the others, and had sacrificed six prisoners to thank Slaanesh for his newly expanded palate.

He had been force-feeding one prisoner spiced crème for weeks, and it was his liver that had preceded this delectable tart.

Revish staffed the fortress kitchen with chefs – human trophies of his conquests – and it was always good to have more than one on hand. After all, they tended to go mad fulfilling his culinary desires.

For Revish the Epicurean coveted taste above all else. In past centuries he had held other fascinations, it was true. The pounding blood-song of his body as he pursued the enemy. Carnal delights of flesh. Exotic intoxicants. Yet for centuries, he'd found no battle glee as savoury as the first bite of a buttered eel, no pleasure of the flesh greater than a gryph-hound grilled with expert precision. Nothing so intoxicating as wine from a good vin-grape, made plump by rich soil and warm sun.

So he'd put aside the shallow, adolescent pleasures of violence, sensuality and athleticism. The tongue was his altar now, and upon it he sacrificed all manner of animals, plants, sweets and men.

And it was well known that the master was not to be disturbed at his meal – which was why his warrior-consort Sybbolith waited patiently, her boot on the neck of the prostrate man.

'Speak,' said Revish, as the concubine dabbed his face with rose water.

'A menial from the pleasure gardens,' Sybbolith said. Her eyes, golden and whiteless like those of a jungle cat, stared at her lord. Her thumb slid tenderly over the hellstrider whip coiled at her belt. 'He broke the rule.'

The menial quaked, bones showing through his translucent skin. Hands filthy with dirt. It was impossible to tell whether he was twenty or sixty – like the cooks, the garden menials did not last long.

'Is this true, filth?' asked Revish.

The question was rhetorical, since as a garden menial, the man's mouth was padlocked shut. But he tried to answer nonetheless, and as he gibbered Revish saw that the muzzle was ill-sized, leaving just enough room to slip a mashed berry through.

'Is it true?' he repeated, but this time, he addressed his question to the figure who stood in the shadows of the audience chamber. 'Did he eat from the pleasure garden?'

The branchwych limped into the light, body creaking like a great oak in a windstorm. A rusting metal collar encircled her neck, its sigils glowing pink. Stone amulets rattled in her wooden antlers.

Her voice, high and melodic, filled the chamber with birdsong. 'I have witnessed this truth, my lord. But he is a good gardener–'

Revish held up a hand and stood, reluctantly leaving the upholstered embrace of his human-leather chair.

'My dear seedling,' Revish said. 'You know I do not like killing. I have as much natural inclination to kill a man as I have to cook my own meals. The fruits of violence, like the act of feasting, I am happy to enjoy. But the labour of death is not to my taste. I am no Khornate barbarian, glorying in slaughter.' Light danced on his mirrored armour as he approached the cowering menial. 'But whether to kill or spare is not my choice. Our gods have laid out their ways of justice. Is that not so, darling Sybbolith?'

'It is so,' responded the Seeker.

'And though those ways are cruel and capricious, mortals can do naught but follow them. You, who have your own goddess-queen, no doubt understand this.'

The branchwych hesitated, nodded.

From the floor, the hollow-cheeked menial stared at Revish's breastplate, entranced by the sight of his own horrid reflection. He tried to speak, and the lord hushed him, placing a long finger close to his lips.

Then he opened his arms, as if accepting the divine burden. 'My Prince Slaanesh, the god of my house, says that there can be no mercy for the disobedient. As a natural insubordinate myself, that is not to my liking, but my Prince says rule breakers must be punished. And we have one rule here.'

It happened so fast even Sybbolith flinched, a cry of ecstatic surprise escaping her shark-toothed mouth.

Revish's hands dropped beneath his cape and the axes came spinning out.

No clumsy woodsman's tools these – they were sharp sickles, like the pickaxes used for scaling ice floes in frozen lands. So sharp were they that even as the whirling blades punched into the menial, the blood did not come immediately. Instead, it seeped slow and languid as if from a razor cut.

There was no sense wasting it, after all. Blood was a valuable ingredient.

So when his precision butchery concluded and the menial ceased to wail, Revish lost no time in asking:

'Can we use this man, seedling? As fertiliser?'

The branchwych shook her head, staring at the slaughtered gardener. 'He will make the fruits bitter, the spices plain.'

'The hog trough, then,' said Revish. 'And I will go to the garden and count the cost.'

The concubine had already brought rose water, and he dipped his hands in the bowl to clear the blood. Aware that the meal and audience had concluded, attendants began to shift and move about their business.

Sybbolith slid up beside him, voice low. 'My lord, a word.'

'Not unless the words are new ones, my little horror.'

She leaned in, tiptoed so that when she whispered, her lips brushed his ear. 'My ships have been probing the Gushing Rapids. The summer rains have made them navigable. If we provision the fleet...'

'We'll speak later,' he said.

'But lord, we agreed that this summer we would return to the search. Our foothold is secure, we can–'

'Can't you see I'm dealing with something, Syb?' He pushed past her. 'Whichever watchman spotted the menial eating my berries, give him a day in the harem.'

He drew up alongside the wych and offered his arm. She ignored it, and he guessed that she did not understand the human gesture.

Indeed, she was so much more than human. Even the issue of her name was aloof and exotic – she insisted that her people did not use forms of individual address, and after a year he still simply called her 'seedling' or 'wych'.

She had fascinated him ever since he had sighted her during a raid on Neos. He could still hear her keening a war song, and picture the grass of the scorched battlefield sprouting anew beneath her bare feet.

And it was then that he knew he must possess her.

In movement and aspect she reminded him of a daemonette – she had the same otherworldly motion, a vaguely human form animated by a non-human spirit – but she exuded a vitality the handmaids of Slaanesh lacked. Daemonettes were hungry. They took you to great heights but left you lessened. This exquisite creature, on the other hand, projected youth and vitality.

Revish had lost control. Cut his way to her, axes gouging deep into the dryads separating them. He still remembered how the blood-sap made his axe hafts sticky and his tabard stiff. How the strange-toothed wyrm living in her shoulder had lunged for him and blunted its teeth on his greave before he knocked it to the ground and pulped it with a stomp. How he'd tackled her, the strange rough bark feeling so odd under his hands as he pinned her down.

He had also taken twenty of her dryads. It had been easy enough corralling them once Sybbolith had torn their branchwraith's head from its body. His warriors had brought nets for the purpose.

He wanted them for his garden. To let him explore all the culinary pleasures of this Realm of Life.

He escorted the wych in silence through the tower's entrance hall, past tapestries that, if one looked at them too long, brought hallucinogenic glimpses of other realms. Her injured leg creaked. Ecstatic moans drifted up the corridor.

'Sounds of the harem,' chuckled Revish. 'My man gets his reward. Everyone will want to catch a thieving menial now.'

'Dost thou visit the harem?' she asked.

'Regularly, yes. It is my harem. And it is expected.'

'Then thou hast many progeny.' She nodded approval. 'Life blesses.'

'I have no children.'

She stopped, turned. As her head cocked, stone trinkets clattered in her branch-horns. 'I am sorry, but I understood that the purpose of a harem was...'

'It is.'

'Then art thou sterile?'

'No,' he said quickly, then laughed. 'The point of the act is not to produce children. It is to become lost in waves of rapture. To briefly feel the euphoric ravishment of our lord Slaanesh.'

'It seems a lot of work for little result,' said the branchwych.

'Children would... distract from the pursuit of pleasure.'

'Aye,' she agreed. 'As they should. Pleasure is not the point of life, my lord. The point of life is to create more life. A being without progeny hath no legacy.'

'Perhaps that is why we do not have children,' replied Revish, climbing the stairs of the north tower. 'To keep us rooted in the now. We are in pursuit of the infinite present. An unending ecstasy beyond time and the Mortal Realms.'

'I see,' said the wych. 'Thou hast strange beliefs, Revish... and thou dost fight hard for a man without a future.'

He laughed as they stepped out on the parapet, following the fortress wall to the pleasure garden. He could see the wych breathe deeper as they stepped outside into the wind. The orchids that spilled down her wood-scalp raised, turning their faces towards the sun. Her amber eyes, dark and flat inside the fortress, lit like lanterns. He knew that here, above the walls, she could hear the songs of nature.

It thrilled him. Seeing its power work upon her. He had never met a thing, even daemons in the Realm of Chaos, that were so *of* a place.

Ghyran and the wych, the wych and Ghyran – indivisible and inseparable.

Below them, docks radiated off the island's shore, jetties pushing into the glass-green sea in a circular pattern, like the spokes of a broken wagon wheel. An enormous star of Chaos, cluttered with the sleek, black hulls of warships.

'Raiding season,' said Revish.

'Berry season,' said the wych, and she took his hand. It was warm, like a polished stone in the sun. 'Let's see what we have grown.'

He let her pull him towards the garden.

'I wish I'd stripped the flesh from his bones,' growled Revish. 'Given him to Sybbolith, told her to take her time about it.'

'I was away,' said the branchwych. Even her inhuman sing-song held a tone of apology. 'I cannot be here when they prune the dryads. Even wearing this.' She gingerly touched the iron collar with its sigils. 'It cannot block the loudest screams of the spirit-song. Not this close.'

A bloodcurrant shrub speared its way out of a dryad's chest. Berries hung in bunches, crimson-black amid the whorls of serrated leaves.

'How many did he eat?'

'Twice the seasons,' she replied, then recalculated. 'Eight, as thou and thine say. Seven more in his pockets. They were served at dinner.'

He nodded. 'This was a terrible violation.'

'Indeed, the garden must always have balance. Clumsy harvesting, overeating, these things destroy the cycle. The garden can sustain one man eating from it, but no more.'

Revish looked at his beautiful cultivation. Twenty dryads, their humanoid forms thrust into the earth and sprouting every kind of summer fruit. Tangberries hung like dewdrops from one, while another's arm-branches had grown long and flowered pink – crimson stonefruit now nested in the leaves. Three others, planted hand-and-foot and woven together, formed a trellis that hung heavy with vin-grapes.

'When will they be ready?'

'Another month more,' said the wych. 'Two, if thou wishest the wine extra sweet.'

He nodded. In this long year, he had learned patience. That the pleasure of *now* was often worth sacrificing for greater delight later. He had forced the wych to plant the dryads in berry season, last year. He'd been pigheaded and eaten the fruit too early.

That had angered her. Indeed, she'd even tried to poison him. A silly thing to do. He went through food tasters almost as fast as chefs, and each morning, he had his chamber pot examined before it was dumped over the fortress wall. He'd given her the limp for that – broken the leg, let it regrow crooked through an iron corkscrew – but they had quickly come to an understanding.

He allowed her to keep her dryads alive, headless and immobile, laced with foreign plants, but still experiencing the yearly cycle so important to the Sylvaneth. The garden was her domain, provided that she keep the peace and provide him with the greatest produce that had ever touched his three-lobed tongue.

Sweet cob in autumn, along with crisp apples the size of babies' skulls. Winter spices and pom-clusters that stained his chin purple when the snows came. Hot crisproot and coiling ferns in spring, cooked savoury alongside venison. And now, the berries he had been too impatient for last summer.

Revish removed his mirrored gauntlet and reached out, feeling a leaf between his fingers. Closed them around a womb berry big as a human eyeball, feeling the tender flesh, yielding as that of a lover.

'May I?' he asked.

The wych nodded.

It left a residue on his fingers, this berry. So tangy that he could not help licking them clean after relishing the juices that burst on his tongue. It was all he could do to keep from plucking another, and he contented himself with sucking the seeds from his teeth.

'Thank you for killing the man,' said the wych.

'You seemed hesitant.'

The wych stroked a dryad, picked a beetle off a leaf. 'My kin do not make decisions in haste,' she said, letting the insect scuttle over her fingers. It was greying, blighted. One of the tainted insects that occasionally rode in on the wind, carried from Nurgle's territory. 'But though thy speed distressed me, thy calculus was correct. All life is precious...'

She trapped the beetle between two twig-like fingers, crushing it, rolling the broken body so it shredded.

'...but pests must not be tolerated in the glade,' she continued, regarding the smear left on her bark. 'My kin and queen understand that. And so does my Lord Revish.'

'So we are starting this absurdity again,' he breathed.

'It is not an absurdity,' she pressed. 'Thy god is not like the Great Blight. Unlike Nurgle, thy god wishes to cultivate. Cultivate pleasure, true, but now my lord sees how pleasure and nature intertwine.'

'This,' he gestured around them, 'is an experiment.'

'A successful one.' She stepped close.

He caught the scent of the wild orchid from the blossoms that spilled down her shoulders.

'But the pleasure garden is not thine only experiment,' said the wych. 'This whole island is a walled garden. On the mainland, Nurgle rules. His rot permeates soil and stream. Nothing grows. But my Lord Revish knows how to be a steward.'

He stepped back, light-headed. It was clumsy, this flirtation, by the standards of a Slaaneshi court. Yet he found it so enticing. Her eagerness and youth. The wholesome exuberance. Revish had spent long years in the company of those dead, those soon to be dead, and daemons who had never truly lived.

'Your Everqueen would not agree to an alliance.'

'Perhaps not the queen, no. But we in the Harvestboon Glade are young and practical. Not so tied down with grudges. If thou wert to expand – take sword against Nurgle in Invidia, cultivate it as you have this island – Harvestboon might approve. Trade peace and the exquisites of our branches in exchange for wild places left alone. And my lord... wild fruits are sweeter than those grown within walls.'

'And if they didn't agree?'

She smiled, an expression that looked both strange and frightening on the moist bark of her lips. 'Then we two could do it alone.'

The wych turned, beckoned towards the small half-cellar that he'd dug so she could grow mushrooms during the wet season. Nothing special, a few planks over a hole in the ground. They had to stoop to get inside, and Revish was shocked to see great, heart-shaped leaves covering the earth floor.

'Dost thou know what this is, my lord?' she said, brushing back the foliage.

His breath caught. Bioluminescent glow radiated from an orb's emerald surface. It was large, the size of a great melon or a new-born child.

'A soulpod,' he breathed. It must be.

'The start of new growth,' she said. 'The first sowing that will bring life back to Invidia. Under thy hand, my lord. Thou said that thou had no children, but it is not true. This can be our progeny.'

Revish knelt and stroked the glassy surface, saw a coil of life move inside at the warmth of his touch. She laid her hand over his.

He could see his own face, reflected in the surface.

Sybbolith brushed past the Chosen guarding Revish's private chamber. She did not ask to enter and they did not try to stop her. Everyone in the fortress knew what had happened to the last man who'd done that – she still wore his skin as a stocking.

She closed the door behind her.

'I've told the fleet to prepare,' she told Revish.

'Excellent,' he said. He tied his silk robe closed and offered a plate. 'Candied lips? Freshly severed.'

'I'm glad we agree,' she said, ignoring the confections. 'If we sail in two weeks, the rivers will still be full. We could hit the Dreamloss Realmgate, or if opportunity presents, take another run at the Gates of D–'

'I have an alternative plan.' He dropped into a chair and rapped a nautical map with his knuckles. 'We sail north, to the Nothing-well Peninsula. Garrison it, prepare to cut off the southern half of Invidia and take it in the name of Slaanesh.'

Sybbolith dropped her chin, studied him with her cat eyes. 'Turn on Nurgle. Stab the Father of Plagues in the back. Why?'

'How better to honour the Prince of Pleasure than by giving him a place in this realm?'

'By finding him and freeing him from his prison,' she hissed.

'This place has twisted you up, Revish. Ever since we came here, you've been eating too much, drinking too much.'

'Pleasure is our god's blessing, my little horror.'

'Pleasure with purpose. Ecstasy that binds us to Slaanesh, and elevates us into his experience.'

'I don't feel our Prince the way I used to,' admitted Revish. 'Centuries ago I loved the flesh, but it no longer thrills me. Then, those tapestries – the sacred art – but I scarce look at them now. Violence holds no interest... but a *legacy*. Syb, if I could create something–'

She raised a hand for silence, sat down across from him. 'Revish, I have seen this before. You have served our Prince for a long while. The same things, the same sensations, do not stimulate us forever. It will come back. You will rediscover forgotten raptures. The important thing is to keep moving, to keep searching. This realm was never meant to be more than a transit to the next–'

'The branchwych has suggested an alliance. Slaanesh and Sylvaneth, giving us a continent if we turn back Nurgle's desolation.'

She paused. 'The plant cannot convince the Everqueen to ally with Chaos.'

'If not, then we need no alliance. She has a soulpod,' smiled Revish. 'We can start our own glade. Reforest the Nothingwell. Raise our own race of Slaaneshi dryads. The land would garrison itself. It is a good plan.'

Sybbolith ran her tongue across the inside of her saw teeth. 'Are you my lord, or not?'

'What?'

'Lord Revish is a conqueror. A reveller. He's no farmer who reaps barley.'

'We don't grow barley–'

'Do you remember last year? We burned everything from the coast to the Jadewound. Made a play for the Gate of Dawn. Took slaves, razed cities. Soldiers screamed your name while in the grip of nightmare. Then that wych came, and you haven't left this island since. She's made herself your gaoler. Removed a Slaaneshi lord from the battlefield for an entire year. She's manipulating you.'

Revish looked at her, really looked at her, for the first time in ages. Sybbolith had changed since she'd walked the path of mutation. It was not the confidence, she had always had that; it was the divine certainty. The fact that Slaanesh had bestowed more gifts on this hellstrider than even her consort-warlord possessed.

'The wych has offered me a future,' said Revish. 'Not an endless search across realms and gateways. She's offered something of herself rather than taking.'

Silence hung between them. Sybbolith dropped a hand under the table, the hooked, retractable claws of her left hand sliding out in case it came to a fight.

'Very well,' she said. 'If you think she's so wholly devoted to you.'

'She is.'

'Then ask something of her. Something important and painful. Tell her you want to eat the soulpod.'

'What?'

'Come now, Revish. Don't claim it hasn't occurred to you. What would it feel like to eat a soul?' She preened. 'Having done it, I can tell you it was... invigorating.'

'It would be a waste.'

'If she's in your power, if she is so *enraptured* of you, she'll give it. And you won't have to take a single bite. But if she resists, you'll know that she has her own agenda. Unless, of course, you don't dare ask something of your own prisoner.'

Silence again.

'I'll give you the night, Revish. But if you don't ask her at dawn, I'm leaving. My riders and I, we move fast. And if we move, you'll never catch up.'

* * *

Revish came to the garden via the parapet, down the tower that connected the garden to the fortress' battlements. It was wider than his private entrance, with enough room for the retinue that came with him.

Sybbolith stood at his shoulder, and four Chosen at his back. The great curved horns on their helmets scraped the ceiling of the tower's spiral staircase.

The dryads rustled as they passed, the tread of armoured feet calling up unpleasant notes of nightmare in their death-dream.

'What is this?' asked the wych. 'We made a pact. No warriors in this place, it disturbs–'

'The soulpod,' said Revish, eyes red from sleeplessness. 'I want it.'

'I need the correct ground to plant it,' said the wych. Her amber eyes darted from the hellstrider to the warriors and their great axes.

'I wish to eat it.'

'Thou wish…'

'To eat. Devour. Consume. I have decided to see how it tastes.'

The wych's keen eyes darted towards Sybbolith. 'This is her doing. She's turned you against–'

'Give it to me.'

'I will not sacrifice the future for today's pleasure.'

Revish nodded and one of the Chosen raised his double-handed axe and turned to the nearest dryad.

'No, please–'

The dryad shrieked as the axe blade crashed into it. It warbled, screamed like an injured raptor with each blow. Even the Chosen, hardened to the death-wails of men, stepped back from the sheer emotion of it. Dark sap flecked the grass. Bunches of bloodcurrant burst, staining the pale interior flesh-wood imperial purple. The screams continued longer than anyone expected.

The wych was on her knees, hands on her face, wailing with

grief and sympathetic pain. She reached a hand out to the dryad, now nothing but twitching roots that whined like a dying hound.

Revish reached behind his cloak and drew his pointed razor-axe. 'The next I do myself.'

The wych brought the pod, cradling it to her chest, singing softly to it as if to calm its spirit. Then she handed it to Revish two-handed, giving the surface a last brush of her fingertips before stepping back.

Revish looked at the soulpod, seeing his reflection in it. Inside, something moved.

She had given it to him, true. But she had resisted. If he handed it back, said it was all a test, his weakness would be exposed.

'Well?' said Sybbolith.

He bit into the rubbery surface, feeling the gooey interior flood his mouth as the internal waters broke. It tasted of loam and dirt. It was bitter.

So bitter.

And then it bit him back.

Bone-hard mandibles pierced his face. Chitinous coils wrapped his throat. Whatever had emerged from the pod, it was strangling him.

A Chosen stepped forward and grasped the wriggling, segmented body and the creature snapped away from Revish, launching itself at the new attacker, burrowing itself between the warrior's pauldron and helmet, into his throat. Blood fountained high, spraying a headless dryad as he collapsed among the roots. Other Chosen dashed forward, stomping and slashing at the fat, hard body as it slithered into the dryad grove.

It was a grub. One of those damn worms the wych had launched at him when they'd fought a year ago. She'd *tricked* him.

He looked into the mirror of his vambrace. From ear to chin, his face was gory ruin. Ivory teeth showed through the ripped flesh of his cheek. One eye, plump and purple with venom, had nearly swollen shut. His three-lobed tongue probed through the ragged flesh, tasting the iron wine of his blood.

Revish snarled at his ruined beauty, gripped his axe haft and looked for the wych.

She was already gone, darting through the grove.

Leaving a trail of laughter behind her.

Kurdwen cackled as she ran. It was no longer the youthful, songbird laugh she had affected for the past year, but the mad, crow-like bark of a wych crone old as the forest.

It had been so tiring to be young, to wear the ebullient mask of spring that Revish found so alluring. That was not who she was. Kurdwen was an autumn hag through and through, with a heart full of dry leaves and chill winds.

Indeed, even as she fled her youthful trappings fell away. The orchids on her scalp browned, shedding petals so they pinwheeled to the ground in her wake. Bark hardened and roughened. The twisted wood of her leg that was trapped inside the corkscrew – the portion she had let go dry and brittle – cracked and fell away, letting the bent limb spring supple to its full length. Her lithe, ancient form thrilled at the cast-off artifice.

And she sang, a full-throated spirit-song that roused the mutilated dryads. They were not alive, or not sentient, at least. Echoes of their former selves, raw nerves responding to their environment much like the revivified skeletons of Nagash's horde. And for a year, she had been filling them with memories of their last battle – the echoes of her war song.

Now, they heard the cry again.

Dryads reached out like sea anemones, swiping at the Chaos warriors behind her. One snatched a Chosen and held him wriggling, crushed against her chest, while her neighbour punched her root claws through his breastplate over and over. Blood fell on the rich earth.

Behind her, Revish and his retinue hacked towards her, battling through the grove like men cutting a trail through jungle.

She was far ahead, nearing the entrance tower with its guards.

And as she saw their look of hesitation, she tore the lock off her nullifying collar.

Humans, even Chaos-corrupted ones, had such foolish faith in the strength of iron. After all, iron rusts. Particularly this close to the sea. Especially when a wych squeezes drops of salt water into its workings patiently, day by day, for an entire year.

The clasp came free, and she flung the circlet at one of the warriors guarding the tower steps, winging it end over end. He raised his shield to deflect it.

He never saw her leap at full run, never saw her coming with her whole body and whole spirit, never saw how she had broken off a tip of her own wood-antler and held it like a dagger.

Gnarled root-feet hammered the shield with the force of a club and he went over backwards. She plunged the antler through his visor slit and he choked on blood and broken teeth.

The other warrior struck at her with a mace as she crouched on the struggling man. She ducked the first blow, got in under his guard and grabbed at his throat, but he struck out with his shield boss and slammed his mace down, crushing her left arm.

She retreated.

Through the visor slit, the man's eyes betrayed fear. But this wych was unarmed and unarmoured. She'd struck at him and missed. She was wounded, sap clotting on her useless left arm. He brought up his shield and advanced on her with deadly steadiness.

But Kurdwen had not missed, and instead of a weapon, she held out something better – a bone totem, snatched from the warrior's throat.

Cold words ran through her smile. Syllables that tasted like bare branches and myrrh resin. Her wooden hand felt the amulet, but her spirit-hand felt the labyrinth of meat within him. Her fingers slithered through the warm, subterranean rivers of his organs, following the pulsing streams of blood until she caressed his greasy heart.

Then she snapped the amulet in two.

The mace dropped from nerveless fingers and she was past him, up the stairs.

She did not need to look behind her to know that Revish and his men were pursuing. Her bittergrub still lived, and through his segmented eyes she saw Revish and his Chosen surrounded, wading through a forest of scathing branches and entangling roots.

And she saw the purple streak of Sybbolith, twisting and sliding between reaching talons.

Kurdwen slammed the tower door and threw down the bar. She leapt up the spiral stairs throwing braziers and torches behind her.

Then she was in the wind, the salt kiss of free air whipping her vine braids wild. Above the walls, able to hear the songs of life, the songs of power and war these obsidian walls made dead.

And she joined the chorus.

> Arise, all ye spirits, arise from your slumber,
> O children of the Everqueen, come to my call.
> From ditch-moat and hog-pen come make thee a war-host,
> To burn their black sea-steeds and crumble their wall.

At the base of Lord Revish's private tower, the ground began to churn and sink. Keening, like the squeal of enormous predators or screeched violin notes, emanated from the sinkhole. Roots speared up, hooked the earth, and dryads pulled themselves free. Dozens of them.

They dug their talons into the curtain wall's black stonework, finger-shoots sprouting to give them purchase between the blocks, climbing upwards like a swarm of beetles fleeing a rising stream. As the wave of them approached, she could feel her reserves increasing – four seasons of magical drought, and now the spring bubbled anew.

'Welcome, sisters,' she whispered.

One looked up at her and shrieked in alarm.

Kurdwen leapt high and away like a stag, the hellstrider's six-tailed whip cracking by as it missed her by a twig's breadth. She landed in a crouch, sprang backwards and vaulted off her hands to avoid the disembowelling follow-up lash.

If she'd had her greenwood scythe, she could have defended herself – but it was hanging up in the audience hall, among Revish's trophies. And while she could spare enough glamour to stop a weak heart, combatting a mighty champion of Chaos was another matter entirely. Especially when she needed the magic for something greater.

So she fled, bolting along the parapet with all the energy of a hare. Got distance. Poured all of herself into her song.

> *The Mirrored One lives, claim revenge for thy sisters,*
> *Cut down in defence of our twice-hallowed glade.*
> *The foe-men sit idle, in unguarded chambers,*
> *So bring them the talon, and bring them the blade.*

Sybbolith followed, ducking and leaping the dryad limbs that reached for her over the battlements. She decapitated one with her clawed hand. Lashed another by the neck and tossed it into space. Grabbed a third that got too close and punched through its oaken forehead with a tongue sharp as an awl.

And when they grew too thick on the parapet, she jumped onto the sawtooth battlements themselves, leaping from promontory to promontory without slowing her gait.

Kurdwen reached the end of the parapet. She yanked at the door to Revish's private tower and found it locked.

She could turn and meet the hellstrider, or jump into the courtyard.

'Run, little wych,' howled the oncoming champion.

Kurdwen jumped, aiming for the soft manure of the hog pen, singing still.

And as she fell, the whole world rocked.

The earth below her erupted, its displacement buckling the wall's flagstones upwards. An upheaval of soil and moss rose to meet her.

She hit hard, rolled, scrambled for a handhold. Felt a sharp spear pierce her thigh-branch. Still, that was purchase enough and she held on, grabbing the great wooden antler as the rest of the earth and stones fell away.

Kurdwen had not known the seed would sprout into a treelord, but she'd done everything she could to tip the chances. She'd hidden the biggest soulpod inside the menial along with every treelord lamentiri she'd hung from her antlers like meaningless trinkets. Tricked the poor man into eating the bloodcurrants. Declined using his body as fertiliser so Revish would send it to the nutrient-rich soil of the hog pen.

Even then, she couldn't be sure it would have the desired effect. Soulpods didn't work that way. But the Queen of the Radiant Wood had smiled, and now she stood on the shoulder of a newborn champion of the forest.

And she whispered what he must do.

The treelord reared his great arms back and speared the defensive wall with his root talons, green shoots unspooling, working their way in between the stonework.

Kurdwen stroked the antler, eye to eye with the champion on the parapet. Sybbolith staggered, thrown from her footing as the growing tentacles of green shifted the wall's stability. Dryads crawled away like lizards, leaving the hellstrider alone on the rocking structure.

In those jungle-cat eyes, Kurdwen saw something that looked a great deal like fear.

'Thou wert right,' she said. 'I was trouble.'

Then the treelord ripped his arms backwards and the wall collapsed in on itself, stones clattering against each other with a sound not unlike the felling of great trees.

Dryads surged through the breach, scrambling over the obsidian blocks – but the hellstrider was gone. Crushed perhaps, her body pinned to the earth under immovable stones.

But Kurdwen was not so sure. Because for a fleeting moment, she thought she'd seen an impossible thing – a figure dancing on air amidst the falling stones. Leaping from block to block with feline precision, tumbling like an acrobat through the debris and towards the dry moat.

Towards the fleet.

Later they would search for Sybbolith among the burned wreckage of the docks, picking through the shattered hulls of ships that the treelord had hoisted clear of the water and hurled onto the rocky shore.

There was no trace, except for a host of dismembered dryads – and the stories.

Stories of coastal ravagers who pillaged and vanished. Riders whose serpentine mounts leapt from the deck of low-hulled ships and plunged ashore through the roiling surf.

Tales of a woman with golden cat eyes, sailing west towards the Gates of Dawn.

Revish the Epicurean strode into his audience chamber feeling *alive*.

He alone had cut his way out. Twenty dryads in the garden, more on the walls. Claw marks scored his mirror-crystal armour. One axe had been lost, lodged in a dryad who'd taken it with her as she toppled off the wall and into the dry moat. He'd left behind the corpses of his Chosen – they had sacrificed themselves for their lord, as was their purpose. The wall had been breached, but walls could be repaired.

The important thing was he'd lost himself in the exuberance of it. He'd never been so close to death for so long, and in that liminal space he found a new passion – the thrill of survival against the odds. Adrenaline, battle-fear, would be his new addiction. His consort would be pleased.

Face bloodied, hands sticky with sap, he called out to the lithe, inhuman silhouette sitting in his throne.

'Syb! You were right. The battle-lust has returned. I feel...'

The figure leaned into the light, grinning. Stone trinkets rattled in wooden antlers.

'Thou wert saying? How dost thou feel?'

He stopped short. 'Deceiver.'

'Harsh judgement from a man who tried to devour our dear child,' said Kurdwen. She stroked the bittergrub that lay around her neck like a fox fur. It cooed softly. 'Not very pleasant of dear father, was it, my lovely? Trying to eat thine egg sac.'

She scratched it under the mandibles.

When Revish took a step forward, it turned its pincers towards him and hissed.

'You bewitched me,' said Revish. 'Fed me sweets to keep me docile. Promised me children.'

'And I have delivered.' She swept a thorny hand around the chamber. Polished wood whispered on stone, and the forest folk emerged from behind hallucinogenic tapestries, baroque screens and captured war banners. 'These are, in a way, our daughters.'

'Absurd.'

'All the things I taught thee, Revish, and thou still dost not understand.' She stood, pushing herself to her feet with her reclaimed scythe. 'Dost thou even know the purpose of fruit?'

His brow furrowed.

'A plant must spread its seeds. So it grows a tasty morsel to attract dumb beasts to eat them. Beasts... like birds, or wild asses, or Chaos lords.'

Revish growled, raised his axe. The dryads drew closer.

'Think of it, Revish. All those fruits that passed your table. Apples in autumn, berries in summer... all impregnated with soulpods. After all, they come in many forms. And every morning, a servant would take thy chamber pot, examine the night soil and throw it into the dry moat outside the window. An army grown under your nose.'

He sputtered.

'I'm Kurdwen, by the by. Wilde Kurdwen. We do use names, I just don't make a habit of giving mine to men that consort with daemons.'

He flung himself at her, wild, furious, screaming at the edge of exhaustion.

She turned his blow and dipped the sickle into his mouth, hooking him through his torn cheek like a landed fish. Dragged him staggering across the audience chamber and threw him into his throne. Vines tightened around his wrists and ankles. His face went white.

'Please, no, please,' he begged. 'I... I can be a partner. Keep clear of your woods. I'm a good steward.'

'A good steward,' the wych cackled. 'This *good steward* defor-
ested this island to build his docks. This *good steward* diverted a
river to build his fortress of pleasure. This *good steward* looked
at us as nothing but foodstuffs.'

'I can be of use, I promise.'

'Oh yes,' she smiled. 'And I know just the role.'

It is known on maps as Hermit Island, but for as long as folk
can remember, the people of the Jade Kingdoms have called it
Wych Isle.

Deep forests cover it, gnarled roots extending to the rocky shore.
Yet despite this abundance, it is tradition that it is unwise to cut
timber there, or spend the night ashore.

Those who beach on the isle by day have seen strange sights.
The broken ribs of great ships tangled in the underbrush. Black
foundation stones, long ago dismantled by root and vine.

But the talented trail master, or unluckily lost, may find another structure. Four walls still standing, closed with a rusted
iron gate set with sculpted ivy leaves. Trees choke the interior,
soaring above the old walls.

At its centre, in the oldest oak of all, can be found a suit of crystalline armour halfway swallowed in the bark, as if melting into
the wood. Long ago, it's said, a warrior died leaning back against
the trunk, and over the long centuries the tree grew around him.
Devouring and digesting him over slow ages.

And atop the armour rests a skull, sunken back into the bark.
Its jaw hangs open, they say, as if in a centuries-long scream.

THE HAMMER OF IMMANENCE

Eric Gregory

Gardus raised his runeblade and squinted into the setting sun of Shyish.

His battalion marched out of the storm and into the light. Every instinct born of his old life told him this was madness, but he wasn't the person he had once been, and neither were his soldiers. Each had lived centuries in the hosts of the God-King; each was accustomed, now, to the jolt of displacement when the armies of the heavens deployed in their thunder.

'Tempestors,' he shouted into the wind. 'At the ready!'

The six silver-armoured riders before him hefted arbalests towards the horizon. White capes fluttered behind them, and their dracoth mounts kicked up the black sand of the badlands.

Ahead, against the dusk, a legion of the dead was on the march. Sepulchral siege engines like the towers of dread necromancers rumbled forward, silhouetted against the low red sun.

'Steady!' Gardus called.

He wasn't the person he had been. He could stare into the light now – he *was* the light. In life, he had been Garradan: healer in a hospice of Demesnus, a man of inquisitive faith and a worker of comforts.

Now he was Gardus Steel Soul, a Lord-Celestant of the God-King's armies, and he dealt in a different trade.

Gardus gripped his sword so tightly that hairline cracks of lightning leapt between the runes on the blade. He stared into the sun and studied the line of dead on the horizon.

The Ossiarch Bonereapers of the Necropolis Mortarch.

The God-King himself had warned Gardus of the enemy, and charged him with his mission.

'*They would make our Free Cities a charnel ground,*' *Sigmar had told him.* '*This is their design – the Bonereapers fashion the bones of the living into the blades of unlife. They forge soldiers out of teeth and spines, and their victims are their reinforcements. They lay siege now on Fort Immanence in Shyish, and if they take it, the Free City of Gravewild may follow. They would raise a new capital city of the dead.*'

'*You would have me hold the fortress,*' *Gardus had ventured.*

'*No.*'

Past the Bonereaper line, Gardus could see Fort Immanence now – the ancient stone monastery-turned-fortress was set upon a plateau overlooking the Sea of Dust. This was the target the Bonereapers marched upon. They too faced straight into the sunset, dead eyes unbothered by the light.

'Steady,' Gardus said again, under his breath this time. And then, when he judged that his line of Tempestors was within range, he raised his voice.

'Fire,' he shouted.

The desert air crackled as his Tempestors unleashed their volley-storm crossbows. Their bolts burned like falling stars, streaks of light searing over the black sands. Gardus permitted himself a grim smile as the bolts converged on the first of the Bonereapers' siege engines, nearly toppling the tower of bone.

'Liberators, forward!' Gardus called. While the Tempestors slowed and reloaded their crossbows, his first rank of infantry advanced: silver-gleaming Stormcast Eternals with warhammers raised.

'Who may prevail in the deserts of the dead?' Gardus asked. The question was strangely quiet, almost philosophical; it might have been intended only for himself. But his warriors knew him – they knew how he spoke, and they knew it was a call for a response. Thuna the Never-Reforged grinned at his side. The rust-haired Retributor-Prime wore the sign of the twin-tailed comet daubed in warpaint around her eyes.

'Only the faithful!' she roared.

Now the Bonereapers knew they were under attack. While the ponderous siege engines still rumbled towards Fort Immanence, their Mortek Guard line infantry whirled towards the Stormcast assault, osseous shields and blades raised. They were skeletons – or rather, bone grafted into the forms of soldiers and braced with ornate armour. There were no eyes to meet here, only a line of skulls, smiling their fixed smiles in unwavering service to the Lord of Death.

The Liberators charged into the first line of Mortek Guard, battering the soldiers aside with their shields. The bulk of the enemy infantry weren't making for the Stormcasts, though – instead, they were crowding around the siege engines, and something else *behind* the engines.

A stray blade lunged towards Gardus' armpit; he deflected it, caught the Bonereaper's skull in his hand, and twisted it from the neck. The construct was stronger and stranger than the deathrattle revenants he had fought before – the skull continued to bite and lash, and Gardus hurled it out into the fray. While his Liberators drove into the back of the Bonereaper ranks like a spear, Gardus fought to catch a glimpse of whatever the line-troops meant to protect.

A sweep of his warhammer cast a pair of unwary Mortek Guard aside, and now he found the answer: riding atop a bipedal, necromantic war-throne was the Ossiarch leader. A *soulmason*, if Gardus recalled the Azyrite intelligence correctly. It was as skeletal as its troops, but slighter, knees pressed up to its chest, the permanent expression on its skull a wry grimace rather than a grin.

'The general!' Thuna shouted, nodding towards the soulmason. 'We got a straight shot. I'll send 'im right back to Nagash!'

Before Gardus could agree, three massive *cracks* sounded across the badlands. Above him, the slender catapult arms of the Ossiarch siege engines snapped and unfurled, hurling death into the skies.

No, not death – *the dead*. The Bonereaper infantry weren't crowding around the siege engines to protect the machines; they were presenting their skulls to the engine artillerists as ammunition. The Ossiarch engineers tore the skulls from their compatriots and loaded them into the catapults, setting the skulls ablaze with necrotic magics… and then hurling them through the dusk towards Fort Immanence.

Gardus thrust his crackling blade through the ribs of a Bonereaper warrior and glanced back at the soulmason, whose slender fingers wrote some eldritch command in the air. The general was reconstructing his soldiers as they fell, or as they broke themselves down for ammunition.

A clap of thunder behind him. The Tempestors were caught in a line of four-armed, heavily armoured Ossiarch constructs whose blades swung in a brutal whirlwind. One of the Stormcasts was going home to Sigmar already – he fell backwards, impaled through the stomach by the Bonereaper's massive sword, before exploding into the sky in a thunderclap.

A dracoth tumbled onto its side, sending another Tempestor rolling into the sand.

'My lord!' shouted Thuna. 'The soulmason!'

This was the moment that arose in every engagement – when any plan of action met the rigours of reality, and a general either adapted or died. This was when battles were lost or won. Gardus felt, sometimes, that he lived this moment in eternal recursion.

Thuna shattered the skull of a Bonereaper with the butt of her lightning hammer, then swung around to bring down holy storm-fire on a mass of dead legionnaires scrambling towards a siege engine.

'My lord!' she shouted. 'Do I have your leave to end 'im?'

The soulmason grimaced over the heads of his warriors. Gardus almost imagined he could hear a deathless whisper in his head:

Yes. End me.

Gardus shook his head, breathed deep, and raised his sigmarite runeblade. 'Fall back to the fortress!' he barked.

Thuna gaped at him. 'We're *retreating?* But the soulmason–'

'Our objective is up there,' Gardus growled, jerking his head towards Fort Immanence on its plateau. 'We must protect her.'

'He's right there! I'm going to take 'im out!' She started towards the soulmason.

'Retributor, you will *obey.*'

Reluctantly, Thuna turned away from the soulmason. 'My lord, Sigmar will protect the mortals!'

Too many of his Hallowed Knights had this peculiar faith, in spite of all they had seen and all that the Stormhost had suffered. This faith as hope, as *expectation*. It troubled Gardus.

'We are Sigmar's hands here,' he said, then raised his voice and shouted across the sands. 'Tempestors, *bring down those engines now.*'

There were only three Tempestors left, one on a dracoth, and those were barely holding their own against the four-armed heavy constructs. The order would be their deaths and reforgings. But they were Hallowed Knights, the unwavering elite of Azyr.

One by one, the Tempestors trained their arbalests on the Ossiarch siege engines, focusing searing streaks of blue fire on the catapults... even as the heavy constructs advanced and cut them down. First the arm of one catapult snapped and toppled, and then a second. Gardus nodded grimly.

The Lord-Celestant cut down the Bonereapers before him, and the thunderclaps of fallen Hallowed Knights sounded around him. His spear of Liberators and Retributors was battered, but it had pierced through the Bonereaper line, and they were moving now in a fighting retreat towards the objective. Night was falling quickly, and before them, smoke rose from Fort Immanence. They needed to reach the fortress quickly.

'Hallowed Knights,' Gardus called. 'Fall back!'

The war-abbess Nawal ib'Ayzah stood atop the battlements of Fort Immanence and watched skulls fall from the sky.

A streak of necrotic fire crashed into the high minaret that rose from the front gate. For a moment, it seemed the tower would stand... and then slowly, slowly, the spiral cap collapsed into rubble. A second shot struck the wall nearby; the fortress shook underfoot, as if in a small earthquake, but the stone held.

The Master of Orisons placed a hand on her arm. 'Your holiness – it's time. Come down to the cellars.' He didn't wait for her answer, but started to draw her back from the parapet.

Nawal jerked her arm away and rested her hand on the haft of her hammer of office, running her thumb over the faded gold of the twin-tailed comet inlaid there. For decades, she had worn this hammer, and she wore it still, though her hip ached with the weight. It was an ornament, now, but there was a time when her ministers and officiants froze in fear at that gesture: her hand on her hammer, and a narrowing of the eyes.

'I'll do no such thing. And neither will you. Are the wizards in the temple?'

Master Diwat paled. 'I... yes, your holiness.'

The man was a coward who had come to his position between the wars. Nawal had little use for this soft and frightened generation of elders – she preferred the young soldiers who had grown up in a convulsed Shyish – but there was no stopping the procession of years.

'We will wait,' she said. And now Diwat looked properly afraid of her.

She turned back to the parapet. Across the black sands, the siege engines and the dead legion had... stopped. Why had they stopped?

'I want every unit you have left surrounding the Sunside Minaret,' she said without turning.

The Freeguild Sergeant Ahram coughed. 'Every unit, ma'am.'

The sergeant was wise enough to voice his objections as confirmations. She didn't mind Ahram. The buttoned-up, moustachioed veteran was going grey himself – his was a face from another age.

'The dead must be contained,' Nawal said. 'It's too soon for a breach.'

'Too soon,' Diwat repeated under his breath.

Why had the march stopped out there in the desert? Nawal raised her spyglass and surveyed the field. Her sight, at least, had remained with her, even as the rest of her body wore down, but the sun had nearly sunk and the dark was coming on quickly. Out there on the horizon... it looked as though the siege engines had collapsed. Well, that explained why skulls had stopped falling from the sky. But here–

A small group of fighters was advancing *past* the Ossiarch line, moving across the desert towards Fort Immanence with weapons glowing in the dark like blue torches, like comets.

'Sergeant Ahram,' Nawal ordered, 'ready the sand teams at the Dust Gate. Bury the skulls at the walls and have your handgunners at the ready.'

While Ahram set about ordering the sand teams along the parapet, Nawal watched the advancing warriors. Apprehension curled in her stomach. The dead took many forms, but these didn't look like the dead, didn't move like the dead. The way their armour gleamed, the way their weapons shone in the dark...

As they drew closer, the figures disappeared behind the lip of the plateau. Abruptly, Nawal marched along the battlements towards the Nightside Minaret, her white robes fluttering in her wake. The stiffness in her knees made her gait uneven, but she moved with determined speed; startled, Master Diwat jogged to catch up.

'Abbess, what are–'

From her new angle, she raised the spyglass again. There – steadily, determinedly, the silver-armoured figures were climbing the escarpment, pressing forward even as it steepened into the plateau.

As the sand teams unleashed their freight on the biting skulls at the base of the wall, quenching the unnatural fires and burying them, Nawal watched and waited. From time to time, she looked up at the constellations circling above, and took some solace from the sight.

At last, the silver-armoured warriors clambered over the edge of the plateau. Swords and hammers crackled with lightning, starlight mirrored in the warriors' armour.

'Ahram!' she shouted. 'I want those handgunners! *Now!*'

'Your holiness,' said Master Diwat. 'What– what is the matter? These are allies!'

'No,' she spat. 'These are Hallowed Knights.'

* * *

Gardus sheathed his sword and gazed up at the vast arched gates and proud minarets of Fort Immanence. Stormcast Eternals strode the realms in heroic proportions, walking at least a head taller than any mortal, always larger than the life that carried on around them. Yet when *he* had lived, when he was Garradan, he had been a quiet, unprepossessing man, and he was sometimes ill at ease in the frame of an immortal. It was a small pleasure to be humbled by the work of mortal hands.

A Stardrake might have walked through these gates, but they were only seven Hallowed Knights. Thuna the Never-Reforged, the child-faced veteran Phaithon, Ekatera, Dahedron, the Twins... this battered group of Liberators and Retributors followed after Gardus, standing tall in spite of their weariness.

On either side of the gate, lines of Freeguilders stood in silent pairs, one partner holding a torch while the other levelled a handgun or a crossbow. Their uniforms were filthy and torn, and some of the soldiers wore no uniforms at all – Gardus suspected they were Collegiate apprentices and novices of the fortress-abbey pressed into service. He tried nodding to one of those, but the boy's face remained impassive, or perhaps betrayed a touch of fear.

As they emerged into the outer bailey of the fortress, the night was silent except for the Hallowed Knights' heavy, clanking footsteps. The air was thick with the scent of charred bone. The forty-odd assembled Freeguilders frowned or looked away as they passed, and where Gardus found hope in a face, it swiftly faded.

'Leave.'

The voice that spoke was crisp and steady. Gardus glanced across the bailey and found the voice's owner.

The war-abbess must have been in her eightieth year, her skin as dry and cracked as the badlands outside the walls. She walked with a stoop and an uneven gait, but her eyes were hard, and she still wore the warhammer of a devoted cleric at her waist.

Nawal ib'Ayzah. His entire reason for being here. Sigmar himself had spoken her name.

Three nervous advisors hovered around her, prepared to steady the abbess should she take a false step, but she advanced on Gardus in a cold fury, staring up at him without a trace of fear.

'War-abbess,' he said, inclining his head. 'I am–'

'Leave. Now.'

Her advisors – a grizzled Freeguilder, a middle-aged devoted, and a miserable-looking wizard of the Celestial College in starry robes – exchanged glances. Gardus suppressed a frown and pressed on.

'I am Lord-Celestant Gardus Steel Soul of the Hallowed Knights Stormhost,' he said. 'I am here on behalf of the God-King Sigmar.'

Mutters passed among the frayed ranks of Freeguilders and novices. But there was a nervous timbre to those whispers. And the war-abbess herself was unmoved.

'You're not welcome here,' said Nawal ib'Ayzah. 'I have received you as befits your station, but I can offer you no provisions, and you are not welcome. I am requesting that you leave us, but I will require it if I must.'

'Ma'am,' murmured the moustachioed Freeguilder at her side. 'If I may... we lost a great many faithful containing the dead from the last breach, and we could use–'

'Hush, Ahram.'

Gardus studied the figures before him, listened to the fear in the quiet that hung over the bailey. He was accustomed to a different mortal reception – hope, gratitude, even rapture. What, precisely, had made these people so afraid? Gardus himself? The abbess?

This would require some delicacy.

'I wonder if I might speak with you alone,' he said. 'Our lord has tidings for your ears. Once I've delivered his message, I'll be on my way.'

The war-abbess narrowed her eyes. 'I have your word?'

'You have my word.'

'My lady,' the wizard began. 'As a representative of the Collegiate–'

She cut him off with a raised hand and turned to her Freeguilder.

'Sergeant Ahram, I want the handgunners to remain here, weapons trained on our guests. The Hallowed Knights are not to leave this spot. Am I understood?'

The moustachioed sergeant bowed his head, his gruffness belied by a genteel deference. Nawal sighed, turned her back on the Stormcast Eternals, and began to stride out of the circle of torchlight and into the dark. After a moment, she raised her hand and gestured for Gardus to join her. The Freeguild Sergeant Ahram gave Gardus a torch, a wry smile, and a sort of half-shrug.

Gardus fell in beside the abbess and walked with her along the inner wall, admiring the brickwork and waiting for her to speak. Immanence had served as an abbey-bastion in the badlands for three hundred years, but the stones were more ancient still – older than the local histories or the survey maps archived in Azyrheim. Civilisations had risen and fallen while these walls stood.

'Well,' said Nawal, 'you wanted to speak with me. Speak, then.'

Here, the bailey between the inner and outer walls was dark and empty, high weeds grown up through the scrub. There were no soldiers along this face of the wall, no torches but for the one in Gardus' hand; the two of them were alone with the night.

'Our God-King has instructed me to remove you from Fort Immanence and deliver you safely to the Free City of Gravewild. He has declared you a crucial strategic asset, and wishes for you to coordinate the Shyish theatres from the high command at–'

Nawal ib'Ayzah cut him off with a bark of a laugh. 'I was *right!*' she crowed.

Gardus frowned down at the old woman.

'Hers is a ruthless mind,' the God-King had mused from his throne.

ERIC GREGORY

Lightning danced in his eyes. 'A mind that can fashion a city into a sword. Our free peoples have some need of such minds.'

'But the fortress is lost,' Gardus said.

Sigmar steepled his hands before him. 'How many of my Hallowed Knights can you spare to aid you?'

After the Genesis Gate, the Stormhost was overextended. Gardus told his lord the number.

'I expect the fortress is lost,' Sigmar said.

Was this truly the woman the God-King meant to save? Even her laughter was in anger.

'Lifetimes ago,' Nawal said, 'I was a novice in a little devoted priory outside Caddow. Hardly a girl, can you imagine? The priory was far enough out of the way that it managed to avoid getting caught up in the wars of the day – until, of course, it didn't. A coven of vampire sellswords happened on our happy priory in the night, and, well...'

Gardus tilted his head to regard her.

'My brothers and sisters prayed for some knights of faith to deliver them. I hid beneath a board in the wine cellar. What do you suppose happened?'

'You lived,' Gardus said softly.

'But my brothers. And my sisters. Do you think their prayers were answered?'

Gardus was silent.

'I'll tell you. Hiding there in the cellar, I heard thunderclaps like the great storm before the world. *Crack* after *crack* after *crack*. I thought the priory was going to collapse around me. I prayed too, just then. Under my breath, I recited all the names of Sigmar that I could remember, over and over and over. When the noise quieted, the footsteps and the snarls of the vampires overhead were gone. I climbed up the stairs and peered into the nave. Do you know what I saw?'

She didn't wait for him this time, but raised a finger to his chest.

'*Hallowed Knights*. Oh, you'd slain the monsters. The novices were dead, too. Some were called home to the God-King, others left to rot. The nave was strewn with the corpses of undead and innocent alike. And your Hallowed Knights just… stared at the ruins. You didn't even realise I was there.'

'No child should experience such a horror,' Gardus said.

Nawal ib'Ayzah scowled. She beckoned him through a gatehouse door built for a mortal frame; Gardus had to duck his head to pass through.

'No. I was *fortunate*. I learned something of the nature of our God-King and his works.'

Within the inner walls of Fort Immanence was a pyramidal keep. Nawal turned to face him, the temple behind her silhouetted in black against the starry sky. A shiver ran along Gardus' spine.

'Ask yourself. Why does the God-King send you to recover an old relic like me when he could' – she snapped her fingers – '*whisk* me up and enlist me in the armies of heaven? Why, do you suppose?'

'It is not my place to know,' Gardus said quietly.

'You Stormcasts are the lesser weapon. I guessed it all those ages ago in the priory, and I was right. There's something wrong with you. A light behind the eyes is missing. You're an army of echoes, an army of ghosts, hardly any different from those reanimated bones outside the walls. Mortals are the sharpened blade, and you are the weapon at hand.'

Gardus stared at his ungloved palm. His veins shone with a soft blue light underneath the skin. He had lived lifetimes at war now, violence that he recalled with terrible clarity – but every time he died and was reforged, his memory of Garradan faded. His old life became less and less of who he was.

No, he wasn't Garradan. Whether he was greater or lesser than the man who had gone before, he was someone else now.

'What you saw as a novice,' he said, 'that could break one's faith.'

She shook her head, turned around again, and started towards the dark pyramid at the heart of the abbey.

'Sigmar is a ruthless god,' she said. 'I respect that. And he tarries in these realms when he might simply leave us to fend for ourselves. I have faith in the God-King.'

'You'll answer his call, then,' Gardus ventured. 'You'll come with me.'

'No.'

Gardus' patience was steel, but for the first time, he was truly wrong-footed. 'No?'

'I will be frank, Lord-Celestant. I have a plan to defeat the Bone-reapers. It is an exacting plan, and it will work, but I must remain here if I am to serve Sigmar and protect the free peoples of this realm.'

'I'm *here* on behalf of the God-King,' Gardus said incredulously. 'I've *spoken* with Sigmar.'

Nawal shrugged. 'So you say. I have faith in my god in Azyr, and I trust in my own mortal hands.' She raised her cracked palms. 'I have neither faith nor trust in you.'

'This fortress will not stand, abbess. You will not survive here.'

'*Only the faithful*, eh?' She grinned. 'I don't need to survive. I only need to win.'

He stared down at her in wonder. But before he could object, the first impacts shook the gatehouse.

'It's started,' she said.

The Lord-Celestant shielded her with his bulk as debris rained from the gatehouse and the inner wall. Nawal craned her neck to search the skies. Dozens of small projectiles streaked into the fortress; her stomach lurched as one glanced off the keep, and another crashed into the side of the barracks.

'Al'akhos has repaired his catapults,' she hissed.

Nawal seized the torch from the Stormcast and started back along the inner wall. Gardus unsheathed his sword, unlatched the warhammer from his belt and followed beside her, watching the sky.

'Al'akhos?' he asked.

'Our quarry, the soulmason.'

'You know his name?'

'Oh, yes. The two of us have corresponded by carrier-vulture. He is quite witty.'

A projectile smashed into the bailey, casting up a spume of dirt and rock. It was an obsidian stele, like the foundation stone of a necromancer's altar, engraved with peculiar glyphs that made Nawal think of every time she had ever glimpsed death. That night in the priory, the fever that had nearly taken her three years ago... a sensation of vertigo nearly tumbled her to the ground.

Another stele fell – this time, straight towards them. The Lord-Celestant wrapped an arm around her. His armour was cold as desert night, even through her robes. He reared back with his lightning-wreathed warhammer, grunted, and shattered the stele in a blow. The eldritch debris clattered against his armour.

As they parted and turned back towards the outer bailey, a towering skeletal form stalked towards them, a head higher than even the Stormcast.

'They've breached the walls,' Nawal whispered. '*How?*'

The massive skeletal warrior wore heavy, spined armour. It bore a shield larger than Nawal, and two limbs gripped a halberd that might have impaled several Stormcasts at once.

Immortis Guard. Al'akhos' elite. If they were here...

The construct screeched and charged across the scrub of the bailey towards Nawal and Gardus, its halberd lowered. Gardus gripped her arm and held the two of them fixed to the spot.

An instant before the Immortis Guard impaled the two of them on its halberd, Gardus whirled to the side and swung his sword in a wide arc. The runes on the blade erupted in lightning as the weapon slashed through the neck of the unliving thing, and its armoured skull toppled into the dirt. The body bucked and thrashed until Gardus ran his sword through the spine, incinerating the vertebrae.

The Lord-Celestant's eyes flashed with storm-light. There was a cold fury in Gardus, Nawal thought, beneath his stoic mien. Like the light that shone under his skin.

'Al'akhos is committing,' she said, catching her breath. 'Unless he harvests *us*, he only has so much materiel to build his constructs. He needs to take Immanence to continue the march on Gravewild. If he's committing his resources now, he believes he'll win.'

Gardus raised his shield again and scanned the sky. 'You learned the monster's mind by exchanging letters.'

'No. I know his mind by the way he commands.'

'Why the correspondence, then?'

She waved the question away as if it were trivial. 'I tried to negotiate for the safe passage of our novices and civilians.'

'Laudable,' Gardus said.

Nawal shook her head. 'It seemed to amuse him. But I needed Al'akhos to believe that we wanted to live.'

Gardus stared down at her. 'What *do* you intend?'

She held his gaze. 'I will draw the Bonereapers here and burn them to ash with the fires of heaven.'

The outer bailey was in chaos. Now Gardus could see how the Bonereaper had got inside: the top of a slender, skeletal siege tower stood against the outer wall, and the soulmason's most elite constructs were dropping inside.

More Immortis Guard rampaged across the parade ground,

while a many-limbed necropolis stalker danced into a line of hand-gunners. Freeguilders scattered and shouted, careful with their shots lest they kill their own. The Liberator Ekatera was doubled over in the dirt, impaled by a halberd; as Ekatera exploded into light, the remaining Hallowed Knights held their weapons aloft, fighting to form a defensive perimeter around the mortal soldiers.

Gardus' mind was a tempest. The violence before him, the fury and fire of Nawal ib'Ayzah's plan. *She means to sacrifice it all.* The abbess was cold, damned cold. She was arrogant, and she was obstinate... and she was brave, too.

A pair of advisors to the war-abbess – the devoted and the moustachioed sergeant – ran towards them, relief and terror mixed with wild hope in their faces. The Freeguilder, Ahram, took the abbess' arm, while the cleric nearly threw himself at Gardus' feet.

'Lord-Celestant,' he pleaded. 'We need more of your warriors, we – we can hold out a little longer, but soon, we need them–'

He flinched as another stele struck the Nightside Minaret.

'Don't be pitiful,' said Nawal. 'No one else is coming. He is only here to rescue me, and I'm not going.'

The men looked up at Gardus with dawning horror. Even behind his helm, he found it difficult to hold their gazes. He felt a swell of anger at her for telling them the truth, and a swell of shame over his anger.

'Sergeant Ahram,' she said, 'instruct your survivors to fall back inside the inner wall. I want every pike, rifle and dagger in Fort Immanence defending the temple. Master Diwat, you will escort me to speak with the wizard.'

Ahram and Diwat exchanged a look, then set about their orders. The war-abbess spared Gardus a backward glance as the Master of Orisons hurried her into the fortress.

'You won't be seeing me again,' she said. 'You carried your

message. There's no shame in leaving the war to more capable hands.'

And with that, she was gone.

Should he follow? No, they would never get the abbess out safely with the stalkers and Immortis Guard rampaging through the fortress. It was madness.

He was making for his surviving Hallowed Knights when the gates fell open under the press of battle-constructs. The crash of the breach stole Gardus' attention for an instant, and when he turned ahead again, he found a necropolis stalker standing before him, blades raised to strike.

The Retributor Dahedron howled and charged, driving his crackling lightning hammer into the stalker's side. The construct's greater blades scythed away from Gardus – but its lower limbs rammed nadirite daggers up through the join in the Retributor's plate, deep into his sternum. Dahedron gasped and spat blood before collapsing into lightning.

Gardus barrelled across the bloody parade ground, heedless now, furious. He realised his Retributors Thuna and Phaithon were at his side, but they asked for no command.

Dahedron's slayer considered its Stormcast-felling blade before regarding Gardus with its triune skulls, all smiling their wicked, fixed smiles. The Lord-Celestant gripped his hammer and runeblade, lowered his shoulder, and charged. Sweat ran down his face, sizzling into steam when it reached his eyes.

Beneath the arch of the broken gate, Stormcast and Bonereaper met. Gardus hammered aside the first blade, caught the second on his pauldron, and seized the tri-skull in his hand; he tore open the nearest jaw and thrust his runeblade deep into its gullet. The sword blazed, and the necropolis stalker shuddered and collapsed in blue flame.

He forced himself to breathe deliberately, to calm his mind.

Everything was wrong. His soldiers were falling. The abbess was a fool, and the fortress was bedlam. He looked out through the open gate, out over the plateau…

'Oh,' said Thuna at his side. 'Oh, no.'

The siege towers and the elite constructs, Gardus thought, were a distraction.

In the desert below, the Bonereapers were building a bridge to the sky. Arches and girders of fused bone rose from the scrub to the escarpment of the plateau. This was no mere siege tower, but a passage for a legion. In the distance, Gardus could make out the figure of the soulmason Al'akhos flanked by a trio of Mortisan boneshapers. Under the soulmason's direction, the necro-architects cast their osseous material into shape, steadily building out the vast ramp while a legion of the dead waited patiently to march.

'We have to destroy it,' Thuna said.

He looked to her. He thought of what the abbess had said: that there was no shame in leaving the war to more capable hands.

This is the moment, Gardus thought. *When the battle is won or lost.*

'No,' he said. 'We don't have the strength. We fall back behind the inner walls.'

'My lord,' Thuna said. 'We are *Hallowed Knights*.'

'We are. And we will fulfil our vows to serve Sigmar and protect the free peoples of the realm. We're no good to them if we fall down there.'

'I'm going,' she said. There was something desperate and defiant in her eyes, within the smeared warpaint. 'You might have lost faith, but I haven't. I'll show you what–'

'*You will fall back, Retributor.*'

Thuna froze. Even the other Stormcast Eternals froze. Gardus had unending patience, and rarely did he raise his voice.

Stony-faced, Thuna bowed her head and stepped back from the precipice.

'Yes, Lord-Celestant,' she said quietly.

On Gardus' orders, the Stormcasts fell back to support the Freeguilders' withdrawal behind the inner wall. By the time they reached the relative safety of the inner bailey, there were five Hallowed Knights and twenty-eight Freeguilders or conscripts remaining.

Once he had ordered his soldiers to their posts, Sergeant Ahram approached Gardus with a solemn expression.

'My lord,' he said. 'I have a proposition.'

The temple at the heart of Fort Immanence had stood for millennia. Longer, according to the Collegiate Arcane's archeo-mystics, than even the fortress walls. It was a harmonic node, so Nawal's wizards told her, between the ley lines of the land and the prevailing constellation in the skies of Shyish. A place of power.

Nawal had never quite grasped the lore and arcana behind the wizards' work – but *power* she understood.

Master Diwat escorted her into the sanctum sanctorum, glancing nervously over his shoulder. *A coward to the end*, she thought. But no matter. The end would come for the brave and the cowardly alike. She smiled sadly as the warmth of the inner sanctum washed over her skin.

At the precise centre of the sanctum, within the eldritch machinery of the Collegiate Arcane, burned a minor star. The mages' celestial orrery whirled around the little sun, a clockwork of orbits that created a cosmos in miniature. Eight wizards – half of them hardly old enough to marry – stood in a circle around the orrery, eyes closed in focus, sweating as they chanted.

And all around them, a desperate harvest. Rows and rows of soil beds overflowed with crops. Vines snaked along the walls, heavy with fruit cultivated by conjured starlight and determined hands.

A star, Nawal had found, could feed an outpost under siege for a year. Or it could annihilate them all in a night.

Oron, the celestial battlemage in charge of the wizard-scholars of Fort Immanence, approached her with a sombre cast to his face. He had always been a sad sack of an old man, even before she had asked this of him, as though every year he'd spent studying the arcane mysteries had made him more miserable. His robes were adorned with stars, moons and comets.

'It's time?' he asked.

'Very nearly,' said Nawal. 'It's very nearly...'

She trailed off as she realised, a moment too late, that Oron wasn't speaking to *her* – he was speaking to Diwat. The Master of Orisons spun around, jerked her arms behind her and fastened manacles around her wrists.

Nawal tried to kick him in the shin, but he dodged, tried to catch her arm again, and knocked her face first into the flagstone. Her knee seared with pain, and she felt blood gush across her forehead.

'Oh,' Diwat said, crouching to try to pull her up, '*sorry*, sorry. I didn't mean–'

'Unhand me, you stupid shit,' she spat. 'What is the meaning of this?'

'Take her hammer,' said Oron.

Wide-eyed, Diwat looked back and forth between Nawal and the battlemage. 'It feels wrong.'

'Take her bloody hammer, you fool.'

Diwat unlatched the hammer of office from her belt, holding it from the haft as if it might bite him for betrayal.

'You're quite certain this is the moment,' Oron said.

'They've breached the outer wall,' said Diwat. 'Ahram gave me the signal. There's a complication… maybe an opportunity? The Stormcast – he wants *her*. He's here to take her away.'

The battlemage pursed his lips. 'I see.'

Nawal felt cold. *Ahram is involved in this?*

'There's risk in it,' Oron said. 'But I see the logic.' He looked over his shoulder at the apprentices circled around the orrery. 'You can stop chanting, idiots. She's down.'

Nawal blinked blood out of her eyes and craned her neck so that she could see the orrery. One by one, the starry-robed wizards around the arcane machine lowered their arms and ceased their chanting, glancing nervously at her. The star at the centre dimmed and contracted into a single pinprick of light – an ordinary star plucked from the sky and suspended here in the temple. Even that small point lit the chamber like a candle.

No, Nawal thought. *All of them…*

Oron frowned down at her, and she realised she had spoken aloud.

'Between my students and myself, there are *three hundred years* of accumulated magical learning in this chamber,' he said. 'Our researches into realm-magics alone… We can't possibly throw that all away because one arrogant old woman believes she is infallible. It's madness.'

'Have you convinced yourself of that?' Nawal growled. 'I suppose it must be quite easy to believe that you are precious.'

The battlemage glowered at her.

'You have to know,' said the war-abbess, 'if you do this, there is no reversing course. You will still die, and as you go to the darkness you will know that you damned cities to die for your self-importance.'

Oron was silent. Most of the apprentice wizards looked away.

'At the ready now,' the battlemage told his students. They raised their staffs uncertainly.

Heavy, armoured footsteps echoed on the temple flagstone. The

Lord-Celestant Gardus Steel Soul strode into the sanctum with Sergeant Ahram at his side. The impassive silver face of Gardus' helm surveyed the scene before him.

'Damn it all,' Ahram spat, rushing forward towards Nawal, 'what did you *do?*'

'An accident,' Diwat breathed.

Ahram tried to lift her up into a seated position, but she bit his hand and he started back. 'Traitor,' she hissed. 'Don't touch me.'

The sergeant exhaled heavily and looked up at Gardus. 'She's all right.'

'And you're prepared to barter her for your lives,' said the Lord-Celestant, his tone flat. He looked from Ahram to Diwat to Oron. He loomed over the mortals. The flicker of starlight at the centre of the room danced on the silver of his helm.

Ahram glanced to his confederates and then up at Gardus, summoning his courage. 'I'll... remain here with my troops. We'll fight to the end. But the wizards, the priest... they don't need to die, any more than she does. If you can exfiltrate them with the abbess...'

'*Fools*,' Nawal spat. 'Sentimental fools. There is no escaping. If Al'akhos takes Immanence, his forces are bolstered and he will march on Gravewild, and the next Free City, and the next. Even if I could leave, I'd risk drawing the Bonereapers after me or raising their suspicions. *There is no leaving here.*'

Gardus was silent. He regarded the celestial battlemage.

'Wizard,' said the Lord-Celestant. 'If I take you with me, do you believe the fortress will fall?'

Oron pursed his lips. 'I... cannot know. Ahram is a fine leader.'

'I see.'

Nawal tried to meet the Lord-Celestant's eyes, but he was unreadable behind his mask. She watched his palm settle on the pommel of his runeblade.

'Free her,' Gardus said.

'Mages,' Oron said, his voice laced with threat, 'staffs at the ready...'

In an instant, the Lord-Celestant crossed the sanctum, wrapped his palm around the celestial battlemage's face and raised him from his feet. With his other hand, Gardus ripped the staff from Oron's hands and smashed it against the floor.

Almost as one, the apprentice wizards dropped their staffs.

'Faithless cowards and mutineers!' roared Gardus. 'You will free her!'

Without another word, Diwat unlocked the manacles and scrambled away from her, shamefaced. Nawal sat up, wiping the blood from her head with her forearm.

Gardus lowered Oron to the ground, and he sprawled faint over the flagstone. The Stormcast walked back across the sanctum, kneeled before Nawal, and unlatched his helm.

Underneath, white hair was plastered to his scalp. His jaw was covered in white stubble gone nearly to a beard. There were creases around his eyes, and yet there was something youthful in his face, too – an earnestness weathered but unbroken.

'Abbess,' he said.

'I'm pleased to see you again.'

'I want to make a compromise,' Gardus said softly. 'It is neither a command nor a condition of freedom. You are free and Immanence is yours. But if you'll have me, I would serve you.'

'And what is your compromise, Lord-Celestant?'

'Permit me to speak with your people. To lead them in a good-faith defence of the fortress. If we succeed, you'll come with me. If we fail, I will do everything I can to support you in' – he nodded to the orrery – 'your approach.'

Nawal licked the blood from her lip. 'My people. You want to give them false hope, eh?'

He smiled sadly and shook his head, glanced sidelong at Diwat.

'Your advisors here – they don't have your faith. Not in the God-King, and not in themselves. Your people... they are *afraid* to hope. They are despairing, abbess, and waiting to die. It's a hard thing to fight with no hope.'

She considered him for a moment and then extended her hand. Tenderly, he enclosed it in his vast palm and helped her to her feet.

In another life, Garradan of Demesnus had known how to ease pain with words. In little surgeries, during a fearful incision or a knitting together of flesh, he would speak to the patient, ask questions. Often, the simple questions were best: asking after children, or hauls from the river, or the news from abroad. There was no magic ward against suffering – there were only words between people, spoken at the right time.

Now Gardus walked the ramparts of the inner wall and spoke to the soldiers there. The Freeguilders and the devoted novices who had taken up arms, civilians fighting to the last and a handful of Collegiate apprentices who brought their staffs of starlight to war.

He didn't make speeches. He didn't speak much at all, except to introduce himself, and to explain that he would coordinate the defence of Immanence with the war-abbess. While they breathed and readied themselves for the assault on the inner courtyard, he asked questions. Where was home? Who was there? How long had they lived in Immanence? And even as dead warriors screeched along the outer walls, they told him.

Thuna walked with him, while Phaithon and the Twins led the Freeguild halberdiers in exercises in the courtyard. The sky purpled with intimations of dawn. The last assault would come soon.

'It's good to hear their names,' Thuna said. 'To know who we are fighting for.'

Gardus contemplated the sky. 'I suppose I see it as honouring the dead before they're lost.'

She frowned. 'You don't think we'll win.'

He hesitated. 'I need to know that I can rely on you to fulfil your orders.'

'My lord,' Thuna said, flushing, 'I've been more than eager–'

'You've been *too* eager. Always to charge into certain death. You're no fool, Thuna, and you've nothing to prove. You're a peerless warrior. Undefeated! You're my Retributor-Prime for a reason.'

The praise seemed to pain her.

'The fear,' she said.

'The fear?'

'It crept up on me. The longer I've gone, the more it's grown. Not knowing who I'll be on the other side. Not knowing what memories I'll lose. I… I suppose I've wanted to get it over with. To at least be done with the fear.'

Gardus stopped, looked down at the shaken eyes within the warpaint.

Understanding dawned.

'I can't tell you that you won't change,' Gardus said. 'You will. I will. Again and again. There is no shame in the fear – I feel it too. I have been reforged so many times, and always I wonder what memories I will lose and what is already gone that I don't know I've lost. But when Sigmar calls you home, I will be there with you, and so will every Hallowed Knight. We will all be together with whoever we become.'

After a moment, she nodded and clasped his hand.

'Only the faithful,' she said.

'Only the faithful.'

Together, they took position in the courtyard and waited. Minutes lengthened into hours; closer and closer came the scrape of bone against bone, the rattle of ribs against armour, the tread of massed steps. The first shout came from a handgunner on the battlements of the inner wall as the purple of the sky softened to pink. Grey clouds drifted slowly from nightside, threatening to consume the coming day.

'The legions are marching through the gate!' called the Free-guilder.

Crossbows and rifles cracked from the ramparts. There was a *crash* against the inner wall, and then the ancient bricks shattered into rubble.

The first wave of Mortek Guard through the wall marched with nadirite shields raised. Soft rain began to fall as the first line of Freeguild spearmen – Sergeant Ahram among them – charged with the Retributor Phaithon at their head.

Before the spearmen reached the line, a strike of Phaithon's lightning hammer incinerated shields and knocked the skeletal warriors from their footing. The Freeguilders roared, impaling the wrong-footed Bonereapers and tearing away shards of bone. As the next rank of Mortek Guard advanced, Gardus loosed the storm magics of his warcloak, lighting little blue fires in the skulls and ribcages of the enemy.

'It's working,' Thuna breathed, rain drumming around her.

All at once, the courtyard was chaos. Behind the line of Ossiarch infantry, two colossal Gothizzar Harvester constructs crashed through the shattered remains of the walls. Each was a walking engine of annihilation and conscription, flensing the flesh from the living as it reaped their bones. Ossiarch banners fluttered from their arched spines.

In the wake of the Harvesters walked a skeletal throne. Seated upon it, his skull-face a grimace, was the soulmason Al'akhos.

Al'akhos raised slender, bony fingers, and the shards of his fallen warriors rattled in the dirt, then whipped across the throats of mortals and Stormcast Eternals alike. Gardus batted away bone shards with the flat of his hammer, and when he looked out on the courtyard again, he watched a dozen Freeguilders, novices and apprentice wizards collapse bloodied in the mud. Thunder clapped as Phaithon and the Twins' broken forms exploded skywards in blasts of lightning.

'Fall back to the keep!' Gardus called, then realised the only person standing alive to hear the command was Thuna. She raised her lightning hammer and looked to him, her hair soaked and warpaint streaming down her face.

'There's no safety in the keep,' she said. 'Those Gothizzar constructs, they'll break open the temple themselves.'

Gardus gazed up at the behemoth constructs. Monstrous jaws – the skull harvested from some leviathan – bellowed, while massive bludgeons swung from their limbs. There were two of them. It was an impossible fight. But if she could buy them time…

'Now?' she asked softly.

'Now.'

Thuna Never-Reforged, Retributor-Prime of the Hallowed Knights, roared forth towards Al'akhos and his Gothizzar. The first Harvester brought down a massive sickle, but Thuna dodged away and the blade planted itself in the mud. Gardus saw her swing holy lightning into the grasping harvester-hands on the behemoths' underside before he fell back into the temple. He didn't look back when he heard the clap of thunder.

Inside the sanctum, Nawal waited. The celestial battlemage Oron was manacled and bound at her feet, but she might as well have been alone in the dim light of the collapsed star, the shadows of vines cast on the walls around her. Gardus found it difficult to read her expression.

'Is this it?' she asked. 'The end of the defence of Immanence?'

'It is,' he said quietly.

'Ah. Well.' She smiled. 'That didn't take long. The wizards who fought… they're dead, I take it?'

'It'll have to be him,' Gardus said, nodding to the battlemage.

'The entrance to the sanctum – that's our choke point. I'll hold it for as long as I can. But we don't have much time.'

The ground quaked, and something struck the walls of the temple, raining dust and leaves down over them. As Gardus fixed himself at the entrance, shoulders squared and runeblade raised, the war-abbess set about shaking Oron awake. 'I'm afraid you haven't got any choice now,' she said, 'you'll have to conjure the star and redeem yourself whether you like it or–'

There was another battering against the temple, and then the wall caved in. Brick and rubble crashed to the ground, trailing vines; Nawal leapt aside and took cover under the wheels of the celestial orrery, which somehow stood proof against the debris. The battlemage wasn't so lucky. A slab of ancient, black stone toppled into Oron and crushed the upper half of his body.

Pink dawn broke in, and the patter of rain. Thunderheads rumbled in the distance. Gardus peered through the debris. 'Nawal!' he shouted.

She stared at the dead battlemage in disbelief.

'Nawal!' he repeated. '*Thunderer! Heldenhammer!*'

Now he couldn't afford to hold her eyes any longer, because the soulmason and his Gothizzar monster-construct – only one of them now – were climbing through the gash in the temple. As he faced them, he continued to recite the names of Sigmar.

'*Chaosbane! Azyrite! Lord of the Storm Eternal!*'

He leapt onto the Gothizzar and grabbed hold of its ribs, struggling to ram his runeblade through the underside of its serpentine jaw. The thing's arms were flails wrought from ribs and spines; with the unthinking bluntness of an automaton, the construct bashed Gardus with its flail, driving him through its own chest and shattering itself in the process. The Lord-Celestant fell to the flagstone, his armour and his legs crumpled beneath him. His runeblade skittered across the ground.

'*Lightning-Eyed,*' he rasped. '*King… of Starlight…*'

The temple fell silent, except for the hollow clack of Al'akhos' throne-legs as he crossed the sanctum.

The war-abbess Nawal ib'Ayzah climbed to her feet and faced him.

'My… correspondent,' Al'akhos whispered, his voice like the rustle of dry leaves. 'You were a worthy… amusement. I want you to know… that I will honour your bones… by taking them into myself.'

Gardus tried to crawl towards the abbess, tried to raise his voice and call to her, to do *something*, but he could feel himself fading. Nawal picked up her hammer of office from amidst the debris where it had fallen.

'Thunderer,' she said.

Al'akhos tilted his head, curious. Behind the abbess, at the heart of the orrery, the conjured star pulsed and brightened. Her skinny arms shaking, the war-abbess raised the hammer level with her waist, and then her chest. Her bloodied robes billowed behind her.

'Heldenhammer,' she said. 'Lord of the Storm Eternal. King of Starlight.'

Gardus stared at the orrery and at Nawal, mouthing along with her now. The Bonereaper laughed.

'Your… god,' he said. 'Where… is he now?'

Shaking but determined, Nawal raised her hammer above her head.

'My god is in Azyr,' she said.

The lightning struck through the gouge in the temple face, alighting on Nawal's hammer. It seemed to linger there for an endless moment before forking across the machinery of the orrery and the star within. The orrery spun, and the conjured star pulsed, and the entire sanctum grew hot and bright.

As the star grew, holy lightning spread throughout Nawal's body.

Eyes wide, Gardus watched it dance across her nerves and through her veins – the storm encompassed her and consumed her. She looked across the sanctum at Gardus in bewilderment that gave way to a wry smile, as if in grudging appreciation of a grand, cosmic joke.

And all at once she was gone. Taken home to Sigmar.

Al'akhos started. Before him, a star groaned into terrible enormity. The sanctum began to burn with a celestial heat that annihilated stone and bone and mountains, temples and armies and certainties.

Gardus had lived lifetimes at war now, violence that he recalled with terrible clarity. Every time he died and was reforged, his memory of Garradan faded, and his old life became less and less of who he was.

But this time, he was laughing when the lightning took him.

YOUR
NEXT READ

PLAGUE GARDEN
by Josh Reynolds

During the greatest battles of the War for Life, the Stormcast Eternals suffered a great tragedy: the Hallowed Knights Lord-Castellan Lorus Grymn was lost to the Realm of Chaos. Now his fellow Steel Souls venture into the domain of Nurgle himself in search of their lost comrade…

BLESSED OBLIVION

Dale Lucas

'Shield to shield, brothers!' the Liberator-Prime barked. 'Close ranks the moment the refugees are through the lines!'

Klytos fell into formation, tower shield at the ready, warblade heavy in his gauntleted fist. He took a moment – the briefest of moments – to close his eyes and summon his last, fragmentary memories of the people he had loved in life.

A woman: sea-green eyes in a smooth, tanned face.

A newborn: small, impossibly fragile in his seemingly enormous hands.

An old man: face eroded like a time-worn cliff, tears on his filthy cheeks.

He stirred his memories before each battle, knowing that if he fell, he would next incarnate with even fewer of them dwelling inside him. He'd already lost their names, most meaningful details of the life he'd lived, even the smallest inkling of where or when that long-ago lifetime had unfolded. When next he was smashed and reforged upon the Anvil of the Apotheosis, there was no telling what might remain, if anything.

That thought terrified him.

A jostling. Klytos opened his eyes. His fellow Celestial Vindicators formed a vast wall of shield bosses, gleaming blades and shining turquoise armour to either side of him. For days they had protected a massive refugee band effecting a desperate retreat across the Hallost Plains towards the sea, mere hours ahead of the trailing Khornate warhost. Now, at last, the servants of the Blood God bore down upon them.

They could run no further. It was time to make a stand, however desperate.

'Prepare to close ranks!' the Liberator-Prime shouted. Klytos' world was a storm of panic and terror as the refugees fled through their spaced ranks. As he often did, Klytos saw the ghosts of his lost loved ones in the faces of the mortals they now stood to defend: there, his wife, as a fleeing mother clutching her infant; nearby, an old man with a face like his father's – or was it his grandfather's? – hobbling along on a crutch. Phantoms. Echoes of a past that every death and rebirth took him farther and farther away from.

The last of the refugees – the lucky ones – were just about to pass through the massed ranks of the Stormhost. Out on the plain, scores of unlucky stragglers were overtaken by ravening Flesh Hounds or cleaved by bloodied hellblades.

The order came. 'Shoulder to shoulder, my brothers!'

The shield wall closed. A shock wave rippled through the Stormhost, Klytos and his comrades absorbing the impact of hundreds of charging, screaming bodies as the Khornate vanguard met them. Barbed spear tips and bloodied sword blades thrust and swiped at Klytos and his Stormcast brethren around their enormous shields.

Barely discernible above the tumult: 'Make them pay, brothers! Strike! Forward!'

The battle line moved as one, the shield wall crushing the forward ranks of barbarian marauders and lesser daemonspawn. Klytos lowered his shield, warblade thrusting and slashing, mowing a bloody swathe through his amassed adversaries. All was chaos and slaughter: a storm of churned soil, clods of torn-up turf, gouts of diseased blood, gobbets of hewn flesh, the deafening ring of steel upon adamant sigmarite. Klytos revelled in the carnage: it filled him with a dutiful calm.

Then, a blasphemy enormous and terrifying advanced from the surging fray: an Exalted Deathbringer, a tower of rippling, knotted sinews and taut, leathery skin the colour of dried blood. Tall and looming, it waded through the massed bloodletters and skullreapers clogging Klytos' vision like a man striding out of a rolling surf.

The monstrosity bore in its hands an enormous, double-headed axe. As it closed on the front rank of the Stormhost – on Klytos – it drew that axe back over its broad shoulders and began hewing, right and left, indiscriminately slashing down foul comrades and shining enemies alike.

Its monstrous blade split Klytos in two, and the holy lightning of Sigmar Heldenhammer stole him from the field of battle...

That night, the slaughter abated and the plain secured, the Stormhost established a perimeter around the refugee camp. Inside that perimeter, the mortals stoked cook fires, fed empty bellies with meagre provisions, tended the wounded and comforted the dying. A chill wind skated over the Shyish plain, now moaning, now sighing, offering melancholy harmony to the hymns of the Knights-Incantor.

The songs, which should have stoked Klytos' courage and focused his warrior's heart, now filled him with a strange sense of disaffected dread. True, he was now reforged, ready once more to rejoin the eternal struggle against Chaos… yet he was nonetheless diminished; thinned, like clouds effaced by the wind.

Klytos had died many times, his very essence torn out of the Mortal Realms and returned to the Chamber of the Broken World, there to be superheated into molten impermanence, smashed by the Six Smiths upon the Anvil of the Apotheosis, and finally reformed. Vague recollections of some of those deaths yet haunted him: the searing pain as his skull was crushed beneath the hammer of a beastlord; the taste of blood as he was ridden down by the thundering hooves of charging gore-gruntas; the panic and terror that gripped him as he was butchered and dismembered by the accursed blade of a laughing daemon prince. He even suffered a recurring nightmare of slowly succumbing to suppurating pustules and a writhing maggot infestation courtesy of the vile plague sorcerers of Nurgle… though he was not sure if that benighted vision was a true memory or only a dream.

He had once tried to keep count of his many deaths and reforgings, but that count was now lost, like so many other expendable bits of him – gaping, bleeding spaces in the fabric of his consciousness that should contain something yet did not, like the persistent itch of a long-lost phantom limb, empty cavities in his memory stirring impulses he could barely understand or articulate.

The woman was a ghost in his imagination now. He remembered the wood-brown colour of her skin, the cool depths of her eyes, but he could no longer conjure features to make her face anything more than a blurred mask.

Or the babe. Was it a boy? A girl? He yet recalled how small it was in his seemingly enormous hands, but that image – a trembling newborn – was all he could summon.

Then there was the old man… Klytos no longer remembered a face, or a voice, or any wisdom imparted. All he could remember, with great effort and concentration, was the feeling of bony, arthritic hands in his own. A presence, not a person.

Why? Why could he not simply forget, and be content to do so? He saw the after-effects of reforging in every member of his conclave: the way Barnavos eternally stared into the middle distance, reciting chains of numbers and formulae; the way Hareggar treated the scouring of his warplate and the oiling of his sword blade as crucial rituals, demanding almost religious fixation; the way Jennaeus, when he thought no one was listening, recited a constantly transforming list of all the ways he had died, making of his many, painful ends a strange, martial litany.

'The sting of a spear, the bite of a blade,' he would mutter. 'Cleft in twain, unwound, unmade...'

Eagerly, hungrily, he listened to the holy hymns of the God-King, praying that the deep and sonorous harmonies of the Knights-Incantor might banish his doubt and grief entirely. He knew that such merciful amnesia, the salvation of an eternal present, should beckon to him, tempt him... but it only filled him with a sense of overwhelming panic and impending tragedy.

A great shadow fell over him. Klytos raised his eyes to find Liberator-Prime Gracchus looming at his elbow. Klytos shot to his feet. Gracchus laid one gauntleted hand on his shoulder pauldron.

'You fought well today, young Klytos,' the Liberator-Prime said gravely.

Klytos nodded. So far as he could reason out, he had been fighting in this Stormhost for several centuries... and yet, to every Liberator-Prime who had ever commanded, he was always 'Young Klytos'.

'I am proud to serve,' Klytos said, and meant it.

'I am surprised,' the Liberator-Prime said, 'to find you back in our midst so quickly. Sigmar must have great need of you.'

In truth, Klytos had been just as surprised. Reforgings usually took longer than several short hours to complete. He had idly wondered if his rushed reconstitution might account for how disordered his thoughts now were, how rattled and empty he felt.

'Sigmar's will is all,' Klytos said, and he meant that too. Or did he? His own feelings defied his understanding.

The Liberator-Prime studied him for a long, curious moment. 'Something troubles you,' he said. It was not a question.

Klytos felt fear stir in him. He could not tell Liberator-Prime Gracchus the truth. Give voice to his shame? His fear? Impossible!

Luckily, Gracchus spoke again before Klytos was forced to. 'Duty,' he said at last. 'Your reforging has left you disoriented, and only duty will restore the sense of order your still-adjusting psyche now desires.'

Klytos nodded eagerly. 'Command me,' he said, all but begging. *Anything but sitting here, contemplating it all.*

The Liberator-Prime turned towards the dark landscape stretching beyond the ragged edge of the camp's firelight. He indicated a cluster of low, rolling hills to the north-east. 'Earlier, patrols reported signs of scouts in those hills. Investigate and report. And if you find anything, your first task is to make the Stormhost aware, not to slay those you find single-handed. Am I understood?'

Klytos saluted his commander. 'Understood, Liberator-Prime. I live to serve.'

Eager for a purpose – a mission – his mind still awhirl with self-recrimination, Klytos took up his shield and his warblade and trudged off into the night, as commanded, each long stride leading him farther from the camp. In truth, he was thankful for the lone patrol, dearly hoping that duty and vigilance might somehow assuage the storm raging inside him.

Having cleared the ragged edge of the firelight, he scanned the doleful, moonlit landscape surrounding him. To the north, the bright crimson bonfires of Khorne's warband littered the plain to the black horizon. He knew their withdrawal after the day's blood-shed was only a brief reprieve before another, inevitable clash.

He was closer to the hills than the camp he had left behind when he heard the sound of excited voices, followed by the unmistakable tumult of a battle: barked orders, pounding feet and ringing steel.

'Take them!' he heard. The voice was throaty, inhuman.

Behind the hill directly ahead of him, there came a flash of bright green light.

Klytos broke into a run, aiming to remain both swift and silent. He mounted the low slope before him, trudging up towards the broad hilltop. The voices from the other side were much louder now, the din of battle more frantic.

Klytos reached the hilltop, took shelter behind a ragged line of stunted, wind-wracked old trees, and took in the scene below.

Seven enormous figures encircled a lone swordsman, trading blows with the trapped fighter and making escape impossible. An eighth large figure stood apart, watching the proceedings. A smaller figure, wrapped in a flowing cloak and cowl and bearing a wizard's staff capped by a scintillating green gemstone, haunted the edge of the melee, two bulky adversaries lying dead at his feet.

The big loner and the encircling forces were easy enough to iden-tify, even at this distance. Only a slaughterpriest possessed such magically swollen slabs of muscle, and only Chaos-tainted skull-reapers could stand beside such a preternaturally massive servant of the Blood God and not be dwarfed by him. The swordsman – lithe and swift amid those lumbering, oversized bodies – stood his ground against the attackers, but it was clear that his defences were flagging.

The cloaked figure suddenly shouted to the swordsman. 'Mala-zar, fall back!'

The voice was female.

The swordsman, Malazar, met three attackers who all rushed

him at once. One felt the bite of his steel. The other two parried the deft, deadly blows he rained upon them. Then, in desperation, the swordsman withdrew. He put his body between the cloaked woman and their slowly closing adversaries.

Part of Klytos bade himself burst from hiding and rush to their aid – but there was another impulse, a subtler one. *Wait*, it said. *Watch. Something in this makes me uneasy...*

As Klytos watched, the still-cowled woman drew a knife from beneath her cloak. She said something to her companion, but Klytos could barely hear the words.

The swordsman dropped his sword and raised his chin, exposing his throat. He acted swiftly, obediently, never taking his eyes off the advancing skullreapers.

'Back, you fools!' the slaughterpriest suddenly roared.

Two of the Bloodbound withdrew, as ordered, but the rest, rendered reckless by battle lust, advanced towards the woman, blades ready to rip and tear.

The woman stepped close to her sword-wielding companion, placed her knife at his offered throat, and sliced it open. As blood sheeted, thick and hot, from the gaping wound, she shouted strange, guttural words in a language Klytos did not recognise. With each word, the gemstone on her staff pulsed, its luminescence intensifying in seconds.

A great explosion of light suddenly erupted from the staff, an expanding corona of emerald energy that tore through the five advancing skullreapers, ripping the life right out of them and throwing their hellishly enlarged bodies to the earth. Then, as quickly as it had appeared, the great cloud of energy dissipated. Its thinned, ragged edges never touched the plot of ground to which the last two skullreapers and their slaughterpriest master had retreated.

Klytos could not believe his eyes. The woman had slain her

own companion – her protector! – and used the dark energy of his sacrifice to fuel that lethal, magical discharge. Nor had the swordsman hesitated. She demanded his life: he gave it.

But now, magical energies spent, the woman was helpless. The two remaining skullreapers charged, eager to subdue her.

'Blood for the Blood God,' one snarled in ecstasy.

'Aelven blood for the Lord of Slaughter!' his companion growled.

Aelven?

Klytos had to help her. He burst through the screen of twisted trees, ready to join the fight.

'Two Darklings,' the slaughterpriest below said slowly, 'skulking about alone in the night, between two camped armies? Why?'

Klytos froze. *Darklings.* No wonder he had hesitated when moving to defend her. He knew well the blasphemies and dark sorceries attributed to the Darkling Covens. Clearly, some part of him had sensed that darkness emanating from the sorceress and her companion.

The skullreapers were upon her. She fought bravely, using her staff as a weapon with practised assurance, but her adversaries were too large, too savage. In moments, one wrested her staff from her and tossed it aside. The other locked the aelf woman's arms in his huge, muscular hands.

The slaughterpriest approached, all but swaggering in the moonlight. 'Tell us what you're after,' he demanded, 'and the master just might make your end quick and relatively painless.'

Darkling or no, Klytos thought, *she needs help. Is Chaos not the greater foe?*

Klytos found his voice. 'Unhand her!' he bellowed.

The Bloodbound all turned towards him. Klytos did not move. Being outnumbered, he knew he would maintain his advantage only if he could draw them up the hillside and hold the high ground.

'What is this?' the slaughterpriest snarled.

'Just out for an evening stroll,' Klytos said coldly. 'And look what I find...'

'I suppose,' the slaughterpriest answered, 'you shall now tell me there are more of your infernal kind waiting, just over that rise? A battle chamber, ready to destroy us?'

'No,' Klytos said. 'Just me.'

'Kill him,' the slaughterpriest commanded. His two lumbering subordinates unhanded the sorceress, eager for a bloody duel with what they considered a more worthy adversary, and advanced up the slope. One bore a nasty-looking hellblade, encrusted with dried blood that looked black in the moonlight. The other wielded a large, lethal warhammer. Only when the first of them was nearly upon him, raising that warhammer and sounding a hideous battle cry, did Klytos finally move.

He thrust his shield forward, throwing it edge-on. The leading edge of the heavy sigmarite slab slammed hard into the mutant marauder's face and sent the hideous creature toppling backwards, blood gushing from its crushed and broken nose. As the first skull-reaper fell, Klytos pivoted to meet its sword-wielding companion, that ugly blade rising high for a killing blow. Klytos blocked the blade with a powerful, two-handed stroke, then swept his own warblade in a broad, sideward arc while his adversary's steel yet rang. The slash bit deep into the creature's muscular torso. The skullreaper roared, enraged by the painful, seeping wound, but its shock was only momentary. With a monstrous battle cry, it charged Klytos, hellblade crashing down time and again in fero-cious hammer blows, its speed and savagery more than a match for Klytos' skill and strength.

As Klytos danced across the hillside, parrying and dodging his would-be killer's attacks and struggling to land his own, he caught sight of the first skullreaper – the one stunned by his shield attack – now creeping in from the right. Below, at the foot of the hill, the slaughterpriest struggled to bind the belligerent prisoner so that he, too, could safely turn his back on her and join the fight. Klytos was fairly certain he could slay the two Bloodbound that he now faced... but if that slaughterpriest entered the fray before the other two were neutralised, any hope of survival – let alone victory – would evaporate.

The shield-stricken skullreaper suddenly charged, bellowing through a face sticky with coagulating gore. Klytos barely avoided a deadly blow from its monstrous warhammer, then ducked under the Khorne worshipper's reach and lunged sidewards, throwing all of his armoured bulk against the charging monster.

The gambit worked. The hammer-wielder crashed hard into its sword-swinging comrade and the two hit the hillside in a tangle of limbs, weapons and rusted armour. Before either could rise again, Klytos rushed to meet them. His warblade sliced the air once, twice. The heads of both skullreapers thumped down the hillside.

Klytos turned, expecting to find the slaughterpriest still trudging up the slope towards him – but the demagogue was already upon him, having closed the distance that separated them with in-human speed. The slaughterpriest bellowed praise to Khorne as he revealed his own weapon of choice: an enormous, broad-bladed battle scythe. The blade flashed in the moonlight, sweeping in a wide, savage arc towards Klytos' head.

Klytos ducked the whistling blade... barely. Half-crouched and unbalanced, Klytos thrust his sword deep into the slaughterpriest's exposed flank. The hellish prophet threw back his head and roared, but pain did not deter him. His movement yanked Klytos' warblade from his grip. Already unbalanced, Klytos was thrown to the ground. As the Stormcast raised his eyes, seeking a means of escape or some weapon close at hand, the slaughterpriest brought his death-dealing scythe down towards Klytos' hunkered form.

No escape. Another death. More pieces of Klytos, soon to be lost.

There came a sudden, blinding, sun-bright flash of emerald light. Klytos shrank from the burst, sure that, in the next instant, he would feel the bite of the slaughterpriest's scythe blade.

No killing blow came. Instead, Klytos heard the sound of sizzling, as of meat in a hot frying pan. The stink of burning flesh assailed him. Then, the night was split by an unholy scream of rage and agony. He opened his eyes.

The slaughterpriest twisted and writhed on the hillside, his enormous, muscular frame smoking as his foul skin blistered and cracked. As Klytos stared, horrified, the slaughterpriest's body seemed to be eaten from the inside out by squirming, devouring worms of pure light. The whole process took seconds. In the span of a breath, the slaughterpriest's scream was cut off, echoing into the void that claimed him as the writhing, devouring glow-worms guttered out like spent embers and disappeared.

Stunned, Klytos turned towards the aelf woman. Her cowl had finally been removed. Her long, dark hair waved placidly in the night winds, the tapered points of her ears now visible. Though she was dishevelled and slightly worse for wear, her stark, frighteningly beautiful face suggested a calm strength – fierce determination and indomitable will in equal measure. Clearly, she was not one to be trifled with.

Klytos stood and snatched his warblade from where it lay among the ashen remains of the slaughterpriest. 'My thanks,' he said, nodding towards her. 'But, I had hoped to do the rescuing, not to be rescued.'

'Such gratitude,' the aelven sorceress said drolly, then lowered her staff and turned round. She moved to the still, prone figure of her swordsman companion – the one slain by her own hand as a blood sacrifice – and knelt beside him.

'Who was he?' Klytos asked. 'A servant? A slave?'

'A friend,' the sorceress said, almost to herself. 'True and faithful. He knew his death could fuel magic sufficient to lay them low. Most of them, anyway.' She laid a single, pale hand upon his still body.

'What were the two of you doing here,' Klytos pressed, 'in sight of a Khornate battle camp?'

The aelf sorceress stood again.

'Don't worry your shiny, empty head over it,' she said. Then, staff in hand, she turned northward and began a confident march.

'Hold on!' Klytos shouted. 'You can't go that way! There are more of them!'

'Your grasp of the obvious is astounding,' she said, not stopping. 'I'll find a way through. I have to.'

'That's folly, and you know it,' Klytos said, following close behind her.

She was not listening. Well ahead of him, she mounted the slope of another hill and trudged upwards towards the ridgeline.

It was at the crest of the hill that Klytos finally caught up with her. She stared down upon the vast, level plain, the Khornate horde's camp blighting the landscape like a festering burn scar. On the soughing winds, Klytos heard the rattle of chains and the crackle of flames, mingled with cruel laughter and mournful lamentations. Beyond the Khornate camp, an eerie blue-green glow marked the place where horizon and sky met.

'What is that?' the aelven sorceress asked, eyes narrowing.

'A procession of nighthaunt,' Klytos said. 'They sometimes follow in the wake of the Blood God's minions here in Shyish, scavenging tortured spirits from the battlefield.'

The sorceress stared, eyes locked on the spectral light. Klytos studied her by the glow of the gibbous moon. Her face was a mask of cold analysis: weighing all options, considering all variables.

'Where is it you're trying to get to?' Klytos asked.

The sorceress turned then and seemed to study him, long and hard. Klytos knew that all she saw was the implacable, unreadable mask of his great sigmarite helm, but there was still a strange, probing quality to her gaze that seemed to penetrate beyond the mask, behind his hazel eyes, into the very locus of his soul and consciousness. Though armoured from head to toe, he suddenly felt naked, exposed.

Instinctively, Klytos took a single step backwards – the only retreat he could remember making since being plucked out of mortality by Holy Sigmar.

'Who are you?' he asked.

'My name,' the aelven sorceress said, 'is Lichis Evermourn. My companion and I were sent by our coven to recover something very precious, lost on the other side of that.' She gestured to the vast Khornate camp. 'I need to reach a citadel back in the foothills. That is what my companion and protector died for.'

'Impossible,' Klytos said. 'Even if you get past the camp itself, the country in its wake will be crawling with the servants of Khorne. And that's to say nothing of the terrors of Shyish itself, both living and dead.'

'Then come with me,' Lichis Evermourn said. 'As you've seen, I have powers of my own, but I could use a strong warrior – a faithful warrior – at my side.'

'No,' Klytos said flatly. 'I cannot abandon my Stormhost – my duty.'

'Your duty is not only to Sigmar,' Lichis said, 'but to Order and Light. Believe me when I say, the artefact I seek is powerful enough to risk anything for its recovery... because if the enemy discovers it, its power will be theirs, and serve their vile ends alone.'

'What is this artefact?' Klytos asked.

'A stone,' Lichis said. 'Pure Shyishan realmstone, calcified and bound into the form of a large amethyst. In the simplest terms, it restores all things – rebuilds that which is broken, regenerates that which was lost. It's remained safe and hidden in an out-of-the-way redoubt in the foothills, but its keeper and her initiates were forced to flee before she could recover the stone from its hiding place. She tried to backtrack and retrieve it, but her attempt was... unsuccessful.'

Klytos barely heard any of the words she said after *it restores all things – rebuilds that which is broken, regenerates that which was lost.*

No, he thought. *Impossible. It is heresy. Betrayal!*

'If it is so precious,' he said, 'so powerful, then go to the Storm-host commander and ask for a full conclave–'

'There is no time,' Lichis snapped dismissively. 'Besides, a larger force would be a larger target. Malazar and I had thought to slip through alone, the two of us, but now, I am forced to continue without him. And seeing what lies before me...'

She stared down at the plain.

'I need your help, Klytos,' she finally said, eyes still on the enemy camp below. 'And I will reward you for your aid.'

He had not told her his name, nor anything about himself. It had not been his imagination. She *had* opened him, examined him, and learned of his secret yearning.

Lichis Evermourn turned her large, dark eyes upon him. There was pity in those eyes now, even understanding.

'I know what you desire most of all, Klytos. The realmstone can provide it.'

He thought of the child. The woman. That rough, wizened hand in his own.

I could have them again! he thought. *In my mind, in my heart, part of me–*

'No,' Klytos said, turning from her. 'I cannot. This is a violation of my oaths... of my duty...'

He started to descend the hill.

'It's true what they say, then,' Lichis Evermourn said. 'You Stormcasts are a horde of mindless automatons, slaves without a speck of self-awareness or free will–'

Klytos stopped. Rounded on her. 'I am no slave! I serve because I was chosen!'

She moved closer, her gaze meeting his. 'Then prove it and help me. I know you want to. You'll remember *everything*, Klytos. Their names. The life you shared with them. If your existence, for all the ages yet to come, is to consist of endless cycles of death and resurrection in the name of Holy Sigmar, should you not be granted the recollection of who you were and what you lived for?'

Their names. Their faces. The woman's dark skin against his own. Songs he sang to his newborn babe. Lazy afternoons among wildflowers under sunny skies. All that, and more, could be his again, his last memento of all they shared...

'The reforging,' Klytos said, mind already turning to the future.

'Immaterial,' Lichis said. 'Once I restore what's been lost to you, it cannot be taken away again. I swear it.'

This is folly, he thought. *Only disaster can come of this. To abandon your Stormhost? To aid this woman? To feed a selfish desire?*

I serve, he reminded himself. *I fight and I have been loyal unto death, a thousand times over. Should I not reclaim this one, small thing?*

Klytos sighed. He had already made his decision, hadn't he?

'Let me recover my shield,' he said, and marched down the hill.

Their way through the hills was slow and treacherous, but they eventually cleared the Khornate camp. Once upon the open plain,

Klytos allowed Lichis to guide them. The only words they shared were pointed, utilitarian: time to rest; time to camp; movement ahead, proceed with caution. The farther they wandered from his Stormhost, the more despondent he became, his hope and guilt at war within him.

It was during their second night on the plain that Lichis made an effort to speak with him.

'You're not much for conversation,' she said.

Klytos raised his eyes. He had been contemplating the crackling flames of the pitiful fire before them. The night was cold and dark, and they had not found food since the day before. Even sufficient kindling was in short supply. He could go a long time without sustenance – any Stormcast could – but the lack of need did not quell the desire.

'I have nothing to say,' Klytos answered.

'That may be the case,' Lichis said, 'but I am hungry and bored. Make the effort, for my sake.'

'For your sake,' Klytos scoffed. 'We have nothing in common.'

'You might be surprised,' Lichis said. 'Do endless reforgings blunt your curiosity, as well? Your ability to empathise?'

Klytos sighed. 'I shall be damned for this. Cast out. Possibly obliterated.'

'Simply for reclaiming your past?' Lichis asked. 'Restoring your soul? I had no idea Sigmar was so cruel.'

Klytos raised his eyes. 'Sigmar is worthy of all praise, all admiration. He is the paragon of virtue. If he punishes me, I well deserve it.'

The sorceress smiled a little. 'And yet, you came.'

'Do not mock me!' Klytos snapped. 'You cannot understand what this feels like.'

'That's a foolish assumption,' Lichis said. 'Let me assure you, Stormcast, I've forgotten a dozen lifetimes and barely wondered what became of them. I know well what it means to lose pieces of oneself, be it to hungry time or soul-flaying trauma.'

'How do you endure it, then?' Klytos asked.

'I remind myself,' Lichis said, 'that I am not what I remember, or who I was in the past. I am only *what I do* in the present. Actions define me, not memories.'

Klytos nodded. He could appreciate that ethos – he truly could – and yet, he still felt she could not wholly comprehend his predicament.

'The memories you've lost were erased by time itself,' he said, 'and ultimately replaced with new experiences. My mind feels like a haunted castle that's collapsed and been sloppily rebuilt a hundred times over. The rooms and corridors keep shifting, changing, yet always, the ghosts remain...'

Lichis studied him in the firelight, like a wizard closely observing a newly fashioned homunculus.

'No wonder you Stormcasts are all so dour,' she finally said. 'You've lost everything that makes you human.'

'You mock me,' Klytos said.

'I pity you,' Lichis countered. 'There is a difference.'

They spent four days trekking steadily towards the mountains. In the foothills, folded into a dreary vale shrouded in mist and shadows, the citadel they sought loomed, dark and ancient upon a craggy promontory, a cluster of gloomy towers, sharp spires and peaked roofs clustered behind high, sheer curtain walls.

Klytos shuddered inwardly upon first espying the bleak old fortress. It was all the darkest essences of Shyish, extracted and distilled into a single agglomeration of sweating, night-black stone, pallid, half-dead creeper vines and brooding shadows. The front gate – tall, narrow and dark as a mountain crevasse – stood wide open, daring them to enter.

'What was this place?' Klytos asked, peering from cover behind a wall of fallen boulders and rocky scree.

Lichis, secreted beside him, met his wondering gaze with her own.

'My coven holds many such redoubts,' she said, 'in all the Mortal Realms. Places where sensitive objects of power can be hidden and guarded.'

Something moved behind the battlements: a figure visible between the crumbling merlons of the parapet. It paused in the gap and glanced out casually, scanning the grey, rocky landscape beneath the wall. It was a man, apparently human.

'Scavenger?' Klytos wondered aloud.

'Not alone, I'll wager,' Lichis said, then pointed. 'Look there.'

Something moved in the citadel's ward-yard, visible through the tall, open gateway. Another man, carrying in his arms an unwieldy pile of some sort: plundered provisions or stolen treasure, perhaps. Above, the skulker on the rampart turned and shouted something down to his companion. An unintelligible answer was given. The man on the rampart withdrew into a corner tower. The one in the courtyard disappeared from view.

'The way is clear,' Lichis said. 'Let's go.'

They hurried over the bleak, open ground before the citadel and shortly arrived at the yawning gate. There before them stretched a deep, dark alley between high, sweating walls, all shrouded in darkness under the looming bulk of the gatehouse. The lower extremities of not one, but two raised portcullises hovered high in the murk above them like titanic jaws, poised to snap. The passage stank of mildew, mould and stale ash.

As they advanced, Klytos more clearly heard voices from the courtyard. He discerned only two of them.

'A good haul,' one of them said.

'How far back to the crossroads?' the other asked. 'A day? Two?'

'It's west for us,' the first answered. 'Over the mountains.'

The second man cursed such a long, dispiriting journey. Klytos was just about to step into the yard, when Lichis suddenly swept past him. Heedless and impatient, the sorceress strode forwards, staff in hand, wearing a narrow-eyed grimace that suggested she deeply disapproved of finding thieves in this place.

'Lichis,' Klytos hissed. 'What are you doing?'

The two men – busy packing the overstuffed saddlebags on their horses – bickered on for a moment before finally noticing that they were not alone.

Lichis stood in the centre of the courtyard, the ferrule of her staff planted firmly beside her. Klytos hurried out of hiding to join her.

'What's this?' the first man asked. 'Some aelven conjuress and her pet Stormcast?'

'Better than a pair of diseased vultures,' Lichis said, 'picking over the bones of a fresh corpse.'

The gem at the head of Lichis' staff pulsed impatiently.

The second man drew a short sword sheathed at his hip, though he looked far too scared to use it. The first man held out a hand, calming his companion.

'Now see here,' he said to Lichis. 'The place was abandoned–'

'So,' Lichis said, 'you thought to help yourself to its treasures?'

'And its stores,' the second man said. 'We were hungry.'

'Lichis,' Klytos said quietly, 'these two are no threat. Settle this peacefully.'

'We don't want any trouble,' the first man said.

'There will be no trouble,' Lichis said. 'Go now, with only the clothes on your back and you shall not be harmed. None of what you found shall leave with you.'

'Just a minute,' the first man said, impatient.

The second man, trembling, suddenly dropped his sword and tried to bolt for the citadel gate.

Lichis levelled her staff. A fat green fireball shot from the pulsing gem and enveloped the fleeing looter mid-stride.

Klytos lunged for his companion. 'Lichis, no!'

The first man stared, goggle-eyed, at his screaming, writhing comrade, now swathed in livid green flames. The looter turned to Lichis, eyes wide, opening his mouth. Klytos guessed he was about to beg for mercy.

Lichis loosed another fireball. The man burst into flame. His words became agonised screams, echoing in the courtyard in atonal harmony with his still-dying companion. Klytos smelled the sickly-sweet stench of burning flesh. Those flames, despite their wholly unnatural green hue, burned forge-hot. In seconds, both men lay still and silent on the debris-strewn earth of the courtyard.

Klytos grabbed Lichis by one thin arm and whirled her round to face him.

'Murderer!' he growled.

'Think of me as an exterminator,' Lichis said. 'Rousting out and eradicating the vermin.' With that, she shook loose from Klytos' grip and marched across the yard. The laden horses had shied from the flames and retreated. Lichis chose the nearer of the two, drew the knife at her belt – the same knife used to sacrifice her companion, Malazar – and slashed the overstuffed saddlebags it bore. The contents tumbled out in a clamorous clatter.

Klytos stared, stunned and silent as Lichis began rifling through the trinkets and provisions and small, second-rate treasures freed from the saddlebags. She seemed to be searching for something but finding no sign of it. Disgusted, she closed on the second horse, some distance away. In seconds, its saddlebags were slashed and emptied as well.

Klytos looked to the two flaming corpses now bleeding gouts of thick, black smoke. Thieves? Perhaps. Small men, of mean character? Certainly. But worthy of death? And such hideous, agonising deaths, at that? Hardly.

He might have been with his Stormhost at that very moment, doing what he was forged to do: slaying minions of Chaos, shielding those innocent, frightened refugees as they raced for the coast and the ships waiting to bear them away. He should have been serving a greater good... but instead, here he stood, a party to murder, serving his own selfish ends.

I've proven Lichis wrong in this, at least, Klytos thought mordantly. *I am no slave. I have free will. I can make my own choices. And I am starting to believe I made the wrong one.*

All at once, Klytos found his Stormcast helm constricting, practically choking him. Irritated, he yanked the helm free and tossed it to the ground. He paced the yard, drinking deeply of the stale air.

He suddenly realised that the sorceress was studying him, her normally unreadable face evincing bewilderment, even a kind of wonder.

'What are you staring at?' Klytos asked.

'Your face,' she said. 'I'm shocked by just how *ordinary* you look.'

'Why did you kill them?' Klytos asked. 'These weren't the servants of the Dark Gods. They were two fools looking for baubles to sell and provisions to see them through a night or two!'

'How do you know who they were?' Lichis shot back, voice cold. 'Or what they were capable of?'

'You read me,' Klytos answered. 'Are you saying you read them? Saw undeniable evidence of the threat they posed?'

'A waste of time,' Lichis said. 'Besides, I had to be sure.'

'Sure of what?' Klytos demanded.

'That they hadn't found it first,' Lichis answered.

Klytos had no reply. His presence here, with this woman, was a blight upon his honour as a Stormcast, a stain upon his soul. Suddenly weary and eager to be away from her, he sighed.

'Where is it, then?' he asked.

Lichis turned and set out towards a gloomy span of wall crowded between a looming keep and a low, squat chapel beside it. Only when Klytos squinted and studied the wall did he realise there was an open doorway set into it.

'Follow me,' Lichis said without looking back.

They descended by way of a narrow stone stairway into a winding catacomb littered with ancient bones and choked with cobwebs bestirred by soft, phantom breezes that slithered up and down the subterranean passage. The only light was the sickly green glow from the gem on Lichis' staff.

'I am starting to believe you tricked me,' Klytos said darkly after a long silence.

Lichis stopped. Turned. She clearly wanted him to see her face – to look into her dark, ageless eyes – as she spoke.

'If I wanted to send you back to Sigmar for yet another re-forging, I could have done so long before now. I brought you with me for a reason, Stormcast. Until your purpose is served, it is my responsibility to protect you, not to endanger you.'

Klytos studied the aelven sorceress. He found her face alternately beautiful and terrible in the garish green light of that jewel on her staff. Her dark eyes appraised him, deconstructed him. All he could do was stand, enduring it like a helpless, scolded child.

'And just what is my purpose?' Klytos asked her.

A strange, sly half-smile bloomed on Lichis' face. 'What you were made for. Come along, now. We're almost there.'

With that, Lichis carried on down the passage. Klytos marched after her.

In moments, they emerged into a large, airy crypt. Its high ceiling was supported by elegant ribbed vaulting crusted with ancient, pale fungi and ragged, long-decaying cobwebs. More tombs for interment were carved into the chamber's widely spaced walls, some of the vaults sealed, others smashed and yawning wide. The centre of the room was dominated by twin rows of enormous sarcophagi, each capped by a massive, carved stone slab. At least one of those princely tombs had been broken into and rifled through, for its slab lay broken beside it and the bones of its former occupant – now cracked and degraded with age – lay strewn about on all sides. Piles of old crates, haphazardly stacked furniture and ancient hogsheads crammed into out-of-the-way corners suggested that those who dwelt in the citadel had, at some point, so thoroughly disregarded the sanctity of this crypt that they'd used it as surplus storage.

But the most troubling sight were the skeletons, along with two corpses that looked – by comparison, at least – rather fresh. These remains were tossed about in various locations and positions, most still wearing scraps of old cloth or rusted mail. A fallen weapon lay close to each: a sword, a maul, a hand axe. Instinctively, Klytos knew these could not be the scattered bones of the crypt's ancient occupants, for the arrangement of each skeleton suggested that it had decayed where it fell. The two fresher corpses, likewise, evidenced signs of distress. One had probably been there four or five years, for it still had skin, though that skin was now dried and wrinkled like old parchment on the cusp of disintegration.

The other corpse, however, looked entirely too fresh. A day old. Maybe two. There was still moisture on the dead man's bulging, affrighted eyes and signs of bruising under his ashen skin. The man's face was a horror, frozen in wide-eyed terror and gape-mouthed disbelief, as if he had died of fright.

Klytos studied the grim tableau as Lichis moved quickly among the sarcophagi, hastily perusing the carved glyphs upon each in search of some sign of her quarry.

'Here,' she said at last. 'Help me.'

'What happened here?' Klytos demanded. 'These dead scattered about – they are not the ones buried here.'

'You're wasting time,' Lichis snapped. 'Help me!'

Klytos, despite his misgivings, hurried to Lichis' side and laid his weight upon the great, heavy slab that capped the sarcophagus. Inch by inch, the slab slid and groaned, revealing dusty, undisturbed darkness within. Overbalanced, the slab pitched sidewards and tumbled to the floor of the crypt with a thunderous crash.

Lichis hesitated for a moment, then clambered over the lip of the open sarcophagus. Inside, she crouched among the old, rotten shroud and long-undisturbed bones of the tomb's occupant. Careless and businesslike, Lichis hastily shoved the old bones and decayed rags aside to reveal a hidden, round carving beneath.

The carving was a seal of some sort, though Klytos did not recognise the swirling, interlocking symbols upon it. As he watched, Lichis planted the ferrule of her staff upon the seal, then gripped her staff tightly in both hands.

'Listen to me carefully,' she said, 'for this is why I need you. I have to open this seal, and it will take a great deal of time and energy for me to do so. The moment I begin, the crypt's guardian will awaken.'

'The guardian?' Klytos drew his sword. 'You bloody, evil witch! You said nothing of–'

'We both have a part to play in this, Klytos,' Lichis said testily. 'You can't get at the stone without my magic and I can't work my magic unless you fend off and slay the guardian. *This* is why I need you. *This* is how you earn your reward.'

Klytos was filled with a righteous, murderous fury. He wanted to yank the Darkling sorceress out of the open sarcophagus and hack her limb from limb. How could he have been such a fool?

Lichis continued. 'The guardian is your shadow, Klytos – a Knight of Shrouds, interred here long ago as penance for his betrayal. Your faith is proof against his wickedness. Let that serve you.'

Then she began her working, murmuring a rapid, tripping canticle in an ancient tongue. The green gem at the head of her staff began to glow. Beneath her, the carven inlays on the seal pulsed, the energies locked within them stirring and intensifying, moment by moment.

Klytos felt a strange prickling at the nape of his neck. The air around him was suddenly cold – unnaturally so. He had also become aware of an eerie glow gathering behind him, casting his own, long shadow on the debris-strewn floor of the crypt. Though encumbered by armour and several layers of cloth, he felt goose pimples rising on his flesh. He even saw his breath, pluming hot from between his gnashed teeth. The very air in the crypt had changed, and something vile now stirred behind him.

It spoke before he ever turned to face it.

'Foolish plunderers!' it boomed in a raspy voice like rusted hinges protesting movement after centuries idle. *'What blasphemy is this?'*

Klytos turned, steeling himself for the horror that was about to reveal itself. He had faced a thousand enemies, slain bloodletters, Chaos knights, gargants and orruks. He had stood his ground against charging razorgors, slavering jabberslythes and snapping, venomous chimerae.

But now, it would appear, he faced an enemy unlike any other.

The Knight of Shrouds materialised above another opened sarcophagus and hovered there, seemingly anchored where it floated. The phantom's leering, skeletal face bore some subtle and dreadful potency – a deeper, more malignant darkness in its gaping eye sockets; a mocking, lopsided set to its rictus grin – that made its visage more frightening than anything Klytos had ever seen. Radiating the same, sickly, blue-green light that all the ghostly damned of Shyish were imbued with, the abomination towered over him, its flowing, spectral robes simultaneously real enough to grasp and as immaterial as swirling smoke. Only the enormous, two-handed blade it held in one skeletal fist seemed truly solid.

Klytos tightened his grip on his warblade. *Sigmar*, he prayed, *forgive me.*

'*Stormcast*,' the phantasm said slowly, as if savouring the very word. '*Quake, fear, for I am your ruin!*'

Summoning his courage, Klytos reminded himself why he'd come here. He wanted his past. He wanted the people he'd lost and forgotten restored to him. He wanted to be whole again. If he had to slay this beast to do that... so be it.

'Creature of the grave,' he said slowly, 'I am Stormcast, a Celestial Vindicator, and I have no master but Sigmar Heldenhammer. To claim what I have come for, I will gladly cast you back into the pit you slithered out of!'

The ghostly knight howled – whether in disbelief at Klytos' bravado or delight in the challenge to come, he could not say. Its foul, shrieking voice stirred a maelstrom of cold, spectral winds in the vast crypt.

Then, it attacked.

The world around Klytos became a storm of frigid, biting air, ghastly cackling and shifting pools of ghastly blue-green luminescence. He spun and pivoted, seemingly beset by the Knight of Shrouds on all sides: in front, behind, to the left, to the right. Its enormous sword sliced the foetid air, again and again, as his own shining sigmarite blade rose and fell with almost painful slowness to fend off its attacks. Here, a lucky parry. There, a blocked thrust. A clumsy dance sideways, narrowly avoiding a death blow. A skating retreat. A scrambling recovery.

Preparing for another attack, Klytos stole a glance at Lichis. She still crouched in the sarcophagus, rooted and unmoving, the gem on her sorcerer's staff pulsing brightly as she recited the alien words of the spell intended to unlock that seal. Every muscle in her body was rigid and tense, her immense concentration and adamantine willpower exhausting to behold.

Then the Knight of Shrouds shrieked and charged again. Klytos barely deflected the monster's first attack, then struck in answer. It was a sloppy but savage blow, his sword blade arcing in a wide horizontal chop. As the bright sigmarite passed through the undead knight's ghostly, insubstantial form, Klytos felt a strange sensation.

Resistance. Solidity. His blade had hit *something*.

Confirming his sudden suspicion, the Knight of Shrouds screamed, whirled and retreated. Its cry was high and maddening, boring deep into Klytos' ears, stabbing at the very centre of his consciousness – but he revelled in it. He had struck the spirit! Hurt it!

The Knight of Shrouds recovered and patiently circled, studying its would-be prey. Its howling shriek subsided to a ragged chuckle, low and ominous. Klytos, glad for the moment's reprieve, began his own slow circle of his aetheric adversary, blade ready.

'Despair, Stormcast!' the knight taunted. *'Look upon my face and see your own! I betrayed my vows to earn my place here! What shall become of you, oh faithless fool, when I strike you down? Can your shining God-King draw your soul back to Azyr even here, at the threshold of the Afterdark?'*

Then, as its taunt still rang in Klytos' ears, the nighthaunt exploded forwards, swift and shark-like through the empty air. Its sword rose for another attack. Klytos started to retreat, felt one of the sarcophagi blocking that retreat, and knew there was only one choice: forwards.

Without hesitation, he launched himself and his upraised warblade straight towards the onrushing phantom. He managed to get inside the knight's sword-strike, but this time, Klytos' own blade seemed to touch nothing at all. He rushed through the bone-chilling cold of the creature's swirling, spectral essence – through the creature itself – before finally breaking free again on the far side. Shivering with a combination of terror and rage, he crashed to the crypt floor.

Impossible! he thought. *Too fast! Too strong! How can I fight it?*

'Your faith, Klytos!' Lichis suddenly shouted from where she knelt, still at her magical work. 'Remember why you came here! Why you trusted me!'

Klytos turned, preparing to meet another charge from the Knight of Shrouds – this attack likely to finish him.

The knight whirled to face him. It hovered in the stale air of the burial chamber, empty black eyes radiating cruelty and contempt. Its notched and ancient blade reflected the sickly blue-green light emanating from it.

'Tiring, are you, Stormcast?' the fiend hissed. *'Come now! Throw down your sword! Let me show you the way to true eternal life! It has been so long since I've known a companion here...'*

Klytos felt a fury suddenly rise in him. All at once, he realised that it was not Sigmar he had no faith in – only himself. His shame, his desire to reclaim his past, had convinced him that he was inferior... lesser... unworthy.

But had not Sigmar *chosen him?*

Whomever he mourned, whatever he desired, it was part of him, the very essence of who and what he was. And Sigmar – his master, his god – knew every dark and shadowed corner of his heart. Sigmar knew what Klytos wanted...

...and he had brought Klytos here, now, into this chamber, to prove his mettle.

To test his faith.

The Knight of Shrouds dived through the air towards him, sword drawn back for a vicious, killing blow.

Klytos sprang to his feet, lunged, and met the falling blade with a mighty blow from his own. The swords rang like bells in the crypt's dank air.

Determined, enraged, Klytos struck before the knight had even a moment to recover. His blade thrust forwards, its razor-sharp point seeking the misty, blue-green heart of the 'haunt's diaphanous form.

And there, it seemed to strike something.

The knight's skeletal jaw fell open and it screeched, a deafening sound drenched in pain, fury and disbelief.

Klytos laid both hands on his sword-grip and twisted the blade.

The knight dropped its sword and the ancient blade hit the crypt stones with a loud clatter. At its extremities, the spectral devil was discorporating, its grasping, skeletal fingers already swirling into the aether, their blue-green light extinguished.

'For Sigmar!' Klytos roared.

He withdrew his blade and brought it round in a wide, powerful arc, slashing right through the centre of the floating knight. Again, he felt the blade pass through something solid – something now hewn in twain by his attack. As the blade cut the Knight of Shrouds in two, the creature gave a last, mortified scream, then dissipated into swirling smoke and vanished.

Klytos waited, half expecting the vile guardian to suddenly reappear. But, no… the phantom did not return. He turned towards Lichis. The sorceress yet recited her eldritch incantations, the rich green light from the gemstone capping her staff now blinding, since it was the only light in the chamber. The seal beneath her glowed angrily, as though it might turn to molten rock and swallow her at any moment.

Then, as though some unseen boulder had suddenly fallen upon it, the seal shattered. Simultaneously, its glow was extinguished. Realising her spell had, at last, succeeded, Lichis lifted her staff and stumbled away from the broken seal. She leaned on the edge of the sarcophagus, gulping air, physically exhausted. As the glow of her gem subsided, her eyes darted about the chamber, searching.

'The guardian?' she asked.

'Destroyed,' Klytos said.

'Well done,' Lichis answered. Her lips curled at the corners in something like a proud smile.

'Where is it?' Klytos asked. 'Let us be done with it.'

Lichis nodded, sighed, and knelt back in the sarcophagus again. She hastily yanked out the shattered pieces of the broken seal and tossed them aside, revealing beneath a shallow depression. In that depression rested a square box of medium size and impressive workmanship. Lichis snatched up the box. Her elegant fingers worked the many cunning latches that held it shut. Inside that box lay Klytos' salvation.

It was a gem, about the size of a closed fist, possessing planar facets, rough edges and occluded depths that made it seem both naturally occurring and wilfully made, as if the earth itself had set out to fashion a work of art. A hypnotic glow emanated from within the gemstone: amethyst light, just like the inherent magical energies that had powered and pummelled Shyish through the ages, as though a small, purple sun burned at the heart of the great jewel.

Lichis displayed the gem in her outstretched hand. 'Do you see?' she asked, evincing something like wonder and piety for the first time in the many days that Klytos had known her.

'Indeed,' Klytos breathed in wonder, then glanced at his companion. She wore a strange expression, as if eager to speak but unsure of the right words. Klytos felt cold rage rising in him. 'Why do you hesitate?'

'That which you ask,' Lichis said, 'you may find that you did not want.'

'*No more games,*' Klytos snarled. 'Do your work now, witch! Fulfil your vow to me!'

'I warned you,' Lichis said, then placed both her hands upon the gem and began a new incantation.

Little by little, the light at the heart of the gem intensified. Klytos instinctively felt that he should look away or cover his eyes, but that light, no matter how bright or blinding it became, all but demanded his hungry gaze. It drew him out of himself. It sang to him. Caressed him.

The light became a void, and Klytos plunged into that void.

The woman, his wife: Nara. His one true love. Beauty and grace incarnate. Her wood-brown skin, so smooth and delicate. Her eyes, green as pale emeralds, deeper than forest pools. He remembered kisses. Lazy afternoons beneath bright summer suns. Seeing dream-beasts in the passing clouds. Lovemaking. The joy that leapt in him when she told him she was with child.

Then, the sights, sounds and smells all changed. He heard the ring of steel on steel mingling with shrill screams. Saw fire and smoke. Smelled burning flesh and the coppery tang of blood. There Nara stood, amid surging, panicked villagers searching for egress from a tightening cordon of bloodthirsty reavers – human and inhuman alike. Klytos was too far away from her. He struggled, feet tugged at by sucking mud, tripping upon hacked corpses, his way barred by fallen, flaming debris.

Nara clutched the baby – Xandia, that was her name! A little girl, swathed in her favourite, hand-stitched blanket. The baby screamed in Nara's arms. Klytos saw one small hand emerge from the folds of the blanket, clutching at her mother's trailing braid.

Gods and daemons of an elder age, he knew what was about to happen!

A reaver suddenly towered over Nara. The barbarian's sword was sharp, his eyes alight with cruelty. Nara screamed. Down came the blade. Nara was silenced, forever.

Xandia still lived, wriggling in her slain mother's arms. The marauder who had cut Nara down bent, snatched up the baby in its bundle and lumbered away, Klytos' only child tucked neatly in his filthy embrace.

It did not happen once. It happened again and again, replayed in Klytos' memory like some foul verse from a catchy tavern song, repeating, repeating, repeating, resisting all attempts to purge it. Klytos tried to close his eyes, to summon memories of love and joy to counter the horror that repeated, time and again, before his unwilling gaze. He tried to recall meeting Nara, courting Nara, holding Nara in his arms on a cold winter's night, watching Nara scream and cry as she brought their daughter into the world.

But those memories were little more than a cloud of swirling gnats – tiny, unreal, ephemeral. They could not banish the horribly *real* sight of Nara dying under that reaver's sword. Of Xandia, borne away to live life as a slave – or worse, as the child of the barbarian that stole her, wholly ignorant that her apparent father had murdered the woman who'd given birth to her. Of Klytos, separated from them by slaughter and ruin, too late to protect them, too weak to pursue and overtake their murderer, to avenge them.

Then the old man returned to him. Phiro, father of Klytos, a simple sort: farmer, village elder, trader in orchard fruits and home-fermented wines. A strong man, a proud man, a good man.

Phiro, ruined by a fall in old age. Phiro, bent and twisted by injury and the indifference of time. Phiro, poisoned by an apothecary's out-of-date stock, rendered speechless and vegetative. Phiro, a twisted, bony marionette lying prone in a bed beside a fire, shivering because he was cold – he was *always* so cold – his cataract-clouded eyes begging his son for a final reprieve.

Phiro's skeletal old hand, thick with calluses, squeezing Klytos' own. The old man had no words left, but Klytos understood well enough. His father wanted the mercy – the dignity – of a quiet end at the hand of someone who loved him. The old man wanted peace, release… and Klytos was not brave enough to give it. He allowed that poor, wizened creature to lay there on his piss-stained bed for weeks, dying in slow, small increments. Klytos knew what the old man wanted – what the old man needed – but he was too selfish, too craven, to bestow it.

No. This could not be. These were not the memories Klytos wanted. These were not what he had fought to reclaim. He wanted love, joy, familiarity, the prosaic; the simple, long-forgotten pleasures of mortal life.

He rifled his memories in search of pleasure – any pleasure – amid the now swirling storm that assailed him. He tore through them and tossed them about in desperation, as a thirsty traveller in the desert might ransack an abandoned camp for a hidden gourd containing the smallest drink of water. Intermittently, he found those delights. Childhood. Innocence. Play. Imagination. Love and romance. Hopes and dreams born of affection and intimacy. He found cherished memories of his father's nurturing love and paternal pride, of laughter and friendship, of adventure and excitement. There was dancing. There were drunken revels.

But these pleasures were all isolated, intermittent, fleeting. Sickly, stunted roses on a malignant, ever-expanding thorn bush. Every petal of memory seemed to hide in its shadows a darker twin, the prick of exposed spines, the scuttle of insects and the stains of lurking rot. Slain friends. Ill relatives. His village wracked by plague. A winter famine that forced a nearby tribe to tear itself to pieces, the strong and cunning feasting upon their friends and neighbours. He even relived the bitter, senseless loss of his mother when he was yet a child; how she died twitching after being kicked in the head by a mule.

All pleasures were tempered by loss and pain. All hope was

swallowed, over time, by sudden, foolish calamities or incomprehensible cruelties.

Klytos heard someone screaming. After a time, he realised the cries were his own.

'Deserted,' Eigrim said, surveying the citadel's shadowy inner ward. His four companions spread out, weapons at the ready, searching the sheltered corners of the courtyard, certain that some danger yet awaited them.

A stone's throw from where Eigrim stood, Torgo poked at a strange, charred mass – one of two – with the beak of his axe.

'What'd you find there?' Eigrim asked.

Torgo's face twisted up mordantly. 'Dead men,' he said. 'Charred to a crisp.'

Rinz toed through a pile of trinkets spread haphazardly over the gravel. 'Looks like someone was here,' he said. 'There's some good stuff. Trade-worthy, anyway. And look at this...'

Rinz snatched up a large, shining object lying discarded on the well-trod earth. It was a heavy, turquoise-hued helm of a very distinct and unique design.

'That's a Stormcast helm,' Eigrim said.

'Aye,' Rinz agreed, turning the big, heavy object over in his hands to study it. 'But what's it doing out here?'

Eigrim offered no explanation. He had seen Stormhosts in battle, if only from a distance. Their warriors were demigods. Order, discipline and inhuman devotion were their hallmarks. They did not simply abandon those masked helms of theirs. His eyes skated sideward towards the dead men. Could one of those be the owner of the helm?

Impossible, he reminded himself. *When they die, their god yanks them back to his holy halls. If a Stormcast fell here, not a trace would remain.*

'Stormcast or no,' Torgo insisted, '*someone* was here, and not long ago.'

Eigrim said nothing. He was ready to bolt right back out of that gate without a single bauble in hand. Something strange was afoot.

'We should go,' he said. 'Now.'

Then, a voice boomed into the yard. 'You there!' it shouted. 'Looters! Thieves!'

The men went rigid where they stood. Every weapon rose in readiness.

A huge figure in shining plate armour lurched out of a low, dark doorway across the yard: clearly, the owner of the helm. The Stormcast Eternal's warplate trailed wisps of cobwebs and shone dully where ancient dust lay caked upon it, as though the holy paladin of Sigmar had just crawled out of a filthy cellar. An enormous broadsword was gripped in one hand but trailed behind the Stormcast, its point cutting a shallow track through the dirt.

His face was ordinary enough – olive skin; a mop of black, curly hair; piercing hazel eyes under heavy brows – but the way he staggered and blinked under the wan light of the cloud-shrouded Shyishan sun made Eigrim uneasy. He looked weary and hysterical at once, like a berzerker whose bloodlust had just abandoned him. His eyes bulged, darting about anxiously.

Eigrim knew a madman when he saw one.

'Stay where you are,' the Stormcast commanded, and raised his sword in threat. 'I have need of you. All of you.'

Eigrim held out a hand. 'We're not looking for trouble.'

'Kill me,' the Stormcast said.

Eigrim blinked. 'What's that?'

'Kill me,' the Stormcast said again. 'Kill me, now, or I'll hew down the lot of you. This has to stop. If I die, maybe… *maybe…*'

The others looked to Eigrim. Eigrim looked to them. He had no idea what to do. They were far enough from the stumbling

Stormcast that they could, perhaps, make a break for the gate and simply outrun him–

Without warning, the Stormcast charged Rinz, sword rising.

'Kill me!' he cried.

Rinz dropped the helm and tried to run, but he was too slow. The Stormcast cleaved him in two with a single stroke.

The others all gasped, shouted, cursed. What was happening? This was insane! A mad Stormcast, begging death and threatening it in the same instant?

Torgo charged, roaring as he went. Rinz had been his oldest friend. Eigrim knew that the warrior had every intention of cutting that Stormcast down where he stood. His big, beaked axe rose high for a mighty chop.

The Stormcast lowered his sword and opened his arms, as if for an embrace.

'Torgo, stop!' Eigrim shouted.

Torgo skidded to a halt. His axe still hovered, but he was several yards from where the Stormcast stood, waiting for the death blow. The barbarian looked to his commander. Eigrim shook his head and gave a simple gesture. Torgo, shaking with rage, fell back.

The Stormcast, denied his hoped-for death, looked to Eigrim. 'You cowards! I slew your companion. Kill me!'

Eigrim spoke, addressing his men. 'We need to go. Now.'

The Stormcast strode forwards. 'No! Kill me, I said! Kill me now, where I stand, or I'll slaughter you all!'

'Friend,' Eigrim said. 'We have no quarrel with you.'

'I have quarrel with him,' Torgo snarled.

'I remember it,' the Stormcast said quietly, almost to himself, then began babbling. 'I remember all of it. *All of it!* Kill me and send me back to Sigmar, I beg you! She said reforging would change nothing but maybe, just maybe...'

'Everybody out!' Eigrim commanded, and began a backward

retreat towards the gate. The men obeyed, all effecting their withdrawals in reverse, keeping their eyes on the mad, raving Stormcast.

'Come back here!' the Stormcast Eternal cried. 'I command you, in the name of Sigmar Heldenhammer, *to kill me where I stand!*'

Eigrim wished he had words. Clearly, this fool was hurting, broken somehow. Stormcasts were, in his experience, creatures barely human. They felt no fear, no hate, no love, no pity – they were simply engines of destruction and wrath, given human form and set against the hordes of Chaos. What could have so bewitched this poor devil to leave him murderous and suicidal in the same instant?

I remember it, he kept saying. What did that even mean?

Eigrim was ready to turn his back, to run for the gate, when the Stormcast's mad ranting dissolved into a fierce battle cry. The great, plated giant charged Torgo. His sword was high. His face was a mask of fury and desperation.

'*Kill me!*' he cried as he ran Torgo through with his shining blade. '*Kill me, I beg you!*'

The others hesitated in the shadow of the gate, staring, confused.

'Go!' Eigrim commanded. 'Run!'

The three of them went pounding out of the bleak old fortress through the long, dark tunnel under the gatehouse. Behind them, they heard the Stormcast cursing them, challenging them, even as he cried to the indifferent sky.

'*Kill me!*' he howled, his voice broken and desperate. '*Kill me, in mercy's name...*'

YOUR
NEXT READ

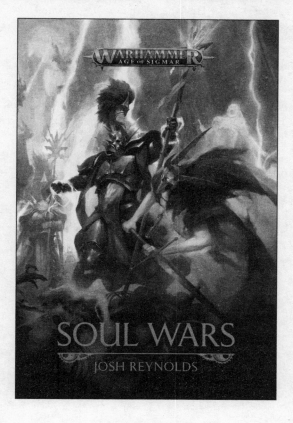

SOUL WARS
by Josh Reynolds

Nagash is rising. As his legions march forth from Shyish to bring death to all the realms, the Anvils of the Heldenhammer stand firm in Glymmsforge, a city of Order in the heart of Nagash's domain…

THE SERPENT'S BARGAIN

Jamie Crisalli

Laila wriggled into the hole dug deep under the hut she called home. The hole was little wider than her hips and she yanked the stone cover over the opening, sealing her in a womblike darkness. Small holes the size of an old Pelos coin let in air. Thin roots tickled her freckled skin and the smell of Ghyran loam smothered her nose. A cache of water and bread in a sealed clay pot sat between her bare feet. In her shaking hand, she clutched a small leather bottle on a string around her neck.

Raw screams and exultant roaring filtered down to her in that tiny hollow. And other, more obscene sounds as the fiends went about their horrid joys. Of all the places in Ghyran, the followers of the Needful One had come to her village of Varna. The new palisade had not kept them out, nor had any fighter that they possessed.

Up above, the hut door banged open and she started, her heart racing.

A man moaned and licked his lips.

'Not much sport here,' he said, his voice melodious.

'This is the first settlement in weeks not tainted by those reeking pus-bags,' said another. 'So, I'd enjoy yourself while you can. These little people are entertaining enough.'

Something crashed over, shards of pottery scattering across the floor. And they talked about what they had done and would do if they found someone. Shuddering, Laila clamped a callused hand over her mouth and pressed herself deeper into the dirt. Her mind shrinking away from the memories of her husband's tortured last moments years ago, Laila worked the stopper out of the bottle and a dusty smell like dead flowers filled the air. She would not die as he had.

Inside was a poison called Blood of the Wight; it was not painless but it was lightning quick. Her mother had given it to her when she was a child and told her to keep it with her even when she slept. There were numberless things worse than dying.

With a hiss, the raiders went quiet. A shadow crept over the breathing holes, sniffing. Laila put the bottle to her lips. Then a shrill hollow tone wended over the town, reverberating in her head.

'Is that a retreat?' one asked in disbelief.

'I would watch your forked tongue unless you want to be the cure for Lord Zertalian's ennui,' said the other. 'Clearly he wishes to save this place for future amusement. So let's go.'

Ceramic crunched under foot and the door banged shut. Yet, Laila could not move. She stayed, holding the poison to her lips, staring at the dirt wall, trying to breathe quietly. Only a buzzing tension remained, as if her head were full of bees. What if it was a trick and they had not left, instead waiting to pounce? No, it was better to stay in here with poison than risk that fate. Even as her sturdy legs cramped and her lips went numb, she held still. Then a familiar voice called her name.

'Stefen!' she called, her voice ragged.

Laila crammed the stopper back into the bottle and clambered out of her sanctuary. Then she paused.

Her home was wrecked, her meagre belongings tossed about and broken, her food stores spilled and trampled. Still, she was lucky – only her things had been touched by the seekers. She would burn it all as was tradition with tainted things. Hopefully the elders would spare the hut itself or she would have to move in with a neighbour during winter.

Stefen rushed in, his dark eyes wide.

She embraced him, trembling and choking back tears. He was an old childhood friend; they had gone on to their separate lives when he had become a hunter and she had married Jonas.

'It's all right, they're gone,' he said, pulling her close. Stefen was tall and well built, though the Rotskin pox had left him with scarred, pallid skin, ruining his good looks. A clutch of scrawny birds swung over his shoulder, along with his snares and bow.

A wash of cold fear rolled through her as the gossip of the raiders rattled in her brain.

'Are the elders still with us?' she asked.

'Yes, they were spared,' he said.

'They need to know,' she said.

Without waiting to see if he followed, she rushed out into the bright light of the Lamp. The palisade gate dangled as men worked desperately to wrench the doors back into place. Homes burned, releasing sweet smoke and pale flames as ashen-faced neighbours watched, making no move to put them out. Others wandered aimlessly, their clothing torn and eyes utterly vacant, while some desperately called out for missing loved ones. Horror seeped through the very air as if some malign spirit had made a home in every hut and heart, a final curse bestowed by the fiends. No doubt it would linger for years.

Laila walked, eyes seeing but unable to understand it, same as it had been then. The horrid memories edged into her mind and she forced them away. Jonas was long dead, praise Alarielle.

By some miracle, the stone elders' hall had not been touched. Some speculated that it was once a temple devoted to a forgotten storm god. Perhaps that was why the fiends avoided it.

Inside, the place was stifling hot, the fires burning high to warm old bones. Yet, the crowd was more meagre than Laila had expected. The hall guards were gone to help with the gate. At the far end, sat in a loose half-circle, were the elders, some hunched and withered, some grey and still robust. The old altar loomed behind them.

'We will rebuild and mourn as we have always done,' Uma said, her voice like a creaking door. 'The dark ones never stay. The seekers will move on and leave us be.'

The other elders nodded. As always, they acquiesced to the ancient crone. Laila suddenly hated the old woman and the sycophants that surrounded her. Of course they felt that way; they sat in the heart of the village surrounded by stone and armed guards. Did they even know what happened out there? No more than they had after the last raid by the seekers.

'No, they won't,' Laila said, her tone cold. 'They're coming back.'

The silence sharpened and Laila blushed as all eyes focused on her. Uma's face crumpled, her eyes narrowing.

'What do you mean?' Uma said.

'They're coming back?' another man said.

The crowd bubbled with alarm, looking around as if the dark ones were going to lunge out of the walls.

'Two of them came into my house while I was hiding,' Laila said, wrapping her arms around herself. 'They were summoned by their leader early. They said that they would return.'

Another rumble of discontent. If Uma could have killed Laila with her gaze, she likely would have.

'I agree with Laila, we can't wait and do nothing,' Stefen said behind her.

'What would the youngsters suggest?' Uma said. 'That we fight them?'

Laila stammered, her thoughts churning. She had no solution to the problem that she had presented. Then an idea popped into her mind. A dangerous endeavour, but better than the alternative.

'The Fair Ones in the Valley of the Oracle's Eye,' Laila said. 'They help people if the foe is right. Is that not correct?'

The crowd murmured. The Fair Ones. Some said they had earned this name because they were beautiful. Others claimed they were hideous, with snakes for hair, and cursed those who did not flatter them. What the legends did agree on was that the Fair Ones hated Chaos more than anything else, especially the followers of the Needful One.

Uma snorted. 'You are not serious,' she said. 'The valley where they dwell is a place of madness and they are themselves not remotely human. The Fair Ones fight on their own terms and no one else's. You are a fool.'

'Says the old woman who counsels that we wait for those beasts to return and finish what they started,' Laila snapped.

Uma blanched, her thin skin turning whiter than the wisps on her head.

'Out! I will not tolerate your stupidity a moment longer,' Uma said, snapping a finger at the door.

Laila spun on her heel and pushed through the crowd, out into the smoky air. Inside the hall, the arguing escalated. Although there was a harvest to bring in, no one wanted to go outside the walls if there was the slightest chance that the fiends were waiting for them. Cries echoed, questioning why they did nothing. Others called for the villagers to resettle elsewhere. Uma shouted back with all the ferocity in her old bones.

'And she calls me stupid,' Laila muttered to herself.

'She's afraid, nothing more malicious than that,' Stefen said. 'This isn't like the pox walkers. It's worse. I should have been here.'

'You would have just got yourself killed, or worse,' Laila said. 'We need to get help from people that can fight. Uma is right, we can't defend ourselves against that.'

'I can lead us to the valley,' Stefen said. 'I've been to the borders anyway.'

'Really, you've seen it?' she said. 'That's forbidden.'

Stefen blushed sheepishly and nodded. 'Once.'

'You will not get there alone, especially if the fiends are still out there,' a stranger said in a hard, growling accent.

They both spun about. A man stood before them in leather and bronze plate. His skin was tanned and aged, and he was built heavily with a round gut that spoke of a steady diet of beer and meat. That he was creeping into middle age indicated either luck or skill, likely both.

'Who are you?' Laila said.

'Ano,' he replied, as if that explained everything. When they continued to look at him in silence, he added, 'I worked for the merchant, Antton. I hope that if I help you, your village will let me stay over the winter.'

'What we're talking about doing is dangerous,' Laila said, suspicious.

'I heard, but what that old woman is suggesting is worse,' he said. 'What you described sounds like something that the fiends do. They wait for your guard to fall. And they can wait a long time. Then they strike.'

While Laila did not trust the stranger, when standing against the Chaos hordes all pure humans had to stick together. What few untainted humans remained.

'The real question is, will Hadlen let us out?' Stefen said.

Laila winced; the reeve was stubborn at the best of times. 'We have to try,' Laila said. 'He might be persuaded.'

Stefen smiled tightly. 'Yes, and lightning men will fall from the sky and kill our enemies.'

They snickered at the old child's tale and made their plans. They delayed as much as they dared, speaking to the few close friends that they knew would keep their peace. With the watch so tense, sneaking out would be a challenge. Carefully, they gathered their supplies – a few loaves of hard bread, dried beans and smoked meat. Then at the light of dawn the next day, they walked to the back edge of the village where the midden heap lay next to the wall. It smelled of rotten grain and human waste; however, there was a gap in the palisade where the beams had rotted and they slipped out into the greater world with no one the wiser.

'So this is how you kept escaping,' Laila said.

Stefen grinned as he brushed off his hands. 'No one ever looked.'

As they walked around the village and onto the road, they saw not a single corpse. Just dried bloodstains and spatters of clear fluid like the trails of slugs. Strange perfumes lingered in the air, faded but potent enough to tickle the nose. Crows fluttered out in the fields, squawking at each other.

Stefen took them off the road towards the east, into the thinning forest. A deep layer of leaves rustled underfoot. Overhead, the skeletal trees rattled in the wind. The glow of the Lamp dimmed with the evening, while the Cinder Disc glimmered, already small and red with the autumn.

It felt almost unnatural to be moving away from Varna. The trees seemed to hide sinister threats, and Laila waited for some pale horror to come pelting out at them. Out here, the urge to leave struck her as impulsive while in the town it had felt brave. Had she misheard the raiders? Was Uma right? With a start, Laila realised that she had never been this far from the walls.

'Second thoughts?' Stefen said.

'How do you do it?' she said. 'Leave Varna I mean.'

'One step at a time,' Stefen said, smiling.

They walked on, the shadows growing long. Stars flickered into being and the night birds started to warble to each other.

'What about you?' Laila said to Ano. 'How did you come to travel?'

'It's tough to do,' Ano said. 'But there are advantages.'

'Like what?' she said.

'Being paid in coin is good,' Ano said.

It was practical, yet there was a mercenary attitude to his response that she did not like.

'We can't pay you in coin,' she said, hoping to gain a clearer sense of his motivation.

'No, but a bed for the winter is priceless,' he said. 'Besides, I could not help my employer.'

She let the subject drop when he looked away from her with a cough.

They travelled for several days, the forest twittering and breathing around them. It had not always been so. Once upon a time, this entire woodland had been a mire of maggots, rot and corpses. Then something had changed. Some said it was just the way of nature to reassert itself after a time. Others said it was a blessing from Alarielle, waking from her long slumber. Still others whispered that it was the Fair Ones that had freed the region of its decay.

Laila found herself dreading the night. Her sleep was long in coming and when she finally drifted off, nightmares haunted her with horrifying blends of past and present. The fiends, all wearing the manic sweaty face of Jonas, chased her through the fields. They always caught her and then cut her apart, ecstatic breathing echoing in her mind. The shadowy pain remained after she bolted awake, lingering in cramping muscles and unmarked skin.

Just as Laila began to think they were going the wrong way, Stefen spotted a coiling vine growing under the dense boughs of a great tree. It was black, like the night void when no other heavenly bodies lit the sky. Laila had never seen such a colour in nature before and marvelled at the glossy black leaves.

'Don't touch it,' Stefen said. 'Most things in the Valley of the Oracle's Eye are venomous.'

'Are you sure you can get us there?' Ano said, shifting his weight.

'Normally this is where I turn around,' Stefen said. 'If we just keep walking, the landscape will guide us. Though it will be dangerous in ways that are unfamiliar to us.'

'We should be more cautious now,' Ano said, gripping his spear. 'Pay attention. Watch your backs. I will take the rear.'

'Why?' Laila said.

'Because I have the feeling that the beasts out here do not attack from the front,' Ano said with a sardonic smile.

Laila shivered. The shadows seemed even deeper and more threatening than before. As they moved eastwards, the land grew bleak. The trees shrank, their limbs struggling upwards. Blood-red leaves coated the earth, filled with worms that slithered alarmingly under Laila's bare feet. Above them, the Lamp grew fat and orange as if seen through a veil of ashes. Animals became quiet and unnatural, with deep black coats, bloated white eyes and long spidery limbs. The world of Ghyran changed, tainted by whatever miasma leaked from the Oracle's Eye.

They trudged onwards until the Lamp suddenly winked out and darkness fell, a blackness so complete that it hurt the eyes. Laila stifled a scream. The night had never come on so fast back at Varna, not even in the depths of winter. A clammy chill rushed in, cutting through their clothes. The sort of cold that would slowly kill if allowed to.

'Light,' Ano hissed. 'Now.'

Leaves rustled under foot as Ano shifted around.

The shadows watched them. This she knew. She felt their gaze lingering on the skin. Something whispered past her and she flinched. Shadows touched her hands, coiled around her legs and brushed her cheeks, light as cobwebs. She stayed still, even as a scream threatened to escape her throat.

Instead, she focused, her ears straining. The whisper of cloth, a soft grunt, a light rattle of stone. Something fell into the leaves. Stone clacked against stone. Sparks flared, stinging her eyes. Then the crackle of fire. The hiss of retreating things.

'Hold this,' Stefen said, handing her the torch before putting an arrow to the string of his bow.

'Where is Ano?' she said, looking around.

Their hearts hammering, standing in the little circle of light surrounded by blackness, they realised that their best fighter was gone without a struggle. How could he have not made a sound? Neither dared to call for the man. Laila crept to the edge of the light, as if she were looking over the side of a boat into a dark sea.

'Ano, say something,' she hissed, then her toes brushed something heavy and wooden.

Ano's spear lay where he had dropped it. There was nothing else. Not a drop of blood, nor a shred of cloth. Not even the leaves were disturbed. With a start, she looked up, expecting some beast but there was nothing but blackness.

'Don't make a sound,' Stefen said, then turned his back to the light and walked out a few paces. Unblinking alien eyes peered from the gloom, disappearing and then reappearing somewhere else. He raised his bow, drew and waited. Then he loosed and something hissed in pain out in the darkness. That he could see anything amazed her.

'We should move, that's not the only thing out here,' Stefen whispered. 'We may be in some creature's territory and it will leave us alone once we're gone. At least that's what I hope.'

Some might have called her and Stefen cowards for not looking for Ano. However, death came quickly or sometimes not fast enough. He was already lost and she would not risk her own life for a corpse.

Laila nodded jerkily, shaking from the fear and cold. She picked up the heavy spear though there was no way she could wield the thing. The idea of fighting was not comforting: more than likely she would die. Still, better that than simply giving up. They moved on, searching for shelter of some sort.

Laila wrapped her cloak about herself. She had thought the greatest danger was the fiends waiting outside Varna; once past them, she imagined that the venture would go smoothly. Guilt crept over her. This journey was her idea. Ano would not have been out here if they had not gone. But what choice did they have, given what they knew?

They needed an army, and if Ano had died to give them that, then his death was not in vain. Yet if the darkness could take Ano, what hope did they have of reaching the valley?

Eventually, the pair found a small ditch within which they took shelter, building a roof of branches over the top and then a fire to stave off the chill. Laila did not sleep, every noise emphasised by the unnatural darkness. The rustling of her clothes, every small cough, even her breathing seemed loud enough that all the world heard.

Dawn came on weak and cold, the air thick with grey vapours. They helped themselves to some beans and bread, then moved on. The earth became hard and stony, the trees shrivelled and the undergrowth thickened with pale white plants that shrank back when touched.

'We're definitely moving down,' Stefen said.

Grey hills rose on either side, shrouded in mist. Laila felt she was walking into a prison that she could not escape. Yet, her nightmares whipped her on. What dangers compared to what the fiends promised?

They walked on and then the rocky earth gave way to a smooth stone street, like the ancients had made before the Plague Times. Tall statues of women loomed on either side. But their proportions were strange, too tall and thin as if they had been stretched out. They wore scandalously little clothing and brandished swords as they silently charged towards an unseen enemy. Laila shuddered at their screaming faces and wild hair. The place seemed abandoned, yet every eye followed them as they passed.

Ahead of them, impossibly tall towers hove out of the mists, clawing up towards the heavens like a clutch of brambles. Laila had never seen anything so vast made by the hands of mortals. Set in the side of the nearest was a huge set of doors that stood open, guarded by another pair of stone warrior women. From over the doors, an idol with a screaming face watched them, grasping a downturned sword in one hand and something small and dripping in the other.

'Maybe this was not the best idea,' Stefen said. 'We should not be here. This place is not for us.'

She found herself nodding in agreement.

'We can't,' she said, more to herself than him.

'That statue is holding a heart in its fist,' he said, drawing an arrow from his quiver.

Laila paced around on the threshold, her fists balled up, trying to summon up her courage. One part of her wanted to yell at him for strengthening her fears, while another part wanted to leave and never return.

'I know what they will do,' she said, her voice shaking. 'I can't let that happen to me or anyone else. This place is terrifying, but not as bad as being in that hole, knowing what they do.'

She looked at the black opening and steeled herself. With a deep breath, Stefen stepped forwards.

'No, not you. Just her,' a hoarse man's voice floated to them out of the darkness.

They both froze like rabbits caught out by a fox.

'And no weapons in this holy place,' the voice said.

Laila swallowed. Reluctantly, she handed the spear to Stefen and then stepped over the threshold. A stifling silence enveloped her and when she looked back, the outside world was hazy and dark. Stefen was little more than an ink blot on a sheet of paper. Pale blue torches guttered, merely enhancing the deep darkness that settled in every corner. The ceiling loomed far above her, arched and covered in sharp, jagged runes. It made the old temple at Varna seem like a hovel.

'Go on,' the voice said.

She caught sight of a gaunt face in the dark, the eyes two black pits. Then it vanished into the gloom.

What kind of place was this? How could a darkness this deep exist? And was this one man all there was? No place this grand stood empty and unprotected. Yet the silence was so deep, and the place so empty. What if this was merely another grandiose ruin?

As she walked deeper, her eyes started to pull phantasms out of the black air, leering faces, flying serpents and skeletal men riding gangling horses.

A glutinous bubbling sound caught her attention and she moved towards it. As she walked closer, the air grew thick with incense and a sweet, coppery stench like cooking blood sausage. A strange altar revealed itself – at least, she thought that it was an altar. Two flights of stairs wound their way up to a vast cauldron held by a statue of a straining man. Steam rose from within the huge vessel. Looming over it was the same idol she had seen above the door. Yet this one was covered in thick red enamel, burnished gold and glittering gems. Its eyes burned crimson and seemed to follow her with predatory focus.

Something stirred in the cauldron, fluid sloshing over the side. A great coil rose, like a leviathan breaking the surface of the sea. Then a small green snake crept over the side, black tongue flicking. She cocked her head, puzzled. Another serpent and then another slipped over, peering at her with unnerving, single-minded interest.

Laila took a step backwards. Why would anyone put a snake colony in a cauldron? And what else was in it? Instinct rattled through her, the overwhelming need to run. There was a predator in here, one large enough to kill her.

Then a bright light leapt to life from her left, stinging her eyes. A woman's voice, deep and rough with wisdom, spoke softly. Whatever was in the cauldron settled back like a dragon lulled to sleep.

'I would come towards the light, young one,' the voice said. 'My sister is not friendly to the curious.'

Laila blocked the light with her hand and stepped towards it, feeling her way with her toes. She stumbled when her feet touched earth and a soft fragrant wind sighed through her curls. With watery eyes, she looked around at an outdoor garden, the surrounding walls gleaming like black glass.

All the plantings, neatly laid out in vivid clusters, were venomous: Strikeweed, Neolinem and Grave-eye. And those were just the ones she recognised. Other plants and trees whispered in the wind, dark and spiky or pallid and ghostly. Even the grass under her feet had a purple cast to it. Above her, the Lamp was shrouded, though still brighter than the blackness within the temple.

In the centre of the garden stood the most beautiful woman she had ever seen. Now Laila understood why they were called the Fair Ones.

The woman resembled a human being only loosely. Long and thin as a blade, she moved with an airy grace, like a great cat. Her pointed ears peeked through her black hair and her skin was dark as a doe's eyes, without blemish or scar. A jewelled leather cloak hung off her slim shoulders and underneath she was nearly nude, though Laila doubted she felt any shame in it. Two strange blades hung from her hips, more like torture instruments than weapons of war. Yet it was her face that was the most unnerving. While her expression was gentle, it was at odds with her sharp black eyes and thin, cruel lips.

Next to the aelf was an elaborately carved table, upon which rested a stone bowl etched with sharp runes and the familiar idol in miniature.

'We have not seen one of your kind in many years,' she said, her accent hissing through the human words.

'Generations, ma'am,' Laila said, her voice scratchy with nerves. 'I am Laila. I represent the village of Varna.'

The woman's eyes narrowed and her smile deepened. No human expression, that. It was like seeing a sicklecat smile.

'I always forget how short-lived you humans are,' she said. 'So, Laila of Varna, do you know who we are or have even your legends forgotten us?'

Laila opened her mouth but then realised that she could not in fact answer the question. Certainly not to this woman's satisfaction.

'Only in the vaguest terms,' she said. 'We know that when the great enemy comes, you will fight for us.'

'For a price,' the woman said, with a tremor in her voice as if she were trying to repress some strong emotion. 'Let us move beyond simple legends, shall we? My name is Cesse, and this is a temple of the Khelt Nar, a sisterhood devoted to the defeat of Chaos under Khaine's holy guidance.'

'So you are a holy order?' Laila said warily.

'Precisely,' Cesse said, her voice bright with fervour. 'We are dedicated to our faith and that is enough.'

'And if you operate on faith, what is this price then?' Laila said, sensing something was off.

'The price is that of blood. Blood buys blood,' Cesse said, drawing a dagger from her belt.

Laila took a step back.

'Please, I will not kill you,' Cesse said, flicking her hand dismissively. 'You have a need of our skills. You need us to kill your enemy. What is this enemy?'

'They worship... um... they worship...' Laila started, then she took a breath and looked up at the sky. 'The Needful One. The Beckoning Prince.' Yet Cesse looked at her, one thin brow arched in confusion. '*Slaanesh*,' she mumbled finally, looking at her feet.

Heat crept into her face at her blasphemy, at speaking that abominable name. She looked up and recoiled. Cesse stared at her, every muscle standing like a cord under her skin. Seemingly unaware, the woman slowly drove her blade deep into the table, the wood creaking. The pleasant mask was gone, leaving a hate that shivered through the aelf's limbs and etched her face into a scowl of furious cruelty.

'Hear my words, human. We will not rest until your dread enemy is slain,' she snarled, her voice a terrible rasp. 'We will kill them without mercy. None of them can be allowed to live.'

Laila fought the urge to run, holding herself still as Cesse wrenched the dagger from the table. Seeing Laila's expression, Cesse's eyes narrowed in suspicion as if sensing some weakness.

'Do you not want them all dead?' Cesse said, her black eyes feverish.

'Yes, of course I do,' Laila stammered.

Cesse smiled. 'Oh, I see. To be as ignorant as you are now. You do not know what they do. You do not know the thing that lurks in the darkness and eats at their souls.'

Cesse's focus turned towards some inner turmoil, her eyes dark and dull. A profound hate flickered there, a self-loathing that was all-consuming and burned eternally. A shame that ever boiled, a pain that never eased, a hurt that never healed. What caused it, Laila could not guess. However, she did not want to be around when that storm of emotion turned outwards.

'You will kill them for blood?' Laila prompted. Now that she said it out loud, it seemed insane. What would a holy order want with blood? What was the significance?

Cesse tossed her head, her black hair shimmering, coming back to the present.

'Of course, that has always been the agreement,' Cesse said. 'And what is blood compared to the tortures that await you if you do nothing?' Cesse leaned across the table. 'Trust me when I say, the agonies and slow death that you envision are only the beginning. It is not just the body that they devour.'

'Whose blood is it?' Laila said.

'Yours, I assume,' Cesse said. 'Who else's?'

Laila blushed. It seemed easy enough.

'Why?'

'All of creation moves at the beating of a heart. All things from the strongest godbeast to the stars themselves. Nothing can be outside it. The heart and the blood it moves are the most sacred of things.'

Laila nodded. 'I agree on behalf of Varna. You will kill the raiders in return for blood.'

'Excellent, now we can begin,' Cesse said, gesturing that Laila should stand opposite her at the table. Then she began to chant, her words like the rattling of swords and spears. The aelven woman sliced the dagger across her palm without even flinching, as if she had done this many times before. Blood leaked into the bowl. Then she crooked a long finger at Laila.

Yet Laila hesitated. Then she shook herself. What was a little cut compared to what those creatures did to their victims? She

413

thrust out a hand. Cesse took it, her skin feverish, and then quickly slashed open Laila's palm. It burned like hot iron and Laila tried to jerk away, but Cesse held her fast until her blood fell into the bowl. At last Cesse released her, still chanting.

Now the blood began to seethe, filling the air with coppery smoke. Shadows crept among the shrubs and flowers. Cesse's voice rose to a shout, darkness seeping around her body like a serpent. Then she clapped her hands together, the sound like thunder. Laila stepped back towards the door. The air became dark, vile and oozing, catching in her throat and lungs, crawling over her skin like spiders. Cesse's eyes were pits of the blackest spite, her hands dripping blood and gloom.

'It is done,' Cesse said. 'You will have our blades, our magic and above all our hate. All is yours for blood yet spilled. Now go, this place is no longer for you!'

Laila did not need to be told. She fled, the shadows hurtling after her. As she burst through the hall, something hissed and roiled up on that dread altar. Laila ran on, things catching and plucking at her clothes and hair. She bolted under that fearsome archway out into the sickly light.

'Stefen,' she yelled, slowing her breakneck pace only slightly. 'We're done. We need to go!'

He was not there. Only the spear, a broken arrow and an ominous spatter of blood remained.

'Stefen!' she screamed, looking around frantically.

The shadows boiled out of the temple, hissing like vipers.

Laila ran as fast as she could. Like any nightmare, it could not catch her if she did not look back at whatever it was that snarled and snapped at her heels. She reached the edge of the forest and hurled herself through the trees without pausing. The seething shadows grew distant and then retreated as if the brilliance of Ghyran was not to their liking.

Once she was certain that she had left the creatures far behind, she dropped to her knees and wept. Never had she imagined that Stefen would perish. She had always thought that it would be her, that Stefen would be the one to carry back the news of their success. After all, she was just another farmer and he was a hunter that went out in the wider world.

Why had she lived while he had not? As if in answer, the cut in her palm leaped to life, stinging like an envenomed lesion. The wound seeped a clear fluid, and the skin surrounding it was a sickly grey. She tore a strip of cloth from her frayed tunic and tied it around the torn flesh.

This done, Laila set off towards home, tormented at night by nightmares and pain, and driven on by terrors of fiends and predators during the day. Sometimes, out of the corner of her eye, she glimpsed thin pale men on dark horses slipping through the shadows. She wondered if she was going mad.

It was twilight on the third day when she came within sight of Varna, long shadows reaching across the fields. A familiar sickly-sweet smell tickled her senses. Had she been too late? Was that grim bargain all for nothing?

Exhausted fear leaped through her and she pelted out across the fields of red-tinged grain. She half expected some terrible shriek or that shrill tone to echo from the trees, but there was nothing.

The gate was already closed when she reached it. She banged on the wood and called out for someone to have mercy and open it, though she knew that they should not. They would leave her out here to survive the night as best she could before opening that door.

Then the gate creaked, opening just enough to let her in. She rushed through the gap and crashed into something solid.

'Laila,' Hadlen said, slowing her down. 'Where have you been? Where is Stefen?'

One of the other warriors took off, running towards the great hall, shouting that she had returned.

She shook her head and told Hadlen what had occurred in a soft voice. Yet, she found herself obscuring details, even as the story spilled out. She lingered instead on Stefen, on his skills, on his calm. As she finished, she noticed a commotion coming towards her.

Uma. Of all the people in Varna, the last person she wanted to see was Uma. Laila had no stomach for the crone's displeasure after everything that she had seen.

'You were forbidden from doing this, Laila,' Uma snapped as she shuffled up to them.

'What would you rather have happen?' Laila said. 'That we just sit waiting to be slaughtered by the worst that this world has to offer? By those beasts. You know what they were going to do to us.'

Laila glanced around. To her surprise, some of the others crowded around rumbled in agreement. Still, many clearly sided with Uma, their faces set hard as stone.

'You know not what you have done,' Uma said. 'Time will tell. The legends say to be cautious of the Fair Ones. Who knows what they will do in the end.'

'They are going to kill all those fiends for us,' Laila snapped, jabbing a finger in the old woman's direction. 'We might learn that we don't have to be so afraid any more.'

It was an empty thing, grasping at surety in the face of Uma's doubts. It was as if the old woman were plucking Laila's own secret worries from her head, when Laila desperately wanted the bargain to work out. Uma had not seen Jonas' body or heard his last wheezing breath. Sometimes the lesser evil was all that remained.

'I doubt that,' Uma said, turning away from her. 'There is always something to fear.'

Uma shuffled away, her back bent more than Laila remembered. Her supporters went with her, scowling.

Exhausted, Laila excused herself when the others pressed in with urgent questions. She stumbled into her house and hurled herself into bed. Yet her nightmares continued, dreams of shadows chasing her through endless halls while the aelves' bloody-handed god loomed over her with burning eyes. Sometimes, Ano and Stefen were with her and they were always devoured by whatever beast ran in the shadows.

As Laila returned to the familiar rhythm of her old life, she remembered the bargain with ever greater unease. She was missing something. But what? Cesse was sinister certainly, but had given her word in front of her god. While that god was no Alarielle, he was still a deity that had rules that were binding. So why did it feel like something had gone horribly wrong?

The days turned into a week and then two, autumn cooled and the rains started in earnest. Fear of famine set in; their stores were lean as much of the harvest had rotted in the fields. Stefen and Ano's funeral came and went, bleak and routine like all the others before it. Normalcy never returned. The cut in her hand would not heal; instead it constantly broke open and bled, the skin ashen and dry. Likewise, the vivid nightmares also continued, an unending torment.

Her neighbours treated her differently, either greeting her with cool politeness or pointedly avoiding her, making holy signs as they did so. Rumours that she was cursed began to circulate. Never had she felt as alone as she did now, surrounded by familiar faces, none of whom trusted her as they had.

Then late one night, a high musical tone sounded through Laila's dreams, reverberating through her bones. Dazed, she opened her eyes as another call went out, louder than the last. Laila clamped her hands over her ears as the sound pierced her skull like a butcher's pick. The horn-blower was real; worse, it was out in the fields. The fiends were outside the walls.

The cut began to itch, then to throb. She clutched her hand tight and felt warm blood. She stripped off the soaked bandage and searched for another. As she looked, another horn call went out, different than the first. Brassy and eerie, it shivered up the spine and set the heart racing. Then there was a high, keening howl.

The Fair Ones had come.

She wrapped her hand and glanced at her bolthole. Disgust at her fears and nightmares rose. She had to see the creatures die. Maybe then she would be free from the monsters that stalked her dreams and the memories of her husband's death. The Fair Ones had promised to kill them all, why not see them fulfil that promise?

She paused. The sounds from the battle filtered through to her, high ululating screams, roars of elation and the metallic bang of weapons meeting. It was almost musical in its own way, rising and falling by some rhythm that she could not discern.

Even as the pain crept up her arm like venom, she stepped outside and looked up at the cloudy sky. No, not clouds. Shadows. They weaved through the sky as though they were living things, tinting the Cinder Disc into a colour like heart's blood.

She climbed the wall to where Hadlen and a couple of warriors stood and looked out with them.

The scene was grim.

Out amongst the rotten grain, a great jewelled chariot lay crumpled like a dead beetle. Clustered about the wreck was a group of heavily armoured men, if one could call them such, bunched up with weapons turned outwards. At the centre was a tall, lithe creature with an elaborate helm, shouting in a silvery voice. All about them, shadowy women probed at the raiders' defence, thin spears piercing through hardened armour, others tearing at shields with hooked blades. A final, bloody last stand.

Something flew out of the trees on the wings of a drake and

circled above the battle. Then it dived down into the heart of the raiders like a hawk. The defensive knot broke apart, revealing a flickering dance between the Chaos leader and a monstrous winged aelf. Blows lashed between them and, for a moment, it looked as though they were equal. Then the aelf skewered the leader through his jewelled breastplate, ending the beast's life.

The winged woman was not the only monster. Other aelves with the bodies of serpents weaved among strange crystalline statues that glittered in the half-light, frozen in mid-flight. Still other warrior women flickered after their fleeing enemies, snaring them with barbed whips or lopping off limbs with long daggers. The crack of breaking bones, the chanting of women and the screams of dying things drifted out from beyond the trees. A strange fire burned out there, throwing up dense, ruddy mist. The stench of blood was so thick on the wind that it gummed in the eyes and throat.

Never had Laila imagined that their defence would be so ugly. Yet did those creatures not deserve it? Did evil deserve evil? Yes, they did. Maybe now, Jonas would no longer haunt her dreams with his screams and pleading.

As they looked on, a shadow walked down the road. It was Cesse. Below them, she stood, strong and cold. A bloody sickle gleamed in one of the aelf's hands, while in the other was that magnificent crested helm. No, not a helm, a head in a helm. She lifted up the gruesome trophy, blood dripping from the severed neck.

'We thank you for this glorious slaughter, which we have carried out in your name,' Cesse said, her voice quivering with a cruel elation. 'This creature will trouble you no more. Now, whose blood shall it be?'

'What? I gave you what you wanted,' Laila said. 'I gave you my blood.'

Cesse blinked and dropped the head into the dirt. All the other aelves stopped and looked towards the village as one. The shadows paused in the sky as if frozen and then seeped downwards like black snow. Out in the forest, something rumbled and that dread altar rolled forwards of its own volition out of the trees, the cauldron the source of the terrible smoke. Around it slithered some terrible thing, a vast serpent.

'It pains me that your kind are so forgetful,' Cesse said, a hint of amusement in her voice as if she were revealing the punchline of a joke. 'You spoke for all, therefore you are all. Your blood stands for your village's obligation to us. Do not worry. We will not take the strong from among you, only the weakest from each household. The ones that you will not miss. Given the state of your harvest, you would not be able to feed them anyway. In time, you will be grateful for the lack of useless mouths. Just as it was before.'

'She cannot be serious,' Hadlen said. 'Laila, you could not have agreed to this.'

'I didn't,' Laila stammered. 'That was not what we agreed to.' She leaned over the wall. 'I gave you blood.'

'No, you sealed the agreement with your blood,' Cesse said. 'A few drops is not enough. Did you really think it was?'

Laila frantically searched her memory for some misstep, some loophole, something. Then a single moment leaped out at her.

For blood yet spilled.

It had been right there in front of her face. She had thought that the phrase referred to the enemy. But no, it had been her own people. That could not be right. She looked at the others, who glared at her with the frightened anger of those dragged into a situation not of their making. She had to fix this.

'The whole point of this was so that the defenceless would live,' Laila said. 'If we could have done it ourselves, we would not have needed you.'

Cesse cocked her head, her sharp brows furrowing. 'I do not understand your motive. We have laws. We do not move our forces on behalf of the weak without payment in blood. The weak must be culled from the strong so that the strong may continue unburdened. If you do not give, we will take what we are owed, no more, no less.'

Cesse did not – no, she could not – understand. She wasn't human. It was inevitable now. Dozens were going to die because of Laila's naïveté, her idiocy. There was now nothing that she could do. There never had been. Someone was always going to kill them; she had merely chosen a different foe.

'You are like the fiends, like a reflection of the Lamp in a lake,' Laila said.

Cesse's face twisted into a depthless fury that no human could know. All the self-loathing and hurt turned outwards. She leaped into the air with a shriek, her cloak falling away, wings like those of a great dragon snapping free. The monstrous aelf crashed into Laila, slamming her off the wall. Laila experienced a long moment of weightlessness before she hit the ground, the breath blasting from her body. Breathless and throbbing with pain, she lay there.

Shadows flitted past her, the gate groaned open and the aelves shrieked in. They bolted right for the hall and the villagers scattered like startled birds from a nest, fleeing in terror. It mattered not, they died all the same: the infirm, the aged, the injured and the unlucky.

Cesse crouched nearby, a fleshy tail flicking, her wings loose over her back, watching the slaughter.

'Please understand, this is not purposeless or merciless,' Cesse said, calm as if the screams mattered to her not at all. 'We build a better world. One that is strong enough to stand against not only the destruction of the flesh but also the entropy of the soul. Illusions like justice and fairness allow weakness to fester. Killing the weak is merciful to the strong.'

Laila pressed herself onto an elbow, still trying to suck in a breath. Pain flared in her palm and then was gone as if it had never been. She looked down. A thin scar was all that remained of the wound.

'The bargain is complete,' Cesse said, straightening up. 'Now you are strong and will survive.'

Cesse leaped into the sky, her wings hitting the air. In the space of a breath, she was gone. They were all gone as if they had never been. Light washed over Varna as the shadows lifted, revealing a village of sorrow and corpses, of wailing and death, of curses and recrimination.

And Laila wept.

GHASTLIGHT

Anna Stephens

They were outnumbered three to one, not that it mattered. Skaven were rarely a significant threat, and against the Dread Pageant, blessed by the Dark Prince Slaanesh, they were laughably out-classed. Glissete paused for a second to watch as Hadzu, the Pageant's archer, who crouched atop a cracked stone pillar, sent an arrow infused with madness down into the nearest ratman. The skaven squealed and kicked, ripping the barbed head from its thigh, but the poison was already streaking through its system. It leapt at one of its own pack and bore it to the ground, yellowed incisors burrowing through thick fur to the other skaven's throat while its back feet kicked, trying to rip through the chainmail so its long claws could disembowel its pack-mate.

Glissete laughed as they rolled and fought, squealing, their thick bald tails whipping about. She shook skaven blood from her glaive and sprinted forward, leaping the thrashing creatures and using the momentum to carry her up the wall of the cavern. Beast-grave's Direchasm was jagged and unfinished, and there were outcrops and ledges and footholds everywhere she could exploit. Glissete twisted back on herself and fell upon another skaven, this one waiting near the back of the pack for its turn to face Vasillac the Gifted, the Pageant's leader, and his slaangor companion, Slakeslash.

'Hiding won't save you, rodent,' Glissete grunted as the blade found the angle between the skaven's neck and shoulder. The backswing crunched the butt of the glaive into its chest, and a third strike took off its bony paw at the wrist. The paw and the knife it held clattered to the stone and the rest of the dying creature followed as she hacked the glaive into its skull.

The skaven's hot, sticky blood sprayed into her face and she shivered with delight as its very life ran down her cheek and neck. She paused to rub the blood between her fingertips; its thick, oily texture like stinking liquid silk to her senses. Two more skaven attacked her in that moment, approaching from either side. Perhaps they thought that, as the smallest member of the Dread Pageant, Glissete would be the easiest to kill. They were mistaken, for the reach of her glaive was deceptive. She twisted between their raking, serrated knives and their slashing claws, leaping to one side and carving the weapon down across chainmail as she passed. It raised a painful screech of metal on metal that made the skaven's ears press back against their heads, but it did not bite flesh.

Glissete threw herself into a tumble to find space and then dived back in as Slakeslash raced up behind one of the skaven and rammed his serrated claw through the ratman's back. The skaven roared and thrashed, distracting its pack-mate. Glissete stroked her blade down the side of its head, removing an ear and laying open fur and scalp. Black blood flowed and the skaven squealed and turned to flee. Glissete swept low and hamstrung it, and the creature collapsed, screaming. The ratman's pain was pleasure nestled in the woman's heart, dark and brooding and begging to be drunk.

Slakeslash was hacking apart his own victim, intent on the almostcorpse shivering and flailing beneath his blade and pincer. Glissete stalked the hamstrung, earless skaven as Vasillac and Hadzu finished the rest. The pathetic creature was dragging itself away, gibbering pleas for mercy lost in the echoes of screams and Beastgrave's own mingled bellowing of triumph and despair. The sentient mountain that crouched like a monstrous predator on the plains of Ghur feasted on those who died within its passages and caverns – or it had.

Not any more, not since the Katophrane curse had infected it, leaking through the cracks in reality between the Realm of Beasts and Uhl-Gysh, resting place of the cursed Mirrored City of Shadespire. And now death was not the end, for the dead rose to fight and run and kill again, forever, and so Beastgrave's appetite went unanswered. The mountain hungered and suffered and raged and begged. A whole mountain, a whole sentient landscape, screaming its want. And if the Dread Pageant were good at anything, it was denying the wants of others and indulging their own.

And so they had. As Vasillac followed the call of the visions of Slaanesh deeper into Beastgrave and the rest of the Pageant followed him, they fought and killed and discovered what the curse actually meant when their victims rose again. They learnt of the mountain's sorrowing, gnawing hunger that could never be sated. Soon, they realised that they could bring Beastgrave even greater despair by finding and torturing victims – tormenting them to the very point of death and potential sustenance for it – and then leaving them alive, even if only just. The mountain lusted after death to feed its echoing emptiness, and so each one they deprived it of was a further layer of anguish for it to endure.

To so tempt and then deny the mountain, to revel in the rage and impotence of a mind so incalculably huge and alien, was the most transcendent experience of Glissete's life. The screams and pain of the victim, the screams and pain of the mountain, combined and multiplied in such a way that it was as if she were breathing sunlight, her every nerve and sense alight and golden and vibrating. It was the closest she would ever get to having the power of a god. And it was addictive.

Glissete stamped down on the skaven's tail as it dragged itself away, eliciting another screech, and then she brought down her glaive with all the strength of her shoulders, back and thighs, severing the ratman's spine. There was less screaming this time as the kicking legs fell still. Now only whimpers rasped their way from its throat amid the bubbling gulps for air. Glissete crouched next to its head.

'Does it hurt?' she asked. The skaven mewled but didn't answer. 'Good,' she whispered, but before she could increase the torment and offer the creature's suffering to the Lord of Excess, a furtive slide of movement caught the corner of her eye.

It was another skaven, neither smaller nor seemingly weaker than its pack-mates, but this one made only a token attempt to defend itself.

'No no no,' it begged as Glissete prepared to stab. 'No no, no no. I show you the stash. You can have the stash, please, Ytash doesn't want it, oh no. Ytash will starve and be glad, beautiful lady. Only don't put the metal in him. I show you the stash.'

The babbling drew the others' attention. Even Slakeslash ceased cutting his victims into pieces and rose to see what was happening. The slaangor paused over Glissete's paralysed victim, staring down at it as skaven blood dripped from the ends of the pincer that was his right arm. He sat on his haunches and reached out to stroke the soft, velvety fur of the skaven's left ear.

'Don't,' Glissete warned as the slaangor's slit-pupilled eyes narrowed. 'That one's mine.'

Slakeslash looked up from beneath curling antelope horns, ears flicking forward at Glissete's words. Glissete tightened her grip on the skaven – Ytash – and growled a low threat.

'Mine,' she repeated, swinging her glaive towards the pair. Almost a threat. Almost a challenge to the slaangor.

Slakeslash tossed his horns and stroked the fur of the skaven's face again. His wide nostrils flared as he drank in the scent of pain and fear and the bitter tang of blood. Then he rose slightly and threw his weight downwards, ramming his pincer into the hole Glissete had made in the ratman's back with a grunt.

The skaven's mouth opened in a soundless scream drowned in blood until, muscles bulging as they flexed beneath the fur of its upper arm and shoulder, the slaangor opened the pincer and ripped the skaven in half. His bleat of pleasure was lost beneath Ytash's wail and Hadzu's laughter.

Glissete threw the gibbering skaven at Hadzu and lunged forward; Vasillac stepped between her and Slakeslash. 'Let me past,' she snarled. 'I'm going to carve its face off.'

Vasillac slapped her. 'Remember who you speak to,' he growled, and the Hedonite shut her mouth on the unwise response that sprang to her tongue. Her cheek stung but she refused to raise a hand to it.

Rage boiled in her veins. 'Lord Vasillac, this is the third time the slaangor has taken a kill from me in the last days. He is a liability–'

'Liability?' the Godseeker interrupted in tones of steel. 'Slakeslash is an exquisite warrior. He has saved your life at least once. How is this a liability?'

Glissete didn't notice the warning in her lord's voice. 'This place. What it's doing to him – doing to us all. He is out of control...'

'Which is itself an act of worship of Slaanesh, the Lord of Excess. Is your faith faltering, Hedonite? Have you found reason to doubt the Dark Prince here in the belly of the Beastgrave?' Vasillac stepped even closer, only the line of his perfect jaw and a few stray tumbled blond locks visible beneath his helm. His eyes were lost in blackness, but they glittered down at her. 'Did I choose poorly when I chose you to accompany me here in search of the truth of the visions of Slaanesh?'

'But were they true?' Glissete demanded. Beastgrave's fury was nothing compared with hers. Vasillac would permit no questioning of the slaangor's place in the Pageant or his loyalty or ability. 'We have learnt nothing since we came here, nothing of Slaanesh or why he absents himself from us. Those were not true visions, lord – they were sent by the mountain. It lured us here and now we're trapped and lost inside it.'

'Then the mountain will rue the day it called to the Dread Pageant, for we turn its desires back on it and use them to our advantage,' Vasillac shouted in her face. Glissete flinched. 'We will make its suffering our delight. We will wring every drop of sensation from this place and despite Beastgrave's greatest efforts, we will be triumphant and it will wallow in eternal anguish. For Slaanesh is our god and we will make him proud.'

The Dread Pageant roared back their faith and their joy at the Godseeker's prayer, and Glissete shouted with them. Vasillac's eloquence always found its way around her defences and her fury retreated – for now – beneath the promise of glory.

Retreated, but did not die. Could not die. Anger was as much a part of her these days as her glaive or her skin. As if she'd been angry all her life, and Beastgrave had unlocked the chamber of her heart where it resided and called it forth. Slakeslash would get them all killed in his recklessness. Hadzu was a rotten tooth, a constant irritant. And Vasillac...

'As to your accusation, Hedonite, I promise you that we are exactly where we need to be,' the Godseeker said. 'Haven't you noticed the difference in our movements the last two days? There is more to sensation than just torture, Glissete. The Dark Prince teaches us to crave intensity in all its forms. Observation. Stealth. The simple pleasure of eating or sleeping or searching for a thing. Have you forgotten what true worship is in your single-minded quest for blood? Is that as far as your imagination stretches these days? I had expected better.'

The whisper of his threat was like fingers over her skin. Glissete shivered, longing to press against him; she did not. Vasillac no longer desired her and the rejection was a bitter wound.

'I have noticed,' she said instead, 'you are following the ghastlight.'

'The crack between realms, yes. The fissure through which the glow of Shadespire shines. We were brought here by visions of Slaanesh – they called to me and I answered, for my purpose is to better understand my lord. Those visions were not a lie, whether or not Beastgrave generated them. The crack between here and Uhl-Gysh is real. It is a door, a passage, as close to a Realmgate as a mindless curse can fashion.' He seized Glissete's shoulders and squeezed, his fingers digging into hard muscle with bruising force. 'Shadespire. The Mirrored City.'

'Home of the Katophrane curse,' Glissete agreed, accepting the pain of his grip and offering it to her god, as she likewise offered the pain of Vasillac's indifference.

'Home of the Book of Pleasure,' the Godseeker hissed, and that stopped her. Hadzu cursed in surprise.

'It is lost,' Glissete said, but her heart was beginning to pound. Could it be true?

'As is Shadespire. Where better to hide the book that is said to tell the secrets of Slaanesh himself than in a place thought impossible to reach?'

His teeth flashed in the shadows of his helm and he let go of her and spread his arms wide.

'The Dread Pageant will cross into Uhl-Gysh itself and find the Book of Pleasure. We will bring it back to the Mortal Realms and with it we will learn all we need to know to bring mighty Slaanesh back to us. After aeons of absence, he will once more have dominion. That is our purpose in Beastgrave. That is our glory and our fate. But if the stolen death of a single pathetic skaven is more important...' Vasillac trailed off and shrugged, and his excited good humour vanished as if it had never been. He gestured to Slakeslash and the two halves of the ratman.

Glissete swallowed. 'No, lord. You chose well when you chose me,' she promised him. 'My life is dedicated to Slaanesh and his teachings. My blade is yours, you must know that. But Slakeslash is–'

'Slakeslash is my creature and he is loyal. Question me on this again and I will ensure you live a long time in agony to regret it. An agony not even you can turn to worship.'

'I too am loyal,' Glissete said, embracing the anger that roiled once more within her. That he would think the slaangor better than her...

Vasillac stopped her words with his mouth, the kiss unexpected and deep and familiar as he wrapped her in hard, scarred arms and pressed his body against hers. Desire replaced anger in a hot rush beginning in her belly, but the kiss was over all too soon and he shoved her away.

The Godseeker stepped back. 'Good,' he said, and the cruel twist to his mouth told her he knew her feelings for him had not faded, and that he relished it. Glissete tried to keep her expression neutral, denying him the pleasure of her pain. It left them both unsatisfied.

'Bring the skaven – it will be useful when we reach a fissure wide enough to cross.'

'Useful?' Hadzu asked.

'He is risen,' the slaangor said. 'Undead. I smell it.'

Glissete swivelled to stare at Ytash; the skaven chittered something that might have been a laugh – or a sob.

'Ytash will wait for his pack now,' he said to himself. 'We will be all together again. They won't cast out Ytash now. Not now they won't.'

'Ytash will come with us,' Glissete snarled, wrong-footed and trying to cover her mistake. She should have guessed, or seen the peculiar glaze in the skaven's eyes that was the film of death only partially lifted. They'd encountered it enough times by now. She looked at her lord, unsure why he wanted the undead skaven.

'About that,' Hadzu said from his place back atop the pillar. 'The ghastlight thread has vanished. We moved a good way from the initial ambush to hunt down this scum, and I had a scout around while you were all bickering, but I can't find it. It's as if the passages themselves have shifted, or the magic, perhaps. Either way, the fissure's closed or moved away from us.'

Hadzu had been with Vasillac for years, yet even their long association would not allow such insult to pass. Glissete's hands tightened on the smooth wood of her glaive, driven by a quick-silver mood change from anger at her lord to anger for him. Vasillac moved first, clenching his fist and then thrusting it to-wards the archer with fingers splayed wide. A blast of purple-edged magic slammed into Hadzu and he was blown backwards off his perch.

Now it was Glissete's turn to laugh as the archer dragged him-self groaning to his feet. He knew better than to look at or speak to Vasillac; he knew better than to respond in any way, for the Godseeker ruled their warband with absolute control and without mercy. He would take the tongue or eyes of one of his own in an instant and dedicate their suffering to Slaanesh if his orders were questioned.

Chastened and yet furious, Hadzu's gaze landed on Glissete. He bared his teeth at her laughter and she raised an eyebrow in re-turn, accepting his challenge. She beckoned and tension heated the air between them. Her acrobatics against his arrows; it would be a glorious battle.

'Be still.' Vasillac's voice was implacable, denying their need for violence. 'Take what you want and get ready to move. We are here for more than our own pleasure, remember that.'

Glissete believed in excess in all things, including extremes of emotion, and Vasillac denying her and Hadzu the opportunity to fight frustrated their bloodlust while stoking resentment. But no one emotion held sway over another, for betrayal could taste just as sweet as love if it was approached with open arms. It was the intensity that was important. And Glissete was intensely resentful. She set it in her heart and fed it patiently, stoking it higher and hotter until she was grinding her teeth and the urge to kill Hadzu faded beneath fantasies of tearing the Godseeker limb from limb.

Glissete looked up. Slakeslash was watching her, his half-antelope face as unreadable as ever. The slaangor had moved between her and Vasillac, a casual repositioning that meant he could protect his lord if necessary.

That the wild and unpredictable slaangor would make such a move told Glissete just how obvious her emotions were – and just how strong. Putting her back to the horned monstrosity, she tied Ytash's front paws and then rifled through the belongings of the newly dead skaven – trail rations and waterskins, thank Slaanesh – and reflected on the increasing loss of control she and the others had been experiencing. It wasn't something they could attribute to the cult of excess: something external was manipulating them, Glissete was sure of it now. That manipulation was one of the reasons she no longer trusted Slakeslash, even if Vasillac did.

Glissete knew the others had the same suspicions, and her private conviction was that the source of their emotional warping was Beastgrave itself. Perhaps the mountain was trying to punish them as they punished it. And yet... *sensation is all. The mountain is simply another route to intensity, perhaps the greatest route after Slaanesh himself. If it wants to aid us in our quest for sensation, I will not try and stop it.*

In fact, she prayed that their route would lead them deeper into Direchasm, the great downward-sloping cavern-and-tunnel complex that seemed to be the heart of Beastgrave's emotions. The psychic rage and suffering from the mountain had grown every time they had descended deeper, until it was as heady as wine, filling all of the Dread Pageant with shivering ecstasy.

A ruby the size of Glissete's thumb tumbled from the sack next to a skaven who'd died while trying to stuff its guts back into its belly. It took the torchlight and reflected it back like blood; pretty enough. She put it in a pouch on her belt. The gold statuette next to it, though, was heavy and pointless. It would only weigh her down. Glissete set it at an angle between the ground and a rock and then brought the heel of her boot down across it. It crumpled, the delicate workmanship folding in on itself, the unique decorations flattening or shearing off.

The skaven prisoner squeaked its distress at the loss, and Glissete smirked. There were few enough pretty things to break this far below ground, if she didn't count the skaven corpses, so angular and wet in their pathetic, jumbled deaths. She took satisfaction from the destruction of the treasures, but more from the knowledge of Beastgrave's fear of the Dread Pageant and their ability to increase its anguish. A sentient mountain feared her; now that was a sensation worth experiencing to its utmost.

'These'll be up soon enough, my lord,' Hadzu said eventually, toeing one of the corpses. Perhaps an offering of apology, though he made no such overture to Glissete. 'No point us fighting them again so soon. We should get moving, maybe? The captive said there was a stash. Might be worth checking out.'

'Others stalk us,' Slakeslash interrupted as he mutilated another corpse. His big ears flicked, but he seemed otherwise unconcerned, his pincer busy lopping claws from ratman fingers and toes. When he had enough, he laid them out in the pattern of Slaanesh's sigil. When the skaven undead rose, they would be whole again and without injury, like Ytash, but until then the sigil would burn with dark magic, scorching Beastgrave's hide and casting an aura of dread for any who might come after them.

'The stash is nothing – we have food and water enough for now. I must find our route,' Vasillac said and sat cross-legged on the floor, his hands on his knees. Glissete imagined his perfect face smooth and serene beneath his helm as he extended his senses into the tunnels around them, searching for the call of the ghastlight that he believed would eventually lead to a fissure large enough to squeeze through, leaving Ghur for Uhl-Gysh and all that it might contain.

She was light-headed at the promise of it. They would discover new sensations, new experiences and intensities in a demi-realm comprised of both light and shadow magic. They would meet undead mages who haunted their lost city in a desperate dance to undo their own hubris and the will of Nagash that had put them there. The pull of both light and dark upon the soul would be exquisite.

But still, Beastgrave too was exquisite.

The crack in the realm was one thing – one destination and one purpose – but it wasn't the only direction they could take. They'd been wandering through the mountain for weeks or more as far as they could guess, unable to tell time down here in the endless gloom, pausing to eat and sleep when they needed to, stopping to fight when they had to or they wanted to. They'd learnt how to torment the mountain; they'd destroyed priceless artefacts in front of the thieves who'd stolen them; they'd fought against overwhelming odds and survived because the Dark Prince willed it.

In a life spent searching for new experiences, new sensations ever more extreme, Beastgrave answered their every craving. Even the gnawing emptiness when they ran out of food, or the thick-tongued, fur-throated agony of thirst, could be relished with the correct attitude, the right approach to existence. Whether fear, lust or anger; apathy, agony or sadness, every emotion and action should be experienced to its utmost. The mountain gave them that and more besides. And so, really, did they need to leave?

Did Glissete even want to?

She lived for the moment, for the next experience, and if one didn't come she created it. For now, their experiences were in Beastgrave and their following of the ghastlight was merely an excuse to move further and deeper into Direchasm, further and deeper into the mountain's own emotional whirlpool. But the truth was, they might be in here for years if they couldn't – or didn't want to – find their way out. For the rest of their lives, however long that might be.

And there was something... alluring about that idea. All the lives they would influence from now on would be the ones they ended in this cursed mountain. The only legends that would spring up about the Dread Pageant would be whispered by other bands of explorers and maddened, starving groups as they fought each other for eternity, first as living offerings to Slaanesh, and then as undead disciples of sensation. And those legends would be glorious.

Logic said they should turn around and flee back the way they had come, ever upwards until they tasted fresh air and saw blessed daylight. Glissete shook her head; logic meant nothing. Where was intensity in logic? Where was sensation and experience in the safe path, the obvious choice? How did one *feel* or *know* or *live* without risk?

The skaven chittered, breaking into her thoughts, and Glissete shook him into silence. Hadzu crept around the closest corpses, pulling his arrows free and examining the heads to see if they were still useable. He took others from a ratman archer and muttered, casting the magic of self-loathing over them. Any enemy struck by one would become desperate to attack themselves and their own instead of the Hedonites.

And then Vasillac rose. He pointed to a branching tunnel with no hint of hesitation. 'That way. I can smell it.'

Slakeslash looked up from his meal of skaven dead, his fur matted with blood, and examined the tunnel down which Vasillac pointed. With a swift clip of his pincer, he cleaved a skaven's leg, tearing off mouthfuls as he went first, not waiting to see if the others followed.

Vasillac followed Slakeslash, then Glissete dragging Ytash, chittering and limping and sorrowing over his bound claws and casting many a longing glance back at the carcasses of his kin, and Hadzu came last with an arrow loose on the string. A deep, inhuman rumbling rose from the walls around them as Beastgrave roared its impotence that the dead they'd made could not feed it. Glissete and Hadzu exchanged grins, their past altercation buried for now.

The archer reached out to pat the tunnel wall. 'So hungry,' he crooned and chuckled. 'How absolutely terrible.'

'Quiet,' Vasillac snapped back and they fell silent, even Ytash unwilling to incur any more of the Godseeker's wrath. Soon enough Slakeslash dropped back and took possession of the prisoner. Glissete bared her teeth at the slaangor, who snapped his pincer under the woman's nose before turning an insulting shoulder to her. Glissete shifted the glaive on her shoulder, picturing how it would feel to ram it through the slaangor's ribs from behind. But the Godseeker had been more than clear in his threats, so she wallowed in her frustration instead, imagining all the myriad ways she would separate the slaangor from life when the time finally came.

Glissete hurried forward past Vasillac to take the lead Slakeslash had abandoned. She had no wish to feel her lord's anger again, and putting space between herself and the slaangor was the wisest thing she could do in the circumstances. Slakeslash's increasing unpredictability was beginning to make her nervous, and even though she was a Slaaneshi Hedonite, that was one emotion with which she had little experience.

The slaangor was losing himself to the warping magics of the mountain faster than the rest of them, and while Glissete couldn't fault the enthusiasm with which he revelled in the experience, it made him less competent as Vasillac's protector, and that was a liability rather than an advantage. This far into Direchasm, this deep beneath the mountain, Glissete didn't trust Slakeslash to be aware of danger to the group while there was a prisoner to torment, let alone honour the bond between himself and the Godseeker.

Striding along at the front, quartering the tunnel ahead for danger, no one could see Glissete's face or the expression it bore. Slakeslash was going to get them all killed – or Glissete was going to kill him. The slaangor's binding to Vasillac was a secret known only to the two of them: Glissete didn't know its terms or limits. What she did know was that she shouldn't come between the two who had agreed such a compact, but Slakeslash was fracturing the trust that united the Dread Pageant and here, in the bowels of the mountain, mistrust was lethal. Glissete would let no harm come to her lord, yet the slaangor seemed more determined every day to bring harm down upon them.

'We're getting close.'

Vasillac's voice was a low rumble against Glissete's skin and she shivered. He'd appeared at her side without warning, stalking silently up behind her and taking her unawares.

'I can smell it. Smell… something.'

'The Dark Prince will honour our endeavour,' she said softly.

'For all we do is in his name. May I ask how the undead skaven will assist us, lord?'

'He can no longer die, but he can be harmed. He can be bled, and I can use that blood to form a corridor between here and Uhl-Gysh.'

Glissete walked in silence as the implications sank in. They were really doing it; they were going to enter the Mirrored City, lost in a demi-realm and crawling with undead magi, and they were going to find the lost and legendary Book of Pleasure that would lead them to their god.

'Slakeslash is not to be harmed.'

Glissete sucked in a shocked breath at the abrupt change in topic. *How does he know? Does his magic extend to reading the thoughts of others?*

'Lord?' she asked, striving for calm.

He didn't look at her. 'I know your mind. I always have and I always will. Leave him be.' The words did nothing to reassure Glissete, but he spoke again before she could think up some excuse or deflect the conversation somewhere safer.

'There.' He pointed a scarred hand: glistening against the amber darkness was an eerie thread of silver and smoke.

Ghastlight. The merest fracture between Ghur and Uhl-Gysh, through which Vasillac intended eventually to pass. The God-seeker hurried to the wall and pressed his face against the silver thread, inhaling.

'Yes. Yes, it's there. That smell. That... presence. We must find a way into Shadespire and discover the secrets it holds. Hurry.'

He bounded forward into the darkness, and Slakeslash shoved Ytash at Hadzu and followed, passing Glissete with a flash of tawny fur and the clatter of hooves.

'Looks like we're hurrying,' Hadzu said in his bland, dead voice. 'Take the rear.'

Glissete watched them hurry into the strange, shifting orange darkness, following the ghastlight down, ever deeper. Down into the mountain's raging, formless, sweeping emotions. A smile split her face as she followed.

The Dread Pageant revelled in the gloom and the ghastlight, the amber walls and outcrops in which monsters from past and present were entombed, mouths stretched in agony. They revelled in the awful, searing heat of magma that had cut across their path and the intense fear that came with having to leap across it.

They were lost in the guts of Ghur now, and Glissete was glad. She gave in to every urge: treading heavily on the skaven's tail at irregular moments to make him jerk and stumble and squeak; rasping her blade across the walls in an unholy screech that flattened Ytash's and Slakeslash's ears to their heads. She taunted Hadzu and smirked into his black, dead eyes. And yet she checked behind every few paces, pausing to listen for the sounds of pursuit. Direchasm might be eating at her soul, but she was a fighter and a killer and she wouldn't let her lord be taken unawares by an enemy from behind.

Glissete was filled with joy that her life had led her here into this cloying, claustrophobic, living rock. Even if they were ultimately unable to reach Shadespire and instead forced to wander this underground hellscape, the Hedonite knew that if she somehow stumbled onto the exit out of the mountain, she would turn her face from that daylight, from the promise of escape, and retreat back into this eternal gloom that provided her every sensation she could hope to experience. Even if the rest of the Pageant left, she would not. Glissete's life down here would be a living monument to Slaanesh, her every movement an act of worship. And she would see out her days here in Beastgrave's belly.

Curse or not, Glissete was home.

But if they stayed in Beastgrave, or even if they made it to Uhl-Gysh, then everything they were and did would remain unknown, hidden from view. There would be no glory for the Dread Pageant if they did not return to the living world, either with tales of Beastgrave or in possession of the legendary Book of Pleasure. They would be just another group of Slaaneshi loyalists who vanished from the realms and were forgotten.

But what did that matter? They would know, their enemies would know, and Slaanesh would know. Glissete's thoughts bounced from one outcome to another and back again, unformed hysteria bubbling in her belly.

They had come to Beastgrave in response to Vasillac's visions of Slaanesh; they had found the tantalising delight of hurting the mountain. And then they had found so much more. Shadespire and the Book of Pleasure was a destiny none of them could have foreseen. Now that they knew of it, to deny that call, that scent which only Vasillac could detect, would be the vilest and most cowardly heresy. Whether their pursuit of a fissure into the Mirrored City led to a lonely and unremarked death and resurrection in the depths of Direchasm or glory beyond telling was unknown. Trepidation warred with anticipation and swirled in a mad dance inside her as the mountain projected its own emotions on top of hers and she drank it all like the sweetest poison.

Glissete embraced her doubts and fears rather than suppressing them, as ordinary, irreligious humans were wont to do. Where her emotions ended and Beastgrave's began she no longer knew; perhaps the mountain had learnt from their torment of it and was returning the favour, manipulating her consciousness as she did its. She embraced that too and drew strength from it, denying the mountain's intention to break her. They were in combat now, Hedonite and Beastgrave, and if she should be killed down here, then she would experience the ultimate of all sensations – that of dying and returning to unlife with the memory of her ending intact.

After that, Glissete could spend eternity drinking the mountain's distress and whipping it ever further into a frenzy. So much raw sensation sparked like lightning across her nerve endings that her breath was high and shallow and waves of heat chased each other through her bones. Everything was so much *more* down here. It was truly a playground for devotees of Slaanesh. Glissete snorted a sudden laugh, the sound echoing back from the weird, blasted rocks that twisted the path so she couldn't see more than a few paces ahead or behind. The Katophrane curse could well be the most delicious gift it was possible to give a Hedonite.

She trailed a hand lovingly across the smooth amber of the tunnel. The threat of the curse was no longer a threat; the struggle now would be focusing on finding the book instead of chasing death and rebirth. But if they could find such an artefact, the power it granted them would outshine even Beastgrave's.

Glissete pulled her thoughts into order as best she could down here in the mountain's heart. They had a job to do. They were the Dread Pageant and they didn't run from anything.

They ran. Fast and hard and back the way they'd come until the tunnel forked and Vasillac and Slakeslash ran ahead with Glissete hard on their heels. Hadzu and the skaven were behind, but she didn't wait for them to catch up.

The Fist of Ironjawz they'd come across had numbered at least twenty, and Vasillac had signalled that they should find another way around; the fight was beyond them and the fissure they'd been following for the last days was steadily increasing in size. The importance of crossing had grown in all their minds until it consumed them, as though the magic pulled at them, seductive and beckoning – or perhaps it was the song of the book that drew them now. Either way, none had regretted slipping past the orruks without a fight, despite their wealth of food and water. But then Slakeslash – again, the fault lay with the supposedly faithful slaangor – had scuffed his hoof on the stone, deliberately, Glissete was sure, and drawn the Fist's attention.

There'd been no option but to run then, despite the Pageant's proudly stated bravado and lust for battle or the smaller groups of aelves, humans and duardin they'd slaughtered down here. Though to stand and face them, four against twenty, would have been glorious.

Glissete skidded around a corner and spotted Vasillac on his knees with the slaangor looming over him. She spun the glaive in her hands and sprinted towards them with a howled war cry, then jumped up onto a boulder and threw herself through the air towards Slakeslash's head.

The slaangor began to turn towards the sound, but it was too late – almost. One of his tall, pointed antelope horns ripped open the underside of Glissete's upper arm from elbow to armpit. It threw off her aim somewhat, but the bladed end of her polearm went into Slakeslash's back and tore him open – chainmail, fur and muscle – from shoulder to hip.

The slaangor bleated his agony and collapsed beneath Glissete's weight, the pair of them flattening Vasillac. Glissete screamed her own pain but also her triumph – the Godseeker wouldn't die at the pincer or hand of his own bound monster – but then purple-tinged magic blasted from beneath and threw her clear. She slammed into a wall back first and bounced off; rolled twice before coming to a dazed and bloody stop ten feet down the tunnel, her glaive lost somewhere between her and the traitorous slaangor.

The blast or the impact of their falling bodies had ripped Vasillac's helm from his head and his handsome face was tight with fury and anguish, pale where his ritually scarred arms and torso were bronze.

'No.' His voice was cold and full of disbelief.

'He was...' Glissete began, groaning. He didn't even look at her. She rolled up to her knees and clamped her wounded arm to her side in a futile effort to stem the bleeding. Down the corridor she could hear running feet. Hadzu and the skaven.

'Don't.' The word was death and winter and implacability. The Hedonite swallowed her explanation and instead watched as the lord of the Dread Pageant muttered in an arcane tongue. More purple-edged magic, a seeping vapour this time, puffed out from his mouth and eyes and drifted about the weakly pawing slaangor. The smoke separated into tendrils and poked into the wound at a dozen points along its gaping, wet-mouthed length.

No tendrils of healing magic curled Glissete's way, and so she pulled a roll of bandage from the pack on her back and clumsily bound her arm. It needed stitching; she didn't think the Ironjawz were going to wait for her, though.

She found her glaive and cut the bandage on its edge. She flexed her arm, cursing at the hot flash of pain and then accepting it, owning the hurt so that it could not own her. Teeth gritted, she took up her weapon and planted herself at the bend in the tunnel. Hadzu and the skaven would have the enemy close behind them, and Glissete would let the archer and his prisoner through and then hold off the orruks as long as she could. She would die so that Vasillac might live.

The slaangor too.

The words were bitter in her mind, but she pushed them away. When she rose again, she would return to the Dread Pageant and face Vasillac's wrath. It didn't matter that she'd acted to save his life, didn't matter that it had been an honest mistake. Vasillac's tone was her death sentence, but that death would be of her own choosing.

'And I choose violence.' Glissete could feel her body, the slow, stale air currents brushing her face, hear the hitches in Slakeslash's breathing and Vasillac's quiet chanting as he healed him. Almost fancied she could hear the healing itself; the hiss of magic knitting together muscle and flesh, dulling pain and restoring blood and sensation and strength.

The hissing grew louder and more urgent. Closer. Glissete glanced back and saw something moving and writhing above Vasillac and the slaangor. The tunnel roof seemed to be alive.

'Above,' she yelled, abandoning her position at the bend and racing back towards them. Vasillac looked up just as a great jumbled mass of... something fell on them. It broke apart and resolved itself into scores of beetles, each the length of her blade, with shiny black carapaces and sharp, clacking mandibles. Vasillac was roaring and Slakeslash thrashing beneath the tide of black chitinous death.

Glissete leapt into the fray, using wide slashing sweeps and the flat of her glaive to clear the giant insects from the vicinity and give the other two a chance to reach their feet and begin to fight back. Slakeslash was up – unsteady, but up – his pincer slow as he grabbed for and crushed the beetles that scrabbled up his legs and armour.

The Godseeker's spear was not the best weapon against the multitude and yet it seemed made for the task, so little was he hindered. Glissete put her back to his, Slakeslash the third point of the defensive triangle, and they hacked and cut and stamped and swatted until they were ankle-deep in cracked chitin and clotted with purple ichor.

The surviving insects abandoned the attack, their feelers questing towards the tunnel instead. As one mass, they headed in that direction, either towards Hadzu and Ytash, or perhaps the Fist of Ironjawz. Glissete wiped her glaive clean of ichor and cracked carapace. Her hands and face and neck were abraded and sliced where the insects' mandibles had closed on her flesh – the others weren't much better, though the healing magic Vasillac had poured into the slaangor was still working within him, for his cuts and scratches disappeared beneath Glissete's envious gaze.

'Lord Vasillac, forgive me,' she said, while she still had the chance before the orruks found them. If this was to be their death, she would have Vasillac's understanding, if not his forgiveness. The Godseeker's expression was hidden beneath his restored helm, but his mouth was tight.

'You were told.'

'I thought he was attacking you!' Glissete tried. 'I came around the corner and he was over you and you were on the floor.'

Vasillac scraped his boot through the beetle debris on the ground, clearing a space. Then, with a swiftness she wasn't prepared for, he grabbed her by the nape of the neck and hurled her onto her knees. 'Look,' he spat. 'Look there.'

The pressure on her neck increased and Glissete crumpled lower, her vision blurry with pain, but still she saw it. The ghastlight. The fissure had widened here, wide enough that she could put her arm in if she wanted to. Fear bloomed in her chest – perhaps that would be her punishment. None of them knew whether they could cross into the demi-realm without being destroyed. What if Vasillac made her shove her arm into Uhl-Gysh to see what would happen? An image of being trapped up to the shoulder in the floor while Ironjawz hacked her apart crossed her mind.

'I sent my magic through, searching. Slakeslash guarded me while my mind was spooling into Uhl-Gysh. Not only did you nearly kill him, you nearly severed me from my body.' He shook her hard by her neck and she whimpered.

'I'm sorry, lord,' she said, her voice tight and high with pain and anxiety. 'It was an honest mistake. Slakeslash has been–'

He shook her again and she bit her tongue. 'Get up,' he snarled, releasing her.

Glissete lurched sideways with none of her usual grace and

stood, knowing better than to massage the crushed muscles of her neck. She kept her eyes down, meek in submission. Seething with frightened rage.

'Where are the others?'

'I don't know, lord.'

'Then go and find them. We're going that way, away from the orruks and following this fissure, and we're not waiting for you. I only need the skaven.'

The casual, cruel dismissal in Vasillac's tone cut at her, but she just nodded and fled. The beetles and the orruks were likely between her and Hadzu with his prisoner, but she could no more argue with her lord's command than she could fly.

She slowed at the bend, holding her breath and listening as the hot, throbbing agony in her arm beat in time with her heart. The scrape of metal and bellowing snarls of battle echoed back to her. They weren't as close as she'd feared, and it definitely didn't sound like they were fighting insects. An alien, unidentifiable trumpeting bounced around the cavern and tunnels, louder by far than the orruks' war cries. Fear slithered up Glissete's spine.

She dared a glance around the bend and found it empty. She exhaled in silent relief, darted into the space and ran back down the twisting tunnel until she came to the fork. The sounds grew steadily louder, and beyond the fork was the large cavern where they'd first found the Fist. Something, some unknown creature, had appeared between the Pageant and the pursuing orruks and then forced the latter back. Glissete didn't want to think about what sort of being was capable of stopping a charging Fist of Ironjawz.

The Hedonite took the dog-leg into the other tunnel and crept along it, glaive at the ready and senses straining. The urge to call out for Hadzu was strong, but it was almost certain death. It was probably not her own urge, but Beastgrave's. The mountain was growing in cunning, as well as brutality.

The swirling echo of battle behind disguised the sound of running footsteps; Glissete rounded a corner and came face to face with an orruk that was half again as tall as her and at least three times her weight. Fear and fury mingled within her and she raised her glaive as the orruk's huge, serrated blade – more club than sword and black with old blood and rust – began to punch forward to cleave her in half. Glissete skidded onto her knees on the rough stone, ripping her trousers and the flesh beneath. The sword split the air above her with a whine, but she was already past it, within the orruk's guard, and her glaive thudded home deep in its thigh.

The orruk stumbled back, its sword falling with a clatter as one huge hand clamped around the spurting wound and the other closed on her face.

The punch sent her sprawling backwards, lights flashing in her head and blood on her teeth, but she scrambled up using the polearm as a crutch and threw herself back at him. Glissete jumped, evading the orruk's second swing. The glaive flashed in the gloom as she brought it sweeping down on the Ironjawz brute's neck. She landed with the weapon in guard, ready for anything and blinking desperately against threatening unconsciousness, but the orruk stood slack and swaying, its eyes glazed as blood fountained from throat and thigh. And then it collapsed backwards like a tree, chainmail and the scraps of stolen armour clattering against the stone.

Glissete fell to one knee, her fingers tight on her glaive, sucking in deep breaths to clear her head. To her right, the direction she'd been heading, she caught what might have been the glint of eyes. The mountain's madness yammered against her skin and senses until she doubted that she'd seen anything, but she forced herself to stand once more. It could be a trap, but whether one laid by orruks or by Beastgrave she couldn't say.

No matter what waits for me, I will taste its death before my own finds me. I will meet Slaanesh with blood on my blade and a surfeit of sensation to gift to him. Excess in all things.

With her vow pumping dark and seductive through the chambers of her heart, Glissete broke into a shambling run towards the gleaming eyes. She was a dozen paces away when the skaven prisoner shuffled out of the gloom, his tied paws raised in front of his snout and his ears back in anticipation of pain to come. The effort required to slow and lower her glaive was almost too much – the urge to slam it through the skaven's chest was a hot need flowing through her chest.

But she slowed. She stopped. She was lowering the glaive as Hadzu sauntered forwards with his habitual grin, at which point it twitched in her hands again.

'You all went the wrong way,' he whispered, and Glissete scowled.

She held her finger to her lips and motioned back down the tunnel. Hadzu gestured her on, the skaven in between them, and they crept back down the tunnel and past the orruk corpse. They had just reached the left-hand tunnel when a wild victory chant echoed from the cavern to their right, a blast of sound and violence.

'Go,' Glissete hissed, ripping her blade through the ropes binding the skaven's paws. She took the turning and put her head down, accelerating into a hard sprint. Every pump of her arm sent a flash of pain through the tear in her flesh, but she had no time to worry about the wound ripping. The ratman's paws skittered after her, and Hadzu came last with an arrow nocked and ready to slow down the fastest of the Fist.

The trio trampled through the shattered corpses of the black beetles that had attacked Vasillac and the slaangor, and continued into the darkness of the passage the Godseeker had indicated. Behind them, the Ironjawz thundered after, not as swift as the humans and skaven, but relentless.

Over her rasping breath and jangling chainmail, Glissete heard the sound change ahead of her. There was a sudden gust of foul air against her face and the passage opened up. Opened and ended in a sheer cliff that spread to either side, as if the ground had been scooped out by a giant hand. She screeched a warning and skidded to a halt. The skaven thumped into her back, graceless, and she tripped and stumbled at the very edge of the precipice. Slakeslash lunged from the darkness and grabbed her flailing arm and dragged her to safety.

Glissete looked up into the slaangor's unreadable face, but he had already let go and was beckoning them out onto a tiny ledge leading around the crevasse. Glissete followed, dumb with surprise. After everything, the slaangor had saved her life without hesitation. Vasillac was farther ahead, his outline lit by ghastlight that glowed more brightly than she had ever seen it. The thread had become a fissure had become a crack they could definitely squeeze through, and there was a wide spit of rock hanging over the chasm where they could perform the ritual that would – should – allow them to cross into the demi-realm.

They hurried around the ledge and to the Godseeker's side.

'This is it,' he said as soon as they arrived. 'This is where we cross. Can you feel it? Feel the magic and the pull of it? The book calls to me.'

Glissete didn't answer. The hungers and rages and bitter hurts of Beastgrave flowed from the pit beneath them, caustic and foul as the air. Despite the glorious promise of what lay ahead of them, she was filled with regret at leaving a sentience so vast and so tormented.

Vasillac gestured and Hadzu shoved the skaven forwards.

Ytash sank onto his haunches and began to chitter. 'Not the bad light, lords. Don't put him back in the bad light with the bad people. Ytash will fight at your side, yes he will, yes, all your enemies. Just don't put him back in the bad light.'

The bad light – the ghastlight – flickered and darkened as if in response to his pleas and then bulged, as if it were a membrane rather than a glow. It deformed and stretched out of the crack and then split open – and a dozen people stepped through. Gaunt and tall, clad in strange armour or flowing, ragged robes with deep hoods, they paused, silhouetted, just this side of the crack.

'Mages and warriors of the Mirrored City,' Hadzu breathed, his voice coated with awe.

Vasillac stepped forwards, using his spear as a staff rather than held ready in threat. 'My lords and high ones, I am Vasillac the Gifted, Godseeker of the Dread Pageant and devotee of the Dark Prince Slaanesh. Tell me, have you come from Shadespire? Is there a book there, somewhere within your famous city, that–'

And then they saw it. Not mages or warriors. These shambling creatures were more bone than flesh, undead skeletons held together with desiccated strips of sinew. A robed one stepped forward and levelled a staff. Green flame burst from the end and raced towards the Godseeker. Vasillac brought his spear down and across, shouting a word of power, and dispelled the blast with one of his own.

The undead attacked, fanning out so that two warriors protected every mage. 'We wish to cross into Shadespire!' Vasillac screamed, but the words were lost beneath three concussive booms of magic discharging, the explosions echoing across the vast chasm. The Pageant dived for safety, the skaven too, and Glissete rolled over her shoulder and came up inside the guard of a spear-carrier. Before the undead warrior could react, Glissete hacked off its arm and slashed through its throat.

It fell, and the Hedonite picked up the severed limb and threw it at another, spoiling the aim of its fireball so that it blasted into another of the undead instead of Hadzu's back. She followed it in, cutting low and shearing through bone even as she ducked its warrior companion's spear thrust. She spun behind the mage-skeleton and ripped her glaive across the back of its neck, severing the spine. It collapsed, but Glissete was forced to somersault out of the way of the next attack.

Hadzu's arrows had no effect, some passing harmlessly through robe or armour, unhindered by flesh beneath. Killing them wouldn't work – they were already centuries dead – but dismemberment might.

Glissete backed away from an undead's snake-quick spear, butt and blade of her glaive both defending and attacking. Slakeslash appeared on her right. He caught the Katophrane's spear in his pincer and snapped the head off it so that it was just a useless stick, and between them they cut the warrior onto its knees and then took off its head. But they were outnumbered against an enemy that could not be defeated.

The Dread Pageant backed farther away from the tiny ledge they'd crossed to reach this point. The edge of the lip of rock over the pit was less than twenty paces behind, and every step in that direction took them farther from the crack into Uhl-Gysh. This, then, was the end of their glorious quest. So be it.

'I will rise again after my death and we will continue this battle for eternity,' she screamed at the undead bearing down on them. 'For Slaanesh I will drink deep of pain and suffering and lust and joy. We will all die and rise a million times, and each moment of our agony will be a joy to him.'

'Down!' Vasillac screamed and she didn't hesitate, throwing herself into a tumble on the uneven stone, her shoulder and hip bruising bone-deep on jagged rock.

A blast of purple magic bigger than any she'd seen before rippled overhead and into their attackers, forcing them back towards the ledge leading around the chasm and into the tunnels. Back from the Dread Pageant and the way into the Mirrored City. Back into the welcoming arms of the Fist of Ironjawz who had followed them to this place of their final confrontation.

The numbers now were more evenly matched, and both forces seemed to forget about the existence of the Hedonites and their skaven sacrifice.

'Quickly,' Vasillac shouted, and the four of them grabbed Ytash by armour and arms and handfuls of fur, and dragged him to the ghastlight crack.

'Not the bad light again. Not the bad light!' He gibbered and pleaded and struggled, to no avail.

There was no time for grace or a protracted undeath; the God-seeker simply dragged his spear tip across Ytash's throat, holding the shuddering skaven in the ghastlight itself. The tips of his fur silvered and his blood steamed within its glow. Tendrils of shadow-magic stroked towards the skaven and his pooling life force.

They touched him and then shoved down through his gaping mouth and gaping throat, and yanked him through the crack.

Vasillac ripped off his helm. He scooped up a handful of blood and smeared it across his face and neck, even licked it from his fingers. Then he reached out with a red palm and grasped the nearest tendril of ghastlight. It curled around his hand and up his wrist, seeming to drink the blood – blood that was not his. Before it could reject him – if such a thing were even possible – the Godseeker stood up, still holding the tendril firmly in his hand, and stepped forward. The crack bulged, light flared, and Vasillac disappeared.

'Lord!' Slakeslash bleated. He copied Vasillac's actions, splashing himself in skaven blood and grabbing onto the magic. Then he shoved forward and muscled his way into the light.

Into the light? Or into Uhl-Gysh? Or just into death, lost between realms in endless black and eternal cold? Glissete didn't know. She exchanged a glance with Hadzu, who shrugged.

'It'll be intense, at least,' he said.

Together, they repeated the ritual and stepped forward. The ghastlight was both bright and dirty, at once the searing heat of a forge and the cold of an ice storm. It battered at Glissete and she lost sight of Hadzu, lost sight of everything, trapped in an eternity of conflicting sensation that assailed her mind and tore her body. It was exquisite.

And then she was on her knees on unfamiliar stone, beneath a sky that hurt to look at and surrounded by buildings of angular, alien magnificence. Surrounded, too, by the other three members of the Dread Pageant and Ytash, still chittering but in rage now, his yellowed incisors exposed and his fur bristling.

Beyond them, hundreds of undead turned as one to regard them, their fleshless faces set in permanent grins reflected in the dull steel of their weapons.

THE SIEGE
OF GREENSPIRE

Anna Stephens

Brida Devholm, captain of the Freeguild company Lady's Justice, watched with dismay as the most incompetent of her new recruits staggered, fell and landed hard on the stone courtyard that made up the ground floor of the watchtower known as Greenspire. The barrel he was carrying slammed onto the flagstones and split, and a cascade of fine black powder spilt forth over him and the stone while clouds of it plumed into the air.

Brida leapt back on instinct. 'Careful, idiot,' she shouted. 'You want to blow us all up? That's gunpowder! Why not just strike a spark while you're at it?'

It was no use. Kende had hit his chin on the top of the barrel as he went down and was sitting in the drift of gunpowder, bleary-eyed and spitting blood from a bitten tongue. 'Sorry, captain,' he managed. He made it to his knees, upended the broken barrel and began scooping the powder back into the hole cracked into it, scraping handfuls up off the stones.

Brida ran forwards and snatched the barrel from him, spilling more onto herself and the ground with the violence of the movement. 'By the Lady, are you stupid?' she demanded, despite the clear evidence confirming her suspicion. She pointed at the ground as he blinked up at her, confused. 'That powder's contaminated now, full of dirt and dust, your blood and sweat, stone chips even. You've just mixed it with the pure still left in the barrel.' He stared at her, still not understanding, and Brida cursed him silently.

'Do you know what happens when you put dirty gunpowder in the firing pan of your musket? Either it doesn't fire, leaving you unarmed against the hordes trying to claw your guts out of your belly, or it backfires and blows your damn hand off. Which would you prefer, Kende?'

Kende wiped blood from his chin with a blackened hand and scrambled to his feet. 'Um, neither?' he ventured.

Brida nodded. 'Neither. Good choice. Now think what would happen if you loaded it into the breech of a cannon.' She cursed again as she peered through the split wood and gave the barrel a tentative shake, judging its weight. It had been full. She groaned and gave it back to him. 'Congratulations. Your first month's wages are forfeit to enable me to purchase more powder, though it's anybody's guess when the suppliers will be back this way. And don't even think about complaining.' She stared him out and Kende closed the mouth that had been about to utter something very unwise.

'Shovel the rest of it back in there and then mark up the barrel with chalk so we know not to use it in the weapons. Might be we can sprinkle it in some of the traps out front, add a little excitement for when the beasts come again. And then sweep this yard – I don't want a stray spark setting my company alight because the ground's dusted with gunpowder. And then report for night duty – no, I don't care that you've just pulled a day shift. And try not to fall over your own feet next time, yes? Alarielle knows what you'll be like in an actual fight.'

The torrent of orders and abuse withered the man like a tree before Nurgle's rot and he nodded, mute, his black-stained face slack with chagrin. Brida bit the inside of her cheek to stop herself saying more, and sighed. She shouldn't be too hard on him; he'd been a farmer before a tzaangor warflock from the Hexwood took everyone he loved and he swore to end his days fighting them. The problem was, he was doing a damn fine job of trying to take Lady's Justice and Greenspire with him when he went.

His was a common enough tale in Verdia and, truth be told, she knew a thing or two about that driving need for vengeance and where it could take a person. She just had to hope Kende could learn weapons easier than he could carry barrels of gunpowder across a flagstoned courtyard. And he wasn't the only one. The last skirmish had left her company under-strength, and they'd replaced the dead with a dozen raw recruits – some barely more than children, the others merchants or farmers like Kende. A dozen who didn't know which end of a sword was safe to hold. One, Raella, who'd discovered she didn't like heights and cried every time she stood watch on the third level, spending most of her time with her eyes screwed shut and clinging to the guard wall until they prised her loose and sent her down to the ground floor again.

A muscle jumped in Brida's jaw, but she managed to keep her frustration trapped behind her teeth as Kende resumed funnelling wasted powder into the barrel. He'd learn or he'd die, all of them would; that was the way of it out here on the Emerald Line, which stretched from Fort Gardus to Hammerhal-Ghyra. Brida's concern was that they didn't take too many seasoned soldiers with them into death.

Above, Greenspire's bell rang the changing of the watch, and Brida left Kende to his task with a final reminder to bathe and change before going near any naked flames. She jogged up the stairs to the top floor of the tower and marched a brisk round of all four sides. This evening the approaches from the Hexwood were clear, although there was a tangle of vine crawling out from the treeline towards them, already closer and thicker than it had been at dawn. Brida rubbed a weary hand across her face. The Lady of Leaves would need to be propitiated and placated before they could hack away the vines; left untouched they would strangle Greenspire, cracking the strong stone foundations and tumbling it into ruin, leaving a gap in the Emerald Line through which the beastkin and tzaangors of the Hexwood could launch attacks.

'A captain's work is never done,' Brida muttered under her breath, though in truth she wouldn't have it any other way. Her hand found the thick gold ring hanging from its cord around her neck and she squeezed it, feeling the reassuring weight and warmth of the metal – more habit than reminder of all she'd lost to bring her to this point. It wasn't often she thought of her life before, but Kende's earnest incompetence and the hesitant, awkward actions of the other recruits brought back an old pain, one never fully healed.

She was relieved when Drigg, her duardin second-in-command, appeared at her side and the memory rolled like a corpse in a river and submerged again. It'd be back, it never left her for long, but hopefully not tonight to steal her sleep. 'All quiet?' Drigg asked. He'd been awake for a couple of hours and already knew the answer, but she appreciated him asking. It signalled the formal transference of power from her to him for the night watch.

'Too quiet, and for too many days,' Brida said. 'I don't like it.'

Drigg laughed, the sound rusty and low in his throat, and shifted the double-headed axe hanging from his belt. 'You wouldn't like it if Sigmar and Alarielle themselves came down here and proclaimed the war against Chaos over, the enemy defeated, and all of us able to go home to peace.'

The corner of Brida's mouth twitched. 'I'm a careful sort,' she acknowledged.

Drigg shook his head. 'You say careful, the rest of us say suspicious and untrusting. And this is a duardin speaking. Careful is what we do.'

Brida glared at him for a long second, but there was no heat in it. 'It's strange how often the two sentiments can be confused. Check floor two for me, would you? Orla reported an issue with cannon one, something about the vent hole being blocked, so I've ordered crossbow emplacements set up at each corner. I know, I know, I'd have told you earlier if I'd known earlier. I didn't. You'll have to tinker with it in the morning, we can't risk moving it now. Even a visual deterrent's better than nothing. Oh, and Kende's pulling a double shift – or maybe a triple if I decide he's on duty tomorrow as well, so keep an eye on him. He's greener than springtime and clumsier than a one-legged tzaangor, but he needs to learn, and fast.'

'Because you have a bad feeling?' Drigg asked.

'Because I have a bad feeling, and because he's fouled an entire barrel of gunpowder,' Brida confirmed. 'You have the watch, lieutenant.'

Drigg saluted and stepped back. 'I have the watch,' he confirmed formally. 'So you can take your bad feeling off my wall,' he muttered, and only their long familiarity allowed him the privilege – and then only when no other soldier could overhear. Drigg and Devholm, backbone of Lady's Justice for twenty years. Other than Brock, Orla and a couple of others, the only surviving members of the company from back when it was formed. Years and battles and deaths and horrors they'd been through, saved each other's lives more times than she could remember, and she'd never once got Drigg to admit her bad feeling had been right. He always insisted it was coincidence.

She listened to his footsteps retreating along the walkway, the crisp commands as the watch was handed from the day to the night units. The wind hummed around the watchtower, warm and pleasant and vibrant with life – and, every so often and only from the west, tainted. The tiniest breath of foulness, there and then gone so fast she almost couldn't detect it. But there.

Brida's scarred fists clenched on the waist-high guard wall and though she was now officially off-duty, she didn't move. There was something wrong.

There was something coming.

The watch changed again at dawn and Kende was found asleep at his post. So was Raella, who should have been preparing the meal that would end the night watch's shift and begin the day watch's. Instead, all of them went hungry for an extra hour while she frantically stoked the ovens and baked, in some cases burned, the bread and scalded the porridge. It was poor fare, and it put the whole company in a mood.

Brida was staring through an arrow slit at the tangle of vine, taller than she was now and closer than ever, when Drigg brought them both to her. He was shamefaced and furious in equal measure – the night watch was his duty, so the failure was also his. He offered to endure the recruits' punishment along with them, in a voice loud and clear that carried across the yard and brought everyone within earshot to a halt. Those recruits who'd managed to stay awake muttered to the more experienced Freeguilders, surprised and a little awed by Drigg's offer. Their respect for him grew, but Brida knew if she agreed, their opinion of her would fall.

She turned him down, but she had no choice but to punish the pair, smacking her spear shaft across their backs three times each and driving them to their knees, welts and bruises springing up on their skin. It was worse than they'd anticipated though less than the proper flogging they deserved, and both shouted in pain; Raella begged to be allowed to resign from the company.

'No. You signed up for a year and a year is what you'll give me. We're under-strength and I can't afford to lose you. You're going to learn to be a soldier, and a damn good one at that.'

Raella burst into tears again and ran for the kitchens. Brida didn't like punishing her soldiers, but Lady's Justice was a tight-knit company, a hard and disciplined company, and over the years they'd all received punishment for similar infractions. Brida herself had the scars that told of her own insubordination back when she'd been a grunt.

Just because Kende and Raella were new and still grieving whatever horrors had led them here, that didn't mean they got a longer rein than the rest of the company. And best to find out Raella's mettle – or lack of it – now than when they were beset by the worshippers of Tzeentch. Lady's Justice didn't break and run. Raella had broken already and Brida couldn't afford sympathy for the woman. Her job now was to take Raella's broken pieces and fit them together into something hard and sharp – a weapon. She hoped she'd have enough time to do it before the next attack.

'We're on the frontier, Kende,' she said. 'We're part of the thin line between Hammerhal-Ghyra and the Hexwood, between civilisation and Chaos. Between joy and despair, and life and death. We're here to prevent what happened to your family from happening to everyone in the realm. I have to be able to trust you and know that you'll follow my orders, that I can depend on you. At the moment I can't. You have ten days to prove me wrong. Shadow Lieutenant Drigg, learn from him, and for the Lady's sake try and stay awake.'

He didn't ask what would happen after ten days. He didn't argue and he didn't beg for leniency or even promise to do better. He just gave her a sloppy salute and walked away too fast for dignity. She watched him go, frowning, wondering if she'd made a mistake. Perhaps it would be better to cull him and Raella now, cut the rot from her company before it had a chance to spread. He'd been sullen, and there was no place for resentment in Lady's Justice. No place for anything except dedication to the cause and belief in the Lady of Leaves.

Twenty years as a soldier had taught Brida much, and she knew with bone-deep certainty that Kende wasn't going to make her believe in him in ten days. But what else could she do? She needed him. She needed them all.

The beastkin attacks had been increasing in frequency of late – increasing in cunning too, which worried her more. Greenspire's neighbouring watchtowers, Highoak and Willowflame, had both reported growing pressure from skirmishes. Couriers were vanishing on the roads strung along the Emerald Line, and the green alchemical flames that burned day and night at the top of each tower were changing to red to signal attacks more and more often. Even on a clear day, the flames were all that could be seen through the miles separating each tower, and usually by the time Lady's Justice had marched to the aid of a red-crowned neighbour, the attack was over.

Part of Brida longed for a full-scale battle, a chance for all the Freeguilders to unite to crush the enemy. This probing of the Line worried her. It suggested an unexpected intelligence guiding the horde's attacks.

Mostly, those dazed and lucky few who survived an attack fled to bigger towns and cities, abandoning their farms and orchards to scrape a living on the streets or as labourers in the sky-docks. Only a very few found the courage to transform their loss into fire and join the Freeguild. Lady's Justice had been under-strength for half a year before Kende and the rest were finally allocated to them and Greenspire. Even if they'd each had the resourcefulness and skill of five soldiers, they would not have made up the shortfall. And if Kende's anger or Raella's timidity infected the other recruits... Brida's gut wound another notch tighter.

'I should have meted out their punishment,' Drigg said from behind, and then yawned wide enough to swallow a cannonball. 'They slept on my watch.'

'No, better they hate me and respect you. Kende's going to need a lot of babying – I've given him ten days – and you're better at that than me. Help him but push him wherever you can. I'll put Brock on Raella – his charm and encouragement might work better on her. We need them all, and none of them are ready for anything except feeding to monsters.' She slapped him on the arm. 'Go on, fix that cannon for me and then get some sleep – we'll speak again before dusk.'

Brida found Drigg at noon. He was hunched over the cannon in his workshop following a complicated hour spent with rope, tackle and pulleys lowering it from the second level to the court-yard, then trundling it into the sooty, alchemical-smelling gloom. The duardin leapt to his feet when Brida's shadow fell over him, and she noted the instinctive dart of his hand towards his axe. A cold weight settled into her stomach.

'Look at this,' he grated. She advanced and took the object he handed her, then looked from it to where he was pointing on the cannon and back again. Brida had always preferred spears and swords to cannons and muskets, but that didn't mean she didn't understand artillery.

Air hissed through her teeth. 'Someone's spiked it?'

'Yes, and done a good job, too. It was sitting flush with the vent, barely visible. On casual inspection it looked fine. Whoever's done this didn't want us to realise we couldn't fire her until we needed to. Say, when we came under attack.'

Brida met the duardin's deep-set eyes. 'You're saying we've a traitor in Lady's Justice?'

'I'm saying it's taken me most of the morning to bore out the spike without damaging the vent. We'll still need to test-fire a few balls and I won't allow anyone near it when I do in case she blows. I don't know who spiked it or why, but after I'm done here I'll be checking the other cannons and the muskets too. I'll be checking firing pans and barrel rifling and everything else I can think of.'

Sweat prickled at Brida's hairline. There was a joke in there somewhere about how he thought her untrusting, but there was nothing funny about the situation. 'You check the cannons, I'll check the rest. Then get some sleep, that's an order. I need your eyes sharp for the enemy.' She gestured. 'Outside Greenspire – and maybe inside it.'

Drigg nodded and bent to the cannon without another word. She left him to it, striding back out into the bright day with suspicions blackening her heart.

She spotted Brock and called him over, reassured as ever by his easy competence, his ready smile. If she was the head of Lady's Justice, Brock was the heart, and his return from Fort Gardus had given them all a boost. A joke and a wink at the right time from him solved most disputes before they escalated, and his easy reminiscences of mistakes made when he first joined up served to reassure the recruits that they, too, could get better with practice.

'What do you think of the new lot, sergeant?' she asked as she led him to the armoury.

'About as useful as you'd expect, captain,' the tall man said. 'Though they're having much the same issues even at Fort Gardus, if that's any consolation, as well as along the Line. Too many youngsters and old folks, not enough steady hands. That Kende's a waste of uniform and I wouldn't be surprised if Raella poisons us all.'

Brida gave him a sharp look. 'Can they be trusted?'

Brock's eyebrows shot up. 'Trusted? That's a strange question, captain. They're young and they're nervous, but they're decent enough. Why do you ask?'

They ducked inside before she answered. 'Someone sabotaged cannon one. Spiked the vent. I trust the rest of Lady's Justice with my life – gods, most of them have saved it at least once, you included – but the recruits? That's a different matter.'

Brock's mouth was hanging open, but he snapped it shut and thought. Brida reached for the first musket in the rack and let him. Slow and steady, was Brock. No point in hurrying the man. She checked the firing pan and cocking mechanism, peered down the barrel.

'I haven't noticed anything so far. I mean, Kende's useless, but I'd have said he was harmless, too, before this. He was stationed by the cannon yesterday – could he have done it then? Would he even know how to spike a cannon? I can fetch his records, check his background.'

Brida selected the next musket, repeated her inspection. 'Vine-town, down west. A small agricultural town that provided wheat, oats and barley to Fort Gardus. Attacked and destroyed by tzaan-gors eight months ago. Kende was one of only a dozen survivors.'

Brida made a point of knowing the histories of every one of her soldiers. For the longest-serving members of Lady's Justice, their histories were hers and as familiar as the feel of her spear in her hand. She'd learnt the stories of the recruits as well, but they didn't open up to their captain the way they would to a friendly, easy-going sergeant, and Brock had been on a supply run to Fort Gardus for pig iron when Kende and the rest arrived.

It wasn't Brock's responsibility to assess the recruits, of course, but over the years she'd come to rely on his judgement and now she needed it more than ever. 'Work your charm with Kende and the others,' she said as she picked up another musket. 'Let me know if anyone seems off to you, but don't make it obvious. You know the drill.'

'Yes, captain,' Brock said. 'I won't let you down.'

Brida found a smile for him. 'You never have.'

Drigg and a team of ten had manoeuvred the cannon back into place, and he'd checked the other two as promised and found everything in perfect working order. It was mid-afternoon before he'd tumbled into bed in the small room in the officers' barracks. Brida could hear his snores from where she sat outside, checking the supply lists in the shade away from Ghyran's fierce sun. Even after twenty years, the sound amused and infuriated her in equal measure.

'Captain?'

'What is it, Orla?' she asked the gunner.

The short woman's freckled face was pale despite her tan. 'Three day watch taken sick, captain. It's coming out both ends, if you get my meaning. They're in the infirmary.'

I wouldn't be surprised if Raella poisons us all. Brock's words rang in Brida's head as she shoved the papers onto her desk and weighed them down with a mug. 'What have they eaten?' she demanded. 'Who made it?'

Orla stepped back from Brida's vehemence. 'Nothing, just the same as the rest of us and we're fine. Do you want–'

She was cut off by the sight of Raella running from the kitchen. Brida's hand went to her spear, but then the woman was on her knees in a corner vomiting. 'Bring her to the infirmary,' she said, and ran for the building herself.

Over the next hour fourteen more soldiers arrived, until there were no beds left and the room stank of vomit. 'Heatstroke?' Brida asked Tomman as Raella sipped from a cup and promptly threw it back up again. The physician shook his head. 'Poison?'

'It seems most likely, but the method of ingestion is unknown. Perhaps they've touched something smeared with it, or–'

But Brida wasn't listening. 'We all ate the same, yes. But you and I haven't drunk from the water barrels on the levels. Orla?'

The gunner shook her head and patted the waterskin slung over her shoulder. 'From this morning,' she said.

Brida slapped a fist into her palm. 'That must be it. Orla, go and wake up Drigg. Brock, with me. You too, Tomman.'

The sergeant hurried after her and they met Orla and a bleary-eyed Drigg in the courtyard. 'We're low on gunpowder, a cannon gets spiked, and now my soldiers are taking sick,' she said to the huddled group. 'Tomman, I need you to test the water barrels on each level for poison, then the well – day watch will have been drinking a lot in this heat. Brock, Orla, see anything suspicious around the barrels or well in the last couple of hours?' They both shook their heads. 'Damn. Fine, Drigg and I will begin questioning–'

The bell on Greenspire's third level began to ring. 'Attack, attack from the Hexwood. Warflock, some hundreds!'

Brida exchanged a horrified look with Drigg. 'All hands,' she said. 'Tomman, get those samples, then Orla, confiscate the barrels. Brock, cap the well. Tomman, do whatever you have to to get the sick on their feet and ready to fight. Powders, potions, I don't care. Just do it, and then find or create me a clean water supply. Fighting soldiers are thirsty soldiers.'

Freeguilders began sprinting to the armoury for muskets, powder and shot. Others stumbled from the barracks, cursing and fumbling with the buckles of their armour. Dusk was beginning to pool in the sky. Brida looked at the duardin, her mouth dry. 'Crimson the flame.' Drigg blinked away the last of his fatigue and broke into a run for the nearest stairwell.

Brida snatched up her spear and took the stairs two at a time, cracking her knee into the wall at the second level turning, and cursing as pain spiked through her leg with every step. She was breathless when she reached the third level and sprinted onto the allure, craving water now she knew she couldn't have it.

The sight that met her eyes dried her throat even further. Tzaangors, their beaks and horns sheathed in steel and reflecting the dying light, raced across the open ground bearing jagged weapons. Beastkin, twisted giant wolves and maddened bear-things with too many teeth, too many claws, thundered alongside.

Brock reappeared. 'Well's capped, captain. And, I don't know, but does it seem a bit too convenient that Orla has a separate supply of water to everyone else on the day they're all getting sick?'

Brida blinked at him, uncomprehending for a moment. 'Orla? I've known her as long as I have you and Drigg!'

Brock wouldn't look at her. 'Of course, captain.'

Brida stared over the wall at the oncoming flock, but she wasn't seeing it. Orla was the gunnery sergeant. She knew how to spike a cannon. Could it be more than a coincidence? Had one of Lady's Justice walked into the arms of Chaos and agreed to betray Devholm and all the soldiers under her command? But why? *Why?*

'Captain?'

'Drigg, there you are. We've got enough powder for a dozen shots each, so get... What now?' A throbbing pain began behind Brida's eyes at the duardin's gloomier than usual expression.

'Flame won't crimson, captain. I've changed the alchemical compounds three times – she just keeps burning green. No one's coming.'

Brida looked up, as though she could see the fire through the stone separating them. 'That's not possible.'

'Sputters crimson for a heartbeat and then greens again. It's trying, the alchemy's there, but something's holding it back. I'd say we've some sort of mage in Greenspire. They've spell-locked the flame, bound it to something living. Or someone.'

'So we kill them and the flame crimsons?' Brida asked, biting back the urge to scream. No one was coming to Lady's Justice's aid.

'Theoretically. Need to know who it is first.' He stroked his beard. 'Come to think of it, I took Kende up there last week. He was curious, asked a lot of questions about the flame – how it changes colour, when we'd signal for help and how long it'd take to arrive. Thought we might've had a budding engineer on our hands until his recent lapses in discipline.'

Brida stared between her two officers and then out at the approaching warflock again, closing fast on their position. She didn't have time for this, but she couldn't let a traitor run around loose in Greenspire, either. She sucked air through flared nostrils. 'Drigg, prime the cannons.'

The duardin blew out his cheeks. 'Orla's gunnery sergeant,' he began, and Brida rounded on him.

'And right now you're one of only two people I trust, so you're gunnery sergeant. Get to it.'

Drigg stepped back from her fury and saluted, then clattered down the stairs without a backward glance, giving no indication of what he thought of her implication.

'Brock, get me Orla and Kende, now.'

The warflock had reached the broken ground and pit traps dug into the rich soil around Greenspire. She had to make this fast. *Please don't be Orla,* she thought as she waited, the tower humming with activity and shouted orders, the controlled panic of a company about to come under attack.

Orla, Brock and Kende arrived at her position. 'Captain? You don't want me on the cannons?' the woman asked, a wrinkle of confusion between her brows.

'Where were you both when people started getting sick?' Brida demanded, turning from the enemy picking their way through the maze. The cannons would open up any minute now, the crossbows when they reached the marker flags that signalled they were in range.

Orla's frown deepened; Kende just looked confused. 'On watch, captain. As always. Forgive me, but didn't we have this conversation in the infirmary? I haven't drunk the water.'

'I was counting supplies with Raella in the kitchen before she felt ill,' Kende said.

'Who replenished the water barrels?' Brock demanded. 'It was you and Raella, wasn't it? And you oversaw it, Orla.'

'I did,' the woman said with stiff indignation. 'You saw me. You watched me do it. What are you saying, sergeant?'

Brock glanced at Brida as though that settled it. Perhaps it did.

'You're both relieved of duty and will be confined to the cells to stand trial once we have repelled this attack,' Brida said heavily. It didn't sit right with her, but they were fast running out of time before the enemy was at the very walls of Greenspire. And the cannons still weren't firing. 'Put your weapons on the floor and step back, keep your hands where I can see them.'

'Captain,' Orla tried, but Brock muscled in between them and wrenched the spear from her. Kende threw his to the stone and put his hands up, his habitual confusion drowned beneath fear. Fear of her, or of discovery? Or of the hordes coming to tear them to pieces?

'Get them out of here, sergeant,' Brida snarled. She didn't turn her back until the trio had vanished into the stairwell, but as soon as they were gone, she ran to the middle of the allure and leant down to see the gun emplacement at the corner. 'Drigg! For the love of the Lady, fire! They're nearly on us.'

The duardin looked up at her shout, then around the men and women standing in tense silence on the wall. None were working the cannon. He pointed to the gunpowder barrel and drew his finger across his throat. 'All of them,' he shouted back.

'Get up here,' Brida roared, instead of the curses that crowded her throat. 'Crossbowmen and archers, start loosing in volleys as soon as the enemy breaches the marker flag. No let up. Independent firing when they're twenty feet out.'

'What in Sigmar's name is going on?' she hissed as soon as her lieutenant arrived. 'We lost one load when that fool Kende smashed it. Didn't he mark it up like I said?'

'There's flour mixed into every barrel, captain. Put that in a cannon and you blow up the cannon. Dropping them on the warflock is about all our artillery's good for now.'

Brida gaped at him, her mind a momentary fizzing blank. *How? Why?* Then she forced herself to think, to plan some way to save her company. 'Get back up to the flame. I don't care how you do it, but crimson it. We're not going to outlast this attack without aid or artillery. Barricade yourself in there, Drigg,' she added, squeezing his forearm, 'and Alarielle guide you.'

'The defence?' Drigg asked, already backing away.

Brida hefted her spear. 'I've got the defence.'

Bows and crossbows were taking a toll among the warflock, finding the joins in armour and punching through them, the ground shuddering beneath the thunder of running feet and falling bodies. The demi-wolves and half-bears, though, shook off the missiles as if they were stinging insects, leaping across the pit traps and sharpened stakes, gaining ground. Without Drigg, Brida was everywhere, running between the second and third levels, shouting down to the ground to ensure the gates were fully braced.

She looked for Brock, couldn't find him, and hoped Orla and Kende hadn't resisted. She was torn between wanting it to be them so they were locked away, and hoping it was all some horrible series of accidents. A small, ugly voice in her head told her to execute them both now. If it was one of them, their death would release the spell-lock and the flame would crimson. She pushed it away and focused on repelling the attack.

The beastkin reached the walls, the still-green glow from above glistening in their eyes and teeth. They roared their pain and hate and madness, and they began to climb.

'Crossbows, down into the beasts. Archers, take the tzaangors!' Brida screamed. Greenspire seemed to rock under the impact of mutated flesh, and she stepped back, let an archer take her place at the wall and spun to look into the courtyard. Three figures sprawled in their own blood in all the indignity of violent death. 'What the–'

She raced for the stairs, threw herself down them two at a time and came out into the courtyard. She whirled around, looking for enemies, but saw no one but Brock at the main gate.

Brock at the main gate.

She ran even as she processed his actions, realised he was clearing the barricade and tearing back the bolts that would let in the enemy. The gate shook as it was charged from outside. 'Brock, no!' she screamed as the awful realisation dawned. He'd fooled her. He'd fooled them all and damned them all.

He turned as if in a dream, exultation glazed across his face. 'For Chaos!' he yelled, and slipped the last bolt free.

Icy fury rose like a hurricane and Brida channelled all of it into the cast of her spear. The weapon hummed through the air and punched into her sergeant's chest, snatching him from his feet and pinning him to the opening gate. He never lost his expression of adoration. She followed the spear and shouldered into the gate with all the momentum of her sprint, digging her boots into the stone and heaving. Seconds later, Tomman the physician joined her. He didn't push, but darted his arm around the opening gate and threw a handful of pellets. The pressure from the other side lessened and now he did lend his strength to hers. 'Quick-sleep,' he panted, 'slow them down a bit.'

'Gate breach!' Brida bellowed, so loud her lungs hurt and Tomman winced. Shouts of alarm from above told her that soldiers would be sprinting down the stairs to help, and across the wall above the gate to rain death on the monsters seeking entry.

It wasn't enough. The pressure on the gate returned and then increased, and Brida and Tomman were shoved back. Shoulders and thighs burning, Brida gritted her teeth and pushed, but the beastkin had the momentum now.

She met Tomman's eyes. 'Count of three, run.'

'We have crimson!' a voice from above blared, and Brida felt a sliver of hope. Brock's death had broken the spell-lock on the flame, and Drigg had added the alchemical compounds to change the colour. It wasn't over yet.

'Stay alive, physician. Help's coming. One. Two. *Three.*'

They let go of the gate and sprinted away as the first half-bear tumbled into Greenspire, falling over itself as the pressure on the barrier released. Those behind clambered over it slavering and howling, each one big enough to tear Brida in half. She didn't give them the chance, hurling herself into the nearest stairwell behind Tomman and slamming the door and locking it. The stairwells were narrow and low to prevent the mutated giants of Tzeentch's hordes from entering. Though that wouldn't stop them rampaging through the kitchen, stores, armoury and infirmary. Anyone found alive in there soon wouldn't be. She had to save them.

She ran into Drigg on the second level. 'They're in.'

'I know. Got half the archers picking them off but there are more still piling through the gate.' He was cut off by a splintering crash and a chorus of desperate screams: a demi-wolf had taken down the door to the infirmary. Drigg directed arrows at it, but it was already too late. The patients were gone, torn apart in seconds as Brida watched in stunned, helpless silence. Ice swamped the fire that had raged in her blood, black and lethal, and Drigg took a step back when he saw her expression.

'You said drop the cannon,' Brida said, the rough edge to her voice all the grief she would allow herself. 'Drop it in front of the gate, crush those coming through so their bodies block the entrance.'

Drigg nodded once. 'Inside the gate,' he corrected, and she trusted him enough not to ask why, just ran for the cannon nearest the gate.

The gun carriage was wheeled, but it still took ten of them to get it moving while another two rigged a hasty pulley system from the hooks hammered into the roof. The tzaangors had cleared the last of the traps and were crowding in behind the warped backs of the beastkin at the gate. The fog of their stink was overwhelming, stinging eyes and clinging like slime inside mouths and throats.

The cannon rocked on its carriage and came free with a chorused grunt from those on the ropes. Brida helped guide it up over the guard wall and into position. She chanced a look down into the courtyard and came face to snout with a half-bear, talons dug into the stone blocks of Greenspire's wall.

'*Drop it!*' she yelled and the cannon vanished, scraping the bear from the wall and thundering into the mass of twisted flesh spilling from the gate. The end of the rope, smoking from the speed it went through the pulley, ripped across the side of Brida's head as it flashed past, laying open her scalp and cheek to the bone. She reeled back, blood sheeting, a screech of pain bursting from her.

There was a wailing-howling-roaring from below as beastkin flailed under the cannon's weight, spines cracked and pelvises shattered. They scratched at the flagstones and each other, straining to free themselves, their bulk blocking most of the gate.

Brida sagged against the wall and blinked blood from her eye, trying to formulate a plan that would see them survive until reinforcements from Highoak and Willowflame could reach them. All around the interior of the second level, the soldiers of Lady's Justice were shooting down into the mass of the enemy choking the courtyard. More half-bears were climbing the walls while a giant wolf was half inside a stairwell and straining upwards, arrows lodged in its haunches.

The mess at the gate began to writhe. Howls rose up as broken bodies were shoved aside and tzaangors began worming through the carnage, hacking any flesh that lay in their path.

'...powder.' Drigg's voice was hard to hear over the cacophony rising within and without Greenspire's walls. She turned. The duardin was roping four gunpowder barrels together. Soldiers were breaking open the lids of the others and throwing powder and the contaminating flour into the air over the attackers until a fine mist hung above the warflock's heads.

'Fire arrow,' Drigg snapped. Brida snatched up a bow, lit the arrow from the safety lantern and nocked as the duardin pushed the bomb over the edge.

Brida loosed. The fire arrow struck home when the barrels were just above the heads of the attackers. They exploded and so did the flour hanging in the air, a roiling fireball that sent those on the wall diving for cover and ripped the warflock to pieces. For a few seconds the world was nothing but noise and searing light and boiling air, and then it started raining blood and flesh.

The tzaangors who hadn't been killed outright were running or dragging themselves away, many falling into the traps and pits they'd avoided on the way in. Drigg set archers to harry them as they fled. Brida gave him a grim nod, handed off her bow and snatched a spear, then gathered a score of soldiers and headed for a clear stairwell. There were still disciples of Tzeentch in Greenspire and it was time for them to die.

* * *

The Freeguilders from Willowflame reached them first, when they were mopping up the last of the enemy and beginning to count their own dead. That included Orla and Kende, killed by Brock instead of imprisoned. Killed because of her short-sightedness, Brida knew, her trust in a man who didn't deserve it. Orla, a friend of decades, who'd never done anything but stand at her side and support her. And Kende, who hadn't been cut out to be a soldier but who'd died one anyway. Because of her.

Captain Sonoth sent half his company to harry the decimated warflock back to the Hexwood, and the rest began the ugly process of piling dead tzaangors and beastkin for burning.

'Lot of corpses considering your flame was only crimson a short while,' he said. 'How did they get the jump on you?'

Brida sat on the well cap while Tomman stitched her face. She'd been lucky not to lose an eye, though part of her ear was missing. She'd refused poppy extract for the pain – her penance for Orla and Kende, the scar a lifelong reminder that trust was a luxury she could no longer afford.

'We had a traitor,' she said. 'Sergeant Brock, a man I've served with for twenty years. Took a supply run to Fort Gardus and when he came back… fouled the gunpowder, poisoned the water, framed a damn good soldier and a recruit for it, and then opened the gate to let the flock in. And I didn't see any of it coming. I just let him back in and he nearly got us all killed.'

Sonoth's face hardened. 'And where is this sergeant?'

Brida met his gaze. 'I killed him, and my only regret is that I didn't do it slowly. Our flame was somehow spell-locked to his life force – when he died it changed colour. Either there's a Chaos cult in Fort Gardus or one of the Emerald Line towers between here and there chose evil and drew him in. But he's dead, so we'll never know.' She hoisted herself to her feet, groaning as wounds and aches made themselves known. 'Captain Sonoth, I'll be sending word up and down the Line about what happened here. Any new recruits, any veterans who leave your company for any period of time, especially if they're sent out alone, they need to be carefully watched on their return. Maybe even quarantined. Tzeentch's plans are subtle, but not even I ever considered something like this. We need–'

'Crimson on the horizon!' came the shout from above. 'Highoak, Gemfire, by the Lady, Dawnspike too! Captain… captain, they're all changing. Crimson along the line, far as I can see!'

Sonoth and Devholm looked at each other. 'Whatever warning you have, captain,' Sonoth said heavily, 'I think you're too late.'

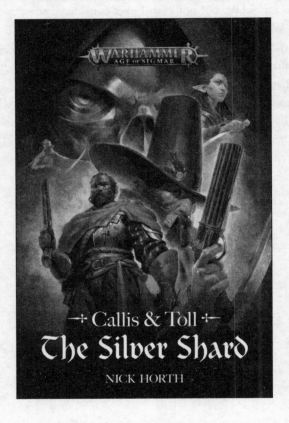

THE GOSSIP
OF RAVENS

David Annandale

The fortified town of Darkhail glowered from the top of a rocky hill four days' march to the south of Nulahmia. Rare among the settlements of Shyish, it was an enclave populated entirely by mortals. More than a thousand souls lived within its outer walls, watched over by the keep that dominated the northern prospect. The land that Darkhail governed as its domain was a rugged, cold moor, a landscape of fog sweeping between tumbled tors and grasping trees bent almost double by the endless shrieks of the west wind.

On the balcony outside the throne room, Lord Raglev made an expansive gesture, as if the land were truly his, and not part of Neferatia. 'Tell me what you see,' he said.

Kyra glanced up at her father. She shivered in the cold, wishing they were back inside, where she could stand in front of the hearth for warmth. Overhead, ravens flew in raucous clouds, shrieking at the wind.

Kyra looked down at the road leading north through the moor, and the line of prisoners marching along it, escorted by horse-mounted guards. Each captive's hands, she knew, were manacled together and linked to a chain that circled the waist of the prisoner in front of them. The miserable caravan was climbing a hill that would take it over the horizon and out of her sight.

'I see your tithe to Neferata,' Kyra said, guessing at what Raglev wanted her to notice.

Raglev gave her a patronising smile, as though she had answered precisely as he had expected, and was wrong precisely as he had expected. 'Why are we sending those prisoners to Nulahmia?' he asked.

'Because we owe our fealty to Neferata.'

Raglev smiled again. 'So she thinks, and it is in that spirit that she will receive this offering of blood. But here is a lesson for you, daughter. The truth is that Neferata serves my purposes without knowing it.'

Alarmed, Kyra looked around quickly to make sure they were alone, and that no one had overheard her father's dangerous words.

The wind gusted, flapping her coat so hard she stumbled. The ravens screamed.

'Father, you don't mean that,' Kyra said.

'But I do. Darkhail has her protection against the forces of the Dark Gods. The tithe gives us further protection against our rivals.'

'Are we certain? They must send their tithes in too.'

Raglev raised a hand. 'I wasn't finished. Do you know who those prisoners are?'

'No,' Kyra admitted.

'What do you know of the House of Fallack?' Raglev asked, apparently changing the subject.

'I know that Orissa Fallack has a habit of suggesting her claim to the throne of Darkhail is as good as, or better than, yours.'

'She does indeed. She has also been growing bolder in her statements as she has gathered allies around her family.'

'You think she might be a threat?'

'Do you?'

'I had wondered,' Kyra admitted. 'But she's been quiet recently. I thought perhaps she had rethought her position.'

'When did you last see her?'

Kyra thought for a moment. 'I'm not sure. It's been a few weeks at least.'

'What about any of the other Fallacks?'

'The same,' Kyra realised.

'That's right. Their threat is ended.'

A raven cawed just above Kyra's head, and as if it had startled the thought from her, she found herself asking, 'Did you imprison them in Greymourn?'

'What?' Raglev sounded rattled. 'Why would you say that?'

Kyra blinked. She shook her head, trying to clear a sudden fog. 'I don't know,' she said. She couldn't say why the thought of Greymourn Tower had suddenly come to her. The tower had been abandoned during the Age of Chaos. Though it fell within the boundaries of the land Darkhail claimed, no one had sought to reoccupy it. No one, in the memory of the Raglev family's reign, had ventured to the tower. During the time of darkness, Greymourn had become a place of fog and shadows and whispers. It was best forgotten. Kyra couldn't imagine why her thoughts had flown at this moment to the tower. She shivered.

'The Fallacks are not in... They are not there,' said Raglev. He cleared his throat, and regained his air of self-satisfaction. 'They are on their way to Nulahmia.'

Kyra stared at the disappearing line of prisoners. 'All of them?'

'All of them,' Raglev said quietly. 'Such is the fate of those who would hurt our family, and seek to claim the rule of Darkhail for themselves, or for some other traitor they serve. With every tithe I send to Neferata, our position in the city grows stronger. This is how she serves me. She destroys my enemies while receiving them as her due. And now you know the secret of our family, Kyra, the one it will be your responsibility to preserve in times to come. We have tricked Neferata. This is my legacy, and my gift to you. That is something worth savouring, isn't it?'

The ravens shrieked again and again. One flew down and hovered in front of the balcony for a moment. Kyra was sure that it stared into her eyes.

Night came to Darkhail with a chorus of screams. Ravens had always been numerous over the town, wheeling between the spires of the keep, chattering from the rooftops of the town and stalking the battlements as if they were the true rulers of the fortress. Tonight, though, they had descended on Darkhail as a storm, the clouds breaking up into winged darkness, their calls deafening and shrill.

Lord Raglev couldn't sleep for their raucous shouts. He paced the throne room, trying to distract himself. Next to the hearth stood a bookcase that held the tomes he had come to think of as the true secret of his family's success. Most of them had been written by his mother, whom he had succeeded as ruler of Darkhail, or by himself. They were writings on strategy – political and military. Raglev liked to take one off the shelf in the evening, particularly one he had written, and pore over the wisdom of its pages, nodding in approval and storing away the lessons that he had invented.

He tried to pick one now, but with the cacophony of the birds he couldn't even concentrate enough to make a choice. Frustrated, he turned away from the books and stormed out of the throne room.

He made his way up a flight of stairs and stopped at the door of Kyra's bedchamber. She had retired earlier, before the coming of the full fury of the birds. He knocked on the door. 'Kyra,' he said. 'Is that noise bothering you too?'

There was no answer.

Raglev knocked again. 'Kyra?'

Still nothing. He turned the handle and opened the door.

Kyra was not in her bed. She had opened her chamber's terrace doors, and she was walking slowly towards the parapet, her silk nightclothes billowing like sails in the wind. Before her, huge numbers of ravens were flying in spirals, creating a tunnel of wings leading from the parapet into the night.

The revolving, jagged lines of the bird spiral seized Raglev's gaze. It pulled him forward, and he had stumbled halfway across the room before he managed to tear his eyes away.

'Kyra!' he shouted. He ran to the door and held on to the wall, frightened a violent gust would pick him up and carry him away. 'Kyra!'

His daughter did not answer. She gave no indication she had heard him. She moved as if in a trance, but purposefully. She didn't hesitate when she reached the parapet. She climbed up, and stepped into the tunnel of ravens.

She did not fall. The whirling tunnel held her suspended in the air. She kept walking, and the birds closed around her, sealing her off from Raglev's sight.

He screamed her name and ran to the parapet, ready to throw himself into the cloud of ravens. He was too late. They pulled away, a huge mass of talons and wings, Kyra invisible inside the darkness, and they flew off into the night, leaving the lord to shriek himself hoarse.

The guards came running in answer to his cries, and Raglev gathered his wits. 'My daughter has been taken by sorcery!' he rasped. 'Send out riders. Search for her!'

'At once, my lord,' one guard said, though she, like the others, looked uncertain.

Raglev turned around and faced the night. It was deep and dark. Anyone out on the moors would be lucky to see the ground in front of their feet. Kyra could be a few yards away and they would not see her.

But he could not wait until morning. He could not. Kyra was his only child. His wife was dead. His only other blood relatives had been rivals, despatched to Nulahmia. Kyra was his one real point of vulnerability, because she was the embodiment of his legacy. Without her, the memory of his name and his accomplishments vanished. She was the guarantor of his fame.

'I will ride north with a company,' he said, striding from the bedchamber. The guards followed him along the hall and down the stairs as he made for the armoury and the stables. The ravens had vanished in that direction. It was a start, at least. 'In the morning, I want searches in all directions. We do not stop until Kyra is found.'

What if she can't be?

He refused the question. He would find her. He would force events to conform to his will. He would not countenance the alternative.

But as he donned his armour, and as he and his company gathered in the courtyard of the keep before the main gate, the questions kept coming.

Who took her?

He didn't think any of his enemies, whether inside the walls of Darkhail or in rival keeps, could summon that kind of sorcery.

Neferata?

Raglev had so completely convinced the people around him that he did not fear the Mortarch of Blood that he had largely convinced himself, too. The fear tried to resurface, but he stamped it down. He had to. If he believed Neferata had taken Kyra, then she was lost.

There was no reason for Neferata to act against him. He had always been loyal. Or at least, visibly so.

The search company rode out of the gates and onto the moor. Raglev's initial impulse was to order the riders to fan out, but that was impossible in the dark. The terrain of the moor was too treacherous, the ground strewn with rocks to break a horse's leg, and riddled with invisible mires that would be deathtraps for the rescue party. So he led a hundred troops up the road the prisoners had taken, and did not divide his forces at all until the first crossroads, five miles north of the city. Even then, he kept fifty guards with him. The sense of riding with strength was the only comfort the night offered.

Raglev kept heading north, the torches of his riders giving just enough light to see the road, its rough surface a patch of grey in the darkness, leading on and on to nothing except more darkness.

Riding beside him, Bertholdt, the captain of the guard, said, 'We can see nothing, my lord.'

'I know that,' Raglev snapped. 'What would you have me do, then? Nothing? If we are out here, there is always a chance.' *There has to be, however small.*

After three hours of riding, they reached another fork in the road. The main road, itself barely wide enough for two riders abreast, angled north-west. The smaller path, little more than a hint of a line over the moor, went due north. Raglev halted at the intersection and stared at the broken road.

'Greymourn?' said Bertholdt. 'You think she could be there?'

'No,' said Raglev. *No, please.* The ravens had flown north. That was all. That did not mean they had taken Kyra to Greymourn.

Even so, dread made him pause and hold a hand up for silence. He listened to the night, and when the cawing of ravens sounded in the direction pointed to by the path, he shivered at the inevitability of things. *Not Nulahmia, at least. He tried to find any comfort he could. She hasn't been taken there.*

'We must go to Greymourn,' he told Bertholdt. 'I hear the cry of her captors.'

'Maybe just birds,' said Bertholdt, visibly reluctant.

'Maybe,' said Raglev. He took a breath, steadying his courage. 'But we have to look.'

Raglev started up the broken road, his troops following in single file. The trail took them uphill, passing a tor that loomed over them like a brooding monument. As they emerged from the shadow of the rock, the clouds parted, and the silver moons of Shyish cast their dead light over the land, framing Greymourn Tower in silhouette on the horizon. Mist began to rise as if in greeting, its movements serpentine in the wind.

It took another half an hour to reach the tower. Midway there, Bertholdt grunted and looked to the west.

'What is it?' Raglev asked.

'I thought I saw another company of riders,' said Bertholdt. He pointed off into the mist, and the land of shifting shadows created by the moonlight. 'Heading south. Maybe I was wrong.'

Raglev looked. Did the fog swirl from the passage of horses? Was that a distant echo of a hoof? He couldn't tell. The crying of the ravens filled the night, hiding other sounds.

'There should be no one else here,' Raglev said. *But borders are porous.* Raiders from a rival keep? Had he done enough to quash the Fallacks and their allies?

'I must have been wrong,' Bertholdt said again.

Raglev grunted. There was nothing to follow, even if Bertholdt had seen something.

They rode on, and finally reached Greymourn, the cold sentinel at the top of a rise, keeping guard over nothing but the wastes.

The ground rose more steeply in the immediate approach to the tower. There might once have been a keep here, though the ruins lying at the base of Greymourn were so worn down it was unclear what structure once stood there, or if they had ever been more than jumbles of boulders, scattered in a rough circle like old bones, some standing, some leaning, others heaped one atop another. Their silence murmured dreams of a shattered past and forgotten rites.

Greymourn stood aloof from the landscape, brooding over its hidden purpose. Its slabs of dark stone fitted together without mortar, almost without seam, yet thousands of cracks webbed over its surface. Scores of ravens perched on the edge of its roof, staring down at the rescue party with unnatural stillness. Fifteen feet below them, still high off the ground, was the tower's single opening, a doorway leading to the balcony. A glow, the same cold silver as the moonlight, came from within, and when Raglev was still a hundred yards from the tower, a figure appeared on the balcony, nightclothes billowing like the fog.

'Kyra!' Raglev shouted. That was her. It had to be her. 'Help is here!' The relief of finding her clashed with the dread of seeing her in this place.

The ravens took to the air and circled the tower, shrieking back at Raglev, their cries a mocking mimicry of his daughter's name, *Keeee-raa, keeee-raa, keeee-raa.*

The figure retreated back inside Greymourn.

'Was that her?' Bertholdt said. 'Her face was in shadow.'

'Who else could it be?' Raglev demanded.

They rode around the base of the tower, looking for an entrance. There was none, not even the trace left by one that had been bricked up. Only the smooth curve of the wall that brought them back to their starting point beneath the balcony.

'I don't understand,' said Bertholdt.

'I don't have to,' said Raglev, thinking, *I don't want to*. Things had happened to Greymourn since its construction. Mortals had built it, once, or so he thought. It was no longer the thing they had built. He was not here to divine its purpose. *Rescue Kyra and get away from here.*

He examined the curved walls of the tower. 'They can be climbed,' he said. The cracks were large enough to pound in spikes and fix ropes. 'Let us begin.'

Bertholdt joined him in the ascent. Raglev had ordered the company to carry all the materials necessary for a rescue, no matter where Kyra might be found, and there were enough lengths of rope and the spikes to hold it to make the climb. Raglev and his captain moved slowly, carefully, wary of the trickery of the night and its shadows.

'Kyra!' Raglev called, again and again.

Only the ravens answered.

'Doesn't she hear?' he said, frustrated.

'It might not be her,' Bertholdt cautioned again.

'It is,' Raglev said. 'I know it is. That's her nightdress. Ravens took her away. That's *her*. Sorcery brought her here, and I don't know whose, or for what purpose. That is for later. All that matters now is that we get her out.'

As he pulled himself up to the balcony's parapet, Raglev felt the sudden passage of something huge overhead. He looked up, hunching down into his shoulders, his grip on the parapet turning slippery. He saw nothing, as if the thing he had felt were too high up to see, yet so powerful it felt as if it had grazed the roof of the tower. After a few moments, the sense of a presence eased, and he could move again. Raglev climbed onto the balcony and helped Bertholdt over the parapet. They hurried through the open doorway, into the chamber lit by the dead, silver glow.

He found himself back in his throne room, and he wavered,

brutally disoriented. He had travelled to Greymourn only to end up in Darkhail.

Wake up. Wake up. This is a dream. Wake up.

'What is this?' Bertholdt's voice shook. The sound of his fear was real. This was no dream.

Not a dream, but also not Darkhail. A nightmare. The chamber was a twisted image of the throne room, a parody grinning like a skull. Raglev saw his throne, and his family's coat of arms over the hearth, and the shelves filled with the flowerings of the Raglev family genius. But the throne crawled with skeletal worms, their small bones scraping against wood. Serpents writhed instead of flames in the hearth, the silver aura emanating from their struggles. The shelves sagged, melting like candle wax.

And the chamber was only partly a throne room. It was also a space of torture and death. Instruments of pain lined the walls. There were racks and wheels, whips and iron bridles, cages and manacles, all of them holding corpses in their positions of final agony, corpses that still quivered in the throes of extremity.

'Kyra,' Raglev whispered, in one last moment of hope that the figure before him was his daughter. It was slumped forward, head down, face concealed by its hair. When Raglev spoke, it raised its head.

It was not Kyra. It wore her clothes. Its hair was long, like hers, and from a distance, in the moonlight, he had mistaken it as golden. It was silver, the same silver as the moons and the chamber's light, the silver of stillness, of the coldest death. Where there should have been a face, there was only a sunken hole in the skull, a maw of shadows. The horror walked towards Raglev, arms outstretched, pale talons grasping for his embrace. The thing moved with harsh, stuttering jerks, like an insect, like a breaking dream.

'My lord!' Bertholdt yelled. He jumped in front of Raglev, sword drawn. 'Go! There is nothing for us here! Please, *go!*'

Raglev snapped out of his horrified trance. He ran from the chamber, onto the balcony, grabbed the rope and dropped over the parapet. He climbed down quickly, recklessly. From above came a terrible scream, and then the sound of rending. Whimpering in terror, his own movements too fast and clumsy, he almost fell twice. He dropped the last five feet and stumbled back from the tower, staring up in fear at the heights of Greymourn.

Then he mounted his horse and ordered a retreat. He abandoned all thoughts of continuing the search. Not during the night. He could think only of racing back to the safety of the walls of Darkhail.

Though it was dawn by the time Raglev and his fifty riders returned to the city, the clouds were so thick and dark it still felt like night. The land brooded in deep shadow, and the mist crawled in from the moors, brushing against the walls of the city like the dragging of a shroud.

Raglev had not spoken to any of his guards on the ride back. Despair pressed down on him like a cloak of lead. But as he drew near to the keep, the cloak fell away. Warm firelight blazed from the open windows of the throne room, and there, on the parapet, was Kyra.

The sight mirrored the vision that had waited for him at Greymourn, and dread clutched his heart. *Not again. Please no, not again.* He stared hard at the figure on the terrace, bracing himself for the absence of face, for the skittering movement. He stared until he was close enough to see that, yes, this was indeed Kyra. She smiled down and waved at him.

All was well.

How? How is she here?

Someone else found her. Reward them for preserving your legacy.

The gates of the city were wide open, the portcullis raised. In celebration, he thought. The city shared his relief.

His joy and sense of wellbeing did not waver until he and his troops were well into the courtyard and the portcullis slammed shut behind them.

That was when he saw that there were other riders already in the courtyard, lining its circumference, and that he was surrounded. This company carried the banners of Neferata. The knights wore heavy, black armour, and their raised visors revealed bare skulls. Their horses, too, were skeletons, jaws open slightly as if they hungered for the taste of living flesh.

The courtyard was awash with blood. From beyond the keep came the distant sounds of clashing swords and the screams of the dying from the streets of the town. His throat tight with despair and fear, Raglev remembered what Bertholdt had seen. There had been riders heading south after all, riding with fell purpose through the night and mist. He remembered, too, the presence he had felt pass south in the sky over Greymourn.

As if in answer to his thoughts, a huge roar reverberated through the courtyard. Raglev looked up to see a skeletal monster coiling its tail around the spire of the keep's central tower. Ravens circled it in worship, answering its roar with their shrieks.

The leader of the black knights rode slowly up to Raglev. He tried to shrink away from the powerful figure of death and war.

'I am Skarveth Lytessian,' the hell knight said, his voice like wind from open vaults. 'And I know the meaning of loyalty.'

'I have always been...' Raglev began, but stopped when Skarveth drew his sword and held the point at Raglev's throat.

'Do not insult me,' Skarveth warned. 'Most of all, do not insult our queen any further.'

Raglev said nothing. He winced at the sounds of the dying in the city.

'You have troops that believe in their loyalty to you,' Skarveth said. 'They are learning now that their loyalty was misplaced. Perhaps they will be given another chance in death. Perhaps not. Will you force your guards to learn the price of defying the Mortarch of Blood?'

His guards had drawn their swords too, but they were facing an enemy they could not defeat.

'Sheathe your weapons,' Raglev croaked.

Skarveth pulled his blade away. 'Perhaps they will not die now,' he said. 'Perhaps they will. The decision is not mine to make. Nor is it yours. Now dismount. Go to what was your throne room. You are awaited.'

Raglev obeyed. The keep felt deserted; he saw no servants or other guards. Shadows clung to the walls and tapestries like deep stains. They shifted as he passed them, and voices whispered within.

'Hello, father,' Kyra said when he entered the throne room. She stood in the centre of the room, one hand on the throne. She had donned her armour, which had been hidden beneath the robes she had worn on the balcony. Though her skin had turned bone white, her eyes shone when she looked over to the being who stood beside the shelves, idly turning the pages of one of Raglev's books.

Raglev followed her gaze despite himself, and beheld the worst. He beheld Neferata.

The queen was armoured too, though her stance was relaxed. She had girded herself for war to make a point – she did not appear to expect to have to enter combat. Raglev's legs turned weak. He feared Greymourn, he had been terrified by the grotesque disguised as his daughter, but those terrors shrank to nothing before what he felt in the presence of the Mortarch of Blood. She was doom. She was the source of all fears.

'This is your work, then,' Neferata said, without looking up from the book.

'Yes,' said Raglev.

Neferata examined the leather binding. 'You are clearly proud of it.'

Raglev said nothing.

Neferata shrugged. She let the book fall to the floor. 'There are those, it is true, who are entertained by the facile. Especially when they produce it themselves.' Her smile was the beauty of predation, and Kyra laughed.

Raglev stared at his daughter. Her transformation seemed more horrible than the creature that had pretended to be her in Greymourn. 'What has she done to you?' he moaned.

'She has rewarded my loyalty,' said Kyra. Now she smiled, and it was a wide smile, a smile of adoration directed at her queen, a smile that revealed the gleam of her new fangs. 'I gave myself willingly to her. I refused to betray our queen for the sake of your pride.'

Neferata ran her fingers along the spines of the books. Her nail barely grazed them, yet she tore a gouge through the bindings. She shook her head in amused dismissal and walked towards Raglev, graceful as the night, unstoppable as loss. 'Your daughter has shown I was wise to bestow the gift of the Blood Kiss on her. She opened wide the gates of Darkhail to my black knights. She knows who is the servant, and who commands. Pride has sown no confusion in her mind. She will rule Darkhail well.'

'I meant no disrespect,' Raglev babbled. 'I meant no harm. I have always been loyal.'

'You have never been to Nulahmia, have you?' Neferata said. 'Never been to the Palace of the Seven Vultures.'

'No,' Raglev said, confused by the change in subject. His voice was a cracked whisper.

'At the top of my palace's Daggersight Tower lies the Chamber of Whispers. Its windows look everywhere, and they have no shutters or glass. Ravens fly in and out at will. They shriek. They chatter. They gossip. They carry the shreds of hopes and the tatters of dreams. They tell me tales.' Neferata paused. 'They told me of you, of your words, and of your pride in your schemes. And so I gave them commands.'

Raglev dropped to his knees. 'Please forgive me, my queen, please have mercy, please spare me from destruction, please...'

'Oh, do be quiet,' said Neferata. She took Raglev by the throat, and her grip was stronger than iron. She squeezed, choking off Raglev's pleas. 'Besides,' she continued, 'I am not here to destroy you. I am here to punish. That is far, far worse.'

Kyra laughed and clapped her hands. Neferata yanked Raglev's head back and buried her fangs in his neck.

The tales that were told, by fire and candlelight, of what it was like to receive the Blood Kiss were legion. Raglev had heard them all his life. The thread that wove many of them together was the hope and fear of final pleasure that accompanied the kiss. The glow in Kyra's eyes, shining from the dead white of her flesh, gave truth to those tales. But there was no pleasure for Raglev. There was only pain, and scouring, and the terrible theft of being. Agony shook him, as though boiling oil coursed through his veins, destroying all that he was, had ever been, and could hope to be. A scream enveloped him, but he could not give it voice, so tight was the cold hand around his throat. All he heard, as darkness took him, was the mocking screams of ravens.

Thirst woke him. Wracking thirst that twisted him in pain. Even his bones writhed, and now he could scream.

It brought no relief.

Raglev opened his eyes to silver light. He lurched forward, doubling over at the torture of the thirst, but chains held him back. He was shackled to the throne in the chamber of Greymourn.

The remains of Bertholdt were scattered over the floor, and the thing that had killed him danced around Raglev in scuttling jerks.

Where the opening to the chamber had been, there was now a barrier of grey stone, the masonry as massive as the outer walls of the tower. There was still a gap at the top, room for one more stone. The dead light of the chamber shone on Neferata's face, gazing at Raglev with a quiet smile.

'Hail, lord of Greymourn,' said the Mortarch of Blood.

Raglev strained against the chains. He moaned, weak with the thirst. 'Mercy,' he gasped. 'I must drink. I will die if I do not drink.'

Neferata laughed. 'You have already died. Is your mind really so dull that you cannot even recognise the nature of your thirst? Has the need for water ever tortured you thus? Fear not, Lord Raglev. You are not destroyed. You have the gift of eternity now. Though you will never have blood to slake your thirst. I do leave you with a companion, to remind you of your daughter.' She raised a huge stone, holding it in the palm of her hand as though it weighed no more than a bird.

'No!' Raglev screamed.

'Farewell,' said Neferata. 'I shall look forward to the news of how you fare.'

She put the stone in its place, sealing the chamber.

Raglev shrieked. He strained against his chains. The Kyragrotesque cavorted around him, its gestures taking on the rhythms of his cries. Its head ticked back and forth, the hole of its face jerking up and down and left and right, as if searching for sound, or searching for prey. Its limbs clicked, its joints scraped. Its dance was spider and serpent, and it came closer and closer for the long embrace.

And somehow, through the stone and over his screams, he could still hear the calling of the ravens, revelling in his fate, gathering the tales of his pain to carry to their mistress.

LAST OF
THE BRASKOVS

C L Werner

Darkness dropped like a curtain upon the ruinous city. It was as if the day couldn't flee fast enough from the onset of night, afraid of the things that stirred from their lairs once the light was gone.

Emelda Braskov hugged her cloak tighter around her as the temperature of the already chilly air plummeted. Despite the heavy sealskin wrap with its ruff of wolf fur, she couldn't repress a shiver. She told herself it was the cold, but in her heart she knew it was the sounds rising from the ruins, the bestial cries of nightmares slinking from their tombs to prowl the streets in search of prey.

Was this really Mournhold? Emelda had posed that question to herself a thousand times since her return to the city three days ago. When she'd left with the army for a crusade against the Chaos-worshipping tribes that infested the lands around Szargorond, Mournhold had been a bastion of civilisation, a light in death-shrouded Shyish. The city's many towers stood proud and tall, the banners of merchant guilds and scholarly societies snapping in the brisk sea-wind. The white walls of a dozen castles glistened in the sunlight, palatial homes of the ruling nobility. The magnificent triple steeples of the Cathedral of the Cometstruck loomed over all, the golden hammers adorning their peaks shining like fire as a beacon to the faithful to hear the sermons of Arch-Lector Stanizlas. The roar from the docks, where scores of whalers, fishing smacks and seal hunters brought their catches to be processed, had been so pervasive that even in the most removed districts that clamour of bustling commerce could be heard. When a wayward wind blew across Banshee's Bay, the odour of whale blubber being rendered into oil washed away the flowery perfume of Mournhold's many gardens.

If she closed her eyes, Emelda could imagine things as they had been. Almost she could convince herself that what was around her was only some distorted dream, a morbid reflection of her home caught in a cracked mirror. Almost she could do this, but that way could lead only to madness.

Amongst her idealised memories she had to confess there were shadows. Emelda remembered the great cathedral to Sigmar, but there had also been the sombre temple of Nagash with its grim priesthood and eerie rites. The castles of the nobles she thought of with affection, for had she not grown up in one of them and visited many of the others to feast and dance? Yet perched upon a spire of black rock had been another castle – the Ebon Citadel, the old fortress that had guarded over Mournhold while it grew from fragile village to mighty city, had been there even then, poised like a vulture waiting for its prey to fall.

No, there had been monsters in Mournhold even then. During the great battle when the daemon prince Slaughn set his hordes upon the city, the siege had been relieved by a creature nearly as terrible. The pirate fleet of Radukar the Wolf arrived just as doom seemed certain. With his Kosargi ogors, he wrought massacre upon the slaves of Khorne and himself slew Slaughn in combat. Mournhold had been saved at the very threshold of conquest, delivered from its darkest hour. But the city's saviour was no mortal hero – rather a being of darkness himself. Radukar, the deliverer of Mournhold, was a vampire.

Emelda had seen the vampire a few times as a child, instances when Radukar would attend one of the parties hosted by the nobles. Often he would shun these gatherings, perhaps finding them as distasteful as the celebrants did the presence of the undead, but always an invitation was extended to him. After the battle, Radukar had claimed a position for himself among Mournhold's grand princes and taken the Ebon Citadel for his stronghold. There had really been no choice but to accept the vampire's terms, for after fighting Slaughn's hordes the city didn't have the strength to drive the Wolf and his ogors back into the sea.

She shuddered again when she remembered the vampire. His pale and lifeless skin making the vivid red of his lips all the more striking. His features were savage, stamped with the ferocity of a true wolf. His eyes burned with a ghastly glow that stared into the very soul of those upon whom he set his gaze. More than his appearance, it was the aura that exuded from him that unsettled Emelda even these many years later. On campaign with the army, she'd seen countless monstrous and horrific things, the mutated spawn of Chaos in its riot of grotesques. But never had she felt such smouldering malevolence as she had on those occasions when she'd been in the same room as Radukar. It was an air of eternal evil that could never be sated, the presence of a famished predator whose belly would never be filled.

Emelda found her eyes drawn back to the Ebon Citadel. So much of the Mournhold she'd known was gone, destroyed by the strange cataclysm that had fallen upon the city. The Cathedral of the Cometstruck was just a heap of broken stone now. The brilliant castles of the nobles were shattered and deserted. The once prosperous waterfront was now a wretched slumland of squalor and misery. But the Wolf's fortress remained, lording over the devastation around it.

Mournhold was gone. This place was now Ulfenkarn.

Emelda shook her head and turned away. She scowled at the darkening sky. This was only her third night since returning to the city and already she'd forgotten the first thing she'd been warned against by the people she'd spoken to: never be outdoors at night. So intent on searching for someone she knew from before she'd joined the crusade against Chaos, she'd let herself ignore the lateness of the hour. She glanced about but could see no sign of life in the dismal street around her. Nearby, erected in a niche between two dilapidated workshops, stood one of the white marble fountains that were in every district and neighbourhood. The basin was broad and filled with blood. A ring of razor-sharp steel circled that basin, the better to facilitate the payment of the blood-tax the inhabitants of Ulfenkarn owed their vampire tyrant. Emelda could tell by the gleam of the blood on the metal that someone had been there only moments before, but of where they'd gone there was no sign.

The hungry howls rising in the distance were but a sample of the dangers that threatened those caught outside at night. Emelda had seen for herself the flocks of blood-bats that flapped above the streets eager for prey, yet strangely shunning the marble fountains. She'd been told stories that swarms of corpse-rats would drag down even human prey when they grew ravenous enough. There were accounts of deadwalkers, rapacious zombies that hungered for the flesh of the living. Any body that wasn't quickly hauled away to the grave-pits by the corpse collectors had the potential to rise again as the undead, regardless of whether they had lived a wicked or virtuous life. The awful power that gripped Ulfenkarn cared nothing for such distinctions.

Faintly, Emelda thought she could hear the sound of someone running in the distance. More distinctly came the slamming of doors and the barring of windows. She'd heard that tumult before, when every building sealed itself tight against the darkness and the inhabitants cowered together waiting for dawn. It was a much different experience to be on the outside hearing the hovels being locked up for the night. To know that she was alone with the creatures that stalked the night.

Emelda's hand closed about the sword hanging from her belt. She eased it a few inches from its scabbard to ensure it wasn't caught fast by the frost. The familiar feel of her blade brought her some measure of confidence. She wasn't like the poor, wretched people who lived in the slums at the edge of Ulfenkarn's ruinous centre. They were beaten and broken, meekly submitting to Radukar's diktats. Though the army was gone and the city they'd fought for was a shambles, Emelda remained a soldier. Whatever horror emerged from the shadows thinking she was helpless prey would regret its presumption.

The swordswoman looked around her, trying to match the decrepitude of her surroundings to the vibrant city of her memories. She'd come this far, she would not abandon her search.

The place she was looking for was called the Shark House, so named because of its distinct doorway fashioned from the gaping jaws of a megalofang. It had been built, so tales said, by a sea captain whose ship had been savaged by the giant shark such that it had to be scuttled in Banshee's Bay. Retiring to land, the captain had vented his hate of the monster by adorning his new house with its remains. Emelda wasn't sure if she really believed the story, but she did put trust in what she'd heard about who was living there now.

Emelda took her bearings from the glowering bronze visage of an old Unterweld guildmaster that she remembered seeing so often when gathering her troops from the taverns along Tippler's Row. She headed down the street beyond the old statue, hoping her goal was as near now as she thought it should be.

It was then that Emelda heard the clatter of armour in the street behind her. She didn't bother to turn around. She knew that sound. Once heard, there was no mistaking the noise of rusted mail rattling against fleshless bone. Bats, rats and zombies weren't the only things the mortals of Ulfenkarn had to fear in the night. Radukar had decreed that his subjects remain inside during the hours of darkness; to enforce that curfew, patrols of animated skeletons marched through the slums. The Ulfenwatch, they had been named, and the punishment those caught by them could expect was the same as that inflicted on all who broke the Wolf's law: exsanguination.

Emelda took off at a run, plunging down one of the narrow side streets adjacent to the bronze guildmaster. No shout rose from the Ulfenwatch, but she knew she'd been seen by the increased clamour of their armour. The skeletons were chasing after her.

Down one alleyway, up another, Emelda gave only the briefest attention to her surroundings now. She leapt over piles of debris and sprinted through areas where the refuse was so deep it rose above her ankles. She startled hunting cats and starving rats, sending the animals scrambling for cover. Once, she disturbed a ghoulish shadow that turned towards her, a low snarl trembling in its throat. Before it could pounce, the apparition raised its head. Hearing the sound of her pursuers, the unknown menace slipped away and opened the path for her.

A turn of good fortune for once, or so Emelda thought until the next turn brought her to a cul-de-sac. Staring at the blank stone wall, she evaluated her chances of climbing it. A grim smile pulled at her face. 'Maybe if I were a cat,' she muttered. The sound of her skeletal pursuers was much nearer now. She turned and drew her sword.

By the ghastly scarlet glow emanating from the Shyish Nadir, Emelda could see the Ulfenwatch as they trooped down the alleyway. They presented a macabre vision: decrepit, antiquated armour strapped to bleached bones, skeletal hands gripping ancient halberds while grinning skulls stared from under rusted helms. Lifeless horrors that knew neither fear nor anger, pity nor mercy, only the imperative to carry out the Wolf's tyranny.

Emelda glowered back at the skeletons, but of course there was nothing to be gained from studying those fleshless skulls, no change of expression or shift of eye to betray the moment when they would attack. She judged that there must be a dozen of them in the alley. Her only way out was through the Ulfenwatch. Her only chance of that was to take them by surprise.

Before the skeletons could advance, Emelda dashed forward into their midst. Her sword flashed out, cutting a skull from a spine before the creature could react. A sideways slash bit through corroded armour and crunched into the knee beneath. The guard crumpled on its smashed leg, crashing into one of its companions and sending both to the ground.

Then the Ulfenwatch began to retaliate, swinging their halberds about. In the close confines of the alleyway and with Emelda in their very midst, they couldn't use the long weapons effectively but had to be content with smacking her with the butts of the hafts. Such tactics might have worked against the typical denizen of Ulfenkarn, but the swordswoman was anything but typical. She had armour of her own beneath the sealskin cloak and it deflected much of the impact brought by their blows.

Driving her shoulder forward, Emelda smashed her way through the armoured skeletons. The undead had many advantages over the living, but even with their mail they lacked the mass to resist her charge. They were knocked to either side as she ploughed through them, imitating a tactic she'd seen a blood-crazed bullgor use once upon a cordon of her soldiers. Like the Chaos beast, she forced her way through the ranks of her enemies and won clear to the other side.

Emelda spun around and brought her sword slashing at the undead she'd just escaped. Her blade hewed through rusty links of chain to break the spine of one skeleton, but the other escaped her attack with just a few broken ribs. Both of the deathrattle pitched backwards and obstructed the others as they turned to pursue their enemy.

Emelda didn't linger to see how much of an obstruction the two skeletons would pose. She turned and ran back the way she'd come, praying there would be no more Ulfenwatch between her and the main street. She was certain she was close to her destination. Whether Grigori truly lived there or not, she intended to take shelter in the Shark House.

She could almost hear the gods laughing when the clatter of armour came from ahead of her as well as behind. Another patrol had been drawn into the alleyways. If she didn't act fast, she would be caught between this new group and those she'd escaped. While the deathrattle might have no independence of their own, she wasn't going to gamble that they were so mindless they'd fall for the same trick twice.

Another course posed itself when Emelda spotted a rotten door in the wall to her right. She hoped it would prove as decayed as it looked. Throwing her shoulder forward, she charged into it as she had the skeletons. The worm-eaten panels splintered under her drive and she spilled into a dank, musty room.

Something snarled at her from the darkness and she could just make out what looked like a large dog rushing down a flight of stairs. When the brute sprang at her, Emelda thrust her sword upwards. The animal's own momentum drove it onto the point of her blade. It continued to snarl and snap at her, its decayed flesh marking it as either already necrotic or well on its way to becoming undead.

Kicking the beast in its ribs, Emelda sent it sprawling while she ripped her sword free from its body. The dog lunged at her again, but this time her sword slashed across one of its legs. The animal slammed to the floor, but uttered no whine of pain. Instead it tried to rise and lunge at her again.

'Stay down!' Emelda shouted at the dog. Her blade clove the brute's head in half, spilling its rancid contents. She gagged at the sickening stench.

The sound of clattering armour turned her back to the smashed door. No time to try to hide her path now. The Ulfenwatch were sure to follow her inside. Her only course was to keep moving.

Emelda raced through the dilapidated warehouse. Its contents had been looted long ago, so she had a clear path through its rooms. She remained on edge lest the dog she'd killed prove to be merely one of a pack of such creatures, but no others manifested to bar her way. A faint outline of light showed her where another door was. She hurried towards it, hoping it would lead outside.

Perhaps the gods had taken a hand, Emelda thought when she reached the door and threw it open. Unlike its opposite, this one was in stout condition and looked like it would have held against her charge. Had the situation of the doors been changed, she would've been caught out in the alley between two Ulfenwatch patrols. As she hurried through the door and out onto the street beyond, her regret was that she had no way of securing it from this side to block the skeletons. Throwing it closed and wedging the bar against it wasn't going to hold her pursuers long.

The swordswoman hastened down the street, looking for anything that might be familiar. She saw the grisly exhibition of a pair of men who'd been executed by Radukar's minions, their bloodless bodies splayed out against a wooden framework. With its grisly adornment, Emelda almost passed it by before she realised exactly what she was looking at. That framework, jutting out into the street, had once been the grogshack of a man named Odenthal who'd somehow connived a lease upon this spot on the thoroughfare that was so legally complicated that everyone who'd tried to have it removed eventually threw up their hands in confused defeat.

If that was Odenthal's grogshack, then the Shark House was not far off. Emelda headed for the next side street, dashing down it just as the sound of the warehouse door being forced reached her ears. Again she disturbed rats and cats as she ran along the lonely path between sagging buildings, past one block of structures and then halfway along the next. Then she saw it. Shabbier and more decayed than she remembered, its balcony stripped away and its windows boarded up, but there was no mistaking that eccentric doorway!

Emelda hurtled up the few steps leading from the street to the Shark House. She banged the pommel of her sword against the stout coffinwood panels. 'Grigori!' she called out. 'It's Emelda – Captain Braskov! Let me in!'

She could hear the clatter of armour in the distance, but drawing steadily nearer. The Ulfenwatch had picked up her trail for certain and were in pursuit. She had only moments before the skeletons caught up to her. 'Grigori!' she shouted again. Now she could hear the sound of movement behind the door. She banged on it again with her sword. 'Let me in! It's Emelda! I'm no revenant!'

'Prove it,' a voice challenged from behind the door. 'Invoke the God-King's name.'

'By Sigmar, I'm no revenant!' Emelda snarled the words. She looked down the street, expecting to see the Ulfenwatch at any moment.

The bar was quickly drawn back and the door opened with such haste that Emelda stumbled inside. She'd barely regained her balance before the door was slammed closed again. She turned to see a young man in a shabby tunic standing beside the portal. His hand gripped a thick board. He hefted it back into place, the manoeuvre awkward because he had only one hand with which to accomplish it.

'Grigori!' Emelda greeted the man. He gave her a sad smile, his eyes sparkling with emotion.

'Captain Braskov! We'd heard the army had been wiped out.' The smile left Grigori's face and the look in his eyes became one of despair. 'Perhaps it would have been better to die than come back to find the city like this.'

Emelda was stunned by the squalor of Grigori's lodgings. She knew she should have been prepared to find him as impoverished and desperate as most of Ulfenkarn's people, but somehow she couldn't reconcile that reality with the image of a man who'd been a priest of Sigmar and had served under the arch-lector at the cathedral. Yet here he was, dressed in tattered clothes and trying to play host with a few pieces of hard tack and some dried-out cabbage.

'I thought I should never see you again,' Grigori told her. He squatted down on the floor, leaving the one rickety chair to her. He noted her frown. 'Not too much use for a priest these days. Most of those who survived the cataclysm have already been killed. Anybody who's left is like me, afraid of their own shadow. I think it must amuse Radukar to leave us the way we are, for the people to see us brought low and more wretched even than they are. Helps crush their faith that little bit more. Kill their hope, if they have any left.' A bitter laugh escaped from him and he shook his head. 'After all, if Sigmar won't help us, why should he help them?'

'You're still alive.' Emelda was stunned by the despair she heard from Grigori. He'd always been an accepting, optimistic man. Even when he'd been injured on the training field and had to have his arm amputated, he'd refused to give up. Unable to join the army, he'd entered the priesthood and thrown himself fully into ministering to Sigmar's faithful. To see a man like him brought low was horrifying.

Grigori slapped the empty sleeve. 'But for this I'd have marched out on crusade and earned an honourable death on the battlefield.'

'Dead is dead,' Emelda reproved him. It was her turn to be bitter. 'There's little enough of honour in war. The only nobility is found in what you fight to protect.' Her hand tightened into a fist, the fingers digging into her palm. 'We fought so that Mournhold would never be threatened the way it was before. My men died, the army died, to make certain the Chaos tribes would be purged from these lands so Mournhold would be protected. Through everything, even when I was the only one left, it was that thought that kept me going.' She wiped her face so Grigori wouldn't see the tears growing in her eyes. 'What do I find when I return? I find desolation. I find a vampire lording over the ruins of my home.'

The last word provoked another thought. Emelda leaned forward in her chair. 'Grigori, what has become of my home? What happened to Braskov Manor?'

The former priest hung his head and stared at the floor. For a time it seemed like he wasn't going to answer her. 'It was destroyed. There's nothing left.'

Emelda had expected that response, but she wasn't prepared for it. She felt hollow inside. She'd spoken of the city as her home, but that wasn't true. Braskov Manor, the ancestral seat of her family, that had been home.

'You know, Grigori, for the first time I regret leaving.' She tilted her head back and stared at the broken ceiling above and the snowflakes that slipped through its cracks. 'I couldn't do what father expected of me. He had everything planned out, primping and preening me to marry off to one of the other noble houses. He thought he knew what was best for me, and so he decided I should have no choice at all.' She looked back at the ragged priest. 'I rejected his plans because he gave me no say in them. That was what made me join the army. I didn't even care that father refused to buy me a commission. I preferred it, to earn my rank on my own.'

'You were a fine solider, Captain Braskov,' Grigori said. 'No one could match your determination.'

'I was determined because I wanted to prove myself to my father,' Emelda said. 'To show him I was more than who and what he thought I was.' She drew her sword and stared at it in the soft glow of the rushlights. 'Before the army marched off on campaign, father came to see me. He gave me this and for the first time he told me he was proud. He admitted he was wrong. That came hard to a man like him. He confessed that he was wrong to try to plan out my life, wrong to try to protect me the way he had because he saw now that I was able to protect myself. That night before the army left Mournhold, he told me I had more courage than any of my brothers. That I was more than just a Braskov in name, but in heart as well.'

'Vratislaus Braskov was a good man.' Grigori bowed his head and made the sign of the hammer.

'*Was,*' Emelda echoed the word. She hesitated before posing a question she hardly dared pose. 'What happened to my family, Grigori?'

Grigori stood and started to pace the room. 'No one knows if Radukar brought the calamity upon the city or not, but there's no denying the Wolf was ready to pounce when it came upon us. His minions ranged across the ruins while everyone was reeling from the disaster.' The priest caught Emelda's gaze. 'The only nobles who survived the purge were those who took the Blood Kiss and joined Radukar's Thirsting Court.'

It felt as though an orruk warchief had driven its fist into her gut. 'Dead. All dead,' she muttered. She gazed again at her sword, that last gift from her father. 'I'm the last of the line. The last of the Braskovs.'

Grigori walked over to her and put his arm across her shoulders. 'I'm sorry, Emelda. I know what it is to lose your family. Of mine, I too am the last, as far as I know.' He shook his head. 'The last of my people I saw was a cousin. His body was dangling from a noose. He'd been informed on by one of Radukar's spies for refusing to pay the blood-tax.'

Emelda only half heard the ghastly anecdote. Her mind was filled with images of Braskov Manor. The happy days from her childhood spent there, sitting in her mother's lap listening to her father play the organ. Her mother had died while Emelda was still young and it was difficult for her to even remember her face. But she could remember her father. She could almost hear the strains of his music as he played 'Dragon of Szargorond' or some Carstinian melody.

'I want to go there,' Emelda decided.

'What?' Grigori looked at her in alarm. His eyes narrowed as he met her determined gaze. 'There's nothing left,' he said. 'Only ruins.'

'I want to see it. No, I need to see it,' Emelda corrected herself. 'I can't believe it until I see it.'

'The only thing you'll find there is pain,' Grigori warned. 'Isn't it enough to see what has become of the city? Do you need to hurt yourself even more?'

Emelda remained adamant. 'I have to see Braskov Manor. Even if it is just a pile of rubble, I have to see it.' Her tone became more sympathetic. 'I'm not saying you have to take me there. I'll find somebody...'

'No,' Grigori cut her off. 'If you're set on doing this, I'll help you. The slums are dangerous enough, but the ruins are worse. Radukar's undead patrol them and arrest any mortals they find there. Too, there are all the monsters that have made Ulfenkarn their hunting ground. Vargskyr and deadwalkers. Even worse things.' The priest paused to see if his speech had dissuaded her. When he saw that it hadn't, he continued, 'I know a secret way into the ruins, a route that will take us to where you want to go. It is dangerous, but it would be more dangerous if I let you go alone.'

'Thank you,' Emelda said, hugging Grigori.

The priest pulled away from her embrace. 'Don't thank me, Captain Braskov,' he reproved her, his face grim. 'Please, don't thank me. Not for this.'

There was a haunting tone to Grigori's voice. For just an instant, doubt crept into Emelda's mind.

What would she find waiting for her in the ruins?

'The Ulfenwatch doesn't come this way,' Grigori told Emelda. The priest was navigating a shallow fissure caused when the street had collapsed into the sewers beneath. Broken cobblestones, smashed wagons and coaches, the skeletons of horses and people were littered everywhere, creating bottlenecks where they had to crawl under or climb over a particular pile of debris. The place was utterly devoid of sound, lending it an eerie ambiance. With so many bones lying around, Emelda was sure rats or feral dogs should be about trying to scavenge the marrow, but there was nothing.

'Why don't they come this way?' she finally asked her guide.

Grigori paused as he was about to duck his head and scramble through an overturned coach. He looked back at her. 'They know what makes its lair here. When the cataclysm hit, much of the city was destroyed. The Ven Alten menagerie was ravaged. Most of the exotic beasts they kept there died, but a few escaped to prowl Ulfenkarn. One of them ended up down here.' He gave her a reassuring smile and patted the sack slung over his shoulder. 'It's all right. It doesn't like to come out in the daylight and it hates the smell of bat-thorn. I know where it hides, so if we put a bundle of bat-thorn in front of its hole, it won't come out until it loses its pungency. A few days at the very least.'

They continued on, scrambling through the rubble-strewn fissure. Even in daylight Ulfenkarn had a persistent chill in the air and this trench was colder still. Where the shadows blocked the sunlight she could see patches of ice. 'How far is it?' Emelda asked.

Grigori stopped. Ahead of them a figure stood in their path. Emelda gasped and drew her sword. There was no mistaking that lean, savage shape with its long claws and fanged teeth. A ghoul, one of the feral flesh-eaters that infested the lands of Shyish! She started forwards, but Grigori held her back.

The ghoul didn't react at all, though there was no chance it hadn't seen her. The cannibal stood as still as a statue. Emelda felt a wave of horror pulse through her when she realised that was precisely what it was. Now that she gave the thing a good look, she could see the stony texture to its skin. Her gorge rose when she saw fragments of other statues strewn about the floor of the trench.

'By Sigmar, what is this?' the swordswoman wondered. She kept her weapon at the ready, but now she wasn't focused on the ghoul but on the surrounding shadows for some lurking menace.

'The prey of the beast we've been discussing.' Grigori walked forward and rapped his knuckles on the statue. The ghoul crashed onto its side and broke into several pieces. Emelda gagged when the odour of rotten flesh spilled from the shattered remains. Within the stony outer shell was an interior of meat and bone. 'A necrolisk. One gaze from its eyes petrifies its prey and draws out their life force, which the beast then absorbs into itself.' He nodded up the trench. 'We're very close now.'

Emelda felt her mouth go dry. She could remember the fables her nursemaid had told her as a child, about the basilisk and the cockatrice and how they could turn their victims to stone. 'Shouldn't we have brought a mirror to turn its gaze back on it-self?' She thought that was how the heroes in those stories had defeated such monsters.

'It would do no good. The necrolisk is an undead thing and its gaze kills only the living.' Grigori kicked one of the ghoul frag-ments. 'Even a thing as corrupt as a flesh-eater. Mind, the beast has claws and fangs and a lashing tail to deal with other undead. It's quite territorial.'

'You're certain this is the best way forward? It seems to me we'd be better taking our chances with the Ulfenwatch.' Emelda stared at the stony fragments.

'We'll be safe enough when I put the bat-thorn outside its hole,' Grigori reassured her. He frowned and gave her an almost pleading look. 'Unless you'd rather turn back.'

Emelda shook her head. 'No, we'll keep going. If you say this is the best way, then that's enough for me.'

Grigori looked a bit crestfallen, but he didn't argue. Shifting his hold on the sack with the vital bat-thorn inside, he proceeded up the fissure. Emelda hurried after him.

It wasn't long before they reached the necrolisk's hole. For some time the litter of stone fragments had been increasing; here the trench had the appearance of a sculptor's rubbish yard. Emelda could see a round hole in the wall of the fissure, some outlet for the old sewer. The stench wafting out from it was indescribable, but it was the aura of lurking evil that made the greater impres-sion on her. She could imagine cold reptilian eyes watching her from the darkness and the terrible fate that would fall upon her if she met their gaze.

The priest showed no trepidation when he dropped the sack

to the ground and withdrew the bat-thorn from inside. Taking up the bundle he brought it to the mouth of the hole and set it down. 'The scent will keep the necrolisk in its lair. We'll be long gone by the time it stirs again.'

Emelda nodded, not trusting herself to talk. Put her against any enemy that could be cut down with a sword and she was braver than most, but the idea of fighting a beast that could kill with a glance was an entirely different prospect. She'd more readily charge a Chaos sorcerer than challenge something like the necrolisk.

Grigori moved away from the hole and glanced up at the buildings around the trench. 'We should reach where we're going by nightfall.' He scowled. 'Emelda, wouldn't it be better to wait for daylight? If we stay near the necrolisk's hole, nothing will come down here to bother us.'

Emelda felt her skin crawl at the suggestion. 'I'm not staying here. If you want to, just point the way out. Once I'm on the streets I'm sure I can get my bearings even if a lot of it has collapsed.'

'I'll not leave you, Captain Braskov.' Grigori motioned her to follow him. 'Too much has changed. You might follow old streets unaware they lead to a grave-pit or a patch of vampire vines. I couldn't let that happen to you.' He looked back at her over his shoulder. 'There and back,' he said, trying to suppress a shudder. 'It would be suicide to linger there after dark.'

Emelda started to ask him what he meant by that remark, but Grigori quickened his pace and she was forced to sprint to keep up. When she tried to speak to him again, he maintained a sullen silence. For the first time she began to wonder if it might not be better to turn back.

It was a little farther along when the sound of shifting rubble brought both of them to a sudden halt. Grigori waved Emelda to take cover behind a crumbling section of wall that had somehow dropped into the trench seemingly intact. Closer up she could see how weak the structure truly was. Anything much bigger than a cat putting its weight on it would see the wall collapse. She made a warning gesture to the priest when he slipped over to join her.

'This path isn't as deserted as you thought,' she told Grigori.

'I'm not the only one who knows about it,' he returned. 'There are a few of us who are either desperate or reckless enough to earn our bread stealing from the ruins.' While he spoke, Grigori drew a dagger from his boot. The implication was clear. Just because the scavengers might be mortal didn't mean they were friends. Emelda kept her sword at the ready. She smiled. The situation reminded her of laying an ambush for barbarians out in the wilds.

A man soon appeared, his raiment only slightly less shabby than Grigori's. He had a cloak drawn about him, the hood pulled up over his face. He picked his way carefully through the rubble, an iron mace clenched in his fist as he proceeded. He had a sailcloth bag slung over his back, bulging from the loot he'd collected. His greed had got the best of him, for he found it tough going over the rugged terrain. Soon he set his burden down and began throwing out various oddments. Emelda's eyes blazed when she recognised the figure of a knight carved from whalebone. She'd given such a toy to her youngest brother when he turned six.

'Thief!' Emelda challenged the man, stepping out from behind the wall. The scavenger turned in fright at the sound of her voice and jumped back a pace. He held his mace at the ready, but as she stalked towards him, he threw back his hood. Emelda stopped, shocked to find she recognised that sharp-nosed visage. Though his appearance had changed a good deal, she was certain this man had been a groom in her father's stables.

'Vladislav?' she asked.

The man nodded, but kept his mace poised to strike if she came closer. 'You... you're Mistress Emelda, aren't you?' When she nodded, it seemed to heighten his tension.

'Captain Braskov was away with the army, or didn't you know?' Grigori came out from concealment. If recognition of Emelda had alarmed Vladislav, seeing the priest managed to ease his fright.

'Of course,' the groom said. 'She went with the crusade.' He turned to Emelda and gave her a bow that had more of mockery than courtesy in it. 'Everyone thought you were dead. The army will have a hard time trying to clear out Radukar. The Wolf's sunk his fangs deep.'

'Harder than you think,' Emelda told him. 'I'm the only one left.' She pointed at the bag Vladislav had set down. 'I see you've been digging around what's left of Braskov Manor. Grigori was taking me there.'

Vladislav looked perplexed. He gave Grigori an uneasy stare. 'You won't make it before night. You couldn't pay me enough to go there at night.'

'It seems I'm already paying you,' Emelda scolded the looter. 'The least you could do is come with us. There's strength in numbers.'

The groom stared at her as though she were an idiot, then he darted a surly look at Grigori. 'What did you tell her about Braskov Manor?' he demanded.

'That it's in ruins and there's not much sense going there,' the priest declared.

'There must be something left if jackals are picking through the rubble,' Emelda snapped at Vladislav.

The looter bristled at her disdain. 'More than rubble,' he said, a sneer in his tone. His eyes shifted between Grigori and Emelda. 'You'd be surprised how much is left. What else did his reduced holiness tell you?'

'I told her all she needs to know,' Grigori snarled, fingers tightening around the dagger he held.

Vladislav smirked at the rebuke. 'Is that so? Then Mistress Emelda knows that her father is still at the old homestead?'

Emelda's eyes widened in surprise. She fixed a demanding look on Grigori. Before the priest could speak, Vladislav cut him off.

'He didn't tell you that, did he?' The groom's smile became cruel. 'I wouldn't say Vratislaus is living in the manor, but he's there just the same.' A malicious gleam came into his eyes. 'You see, he took the Blood Kiss. He's a vampire now.'

Emelda lunged at the groom. 'Liar!' she snarled as she thrust her sword at him. Vladislav jumped back, narrowly avoiding her blade. Before she could strike again, Grigori darted in and grabbed her arm. While the priest held her back, Vladislav turned and fled, abandoning the sack of loot as he scrambled down the rubble-strewn trench.

'It isn't true!' Emelda raged, trying to twist free from Grigori. The priest struggled to restrain her.

'Of course it isn't. The swine was just trying to say something that would hurt you.' Grigori tried to calm her down. 'Don't waste the effort chasing him. He's not worth it.'

'My father wouldn't join Radukar,' Emelda swore.

'Of course he wouldn't. Vratislaus was a good man.' Grigori tugged at her arm. 'Now that you know scum like Vladislav have been stealing whatever they can from the ruins, maybe you understand there's no reason to go to the manor.'

Emelda glared after the vanished looter. 'I have to see what's there. I have to see it, Grigori.'

'The pig was lying to you,' Grigori assured her. 'That abominable story he told you isn't true. We'll go back...'

'We'll go ahead,' Emelda countered. 'I have to see Braskov Manor.' She looked at Grigori with imploring eyes. 'Maybe when I see it, then I'll be able to accept it.' She slammed her sword back into its scabbard.

'Maybe then I can accept what Radukar has done to my home.'

* * *

Braskov Manor was more than the broken heap of rubble Grigori had let her think she'd find. It had suffered in the cataclysm, to be certain. The wall around the grounds had fallen down in several spots, the gardens were overgrown with weeds and even more noxious vegetation, the stables had collapsed and it looked like fire had gutted the whole of the west wing, but the central structure looked comparatively intact. Emelda could even pick out the window high up on the facade where her room had been. The glass was shattered, the shutters drooped from broken hinges, the iron balcony was twisted out of any semblance of shape, but it was familiar just the same. A shiver undulated through her skin. Looking at the house like this was like stumbling on the decayed corpse of a family member. Horrible on an intimate and personal level that magnified its innate ghastliness.

'There it is,' Grigori said. They'd come as near as the rubble pile that marked where the gatehouse had once stood. The priest was pale and every sound magnified his uneasiness. Night had closed in upon Ulfenkarn and once again the monsters that infested the ruins were emerging from their lairs to send their hungry cries into the dark.

Emelda slowly nodded her head. 'You were right. I shouldn't have come here.' Her voice was thin and strained as she fought to repress the emotion churning inside her. Her eyes glistened as she looked at the manor. It was so lifeless and empty, steeped in the black shadows of Ulfenkarn. 'If I'd kept away I could have remembered home the way it was.' She waved angrily at the desolate structure. 'Now I'll always remember it like this.'

'Come along,' Grigori told her. 'We'll go back now. There's no sense lingering here.' There was an urgency in the priest's tone that puzzled Emelda. He was afraid of something. Not the ambiguous threat of some prowling creature finding them, but something more immediate and certain. Something he knew and expected to strike at any moment.

Then she heard it, sounding out from that dark bulk of stone and plaster. Music! The melodies of an organ! But such music. It was wild and twisted, swelling with mad cadences and crashing with tumultuous strains. She'd never heard anything so sinister and macabre, at once menacing and forlorn. Yet, as she listened, there was a strange sense of familiarity.

'We must go.' Grigori's face was more pallid than ever and sweat beaded his brow. He pulled at Emelda's cloak, but she shook him free.

'Someone is in there, playing father's organ.' The statement came in a low growl. Outrage surged inside Emelda as she imagined some looting filth like Vladislav in there defiling what remained of the Braskov legacy. Then her anger came crashing down as suddenly as it had risen, blotted out by a fresh shock that pulsated through the core of her being. She *knew* that music! Distorted as it was, now she recognised the melody. It was 'Dragon of Szargorond', the favourite piece of Vratislaus Braskov!

Emelda felt as though all the warmth had drained out of her body when she turned to Grigori and put a question to him. 'Who *is* in there?'

Grigori clasped her arm and tried to draw her away. 'Forget it,' he told her. 'The ghosts of Ulfenkarn play malicious tricks...'

'I want to know,' Emelda reproved him, drawing away. 'I need to know.'

'Don't go in there.' Grigori was begging her now. He stamped his boot on the ground like a petulant child. 'If you go in there, I'm not coming with you.'

'No one's asking you to,' Emelda said. She regretted the coldness in her voice the moment the words left her tongue, for she could see how they hurt the priest. But there was no taking them back and no time to frame an apology. She had to get into the manor before whoever was playing left the conservatory. She spared Grigori a cursory nod and started across the ruined gardens for the abandoned husk of her ancestral home.

A husk from which the maddened strains of an organ continued to emanate.

For Emelda it felt like an iron fist was tightening around her heart as she crept through the empty halls of Braskov Manor. The finery she remembered so well was gone, looted or destroyed. Cobwebs clung to the corners and bats fluttered around the windows. A pall of dust coated such furnishing as remained, recalling to her ancient ruins she'd seen on campaign after the forest reclaimed them and covered the old columns in moss. This, however, wasn't the handiwork of fecund vitality, but of necrotic decay. There was no life here, only death.

Yet still the organ played, its wild music echoing through the halls. Emelda was drawn by it, enraptured as any mariner who succumbed to a siren's song. She felt on the verge of a great discovery, one that she feared as much as she anticipated. Dread and hope, flowing together into a concoction that tormented her every step.

The conservatory was before her now, its great doors drooping on their rusted hinges. For an instant Emelda pictured the room as it had been, lit by hundreds of candles with liveried servants standing to attention along the walls. There were her brothers in the chairs, the youngest bored and anxious to leave, the others attentive and appreciative as they listened to father play. She was there too, at first sitting on her mother's lap, then taking over her mother's chair when a carriage accident took her from them. She was looking to the massive organ with its fan of gigantic pipes and its ivory keys, her father poised before it on his bench and pouring his soul into his greatest delight, the escape in which he sought re-lief from the burdens of power and the responsibilities of family.

The illusion of the past faded, but Emelda was surprised to find the room was far from empty. She could see the organ, far too magnificent for looters to cart away, and before it a bench on which sat a figure cloaked in black. It was those hands that played across the keys and those feet that worked the pedals, yet she had no more than the most nebulous impression of who this stranger was that dared make music in her father's house. Her attention was diverted elsewhere – to a threat that converged upon her from every side with grasping claws.

The conservatory wasn't deserted at all. From where they'd been standing against the walls, a cadre of hideous shapes lurched to-wards Emelda. They were the rotten shells of people, their flesh tattered, their eyes staring with the glassy oblivion of the grave. About their desiccated frames they wore soiled rags foul with dirt and decay. It was only when she saw the frayed Braskov crest on the tunic of one of the creatures that Emelda realised they were wearing the livery of the vanished household.

'Stay back,' Emelda warned the undead as they came towards her. She ripped her sword from its scabbard, only too aware that the zombies were oblivious to any kind of threat. As the first of the worm-infested corpses reached for her, she slashed at it and removed the hand from its wrist. A backhanded sweep clove through its skull and sent the thing crashing to the floor.

It was merely one of a dozen of the decayed horrors.

The only sound the zombies made as they closed upon her was the shuffle of their feet on the floor. The organist continued to play, the maddening music providing morbid accompaniment to the undead attack.

Emelda stepped back into the hallway and kicked one of the sagging doors inwards. It snapped from its already strained hinges and slammed down onto three of the advancing zombies, pinning them to the floor under its weight. The rest of the grisly troop took no notice of the plight of their fellows, several of them even striding across the toppled portal and the struggling bodies of the other undead in order to get closer to their prey.

Emelda stared past the advancing zombies, fixing her attention on the organist. She felt a sudden rage for this intruder who defiled the husk of her home and made a mockery of her memories. Steeling herself for an action that reason told her was reckless and her emotions told her was necessary, Emelda charged back at the zombies.

It was almost a repetition of her fight with the Ulfenwatch in the alleyway. Emelda plunged through the gap in the ranks of her enemy where the door had slammed down. Her blade cut a groping arm from one creature, shattered the knee of another. Then she was clear and dashing across the conservatory. She could hear the zombies turning to pursue her, but for the nonce, her only interest was seated at the organ.

'Who are you to defile my father's memory!' Emelda shouted at the organist. Another few steps and she could have rammed her sword into the cloaked back, but a sudden trepidation made her hold back.

The wild music died and the organist turned. Supreme horror filled Emelda when she saw his face. She, Captain Braskov, who had fearlessly confronted mutant formoroids, gorkin and even the daemons of Khorne while fighting Chaos, now knew the ultimate terror. Her senses reeled, threatening to overwhelm her mind and send her consciousness into oblivion's refuge.

The organist was no stranger. He was Vratislaus Braskov!

Emelda knew at once the horrible change that had come upon her father. The pale flesh, the vivid lips, the burning eyes. She'd believed Grigori, but she should have believed Vladislav. Now she knew why the priest had tried to keep her away. This was the ghastly truth he'd tried to hide from her. Vratislaus had become Radukar's creature and joined his Thirsting Court.

The vampire rose from the bench, his face broadening into a smile that displayed his sharp, pearly teeth. He made a dismissive motion of his hand and the zombies that only a moment before had been stalking closer now shuffled back into the shadows.

'Emee,' the vampire said, invoking the diminutive Vratislaus had always used for his daughter. 'You've come back to me, as I always knew you would.' He moved away from the organ and swept towards her in a few fierce steps. 'Come to me, daughter. Let me embrace you.'

As the vampire opened his arms to her, Emelda felt a compulsion to throw herself into them. She resisted the mad impulse and recoiled from the undead in horror. 'No! Keep back!' The sword in her hand felt like a slab of stone, too heavy and ponderous to raise against the creature that now faced her. She retreated before his advance, but was unable to pull her eyes away from the vampire's gaze.

The tableau held for only a moment, father pursuing daughter in a slow dance across the conservatory. As though tiring of the game, Vratislaus suddenly pounced and caught her in his arms. The cloak folded around Emelda like the leathery pinions of a terrorgheist. Her body shuddered as fear and disgust raced through her veins, yet still she couldn't lift her arm to bring her sword against her father.

'All will be well, Emee,' the vampire promised. The closeness of his cold flesh seemed to drain all the warmth from Emelda's body. She felt as helpless as a little girl in the monster's grasp. He noted her fear and a strange mixture of enjoyment and regret pulled at his dead face. 'Everything will be all right,' he said. 'You are a Braskov and destined to rule over this city.' His eyes gleamed and he drew back his head. 'And after you join the Thirsting Court, you shall.' Emelda could only watch as the vampire's wolfish fangs hurtled towards her throat.

'By the might of Sigmar God-King, you will not do this!' Grigori's voice thundered through the room. The vampire pulled away, flinging Emelda from him as he threw up his cloaked arm to shield himself from the golden light that blazed from the priest's hand.

Emelda crashed to the floor, her mind reeling. She realised now she'd fallen under some terrible fascination, the vampire's hypnotic influence. Even with that knowledge, she found herself unable to leap up and slash at the creature with her sword. How could she use that weapon against the man who'd given it to her? Whatever he'd become, he was still her father.

'Captain! Hurry!' Grigori shouted at her. Emelda saw now that what the priest held in his hand was an icon of Sigmar's hammer... and the brilliant light surrounding it was starting to dim.

Emelda turned from the recoiling figure of Vratislaus. For an instant, she hesitated, trying to nerve herself to confront the monster. She knew there wasn't time. Already the vampire's undead minions were starting to move, poising themselves for the moment the divine light faded from Grigori's talisman.

'All right, Grigori,' Emelda said as she rushed to join the priest. 'You warned me to stay away...'

The priest slowly backed out of the conservatory, his eyes fixed on the vampire and the shuffling zombies. 'That isn't important,' he said. 'Right now we have to concentrate on getting out of here. Sigmar grant I can hold them back long enough for us to escape.'

Vratislaus lowered his arm and his hungry gaze fastened upon Emelda. She felt her stomach turn. Even if they escaped the manor, now that the vampire knew she was in Ulfenkarn she was certain the fiend wouldn't rest until she'd joined him in undeath.

* * *

They didn't speak until they were far from Braskov Manor and back down in the fissure. Grigori was confident that however much Vratislaus wanted Emelda, the vampire wouldn't risk meeting the necrolisk.

'I should have told you,' the priest confessed as they navigated the rubble-choked trench. 'I simply didn't have the heart to do it.' He looked up when the clatter of stones reached them from above. Something like a melding of wolf and ogor glared down at them with ravenous eyes, but it made no move to come after them.

Emelda shook her head. 'Do you think I'd have believed you unless I'd seen it for myself?' She patted the sword at her side. 'I was ready to murder Vladislav for telling me my father was a vampire.'

Grigori waved his hand at the ground ahead of them. 'There's where you caught him,' he said. He shook his head. 'I don't see the bag. He must have come back after you drove him off. Probably down at the Black Ship drinking himself into a stupor after selling his loot.' A frown worked itself onto his face and he gave Emelda an apologetic look. 'I mean, what he stole from your home.'

'It isn't my home any more.' Emelda's eyes were filled with bitterness. 'That thing that haunts it isn't my father. Not now. Radukar has taken all of that from me.'

'What will you do?' Grigori asked, a note of worry in his words.

'I don't know,' Emelda said. 'I don't know if I can take a sword to my own father, but I also know I can't leave him like that. Even if I could, he wouldn't let me. Sooner or later he will come looking for me if I don't do something first.'

'Then there's no oth–' Grigori's speech simply stopped.

Emelda turned to her friend and instantly threw herself to one side, ducking her head beneath her arm as she did so. The priest was dead. In that quick glimpse she saw him standing, rigid and frozen in place. His skin had taken on a grey sheen, its texture hardening into stone. From his eyes, the glowing wisps of his soul were being drawn out. She had only a faint impression of the squat, loathsome thing Grigori's spirit was being absorbed into.

Necrolisk! The horror from the Ven Alten menagerie was free from its hole! Either the reptile had another means of egress or something had happened to the bat-thorn. As she scurried behind a pile of rubble, her every sense alert for the sound of the monster pursuing her, Emelda thought of the missing bag of loot. If Vladislav had come back, perhaps the bag wasn't the only thing he'd taken with him.

A hissing kind of bellow rumbled from the monster as it fed. Emelda couldn't think of Grigori. No time to mourn her friend, because at any moment she might share his fate. There was a gap between herself and the next pile of rubble. Biting her lip so that she wouldn't cry out, the swordswoman threw herself across the span, desperate to get back into cover before the lizard noticed her.

The lunge turned into a sprawl as her foot turned under her, and she crashed to the ground. Before she could think, Emelda turned her head and stared in the monster's direction. The necrolisk was more hideous than her imagination had made it. A huge lizard as long as a horse with eight clawed legs sprouting from its sides, its tail was a rotten stump, the end ragged where something had torn it away. The body had once been coated in thick grey scales, but now much of it was decayed and had sloughed away to expose the putrid flesh beneath. Its head was broad with a blunted snout, and a sharp horn jutted from its nose. The creature's eyes... but here Emelda was able to recover her senses and look away. Had the beast not been distracted by absorbing Grigori's life force, she knew that quick glimpse would have destroyed her.

The necrolisk seemed to know it too. The reptile vented an angry hiss. A ghastly wail whipped through the trench as it abandoned Grigori and scurried after new prey.

Emelda picked herself off the ground and ran. She dived towards the old wall just as the necrolisk's jaws snapped closed behind her.

The swordswoman didn't risk turning to fight the beast. Instead she threw herself against that section of wall, the force of her impact sending the whole thing toppling down. She'd thought simply to distract the necrolisk, but when she heard the crunch of splintered bones, she knew the beast had been caught in the collapse.

Whispering a prayer, Emelda raised her sword and spun around to slash at the beast before it could free itself. Her blade scraped across the cracked stones, missing the reptile's body by several inches. She pivoted and struck again, this time slicing into the monster's wormy flesh. The sword was nearly knocked from her hand as it glanced off the lizard's bones.

The necrolisk didn't react to her attack. Emelda backed away, releasing the breath she'd been holding. There would be no reprisal from the lizard. It was truly dead now, its decayed head crushed under the fallen wall. Grigori was avenged.

Or was he? Emelda walked over to the priest's body. The same crash that had finished his killer had knocked the petrified body over. Like the ghoul, his remains had shattered. It was hard for Emelda to look on the broken pieces; instead her eyes fell to the golden hammer of Sigmar that Grigori had used to save her. She picked it up from the ground.

'I killed the necrolisk,' she said, hoping whatever part of Grigori's essence had escaped the lizard would hear her. She tucked the Sigmarite talisman under her belt. Her eyes were like slivers of steel as she made a promise to the dead. 'If I see the bat-thorns are gone from where you left them, I'll find Vladislav and make him pay for freeing the beast.'

She turned from the shattered priest and hurried down the

trench. Grigori had mentioned the Black Ship. If she didn't find the bat-thorns, at least she knew where to look for the looter.

Vladislav lifted his bound hands to his forehead and wiped away the blood. The cut had started to bleed again and it was unwise to let the smell linger in the air. There were too many things in Ulfenkarn that would be drawn by the scent.

Emelda had no sympathy for the rogue. He'd done exactly as she'd thought, taking away the bat-thorn so the necrolisk would get revenge for him on her and Grigori. It was only by the merest chance that she'd escaped the reptile.

Chance had spared Vladislav this far. He'd have been dead in the alley behind the Black Ship now if he hadn't told her the right things when she'd confronted him. He knew what she'd found in Braskov Manor, and he knew the one thing that would keep her from running him through with her sword. He claimed he knew where Vratislaus hid his coffin.

So Emelda tied up the looter and dragged him back with her into the ruins. It was hard going with Vladislav trying to get away any time an opportunity presented itself, so the hour was much later than it had been when Grigori had brought her here. She was only thankful that the monsters prowling Ulfenkarn were still avoiding the trench. It seemed they weren't aware yet that the necrolisk was dead.

When they'd emerged from the fissure, it had been a different prospect. She was almost certain something had been stalking them on their way to the manor.

'I can tell you as easily as show you,' Vladislav pleaded with her, not for the first time. 'You know the place as well as I do. You could find it easy.'

Emelda's hand clenched a fistful of dust. Was it only last night that she'd crouched here with Grigori in the old gatehouse watching the darkened husk of her home? She turned cold eyes on the rogue. 'You'll take me there. I don't trust you as far as I'd trust Radukar himself. You'll take me right to where my father's coffin is. Then I *might* let you go.'

It was a desperate plan she'd devised. Vampires of Radukar's line weren't destroyed by sunlight, as some hopeful superstitions claimed, but many of them feared it and would flee back to their coffins to wait for nightfall again. Perhaps, she thought, they'd been raised listening to the same superstitions. Whatever the case, she hoped she could catch Vratislaus when he was helpless in his coffin. Maybe then she'd be able to do what had to be done.

'You promised,' Vladislav whined. 'You said you'd spare my life if I showed you where it was hidden.'

'I didn't kill you on the spot,' Emelda snarled at him. 'I've already spared your life. Now you pay your part of the deal.'

The eerie strains of the organ rose into the fading night. Emelda stiffened, her whole being focused upon the sounds, her mind assailed by the knowledge of who was playing the piece.

Vladislav seized on her distraction. His hands closed about a piece of rubble and brought it slamming down on Emelda's head. She wilted to the ground, shaken but not quite stunned. She glared at the rogue as she rose on wobbly legs, sword clenched in her fist.

Vladislav didn't try to talk his way out of this new act of treachery. He turned and sprinted off to the street, trying to outdistance any pursuit. Emelda saw at once that she wasn't going to catch up with the man, so after a few steps she stopped and simply cursed at him.

It proved a wise choice not to chase Vladislav. Emelda saw a dark shape bounding through the rubble off to the rogue's left. The creature that had been stalking them for so long must have been afraid to follow them to Braskov Manor, but now that the man was running away from the place, it felt confident enough to attack.

Out from the shadows the hulking beast pounced on Vladislav

and crushed him to the ground. Its appearance was much like that of the wolfish creature that had watched from the edge of the trench the night before, a decaying hulk with long claws and a lupine head. The vargskyr ripped and tore with those claws, pulling chunks from Vladislav's screaming body to hold above its mouth, so that blood from the flesh might drip down into the beast's throat.

Emelda turned from the grisly sight and closed her ears to Vladislav's screams. Fate had bestowed on the murderous cur a death more terrible than anything she would have done to him.

Concerned that the taste of blood would cause the vargskyr to forget its earlier timidity, Emelda abandoned her original plan and headed into the ruined manor. She couldn't wait for daylight; she'd have to move now. The task ahead of her was daunting. She knew how big the house was and how many places a coffin could be hidden. But, as Vladislav had said, she did know the place and that gave her an advantage. It would be quicker if she had a guide, of course.

Then her hand fell to Grigori's Sigmarite talisman, still tucked under her belt. A bold idea came to her. Perhaps she *could* use a guide to show her the way.

This time Emelda didn't rush headlong to the conservatory to confront the organist. She used the network of hidden passages that burrowed through the manor's walls to reach her goal. Through a narrow peephole, she observed the room within.

Vratislaus had yet to replenish his zombies. Emelda could see only four in the room, but each of these bore the marks of last night's battle. The others, she imagined, were scattered about the manor, lying in wait against her return. The vampire had forgotten, it seemed, that she knew the building's secrets too.

Her father sat at the organ, playing away. Emelda could almost imagine him as the man she'd known until her gaze drifted to the pale figure shackled to the wall. Some woman from the slums, her clothes stained with blood. Her skin was ashen and her head sagged against her shoulder, a great gash in her throat. Emelda had seen death often enough to know she was looking at it now, and it did not take a second guess to know why the woman had been killed.

Loathing for this abomination that had been her father filled Emelda. She pressed the lever that slid back the secret door and stepped from the wall into the room. Before they had even started to react, her sword cut down two of the zombies, dropping them to the floor in a welter of their own rancid guts.

Vratislaus swung around at the noise. Surprise twisted his face for a moment, then his expression hardened into one of smug authority. He rose from the bench and lifted a goblet that had been resting on the organ. He held it up in mocking salute.

'I knew you couldn't keep away,' the vampire declared. He took a sip from the goblet and a little rivulet of blood fell from the corner of his mouth. 'You're my daughter. This is where you belong.' He made a gesture and the remaining zombies backed away from Emelda.

'I came here to end this,' Emelda said, her voice cold with rage. Her eyes darted to the vampire's last victim chained to the wall.

Vratislaus followed the direction of her gaze. A cruel smile curled his lips. 'That? That is what disturbs you? What is *that*? A worthless low-born wretch. Such riff-raff existed only to serve their betters even before the city fell to ruins. They will continue to exist only to serve us as we rebuild.' He chuckled as it became Emelda's turn to be surprised. 'Yes, Emee, rebuild. Do you think I meekly bow and scrape to the Wolf? Bah! I've simply used Radukar to gain power. Power the likes of which you never dreamed.' He emphasised his point by crushing the pewter goblet in his hand until it was flattened. He dashed the vessel to the floor.

'This power is yours,' the vampire assured her. He took a gliding step towards Emelda. 'Share in it with me. Father and daughter, together as family. We'll be the most powerful in all the Thirsting Court, the right hand of Radukar.' His eyes gleamed with savage ambition. 'Then, when the time is right, we'll cast down the Wolf as he cast down the Vyrkos after they gave him their power. We'll rule Ulfenkarn. To rebuild or to destroy as we see fit.'

Without realising it, Emelda had been walking towards her father. A lethargy weighed upon her mind, dulling her to her peril. Again, the sword felt too heavy to lift. It was too much effort to oppose the vampire. She should submit and embrace everything he told her, even if she knew it was lies. No thrall of Radukar could ever break free of the Wolf's domination.

Emelda's hand fell to Grigori's talisman. Touching the holy symbol filled her with new strength. She pulled away from the vampire's mesmeric influence, stumbling back from Vratislaus. Her father's eyes flared with anger. 'Spurn me?' he snarled. He started for her. 'Fool! You have no choice!'

Emelda pulled the hammer talisman from her belt and brandished it before the vampire. Golden light erupted from it as she held it before her. Vratislaus flinched away from her, shielding his face with his arm. 'Destroy it! Throw it away!' he commanded, but Emelda was immune now to his control. She pressed him further, driving him back towards the organ.

There were others that would obey Vratislaus. Focused upon her father, Emelda nearly failed to notice the zombies closing in on her. She spun around, lashing out with her sword. One of the undead fell with its leg ripped in half. The other staggered back, chest gashed. The creatures had accomplished their purpose, however. They'd provided a distraction for their master. Whipping around, Vratislaus fled from the room, his cloak billowing behind him as he sprinted into the hall.

Emelda turned her back on the zombies and chased after her father. One way or another, she was determined this night would see an end to it.

Daughter and sire ran through the empty halls of Braskov Manor. Vratislaus led her on a winding chase through desolate rooms and abandoned corridors. The despoiled reminders of childhood rose up at every leg of her pursuit, clawing at her with despair and loss. None of it could be reclaimed. All of it was gone. All of it except her father.

Emelda cursed the defeatist feelings that sought to overwhelm her. What had been lost couldn't be changed. The only thing that could was what her father had become. *That,* she could put an end to and free him from the blight of undeath.

A pattern began to develop as Emelda hunted her father through the manor, something that any other pursuer would never have noticed. She became aware that Vratislaus kept trending back towards the library, but would always veer away before getting too close. She realised then what he must be doing. He was trying to lose her before diving back into his refuge. When he found she was still on his trail, he diverted and led the chase in another direction.

She remembered the long hours she'd spent in the library. She remembered too the hidden vault where her father kept his most valuable books. Emelda knew what the vampire was keeping there now.

Once Vratislaus had led her far away from the library, Emelda let him think she'd made a wrong turn and lost his trail. She expected him to take a circuitous route back to his refuge to make sure he'd truly slipped away from her. She, on the other hand, would strike directly for the room and be waiting for him when he returned.

The library had been utterly ransacked by Vladislav and other looters of his ilk. It pained Emelda to see the litter of books strewn about, tossed aside by thieves who'd decided they were of no worth. The shelves that lined the walls were bare, denuded of the tomes that had occupied them for generations. Another memory of her past despoiled and lying in ruins.

Emelda hastened to the shelf with the hidden catch. The looters had missed it in their ransacking of the room. Her fingers jabbed the button and the shelf swung wide to expose the little vault behind. The swordswoman gasped when she saw her supposition confirmed. Resting on a bier was a long black coffin, its lid upraised.

Emelda dashed over to the coffin and set Grigori's talisman inside. It had repulsed the vampire when they'd held it in their hands, and she was depending on it to do the same now and keep Vratislaus from the safety of his grave.

Almost as soon as she'd set the talisman in place, Emelda sensed the approach of her father. She turned to see him hurrying through the library. The first rays of day were shining through the windows and his face was filled with panic. When he saw her standing in the vault, he drew back and glared at her.

'Out of my way!' Vratislaus growled.

Emelda continued to bar his path. 'This has to end,' she told him, her voice cracking with emotion. Before she could even try to raise her sword, the vampire lunged at her. His hand swatted her across the vault and she slammed against the stone wall.

'Petulant whelp!' the vampire hissed. He stalked towards her, fangs bared. 'I'll suffer no more of your defiance.' Then his expression changed to one of horror. He had noticed what she'd placed in his coffin. He reeled away. He might have fled back into the library, but now the room was bright with sunlight. He spun back around.

Emelda pushed away from the wall and met her father's enraged stare. 'Can't go back in your coffin,' she said. 'What will you do now?'

The vampire sprang at her. She struck him with her sword, but his hand closed about her wrist and forced her arm down to her side. 'Take that filth away! Take it away!' he howled. When she refused he drew her close and forced her head back, exposing her throat.

'Kill me and there will be nobody to remove Sigmar's hammer,' Emelda challenged him. She saw the fright that twisted his face. Yes, he certainly feared the sunlight. Desperation filled his eyes.

'You are my daughter, Emee,' Vratislaus said, releasing his hold on her. 'Don't do this to your father. You and I, we're the last of the Braskovs.'

Emelda felt the vampire's hypnotic power closing upon her once more. She fixed her mind on the horrors she'd seen inflicted on Ulfenkarn's people by Radukar and his Thirsting Court. She thought of the woman, chained to the wall and bled dry by this creature wearing her father's flesh.

The sword flashed in the growing light, hitting with a strength Emelda didn't know she possessed. The blade hewed through the vampire's neck and sent his head rolling across the floor. The body shuddered for a moment before wilting to the ground, stolen blood spurting from its severed veins.

Emelda looked down on the destroyed vampire with disgust as it rapidly began to decay. 'No,' she told the dead creature, '*I* am the last of the Braskovs.'

YOUR
NEXT READ

CURSED CITY
by C L Werner

When a series of vicious murders rock the vampire-ruled city of Ulfenkarn, an unlikely group of heroes – a vampire hunter, a vigilante, a wizard and a soldier – must discover the truth even as the city's dread ruler takes to the streets and the bloodletting increases.

STRONG BONES

Michael R Fletcher

Stugkor sat at Old Tooth's feet, listening to the fat ogor ramble on about how great everything used to be for the Fangtorn, back before the Everwinter separated them from the main bulk of their clan.

Leaning back so he could see past Old Tooth's belly, he studied the wizened face, skin like dried mud left to freeze. Was he called Old Tooth due to his age, the fact he only had one tooth – a prominent fang jutting from his lower jaw that always looked like it might get caught in a drooping nostril – or because that lone tooth, cracked and brown, looked ancient like… like…

'What's the oldest thing you can think of?' Stugkor asked, interrupting.

The big ogor blinked down at him, eyes narrowing. 'The sun,' he said finally, hooking a thumb in the direction of the cold yellow light barely peeking over the horizon. Noon, this was as high as it would get at this time of year.

That tooth sure as blood didn't look like the sun. 'A real *thing*,' said Stugkor. 'An object.'

Old Tooth sucked in the fat thickness of his lower lip, chewing on it like he meant to devour his own face. A mass of scars and ill-healed wounds, it looked almost as old as the tooth. 'Saw an Icefall yhetee trapped in a glacier. Looked alive, eyes open, teeth bared. Like it might step out and start killin.'

An old thing that wasn't really dead and looked alive anyway? No help at all. 'What's the oldest–' Stugkor stopped when he realised he couldn't remember why he was asking.

'What was I talking about before you interrupted?' demanded Old Tooth.

'How the Fangtorn used to be a great tribe,' answered Stugkor. 'How the 'umans used to scatter before us like frost mice, and how we'd mash them with clubs and then eat them while they screamed.'

'Right. The good days.'

'If they was screamin,' said Stugkor, 'don't that mean you did a bad job of the mashin'?'

'Naw. You mash the legs so they can't run, but can still scream and kick when yer eatin' 'em.'

Made sense, Stugkor decided, as he glanced about the camp. A score of ogors bustled about, either busy at something like sharpening weapons, or eating something from the last raid. Kthang, the tribe's frostlord, had returned from raiding just two days ago and already supplies were dwindling. Off to the east the Everwinter, a twisting swirl of ice and snow, moved ever closer. They'd move soon, before it devoured them, before it buried them in the long-not-quite-death. Like that Icefall yhetee: not quite dead, but not alive either.

'Think Kthang will let me come on the next raid?' Stugkor asked.

'Nope,' said Old Tooth.

Not even a moment's hesitation, not even the briefest pause for thought. Not that Old Tooth was famous for thinking.

'Why not?'

'If you 'ave to ask...'

What the blood did that even mean?

'I'm tired of leftovers. I want fresh meat. Warm marrow from a just-snapped bone. Blood, hot and salty.'

'Y' ate the bear.'

'Not the same, eatin' something dumb.'

Old Tooth nodded, almost looking wise. 'Troof. Best meat *knows* it's being eaten. Best meat had other plans for the day.'

Humans always had plans. It was an ongoing mystery to Stugkor. Why plan for tomorrow when you were probably going to get eaten? Strange creatures. If they hid in the trees, they'd be so much harder to find! But there they were, building walls and making buildings. If an ogor saw a wall and a building then the one thing it knew for sure was that there was a meal inside.

'What was I talkin' about before you interrupted?' Old Tooth demanded, again.

Rolling his eyes, Stugkor pushed to his feet with a grunt. 'Can't remember.'

'But it was important?'

'Very. Life lessons 'n all.'

Nodding, the ancient ogor turned and shambled away, limping on his bad leg. Someday he'd slow enough the Everwinter would get him. Unless the rest of the tribe was hungry enough to eat the leathery old beast first.

Stugkor's belly, hanging far over the heavy leather belt he wore for decoration, rumbled. Fetishes, bear scalps, frost sabre teeth and assorted trinkets taken from things the young ogor had mashed and eaten and forgotten, hung from the belt, swaying as he lumbered off in search of his mates, Chidder and Algok.

He found them toying with a hare, fur white like the snows, eyes wide and black like the night. They'd cornered the little creature in an ice dell and were stomping the ground, blocking its every attempt at escape. The thing quivered in terror, chest heaving. They'd keep this up until either it fell over, too exhausted to move, or one of them misjudged and accidentally mashed it flat. Such a dumb little life, hardly worth eating. No plans. And if Chidder, who'd always been clumsy, mashed it flat, it wouldn't even wriggle when you swallowed it.

Sometimes, decided Stugkor, the game was better than the meal.

'Stug,' grunted Algok, spotting his approach.

'Old Tooth says Kthang ain't gonna let us go on the raid,' he told his friends. He hadn't specifically asked about them, but seeing as he was the oldest, it seemed a safe assumption.

They grumbled but seemed unconcerned.

The hare, sensing their distraction, made a dash for freedom and was mashed flat by Chid, who'd rather see it squished than let it escape.

'I've been thinking,' said Algok, dead hare already forgotten.

In Stugkor's opinion she spent way too much time doing that. He never said anything though because she had a temper and liked to sit on people until they lost consciousness.

'Yeah?' he asked. 'And?'

'Aelves,' she said, crossing her arms.

'Why the blood you been thinking about aelves?' demanded Chidder. 'Ain't none here.' He looked around, beady eyes squinting. 'Are there?'

'No,' said Algok. 'None. But you know how Kthang and the other raiders always say that the best meat is smart meat, meat with plans for tomorrow?'

Stugkor and Chidder nodded.

'Well, aelves,' she said, waiting expectantly.

Chid scowled at his friend. 'What in the blood?'

Stug understood. 'They live a really long time. They're supposed to be even smarter than 'umans.'

'Imagine how many plans a thing that lives 'undreds of years has,' said Algok.

Chid frowned, looking at his huge blunt fingers like they might provide an answer. 'So...'

'So,' said Stug, 'they're prolly the tastiest thing in all the world.'

''Cept for gods,' said Algok. 'Immortals have plans for the big.'

She was right, as always. Gods probably tasted great.

'Old Tooth say why we couldn't raid?' asked Algok. Quicker than most, she bounced from subject to subject with alarming speed.

'If you 'ave to ask,' said Stugkor, repeating Old Tooth's words. He blinked. He'd thought Old Tooth meant that if he had to ask, he wouldn't understand the answer. But what if the ancient ogor meant that if you had to ask, you couldn't come? What if he meant that the way to go raiding was to *not* ask?

'I,' said Stugkor, feeling rather pleased with himself, 'have a plan.'

It was, he decided, a rather brilliant plan. The ingenuity! The cunning! The clever details! By the blood, maybe Algok wasn't the smartest ogor after all!

'So?' Algok demanded.

'We go raiding. Just us.'

'Blood,' swore Chid, clearly impressed.

Even Algok nodded in appreciation.

Stugkor had another thought. 'If we get eaten by some other ogors,' he mused, 'I bet we'll taste better than we would have before.'

Algok understood, eyes widening. 'Cuz we got plans!'

Shard, Stugkor's young, grey-white mournfang, moved effortlessly over the endless wastes. Even through the heavy bone-and-hide saddle, he felt the beast's coiled strength. Ever alert, Shard prowled, massive head low and swinging back and forth as she sought the scent of life. She might not see much past the length of her monstrous tusks, but her sense of smell was second to none. At least when it came to meat and blood.

Algok, riding to Stugkor's right, picked at a scar on her black mournfang's shoulder. The creature's eyes, bloody sparks of hate, never left Shard. There was a harsh hierarchy to the pack, and Stug's mournfang ruled tooth and claw.

Chidder, not paying attention, allowed his red-tinted mount to edge past Shard. The lead mournfang swung her tusks in his direction with a guttural growl, and Stug eyed the other ogor. Was Chid ready for a fight? Had he already grown bored with the raid? While Stug desperately wanted to mash some humans, shove great quivering gobs of fresh meat into his mouth and drool blood down his belly, a mad brawl in the snow would be fun too.

'Go on, Chid,' he said, grinning. 'Go for it. We can always raid another day. After yer mournfang has healed.'

Chidder grunted, and slowed his mount so Shard was once again in the lead.

Snow. Ice. The howl of wind whipping across land broken only by jagged peaks of glacier. The bone-crunch of frozen snow beneath your feet, and the endless expanse of blue, deeper than a glacial lake, overhead.

The sun peeked over the horizon, did little to warm the world, and slunk back down, defeated.

Stomachs growled, and tempers rose.

Another day without food, without mashing anything.

Boring. So boring.

Another day.

So hungry.

Snow gave way to occasional patches of frozen mud sprouting tufts of hardy grass that still mostly looked dead. Sometimes they found copses of stunted trees, gnarled and bent.

How long had they been out here? Was it two days or four? Stug had lost count. He was about to ask Algok, when Shard raised her head, keen nose testing the air. Studying the horizon, Stugkor grinned at what he saw.

'I've forgotten the plan,' admitted Chidder, eyes slitted against the harsh wind.

'Find 'umans,' Stugkor explained patiently. 'Mash 'umans.'

'Blood,' swore Chid in awe. His face crumpled in thought. 'How we find 'umans?'

Stugkor pointed south with a thick finger. 'Smoke. And where there's smoke there's...'

'Stuff burnin'?' asked Chid.

'No, idiot,' said Algok. "Umans.'

'Ah,' he said. 'Burnin' 'umans.'

Cresting a ridge of stone and dirt, Stug spotted the human settlement. It sat in the bottom of a shallow valley. He slowed to examine the distant wall. Made from bundled twigs and branches bound together by wound grass and packed with mud, it was an embarrassing effort at best. Really, all it had going for it was height, standing maybe his own height and half again. Since it didn't look sturdy enough to climb, they'd have to bash their way through.

Rickety wood watchtowers stood at each corner, but they were empty.

Such a strange human thing, he thought. Like knowing you were about to be mashed and eaten somehow made things better. Wouldn't it be better to be surprised? You know, dead and half-digested before you really knew what was going on. Seeing as there was no one in the towers, maybe the humans had figured that out for themselves.

Reining in their mounts, they stopped to study the town.

'Never seen a 'uman village before,' Stug said.

Much like the wall, their homes were built of pathetic twigs and patched with grey clay. Cobblestones lined the main street, the rest being little more than mud paths.

'Something doesn't look right,' said Algok.

Stugkor blinked at the sight, struggling to comprehend. While not mashed, the 'umans were already dead. Some lay scattered and leaking blood into the snow. Others had been torn apart, their limbs gathered in one pile, their torsos in another.

The really strange thing, however, was how many of the dead were still marching around doing stuff. Stripped of flesh and blood, corpses in strange armour or long decorative robes worked at incomprehensible tasks.

There were so many of them, hundreds and hundreds of dead hard at work. Some gathered together corpses, sorting them for reasons beyond Stug's understanding. Others collected what little metal the 'umans had, tossing it into piles.

'This ain't right,' said Algok. 'Town is full of deaders.' She leaned forward in the saddle, eyes narrowed. 'They've already butchered all the 'umans. Nothing to mash. Maybe...' She glanced at Stug. 'Maybe we should go?'

Chid looked ready to argue but less ready to dare Algok's temper.

Stugkor's stomach grumbled complaint. It had been looking forward to digesting living planning things, and let him know just how unhappy it was with the thought of more leftovers.

A gaunt corpse, garbed in the shredded remnants of long green robes and finely crafted armour of a type he'd never before seen, stalked the savaged town. It wore a great fanned crown of curved bone and bore a colossal jade scythe wafting foul smoke from the blade. The other dead stepped from its path. Somehow the scene reminded Stug of the ants that came out during brief thaws. They moved as if perfectly united in purpose, driven by a single will.

'Deader sorcerer,' said Algok. 'Prolly invaders from another realm.'

Never having left the northern wastes of Ghur, the Realm of Beasts, the young ogor had little experience in such things.

That was bad. Sorcerers were supposed to be easy to mash if you surprised them, but dangerous if they knew you were coming. This one, with its strangely shaped bones and smoking scythe, definitely looked like the kind you wanted to drop a large rock on. Preferably from a great height.

An odd feeling shivered through Stug, and for a moment he wished he was somewhere else.

Ain't nothin', he told himself.

That thing was no taller than a man, barely came past Stug's belt.

Just my gut saying it wants to go 'ome and eat somethin'.

By the Lord of Predators he wished he was back with his people.

A massive creature constructed of bone and metal lumbered into view. It bore massive ribbed baskets upon its back, and had a spine of barbed bone. Grasping finger-like appendages protruded long past its terrible body. Twisting coils of greenish smoke leaked from its death's-head maw. Sometimes it walked on the four largest legs, but sometimes it reared back, head raised as if testing the air, the great jagged rune-cut sickles of its forelegs flashing in the pale sunlight.

'It's got too many limbs,' whispered Algok.

She was right. Spindly arms, at least in comparison to its powerful legs, twitched and spasmed, bone hands reaching out to feel the earth beneath it. The whole thing reminded Stugkor of those many-legged carrion wyrms that burrowed into rotting corpses. Except much bigger. Much, much bigger.

The beast stopped over one of the neat piles of body parts, its thin limbs blindly feeling about, grasping severed arms and legs.

'No way that thing is gonna leave any for us,' moaned Chidder. 'Look how big it is!'

The ogors watched in appalled horror as the meat and muscle and blood was stripped off and tossed aside to land in a steaming pile. The arms then passed the bones along until they could be tossed into the massive baskets.

Stugkor struggled to understand. 'Didn't even eat it!'

Of what possible use could stripped bones be?

He stared at the dead creatures. Some were made of bones he recognised. The spine of a bear. Legs of a frost sabre. He tried to comprehend. These things were *made?*

The lumbering beetle-like beast tossed aside more parts than it stripped, littering the snow with perfectly good food.

'I'm hungry,' said Chidder. 'I say we kill the deaders and eat all the meat. They're just gonna throw it away!' His stomach growled. 'Maybe eat the bone-things too.'

'How do we kill dead things?' asked Algok, ever a source of smart stuff.

'Mash,' said Chidder. 'Mash and mash and mash.'

Perhaps he wasn't so dumb after all.

'That's an army in there,' Stug said. 'If the clan was 'ere, we'd mash 'em in a heartbeat. But just us three?' He studied his friends. 'Might be difficult.'

Difficult.

No way these corpses could defeat the Fangtorn. And yet the thought of that fight didn't sit well in Stug's gut.

Just hungry, he told himself.

He found himself staring again at the sorcerer, the smoke curling off its jade scythe. It moved wrong, like it had a will. Like it was a living thing, a twisting wisp of souls.

The deader sorcerer lifted a bone hand, fingers splayed wide. All movement ceased in an instant. Stug watched, helpless, dreading, as it turned its skeletal face to focus on him. No hesitation. No searching. It knew *exactly* where he was.

Not good. Not good. Not good.

Hand raised, it studied him. Even from here Stug saw the stuttering sparks of green fire lighting the empty caverns of its eye sockets.

We have to... We have to go.

He opened his mouth, said nothing.

Chid said something, but he couldn't hear it.

Those eyes that weren't eyes saw him, saw through him. They held Stug, crushed his heart in a bone fist. He couldn't breathe.

We...

Finally, the sorcerer turned away and Stug drew a shuddering breath, his heart slamming in his chest.

'We have to–'

The thunder of hooves interrupted Stugkor, and he turned to see an armoured corpse wielding a sword, blade the same smoking green-black jade as the scythe, and mounted on a similarly armoured dead horse. Iron hooves kicked sparks as they crossed a stretch of exposed stone.

Chidder grinned yellowed teeth. 'Finally!'

Whooping a war cry, Algok and Chid unslung their warclubs, and kicked their mournfangs into a roaring charge.

Unease bubbled deep in Stugkor's belly. He hoped it was just the squashed snowrat he ate last night. Screaming his own war cry, he followed after his mates.

'Look how small it is!' bellowed Chidder as he tried to crash his mount into the armoured corpse.

The dead warrior easily evaded Chid's charge, his bone-and-iron horse neatly sidestepping. That smoking jade sword darted out, punching through the side of Chidder's mournfang's neck. The beast crumpled with a wet cough of blood, forelegs folding beneath it, sending Chid somersaulting forward. He landed in an awkward pile, winded and moaning.

Algok went wide, hoping to attack the corpse from the far side, but its torso twisted alarmingly. Parrying her massive club with smoking steel, it spun the weapon in bone fists and decapitated her mournfang with a single stroke. Algok, too, was thrown from her mount. Unlike Chid, she broke her fall mostly with her face. She lay motionless.

That feeling in Stug's gut definitely wasn't the snowrat. Already committed, he drove his mournfang at the warrior. Even though Shard was only young, sitting on the beast's back Stugkor towered over the undead warrior he faced. The thing should have cowered like those weak little humans. It should have trembled before his might, fled before his ravenous hunger. Instead, it ducked under what was supposed to be a skull-shattering backhand, and skewered Shard with a single neat thrust through the chest.

Having seen what had happened to Chid and Algok, Stug leapt free, rolling across the hard ground and regaining his feet.

The deader made no attempt to follow him. Instead, it studied Stug. Faint sparks of green fire flickered in the hollowed sockets of its eyes. Neither it nor its mount moved or twitched.

For a moment all was still. Only Chid's groan of pain broke the silence. Algok hadn't moved, hadn't made a sound.

The deader dismounted. Its horse backed away and waited, even though it had received no command.

Lying at Stug's feet, Shard made a strange noise, half grunt, half annoyed whine, and died. That uncertain, unhappy feeling in Stug's gut was gone. Something new replaced it. Something hot. Rage.

Stug bellowed and charged the corpse, swinging his warclub in mighty, crushing blows. He hit nothing but air, the deader always swaying just beyond reach. Instead of stabbing or hacking his head off, it used its sword to trip him and he sprawled into the mud.

'Slow,' it said, voice dry and squeezed like someone was choking it.

Regaining his feet, Stug went after his enemy. Either he killed it, or they were all doomed. Chid lay stunned and mumbling, and Algok still hadn't moved.

Unhurried, as if the ogor offered no threat, the deader avoided Stug's every attempt to mash it. Over and over it stabbed that foul sword at him and Stugkor retreated, desperately looking for an opening. Flashing jade left trails of writhing smoke as the corpse followed.

This wasn't at all how fights were supposed to happen. Where was the joyous mayhem, the crunch of bone and spray of blood? The only blood being spilled here was his.

The deader lashed out, leaving a long bloody gash in Stug's belly.

'Slow and stupid,' the corpse ground out, accent harsh.

Seeing the decapitating attack coming but too slow to avoid it, Stug blocked it with his arm. Smoking green steel cleaved through flesh and muscle like it was nothing, and stopped dead, lodged in bone.

Pain, unlike anything the young ogor had ever felt, smashed through Stug's thoughts.

With a scream, he yanked his arm away, dragging the sword from the corpse's bony fists.

The deader stepped back, appraising. 'Strong bones,' it said.

And then Algok hit it from behind, smashing it to the ground with her bulk. Pinning it beneath her, she roared and punched it in the chest, cracking ribs. The dead thing struggled beneath her, fingers of bone and steel clawing long rents in her flesh. She punched it in the face, snapping its head to the side and shattering its jaw. And still it fought, heedless of the wounds it suffered.

Stumbling forward, Stug stomped the thing's legs over and over until its knees broke. It might be made of bone, but it was unlike anything he'd felt before. Any mortal creature would have been dust. Algok still keeping it trapped beneath her, Stug went after its arms next. He had better luck bending the joints until they popped.

Finally, when he'd reduced the warrior to little more than a crumpled torso, Algok rolled free. She pushed to her feet and wobbled unsteadily.

The deader watched them, calm.

Glowing jade sparks focused on Stug. 'Strong bones,' it said again, though its shattered jaw made it sound like *Shton omsh*.

Turning, Stugkor saw Chid, too, had regained his feet. Algok bled from a dozen wounds, tongue protruding as she tested the tooth she'd snapped off landing on her face.

'I don't wanna fight two of those,' said Chidder, collecting a shattered femur from the ground and gnawing on it. Growling, he tossed it aside when his teeth left only shallow scratches in the bone.

'You didn't even fight one,' grunted Algok, stomping on the deader's skull until it came apart. Leaning low, she peered into the ruin. 'Not even a brain.' She glanced at Stug. 'Must be dumber than Chid.'

Stugkor wasn't so sure.

All three mournfangs lay dead. It was almost like the corpse had been more interested in killing their mounts than killing the ogors.

Why? Why would it do that?

He looked north, back towards the tribal lands. A storm brewed there, black iron clouds blanketing the horizon. It was going to be a long walk. Looking back to the human settlement, he saw movement in the town. The deader army looked to be preparing for travel. There was no haste to their actions. Even though Stug and his mates had just mashed the warrior it had sent, the sorcerer still stood where it had before, head tilted back, staring up at Stug.

'To slow us down,' he said, with dawning comprehension.

'What?' asked Chid and Algok.

'It killed our mournfangs to slow us.'

His friends looked doubtful.

Strong bones, the corpse had said.

The deaders were *all* bone, no meat. But they weren't *just* the bones of a corpse given life, they were... He searched for the word. *Constructed.*

Stugkor had pulled enough living things apart to know what they looked like on the inside, and nothing looked like these creatures.

'Bones of lotsa things in there,' Stug said. He thought about that huge armoured beetle creature with the ribbed baskets, shucking the dead humans of flesh and collecting their bones.

Strong bones.

Chidder squinted at the distant sorcerer with a look of deep concentration. 'So?' he asked.

'We 'ave to go,' said Stugkor. 'We 'ave to warn the clan.'

'Why?' asked Chid.

Strong bones.

'They want to kill us,' explained Stug. 'Pull off our skin and muscle. Feed us to that big armoured thing with the baskets.'

'Don't want my skin pulled off,' grunted Chidder. He flexed a massive arm. 'Muscles neither.'

That bad, sick feeling deep in Stugkor's belly festered. His arm hurt, leaked blood where the deader had cut him. It'd be a great scar when it healed.

He wasn't afraid. Of course he wasn't afraid.

'We're leaving now,' said Stug.

Chid and Algok nodded agreement.

'Hungry,' said Chid, eyeing his dead mournfang. With a shrug, he tore off one of its rear haunches.

Equally hungry, Stug and Algok copied him.

* * *

The three ogors walked north, the *crunch crunch* of their plodding steps in crumbling ice the only sound.

Heavy with cloud, the sky looked like it was so low they might reach up and grab it. Fat flakes of damp snow fell to collect on their shoulders. The temperature plummeted, and each breath became great plumes of steam. With each passing hour the sky darkened and the snow fell harder.

Shard's leg having already been devoured, hunger gnawed at Stugkor's every thought, a constant reminder of his failure.

His first raid. Could it have gone any worse?

'Storm,' said Chidder.

'Bad one,' grunted Algok.

Freezing to death on the way home might be worse. When he closed his eyes for a moment, the lashes froze together.

'What we gonna tell them when we get back?' asked Algok.

That, Stug decided, was a good question. Chances were high everyone would want to charge off and do battle with these strange dead. Stugkor didn't want that.

One deader almost killed all three of us. If it hadn't been for Algok surprising it, it probably would have.

It wasn't even one of the bigger ones, just regular puny man-sized.

There were hundreds in the town. An army.

The ogors would lose. They'd lose and they'd die and they'd all be turned into more dead things.

He stopped walking. It was easier to think when motionless.

Could he convince the clan to flee?

No. Ogors never ran from anything.

Yeah? Then what are we doing now?

Should they say nothing, make no mention of the bone collectors?

Algok might see the wisdom, but no way Chid could keep his mouth shut. And anyway, someone would eventually notice their mournfangs were gone and they'd have to explain.

Too hungry. Hard to think. All that wasted meat the deaders were tossing aside, all that fresh muscle and hot blood, soft fat and tender brains.

Stug turned to look back towards the human settlement.

His heart fell.

'Algok,' he said. 'Chid.'

The other two stopped and turned.

Dim silhouettes barely visible through the snow. That huge armoured beetle thing with the arms and the massive baskets lumbering in the middle.

'That's bad,' said Algok.

The deaders were following them. And not just a few. All of them. So many hundreds of hundreds. More dead than Stugkor's tribe could ever hope to mash.

Struggling to make out details, Stug squinted into the storm. Some of the dead rode great skeletal horses that looked like they'd been dipped in molten steel. Other sat in monstrous chairs of bone and iron that walked, striding effortlessly across the barren landscape. Weapons of smoking jade were everywhere.

The dead moved as if one mind controlled them all.

Clean bone.

Bright iron.

An army of perfection.

Strong bones.

For a moment Stug imagined all Ghur covered in corpses, slaughtering the ogors, flaying them of flesh and muscle, admiring their sturdy skeletons, turning them into something new.

Strong bones.

'There aren't *that* many,' he whispered.

There might be enough to make short work of his tribe, but when word spread, the ogors would crush these strange new dead creatures, mash them to bone dust.

'They're small,' said Algok. 'Short legs. We can outrun 'em.' She looked tired, staggered sometimes, like she still suffered from landing on her face.

Stug nodded, looking back at the long path he and his friends had left in the snow. They'd be easy to follow. At least until the storm filled their tracks. But the deaders weren't that far behind. Maybe if they ran, put more distance between them and the army. He didn't like that. The dead marched on, ceaseless and untiring.

'At some point we'll have to rest,' he said. 'They won't. They'll keep comin'.' He imagined the dead finding him as he slept. 'We're days from the tribe. Longer. We rode here but we're walkin' back.'

'They'll catch us,' said Algok. 'Day by day, night by night, they'll gain on us. And we ain't got no food.'

She was right. Hunger and weakness would slow them. And if they fled back to the tribe, the dead would follow and everyone would die.

'We can't go 'ome,' said Stug.

His mates understood; he saw it in their eyes.

'Leadin' them away from the clan ain't enough,' he added. 'We gotta warn our people. And not just *our* people. These deaders are somethin' different, somethin' *new*.' He felt it deep in his co-pious gut. He imagined Ghur populated only by dead things made from the bones of other dead things.

'They're a threat,' he said. 'To everything. Ogor. 'Uman. Everything.'

Stug watched the tight-knit army march ever closer. Was he right, was a single creature controlling all of them?

If the dead stayed together, for whatever reason, then maybe this was the chance he and his mates needed.

'I have an idea,' he said. 'We gotta split up. Mebbe they'll only follow one of us. We run 'ard for as long as we can. Whoever escapes returns to tell the clan, to warn 'em.'

His mates agreed.

For a moment they stood, awkwardly unable to meet each other's eyes. Stug saw the truth: each hoped they would be the one to escape, that they would survive to tell the tale. Even Chidder seemed to understand.

The dead marched on.

'I'll see you back at the clan,' said Stug, unable to think of anything else.

'I'll save you somethin' to eat, if I get there first,' said Algok, looking away.

'I won't,' said Chid, examining his hands. 'I'm so hungry I'm gonna eat everything.'

Nodding to each other, the three set off in different directions, jogging into the endless wastes.

Stugkor ran.

One foot in front of the other.

Snow fell so heavy he saw no more than half a dozen strides in front of him. It clogged his nose, piled on his head, and threatened to freeze his eyes closed. Even his nostrils felt like they were about to freeze shut.

The muted *crunch crunch* of dry snow, like brittle bones crushed in teeth.

The dead nothing sounds of Ghur.

The soul moan of a wind that's claimed a thousand lives.

The groan of eternal ice.

When he slowed, unable to maintain his pace, he walked.

Head down. Going nowhere.

Forever.

The sun rose and fell, the temperature dropping until icicles hung from his nose and ears. Stopping, he stooped to scoop up a fistful of ice and snow and jam it in his mouth. Again and again until his belly grumbled. But it wasn't food.

Looking back the way he'd come, he saw his meandering footprints weaving off into night. Of the dead there was no sign. His was a world of snow. They could be a score of strides away and he'd never see them. He wanted to lie down, to rest. Even if just for a moment. He'd never been this tired – this *hungry* – in all his life.

There, beneath the sighing wind, the rumble of a hundred hundred dead, marching lockstep.

Stugkor pushed on, staggering with exhaustion, falling often.

Strong bones.

They would not take him. They would not make him into some deader monster.

The eastern horizon brightened, and Stugkor saw the dim shapes of a great host. They followed, relentless. Tireless.

Exhaustion ate his strength, drained his will far worse than any freeze.

The dead drew closer.

'I can't.'

Corpse eyes watching, flickering green sparks in hollow caves of bone.

Empty sockets following his progress, waiting for him to fall.

He knew then he would never escape. 'They followed *me*,' he said to the northern wind. It wasn't what he'd wanted, but if it meant his mates escaped to warn the clan, it was still a victory.

For a score of heartbeats he watched the dead advance. He found himself remembering that terrified hare Algok and Chidder had cornered when he'd first dreamed up his fantastic plan to go on a raid. He thought about the little creature's pointless attempts to escape. Maybe it wasn't smart enough to have other plans, but it still wanted to get away. He recalled Chidder mashing it flat.

The dead would never stop. They would follow until exhaustion felled him and he lay helpless in the snow.

'No,' he told the rising sun. 'I will stand here.'

He'd bought his mates time to escape. Now it was time for these dead to learn the true might of the ogors!

The great host parted as the creature with the smoking green scythe stepped to the fore. It studied Stugkor for a long moment before gesturing.

A warrior of iron-wrapped bone stepped forward, a massive greatsword hanging in its skeletal fist. The weapon oozed sickly green smoke that ignored the northern wind, twisting with a life of its own.

It came at Stug, poking and prodding. Icy steel left long gashes in his hide that burned like fire. Stug fought on, unwilling to fail, sheer will keeping him on his feet. His warclub grew heavy, each swing coming slower until he stood, bent over, wheezing great sucking breaths of air.

Seeing his weakness, the deader moved in for a killing blow. Instead of trying to mash it, Stug lunged, catching it by an arm. It stabbed him, drove steel into his gut, as it struggled to break free. But he had it. Raising his club with a roar, Stug smashed the corpse. It felt like he'd struck the frozen ground, the shock of the blow slamming through his arm.

Tossing the broken deader aside, he spat blood and showed the army his teeth in a feral snarl.

More came, and he fought, sometimes smashing them apart with his club, but always suffering dozens of wounds before he managed to finally dispatch them. Shattered bones littered the trampled snow, long lines of his blood drawing strange patterns. His lungs rattled, his heart banging away like it sought to break from his ribs.

So tired. Weak from long days of hunger.

One at a time they came, testing.

Cursed knives left long wounds in his flesh. Over and over they slashed and stabbed, until blood slicked him and his thoughts grew dim and pale.

Another quick-moving corpse, this one with four arms bearing two spears and two swords. Unlike the others, it was Stug's height. It stabbed and slashed as it danced circles around him. Too fast. Too many weapons for him to defend against. It bled him, making no attempt at a killing blow.

Gore spattered the snow, bright crimson slashes in hard white.

Stugkor fell to his knees, and the four-armed corpse stood over him. Where he drew ragged breaths, great sucking gulps of air, his chest heaving, it stood motionless. When it glanced towards the scythe-bearing undead with the fanned crown of bone, Stug lashed out, grabbing its ankle. It stabbed him, over and over, as he dragged it closer. One of the spears broke, leaving an iron tip lodged in his flesh.

Stug broke its knees. He cracked its thick bones, crushed its skull in his fists.

Toppling backwards, he lay in the snow. Ice in raw wounds. Life bled out at a terrifying rate. He couldn't rise, couldn't move. His strength was gone.

The corpse sorcerer strode forward to stand at Stug's side. Strange bones, twisted and melted like forged iron. It examined him, sparks of nacreous green glowing deep in hollowed eye sockets.

'Very strong bones,' it said. 'Your kind will be a fine harvest.'

'Never,' Stugkor said, coughing blood.

'All must pay the tithe. In the end there can be only death. In the end there can be only Nagash.'

'I piss on yer puny god!' Yelling hurt, felt like it tore something deep inside. 'Anyway,' whispered Stugkor, 'you failed. My mates escaped. They've warned the clan by now. They'll be ready. The Fangtorn are mighty! We'll crush you!'

Unconcerned, the bone sorcerer straightened as two more dead-ers approached. These were different, taller, their bones thicker than the others.

'As I said, strong bones. Your kind make fine Immortis Guard.'

His kind?

Stug recognised what remained of his mates. They'd been harvested, broken apart and remade, but there was no disguising who they'd been. The sloped brow of Chidder's thick skull. The broad shoulders and powerful fingers of Algok. Stripped of flesh and blood, they were clean bone.

They'd failed.

No. Not yet. Not completely.

Stug coughed a bloody laugh. 'You followed me far into the wastes. You'll never find my clan now.'

'We are the Ossiarch Bonereapers,' said the undead. 'We flense the useless from the useful, carve meat and sinew from bone, souls from life. We harvest the best of you, waste nothing. Your memories are useful, we shall keep them. Your loyalties are not, they shall be cast aside.'

Stugkor reached for the undead creature, but it stepped back.

'You and your friends will lead us to your people,' it said.

The bone sorcerer raised its scythe, green smoke wafting from the blade. 'It is time,' it said, 'to carve away the weakness of life. We have plans for your soul.'

That hare, eyes wide with terror, darting for freedom. Doomed. Just like Stug's tribe.

It couldn't end like this. He wanted more. More life. More talking to Old Tooth. More mashing and more eating.

There wasn't going to be more.

This, he realised, *is what it feels like to be prey.*

Jade steel flashed in the pale sun, slicing free Stug's soul from the meat and bone of his body.

MOURNING IN RAINHOLLOW

Dave Gross

After tearing down all the wanted posters she could find to delay the competition, Janneke Ritter traced the deserter's path from Glymmsforge to Satyr's End. There she trusted a hunch and bought passage on a duardin longboat across the Nihilus Reach.

During the voyage beneath the weird, amethyst skies of Shyish, she fought elbow to shoulder beside the crew when they disturbed waterlogged ghouls aboard a wreck boarded for salvage. Along with her fellow survivors, she reached Sendport alive but no richer than when she set out.

Her hunch rewarded her with three independent sightings of her quarry: he'd struck north days earlier. Disguising herself in a grey shroud, black cowl and red sash, Ritter joined a procession of Morrsend pilgrims returning to their ancestral city.

After passing beneath the tattered banners hanging from the city's gate, Ritter abandoned the petitioners before they began their seventy-seven-day purification. She had no wish to join the next leg of their sojourn, at the end of which they would offer their blood to the ancient vampires who once defended their home.

Two Morrsend residents recognised the deserter's face from the bounty poster. One had sold the man a donkey and claimed he had ridden it into Modrhavn, despite warnings of the deadly creatures infesting those lands. Biting her lip at the cost, Ritter traded for an ageing grey palfrey and a worn saddle and bridle. A pair of used saddlebags and a week's provisions further depleted her funds. At this rate, she grumbled, she'd be destitute by the time she could collect her reward.

Three days out of Morrsend, Ritter rued her decision to buy the horse. While the beast had an agreeable amble, it baulked at every sharp turn in the stony trail. When Ritter kicked its flanks, the horse bent its neck to look back at her with a comical expression of exasperation.

'Horseface,' Ritter snapped. It was a nonsensical name dredged up from memories of childhood tormentors, but saying it to an actual horse gave her a bitter satisfaction. Anyway, it was slightly better than calling the animal 'horse', and she had no desire to invent a better name for a beast she'd soon trade again.

She walked Horseface over the difficult terrain, consoling herself with the notion that travelling on foot would increase her chances of noticing signs of spoor. When she spotted the first, it was just as well she was already on foot so she could feel the dung to get a sense of how long it had lain on the ground. Cold and starting to form a crust, the turd suggested Ritter was a day or so behind her target.

She returned to the saddle and goaded Horseface until the animal showed it hadn't forgotten how to trot.

They continued for a few more days, resting when they found untainted water or a shelter from the cold winds. As the saddlebags grew slack, Ritter regretted not filling a backpack with horse feed. She preferred to leave easy access to the modified weapons she carried on braces down her back: two guns and a sword.

Like most of the names Ritter chose for things, they were self-explanatory. The Cutter was her heavy broadsword, wider and shorter than military standard. The Catcher was a modified duardin bolt thrower that propelled nets and lines. The Blaster was the multifunctional firearm cobbled together from salvaged Iron-weld and Kharadron weapons. It could discharge several kinds of hell at varying levels of reliability. The scatter shot was both the most reliable and the one she least liked to employ. Bringing back her bounties alive was not only more profitable, it had become a point of pride.

Once Ritter began rationing feed, Horseface wandered off the trail whenever it smelled the rank flora of this desolate realm. Ritter hoped they weren't poisonous. Fortunately, Horseface seemed to know which ones to avoid by scent.

'Smarter than you look,' muttered Ritter. She decided that sounded too friendly and added, 'Horseface.'

While the horse gnawed on a sedge, Ritter took the opportunity to relieve herself. It was while she was squatting that she noticed the plume of smoke in the distance. She squinted at it, still unused to the purple light of the realm. Something about it made it hard to judge distances, much less colours. As she finished her business, she realised what she was seeing wasn't smoke. It was a plume of dust.

Horseface resisted as Ritter pulled her away from the grass, but a few sharp, loud commands reminded the beast who was in charge. Soon they were trotting, then cantering towards the disturbance.

The source was a wagon drawn by two animals, ponies or donkeys judging by their relative size. There was something wrong with their hitch, and one kept pulling the vehicle to one side, forcing the driver to correct course with a jerk of the reins.

Behind the driver, a patched canvas bonnet had torn away to reveal the wagon bows, exposed like the ribs of a skeleton. Below them cowered three figures. One adult-sized, like the driver. The other two were much smaller.

The dust cloud obscured whatever they were fleeing.

Ritter couldn't imagine her target would chase a family across the plains. If he had designs on them, he had only to clap his hands and destroy their vehicle or slay their beasts with a slash of lightning.

There'd be no reward for helping these strangers. Perhaps they weren't running from anything. Maybe the driver had simply lost control of his team after one of the beasts spotted a pale adder.

A distant shriek carried across the wind. Horseface curled her neck again, the irises of her wild eyes straining in what felt like an accusation to Ritter. She cursed as she remembered the other factor in her calculation.

The children.

'Damn it.' She kicked Horseface into action.

Horseface surged into a full gallop before Ritter realised the animal had been holding back.

They drew close enough to make out the individuals on the wagon. A woman had the reins in one hand and a lash in the other. She fixed her full attention on the terrified donkey whose panic kept pulling them off course. It didn't help that the beast was bridled with a make-shift length of rope. Its teammate, a pony, distinguished itself both with obedience and a proper harness.

A box bounced out of the rear of the wagon, falling on the trailing remnant of the wagon's canvas cover and tearing the rest away. The man in the back reached hopelessly after it; Ritter saw he had a stump beneath his left elbow. The man crouched again, arms curling around the children as all three stared into the dusty wake. Ritter peered with them as Horseface slowed, apparently sensing a presence she no longer wished to meet.

Ritter saw it deep within the cloud. A shape darker than the dust leaped over the fallen crate and ran closer to the wagon. Ritter discerned a lupine hunch in its shoulders, but its gait was pure feline. An abhorrent tickling filled Ritter's throat, and a tooth-shivering drone rose above the racket of the wagon wheels.

Just as they were about to pass the wagon, Horseface reared. A second pursuer leaped out of the dust cloud. The size of a grown wolf, it pounced like a mountain cat, yet its shape remained obscured in a dark, murmuring nimbus.

Ritter reached for the Blaster. Her fingers closed around the stock as the impact knocked her off the screaming horse. She hit the ground perilously close to the rear wagon wheels. Rolling, she regained her feet, the Blaster in her hands. The blinding dust washed over her.

She closed her eyes against the grit, listening for a growl or a footfall.

Her hand released the safety on the Blaster's shot cylinder, already in firing position. She heard the click of the mechanism, the clamour of the wagon, and Horseface's frightened squeals – fortunately not the sounds of being devoured, but those of knowing a predator is close.

Ritter opened her eyes.

In the dissipating dust, she saw the monster. It glared at her with empty eye sockets, half its skin rotted away to reveal a cracked skull. Where ears had been, only scabrous stumps of cartilage remained, crawling with fat white maggots. The creature's mottled pelt suggested a leopard, but the spots were nothing compared with the jagged rents in its flesh. The wounds exposed desiccated muscle and fat between wind-scoured ribs. Worse were the black hollows where all flesh had collapsed inward. The buzzing sound originated in those dark cavities.

A crepuscular sheath flowed out of the rotting stalker. It

thickened into a furious cloud. At first, Ritter couldn't comprehend what had emerged from the beast, but then she realised it was a cloud of corpse flies.

The swarm moved with a collective purpose, more like a single parasite than ten thousand individuals. When the monster uttered a dry cough, more insects emerged from the concavity of its skull. As the cloud of corpse flies thickened, the beast tensed to leap.

Ritter raised the Blaster, but a heavy weight knocked her to the ground. Foetid breath gushed over her face as fangs snapped at her throat. She felt hundreds of stings through the gaps in her armour. Rolling, she raised her shoulder to shield her neck. Reeking jaws clamped down on her pauldron.

Ritter thrust the Blaster into the animal's chest and fired. She felt two separate halves of the beast fall away as flecks of bone and gore rained down on her.

She rolled again, knowing that predators using pack tactics seldom pause before a kill.

Sure enough, the first beast landed beside her. She rolled farther before rising to a low crouch. She shifted the gun's selector from shot to flame canister and pumped the primer twice. There wasn't time for more.

She kept the stream trained on the monster as she let herself fall backward to avoid its pounce. The stream was weak, and flecks of hot oil touched her face. For a moment she feared she would immolate herself, but as the igniter snapped, the insects' shivering wings fanned the flames across themselves.

A torrent of incinerated flies fell over Ritter as the animal struck the earth, legs twitching. The stench of its burning pelt wet Ritter's eyes.

She rose to one knee and raised the Blaster, turning to scan the area. She saw no sign of a third predator. The buzz of flies dwindled to a whisper.

Ritter sighed with relief when she saw Horseface stamping around, tail lashing her flanks. Ritter jogged over to help, peeling off her cape to slap at the horse's neck and shoulders until the last of the flies dispersed. With the destruction of their hosts, they no longer acted as one.

The wagon returned, the driver still struggling to keep the donkey pulling in a straight line. Her children stood up behind her, peering over her shoulders. Ritter couldn't tell whether they were boys or girls or one of each. Their faces were little replicas of their mother's but for the bright eyes and curly hair of their one-handed father, who hopped off the wagon to examine the fallen crate.

'You have our thanks,' said the driver. Ritter guessed she was in her mid-thirties, but it was hard to judge the age of those who lived in Shyish. Many died young, and those who survived often appeared decades older than they were.

'It's intact!' called the woman's husband. He pulled an unbroken sack out of the fallen crate and shrugged it over his good shoulder.

'Let's leave her one,' said his wife.

The man nodded. Lugging the sack over to Ritter, he let it fall to the ground. 'Feed for your horse. We have enough to reach Morrsend.'

'Thanks,' said Ritter. She patted her stomach. 'And maybe a little–'

'Yes, of course.' He gestured to the children with his stump. 'Breen, fetch us some of that bread.'

'One other thing,' said Ritter.

'We have little,' said the driver. Ritter could almost hear the woman's hackles rise.

'Just information.' Ritter unfurled one of the wanted posters. 'Have you seen this man?'

The look that passed between the man and woman told her

they had. Neither adult spoke as one of the children – a girl, Ritter decided now that she could see her close – brought over a grease-stained parcel.

'Thank you, starling.' The man passed the food to Ritter. He watched his daughter skip back to the wagon. He turned to Ritter. 'You should let him go.'

'Can't,' said Ritter. 'It's my job.'

'It doesn't have to be,' he said. 'You're no different from him.'

Ritter bristled. Many looked down on bounty hunters, but she was no deserter. 'What do you mean by that?'

The man's wife put a hand on his shoulder and inclined her head towards the wagon. Before he left, the man fixed his gaze on Ritter. 'Our pony could barely pull the wagon,' he said. 'He gave us his donkey, even though he was in a hurry to reach Rainhollow.'

The man's wife shot him a stern look. 'Go on,' she said. As the man returned to the spilled supplies, the woman looked Ritter in the eyes. 'Just follow our trail if you must find him. But the Nighthaunt are already there.' She walked away.

Ritter unfurled the wanted poster and studied the deserter's face.

Usually the artists exaggerated the features to make a bounty target look more villainous, but this one had a pleasant face, even a wry half-smile that made it look as though he'd just said something amusing or charming. The one sinister mark about him was a half-star-shaped scar over one eye, and even that looked more rakish than criminal. The way his hair flopped over his brow seemed incongruous for a portrait of a deserter. Ritter had a hunch the artist fancied him.

After a careful double-fold, Ritter tore off WANTED: ELDREDGE DUUL, surrounded by stylised lightning bolts, from the top and the warnings from the bottom. It might be better not to advertise that she was looking to arrest a man who made a good impression on strangers.

Horseface nipped at the discarded paper. Ritter gave the beast a few handfuls of grain instead before filling the saddlebags and following the refugees' path.

Ritter found Rainhollow at the base of the Modrhavn Mountains.

She passed a few plots of farmland before spying green streaks of moss and ivy that marked the crooked streams running down the eastern cliffs. The run-off pooled in reservoirs too small to be called lakes before following irrigation channels or tapering off to brooks vanishing into pale and lonely woods.

Two of the little pools flanked a great cleft in the cliff wall. Ritter realised the village lay not at the foot of the mountain but within it. The entrance created an illusion: the cleft formed a gentle spiral from the outer edge of the cliff into a gap sheltered by walls shaped like a pair of hands cupping a candle flame. Inside, the village of Rainhollow hid from the plains of Modrhavn.

Fortified ledges formed 'fingers' on the curtain walls. Motionless guardians stood between crenellations built of irregular stones. Ritter could just make out the wooden frames that supported the withered corpses, the wire that lashed their wind-mummified limbs to their spears, and the awkward tilt of their rusty helmets over naked skulls. Here and there, a living watcher patrolled among the sentinel dead.

Ritter followed the sound of a ringing hammer to a double gate spanning the 'fingertips' of the outer walls. One half stood closed, prominently displaying the grim visage of Nagash. The wreckage of the other half had been dragged to the side while workers hurried to construct a makeshift replacement out of scavenged wood and the salvaged iron frame. Whatever had demolished the gate had shredded wood and shorn metal alike.

Ritter reined Horseface to a halt and showed the deserter's face to a man hauling a keg of nails. 'Seen him?'

The man indicated the third of four lanes leading into the village. 'Straight on to the second reservoir.'

She nodded.

'You'd better hurry,' said the worker. 'He could use the help.'

For the second time, Ritter felt a pang of resentment. He's a deserter, she reminded herself.

Meagre light eked its way down into the deserted lanes of Rainhollow. Woodfires flickered in every third stone brazier, but they cast long shadows above the awnings. The doors and windows were all shut tight. Ritter noticed two doors were chalked with skull-shaped symbols.

She heard the dogs barking before she saw them skid around the corner. Three mutts of different sizes, all dirty and wide-eyed, barely glanced at Horseface while peeling off to either side to continue their retreat. With them came a strong scent of bitter smoke and the sound of splashing water. A flash of blue-white light suggested lightning.

Ritter's target was near.

She dismounted and led Horseface to a water trough fed by one of the dozens of ducts catching run-off from the cliff walls. She thought of the frightened dogs and looped the horse's leads loosely, unslung the Blaster, and approached the corner.

Around the bend, the street opened into a plaza bordered by two other streets and a cliff dotted with grey-and-yellow lichen. Light flickered from three fires on the surrounding houses, apparently the result of lightning strikes. No one fought to quench the flames.

In the centre of the plaza was a circular pool fed from the cliff run-off, redirected by a series of flat stones suspended on an iron brace. Around the lip of the pool lay abandoned buckets and pots, and two corpses surrounded by expanding pools of blood.

The cause of their deaths came whirling across the pool. Waterspouts rose beneath the shadow of a dark blur and fell back again in its wake. The thing spun so fast that Ritter could make out little more than a black shroud and chains. Staring, she perceived a grim iron mask beneath the hooded shroud and a greatblade in the grasp of a fleshless hand.

Ritter had never seen a gheist before, but she'd heard them described by Stormcast Eternals who counted themselves blessed to have survived. She faced a Bladegheist Revenant.

The Nighthaunt flew towards a man who was only just rising to his feet. The broken shutters behind him suggested he'd been thrown hard against the wall. Judging from the damage, it was a wonder he could stand at all.

Despite his bloody face and wet hair, there was no mistaking Eldredge Duul. A week's beard darkened the mage's cheeks. Dusty grey robes covered more colourful garments exposed only at collar, cuff and hem. His fingers glittered with jewels. As he stood, he glanced ruefully at the remaining half of his staff before tossing away the useless stump. His fingers sketched esoteric signs in preparation for the gheist's charge, but then he noticed Ritter's arrival.

'Stay back!' he shouted.

The warning had the opposite effect. The Nighthaunt turned its eyeless mask towards Ritter. The blur of chains and blade rushed at her.

Ritter fired. Most of the shot passed harmlessly through the Nighthaunt, despite the dull sound of impacts on metal. The black shroud shuddered, but Ritter saw only a few holes to prove it had been struck. The gheist appeared unperturbed.

Eldredge Duul's voice rose in an arcane language Ritter had heard but never understood. With the first three long syllables, the water from the reservoir rose higher than the rooftops. Duul paused, letting the gheist close with Ritter. The final syllable was thunder. An immense weight of water crashed over the gheist the moment its ethereal form took substance, smashing it against the cliff wall.

The breaking wave forced Ritter back. She tripped over a raised herb garden and cracked her skull against a windowsill. She heard the Blaster skitter across the pavestones, but she could see only bright yellow starbursts. Trying to stand, she fought a wave of nausea. She decided to sit a moment, but that felt only slightly better.

'Here, chew on this.' A warm hand pressed something root-like into hers. Ritter blinked, but Eldredge Duul's face remained a blur. 'Try not to move.'

A whispery voice rose across the plaza. '...never... drown... again.' Chains rasped against cobblestones. 'I'll smother your soul!'

'Get down!' hissed Duul. He spoke a single word of power. The rising screech of the gheist was muffled as an unseen barrier appeared between its descending tomb blade and the mortals beneath the mage's shield.

Terror sharpened Ritter's vision. She watched as the Nighthaunt raised its blade to slash again and again. Each time, the blade stopped inches from Duul's outstretched hand.

'Can you reach your gun?' Duul winced as another blow tested the strength of his spell. Judging by his pallor, Ritter didn't know whether he could withstand another.

She nodded, waiting for the moment the Bladegheist raised its weapon. Rolling towards the Blaster, she sensed Duul moving with her. He kept the shield between her and the Nighthaunt, exposing his own body in defence of hers.

'Wait for it,' he said. 'The moment it strikes, it must be tan–'

'Do it!' Ritter aimed, Duul stepped away, and she fired. The shot blew the blade out of the gheist's grip and shattered the bony hand wielding it. Half the iron mask flew away, the shot pellets leaving a ragged border resembling tooth marks.

The amethyst energies of Shyish continued to sustain the maimed horror. It groaned an inarticulate threat and reached for the mage.

Duul spat out another spell as the gheist's claws closed around his throat. A bolt of energy exploded between them, throwing each combatant backward. Duul hit the ground flat on his back. He rolled to one side, rising on one elbow to brace for another attack, but none came. The last tangible fragments of the depraved soul twitched on the pavement until, at last, they lay still.

Ritter felt the subsiding terror like liquid silver through her veins. Standing beside Duul, both panting with hands on knees, she noticed she was a good six inches taller than he. She was taller than most men, but not usually by so much.

A clatter of hooves caught her attention. Rather than fleeing, Horseface had come to investigate. The palfrey walked up and nosed Duul in the shoulder.

'Aren't you the valiant one?' said Duul. He stroked the horse's nose. He looked at Ritter. 'Your protector, I assume?'

Ritter felt an unexpected indignation that the horse had gone to Duul. What did she care who a dumb animal favoured?

'I'm grateful to you both,' said Duul. 'I was starting to worry that gheist was too much for me. Good thing you showed up when you did. Thankfully, that was the last of them.'

'Umm...' Ritter looked away. He had saved her as much as she'd helped him.

'Oh,' said Duul, noticing something on the flooded street. He reached towards a soggy scrap of paper. At his gesture, it flew from the wet pavement to his hand. He blew on it, and a minor spell dried the bounty poster. He grimaced. 'Bounty hunter, eh? You must be good to have found me so soon.'

Ritter wondered whether she could reach the Catcher and fire a net before he could hit her with a spell. She tensed as he raised a hand to his lips, but he only blew her a kiss. Before she could object, a warm magic breeze dried her clothes and hair. Duul waved his hand as if fanning himself, and the same magic blew back his hair and tidied his soiled robes.

He smiled again. She could barely stand to look at it. She knew he was manipulating her, but he seemed so genuine. Was there magic in that smile?

She shouldered the Blaster, trading it for the Catcher, finger on the trigger. 'Eldredge Duul, I'm taking you back to Glymmsforge to face charges of desertion.'

He grinned. Ritter couldn't tell whether that was a sign of madness or another misplaced attempt to charm her. Suspicious of a trick, she watched his hands for any arcane gesture.

Instead, he showed her his palms. 'Just give me a little time to do what I came here for, and I won't resist. Say, what's the reward for my capture this time?'

'This time?' said Ritter.

Duul pinched his fingers along each torn edge of the poster. An orange-white glow appeared where he touched the paper. Like a cigar burning in reverse, the missing strips reappeared. Duul whistled appreciatively. 'Desertion, is it? The old man isn't fooling around this time.'

'It's a no-kill bounty,' said Ritter. Duul beckoned her to follow as he strolled towards the centre of Rainhollow. Ritter grabbed Horseface's reins and marched after him.

'Lucky for me.' Duul appraised her. His eyes lingered on the butts of the weapons protruding from behind her back. It made her feel uncomfortable. She slung the Catcher over her shoulder. 'You wouldn't happen to be Janneke Ritter, would you?'

'How do you know my name?'

'You caught an old friend of mine a few years back.'

She set her jaw. 'Well, I'm not sorry about it.'

'Nor should you be,' Duul laughed. 'Dorren Tael is as testy as an orruk, and twice as easy to goad. After killing those soldiers in that brawl, he deserved his punishment. I'm just surprised you brought him back alive.'

'It wasn't easy.' Ritter tried not to look as pleased as she felt at the compliment.

'They say you brought in a Stormcast Eternal once.'

Ritter said nothing as they walked for a while. More people emerged from their homes. They looked hopefully towards the plaza, where the residents had finished quenching the fires. No one cheered or thanked them. They merely returned to the task of waiting to die.

'*Did* you bring in an Eternal?' Duul raised an inquisitive eyebrow.

'I never take bounties on the Stormcasts.'

Duul mulled it over. His annoying smile returned. 'Yeah, what kind of maniac would try something like that?'

'Where are you taking me?' said Ritter. 'I haven't agreed to anything. I'm still taking you in.'

'Just up ahead, on the street of yellow doors. That is, if they haven't moved. I need to bring them back to Glymmsforge now that it's clear of Nighthaunt.' His voice darkened, and again the smile faded. 'As you can see, bands of Nighthaunt have scattered from the main armies. What we drove out of Glymmsforge is now finding its way into villages like this one.'

'And you were just going to turn yourself in when you got back to Glymmsforge?' Ritter had had just about enough of Duul's easy charm.

'I hadn't given it much thought,' he said. 'When I heard the scattered Nighthaunt forces had begun preying on villages, I knew I had to get back here. And I knew the commander wouldn't give me leave, so I just took it.'

'You're out of your mind,' said Ritter. 'You can't just leave your garrison to check in on someone.'

'Not just someone.' Duul's smile returned. 'She's going to like you. Anyway, she always said I'd wind up in prison.'

Of course, thought Ritter. A woman. Wizards might be cleverer in some ways, but when it came to women they were still as foolish as other men.

They stepped aside to let a trio of mourners and a corpse-bearing cart pass on the way to the front gates. Ritter wondered what rituals the people of Rainhollow used to propitiate Nagash. She glimpsed Duul sketching a sigil over his heart. Whether it had mystic or religious significance, she had no idea.

Ritter shook her head to clear out the cobwebs. She ought to knock Eldredge Duul over the head, tie his hands, gag him, throw him over Horseface's back and get back to Glymmsforge and her bounty payment.

Horseface nickered as they turned onto the street of yellow doors.

'There it is,' Duul said. His pace accelerated as they approached a corner house, but he paused when he saw the skull chalked on the door. His grin perished.

Ritter felt an unwelcome pang of sympathy. 'Perhaps she moved to another house.'

Duul's expression darkened as he scanned the flowers in the window boxes. 'No, they're still here. Zora would never leave her lilies behind.'

They went to the door, which opened before they could knock. There stood a man thin with grief. His eyes welled as he took in the sight of Eldredge, his fists closing and opening. Ritter braced herself to break up a fight, but the man lunged before she could act. He hugged Duul tight.

'I'm sorry, Gerren,' said Duul. 'I came as soon as I heard the Nighthaunt remnants were starting to maraud.'

'No one is swifter than death,' said Gerren.

Ritter waited with uncomfortable patience.

'This is my friend Janneke,' said Duul. 'She helped me finish off the last of the gheists.'

We're not friends, Ritter reminded herself, but she managed not to utter the thought.

Gerren led them inside the simple home. He gave them thistle tea and slightly stale oat cakes. Duul set aside some of his cakes, and Ritter realised he was saving them for Horseface. She set aside all of hers, thinking, *we'll see who that horse comes to next time.*

'I taught her this recipe shortly after we were married,' Duul said, nibbling on a cake.

'What?' said Ritter.

'Zora had a taste for scoundrels back then,' said Gerren.

'She came to her senses eventually,' said Duul. 'She threw me out long before marrying Gerren.'

'She'd had her eye on me since we were kids,' said Gerren. 'She knew she'd made the wrong choice the first time you went off to war. You never should have learned magic, Eldredge.'

'Lucky for you I did,' said Duul. 'Bad luck for me.'

Despite the situation they were describing, the men didn't seem anything less than friendly to each other. Ritter shrugged, deciding it was none of her business, even if it would have made good gossip in most places she'd visited. Here, it just seemed like a fact of life.

Gerren had made a shrine of Zora's favourite belongings. Together, he and Duul picked them up one by one, sharing their memories of the woman they'd each loved in their time.

Gerren unsheathed a long, double-bladed dagger. 'She once pulled this on a greedy merchant in the market. He learned to barter fairly after that, let me tell you.'

'She once broke this plate over my head,' Duul said, holding up the dish. 'If you look close, you can see where the glaze is lighter where the spell rejoined the shards.'

'She never broke things around me,' said Gerren. 'She knew I couldn't snap my fingers and repair the damage. You're right. I'm glad I never learned magic.'

'And you never provoked the damage.'

They laughed a little.

'How did it start?' said Duul, his lower tone indicating a change in subject. No one needed him to say what he was talking about.

'There was only one at first,' said Gerren. 'An outsider came to the gate. No one realised what it was. It asked to be let in long after dark. Of course, no one opened the gates, but it kept asking. We thought the spells would keep it out. Maybe it had to ask permission a hundred times to wear down the magic. Maybe if we had a mage here... Sorry. I didn't mean you.'

'I know,' said Eldredge, but his voice cracked.

'Eventually it tore down the gate. We tried to fight, of course. You've seen how little use that was. There was something different about this Nighthaunt. Those it slew rose as all sorts of gheists the next night.'

'And Zora fought it?'

'Zora always fought,' said Gerren as he looked away to the window. 'It's almost nightfall. The others that have risen came for their families first. That's why we've been marking the doors.'

'Where is this outsider now?' said Duul.

'It moved on. Maybe it was bored with us. Or maybe it thought it had done enough to ensure we'd all die. Thanks to you, the gheists are all destroyed. All except one.'

'Maybe she won't be like the others.'

'No,' said Gerren. 'She'll come for me. Now that you're here, she'll come for both of us.'

Ritter stood up. 'Then let's get out of here. There's no time to lose.'

The men shook their heads.

'We can't leave her like one of them,' said Gerren.

'Think of the other souls she'll claim if she's a Nighthaunt,' said Duul.

'Think of the reward I won't earn if you die here!' said Ritter.

Gerren looked at Duul.

'We can take you with us,' said the mage.

'We don't even know whether she'll come back,' said Ritter. 'You said it yourself, no one has seen the stranger since yesterday. Maybe it has to be present to transform Zora into a gheist.'

'I don't think that's how it works,' said Gerren. 'The priests say–'

'The priests don't know anything,' snapped Duul. He caught himself from continuing in that testy tone. 'They only tell us what we hope is true.'

'Eldredge, you know magic,' said Gerren. 'What do you think will happen?'

'I think we owe it to Zora to be sure before we leave.'

For a few moments, each of them started to say something before thinking better of it. There was no point in arguing. Ritter tended her weapons, priming the flame reservoir and refreshing the spent cartridges in the Blaster. Duul applied salve and fresh bandages to Ritter's wounds and his own. He knew what he was doing. Gerren cooked a meagre meal and spared some fresh oats for Horseface.

Duul inclined his head towards the door. Ritter followed him outside.

'Look after Gerren, would you?'

Ritter scowled at him. 'Don't think you can slip away that easily.'

'Never crossed my mind.' For the first time, his smile seemed forced. Ritter suspected it wasn't because he was lying but because of what he was planning to do. 'If I can draw her attention, you can get a shot before she knows you're there. You don't even have to take your eyes off me. I'll be right out here with your bodyguard.'

'Horseface.'

Duul looked perplexed. 'You call the horse Horseface?'

'Never mind that,' said Ritter. 'I'll be watching you.'

'Good. If she appears much like the living Zora, I might hesitate. I trust you won't.'

'You know better than I that the Nighthaunt don't look the same in death. You won't be seeing her pretty face.'

'You're right,' said Duul. 'Beauty isn't in the face, though. It's in the action. The way she came to check on us earlier, I think Horseface here is beautiful. She deserves a better name.'

Ritter scoffed. 'What do you plan to do out here all alone, anyway?'

'I will cast a mighty spell,' he said in a pompous voice that made Ritter think he was imitating someone he knew personally.

'I bet you say that to all the girls.' Ritter regretted the remark at once. It sounded too much like flirting, a talent she had never mastered.

'I do say that to all the girls.' Duul winked. 'Right before I cast a mighty spell.'

Now that was flirting, and Ritter wanted none of it. She retreated before things became any more uncomfortable.

They stood vigil, two inside without candlelight, Eldredge on the street lit only by the glow of the stone lanterns. Veins of frost began to form on the windowpanes but almost instantly melted into rivulets of blood. Somewhere on the rooftops a cat wailed a long, sustained note that set Ritter's teeth on edge. When a horrid screech of pain marked its unseen death, Ritter found the silence that followed far more dreadful. Soon she could hear the distant splash of water from the reservoir plaza. Eventually, even that formless noise coalesced into a rising moan – the voice of a woman in mourning.

But not a living woman. A gheist. A banshee.

'*Gerrrreeeeeen!*'

'Zora!' Her widower clamped a hand over his mouth, too late to stifle the unbidden name.

'I came back for you, Zora!' Duul shouted on the street.

'*Ellldredge,*' the bodiless voice keened. '*I can smell the magic on you, the magic you always took with you when you left me alone.*'

Ritter scanned the street for any signs of an ethereal presence. Only shadows trembled as Eldredge paced back and forth. He called out again, trying to fix the banshee's attention on himself.

'No!' gasped Gerren inside the house. He stared at the shrine of Zora's belongings. Her dagger floated above the tabletop, its blade shining frost white.

'Get back!' Ritter said. She aimed at the dagger but held her fire, reasoning that harming the weapon wouldn't stop the gheist. She had to wait for it to materialise.

Gerren took a step away from the shrine, inadvertently blocking Ritter's line of fire.

'Out of the way!'

A spot of blood appeared on the back of Gerren's tunic, then another and another as a rapid succession of thrusts cut through his slim torso. As the dagger withdrew for the final time, his body slumped to the floor. The spectre of Zora hovered before him.

Draped in a shroud that faded from incarnadine at the crown to lily white at the hems, the banshee held the dripping dagger at arm's length as if it were a rat pulled from the porridge. Where a face should have appeared under the cowl, only a jutting metal jaw stood in place of bone. The Nighthaunt's only ornament was an hourglass hanging from a leather jerkin. The sand inside had stopped spilling.

Ritter fired. Her blast destroyed Zora's shrine, but the ethereal foe escaped. The banshee flew through the closed door. Her passage left a rime of frost on the yellow paint.

Ritter started to follow but thought better of it. The Nighthaunt were cunning. Ritter dived through the open window instead, rolling on her shoulder to come up ready to fire, but she did not see the banshee waiting at the door. What she saw frightened her more.

Eldredge Duul stood two doors down the street, feet spread wide as his arms swayed in arcane patterns. Above him, an enormous purple sun materialised, its dark light casting weird shadows along the lane of yellow doors. Upon the face of the sun shrieked an enormous skull, its wail far louder than that of the banshee cowering before it.

With a graceful gesture, Duul asserted control of the great sun and propelled it towards Zora.

The banshee dropped her dagger and reached up with both arms as if to embrace her doom. Instead, her wail caused ripples to flow through the amethyst spell. The sun shivered and contracted, pouring itself between Zora's open arms and in through her widening mouth. Where it went, Ritter could not tell.

'*You feed me, Eldredge,*' she laughed. Bulging veins appeared in her shroud, as if it were flesh. She had paid a price for consuming Duul's mighty spell. '*Show me more of this magic that you loved more than your own wife! Let me feast upon it as I will soon feast upon–*'

The gheist turned suddenly and flew wailing towards Ritter.

'Zora!' Duul flicked his hands towards the gheist. Witch-light flew from his fingers like beads of water from wet hands. Zora's cowl turned towards him just as one of his arcane bolts struck her full on.

She hissed and spat, angry enough to forget her previous target. The banshee flew towards Duul as his second bolt passed through her intangible body.

'Duul, protect yourself!' cried Ritter.

Zora's dagger thrust deep into his chest. Duul twisted, enough, Ritter hoped, to make the blade miss his heart, but a stab to the lungs could also be fatal.

Ritter felt a heavy weight on her shoulder. Horseface nudged her, whether for the animal's comfort or to suggest running away, she could not tell. Slinging the Blaster, Ritter pulled herself up by Horseface's mane.

Without so much as a kick to prompt her, the horse ran towards Duul. One hand pressed against his wound, the mage staggered back from the banshee. Gripping the mane in her fist, Ritter reached down to scoop him up. Thankfully, he was as light as he looked.

'To the reservoir,' he gasped. A red bubble burst, colouring his lips.

'*Run wherever you wish!*' screeched Zora. '*I shall catch you. When I do, I shall take my time. Oh, how I shall linger. How I shall savour...*'

The banshee flew after them, soon shortening the gap between them as Horseface slowed for turns.

'Other side of... water,' wheezed Duul. By lantern light, Ritter saw the basin had been replenished in the hours since Duul had drained it. She started to suspect what he had in mind.

She set him down gently and joined him on the street, debating which weapon to use. She'd had limited success with the Blaster, but she hesitated to let the banshee get close enough to use the Cutter – assuming she could time her strikes to hit the gheist in a moment of solidity.

Horseface shied, torn between fight and flight. For unknowable reasons, she decided to stand fast.

With a few halting gestures, Duul conjured orbs of light against the corner houses just in time to illuminate Zora's arrival.

'*There you are, my wayward husband,*' she crooned. She glided forward but hesitated at the water's edge. *'Ah, ah, ah!'* The banshee glided around the perimeter of the reservoir rather than over the open water.

'It was worth a try,' said Duul. 'She remembers my favourite spell.'

'Lightning,' said Ritter. 'You wanted her over water.'

'We'll just have to do this without the extra oomph.'

'Not necessarily,' said Ritter. She pulled the Catcher from its holster and ensured it was set to the proper cylinder. Then she plunged the apparatus into the water, giving it a good dousing.

'What are you doing?'

'This is going to be tricky,' said Ritter. She took the reins and led Horseface away from Duul. 'You'll need to let her hit you first.'

'I don't think I can take another–'

'On your magic shield, idiot!'

Duul opened his mouth and shut it again.

'Then quick with the thunderbolt. You'll know when.'

'Got it.'

The banshee crept closer, baulked, and moved towards Ritter instead of Duul.

That complicates matters, thought Ritter. Beside her, Horseface snorted and stamped. By all rights the beast should have fled screaming, but something defiant had got into her.

Maybe she too had noticed how often the banshee feinted.

Zora snarled at Ritter, her cowl pinched as if in a wicked smile, and instead flew towards Duul. The mage conjured his magical shield and crouched behind it. Ritter knelt for a better angle to allow for the heavier load in the Catcher. When she squeezed the trigger, the sodden net shot forward with a plopping sound. It rose in a short arc and fell heavily across Zora in the instant her chill dagger struck Duul's shield.

The mage rolled back as the net covered the gheist, and his

arcane barrier dissipated. Immediately, he shouted the eldritch syllables of storm. Lightning flared in his eyes and leaped from his fingertips. The coruscating energy suffused the drenched net. Steam exploded in all directions, its hiss drowning out the doleful sound of the banshee's last wail. At last, all the semi-tangible remains had vanished, leaving only Zora's favourite dagger.

Duul crawled over to the blade but stopped short of touching it. He knelt there on the cobblestones, palms over the hot blade as if gathering the last of its warmth into himself.

Ritter walked up behind him. She stopped herself from putting a hand on his shoulder but remained beside him a long while, listening to his muttered farewells to the woman he'd loved and the friend who'd loved her after.

Four days later, Duul was well enough to walk with a limp.

Since burying Gerren, they had taken shelter in the home he'd shared with Zora. Duul tried to conceal his misery, but Ritter observed the way he moved about the house, sitting near a particular window for a time or studying a simple painting over the hearth as if reminding himself of happier times and trying to fix them in memory.

He removed a stone from the hearth and revealed three leather purses. He opened one to reveal a small quantity of realmstone. 'A little more than I remembered,' he said. 'You should be able to exchange it for enough supplies for a comfortable return to Glymmsforge.'

'About that,' said Ritter. 'I was thinking first we should find this outsider who caused all this trouble. Think of how much horror the thing visited on Rainhollow in a single night. If it gets far ahead of us, we might find an entire procession of Nighthaunt.'

'I thought you were in a hurry to collect the bounty on my capture?'

'Who knows how many souls this outsider will claim before you get out of prison?'

'Oh, I never stay long in prison.' He winked, crinkling the half-star scar above his eye.

'Even so, I'd feel better if we went after him first. Horseface agrees.'

'And then back for the bounty?' Duul's smile softened, and Ritter knew she wasn't fooling him. Something was changing between them, and each was content to leave it unspoken. 'The city elders have found someone to bless their gate, and I think they'll be glad to see the back of us. There's word a stranger was seen on the road to Bitterstone.'

Ritter remembered what she could of the local maps. 'If we take turns riding, we could be there in two days.'

Duul nodded, gesturing for Ritter to mount up. She stopped herself from insisting he ride first. Whoever walked the first stretch would enjoy the relief of a ride later. She hooked a foot into the stirrup and swung herself into the saddle. Duul led the way, pausing only to trade a pinch of realmstone for a sack of fresh fruit and salted meat at the town's tiny market. Horseface followed him out of the repaired gates of Rainhollow, occasionally nudging his shoulder. 'You know,' said Duul, 'I've an old friend in Bitterstone who might like to relocate to Glymmsforge.' He tossed Ritter an apple with deep-purple skin and mimed taking a bite out of another. When Horseface whinnied in protest, he grinned and surrendered the treat to the animal.

Ritter suspected the wizard was teasing her as well as the horse, and a suspicion arose in her imagination. 'Don't tell me you have another former wife.'

'All right,' said Duul. He plucked a third apple from the bag and polished it on his sleeve.

'All right what?'

His only answer was the crunch of his apple.

YOUR
NEXT READ

LADY OF SORROWS
by C L Werner

In Shyish, twin towns face horror – the spectral hordes of Lady Olynder will soon rise and devour their souls. One hero must stand against them – but can he face the Lady of Sorrows?

WATCHERS OF BATTLE

Ben Counter

'We're a long way from Carngrad,' said Kyryll as he trudged up the sludge and shale of the mountain slope.

Voleska looked up towards the sky and the peaks of the Fangs that surrounded them. 'Not so far,' she said.

'Camp's up ahead.' Kyryll peered towards the scattering of bonfires and torches on the shoulder of the mountain above them. 'Looks like the Blackblades and the Mercy Slayers made it.'

'More to watch us,' said Voleska. 'More to weep.'

It had rained blood that night. Bonebreak Pass was clotted with coagulating gore. It formed a slow, black river along the pass, draining into the foothills of the Fangs, a sluggish bloodletting that formed a portent for what was to come. The pass was one of the few relatively stable ways past the Fangs and into the regions of the Bloodwind Spoil closer to the citadel of the Varanspire. Control of it had passed from one bloody hand to the next hundreds of times over the generations. Bones and shattered skulls mixed with the loose shale and formed natural cairns, pulled apart by the coagulating flow.

A lot of people had died there. A lot more were about to.

Voleska and Kyryll made their way through the encampment towards the hide tents and bivouacs of the Red Sand Raiders. Warbands from across the Bloodwind Spoil had gathered for the coming battle over Bonebreak Pass, and the banners of several Spire Tyrants bands hung from the spindly trees clinging to the upper slopes. On another day, they would be butchering one another for the right to be called the best among the Children of the Arenas. Tonight, they were allies against a common enemy.

Voleska pulled back the flap of the largest tent. Inside, Ferenk Sunder-Spine was scratching battle plans into the loose dirt. The Head-Taker of the Red Sand Raiders was a huge man with hundreds of finger bones piercing the skin of his arms and shoulders, each taken from a kill in the arena. He looked up at Voleska's intrusion.

'What do you want?' he demanded.

'Scouted, like you said,' replied Voleska.

Ferenk grunted and poked at the battle lines he had scratched. 'What have you got?'

'The Crows have the high ground at the northern end,' replied Voleska. 'They reckon they'll swoop down on us and peck out our eyes.'

'How many?'

Voleska shrugged. 'Six, seven warbands. Couple of thousand ears hanging from the trees. Flocks of birds everywhere.'

'Were you seen?'

Voleska smirked. 'Look at me. Course I was seen.'

Ferenk looked at Voleska as if seeing her for the first time. She was huge. Most of the time the really big competitors failed to make their mark in the fighting pits of Carngrad – they were too slow and cumbersome, and a leg tendon got cut or a gut was punctured before they could bring their bulk around to face a faster enemy. The crowds whooped when they emerged onto the sands, and they cheered when they fell. But Voleska had climbed the ladder of victories to challenge the very best, all while carrying more heft than anyone in the Red Sand Raiders. She carried a stone-headed hammer over her shoulder – a less than ideal weapon for a pit fighter, but one she wielded as if she had been born with it in her hand. What skin showed beneath her heavy garb of lay-ered animal hides and splint mail was tanned and battered, and her lank black hair was tied severely back to show off the scar taking up the right side of her scalp.

'Not like they don't know we're here,' mused Ferenk. 'What about the Unmade? The Scions?'

'The faceless mob are on the west side of the pass,' replied Voleska. 'Opposite the Splintered Fang. Doesn't look like the Scions made it.'

'Too busy annoying the gods,' said Ferenk. 'Here. Come.'

Voleska walked up to the battle plans Ferenk had scratched out. The torchlight in the tent cast flickering shadows across a crude diagram of Bonebreak Pass and the positions of the warbands. 'What's the plan?' she asked.

'Spire Tyrants don't do subtle,' said Ferenk. 'No feints. No secret paths. No false retreats. We're going straight down the middle. Storm the heights, hit the Cabal, kill them.'

Voleska nodded. 'They think they own the mountains. They're arrogant. They'll try something. But we won't fall for it. Straight down the middle.'

'I saw you,' said Ferenk. It was unexpected. He rarely said anything that wasn't strictly necessary. 'At the Gutripper Pits. Slavemaster Barakhor's games. You killed four men.'

Voleska shrugged. 'They were only small.'

'The last one, you knocked his head clean off.'

'Yes, that I did. Went right into the crowd. They called me the Gift-Giver after that.'

'You fought well for us, Voleska. It was obvious enough, never had to say it. But a lot of us are going to die this dawn. Maybe someone important. Maybe me. The Red Sand Raiders will accept you if you want to step in. Do you want that, Gift-Giver?'

Ferenk looked at her now, piercing and intense, in a way he never had before. Voleska felt herself tense up, as if aware of an assailant trying to flank her. 'I want... I want more,' she said.

'More than what?'

Voleska was rarely lost for words – like Ferenk, she didn't use them when she didn't have to. Now she had to fight to turn her thoughts into speech. 'More than being... one among many. That's what I fought for in the arenas, to be on my own at the top. That's what it means to be a Spire Tyrant – we got to the top in the arenas and now we're doing it in the Spoil. I'm not going to live and die as just another Red Sand Raider. That's what I want. Something more.'

Ferenk nodded. 'Maybe they'll follow you, if it comes to that,' he said. 'But whether they will or not depends on tomorrow. Take some heads, give some gifts, I can make you my right hand. You want that?'

'I'll take what the Spoil gives me,' replied Voleska.

'Good,' said Ferenk with finality. 'Of course, first of all, you'll have to survive.'

'Not planning to do anything else,' said Voleska.

'With the dawn,' concluded Ferenk, and he turned back to his map of Bonebreak Pass.

'With the dawn,' agreed Voleska.

Outside, the night was turning chill. The moons were sinking as the night kept a jealous grip on the Fangs against the daybreak. The Spire Tyrants of their various warbands were resting, but few were asleep. They sparred and gambled, because the habits of the fighting pits never really left them.

'What did you mean earlier?' said Kyryll as Voleska emerged from the tent.

'When?'

'You said we weren't so far from Carngrad.'

'Because we aren't,' replied Voleska. 'Back in Carngrad, we fought for the eyes of the audience. For the lords who might hire us. The crowds. Even each other, so we knew who to respect. You think it's any different now?'

'Not many arenas round these mountains,' said Kyryll.

Voleska clipped him around the back of the head with her meaty palm. Kyryll wasn't small, but he was smaller than her, and he cringed at the impact. 'You're an idiot,' she said.

'So who are you fighting for?' retorted Kyryll. 'For Ferenk?'

'Him, among others,' she said. 'These other warbands will know not to stand in the Raiders' way when they see us tear apart the Cabal. The Cabal will remember us, too, if we let any live. They'll talk about the Ones Who Make The Sand Red, and the Gift-Giver. The Bloodwind Spoil will know we're coming. They'll beg to be the first to kneel to us. And then...'

Voleska gripped Kyryll's shoulder and turned him to face one of the nearby peaks. Bloody snow clung to the highest point, well above the line where the spindly thorn trees thinned out to nothing. On one of the peaks, against the deep dark of the night, a sharp black outline was just visible.

It was a human of immense size, bulked out by plates of spiked armour and a massive tower shield. One hand held a halberd with a bundle of skulls strung around its point.

'One of Archaon's Chosen,' said Voleska. 'Saw them while we scouted. You were too dim to notice. They're watching. Not just us, the Cabal, the Unmade, the Splintered Fang. Why do you think we're here, Kyryll? To be the biggest dogs in the Blood-wind Spoil? Maybe that's enough for you, but not me. They're watching for warriors to take to the Varanspire. For Archaon's army.'

The lone warrior didn't move. The face was hidden behind a solid steel visor broken only by a black eye slit.

'You think they're watching us now?' asked Kyryll.

'Me, maybe. You? Not so sure.'

Down the pass, in the direction of the distant Varanspire, the Corvus Cabal's warbands held the upper slopes. They hadn't set up bonfires and torches as the Spire Tyrants had. Their presence was betrayed by the trophies they strung up among the trees. Their Great Gatherer demanded trophies be taken from their dead. The Corvus Cabal cut a memento off every corpse they left in their wake, and hung up those orphaned ears and fingers everywhere they settled. The Cabal thought Bonebreak Pass and the Fangs were theirs, and they had been labouring under that misapprehension for far too long. With the dawn they would learn the truth.

And the watchers of battle would see them fail.

They swept down from the heights in a storm of bloody feathers, shrieking as they ran. Beneath the clouds of an impending storm, at the breaking of the lightning-touched dawn, the warbands of the Corvus Cabal made their charge.

Across the pass, the Splintered Fang and the Unmade had their own battle to fight, and perhaps the victor of that slaughter would survive in sufficient numbers to challenge for command of the pass. The winners' blood could be shed another time. For now, the Spire Tyrants had the enemy ahead of them to fight.

Ferenk held his spear high. He had used it to kill his way to fame and glory in Carngrad, and then killed his owner with it when he led the breakout of pit fighters who had become the core of the Red Sand Raiders. 'Life kept the prize from us,' he yelled. 'Now we take it!'

The Red Sand Raiders gathered in front of him cheered. They were men and women of every kind, small and fast, strong and brutal, cold-blooded killers and frenzied murderers. They were united by the old marks of combat on them, and the ugly functionality of their wargear. They carried the weapons with which they had learned to fight in the blood pits and amphitheatres. Hooked blades, nets and tridents, scythes, twinned daggers. They were united by the same fury that had seen them earn or steal their freedom from the pits.

'I heard a rumour that we're here to take the pass,' continued Ferenk, which was met by a muttering of dark laughter. 'I say we're here to take some heads! Let the rest squabble about who owns what. We are Spire Tyrants! We turned the sands of the arenas red, and we do the same to the Bloodwind Spoil! We kill and break and tear, and when there's no one else left, we take what we want!'

The other Spire Tyrants warbands had their own leaders, and they were stoking the fires in their warriors just as Ferenk was. Some of them had started their careers doing the same thing in the arenas, in Carngrad and elsewhere in the Bloodwind Spoil, whipping the crowd and their fellow fighters into a fury that could only be sated by blood.

Their words mingled with the howl of the coming storm's winds and the shrieking of the Corvus Cabal. The crow-warriors were a dark tide descending from their high ground onto the treacherous slopes above the blood-clotted pass. They had been expected to hold the heights and wait for the Spire Tyrants to come to them. They had instead chosen to force the battle and, by advancing, join it on their terms.

It did not matter. The battle plan still held. Straight down the middle, and kill them all.

The leaders of the Spire Tyrants couldn't have held them back any longer if they had wanted to.

Voleska felt the ripple of fury running up and down the Spire Tyrants' lines. The ex-gladiators broke into a charge down the slope towards the advancing Corvus Cabal. She was a part of it, carried along on their tide, and she felt her heart hammering with anticipation. It was the same sensation she had once had when the doors of the arenas were hauled open and she saw the enemy for the first time. A hot, tingling spark of anticipation that ran from her core down her arms and legs, a cousin of fear but something rooted far more deeply in her mind.

'They're fast,' gasped Kyryll as he ran beside her, his twin jagged swords in his hands. 'They'll go for the tendons.'

'Not my first tumble, little Kyryll,' replied Voleska.

The distance closed. Voleska could hear the birdlike shrieks and caws of the Cabal, a battle-tongue other warbands could not understand. They wore black feathers and avian skulls. Their faces were smeared with black warpaint. She hauled her hammer up onto her shoulder and felt its familiar, comforting weight on her.

The two forces slammed into one another. The Cabal were fast and cunning. The Spire Tyrants fought with a straightforward brutality. Blood sprayed across the shale and a dozen people died in the first seconds. A gladiator's head was sheared clean off by a razor-sharp blade. A feather-clad Cabalist was rammed through the gut by a jagged two-handed sword. A Spire Tyrant a few strides from Voleska fell back, screaming, his face torn wide open by the finger talons of the Cabalist who had dived under his guard.

With a howl, one of the Cabal leapt off an outcropping of rock. He dived down at Voleska feet first, and the murky sun glinted off the talons built into his boots.

Voleska was faster than he thought.

She swung the hammer to meet him in mid-air. The weapon's head slammed into the Cabalist's midriff. It was a blow the crowd had always adored. They loved the crunch of the spine and pelvis, the elongated grunt as the air was forced out of her opponent's lungs. They loved to see the body, lifeless as a rag doll, thrown down to the bloody sands. She flung the Cabalist's body off the head of her hammer, and she could almost hear the cheering.

Kyryll was alive, wrestling with a Cabalist who had rushed him. The two rolled on the gory slope, in danger of tumbling down into the pass. Their weapons were pinned at their sides as neither was willing to let go of the other. Voleska grabbed the Cabalist's feathered cloak and hauled him up into the air. The Cabalist dropped Kyryll and slashed at Voleska, but her reach was such that the dagger's points skimmed past her throat.

Voleska slammed the enemy back into the ground. He rolled to a kneeling position from which he could stab and slash at her abdomen. But Voleska was wise to it. She was already in mid-swing by the time the Cabalist's head was up, and there was no time for him to even throw out a hand in defence.

The hammer smashed into his face. Voleska angled the blow upwards, into the chin, a trick she had learned in the arenas when the gladiators had been given the maimed or condemned to fight for the crudest entertainments of the crowd. The Cabalist's head snapped back, the neck gave way, and his head was smacked clean off his shoulders.

If there had been an audience, thought Voleska, they would have screamed with joy and bloodlust at the decapitating blow. They would have chanted the name of the Gift-Giver.

She corrected herself. There was an audience. They were watching from the peaks overlooking Bonebreak Pass.

'Get up, little Kyryll,' she scolded. She turned to the rest of the battling Spire Tyrants. 'Onwards! Straight down the middle! Don't give these vermin the time to draw breath!'

The Spire Tyrants surged. Bodies tumbled down the slope into the coagulating gore flowing down the pass. The Corvus Cabal fell back and counter-charged, some finding soft flesh for their blades, others finding only a swinging sword or a shield boss to

the face. Voleska swung her hammer in a huge arc and the Cabalists scurried away from her. The Red Sand Raiders ran into the
gap she opened up, and they set about the fleeing Cabal with an
efficiency born of a lifetime of killing.

Ferenk was among them. The jagged steel head of his spear
found a Cabalist in the back and he pinned her to the ground,
rushing up to her and slamming his foot down on the back of
her head.

Voleska had a split second to gather her thoughts. She risked
a glance away from the carnage, up the slope towards the peaks
surrounding Bonebreak Pass like the spires of a crown.

The watchers of battle were there, unmoving. In the flashes
of lightning she could see how their black armour was banded
with steel. Their shields were inscribed with glowing runes and
hung with strings of skulls and severed hands. Every peak in the
Fangs seemed to have one of Archaon's warriors atop it, watching the various fronts of the battle unfolding in Bonebreak Pass.
Some were observing the bloodshed on the other side of the pass,
where Voleska knew that the Unmade and the Splintered Fang
were butchering one another. Others were watching the Corvus
Cabal and the Spire Tyrants.

They were watching Voleska. They had seen her pair of kills.

'Killing is not enough,' said Voleska to Kyryll, who was scrambling to his feet to join Ferenk's advance.

'What?' Kyryll struggled to understand her above the din of
clashing steel and screams.

'They're watching. Killing isn't enough. We have to show them.
Like in the arenas! We are the spectacle!'

She shot her friend a grin. His face showed only confusion,
which passed as he refocused on the battle unfolding around
them.

She knew now what she had to do. She understood why she

had fought in the arenas, and why she had broken out in a night of anarchy and bloodshed on the streets of Carngrad. Why she had joined Ferenk and the Red Sand Raiders, welding a coherent force out of so many disparate killers. It was because one day, in the chill and storm-lashed Bonebreak Pass, the eyes of Archaon would be on her at last.

'They're falling back!' gasped Kyryll. The Corvus Cabal were scurrying back towards the heights, leaving dozens of dead and maimed in their wake. The slain tumbled down the slope into the thick gore, which was swelling and foaming with the rain.

'It's a feint!' shouted back Ferenk as he finished off a Cabalist on the ground with spear thrust to the throat. 'They want to draw us in.'

'Then let them!' answered Voleska. 'Tyrants! They are watching! Finish these vermin! Fill up this valley with the dead!'

She held her enormous hammer high over her head. The whole Spire Tyrants force could see her – she was a head taller than most of them and her gore-clotted weapon was like a standard of war brandished as a rallying point.

Some recognised the Gift-Giver from their days in the Carngrad fighting pits. Others just roared in appreciation of the bloody hammer and the toll it had reaped. They surged forward again in Voleska's wake as she ran after the retreating Cabal.

Some of the Cabalists were too slow. They were trampled underfoot or killed with blades when they stumbled. Voleska slammed her hammer down on the crown of one Cabalist's head and drove his shattered skull into his chest. Kyryll kept up with her and slashed at the hamstrings of another runner, sending him face first into the bloody scree to be despatched by the Spire Tyrants behind him.

The Corvus Cabal scrambled up the slope to the heights. They had banked on the Spire Tyrants waiting to exult in their victory, licking their wounds and regrouping, not pursuing them heedless of the trap the Cabalists were trying to spring. They never made it to the eyries strung with battlefield trophies, where thousands of crows roosted among the thorny trees of the Fangs. The front ranks of the Corvus Cabal were forced to turn and face the Spire Tyrants before they were overrun, well short of the ridge where they had hoped to mass for their counter-charge

The warriors on the peaks were still watching. They had not moved, save to turn their heads and keep the thickest of the fighting in view. They showed no reaction to the bloodshed.

Voleska had to get their notice. She had to go further.

A leader of the Cabal stood proud of the enemy lines. He stood on long steel legs, like stilts strapped to his shins. They ended in talons that he wielded as skilfully as a bird of prey, clotted with torn flesh and hair. He carried a pair of hooked blades and he shrieked in anger beneath his bird-skull helm. His arms were pierced with hundreds of feathers so that he seemed to have a pair of bloodstained wings.

Voleska had seen other Spire Tyrants killing with a flourish – a skilful decapitation, a flamboyant disembowelment – and she knew her spectacular hammer kills had competition. There was only one target for her in the unfolding bloodshed.

Voleska ran right at the Cabalist leader. He loped towards her, towering over even her prodigious height. He leaped with improbable agility, stabbing his talons down at her. She pivoted to one side and felt the claws raking down her shoulder. She roared in pain and let it fuel her, as she had learned in her first few hours as a killer in the arenas. She would always be hurt. She would always be wounded. It was her choice to use it, and not let it defeat her.

Voleska had the strength and the enemy had the speed. As fast as he was, he could not fly up out of the reach of her hammer. She held the weapon near the butt-end and swung it in a wide, circular arc, ignoring the Spire Tyrants who scattered out of the way. With a clatter the hammer knocked one of the Cabalist's stilts out from under him.

He hopped onto his remaining stilt and let out a series of staccato, shrieking syllables, a war cry in the battle-tongue of the Cabal. Voleska shifted her grip on her hammer and lunged at her enemy, driving the head of the weapon towards his midriff.

The Cabalist easily jerked sideways out of the way of the blow. His twin blades ripped into Voleska's unwounded shoulder and down her upper arm. He spun on his stilt and lashed out again, slicing a deep gash into her cheek and another into her other arm.

She had known she would be hurt. There was no way, with her relative slowness, to get into position. She had made a career in the arenas taking blows and refusing to let them debilitate her. She would feel the agony later. For now, she was right next to the Cabalist leader, his bloody wings unfolded over her, his wicked beak grimacing down.

Voleska swung the hammer down and up again, feeling her torn muscles fighting to power it out of its lowest point.

The hammer arced up and slammed into the Cabalist's groin.

Bones crunched. The Cabalist's pelvis shattered. The roar of an imaginary crowd filled Voleska's mind. Severed heads and heart thrusts got boring eventually, but every crowd loved to see a kill-shot to the groin.

Voleska couldn't leave it to chance. She had to confirm the kill before she could play to the stands and exult in her victory. The Cabalist toppled off his stilt and landed on his knees. Voleska hefted the weight of the hammer over her head and swung it down like a labourer driving a post into the ground. The hammer came down on the back of her foe's neck.

The blow compressed the enemy's body, folding it in half. The ribcage collapsed into the abdomen. The spine was turned to pulp.

Blood and gore spurted out through the Cabalist's torn torso, spraying to either side in crimson wings to complement the false pinions of black feathers.

Every kill needed a final flourish, an exclamation mark. Voleska swung an underhand blow into the shattered mess that remained of the Cabalist leader. She caught him under his ruptured chest and flung him high over the battlefield. He trailed blood like the tail of a comet and thumped into the middle of the Corvus Cabal.

Voleska could feel the tide of despair that rippled out from the corpse's impact. The dismay of the opposition was as sweet as the appreciation of the crowd. Whether they loved or hated her, it was the reaction, the emotion she sparked in the hearts of the onlookers, that drove her on.

The Spire Tyrants roared at the death. They rushed in around her and dived into the Corvus Cabal. The enemy were shattered, their feathered bodies beaten down to the scree or held aloft impaled on spears and blades. They fought back till the end, and there were Spire Tyrants whose throats were cut or whose hearts were pierced even in the moments of victory, but for every fallen gladiator, five or six of the Crows were left butchered in bleeding heaps.

Drops of blood pattered down onto Voleska's shoulders as she paused. The thunderclouds overhead swelled deep crimson, and the storm broke. With a hiss and a roar, the blood rain fell again.

It trickled down the scree in hundreds of tiny streams, mingling with the river that now flowed through the pass, foaming pink around rapids formed by piles of bodies. It streamed down the faces of the Spire Tyrants and spattered against the armour of the warriors on the mountain peaks. It sluiced down the mountainsides. The sky was rent and bleeding, as if the fury of the battle below had dealt a mortal wound to the sky itself.

Voleska panted with exertion and leaned on her hammer. The

pain of her wounds was starting to hit her now. Both arms were streaming with blood, and not only from the crimson downpour. She looked up through the red rain at the watchers on the peaks.

Would that be enough? Did they care? Had they even seen her butchery of the enemy amid the swirling bloodshed? Plenty of Spire Tyrants had made spectacular kills in the last few moments alone. What made her stand out compared to them?

And then she knew.

A Spire Tyrant fought alone. They might form alliances in the arenas, and then join greater alliances outside it, banding together under leaders like Ferenk for mutual protection. But they were not born to such allegiances. Even her friendly rivalry with Kyryll had its roots in a genuine desire to outdo, to defeat, to step over on the way to something greater.

There was nothing for her on that bloodstained slope, nor in the camp where the Spire Tyrants would drink and boast past nightfall. A true gladiator did not make herself a part of that. She stood alone.

She knew what she had to do. She had never been more certain of anything in her life.

She turned to Kyryll. He looked similarly exhausted. His flesh was covered in nicks and cuts, and his arms were slathered in gore to the elbow. He grinned up at her, smearing the blood rain out of his eyes with the back of his hand. 'You were right,' he said. 'Not so different from Carngrad after all. Never gave them a show quite like this, though.'

Voleska felt the weight of her hammer as if she were lifting it for the first time. No one else in the arenas had the strength to wield it. No one had thought she could either. She had proven them wrong.

Kyryll never had the time to let the smile fall off his features. Voleska's hammer blow caught him square in the face.

It was good that she started with him. He was the hardest to kill. Once he was down, his face staved in and ruined, the rest were easy.

It took the other Spire Tyrants several fatal moments to realise what she was doing. They were drunk on victory and their bodies were sluggish with the fatigue suddenly catching up with them. Voleska crushed the skull of one who had his back to her, then knocked the legs out from under another and finished him off with a stamp to the back of the neck.

The first Spire Tyrant to react turned to her and wrestled his blade back out of its scabbard. 'What are you...?' he gasped before Voleska rammed the head of the hammer into his chest, driving the air out of him. She swung the hammer up under his chin, shattering his jaw and snapping his head fatally back with the crack of snapping spine.

They tried to swarm her. When they came into her guard, they were mown down by the swinging arc of her hammer. They leapt at her and she swatted them out of the air where they could be killed down in the scree.

Surviving Cabalists took advantage of the sudden confusion among the Spire Tyrants to leap into the fray. More died in one-on-one struggles with the Spire Tyrants. Others were caught within the whirlwind of blood that surrounded Voleska. Crowded around by enemies, stronger than any of them and with a greater reach, she could not help but catch an enemy or three with every swing of her hammer.

The pain was gone. Her strength flowed back. The hollow inside her, that had been temporarily filled with the adulation of the crowd and the rush of victory, was brimming over with a certainty of purpose.

Ferenk faced her through the carnage. He loped over the broken bones and pulped torsos towards her. His face was a furious mass of scars twisted with anger. He led with his spear, blinded by his anger at Voleska's betrayal.

'Witch!' he snarled. 'You betray! You break us!'

'Give them a show, Sunder-Spine,' said Voleska with a blood-flecked grin.

Ferenk led with a spear thrust. Voleska shifted out of the way but he knew her too well to be wrong-footed. He snapped an elbow up into her face and caught her square on the jaw. Sparks flared in front of her eyes as her head snapped back, and she felt herself drop. She threw out a hand to break her fall, dropping her hammer, and felt Ferenk's spear grazing her cheek as he just missed a fatal stab to her face.

Voleska grabbed the haft of the spear and pulled. Ferenk came down on top of her. She wrapped a meaty hand around the back of his head to keep him from getting back up and the two rolled, wrestling, slick with blood and fighting for a grip.

Ferenk rolled on top. He tore an arm free and punched it down at her. She twisted her head and the blow slammed into her collarbone. The flash of pain told her it was probably broken. Ferenk's teeth were gritted and every ropelike muscle stood out on his lean, battle-carved body. He drew his fist back again and slammed it into the side of her head.

Ferenk's eagerness to punish her had let Voleska free one of her arms. She grabbed a handful of his lank black hair and pulled his head back. He was forced backwards and Voleska had the room to force herself up into a seated position. She wrapped both her arms around Ferenk and held him in a bear hug.

She could feel his ribs creaking against her biceps. He hissed through his teeth as he fought to draw a proper lungful of breath. He pounded against her back but she cinched him in tighter, locking her fingers and grinding his torso. He thrashed and struggled, and his fingers found the haft of the stone dagger in his belt.

Voleska had killed men with this death grip before, but not often. Any competent fighter had a backup blade to slide between her ribs in such a clinch. Even as Ferenk pulled out his knife, Voleska powered up to her feet and threw the leader of the Red Sand Raiders away from her.

Ferenk landed heavily on one shoulder. He rolled to standing, panting down a breath, knife in hand.

'Who paid you to betray us?' snarled Ferenk. 'What did they offer you?'

'No one offers anything,' said Voleska. 'Not on the Spoil. You have to take it.'

'When I leave this pass, I will be wearing your skin.'

Voleska spat out a gobbet of bloody phlegm. 'You'll never leave.'

Ferenk ran at her, but his fury made him sloppy.

Voleska took the dagger thrust on her forearm. It sliced down to the bone, but it was just one more wound among many. Ferenk rushed into her, and she rammed a knee up into his stomach.

He folded and wheezed, almost pitching face first into the scree. Voleska drove her elbow down into the back of his head and felt the skull crack.

Ferenk was on his hands and knees now. Voleska picked up her hammer and shifted her grip to hold it just below the head, with the gore-encrusted lump of stone facing groundwards. She looked up at the closest watcher of battle, whose armoured visor was facing down at her.

'The Gift-Giver has a gift for Lord Archaon!' she yelled, and slammed the hammer down.

The blow crushed Ferenk's skull flat against the scree slope. The Sunder-Spine's brains sprayed out of his sundered cranium. His legs twitched with some primeval instinct of death, and then he was still.

No Spire Tyrants rushed in to avenge their fallen. No spat curses came her way. Voleska turned to look behind her, but through the falling rain she could see only bodies littering the slope.

They were all dead, or fled. She had done it.

She was the last one standing.

They descended the slopes as the last embers of the battle died down. Most of them turned away from the carnage and walked off into the labyrinthine peaks of the Fangs, uninterested in what the warbands had to offer them. But two of Archaon's warriors descended to the place where the Corvus Cabal and the Spire Tyrants had fought, and where only the dead and wounded remained. Save one warrior who waited for them, leaning on her giant hammer. They looked her up and down, sizing up her wounds. Up close they were huge, taller and broader even than Voleska. If they had found her wanting or too badly hurt to be used, they would have despatched her then and there. But they did not.

They turned away and headed for the northern end of the pass, in the direction of the Varanspire. Voleska gave silent thanks to the Dark Gods, and followed them.

Outside the Varanspire was a complex of dozens of forges, each one a structure of black stone and iron belching smoke. The region was bathed in infernal heat and the air was almost unbreathable with smoke and ash. Pale, skinny slave-things scurried about carrying ingots or hauling sleds loaded with swords and armour. The warriors led Voleska through the forges to one where the black iron doors hung open, revealing the glowing throats of the fires inside.

Segments of armour hung on the walls. Hundreds of swords were lined up in racks, with others in the process of being forged by a malformed smith whose enormous, lopsided musculature drove the hammer he used to beat the blades into shape. His face was hidden behind a caul of chain and it looked like he had never left his place at the anvil. He took a blade he had finished beating and plunged it into the water trough running the length of the room. A blast of steam filled the air as the superheated metal was suddenly cooled and hardened.

Voleska let her heart fill with anticipation. She had not dared believe she would join the ranks of Archaon's armies, not truly, until she saw it happen. Now she was to be fitted with the all-enclosing armour of a Chaos Warrior, ready to join the legions marching out through the Realmgates to conquer and despoil.

One of the weapons racked up for inspection was a hammer. It was the length and heft of her own, but of infinitely grander construction. Its iron head was faced with spikes and its haft was bound with the warted skin of some leathery beast. Voleska reached out to touch the weapon, imagining its killing power in her hands.

An iron-shod foot kicked her in the back of the leg. She fell to one knee, grunting in surprise. She reached out to arrest her fall and her hand found the edge of the trough containing the water used to quench the forge's blades.

But it was not full of water.

Voleska was looking into a trough full of blood. A gauntleted hand fell on her shoulder and kept her down on her knee. She struggled, but the grip on her shoulder and the weight pinning her down did not shift. It was like being held in an iron clamp. Voleska had never encountered anyone as strong as she was, but the warrior holding her was stronger by far.

They were not like her. They were not men and women. They were something inhuman. It was no gladiator of Carngrad or brave of the Corvus Cabal beneath that armour. It was no Unmade or Splintered Fang. Perhaps it had once been, a lifetime ago, but now it was something very different.

Voleska had thought the watchers of battle were searching for a warrior who was their equal, but she was not an equal.

She was not strong enough.

Panic rose in her. She had never truly felt it before. This fear was an alien thing, like a ghost that stole into her heart and turned it to ice. She tried to reach up and grab the arm pinning her down, but another hand seized her wrist and she was held fast.

Not strong enough to be one of Archaon's warriors.

She felt the sword point touch the back of her neck. The trough of blood was used for quenching the blades of Archaon's soldiers, but no mundane blood would do. It gave its strength to their arms and armour, imbuing them with the ferocity and anguish of the warbands of the Bloodwind Spoil. These facts rushed through Voleska's mind as she desperately sought a reason why she might live.

Not strong enough to serve Archaon. But strong enough to be a sacrifice.

The Gift-Giver, the Butcher of Bonebreak Pass, was chosen not to march with the armies of Archaon, but so their newly forged swords could be quenched in her blood.

The tip of the warrior's sword pierced the skin of her neck. The first trickle of it ran down her throat and dripped into the trough. The malformed blacksmith grunted in acknowledgement as his hammer rose and fell in a deafening, unceasing rhythm.

The sword punched through Voleska's neck. Ice ran through her as it cut her spine. Blood sluiced into the trough in front of her. Blackness flickered around the edges of her vision.

The last thing she saw was her lifeblood flowing into the trough, the only thing of value the servants of Archaon had seen in the Gift-Giver. Her last thoughts, before they were cut off by the passage of the blade through her brain stem, were of emptiness.

BLOOD OF
THE FLAYER

Richard Strachan

She came to him in the wreckage of another Muspelzharr town, a petty settlement of rough farmland where they tilled the ore and sold it on to the Freeguild furnaces in far Andar. Through the choking smoke she moved, past corpses smeared across the dusty grass. By a tent of skinned hides there was a mound of severed heads, and carved on each was an eight-pointed star. There was lament on the air, the old blade-song of widowed women and old men mourning their sundered sons. They would follow them soon enough.

The warlord stood with his back to her, staring up into the cobalt sky. High up there, like meteors, moved specks of light.

'You waste your prisoners, Lord Huthor,' she said boldly. 'They can last for days in the sweetest agonies, if you know how.'

He was a large and brutal man, she saw, scarred in the face, his skin battered by decades of Chamon's flensing winds. He pointed at the lights.

'Do you know what those are?' he asked.

'Yes, lord,' she said, coming near. 'Duardin sky-craft, trading vessels of those who style themselves "Overlords". They come from the Ashpeaks and make for Barak-Zon, if I am not mistaken.'

'Barak-Zon?'

'Their sky-port.' She bowed. 'As I understand these things.'

'Overlords... I thought so. I've seen them often in the last few days. I thought them an omen, at first...' His voice trailed off, and his hand was white-knuckled on the hilt of his sword.

'I do not know if they are an omen, my lord,' the woman said. 'But if they are then they must be a good one. For I am Dysileesh, and I bring you great tidings.'

'If I could but reach up,' he said softly, 'and pull them down from the aether, I would do so... But you have to marvel at them,' Huthor laughed. 'With sweat and toil, to put a crafted thing into the air and sail it like that through the mineral tides – such courage!' He turned to the man at his side. 'Don't you think, Vhoss?'

Vhoss, a hard and compact warrior, his shaved head flecked with scars, gruffly agreed. 'Aye, Lord Flayer' he said. 'You can't doubt their courage.'

'And for what?' Huthor spat, his mood shifting. 'Coin. *Trade*. Lives ordered by the numbers they scrawl in a ledger.'

Dysileesh, seizing her moment, moved forward. She stroked his forearm. 'And wouldn't you like to tear those lives down, my lord? Wouldn't you like to seize those riches for yourself? Fame you shall have, as well as power. Come,' she said, and into that one word she put all the art of her influence, her intoxicating presence. 'Let us talk. I bring tidings of the Dark Prince, the Lord of Excess... You have drawn the eye of Slaanesh, and power untold is yours if you pledge yourself to him.'

Huthor stared down into those violet eyes, and for the first time he took her in entire – the single dark lock cascading from her crown; the chain that linked the silver hoops in her ear and eyebrow and nose; her sickening smell, more alluring than the stench of battle.

'Sweet tears have you spilled on the altar of Ruin,' she whispered closely, 'but the Dark Gods are jealous, and generous to those who dedicate themselves to their service. Make obeisance to the Prince, and all things shall be yours to savour and command. Does not your eye crave more luxurious sights, your tongue crave finer tastes than cheap fare and peasant women? And does not your lust run deeper than simple murders in the dirt... Seek Slaanesh with me and I will show you the thrill of torments untold, the *ecstasies* to be found in the depths of gluttony and starvation...'

Her tongue, a purple, serpentine thing, flicked madly from her lips, and her eyes blazed with lilac fire.

Others to whom she had made this entreaty would have strained to possess her by now, or would have been lost in greedy dreams of power. But the Flayer only took her arm in his iron grip and pulled her close. His face was a mask, grim and unyielding, scarred by battle. He drew her towards the tent. 'Come then,' he said. 'Let me hear what the Dark Prince has to offer...'

It was on a whim, he told himself later. No more than that. A woman as devastating as any he had ever seen; his soul smouldering with black fire and eager to expand into new experiences; a grasp that exceeded his reach – all these things made him take the Godseeker into his tent. He would walk her path for a while, he told himself. Why not? A gift freely given is seldom scorned. And when he was bored of it, he would kill her and cast her body to the dogs.

With blasphemous orgies and sickening violence, with ecstasies of wine and song, the Raging Tide followed Dysileesh's teachings, scouring the plains of Gazan Zhar in a decadent whirlwind. They raided the caravanserais of the Free Cities, looting fine silks and

precious jewels to decorate their wargear. They made cloaks from
the skins of their victims and found the most intense pleasures
in the limits of their endurance. A troupe of hellstriders on their
freakish reptilian mounts soon swelled Huthor's ranks, and the
warband's savage tribal marks were slowly replaced by sinuous
tattoos, kohl-rimmed eyes and mocking smears of perfumed oil.
Across the plains they plundered for a while, leaving in their
passing a sweet and cloying musk, the wail of grief and torment.

Dysileesh was owned by no man or woman of the warband,
and although she stayed most often in Huthor's tent she lavished
her attention on Elizha too, one of Huthor's charioteers, riding
with her as the warband raided across the plains. Soon she took
up with Vhoss, Huthor's most trusted lieutenant, although when
she announced that she was pregnant Huthor did not reveal his
suspicions. Vhorrun, born on the plunder-path, came screaming
into the Mortal Realms like a true son of Chamon. His pale skin
gleamed like silver, and the thick spikes of his black hair were
dusted with gold. Violet eyes looked from an unforgiving face, but
Huthor couldn't say who his father might be. No matter. Like his
own father, Huthor thought, he was not made to suffer children.
So the warband grew, and the further they went on this path, the
deeper Huthor plunged into the worship of Slaanesh, dedicating
his pains and his pleasures to the Dark Prince and yet in his pride
never straying too far from the road of his own self-made fate.

No god ordered his path, he said. He made his own.

They raided on impulse, moving through the mutable land as
plateaus melted and reformed around them, as valleys raised themselves into rough, sawtoothed spines that marked the plains like a
godbeast's grave.

After a season they found themselves straying towards the Beryllium Coast, where the pickings were richer. It was there, in a chill

dusk, that they first came across the ruins of the Golden Fortress. As the warband marched through a desolate landscape, the sultry plains behind them and the Onoglop Swamps to the north, the walls of the shattered stronghold rose from the sea mists to meet them.

'What is this place?' Huthor asked Dysileesh as he swung down from his horse. The warband dismounted around him. Elizha reared back the mounts of her chariot and coiled her silver whip in her hand. 'I don't like it, lord,' she said. 'The wind smells of sickness and death.'

'That's just the swamps on the breeze,' Dysileesh said. She stepped from the chariot, drawing her silken robes around her and gazing with wonder at the tarnished gold of the fortress walls. They were hazy and indistinct in the mist, like the dream of something vaster than the eye could understand. Weeds and scour-grass choked the pathways that led to the massive iron doors, which listed on their hinges. The fortress, Huthor saw as they drew nearer, had not been built, as such. No mortal hand had cast this place. Rather, the land itself had reared it into being, extruding it from the dark and granular soil like a tooth from a gum.

'In truth, I'm not sure,' Dysileesh admitted to him. 'I have heard rumours, but I have never seen it for myself. A fortress made of purest Chamonite, some say, although we see now that it is not the case. Gold, my lord. The Dark Prince gives, and you shall receive! Gold and splendour beyond your wildest dreams!'

'You cannot imagine,' Huthor said, 'how wild my dreams really are.'

The fortress was silent and empty, its cavernous halls looming around them as they led their steeds through. Rotting tapestries depicted scenes from the Age of Myth – Grungni forging the Nineteen Wonders, the lode-griffon uncoiling above the God-wrought Isles. Of the original inhabitants there was no other sign, and whatever race or nation had secured this impossible bastion had been lost in mists of time as dense as the mists that billowed from the Beryllium Sea.

The warband made camp, and they stayed for years. The Golden Fortress became their keep.

'When I was a boy,' he told her, 'I lived alone with my father. He was a simple man, earning a meagre wage from cutting ironthorn branches in the forest and melting them down for slag – he had no more skill than that. He was a brutal man, who feared Sigmar.'

Huthor leaned over the side of the bed and spat on the ground at the God-King's name. Dysileesh drew languidly near across the sheets. Above them, a polished gold ceiling cast back their reflections, distorted by the metal so that they both looked strangely elongated, like pale snakes basking lazily in a savage sun.

'He beat me every day of my life,' Huthor went on, 'and then one day – whether from drunkenness or poverty or simple indifference – he abandoned me deep in the woods. He hoped I would die and free him of responsibility. He craved order in his life, and children are nothing if not disorder personified... I had no idea how to get home. It was cold, silent. No light came through the canopy. High above me I could hear the crackling of the mantys-birds, hopping through the branches, sharpening their copper beaks.'

'How did you escape?' Dysileesh asked him. She trailed her fingers over his chest, tracing the lines of the torture scars she had given him. The air stank of the young man they'd recently skinned, whose body lay cooling on the chamber's marble floor. Three days he had lasted; it had been exquisite.

'I didn't. I found an ironthorn branch and armed myself, fighting off the mantys-birds whenever they came too near. I hacked my way through the forest for days, on and on. I was starving. I had never been so scared.'

'How old were you?'

'Seven.'

'So young...'

'Old enough. Eventually I came to a path I recognised, and at the end of this path was a crossroads. I stood there. I knew the choice had been laid open to me. One road led back to our hovel in the woods, the other led on towards the outer realm. One road to Order, the other to Chaos.'

'And so, you left that miserable life behind,' she whispered in his ear. 'You left for greater things.'

Huthor laughed, without a trace of humour. His lip curled at the memory.

'Not at first,' he said. He reached for a goblet, brimful of the skinned young man's tears. He drank deep. 'No, first I took the path back home. Armed with my iron branch, I went to say fare-well to my father...'

He had often wondered what would have happened if he had taken the other path instead. What if, at the end of his journey through the woods, he had not stood in front of his blazing home, exulting in the flames while his father's flayed body burned inside?

But he had made his choice. He had taken his first, faltering steps on the road of Ruin, and he had been walking that path with grim rejoicing ever since.

The years passed for Huthor in a blur of excess. Nightly the war-band indulged its most perverted desires, breaking off to launch savage raids into the surrounding territories. Before long, fright-ened towns and settlements along the coast paid them desperate tribute. Warriors flocked to Huthor's silken banner, and every-thing unfolded as Dysileesh had promised. He was carving out an empire, a legacy, but daily the Godseeker pressed him to commit himself totally to Slaanesh.

'You still hold back,' she pleaded. 'You have seen what the Dark

Prince is capable of, and now surely you must pledge yourself to him?'

'Did your Prince give me this?' Huthor countered. They strode to the fortress' half-melted battlements and he swept out his hand to indicate the wild lands before them. Impaled prisoners writhed and groaned across the frontage of the fortress grounds. From the golden corridors beneath them came screams of pleasure and pain. Behind them churned the mercurial sea, lapping in quicksilver waves at the crumbling shore. 'Or did I take it for myself?'

'Could you have gained this without his favour? You speak blasphemies to claim otherwise, lord.'

'Blasphemies? Then let him strike me down – if he can. He languishes in chains, does he not? Why should I follow a chained god, too weak to free himself? It serves me for now to follow your path, Godseeker, but don't think it is a path I will follow forever. The lord of the Golden Fortress makes his own fate. He worships the hurricane of Chaos, the maelstrom. No god commands me!'

She hissed at him, but Huthor replied only with scornful laughter.

All nearby bowed to the Golden Fortress, but in the north, there was one territory that refused them tribute. In the brooding miasma of the Onoglop Swamps, Rotbringer cults met Huthor's scouting parties with axe and blade. Huthor had dispatched a small force to quell them, but this band of hellstriders and marauders had been swallowed by the swamp's glistening mists and no word of them ever came back.

Mounting his steed and unsheathing his sword for the first time in what felt like years, Huthor personally led a sally from the fortress into the dark lands. For days they marched north, the sky above them whipped with glittering tendrils of teal and cyan, streaked with the corposant of harvested aether-gold as the Kharadron sky-ships plied their vertiginous trade. Huthor had watched them as he rode, straining to catch a glimpse of those impossible craft, willing each to catch fire and plummet to the ground so he could crack them open with his blade. Something about their sheer distance offended him, but his mind was soon taken off the duardin by the gloomy edgelands of the Onoglop Swamps.

Flies buzzed in the reeds. A smell so rank it almost made him sick came pouring from the stagnant waters. Strange, greasy blooms quivered in the rancid breeze. His warriors, drawn up in their battle lines, looked at each other uneasily.

'Do we enter?' Dysileesh asked. She snorted a pinch of emerald snuff. 'This doesn't feel right, lord.'

'You'd have me turn back?'

'The lord of the Golden Fortress turn back?' Vhoss laughed. 'I shouldn't think so. The Flayer doesn't run from a fight.'

'The Flayer...' Huthor said. 'It's been a while since you called me that.'

'I was there when you earned that name,' Vhoss said. He slapped Huthor's shoulder. 'The day we met.'

He smiled at the memory: those ancient days, two lost boys scavenging on the fringes of a warband's camp. Slaves to darkness, brooding in their armour; tribal marauders, fleet horsemen scouting the steppes for villages to raid.

'You stole that dagger from a chieftain's tent, do you remember?'

'Aye. He sent two of his best men into the hills to track us down.'

Vhoss cackled at the memory. 'And you sent him their skins in return!'

'Not the first men I'd flayed,' Huthor admitted.

'No. Nor the last.'

The Flayer. Now there had been a fate worth fighting for.

Huthor reared his steed and drew his army up in fine array. Slowly, silently, he led them into the pestilent darkness.

* * *

'The lord is wounded!' Vhoss screamed, bursting through the iron gates. 'The lord of the Golden Fortress is wounded!'

They brought him on a bier of scented cushions and fine coverlets already soaked with blood. The savage wound in his chest pulsed with the beating of his heart, and as Huthor slipped into darkness he heard the frantic pattering of feet along the gilded halls. Healers rushed to attend him. Retainers, those who had not gone out to the fight, roused themselves from debauchery and ran to prepare boiling water laced with Chamonite to tend his wound. Vhoss lashed out at those who were slow to react, beating them with the pommel of his axe.

'Prepare the lord's bed, at once!'

Huthor felt himself being carried to his chamber. The wound tore at him like a lance, darkening his mind, drawing strange fevers into his blood. He felt someone take his hand, wetting it with eager tears – Dysileesh, delighted at this opportunity to indulge herself in the deepest griefs.

'Elizha...' Huthor groaned. He had seen her chariot tip over and had watched in horror as the Rotbringers tore her to pieces. Mishkhar, his luck run out at last, had thrown himself into them, his lacquered topknot spinning as wildly as his blades, but the weight of numbers had brought him down. Hharag was gone too, shouting his lord's name as the swamp water took him, pulled to his doom by whatever infected creatures lurked in its depths. He had laughed as he died. As Huthor led the retreat, hacking through the press, an axe had swung from the gloom and struck him in the chest.

'Vhorrun...' Huthor tried to say. 'My... son...' He caught a glimpse of the boy staring at him from the shadows, his axes spattered with rancid blood, a murderous look in his eyes. Ten years old, and already a great fighter; he had lived, at least. But then the image was gone, and in its place as they lowered Huthor to his deathbed came a vision of placid decay – a hunched and horned figure in a mouldering cloak, atop a rotting steed. The figure slowly raised an armoured hand and hissed.

Your time has come, Lord Huthor. The Grandfather awaits you.

Light broke through the shuttered windows, painting pale, thick stripes across his bed. Huthor woke, drenched in sweat, his skin clammy and chill. The fortress was silent around him. He reached with a flabby hand for the goblet of water on the table at his side, but he knocked it to the ground.

'Help!' he shouted. Only silence greeted him. The wound in his chest, he saw, had been cleaned and raggedly stitched. It throbbed with a dull, low ache.

Wrapped in a sheet as close as a grave-shroud, Huthor trembled on the golden stairs, supporting himself on the bannister.

'Vhoss?' he shouted. There was no reply. 'Dysileesh!' Scattered goblets and spilled wine littered the ground. At the bottom of the stairs lay a twisted body, its stomach burst open, a foul slurry spattered on the marble floor. The expression on the corpse's face was one of sheer, transported joy.

There was a smell in the air of rotting meat and mouldering fruit. As weak as he had ever felt in his life, Huthor followed the smell into the banqueting hall, the stage where his warband had performed some of its most hideous debauches. He stopped at the door and looked onto a scene of utter devastation.

The long, silver table was piled high with decaying food – haunches of meat that were boiling with maggots, platters of fruit and fine pastries now curdled and stale. Crystal decanters of emerald wine were broken on the floor. Chairs were tipped over, the luxuriant curtains pulled from the high windows. Sprawled on the table, or contorted on the ground, were dozens of Huthor's warriors. All of them clutched brutally distended stomachs, their mouths flecked with the vomit that had choked them. They were all dead.

It was a scene replayed throughout the fortress. The mourning feasts held for their lord, who they assumed had died in his chambers upstairs, had turned, as all Slaaneshi rites must, into a crazed pursuit of excess. They had gorged on food and drink until it killed them.

He found Dysileesh lying in an antechamber off the main hall. Her face was blackened with suffocation; she had forced sweetmeats down her throat until they blocked her windpipe, and in absolute euphoria she had died. He knelt at her side and drew a sheet over her body. The Dark Prince had her at last.

'My lord!' came a voice, echoing across the silent hall. Huthor stood and looked back. Vhorrun gazed at him sullenly from the corridor, and in the subtle light, burnished and enhanced by the golden walls, his skin glowed with faint silver. 'My lord, we thought you were dead.'

'Where is Vhoss?' he croaked. He took a step forward and stumbled, and when he looked up he saw for the briefest moment the pale horseman on his rotting steed, beckoning him forward.

The Grandfather awaits you...

It was as if the voice came from inside him, from his very blood, now thick with poisons.

You called and have been answered, and out there great bounty awaits you, life eternal, free of pain...

Huthor shook his head. When he opened his eyes, Vhorrun was leaning over him.

'Vhoss?'

'My father lives,' the boy said. 'Come, I'll take you to him.'

Not everyone had indulged with such desperation. There were perhaps a hundred warriors left, and although Vhoss had joined the frenzy he had not stepped over that final line. The path of excess was over for them now; they all knew it.

Vhoss, dressed once more in his dracoline-hide jerkin, his silken robes cast aside, was waiting in the main hall. Huthor, still clad in his deathbed sheets, came limping to embrace him. The sickness roiled and brewed inside him, fermenting his blood.

'What now, old friend?' Vhoss asked him. Huthor paused, and the pale horseman rose again before his eyes, mouldering and grey.

'We leave this place,' he said. 'We go back.'

'Back where, lord?'

'To the Onoglop Swamps.'

Vhoss stared at him in horror. 'Huthor, we're in no fit state to fight, we'll be slaughtered!'

'Not to fight, no...' he said in a hoarse and drifting voice. 'Don't you see? We're weak here, vulnerable. We've followed this pampered god for too long. The Grandfather calls us, and he can give us freedom from pain, freedom from weakness and death.' He walked towards the iron doors, beyond which was the long road to the north. 'They're expecting us,' he said.

They marched in a ragged train from the Golden Fortress, making the pilgrim journey to the Onoglop Swamps. Huthor staggered on with the guiding light of Nurgle's bounty fore and centre in his mind. The Harbinger met them at the border and, plodding in the muck on his desiccated horse, led them deep into the sweating chambers of the mire. The Rotbringers stood chortling at its centre, like rotting tree-stumps glazed with filth. They welcomed their new brothers and sisters, eager to share the abundance that brewed and boiled inside them. Huthor, aching for eternal life, seized the offer with both hands.

Here, he thought, *here* was true power: to shrug off blows that would kill lesser men; to grow and fade and grow inside the play of constant disease; to never really die but be born anew, again and again. He laughed, and the days of the Golden Fortress fell far behind him.

Those weeks, or months, or years, or however long it was, were feverish and indistinct. Most of all, Huthor remembered the sickness flowering in him, until his skin swelled and split, the wet, bubbling voice of the disease always muttering in his head. There was jubilation and glee, such joyful certainty that they were on the right path at last. Vhoss watched his skin slowly slough away with equanimity, and cheerfully Vhorrun stroked the tentacles that were sprouting from his side. There were so few of them left from the horde that had launched their sallies from the fortress. Now, trudging from the muck, they raided small villages on the swamp's edge, merrily bludgeoning the inhabitants with their poisoned weapons and watching as the bodies cracked and burst apart with putrefaction. Life roiled and flowed in a perfect, sinuous wave. 'The Bringer of Sickness', they called him, those huddled communities. He was a spirit of the swamplands, a nightmare tale to frighten children to sleep.

Who knew how many more weeks, or months, or years, Huthor and his warband would have stayed in the Onoglop Swamps, reiving and raiding, affably spreading the Grandfather's gifts? Time had no real meaning for them any more; but then, one pallid dusk, Huthor's path took an unexpected turn.

The borders of the swamp bristled with energy. There were flashes of sinister light, and the stagnant waters boiled and steamed. Skimming over the reeds on a gnashing disc came a spindly figure in teal armour, his robes streaming out behind him. His head was crowned with two pale horns, and in the middle of his forehead blinked a golden eye. The staff he held blazed with blue fire, and behind him flew a train of razor-beaked beasts on discs of their own.

'I am Tyx'evor'eth,' he said in a crackling voice. 'Magister of Tzeentch, humble servant of the Great Conspirator, and I have come for you, Lord Huthor. The Master of Fate has turned his eye towards you, and offers majesty and power the likes of which you have never experienced.'

'The Grandfather's gifts are all the majesty I need,' Huthor burbled. 'Come to us instead, trickster, see what gifts Papa Nurgle gives to his faithful.' He waved him away with his rusted blade.

Eight times Tyx'evor'eth came to make his offer in the stagnant edgelands, and each time Huthor sent him on his way. The magister showed him visions of plenty – mountains of gold and jewels, hordes of slaves stretching across the plains, the tribute of a thousand tyrannised cities. He demonstrated terrifying magics, spells and illusions that could be Huthor's for the asking. But Huthor was not moved. He had decay and disease, the pleasing dankness of the swamps, and he feared no blade; what more could he need?

'I follow this path,' Huthor told the magister. 'I see no end to it yet.'

On the ninth occasion he visited, Tyx'evor'eth promised nothing of riches or power. He came alone, his warband of Enlightened left behind at his camp. He didn't dazzle Huthor with magic or try to seduce him with visions of the future.

'All I come to offer this time, my lord,' he said, 'is a single word.'

'And what word is that, trickster?' Huthor laughed. The sound was like the stagnant swamp waters bubbling in the stench.

Tyx'evor'eth bowed low. His disc bobbed under him.

'*Legacy*,' he said. He spread his arms to indicate the swamp around them, and his third eye blinked. 'Is this really where Huthor the Flayer will end his journey? Or will his name yet be writ large across the blazing plains of Chamon, remembered for ever more? Come with me, lord, and you shall make it so. None shall ever forget you.'

'Aye...' Huthor said slowly; and then the swamp around him suddenly seemed a mean and shabby place, not fit to have held him so long. He looked down at his bloated skin, his rusted blade that he had carried since he was big enough to hold it.

'Fear not, my lord,' the magister said. 'Form is a malleable thing to those with the power to change it...'

And so Tyx'evor'eth wove his magics, unravelling the tendrils of disease from their bodies. Over the years he guided them far on Tzeentch's path, teaching them his arcane knowledge – until the Ashpeaks, and a bitter duel under the sun.

The night before the duel, Huthor sat in his tent, scrying the future. In the prismatic jewel known as the Unclouded Eye, he watched tomorrow's combat. He knew he must cast an absurd image to anyone who saw him: a born killer, bearded and uncouth, clad in soft teal robes and hunched over a crystal no bigger than a rust-apple. In its shifting light he saw the Khorne warband they had clashed with earlier that day advancing onto the lower slopes, saw the enveloping strike by his own army, the pyromantic cascade of unleashed spells. He saw glimpses of his forthcoming fight with the Khorne champion: the clash of blades; the inspired stroke that saw Huthor feign a stumble then come cutting up from right to left with incredible force, the blow shattering the champion's face and sending his helmet spinning into the dirt; the counterstroke sweeping laterally to disembowel him. It was a move honed by years of combat, and he looked forward to performing it the next day – at dawn, early, on a hard-packed apron of land beneath the looming Ashpeaks. Tyx'evor'eth had been incredulous that Huthor was willing to risk the fight, but the Khorne champion had made the challenge and it couldn't go unanswered.

In the old days, he thought, it wouldn't even have been a question.

At that moment, the old days pulled back the flap of his tent and entered – Vhoss, his seamed face twinkling with amusement. Like

Huthor he was wearing teal robes, but underneath was the old boiled leather of his dracoline-hide jerkin. He smelled of aether, of sorcery. The magister had been tutoring on the eve of battle, it seemed.

'Single combat?' Vhoss scoffed. 'Are you sure about this?' He pulled up a camp stool and sat down, reaching with easy familiarity into Huthor's store-box for a bottle of zephyr-wine. He unplugged the cork with his teeth, spat it out and drank deep.

'You think I'm not up to it?' Huthor said.

'Did you see that vicious-looking sod? Teeth filed to points, eyes bloodshot with rage – even his muscles had muscles. He's going to chop you in half, lad.'

'We'll see,' Huthor said. When their two forces had first skirmished, the Khorne champion had marched fearlessly into their camp, throwing his challenge down. He did not fear death, Huthor had thought. He would die fighting, gladly.

He slipped the Unclouded Eye into his robes. He knew his old friend was half-teasing, but even without the prism's reassurance he would have felt confident. He couldn't say why, but he knew – he *knew* – the duel would go his way. His path did not end here. 'It may be a while since I last fought man on man, but I've no doubt I've forgotten more tricks than that scum will ever know.'

'Just make sure you haven't forgotten all of them, that's all I'm saying...'

Vhoss passed him the bottle. After a moment's hesitation Huthor took it. He sipped the zephyr-wine, feeling its slow and airy burn deep in his chest.

'Not too much, night before a fight,' Vhoss said, winking at him. Huthor smiled and passed the bottle back.

'Ah, it's been a long road, has it not?' Vhoss sighed.

'It has indeed.'

'When did it change, eh? What was the first step?'

'Dysileesh,' Huthor said quietly. Vhoss closed his eyes, luxuriating in the memory.

'The Godseeker, of course, of course... I've still got the scars she gave me. And the son.'

'Young Vhorrun's done you proud,' Huthor said.

'He has. He looks at me with those violet eyes sometimes, and I see her in him still. You know, I sometimes think it was a path we should have stayed on. The Prince of Excess was a pleasurable master.'

'He was no master of mine,' Huthor said. 'Just a guide for a while.'

'No,' Vhoss agreed sadly. He put the bottle at his feet and stared at his open hands. He looked at Huthor, his oldest friend. 'But then you never could commit to anything for long, could you?'

The Unclouded Eye, Tyx'evor'eth had called it. The Jewel that Sees, the Prism of Foresight. 'In this,' the magister had told him, 'a scholar of the arts will catch echoes of the future, but echoes are all they are. They are the shape of moments cast back from their origin, but not the moments themselves. Do you understand?'

'I understand,' Huthor had said.

'The skill is in reading those echoes, understanding those shapes, and seeing where the shapes fit into the puzzle of the present. Once a scholar can do that, he will see events before they happen, before they can disarm him. Yes?'

'Yes.'

'Good,' he said, the proud tutor gazing at his pupil. And his three eyes, which missed nothing, blinked one by one.

Vhoss moved quicker than was humanly possible; he had cast an incantation of fleetness, it was clear, but he was no true scholar and the move was betrayed in advance by a faint nimbus of dark energy around his eyes. The blade came up, dripping with poison, but Huthor had already seen it in the Eye. He had woven a protective ward before Vhoss had even entered the tent, and as the blade bent and refracted against the sorcerous energy that surrounded him, Huthor brought up his own stiletto and plunged it into Vhoss' stomach. Through the robes, through the dracoline-hide jerkin, deep into the flesh of the man who had been his lieutenant for decades; his brother in arms, his friend – his fellow slave to darkness on the road to red ruin.

Vhoss gasped with pain, dropping his own knife, his spell breaking apart in a faint smear of discordant colours. As his eyes widened in agony, Huthor saw some aspect of the old friend he had known, before any god had demanded their loyalty; when to worship on the altar of Chaos was to worship the violence of the storm, the unyielding power of the earthquake – everything that could reveal just how fragile the notion of Order really was. He had been right. It had been a long road from there to here.

Vhoss slipped to the floor. His eyes fluttered as his life left him. Before he went, Huthor resisted the urge to ask him why. The answer would have been inexplicable. Since Tyx'evor'eth had been tutoring them, such fatal feuds had become commonplace. Always at the heart of them was some twisted maze of half-understood portent and prediction. Assassinations, denunciations, stabbings and poisonings – it was a daily event. Who could untangle the web of Tzeentch? Who knew which thread led to which outcome, and which outcome disguised further eventualities unguessable to those without the insight to see them? It was futile.

He looked down at his old friend, the body cooling on the ground, and he was surprised at how little he felt. Only boredom and fatigue, and something very close to shame.

He called for his servants and they took the body away.

'Wake me early,' he told them. He packed the bottle of zephyr-wine in his store-box. 'I have a fight to win, at dawn.'

* * *

The Ashpeaks, like new-forged steel still glowing from the furnace, cast their shadows on the dusty plain. Up there, beyond their distant caps, a glinting speck of light cut with patient industry through the cloud, a contrail of disturbed silver unspooling behind it. A sky-craft of the duardin, she had told him once. He remembered Dysileesh standing by his side with her musk of dead flowers and stale incense, the looped rings of oiled silver in her ear, eyebrow and nose, the thrilling stench of her. Her silk robes had hung from her body like sheets of ruby wine.

'Those who style themselves "Overlords"', she had said, and he had gripped the hilt of his sword.

He held that sword high now, ready to administer the killing stroke. It had been a worthy fight. The Khornate champion writhed in his death agonies, blood frothing on his lips. Through shattered teeth and scraps of gum he laughed, one hand scooping up the ropes of his spilled innards, the other still scrabbling in the dirt for his axe.

'Wait,' he gurgled, spitting blood.

'I send you to the Brass Citadel. Isn't that what you want?'

'What I want means nothing,' the dying champion scorned. 'It is… what *you* want… that matters now.'

He spewed out a stream of black blood. His face darkened with the approach of death, but the closer it came, the more fiercely blazed his remaining eye.

'What I want?'

'You are the one they call the Flayer, are you not, Lord Huthor?'

'The Flayer?' He lowered his sword. 'I had that name once… an age ago.'

'You have had many titles – Lord of the Golden Fortress, Bringer of Sickness, and now Aspiring Magister of Gazan Zhar… Your name is known,' the champion said, grimacing. 'Across the Spiral Crux, men speak of you in awe and cower in their hovels. We have seen your face reflected in the blood we spill, heard your name whispered by the dying when we cut them down. Khorne guides us to you, Huthor the Flayer. Three paths have you walked since turning from Chaos Undivided. But I say to you the fourth has yet to feel your tread, and it is a road waist-deep in blood and fire…!'

The wind from the Ashpeaks, gritty and with a scent of stale smoke, brought with it the distant roar of the warrior's warband. The duel of champions was over, but Huthor had never expected the Khorne fighters to abide by the compact. No matter; already, Tyx'evor'eth's fleet of Enlightened were skimming over the foothills to flank them, while Huthor's warriors formed up in illusory ranks to the front. Vhorrun's force was masked by glamours in the low ground to the east. The battle would be brief, violent, the outcome certain. He had seen it coalescing in the Eye last night, before he had killed Vhoss – the caged green flames interlocking inside the prism, forming a picture of just this moment.

Just this moment – apart from the entreaty of the dying champion at his feet. He had not seen that at all.

Tyx'evor'eth came gliding swiftly over the rusty ground, stinking of ozone. The magister was eager for the fight.

'Huthor, lord,' he said. 'The moment is near. The arc of Fate bends once more to your bidding. Let us be on our way.' His three eyes blinked in a disjointed relay.

Huthor turned once more to the prostrate warrior. He thought of Vhoss last night, clawing at the knife in his guts, lips twitching to speak a final version of the spells he had never really mastered. None of them had, if truth be known. The weaving of magics had always left Huthor himself feeling drained and hollow, a brackish taste of metal in his mouth. Long had Tyx'evor'eth extolled the virtues of the Weaver of Fate, tutoring Huthor in sorcery and revealing the scale of power and influence that would open to him if he walked the Path of Change. He had given him the Unclouded

Eye, the jewel that reveals the future. He had brought his tzaan-gors and his Enlightened to swell Huthor's ranks, until what had been a powerful warband had become something more like an army, with territories and thraldoms of its own, as powerful as it had been in the days of the Golden Fortress. But for too long now had he been on this road, dabbling and learning but never fully committing to the lure. Had all the magister's work been for nothing, in the end?

All this trickery, he thought. These treacherous plots and labyr-inthine plans that curve in on themselves and lose their purpose in the twists and turns of their interminable execution. And here was this fine warrior dying in the dust, mortally wounded, who had thrown himself at Huthor like a hurricane, Chamon's silver sunlight gleaming on his brass plate. In his snarling face had been a look of purest exultation – it had been the most exhilarating fight of Huthor's life. Such simplicity, such purity of purpose: to kill and be killed, and to treat each outcome as a glorious vindi-cation of his brutal god. A trophy for the throne of skulls, deep in a citadel of brass...

'You see it,' the warrior choked. 'I know you do. Why do you think I sought you out if not to see that look in your eyes? You see the Lord of Skulls fuming in the reek, the piled heads, the screaming of the damned. You felt it when you opened me up and saw the blood spill from my guts.'

'I see it,' Huthor mumbled. 'I... I *feel* it.'

'This path shall be your last, Lord Huthor. It has been seen. Follow him, follow Khorne, and I swear you will cover the lands in blood! It has been seen! You will cover them in blood!'

'Lord Huthor!' Txy'evor'eth demanded. His disc slavered and moved agitatedly under his hooves. 'Battle draws near! Kill this savage and let us be on our way.'

Black dust rose in heavy plumes beyond the foothills. The

Khornate warband was advancing from their camp. Huthor could hear the screaming ululation of their war cry, the clashing of swords and axes.

'I give you the mercy stroke,' he said, raising his pale blade. The Khornate champion sneered. His feet kicked at the dust. Death was near now, very near.

'No mercy!' he spat. 'Only blood! Blood! And Khorne cares not from whence–'

The Flayer brought down his sword.

'It is done!' Tyx'evor'eth laughed. 'Now quickly, lord, let us be away. The savages move ever closer into our trap!'

To cover the lands in blood…

'The Flayer', they had called him once. He recalled his camp tent back then, pitched like a flag of his conquests, every panel the skinned hide of whichever warlord, chieftain or elder had opposed him. He remembered his raiders, the Raging Tide, breaking like a thunderstorm over the Muspelzharr plains, drenching them in blood and tears. Vhoss at his side… Aye, those had been simpler days indeed.

'When this is done, Tyx'evor'eth,' Huthor said, 'we will be parting ways.'

'…My lord?'

'I have come to the end of the path, magister.' He cleaned his sword against his cloak. His muscles were aching; it had been so long since he had had a proper fight. 'Fate now takes me down a different road.'

'But, Lord Huthor, have I not fulfilled all the promises I made? Has not the Great Architect twisted the thread of your fate in ways that please you?'

'It pleased me for a while. It pleases me no longer. The thread is broken. I shall make a new one.'

'You return to the Undivided path?'

'No,' Huthor said. 'There is one road yet for me to take.'

He had expected anger, disbelief, but instead the magister cackled on his disc and rose higher into the air. His black eyes frosted with foresight. He pointed his staff and Huthor prepared the equations of an unbinding in his mind, drawing energy from the Chamonian wind, but the sorcerer cast no magics.

'Go now, tempter, or I will cut you down as well!' Huthor said.

'You will indeed cover the lands in blood, Lord Huthor... I see it now. That will be your fate, my lord!' He screeched with laughter as he sped away, blue flame flickering from his staff. 'It is all unfolding as the Architect has planned. You think you walk a path, a road of your own making, but you are mistaken, my lord. It is not a path. It is a maze. A labyrinth!'

The tzaangors and Enlightened would be lost to him now, he realised. Already he felt his own powers diminish, the forms of magic fading inside him. The Khorne warband would be on them in moments and he had lost near half his army.

No matter. He sheathed his sword. He dipped his hands into the dead champion's guts and anointed himself, marching off to join his warriors as the blood cooled on his forehead. The Khornate army was breasting the rise and clashing their swords and axes. He took the Unclouded Eye from inside his robes and cast it far off into the rusty scrub.

'We will do this the old way!' he roared to the sky, and up there, beyond the peaks, the last glint of the duardin ship went sailing on, far from the sun's bold and grasping light.

The shrieking of chained beasts tore the air. Huthor felt it in his chest, the low bass rumble of the chimeras' leonine heads, the roar of the manticores lashed to the ground by brass anchors and hard-wrought steel. The frantic hissing of the cockatrices was like a foul rainfall, and the ochre ground was scrabbled with claw marks and spattered with blood. He had lost a hundred men corralling these creatures. He did not care.

Vhorrun approached him, snarling, trembling with the urge to kill.

'We're almost ready, lord,' he said. His voice was harsh and grating, an angry rasp, the consequence of a blade he'd recently taken in his throat. Huthor regarded him coolly, one hand resting on the pommel of his sword in case the boy finally made his move. Young, as taut as rendered steel, he was the most perfect warrior among them. Of all the Raging Tide, save Huthor himself, Vhorrun had embraced Khorne with the most fervour. He despised the trace of Dysileesh in him, sickened that even a shadow of her pampered god could lie on his fate. He so scorned his violet eyes that he had plucked one out, only keeping the other so he could still see for combat. His silver skin was a latticework of angry scars, and he had long since shaved off his gold-dusted hair. He was born to kill, born to die, although it puzzled Huthor that in all the long months since Vhoss' death, Vhorrun had never made a move to avenge his father. Perhaps, the warlord thought, he realises the truth of his sire? When he stares with such hatred at me, does he know he stares at the man who gave him life?

Huthor grinned at the thought. He looked forward to killing the boy.

'Now hear me!' Huthor shouted to his men. From across the burnished steppe, his army began to gather: Blood Warriors in their battered crimson plate; bloodreavers in their hundreds. Kh'ezhar, his slaughterpriest, ritually slashed at his skin with his sacrificial knife. 'Today you will gorge yourselves at the Dark Feast! You will rend flesh and tear skin, and you will feast on duardin! You will prise them from their metal ships and spill blood for the Blood God!'

To the exultant roar of the crowd, which drowned out even the screaming beasts he had gathered to serve them, Huthor raised his blade and pointed it skyward. Up there, where the Kharadron ships flew to Barak-Zon, black clouds gathered. The storm was upon them; the deafening murder-song.

You will cover the lands in blood...

He had certainly done that. Since dedicating himself to Khorne, he had done little else, and now his army dwarfed any he had led as lord of the Golden Fortress. Swathes of land had fallen under his bloody footprint. Thousands had died, and hundreds more scrambled to join his brass banners. The scum of Gazan Zhar had partaken of the Dark Feast and were his to command.

Now, madness quivered behind Huthor's eyes. Rage made his fingers tremble always for his sword, and, if no enemy was to hand, he seized whomever was near and butchered them without a thought. He felt Khorne's smouldering brass throne as a colossal weight on his shoulders; the citadel burning with sulphur was like a liminal presence before his eyes, ever-shifting in his mad-dened sight. In the wake of the fight at the Ashpeaks, won by the narrowest of margins, Huthor's warband had become the Raging Tide once more. Casting off their Tzeentchian glamours, they had stripped the bodies of the Khorne warriors and clad themselves in their spattered armour. None doubted who had led them to vic-tory that day, who had guided Huthor's frenzied blade. Khorne had willed it. The path was freely taken, and the journey since had been one of uncompromising destruction. The further they went on that road, the more their days as dabblers in the other gods' service faded, like sallow dreams dispatched by the light of day.

The central lands of Gazan Zhar receded, hurtling away from him – an ochre smear of oxide and rust. The Ashpeaks stabbed like fangs into the sky, wreathed in steam and dusted with a sooty snow. They loomed and fell back, and then the immense and mind-bending helix of the Spiral Crux seemed to spread itself out below him. The air was freezing and cut like cold steel, but Huthor the Flayer boiled with rage. The manticore beneath him growled with a sound like the mad alloys of Chamon's sub-realms grinding together, and the carrion reek of the creature enveloped him even as the streaming aether-winds plucked his breath away. He screamed with savage joy, turning in his rawhide saddle to see his warband spread out across the sky – hundreds of them clutching to the feathered crests of swooping cockatrices, or grimly lashed to the snarling fury of the chimeras. It was an impossible fleet, murder on the cutting wind. It was the last thing the Kharadrons would see coming.

Kh'ezhar's unholy invocations had slaved the creatures to their new purpose, but some, unleashed once more into their element, soon turned on their masters. Huthor was amused to see the draconic head of one chimera twist round and snap furiously at the bloodreavers on its back, their mangled bodies slipping off to tumble thousands of feet to the ground. A cockatrice spun round and loosed its riders, darting down to snap at their falling bodies with its vicious beak. In contrast, Huthor's manticore seemed not only to tolerate his presence, but also to welcome it; the creature had purred as he mounted it, and only the slightest pressure on its greasy, blood-flecked mane was needed to guide it in the right direction.

'The Enlightened would have been useful now,' Vhorrun had said as they'd readied themselves to fly. Huthor hadn't been sure if the boy was mocking him. But it was true, he conceded, gaining the saddle; this would all have been much easier with a Tzeentchian disc underfoot.

As they swooped onwards, breaking through the cloud, Huthor saw a dozen elongated shapes ahead. Draped in a sparkling mist from the harvested aether-gold, the Kharadron ships grew more distinct, their strange nautical hulls suspended from globular metal balloons, some of them like vast armoured behemoths and others no more than agile little escort craft. So far, none of them had seen the bestial fleet in their blindside.

'Overlords'... Their very name was a provocation. Wherever Huthor had cast his gaze in the long years of his conquests, the Overlords had always exceeded his grasp. The lands groaned under him, but the sky was pure. Well – no longer. He would stain it with their blood.

'Dive!' he screamed, and the manticore beneath him roared. Even in the slicing wind he could hear the war cry of his airborne army swooping in for the kill, thrashing their mounts and straining for the fight, axes bared, spears raised.

And then the Kharadron responded.

The first wave of bloodreavers vanished in a puff of red mist. The ragged bodies of their mounts listed and fell, keening in pain and trailing ribbons of blood. Ahead, the hulls of the airships were smeared with smoke, crackling with shot from broadside cannons and carbines. Huthor saw a buzzing flock of tiny figures unlatch from the bigger ships, duardin suspended from their own individual balloons, bearing vicious-looking pikes. They sped towards the lead chimeras and engaged, slashing and stabbing and swarming with incredible agility. More of Huthor's army was torn apart when the smaller ships came through on attack runs that peppered their flanks with shot.

'You didn't say it would be this hard!' Kh'ezhar shouted as he wheeled his cockatrice beside Huthor. He laughed with manic fervour before the upper part of his body exploded in a steaming gout of blood. The cockatrice, mortally wounded, screamed and fell, a feathered rag.

This wasn't going to work. Huthor saw his army picked apart in moments, scoured from the skies by the duardin's incredible firepower. Fully half his men were already dead, eviscerated by gunfire or knocked from their perches by their panicked animals, cast down on the long journey back to the plains of Gazan Zhar. The beasts they had so painstakingly herded together were being destroyed.

And yet, it was not all going the Kharadrons' way. Huthor launched his manticore at one buzzing interceptor and laughed at the pilot's panicked reaction as he tried to haul it around. The beast severed the rigging with one sweep of its claws, the ship's hull dropping like a meteor to the earth. He saw one bloodreaver leap boldly through the air from the back of his chimera with a maddened war cry, twin axes in hand, crashing onto the bridge of another escort craft. He hacked the crew to pieces and twisted its wheel to send it slamming into the hull of a bigger ship with a blinding explosion. The larger Kharadron ship split apart with a scream of rending metal. Trailing long streamers of superheated aether-gold, each part slowly listed and fell like a boat succumbing to the pull of deep waters, the bodies of burning duardin spinning from it like falling stars. Other beasts had gained the Kharadrons' main line and were rampaging across the decks, vomiting flame and ripping the deck crews apart. Huthor knew the attack was doomed, but he had never run from a fight. Death was nothing; blood was all. And Khorne cared not from whence the blood flowed.

He guided his own beast towards the deck of the flagship, a vast ironclad bristling with weaponry. He saw the deck crew prepare themselves to repel boarders, scurrying to the gunwale with their carbines raised. A hail of shot enveloped him, striking the manticore in a dozen places and sparking off his shoulder guard, but the Blood God was looking on his favoured son – not a single shot had wounded him. As Huthor drew his sword he grinned to see the duardin run for cover.

The manticore, expiring at the last, hit the deck like an explosion.

In its thrashing death agony, sweeping the deck with its barbed tail, it scattered some of the crew into the open air. Huthor was thrown wildly from its back, crashing into the cupola of the ship's sky-cannon and knocking the gunner over the edge. Dazed, bleeding from a wound across his forehead, he still laughed to hear the duardin's horrified scream.

A dozen duardin in red armour and dark blue fatigues came charging towards him, but before they could even arm their pistols Huthor was on them. He leapt from the cupola with a frenzied scream and barrelled into the stunted figures, hewing left and right in great scything sweeps, like a crazed artist painting the deck in streams of red. He snatched one duardin up and hurled him overboard, grunting then as a pistol shot smashed into his shoulder with a spray of blood and meat. His left arm lifeless at his side, Huthor threw his blade and skewered the duardin who had shot him, pinning him to the fo'c'sle wall.

The deck was littered with bodies. Eddies and swirls of the metallic wind threaded the rigging, and beyond the sky-ship he could see puffs of black smoke, drifts of red mist, screaming warriors and enraged beasts falling to their deaths. What little of his force had made it to the ships was being systematically exterminated, blown from the decks by the Kharadrons' disciplined crews. As the last few airborne beasts were sniped from the sky, Huthor knew it was over. He heard the tramp of approaching boots and pulled his sword from the hull, preparing himself for death, rejoicing that so many had wetted the throne of the Brass Citadel.

'Let them come,' he spat. He held out his sword. 'The path is ended, and it has been a long, strange road indeed...'

But as the duardin charged up the deck towards him, they were immolated in a blaze of fire. Some, maddened by pain, threw themselves over the edge; others kicked and screamed as the flames consumed them. Huthor turned to see Vhorrun's chimera, bleeding from gunshot wounds, spew fire and launch itself at the remaining crew even as the buzzing gunhaulers banked and strafed it with shot. Vhorrun himself leapt to the deck, his axes drawn, but before Huthor could say a word the young warrior had launched himself at him.

It was like the duel in the sun once more, when the Khornate champion had fought as if the world were ending. Vhorrun's blows were both wildly savage and icily precise, a flurry of axe strikes followed by feints and parries that were then converted into devastating cross-cuts. He hooked at Huthor's sword and drew his guard away, then blazed in with elbows and knees, hammering the warlord back against the gunwale. Huthor, the wilier fighter, who had fought and killed for more than twice Vhorrun's lifetime, was as hard-pressed as he had ever been. He couldn't gain the advantage, each parry and riposte easily swept aside by the whirlwind of Vhorrun's assault. His left arm was ruined, his sword arm was weakening, and the wound on his forehead was leaking into his eyes. Huthor raised his sword to block a twin-handed strike, but Vhorrun's axes shattered the blade and plunged into the meat of his chest. He screamed, his sight blackening, and as he dropped to his knees Vhorrun felled him with a vicious punch to the face.

Huthor coughed blood and rolled onto his back. 'I've… had that sword longer than you've been alive, boy,' he groaned. With superhuman effort, hooking his arm to the gunwale, he hauled himself up. He'd be damned if he'd die on his back, or on his knees. 'Well, it came at last,' he said. He clutched the wounds in his chest. 'Revenge for your father's death.'

'Vhoss was many things to me,' Vhorrun said, prowling the deck. He held his axes ready. 'But I know he was not my father.'

Huthor laughed, and the pain was a torment. 'How long have you known?'

'I've always known. I've always known it was you.'

'And you'd kill me still? You're blood of the Flayer, boy.'

'And it's the only blood I reject! I have always hated you, Flayer. Your greed for glory has ever poisoned my fate. You sired me on some foul Slaaneshi cultist, forced me to moulder for months in those cursed swamps, and then dragged me into a labyrinth of cowardly magics!'

'You make it sound like you had no choice, no will of your own!'

'No,' Vhorrun snarled. 'Only your will mattered! When we still followed the Trickster, I tried to get Vhoss to kill you. Plans within plans, schemes within schemes in those days, but instead you killed the only man who had ever showed me kindness or respect.'

Huthor gave him a bitter, mocking laugh. 'I brought you to Khorne though, didn't I? You seem to have taken to his service.'

'Yes...' Vhorrun said. 'Fair is fair, I follow the one true god now. And by my own hand must it be done.'

'A family tradition,' Huthor said. 'I killed my own father, you know. All sons must, in the end.'

Ferried by their floating comrades, more Kharadron were boarding the vessel at the prow. Vhorrun's chimera expired in a murderous fusillade, and of the Raging Tide only the two of them were left. All were dead. Huthor stooped for the broken hilt of his sword. He would die fighting, with a weapon in his hand.

'I live still,' Huthor said. He grinned. 'The enemy approaches. Will we die together?'

Vhorrun looked at him then, smiling. His lone eye sparkled with violet.

'Huthor the Flayer,' he said. 'You won't have the honour of dying in battle.'

As the Kharadron troops opened fire, Vhorrun shoved him in the chest, pitching him backwards over the edge of the ship. Huthor saw his son break apart under the crossfire, and then the world was a spiral of light and darkness, of lustre and pitch. The wind pummelled him, the sky-ships sinking into the depths of the coruscating sky even as the ground hurtled up to meet him. He fell faster than he would ever have believed possible, the mad tangle of Chamon's uncoiling landscape speeding towards him with its eager embrace, the wind roaring like the apocalypse in his ears. And as he fell, his mind, darkened by his wounds, fled back to that duel in the sun, the Khornate champion dying at his feet, his muttered promise. *You will cover the lands in blood...* And then Tyx'evor'eth spinning away on his disc, cackling, gaze frosting with arcane foresight... *That will be your fate, my lord!*

He had seen it. He had seen it all happen. Every step on the path had brought him to this point.

Yes, Huthor thought as the ground came near, and as the promise of his fall came closer to its violent fulfilment. *I will indeed cover these lands in blood...*

But Khorne cares not from whence the blood flows!

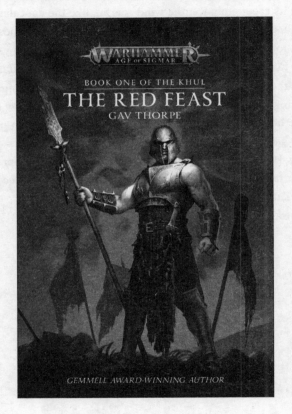

ABOUT THE AUTHORS

Richard Strachan is a writer and editor who lives with his partner and two children in Edinburgh, UK. Despite his best efforts, both children stubbornly refuse to be interested in tabletop wargaming. His first story for Black Library, 'The Widow Tide', appeared in the Warhammer Horror anthology *Maledictions*, and he has since written 'Blood of the Flayer', 'Tesserae' and the Warcry Catacombs novel *Blood of the Everchosen*.

Eric Gregory's fiction has appeared in magazines and anthologies including *Lightspeed*, *Interzone*, *Strange Horizons*, *Nowa Fantastyka*, and others. For Black Library he has written 'The Fourfold Wound' and 'Bossgrot'. He lives and works in Carrboro, North Carolina.

David Guymer's work for Warhammer Age of Sigmar includes the novels *Hamilcar: Champion of the Gods* and *The Court of the Blind King*, the audio dramas *The Beasts of Cartha*, *Fist of Mork*, *Fist of Gork*, *Great Red* and *Only the Faithful*. He is also the author of the Gotrek & Felix novels *Slayer*, *Kinslayer* and *City of the Damned* and the Gotrek audio dramas *Realmslayer* and *Realmslayer: Blood of the Old World*. For The Horus Heresy he has written the novella *Dreadwing*, and the Primarchs novels *Ferrus Manus: Gorgon of Medusa* and *Lion El'Jonson: Lord of the First*. For Warhammer 40,000 he has written *The Eye of Medusa*, *The Voice of Mars* and the two Beast Arises novels *Echoes of the Long War* and *The Last Son of Dorn*. He is a freelance writer and occasional scientist based in the East Riding, and was a finalist in the 2014 David Gemmell Awards for his novel *Headtaker*.

Gav Thorpe is the author of the Horus Heresy novels *The First Wall*, *Deliverance Lost*, *Angels of Caliban* and *Corax*, as well as the novella *The Lion*, which formed part of the *New York Times* bestselling collection *The Primarchs*, and several audio dramas. He has written many novels for Warhammer 40,000, including *Indomitus*, *Ashes of Prospero*, *Imperator: Wrath of the Omnissiah* and the Last Chancers series, including the most recent title *The Last Chancers: Armageddon Saint*. He also wrote the Rise of the Ynnari novels *Ghost Warrior* and *Wild Rider*, the *Path of the Eldar* and *Legacy of Caliban* trilogies, and two volumes in The Beast Arises series. For Warhammer, Gav has penned the End Times novel *The Curse of Khaine*, the Warhammer Chronicles omnibus *The Sundering*, and, for Age of Sigmar, *The Red Feast*. In 2017, Gav won the David Gemmell Legend Award for his novel *Warbeast*. He lives and works in Nottingham.

C L **Werner**'s Black Library credits include the Age of Sigmar novels *Overlords of the Iron Dragon*, *Profit's Ruin*, *The Tainted Heart* and *Beastgrave*, the novella *Scion of the Storm* in *Hammers of Sigmar*, and the Warhammer Horror novel *Castle of Blood*. For Warhammer he has written the novels *Deathblade*, *Mathias Thulmann: Witch Hunter*, *Runefang* and *Brunner the Bounty Hunter*, the Thanquol and Boneripper series and Warhammer Chronicles: The Black Plague series. For Warhammer 40,000 he has written the Space Marine Battles novel *The Siege of Castellax*. Currently living in the American southwest, he continues to write stories of mayhem and madness set in the Warhammer worlds.

Darius Hinks is the author of the Warhammer 40,000 novels *Blackstone Fortress*, *Blackstone Fortress: Ascension* and the accompanying audio drama *The Beast Inside*. He also wrote three novels in the Mephiston series: *Mephiston: Blood of Sanguinius*, *Mephiston: Revenant Crusade* and *Mephiston: City of Light*, as well as the Space Marine Battles novella *Sanctus*. His work for Age of Sigmar includes *Hammers of Sigmar*, *Warqueen* and the Gotrek Gurnisson novel *Ghoulslayer*. For Warhammer, he wrote *Warrior Priest*, which won the David Gemmell Morningstar Award for best newcomer, as well as the Orion trilogy, *Sigvald* and several novellas.

Robert Rath is a freelance writer from Honolulu who is currently based in Hong Kong. Though mostly known for writing the YouTube series *Extra History*, his credits also include numerous articles and a book for the U.S. State Department. He is the author of the Black Library novel *The Infinite and the Divine*, and the short stories 'The Garden of Mortal Delights' and 'War in the Museum'.

Dale Lucas is a novelist, screenwriter, civil servant and armchair historian from St. Petersburg, Florida. Once described by a colleague as 'a compulsive researcher who writes fiction to store his research in', he's the author of numerous works of fantasy, neo-pulp and horror. When not writing or working, he loves travel, great food, and amassing more books than he'll ever be able to read. His first story for Black Library, 'Blessed Oblivion', features in the Age of Sigmar anthology *Oaths and Conquests*, and he has since penned the novel *Realm-Lords*.

Jamie Crisalli writes gritty melodrama and bloody combat. Fascinated with skulls, rivets and general gloominess, when she was introduced to the Warhammer universes, it was a natural fit. Her work for Black Library includes the short stories 'Ties of Blood', 'The Serpent's Bargain', and the Age of Sigmar novella *The Measure of Iron*. She has accumulated a frightful amount of monsters, ordnance and tiny soldiery over the years, not to mention books and role-playing games. Currently, she lives with her husband in a land of endless grey drizzle.

Anna Stephens is a UK-based writer of epic, gritty, grimdark fantasy. She is the author of the Godblind trilogy and her first story for Black Library, 'The Siege of Greenspire', featured in the Age of Sigmar anthology *Oaths and Conquests*.

Ben Counter has two Horus Heresy novels to his name – *Galaxy in Flames* and *Battle for the Abyss*. He is the author of the Soul Drinkers series and *The Grey Knights Omnibus*. For Space Marine Battles, he has written *The World Engine* and *Malodrax*, and has turned his attention to the Space Wolves with the novella *Arjac Rockfist: Anvil of Fenris* as well as a number of short stories. He is a fanatical painter of miniatures, a pursuit that has won him his most prized possession: a prestigious Golden Demon award. He lives in Portsmouth, England.

David Annandale is the author of the Warhammer Horror novel *The House of Night and Chain* and the novella *The Faith and the Flesh*, which features in the portmanteau *The Wicked and the Damned*. His work for the Horus Heresy series includes the novels *Ruinstorm* and *The Damnation of Pythos*, and the Primarchs novels *Roboute Guilliman: Lord of Ultramar* and *Vulkan: Lord of Drakes*. For Warhammer 40,000 he has written *Ephrael Stern: The Heretic Saint*, *Warlord: Fury of the God-Machine*, the Yarrick series, and several stories involving the Grey Knights, as well as titles for The Beast Arises and the Space Marine Battles series. For Warhammer Age of Sigmar he has written *Neferata: Mortarch of Blood* and *Neferata: The Dominion of Bones*. David lectures at a Canadian university, on subjects ranging from English literature to horror films and video games.

Michael R Fletcher is an author and grilled cheese aficionado with several dark and grim science-fiction and fantasy novels to his name, including his first story for Black Library, 'A Tithe of Bone'. He lives in the endless suburban sprawl somewhere north of Toronto.

Erstwhile editor of various publications including *Star Wars Insider*, **Dave Gross** also dabbles in tabletop and video game design. He is the author of various fantasy novels and is perhaps best known for his Radovan & the Count series. He lives in Edmonton, Canada.